THE
PIRATE
CAPTAIN®

CHRONICLES OF A LEGEND

KERRY LYNNE

CompassRose Books
By the Board Publishing

"Nor Silver"

...for not all treasure does silver or gold make.

To DrT and Eleanor:
You are the sea which kept this ship afloat

ACKNOWLEDGMENTS

Where does one begin listing all the help received over a six-year process? A thousand apologies to anyone I might overlook.

To my husband, Jerry, for 35 years of sailing and enabling me to pursue this dream.

To my son, Scott, for tolerating his weird mom and answering all her even weirder questions.

To my Flat-coated retriever, Kate, for her unconditional love through it all. To my family, for waiting until after I left the room before laughing when I told them I was writing a book about pirates.

To Lucy Barker Todd, for convincing me of how "bad" the top-sellers were.

To Rebecca Schoenfeld, for making sure all my "i's" were crossed and "t's" were dotted, and Tabatha and Glendon at Streetlight Graphics. You guys are wonders.

To Sharon Klug, for showing me after a 25-year absence how to construct a sentence and being the gracious friend who gave me a set of O'Brian's audio books. What a treasure, both her and the books, that is.

To Dr. Richard Traitel... It's a shameful thing for a writer to be without words for all the miracles he has wrought. None of this would have been possible without his weekly readings, updates, pep talks, scoldings and hand-holdings. A fellow libro-fiend, he shared his enthusiasm for history and his father's model shipbuilding collections.

To Eleanor Holman, for being a steadfast fan first and friend later. It was her love of Captain Nathanael Blackthorne (even greater than mine, if that is at all possible) that made all this possible. Her vision and dreams far outreached mine, and kept the creative fires burning. She has endured the innumerable evolutions and been the voice of conscience I didn't want to hear.

And last of all, to Jerry Bruckheimer and Johnny Depp, for giving us something beyond Captain Blood and Long John Silver to play with. It would be too much to hope that you might one day read this.

Thank you, one and all...
Kerry Lynne

*"Me hair is silver and me bones creak, but me
cock still rises and I remember why."*

*Wisdom of the ages you seek, lad? I offer but one word: treasure.
At what price does this treasure come, you ask,
for not all does silver and gold make?*

*To pose the question means you've not found yours, for when you do,
'tis no longer a question of the cost to keep it.
"Anything" becomes your creed."*

1: JOURNEY

May, 1753

O N DECK THERE. SAIL HO!"

"Where away?"

"Larboard abeam, sir, 'bout three points."

Ezekiel Pryce looked to the tops. It was Damerell up there, what sung out. An extra ration of rum and the best pistol on the prize would be his, *if* he be correct. Heaven help the blundering bastard if he weren't, and the Cap'n not obliged to raise a finger.

The Cap'n stood peering through his glass.

"What be in yer mind, sir? Be it them, are ye thinkin'?" Pryce asked, coming up alongside.

"The bearing is fitting," the Cap'n said, intent on the speck of white against the east Caribbean blue.

"Nary a ship from England what don't come from that a-ways."

The skipper lowered the glass. A cat on the prowl, he was, and no prey was safe. "Then they're fair game, are they not? The last two proved to be a hare's chase, but fat prizes, indeed. If nothing else, the lads need the practice. We'll burn the rust out o' the guns, eh?"

"Aye, Cap'n."

"Bearing sou'west," Damerell called from his roost.

The Cap'n raised his glass, looked to the compass, and then said to the helmsman, "Make it so, Mr. Squidge."

"Sou'west, aye."

"Prepare to bring her about. Full cover!" The Cap'n was in high spirits, now. "Fly every rag she'll bear."

The ship beneath Pryce's feet quivered. Aye! She knew. She smelled the prey. She'd throw her shoulder to the wind, take every bit of canvas and beg for more.

"It makes for a fair night, Master Pryce," the Cap'n said,

looking skyward. "Light every lamp, so we'll glow like a damned fireship. We'll allow them the night to think about the hell what is about to be visited upon them. She might try to duck and run under the cover of dark, so double the lookouts, and we'll rig the grates for the first slaggardly lout caught napping."

Clear skies, a steady glass and fair course: no creature of the sea could ask for more. Only a dirty night could save the hapless prey.

"D'ye think she'll turn and fight, sir?"

"How often does the rabbit bite the fox, Mr. Pryce? If they opt for blood, then it shall be theirs what runs the decks."

"The last ones we stripped to nature's own and burned to the water line."

"Aye, well, 'tis the price of resistance, is it not? Pass the word to the Master Gunner to pray have his guns ready by... make it eight bells of the morning watch."

"Hands to yer stations," Pryce bellowed over the break of the quarterdeck. "Clear the braces and stand by to come about!"

Staring at the line where sky and water met, the Cap'n went uncommon quiet, a rare sight indeed when sniffing prey.

"I've the feeling on this one, Pryce. The Devil burn me, I don't know why, but this one... this one is different."

✦

A few days earlier
Cate Mackenzie watched the oily sea roll past and wondered if this would be the night to finally end her misery.

Behind was England and everything that constituted a life, everything she had ever had—home, husband, family—and everything she had lost.

Ahead, nothing.

The *Constancy*, a merchant ship, had been riding the trade winds for nearly two months, bound for Kingston, Jamaica, the West Indies. There was little reason to believe the long arm of King Georgie's courts couldn't reach there. Worse yet, there would be no one there either, no one to know whether she lived or otherwise.

Looking down from the rail, the black water was alluring. Voices whispered. Beckoning from the depths, they offered not euphoria, just... peace. She wondered what it would be to step off and allow the stillness to take her. The dark water couldn't be any more chilling than huddling in garrets. She considered dying to be the easy part. Living destitute and alone had been a five-year struggle.

With the impact of her body hitting the water, there was the possibility of pain, an intriguing prospect to be sure. Numbness had been a permanent state of being, moving woodenly from one day to the next. To feel anything apart from wretchedness was well worth the risk.

Captain Chambers emerged from the flickering shadows and drew up beside her. The weather rail was the reserved domain for the ship's captain, but there he was at the lee side, seeking her out once again. He nodded a silent greeting, the sharp green eyes narrowing.

"You must be anxious to meet your family in Kingston," he said around the stem of his cold pipe.

For a while now, he appeared to have a sense of what she was about, always watching. His attempts at small talk were maddeningly awkward. It was all a part of their jousting game: he trying to learn as much as possible, while she strove to tell him as little as could be managed. She cringed. On the docks in Bristol, she had told him there would be family waiting, a necessary lie to be allowed passage. Since then, she had come to understand it had been her coin which spoke the loudest.

She looked away into the darkness, lest the keen eyes see the deception. "Yes, my brother will be most anxious."

Cate spoke with the conviction of an oft-told lie. The game of maintaining it for so long, however, had grown tiresome. She dreaded the same questions posed over and over, the resulting weariness undermining her will to carry on the charade much longer. The worse the Captain could do was throw her overboard, not an all bad prospect.

She shifted uneasily under Chambers' scrutiny, dreading the inevitable line of questions to come.

"You seemed to have gotten on quite famously with Mrs. Littleton and her daughter."

Ah, yes, her traveling companions, the only other passengers. The wife of the new King's Commissioner of Jamaica and their daughter, just coming of age, had been the initial purpose of the *Constancy's* journey. Commissioner Littleton had gone ahead the year before to report to his new post and set up a household. Through some intrigue or *malchance* regarding a Royal Navy ship, exclusive passage had been arranged on the *Constancy* to deliver said family to the Commissioner's waiting arms. They would have, should have been the only passengers, but Cate had arrived at the last minute, coin in hand, eager to leave England. The good Captain Chambers wasn't above a little extra profit, and since they were to be aweigh immediately, no one to be the wiser.

There had been one overshadowing flaw: Mrs. Littleton and Lucy, her daughter, sickened and died barely a month from England's shores.

"They were both very dear," she said, straining to glean the desperation from her voice.

Falling into another one of his torturous pensive pauses, Chambers drew deeply on the cold pipe, the dry rasp sharp over the backdrop of ship and sea.

"We're in pirate waters, now," he said.

"Here?" Startled, Cate looked around, wondering how amid hundreds of miles of ocean this particular track could be different.

"Caicos Passage is just ahead; virtually every ship bound for the Caribbean passes through there. Makes every vessel an easy target, ready for the picking."

"You sound as if you've a bit of experience on your side." she said, scanning the water.

"A bit. I've only been boarded once, and we fought 'em off. We barely made port. Three feet in the well, and only jury-rigged jibs and staysails to fly, but we lived to tell of it."

He stared across the water, seeing far beyond the horizon, his voice shook with uncharacteristic vehemence. "Be bloody goddamned if I was going to allow those black-hearted bastards have my ship. Pardon the language, ma'am," he added, ducking his head.

"They'll take your ship, if they can," he continued, much composed. "And give the crew option to either sign on or join Davy Jones. If one among them is prime for captain, the ship is his and sails as consort. Some have built up nigh on to a fleet. Or, they take what they desire and scuttle her right before your eyes. Couldn't allow that to happen to the old girl, either way," he said, lovingly stroking the rail.

"So, you fought them off?" she asked with growing interest.

"Wasn't easy, mind. I'll carry the scars to my grave. We lost our share of men; we figured we were all as good as dead, anyway. Most vile, black-souled, murderous lot you'd ever face. They'd kill their own mother for the gold in her teeth. They don't call 'em sea wolves for nothing; like a pack of rabid dogs, they are."

He contemptuously spat over the rail. Mr. Ivy, the First Mate, softly cleared his voice, indicating ship's business. While Chambers was thus occupied, she slipped away.

Her cabin was a rabbit-hole of a place: a bunk and the necessary foot space to reach it. She threw open the port and inhaled deeply. Compared to the heat, stench and stuffiness of below deck, the night air was exhilarating. Thanks to the steadiness of trade winds, the cabin had been to windward for most of the voyage, allowing her a bit of moving air when the seas allowed it to be open.

The lantern's golden halo curved up and down the bulkhead as it swung. She pulled a small, often-mended bag from its hiding place between wall and mattress. As was her evening ritual, she set its contents with reverential care before her: a hairbrush — actually a discarded horse brush, but serviceable — and a tin can containing several pebbles — a tried-and-true alarm for one sleeping alone — a needle, its tip secured in a bit of cork, and a stick with a length of thread wound around. A few bits of ribbon lay at the bottom. Too short to be of any use, they were treasured for their color and silkiness, as reminders of a genteel life.

A piece of green - and - white tartan was next, the colors of Clan Mackenzie. Shrinking with the passing of each year, it had been cut from her husband's plaid. Wrapped inside was a shard of broken mirror. In the flickering light, she gazed into the fragment. Barely the size of her palm, she held it first one way and then another, in order to view her entire face. It wasn't an exercise of vanity, but to see if someone looked back.

Haggard and thin, a face there was barely familiar. The eyes — a blue-green color to which no one could ever assign a name — showed the merest spark of life. Her brambled hair defied description as well: copper or brown? Her father had compared it to his favorite blood-bay mare, her husband referring to it as "time-mellowed cherrywood." The wide brow was the same, as was the mouth, its corners still tending to curl independently into a smile. It was a trait which had brought many a reprimand for impertinence in her youth.

A few coppers, a couple of wood buttons, all just for the sake of possession, the last two items were the most treasured: a *sgian dhu*, a stocking knife, and a bit of parchment folded. She clasped the knife's staghorn handle, recalling its warmth from her husband's hand upon presenting it to her. Crackling to the point of near disintegration, the parchment's contents was too precious to be opened, lest the strands of auburn hair, snipped off their last night together, be lost. She pressed the paper to her cheek and closed her eyes to conjure his image once more.

There were no tears; those had been used up long ago. Dry-eyed, she reverently returned each token to the bag, blew out the light and curled on the bunk around what was left of her life.

⌘

Rough crossings.

The term had been heard many times, but Cate had only a vague inkling as to its meaning. She had listened to the stories of violent storms, towering rogue waves capable of smashing masts into kindling, and winds that could pick up a piece of said kindling and drive it through the next mast. There was no reason to doubt such testimonials, but the most intemperate weather she had thus far experienced had been a several days, thin drizzle, the sails hanging as limp as her sodden hair.

Now the day came with howling winds shrieking through every crevice and waves that pitched the ship from dizzying heights to plunging depths, often seemingly at the same time. Nature now seemed determined to make a point of showing the extent of its benevolence of these weeks past. Cate's first lesson was the importance of the berth's raised edge, that single plank her sole salvation from being thrown to the floor. If she didn't wish to roll about like a pencil, she was obliged to plant a foot against the bulkhead and jam a shoulder into the opposite corner. Luckily, she wasn't given to sea illness, but she was very conscious of the peril in closing her eyes.

Braced against the bulkhead, she worked hand-over-hand down the narrow passage to the mess area. The men ordinarily took their meals on deck, preferring the fresh air to the cramped spaces 'tween decks but, in deference to the storm, ate below. Her nose pinched at the combined smells of wet men, fried fish, beer and bilge. Lounged and perched on every surface, they balanced their battered trenchers on their knee, eating and chatting, riding out the weather with the same ease as most rode a horse.

If they're calm, I'm calm, she thought stubbornly.

With both hands for the ship, she gingerly tiptoed through the maze of benches and outstretched legs on her way to the captain's table, the men nodding in amused politeness as she lurched past. Once landed on the bench, remaining there required a foot hooked around the leg. The men at the table dutifully rose at her arrival, ducked the briefest of nods, and then settled back to their meal.

As a paying guest, she ate at the captain's table with Ivy, the first mate; Coombs, the boatswain; Sullivan, the supercargo, and Humphries. An albino, Humphries loved the sea, but the sun had proven too brutal for his pale skin, and so he had found his niche as the Captain's steward. Nicknamed "Mole," it was difficult to say whether the appellation was prompted by the fact that he rarely came from below or his remarkably small round eyes — disquietingly pinkish — and bucked teeth.

She ate out of obligation. To do otherwise would be an insult to Chambers' hospitality. Eating her fill wasn't an issue; for the best part of five years, food had been a sparse commodity, any ort to be portioned out to last for days. Such entrenched behavior was difficult to break. The food was much better than anticipated. Mr. Grogan, the cook, prided his creativity, but there was still a limit as to what could be done with the basics of cheese, dried fruit, peas, pickled and salted beef, pork or fish, with the occasional augmentation of fresh turtle. Her lack of appetite added its own layer of monotony.

"We have rats that eat more," Chambers had observed early on. "Don't be expecting a reduction in your fare, just because you've ate so little."

The jibe was made good-naturedly enough, but his point was made.

Grogan gave her a suffering look as he came around the table. An Irishman with an elf-like face on a hogshead body, he walked the pitching decks with mind-boggling ease in spite of his peg leg. One hand was perpetually occupied by a handkerchief with which to mop his red face.

As with most mornings, Grogan stood pugnaciously at Chambers' elbow, overseeing the meal. The moment she sat, he gestured impatiently to Fitzgibbons for the tarred leather tankard before her to be filled. A Lowland Scot, Fitzgibbons was a gangling lad, with a face full of spots and sooty smudges of hair on his lip.

"You're late," Grogan sniffed.

"I beg your leave," Cate murmured over her ale.

Grogan was a strong advocate of the benefits of small ale for one's digestion first thing of a morning. The drink was palatable enough, but she longed for the bracing effects of a good cup of coffee.

With the hatches bonneted against the weather, the lamps were lit in spite of it being daytime. As they pendulumed over the table, the dinnerware performed a nautical ballet back and forth. The table's lip prevented the plates from shooting off. The men's hands followed what they sought with a second-natured ease. Grumbling under her breath, Cate snatched at a bowl as it passed. Mr. Ivy, at her elbow, ducked his head to hide a smirk.

"Nor'easter," he said into his drink. "Storm blowin' up on the Banks."

She knew of only one "Banks": the Great Banks, rich fishing waters off the coast of Newfoundland.

"Isn't that leagues away?" she asked.

He nodded approvingly at her token bit of sea-going

knowledge, the unspoken implication being perhaps her lubberiness wasn't a total lost cause.

"Coupla hundred, aye, but 'tis nothing to stop a wave out here," he added, gesturing with his tankard toward the unseen beyond.

She had been aware of the conversation taking a sudden shift when she entered. It was a common occurrence. Cursing or coarseness didn't bother her—five brothers and husband had all possessed a very colorful turn - of - the - tongue—but the men assumed as much. Once she was seated and quiet, they would soon come to forget she was there, and the dialogue would return to its natural state. Such conversation always took the same path: speculation on how far they had traveled, when to expect to make land, past voyages, and ultimately working around to storms, best and worst captains, mysteries of the deep, and inevitably, pirates.

Pirates.

The word conjured images of something between sinister mythological creatures of the sea and marauding thieves. In London, she had heard of hangings at Tyburn, their piked heads and tarred, rotting bodies left in public display of the fate which awaited anyone who chose a similar, lowly path. There had been literary attempts to idealize them, but their corruption and savagery were difficult to whitewash. Unwholesome dregs of society that, unfit to live among the civilized, had chosen to live as drunken scavengers. Violence, mayhem and gore seemed the pirate trinity. Life having already served up far too much of that for her tastes, she felt little tolerance or sympathy toward them.

Cate toyed with the dried apple slices and claret-soaked currents on her plate, trying not to focus on its motion. The metered passes had a mesmerizing effect. Blinking from one such trance, she straightened and focused her interest on the conversation.

"How do you know someone is a pirate?" she asked during a lull.

"He'll be the one holding the knife to your throat," Fitzgibbons grinned as he plunked fresh pitchers of ale on the table.

The men hunched forward with enthusiasm, their tales involving such dubious names as Black Bart Roberts, Long Ben Avery, Stede Bonnet, Calico Jack Rackham, and Blackbeard.

"A man signs on as soon as he boards, a-swearin' to the ship's Code," said Coombs around a mouthful. "Equal shares for everything that's taken—*everything*." A meaningful arch of his brows emphasized his point.

"Aye, 'tis true." Ivy leaned closer. "Blackbeard hisself took a wife; shared her with the entire crew. T'weren't enough left for the cabin boys after that."

"The captain gets double, o' course," added Coombs judiciously. "And then so on down the line, from First Mate to the lowest."

The finer details of such a fate for the unknowing bride flashed quickly through her mind.

"Everything?" she asked a bit faintly.

"Everything!" came a chorus of voices. A clap of thunder punctuated the chilling thought.

She quietly put down her fork, what little appetite she had suddenly gone. She dabbed her temples. With barely headroom to stand and stores stacked in every nook, under the best of circumstances the mess area was close quarters. Now, with the hatches closed against the weather and the mass of bodies mixed with the smell of fish, treacle, bilges and beer, the air became oppressing.

In the midst of the sagas and tales, one name continued to dominate the conversation: Captain Nathanael Blackthorne.

It couldn't be overlooked that Blackthorne was something of an exception. As regularly as his name came up, the reaction was always the same: spitting and touching of their charms, making horned signs as if he were the Devil incarnate, while lauding him praises that rendered him almost mystical. A bit of competition almost always ensued in reference to Blackthorne, each participant striving to best his predecessor with stories about the man, each weaving another thread into a thicker cloth that made up what could only be seen as a legend.

"Charmed he is," Humphries said importantly. "'Tis like a guardian angel a-watchin' over him. Been shot thirteen times."

"And wears a bell for every virgin he's taken," called a voice from a dim corner.

"Others claim he can beckon the sea," Humphries went on, "Neptune and all his creatures. Some say it's just pure dern delight Blackthorne takes in makin' a fool outa the Commodore."

A hum of approval came from all around.

"Stole a ship o' the line, by making them think there was wharf fever aboard," put in one from the table behind her.

"Ol' Nathan had taken the Royal pay chest." Coomb's cornflower eyes brightened at the thought of such riches. "The Commodore tore up the waters for months trying to get it back. Finally, he out-foxed Ol' Nathan and got it. The Commodore held a big ceremony at Fort Charles, had the Governor and all the muckety-mucks there. Come time to open it, t'was full o' rotten horsemeat and a note congradulatin' the Commodore on his successes, signed Captain Nathanael Blackthorne!"

The roar of laughter filled the small space, their enthusiastic appreciation for such chicanery punctuated by the pounding of fists and utensils.

"Blackthorne's been a-tweekin' Creswicke's nose and tauntin' Harte, makin' fools o' the both of 'em," said Coombs over the scream of the wind.

"Royal West Indies Mercantile Company, Lord Breaston Creswicke, Governor; that's the power in these waters," Chambers said coldly. "Not a captain, honest or otherwise, don't feel the weight of their yoke, most especially Blackthorne."

"I should have thought the East India Trading Company would have had something to say about them," she said.

It was no secret that the East India Trading Company was all-powerful, ruling the seas' trading lanes with an iron fist on the one hand and an endorsement directly from Parliament and the King in the other. Virtually nothing came or went from England's shores without their stamp of approval.

Ivy snorted in disgust, gesturing sharply with his knife. "Not enough in these waters to entice them thus far. That blessed Lord Creswicke managed a charter from the Crown. What with the Crown always looking to turn a coin..."

"And Creswicke has certainly given them that!" Chambers broke in with unfamiliar vehemence. "Between port tariffs, docking, drayage, wharfage, piloting, victualling fees and the like, a soul can barely make a profit."

They shifted uncomfortably, glancing furtively over their shoulders as if they expected the fiend to materialize.

"Extortion is what it is," Ivy grumbled darkly over his plate.

"And lo unto the one what tries to slip a bondsman past him!" Coombs intoned. "And if someone is so bold as to complain or evade, he'll be boarded within the week."

"Boarded? You're saying that it's more than coincidence?" she asked, looking from one man to the next.

"Oh, aye!" Ivy gave a conspiratorial wink. "Pirates, for sure. Complain a little more, and be declared a pirate yourself, dancin' the hempen jig for yer efforts."

"Just don't scrape the paint too hard on the ship, nor ask to see her log. Ye might be findin' out what's more than healthy," Chambers said, exchanging knowing looks with his crew.

"Or a quick-like visit to Davy Jones," said Ivy.

Her evident failure to comprehend brought Ivy to bend closer. "There be pirates in these waters, to be sure, Blackthorne bein' one o' the best. But one can't help but notice that several are a mite peculiar."

"Privateers," hissed Coombs over his porridge.

"Pah! White-water pirates, bought and paid for by Lord Creswicke," Humphries said, tapping his spoon on the table.

Cate looked from one man to the other, confused. "But I thought you said that Creswicke... or, the Company was killing pirates."

"Aye!" Ivy nodded, chewing industriously. "But the best way to be a good physick is to supply the very illness what you know how to cure."

"What better way to keep everyone under your thumb than to scare them into thinkin' they ain't safe without you?" Humphries asked around a mouthful of porridge. "Including the Crown!"

"To make himself to appear more important and successful, Creswicke has his own fleet of pirates..." Sullivan said, reaching for the pot of treacle.

"Sailing on the very ships he's confiscated..." Coombs said into his drink.

"And selling the plunder for a very nice profit," finished Ivy. "And London is thinking the only way to protect their shipments is to give Creswicke more of whatever he wants to fight off the pirates."

"Surely someone has complained," she said.

Ivy's feathery brows shot up as he stabbed another kipper from the platter. "To who? If the Company succeeds, England succeeds. Lord-on-High Pelham and King Georgie aren't going to tamper with what's bringing them a sack full o' money. There be rumors of war again, and the Crown will be lookin' for every pound it can lay its hands on."

"And the Royal Navy's high command in these waters is of no disposition to listen or intervene," put in Chambers grimly around the stem of his pipe.

"Aye!" Sullivan smirked. "Harte can't hear anything over the rattle of Creswicke's coin in his pockets."

"Harte?" she asked, fork hovering over her plate.

"His Lordship Roger Harte, Commodore of His Majesty's Royal Navy!" Humphries announced striking an imperious pose.

"So Blackthorne works for the Company and this Creswicke?" she asked, still straining to follow.

Derisive laughter burst from all.

"Creswicke hates Ol' Blackthorne with a passion what goes beyond human. No one knows exactly what it was all about, one of those blood feuds that run for a lifetime. Blackthorne hasn't done hisself any favors," Ivy pointed out with a warning wag of the finger. "He's robbed, ransomed, hostaged, pillaged, and plundered. Cost the Company a fair bit o' profit, that one has."

"And made fools of Commodore Harte *and* Lord Creswicke," Humphries said, snickering into his ale.

The storm exhausted itself by midday, the clouds withdrawing to reveal a remarkable day. Cate stood at the rail smiling. Life appeared above and below, giving a sense that perhaps the ship hadn't fallen off the Earth after all. With nothing but weeks of wave and sky, one readily came to believe the world had been swept away in a flood of biblical proportions. The speck of a bird high overhead was proof that something else still existed. A high point was a school of small, greenish-silver fish swimming alongside, or coming upon a great mass of seaweed teeming with myriads of small crabs and jellyfish.

For all its adventuresome sound, the bare truth was that sailing was insufferably boring, a mind-numbing constancy of sky and water. Caught between the dread of what awaited at Port Royal and the staggering boredom of the sea, the desire for land was beginning to win. The ship's time was marked by watch bells, a baffling sequence of peals which she soon grew to ignore, measuring time instead by the sun or moon. As the bells counted off the hours—two rings not necessarily meaning two o'clock—she spent vast amounts of time contemplating the different aspects of waves: how one compared to another, compared to those from the day or week before. When Cate's neck grew stiff with looking down, she looked up through the rigging and sails, and sought hidden shapes in the clouds. At night, she gazed through the port to see how much farther the North Star had shifted since the night before. Too dark, too cold, too tired or too wet were her motivations to retire to a cramped bunk, where she stared out the porthole at the stars, waiting for some shift in the universe to change them.

Idleness having never been her nature, she had tried to become more involved with the ship itself, but soon surrendered in the face of a language that defied comprehension: cat's head, sheave holes, cheek blocks, cringles, fish pendants, and lizards, with a fore bowline not to be confused with the foretop bowline, which was entirely different from the foretop gallant bowline. She was only slightly confused at being told—with little patience—that there were no ropes on a ship; those things hanging everywhere were called sheets. Let one not overlook, however, that a sheet could be a tack, a simple change in the wind making it a leech.

And so, Cate watched the antics of a troop of sea hogs cavorting in the curve of the bow wave. Their silvery backs arching through the indigo water, they almost seemed to smile up at her before streaking away, only to return to frolic alongside once more. She shielded her eyes from the sun to watch a small covey of birds, their black, tapered bodies sharp against the sky. Swooping, they touched their feet to the water, hovered, and then spiraled skyward.

Chambers came beside her and inclined his head toward the birds. "Mother Carey's chickens; the wife of Davy Jones. They fly forever, never touching land, hatching their eggs under their wings. Harbingers of storms they are: the more you see, the worse the storm is to be. They say the sea hogs will lead a shipwrecked mariner to shore. If they leap entirely out of the water, 'tis a gale coming."

"You say that as if you don't believe it," she said, intent on the fish.

Her experience with mariner's superstitions had begun early. The day she purchased passage, she had been hustled aboard, Chambers anxious to weigh anchor that day, since the next was the thirteenth of the month, and no ship sailed on such a date. Sharks had been sighted at the stern "smelling death." The subsequent fever and death of Mrs. Littleton and her daughter came as no surprise, and was met with not a little relief. Their bodies were quickly commended to the sea, being bad luck to have them aboard. Women aboard was the worst of luck. The tension had failed to lessen with the passing of the Littletons. One would have thought fewer women would be good news, but it was quickly pointed out that two people had just died. What stronger proof of bad luck did one require?

Calypso, a woman, was goddess of the sea, her name often invoked for protection, as was St. Bride. The bowsprit was the bare-busted figure of a woman, mermaids—harbingers of good luck—were the hope of every sailor, and the ship was referred to as "she." And yet, women were bad luck.

It defied all logic, but made perfect sense to the men. Not much more could be said.

Chambers' shoulders moved faintly under his coat. "I've been at sea since I was a squeaker near Fitzgibbons' age. I've seen enough to know anything is possible, and nothing is impossible. Whether by the hand of God, or some other power, who's to know? This humble soul is in no position to question."

He stood quietly watching the fish, falling into one of those pensive silences of his that always left her feeling a bit off kilter.

"We'll be making Kingston in three, mebbe four days."

The announcement was a bit redundant. It had been the subject of conversation every meal since sinking England. Still, the prospect of the seemingly endless journey coming to an end left her feeling a bit odd.

And then what?

"We'll be putting on cargo — molasses and sugar and such — bound for the Virginia Colony." He drew thoughtfully on the cold pipe. The green eyes darted from the fish briefly to her and back. "I was thinking... perhaps if your brother has no place for you, I have a sister there in the Colonies, with a household. I was thinking perhaps if you wished...?"

The suggestive lilt in his voice said everything else. A cold pit grew in her stomach, Cate's knuckles whitening as she gripped the rail. "How long have you known?"

Chambers smiled around the pipestem. "If there's one thing you learn at sea, it's to judge a person. You're running from a husband?" He pointed his gaze at her wedding ring, the silver gleaming as brightly as the dolphins.

"No, not exactly." She protectively clutched her ring. His concern seemed sincere, but she worried of how far he intended to probe.

A cry came from the foretop followed by Mr. Ivy appearing at Chambers' elbow.

"Beg pardon. Sail, sir."

"Where away?"

"Larboard quarter astern."

The news was received with no more than the lift of a sandy brow. More revealing was the flexing of his jaw muscles and lips tightening to white around the pipe.

"Tell your man there's an extra half-ration if he's correct. The eyes can play tricks on a man out here; no sense in rewarding false alarms."

Heart pounding, Cate's attention had swiveled instantly to the horizon behind them. It was one of those days when the running seas took them to the top of the world one moment, only to be surrounded by water the next. The ship maddeningly seemed doomed to the latter just then, a wall of deep blue blocking her view.

Chambers looked up once more at the soaring petrels. "Seems they brought a storm after all."

Reports came throughout the day. The moment finally came when the *Constancy* and the distant ship crowned a wave simultaneously, and Cate saw the ship for the first time. A speck barely the size of her thumbnail, the sails stood strikingly white against the backdrop of deep-colored ocean and gunmetal clouds. The next instant it was gone, leaving her to wonder if she had actually seen it or, after having strained for so long, her eyes and imagination had obliged.

Cate closed her eyes. The image was there. It was no figment.

Once seen, the ship was twice alluring, and she stood through the intervals of watch bells, waiting and watching. As wind and water allowed, she spotted it, always at the same angle, always incrementally closer.

In the last rays of daylight, Chambers sent a man aloft with the spyglass, pacing the decks until the report finally came in breathless, eye-rolling gasps.

"'Tis the *Sarah Morgan*, sir!"

"By what means?"

"Black ship with blood dripping the sails, sir."

"Blackthorne's ship," was Ivy's whispered aside to Cate. "Her decks run red with the blood of her victims. She's carried on the back of Calypso."

"Nay, 'tis Neptune hisself, a-risin' on a prodigious sea-horse a-pullin' her. I spoke with a tar what seen it with his own two eyes," came from somewhere behind her.

Chambers swore an uncharacteristic obscenity as he looked aft. An awed murmur emitted from those nearby and word echoed down the deck. He glanced west toward the impending sunset and then told Ivy "Douse the lamps. They've spotted us, but no sense in advertising our whereabouts. They'll lay off for a bit to size us up," he explained to her questioning look. "See who we are, how we're armed or if we're worth taking. 'Course, it could be just another ship, crossing paths. It happens," he added without conviction.

It seemed a blessed unlikely proposition: since sighted, the ship had veered straight for them like a hound on a hare.

"We can only pray for a dirty night in which to hide. Otherwise, we're as plain as a... a... as black on white," he finally managed to a stumbling conclusion.

Contrary to Chambers' hopes, the night was regrettably clean with friendly winds and forgiving seas, the water no more than a rustle at the hull. Once the sails were reefed and trimmed for the night, the decks fell quiet, leaving everyone with nothing but their own thoughts. Sails aglow in the moonlight, the pirate ship was easily spotted, steady and constant as an ever-nearing North Star.

The crewmen off-duty hunched on the hatch grates. There was no pretext of merriment. The grog ration proved woefully inadequate at lifting their spirits; if anything, they grew more melancholy. On land or sea, a storyteller was worth his weight in gold. The cook served the body, but the storyteller kept the spirit. The *Constancy's* resident narrator was a man by the name of Barnstable, also the ship's eldest. A remarkably deep orator's voice emitted from his spare, horse-faced frame. The men tended to follow him like chicks after a hen to perch around him, eagerly settling in for the evening's entertainment. In desperate need of distraction, Cate hung nearby to listen.

That night, Barnstable was in his glory. With a mind like the Library of Alexandria, he called upon his cornucopia of pirate tales. Each darker than the one before, his stories painted a picture of violence and inhumanity which bordered on madness. The individual pirates became lost in a jumble of barely familiar names, some remarkable only by virtue of their horrific uniqueness: Low, who cut off a man's lips and cooked them in front of him; Montbars, who nailed a captive's gut to a tree and then made him dance.

And then, there was Morgan. Harboring a hatred of women, he had married fourteen times, throwing each overboard when he was finished with them.

Cate shuddered and not from the chill in the air. "Vile and inhuman," she aloud.

"'Tisn't the half of it, missus," said Sullivan with a roll of his eyes. "If only that were all. Heaven help any woman what's taken by those slavering curs."

Cate stepped on deck the next morning and her knees sagged. When last seen, the pirate ship had been a foreboding blotch in the night. Now it loomed large.

The ship unfurled her banner into the sun's early rays, panic surged. Larger than the ship's asymmetrical aftersail, the massive black banner bore a white skull with a rakishly angled halo framed angel wings.

One of the men swore vehemently. "It's the *Sarah Morgan*." He swore again and spit, making horned signs with his fingers. "Blackthorne's ship."

"It's his flag," said Ivy, resigned. "The Angel of Death.

Not even the *Dutchman* can catch her. Ol' Blackthorne's outrun the Devil."

"Some say he *is* the Devil," hissed Barnstable.

There was no further discussion. Meaningful looks were exchanged agreeing not to unduly alarm her. She appreciated the concern, but it was a bit late.

In many ways, seeing the *Sarah Morgan* up close was a relief. No expert on ships, Cate knew beauty when she saw it and the ship was all of that. Three-masted, with elevated stern and forecastles, she was a bit of a throwback to another era. With an ornate roundhouse and bowsprit, she was by no means fancy or ostentatious. But she was a glorious vessel, nonetheless, a lady who knew the value of discretion in her appointments.

In spite of the forewarning, the sight of blood dripping from her deck and sails was still disconcerting. On closer inspection—and small application of logic—the tops had been reddened, but certainly not with blood; it would have taken butchering of several oxen to manage that. Instead of the traditional bands of colored trim, the sanguineous drool between the gunports was actually red paint.

With her guns staring like eyes, the ship was very much alive, exuding a palpable presence.

"Sixteen pounders," announced Coombs at Cate's elbow, nodding toward the black maws. "She outranges our nine-pounders by a good measure. Another reason Ol' Black Nate prefers his big ship: those guns would shake apart anything smaller."

He made a skeptical noise, shaking his head. "Goddamned difficult to fight when we can't even get close enough to strike, beggin' yer pardon, Ma'am."

Cate now knew what it was to be in the water with a shark. She made a game of how long she could go without looking, all the while knowing the longer she held out the closer the ship would be, her sails a little larger, the details of her rigging a little clearer. At one point, she turned to find instead of squarely astern the ship had slipped off to one side.

"What are they doing?"

"Going for our wind," Chambers said with measured gravity. "He'll come around behind, starve our wind and..." His fingers snapped in finality.

"Can't you just sail faster?"

He laughed, a little derisive and a lot pained. "We're heavy and she's light. We're out-sailed, out-gunned and out-manned. We've uncaulked the gunports, but to what purpose? If we show one gun, she could rake us. If we surrender, I might be able to negotiate... something." The green eyes darted guiltily toward her and then away.

The black ship's aftmost gun belched smoke, the retort reaching the *Constancy* a fraction before the ball splashed harmlessly astern. Another was fired across her forefoot.

"Warning shots," growled Chambers. "The next ones will find home."

Time. It was all the *Morgan* required to draw closer. Looming larger and larger, her yards and sails towered over the lesser ship. As if gut-punched, the *Constancy* suddenly staggered and then slowed. Sails sagging, her substance-of-life was robbed, her wind gone.

"Helm's a-lee! Douse the tops and lay 'er in irons!"

Sails luffing, *Morgan* drew up and sat like a dark huntress. Cate knew little of sailing, but could appreciate the seamanship involved as the black ship slowed at the *Constancy's* exact rate, the red-crowned sails blanketing her wind.

"Stay by me." Chambers' impassioned voice drew her attention. "They'll take the ship, so there's no sense in you hiding. Perhaps, if you're with us... me... I... we might afford you protection, at least for a bit." He gulped and added bitterly, "If I had the stomach for it, I'd end it for you now. But I'm not that much of a man."

All hands gathered amidships. The weapons earlier dispersed were collected and displayed on the deck before them, notably still within reach should there be treachery. Cate, as did everyone, craned her neck, searching the pirate ship, hoping for a first glimpse of her famed captain, but no single one seemed to stand out. Her decks teemed with men, so many, many men.

Time could indeed be an unmerciful enemy. Cate's heart hammered to deafening proportions, breathing was no longer a natural thing. By the time the longboats drew alongside and hooked on, she was in a complete state. Wiping her palms on her skirt, she discovered that in spite of the tropical sun she was swathed in a cold sweat. Every bone in her body screamed to run, but where? She scanned the horizon, expecting to see only water and was surprised. So preoccupied with the pirate ship, she hadn't noticed the thin line of green marking an island, the first land in over two months.

So near, and yet so very, very far.

"Hoy on deck?"

Cate jerked at the baritone call from alongside.

"Pray pass. We are unarmed," was Chambers' level response.

All vows of bravery dissolved at the sight of the pirates pouring up the side. Circling like a pack of predatory wolves, they were bizarre, many half-naked. What set these men apart was the bristle of weapons and the ease with which they brandished them. She had seen her share of thieves and murderers; never had she witnessed such en masse collection of sinister depravity. Eyes glowing with the prospect of prey, they sniffed for the first weakness, restrained only by the thin leash of decorum. Coiled for attack, they brought the smell of sweat, rum and gunpowder.

"How do you know if someone is a pirate?"

Cate knew now the naiveté of that query. Like a poisonous snake, you knew one when you saw it.

She fell back a step. Chambers squared his shoulders and sidestepped before her. The pack leader stepped forward. He scanned the Constancies, ultimately settling on Chambers.

"My name be Ezekiel Pryce, Quartermaster and First Mate of the *Carrie Morgans.*"

Cate glanced about, but no one seemed to take notice of the disparity in the ship's name.

Barrel-chested with sharp grey eyes, Pryce's bearing made him seem taller than his slightly above average height. In one hand he bore a pistol nearly the length of his arm, a cutlass in the other. Gleaming in the morning sun, its ornate basket and gold filigree a stark contrast against his otherwise inelegance.

"Captain Nathaniel Blackthorne sends his compliments."

"Mordecai Chambers, master of the *Constancy.* Your servant, sir." He ducked an abbreviated bow. "What measures might be taken to spare my crew and ship?"

"We seek captives." The announcement was made with the same casualness of ordering ale. The keen eyes fixed on Cate, a cat zeroing in on a mouse. "Women, to be exact."

Now tucked behind Chambers, Cate felt the weight of every pirate eye. In the face of pistol and sword, she was grateful for his protection, but a fragile shield he was.

"We're a merchant. We've no passengers," Chambers replied, adding offhandedly, "There's none here, except my wife."

Cate held up her hand to exhibit her wedding ring, widening her eyes for an added bit of innocence.

"We were told there would be women," Pryce said unperturbed. If anything, he appeared to have expected a ploy of some sort.

"Then you were told wrong."

"Cap'n's expectin' wimmen." Pryce's glare hardened. "Give 'em now, and you'll be given quarter."

"I assure you," Chambers began. "We've no...."

Somewhere between annoyed and bored, Pryce angled his head. "Get 'er."

Cate yelped in surprise at being roughly snatched from behind. A forearm around her neck brought her up hard against her captor. She cried out again at her arm being given a cruel twist up behind her back. A low growl of protest came from the Constancies but died quickly in their throats.

Pryce stepped closer to Cate and inhaled loudly. "Ah, the smell of a woman!" He dramatically rolled his eyes. "'Tis been a long time, has it not, gents?"

The pirates' leering snickers and a cackling laugh set her skin crawling.

"We were told there would be a Commissioner's wife." Pryce raked Cate with the same appraising eye as one might survey a horse. "A might young, but fair enough. There should be a daughter, as well."

"She's none of those," said Chambers in a low voice. "The Littleton women died a month ago."

"Aye, as sure as black's the white o' me eye," sneered Pryce.

Pryce gave the barest of nods. A Chinaman stepped before her. Half a head taller than she, his broad features were stony save for the cold glint in the near-black eyes. He drew a knife and brandished it, so the wicked thing gleaming in the sunlight. With its elegantly curved hilt and blade, if one were an admirer of knives it would have been considered a beauty. Cate, however, had a particular loathing for knives, any wielded blade. She jerked, but was held firmly as the tip came to rest at the hollow of her throat. The grasp on her arm tightened until the bones were ground together.

"He'll be the one holding a knife to your throat." Fitzgibbons' prophecy was too ironic.

Cate held her breath, afraid to move.

"Get 'em," Pryce demanded.

"There. Is. No. One." Chambers said, now somewhere behind her.

Pryce drew an annoyed breath. Another bare nod and the knife slipped to the edge of Cate's bodice. There was a slight pressure, and then the soft sound of fabric ripping and the periodic pop of laces. She felt the cold sting of the blade brushing one breast. She twisted, her shoulder burning from the horrific angle of her arm. The progress of the knife could be tracked in the reflection of the flat black eyes. As her exposure increased, the pirates snickered, leering.

"Can't imagine what sort o' gent would be a-wishin' to see his wife naked out here for all to see. Can't be a promisin' what might happen. 'Tis been a good while since we've made port, has it not, mates?" said Pryce.

"You damned bloody bastards," rumbled Chambers.

Pryce's laugh boomed across the deck. "Damned and bastards, indeed. Motherless to the man. Perhaps t'were the lack of mother's milk what rendered us so heartless."

Cate's cheek was tight against the pirate's sweat-slickened chest. His hot breath on her neck quickened with excitement, the hard body straining against hers. He stunk of sun-baked sweat and rising lust. A droplet of moisture—saliva or sweat—dripped on her chest and began a slow journey downward. She squirmed; the arm at her neck tightened. Her blood pulsed and her eyeballs grew tight, as if too large for their sockets.

She slid a sideways look to where the Constancies stood and saw everything from ashen-faced fear to quaking with pent rage. Some looked to the weapons piled before them, measuring their chances. A few looked caught short, as if their bowels had gone to liquid. Ivy bore a bullish scowl. Fitzsimmons gaped as if seeing his first circus.

The rush of her own breathing filled her ears. She swung from one emotion to another, one overpowering the next: fear, anger, mortification, resentment and above all, rage, pure, devouring, gut-tearing rage. She strove to remain calm, in order to measure her options. Bite? Kick? Claw? Run? There were wretchedly few, and each instantly dismissed as futile.

All rational thought dissolved under a wave of panic. From deep in her gut, it surged like a rising tide, each wave stronger than the last. The sweating brute holding her merged with others from another time, when the press of slavering male, restraints, the bite of steel and the smell of her own blood had been a part of a nightmarish scene. The knife inched lower and her belly contracted in recollection of abuse and mutilation by another blade.

She writhed. The knife nicked her ribs and the bubble burst. She screamed, high-pitched and piercing, aiming it directly into her captor's ear. He and the Chinaman jerked and fell back. The grip on her loosened and she wrenched free, ripping the last bit of her bodice. She scooped up a cutlass from the pile on the deck. Swiping up and out as she rose, she caught the Chinaman in the leg with the first swipe. He went down with a surprise, high, thin yowl.

The Constancies had taken her cue and seized their weapons. The entire deck was now in full motion. From all around came the clash and mayhem of hand-to-hand fighting. Pistols fired, the air growing thick with smoke and smell of blood. In a two-fisted grasp, Cate slashed from side to side, sending the pirates scattering.

Follow the lead. Anticipate! Focus! she thought, recalling lessons of long ago.

Steel screamed, blade against blade. Pain shot up her arms with each blow. Lacking the strength and skill for offense, defense was her only ploy: swing and block, swing and block, up and block, sideways and block, time to time feeling the impact with flesh. She saw the deck in small vignettes like framed pictures: a storm petrel darting overhead through the forestays, a pirate and a Constancy diving for the same pistol. Another clutched his gut, the blood vibrant between his fingers. A severed finger landed at her feet. In a strange disjointed sort of way, she could see herself: a half-naked, half-crazed woman wielding a sword.

The pirates maneuvered to circle her, lunging at every chance. Dodging their clutching grasps, she inched away. Her skirt was yanked, and she stumbled and fell, the back of her head slamming the deck. The surrounding mayhem faded, her stomach knotted, and then lurched as if she was going to vomit. Internal voices screamed for her to move. By some miracle, she still held the sword. She rolled to her knees, and then stood on rubbery legs, blocking and beating back those who came at her.

"For God's sake, run! Don't let yourself be taken!"

As the pirates closed in around her, the warnings grew to screams. Arms burning, she couldn't last much longer. Away, off the ship suddenly seemed the only answer. From the corner of her eye, she saw once more the dark outline of the island.

Run!

Not quite running, but the effect would be the same. She hitched her skirts and leapt for the rail. Seizing a shroud, one of the wrist-thick ropes supporting the mast, she slashed down her pursuers. A blow to the hip spun her around, jerking the thick rope from her grasp. Her skirts tangled in the dead-eyes and she clawed the air. The sky was blocked by the side of the ship going by. She looked up at the stricken pirate faces over the rail...

And then she hit the water.

2: PURGATORY, OR JUST HELL?

Hitting the water was painful. Worse than falling from a speeding horse, the impact knocked Cate's breath away. The sea was surprisingly warm, the comfort she had sought, a mother's embrace. The chaos and smoke now gone; she was enshrouded by the peace so long sought. The weight of her skirts dragged her down and the sun's brilliance faded.

All would be well; it would all be over soon. She bore no fear: as a child, she had been told Heaven meant floating. Spreading her arms as an angel might, she leaned her head back. High overhead, the *Constancy's* keel was a diminishing dark wedge, the pirate boats gathered at her sides like chicks.

Time came in blissful increments. Her heart pulsed, a hollow echo of itself, once... twice... slower... thrice...

A voice, deep and so very familiar, said "Not yet."

She yearned to remain, but knew she must go. It was what he wanted. She allowed the hands, ones she knew as intimately as the voice, to propel her upward, back to the light.

Rough handling shattered her euphoria.

A bit more gentleness was to be expected in the Dear Beyond, she thought crossly, as she was lifted and pulled. As if her complaints had been heard, peace was returned, gently rocking. Her hopes soared anew. She was being taken. This was the journey of which she had been told. Her heart raced with the anticipation of waiting glories, reunions with loved ones.

The journey, however, came to an abrupt end. She was manhandled once more, coarsely passed through a progression of hands. She thrashed in protest, desiring to be returned to the blessed exultation. To be shown such rapture only to have it taken was too cruel. The unpleasantness increased. She was dropped on a hard surface with the same care as the day's catch.

Her senses congealed enough for her to know that she laid half on her stomach, one arm pinned under her in a growing pool of water. The vibration of approaching footsteps was felt through the wood under her cheek.

Through water-clogged ears she heard, "She breathin'?"

"Barely," came in a male voice.

Breathing. Air!

Her chest spasmed, and she was caught between the gurgling wheezes of inhaling, while at the same time retching up sea water and bile.

"Aye, well, she lives now," said the first.

On the small hope that she had been returned to the *Constancy*, she opened her eyes to a sideways view of a deck, but an unfamiliar one. Feet, bare and shod, surrounded her. She looked up into the faces of strangers staring down with expressions of everything from curiosity to bemusement. A touch on the shoulder startled her, and she swung out. With one arm pinned, however, she could only squirm like an exposed worm in the wetness, the feeble efforts bringing a chuckle from the onlookers. The hand returned to run from the crest of her shoulder down her back.

"Great Caesar's ghost, lookit this, Cap'n."

"Bloody hell! What the...?"

"Looks like a sword blade," murmured another voice, gruffer than the first.

"Looks like she's been through a war."

Amid their wonderment and shock, came an inner voice.

"Run!"

She sprang up and fled. In a part of her mind, she sprinted like a startled deer, evading those giving chase. Another part knew she was but floundering, rubbery-legged and heavy-footed. Whether her path was aft or forward she had no notion. Foremost in her mind was the rail and then the water beyond. The pirates readily caught up and ran alongside, herding her away from her goal. Taunting, they plucked and snatched, shouting insults, until she came up against the raised face of the forecastle. She was trapped.

The pirates closed in. She elbowed a tall one in the throat and kneed a smaller in the gut before she was seized and pressed against the wall. Ducking away from the mouths seeking hers, she screamed, a pitiful half-choked thing. They tore at her meager scraps of clothing to grope her breasts and plunge their hands between her legs.

A shout from somewhere amid them caused them to fall back. She was held pinned to the wall as if in presentation to the single man who approached. A scar angled from brow to jaw across his brutish face. The thick braid hanging from the side of his head, studded with beads and bones, swung with his step as he strolled forward. Fondling his crotch, his intent gaze slid from her face downward. She felt sufficient breeze to know one breast was exposed. She angled an eye down to see her belly was bared, revealing the web of scars there. Mortified, she tried to draw up a knee, but it was seized and forced back down.

Scarface's gaze returned to her face. His lips drew back into a leering smirk. "So, you like knives, do ye? I'll part that pretty flesh with somethin' what will make you smile."

Her breath coming in ragged gasps, she thought to spit in his face, but a mouth once filled with seawater had gone dry. He twisted up a handful of her hair in his fist, wrenched her head back and kissed her. His tongue plunged to gagging depths as the onlookers cheered.

"Hold fast. Belay, there! Belay!" came a shout, nearing with each word.

"Aye, Cap'n!" the pirates chorused and fell back, snapping to attention.

Only Scarface held her now. She writhed under him as his assault continued. She caught a glimpse over his shoulder of a face and a thunderous expression.

"Release her, I say. That. Is. An. Order!"

Scarface was jerked away, growling in protest. Now left to stand on her own, Cate swayed and staggered. Her legs folded, and she crumpled to the deck. She tried to push up, but her arms were rubber. Head hanging, her hair in wet snakes about her face, she could only see the feet of the two men squared off over her. Scarface struck a belligerent stance. The "Captain" stood so near, she had to move a hand to keep from being stepped on.

"You bunch of rutting, unhung, clam-for-brains. Your mates are over there risking their asses for your pockets and all you can think of is your quim-wedges?" bellowed the Captain.

Something was dropped on her. A coat. She clutched it, rolling into it like a crab into its shell. A violent siege of coughing overtook her; the two men's words came only in broken spurts. Their tone was telling enough: Scar-face's defiant, the Captain's furious.

"She's a hostage, not plunder. Can't you bunch of slavering curs remember that or did your brains drain into your cockstands?" the Captain shouted.

She was jerked to her feet. Much to her relief, it was the Captain who propelled her from behind, catching her when she stumbled. Unlike the flush decks of the *Constancy*, this ship had a raised afterdeck and cabin. It was there she was taken.

"What cursed piece o' slime fouled that goddamned deck. Swabbers!" came a bone-penetrating bellow from outside as she was shoved inside.

Stumbling, she caught herself on a mast which passed from the ceiling down through the floor.

"Stow yourself over there," he said, pointing to a far corner.

She squinted into the cavern-like room. She had the impression of dark walls, but it was impossible to see past the blaze of sunlight streaming through the skylight. Shielding her eyes against the glare, she felt her way around to where she had been sent. Every few steps she was stopped by a gurgling hack of a violence which seemed to originate from somewhere near her toes.

"And put a stopper in your gob. I can't abide a yammering woman."

On deck he had been but a blur. Her eyes still unaccustomed to the darkness, he was no more than a dark blot against the light. Still, she could feel his malignant glare. Light-headed from coughing, she thought to at least nod an acknowledgment, but even that small gesture threatened to be an affront. She stood gripping her elbows against the shivering which now beset her.

The light failed long before it reached the room's corners, but it felt considerably larger than Chambers' cabin. Under the skylight sat a large curve-legged table. Its surface was barely visible under the clutter of paraphernalia and charts, their curled edges weighted by everything from a candle sconce to something that resembled a dried cloven hoof. Pencils, dividers and all manner of navigational tools were scattered about as well. The captain stood there now, over a chart. Head bent, he walked the dividers across the parchment, the fingers of his other hand tapping the wood as if in calculation.

While he was thus occupied, she wormed her arms into the sleeves of the coat and nestled deeper into it. It smelled of male and sweat, with undertones of orange oil and cinnamon. Styled without lapels, the deep cuffs reached nearly to her elbows, the coat had the feel of having once lived a life of privilege. As her eyes adjusted to the darkness, she could trace its original rich burgundy where soutache or other decorations had once laid. Now faded to the point of near colorlessness, the garment bore few embellishments other than horn buttons.

The knife scrape on her breast burned horribly. She twitched at the sting of the nicks on her ribs and belly. Water dripped from her, pattering on the floor with the regularity of a ticking clock. She ventured a hand to wipe the wetness from her face, quickly tucking it back into the coat before the movement was noticed. The tremors increased, threatening to tear her joints, with the realization of what had just happened, or nearly so. She kept a sharp eye both on the captain and the door, half-expecting the snarling pack to burst in and finish what they had started.

"Would you mind not staring at me with those damned eyes?"

She started at being spoken to. His voice held a timbre that could have been quite fearsome had it not been so throaty and ragged. It took her a moment to find her voice.

"I beg pardon. I didn't realize—"

"Aye, well, you are," he huffed indignantly. "Seeking to curse me, I'll wager. I've only seen eyes that color once. On a jaguar idol in Vera Cruz, they were. Cursed me the bloody thing did."

He ended with a dramatic shudder. A squat brown bottle sat amidst the table's clutter. He snatched it up, uncorked it and took a long drink.

Cate ducked her head to hide a smile. It wasn't the first time such comments had been made, most especially while living in the Highlands. Nearly as superstitious as mariners, the Highlanders had more than once accused her of casting spells and curses.

He continued to work, while she continued to stand, her gaze fixed on a point at her feet where rug and floor met. From the corner of her eye, she saw him dart a glance at her now and again, presumably in hopes of catching her evil eye.

If only putting a curse on him would be that simple.

"What are you—?" She was cut short by another fit of coughing, this one full of fluid.

The captain straightened. His scowl was visible even through the dimness. "You look bloody awful!"

She cleared her throat, a wholly unfeminine sound. "I feel like I've swallowed half of the Caribbean," she said more crossly than intended.

"Rum will answer." He seized the bottle, and then glanced about, muttering darkly under his breath. "Ah," he said at finally locating a glass atop a desk. "I knew I'd seen one somewheres or another."

Looking up from pouring, he was disconcerted to find her still standing. "Well, don't just stand there gaping. Sit!"

Cate came up against something hard and cold, and realized she had been inching backwards the while. It was a cannon, one of a pair, *"Merdering Mary"* roughly carved in its carriage.

"Jump and I swear I'll cheer whilst you drown," he said.

"Excuse me?"

"Come the bloody hell away from the damned window!"

Another glance showed she was indeed not much more than an arm's length from a gallery of windows. Running ceiling high, they angled out at the top, with a broad sill at their base.

"I didn't mean... I mean, I wasn't—"

"Seems once in a day would be enough, but mark me, I shan't raise a finger to preserve you from Jones's locker. Most of the men believe 'tis the hand of God on a drowning soul. To save one is to deny God, so t'will be no matter to watch you go."

By the sound of his voice coming out of the shadows, he was pacing.

"Then why did you pull me out?" She considered how much easier things would have been if they had just let her drown.

"Because you are valuable," he said coldly. "At least for now. But pressing the point could prove unwise. Value can be ever so relative, don't you think?"

She had the impression the inquiry wasn't meant to be answered.

"Pray, would you not oblige me to shout like you're a f'c'stleman. Sit there if you like. Oh, hell, I don't really give a damn," he grumbled with an irritated swipe.

Minding the coat, Cate reflexively sat on the nearest thing: a chest beside her. Gripping the wood beneath her, the urge to cough built like a rumbling bubble in her chest. She gulped several times, breathing quickly in and out hoping to squelch it.

"Be warned: puke on me deck and you'll regret it. And take those rags off before you catch your death," he said.

Squinting at him, she searched for any sign of lustfulness, but found none. Turning her back, she did so, the shift, now so torn, nearly falling off on its own accord.

His path around the table brought him into the full light for the first time. She sucked in sharply at seeing him. Her first impression was of black eyes and a leonine head of black hair and beard. The back of her neck prickled as the name "Blackbeard" sprung to mind. She stoutly reminded herself that infamous personage was long since dead. Of average height and slimly built, his hair was bound by a faded blue headscarf. The remainder of his features being so buried in beard, it was blessedly difficult to tell much more about him, other than he was probably not much more than her score and a half in years.

In spite of the bucket boots he wore, he moved like a great dark cat as he brought the drink around, barely making a footfall, a predator, lithe and lethal. She drew her legs up underneath herself and tucked in the coattail more snuggly around her, then shakily took the proffered glass, murmuring "Thank you."

She took a drink.

Her throat constricted, requiring her to swallow several times before it was allowed to pass.

"Rum!" Cate shuddered. "But, it's fine. I'm grateful for anything, if it will allow me to warm up."

A fortuitous fit of coughing helped make her point.

The captain eyed her with suspicion then took a drink, closing his eyes to anxiously await its effects. She eyed him, trying to judge his level of drunkenness. Drink could bring a man to do many things not done when sober. His step was solid, but his speech seemed thickened, almost slurred, although that could have been resultant of its graveled quality.

In spite of its noxiousness, she took another sip. If nothing else, the liquor helped erase the nasty taste in her mouth left by seawater and vomiting.

He flopped in the ornate captain's chair across the table from her.

"Rather foolhardy to jump, don't you think?" he asked, gesturing toward the *Constancy*, visible through the stern windows.

"There was an island," she said with far less conviction than intended.

He snorted. "That would have been a bloody long swim. I'd be hard pressed to find two hands what would be willing to row it, let alone swim it. You do know there are sharks in these waters?" he asked conversationally.

Cate's stomach took a sickening lurch. "No, I hadn't thought of that."

His mouth hovered at the bottle's rim as he cut her a sidelong look. "Can't imagine why anyone would do something so half-crazed."

The implication that she was either mad or lying wasn't lost, nor was it appreciated. She flexed her hands, aching from being clenched for so long.

"I'd been told under no circumstances should I be taken by pirates."

He smiled at that, a dazzling display of white and gold teeth splitting the ebony mat of beard. "I've been told the same thing. Nasty rumor, luv."

Rising to cruise the room once more. His path weaving through the light, he popped in and out of sight like a sword-bearing wraith.

"The warnings were very convincing," she said evenly. "The *Ciara Morganse* and Captain Nathanael Blackthorne were enough to scare anyone."

"Ah, then you know of me. Spent the best part of me life propagating that image." Lost in the gloom at that moment, the smile in his voice couldn't be missed.

"Then may I assume that you are...?" She tensed. On deck, she had heard him called "Captain." For formality sake, however, it was best to be sure. Amid the swirl of unknowns, a solid bit of information seemed essential. Liquid slopping on her hand broke her stare; she was shaking harder than she had thought.

"Oh, I beg your leave. Wretchedly uncommon to be introducing meself on me own ship."

He drew up and struck a formal pose. Doffing the battered leather tricorn, he swept a surprisingly elegant bow. "Captain Nathanael Blackthorne. Your servant, mum."

He scowled at seeing her shiver. She felt thoroughly sodden, the wetness of her hair having soaked through the coat. Chillbanes now set in. It seemed impossible that one could be so cold in the West Indies.

"Here, have another drink. I can hear your teeth clacking clear over here. Doomed to never have back me peace," he grumbled as he poured.

A plan seemed required, she thought, as she stared into her glass.

As in what?

Now at his mentioned, jumping carried its merits. Cate cut a clandestine look through the window and the *Constancy*, rising and falling on the swell. Boats plied in a steady flow between the two ships as pirates looted the ship. She was a strong swimmer. Surely once she was alongside, the Constancies would pull her aboard.

And what about the pirates over there?

And the sharks?

Hmm... Yes, well, every plan has its flaw.

The island she had seen earlier was still in view, but now seemed so very out of reach.

A boat then.

And do what?

There was no hiding on open water. She considered waiting until dark and then stealing a boat. It would mean finding the distant island in the dark. To miss, however, would doom her to open seas, there to die of starvation and thirst. She secretly eyed the mizzenmast, collared by a rack bristling with cutlasses and sabers.

And do what? Your arms still hurt from the last sword dfight. You plan to fight your way off the ship, and then what, escape? To where?

Pressing her fingers to the bridge of her nose, she thought

longingly of lying down in a dark, quiet place for the next fortnight. The saltwater, gurgling in her ears and filling her sinuses, rendered her too thick-headed to effectively think anything through. If she had been surrounded by a forest, mountains or wilds, she would have known what to expect, how to survive. With nothing but water around her, hope of escape verged on impossible.

"What do you plan to do with me?" she ventured to ask again, a bit more steadily this time. In lieu of her own plan, knowing his might help.

Blackthorne closed one eye as he strolled around her, shrewdly evaluating her as one would when purchasing a horse. "Scrawny and a bit old aside, a thing such as you could bring a good price at several markets. However, Miz Littleton—"

"My name is not Littleton."

He batted his lids with affected patience. "Aye, but it is. You shall enjoy our hospitality until your father is contacted—"

"My father? He's been dead for years."

"Come now, luv." He virtually purred as he slinked nearer. A wolf circling its prey, the black eyes and wild hair only added to the impression. "Your father is in Kingston. We'll send a messenger with a—"

"No, no, no." She might have been suffering from a number of uncertainties, but on this she was clear. "My father is—"

"Your father is the King's Commissioner—*new* King's Commissioner, that is—of Jamaica, and as such shall pay more, a good bit more than what might be gotten at the markets, for the return of both you and your mother, as soon as those thick-pated, offscourings find her," he added with a malignant look toward the *Constancy*.

"My moth...? You mean Mrs. Littleton? She and her daughter are dead."

It was sobering to hear two lives memorialized so coldly.

"Some kind of fever," she said dully. "It took Lucy first, Mrs. Littleton but hours after."

"Why didn't you sicken?"

"I suppose I was healthier," she said, evenly.

"Can't argue with that," Blackthorne muttered more to himself. "No explaining sickness, especially on a ship. I've seen entire crews decimated, whilst others remained in the pink."

None of this came as good news. He stalked the room, uttering a black-sounding tirade in something other than Spanish or French, and took a long pull off the bottle still clutched in his fist.

"This wasn't my damned plan to begin with. I tried to tell

those oysterheads this wouldn't answer. And now..." He broke off, thinking better of what he was about to say.

He came at her, shaking his fist, the bottle's contents sloshing. "I'll have you know, I do *not* approve of women aboard. Noxious creatures! Nothing but problems. It puts the men's minds on nothing but their cocks, as you already may have noticed." He canted his head toward the main deck where Scarface and his men would still be.

Blackthorne drew up before the window, swallowing back several more remarks that bubbled to the surface. Her heart leapt at seeing his hand come to rest on the pistol at his belt. She braced, chanting inwardly that death might be the blessing she had hoped for.

"What is your name then, luv?" he asked over his shoulder.

It was a bit disconcerting that he needed to know her name just before shooting her. She lifted her chin, determined to meet her end with grace. "Cate."

"Catherine?"

"No, Cate will do nicely."

He pivoted around on his heel. "Very well, *Cate...*"

A firm rap at the door caused her to start. A man's silhouette, a dark blot against the glare of daylight, filled the doorway.

"Cap'n?"

Cate shrank back at recognizing the voice. It filled the room the same way it had echoed across the *Constancy's* deck.

"Yes, Master Pryce?" Blackthorne beckoned him in with a wave.

Pryce advanced several steps before he pulled up short at the sight of her. She snugged the coat tighter around her under his cold stare.

"Wishin' to report, Cap'n," Pryce said, averting his attention. "The prize has give over."

"Readily?"

"None so much as might o' been. Their weapons were already laid, until the Cap'n's wife there called the charge." Pryce cut her a look, now a heated glare. "Took Chin directly in the leg, she did, and then managed to draw blood on several more afore..."

Blackthorne whirled around on Cate. "I could have you hocked-and-heaved or flogged for drawing the blood of another."

At some point, she had risen to her feet. She shrank back, coming up hard against the gun carriage as he stalked toward her. He grabbed her by the arm and towed her around the table. Releasing her, he went out on deck, where a number of pirates churned through trunks taken from the *Constancy*. Shoving them aside, he pawed through the contents, seized something and stomped back.

"I don't give a damn about you, but that's me number one coat and I'll not have it bloodied up. Here," he said and flung a garment at her. "Put it on or parade about half-naked, I don't give a rat's arse."

The garment turned out to be a shift. She turned her back and wormed out of the coat while donning the other. The hem was barely over her hips before the coat was yanked away. Blackthorne reached, meaning to snatch her by the hair. Thinking better, he took her by the wrist instead, the force grinding the bones together, and half-drug her to the steps below. In morbid dread of stumbling, she concentrated on her footing as he pushed from behind.

At the bottom, a shove propelled her much faster than her feet could manage. She stumbled several times. The passage wasn't unlike that of the *Constancy's*: narrow and lined with a couple of cabins to one side, and the galley the other, the cook, ladle poised in hand, watching them pass. They came out of the passage into an open space one could only call the gundeck. As low-ceilinged as the *Constancy*, the t'ween deck was cavernous. The pirate ship was no more than a platform for the double phalanx of guns, crouched in their carriages like silent black sentinels. The ports stood open, the fresh air thankfully stirring the miasma of bilge, stale gunpowder and soiled hammocks.

She balked at the sight of the large number of men gathered at the foot of another companionway. It was only Blackthorne's presence, pushing from behind, which kept her from turning and running, that and the recollection of what had happened the last time she tried to do so. The smell of blood grew sharp. It mingled with that of sweat and gunpowder, as they neared. It was then that she saw the injured being helped down the steps. The wounded sat where they could, the more serious lying on the floor. Some glared at the sight of her; others looked on with mild interest.

Pryce's voice rose over the commotion. "By the saints, Chin. Any chuckle-headed fool could see a thing like that won't close on its own."

A final shove from Blackthorne put Cate squarely before the man Pryce addressed. Hunched on a stool, his sweat-soaked shirt clinging to his chest, the man clutched his thigh, the blood seeping between his fingers pooling on the floor. He looked up, and she found herself looking into the same impassive broad face and flat black eyes of the one who had held the knife to her throat, the one she had slashed with her sword. Her stomach lurched, the rum she had drank now an icy cannonball. Chin's face twitched with recognition and then settled into malevolence.

"He be refusin', Cap'n," Pryce said, his hands propped on his hips. "You know how he is about bein' sewed."

"Sorry for it, Cap'n. In wrong place," Chin said in stilted English. The admission of having been done for by a woman didn't come easily. The glare he directed at her suggested he desired the favor to be returned.

Blackthorne knelt next to Chin and clapped him on the shoulder. "Word has it someone thought you a fish and sought to dice you up for supper. Appears to be a tough one what needs throwing back, eh, mates?"

The pirates laughed, the tension lifted. The change in Blackthorne was so remarkable she had to look again to make sure it was the same man. Like an actor shifting roles, he was suddenly amiable and even caring. Judging by the surrounding faces, this version was a familiar one.

He gently pried open Chin's grasp to inspect the wound. A surge of guilt struck Cate at seeing the gash through the rent in Chin's breeches. Longer than one's hand, it ran diagonally across the fat of his thigh, the blood welling to a steady flow once the pressure was removed. Pryce's analysis had been accurate: with the edges curling back, a wound such as that would only fester, eventually costing him his leg.

Blackthorne clucked his tongue as one would scold a child. "'Tis going to have to be sewn."

Sweat beading on shaven head, Chin clamped his hand back in place and bit his lip against the pain. "All respect, sir, I can't bear thought of stitch, especially by any o' you."

He took the rebuke in stride. "You've seen Pryce and Kirkland both mend many a man."

"Aye, many fester and die—lucky ones, at least. So, Crooks?" Chin directed his question to a man who stood against the bulkhead, his semi-empty sleeve knotted off just below the elbow.

"Can't say t'were Pryce's fault entirely," Crooks said, laconically.

Blackthorne fixed a minatory eye on her. A drama was being played out in which she was expected to take part, but how she couldn't tell. Chin's reluctance seemed to be feeding Blackthorne's irritation with her. Judging by the intent and worried looks, Chin was held in high regard by all. The sense of brotherhood was striking, no different than among the Highland clans.

Wiping hands suddenly gone sweaty on her shift, she looked

from one grizzled face to the next. Bearded and sun-beaten to evenness, they could have all been of one family. In full daylight, they had been a barbarous and menacing lot. Now, clustered in the cramped and dim space, they were even more intimidating. The sight of Chin set the cut on her breast to sting anew. It was either play along with the drama, or face Blackthorne's wrath.

She glanced judiciously at Chin's leg, not without sympathy. "You can try binding it, but you know that won't answer, don't you?"

The pat of blood dripping on the boards marked the seconds as she held Chin's gaze. His defiance faltered, his lids lowering. They snapped open, only to close once more.

"Bleeding like that for another hour or two," she said, "you'll be half out of it, probably verging on delirium. By then, weakened by all the blood lost—"

"Right she is!" Pryce shouted. "I ain't never seen a gash what benefited with the waitin'."

Pryce's declaration was endorsed by encouraging murmurs from all around. From behind Chin's back, Pryce moued at being obliged to agree with her. She looked to Blackthorne for some sign of having done right, but he was too intent on Chin to notice.

"What man would pass up the chance for a lady's hand on his leg and not have to pay first?" Blackthorne winked, prompting a lewd chuckle from the rest. "Hell, I'll throw in all the rum you can swallow."

Chin's increasing struggle to keep his eyes open gave credence to her prophesy. Through a haze of pain, he regarded her with cold suspicion, trust apparently a scarce commodity among the pirates.

"I'll warn ye, Cap'n," Chin said at last. "That could be a fair bit."

"I've a quid in me pocket what says you can't make a pottle," said Blackthorne as he rose to his feet.

Catching their Captain's spirit, the men made their wagers, bringing forth coppers, shillings, shares of grog and other tokens of value. Blackthorne turned and clapped a hand on Cate's shoulder. To the idle observer, it would have seemed a genial gesture, but he squeezed the soft muscle until she winced.

"A life for a life 'tis our motto, so have a care," he said, low-voiced in her ear. "And hark ye well: there are no secrets on a ship, so I shan't advise foolery."

Chin made it eloquently clear to all within hearing that he would not be touched until properly numbed. He ground out black-sounding Chinese at being lifted to a table. He beamed, however, when the promised rum arrived and drank with determined purpose.

As it turned out, Pryce and Kirkland, the cook, shared the duty of ship's chirurgeon. A medicine chest was brought containing a sharpened sailmaker's needle and a spool of cord-like thread.

"That'll never do," Cate muttered poking a finger at them. "There should be a sewing kit in those trunks from the *Constancy*. In the smallest one, I believe."

"Fetch it!" barked a faceless voice.

"Bring some of those petticoats, too," she called after the hand scrambling away.

The remainder of the medicine stores was disappointingly sparse: a few rags, a bottle of liniment smelling of things long-gone bad and a jar of innocuous salve. That, plus hot water from the galley and rum, composed the total of her weapons. Meager, yes, but she had gone into battle against injury with far less.

An ebony *etui* was delivered. It bore a silver family crest with the initials "LL": Lucy Littleton. Cate stroked the glossy wood, seeing once more the slip of a girl. Barely fifteen, Lucy had possessed all the innocent sparkle of youth, breathily anticipating her coming life, a husband her greatest aspiration. She would have been stunned to see her symbols of ladyhood being put to such brutal use.

But Lucy was gone, now.

Cate flicked open the small case, and extracted two silver needles and the ivory bobbin of black thread.

Next to where Chin laid appeared a man. As tall as he was broad, he seemed a mountain in the low-ceilinged space. Black of hair and eye, his body was so encased in bands of geometric tattoos it was difficult to discern his skin's natural tone. He shifted as she did, always taking a position directly in her line of sight. Arms crossed over a hogshead chest, he stood disquietingly still, except for a length of rope, a fist-sized knot at its end. He swung the bludgeon-like thing with well-practiced ease, passing it several times closely enough for her to observe the knot's discoloration, looking too much like dried blood. The knot was periodically struck with startling force against whatever surface which happened to be within range.

At one point, there was a subtle shift in the press of men around her, parting to allow a single figure forward. The dry old stick's rheumy eyes regarded Chin's leg, the withered mouth pursing in consideration.

"Huh! I've seen worse." The creaky-voiced pronouncement came with the same significance of a verdict handed down at Old

Bailey. And then, he was gone. Puzzled, Cate forbore inquiring as to what that performance had been about.

While waiting for Chin's rum to take sufficient effect, Cate inspected the other casualties, those who would allow her, that is. A good many would not deign to subject themselves to the hands of a woman, preferring to bind their wounds themselves or by their mates with whatever bit of rag might be to hand, in spite of her protests.

"Eye fer an eye," came a low-voiced rumble from somewhere behind her.

"Justice," hissed another.

She spun around to where several men sat with a unified mask of malice.

"We'll see whose blood stains the deck next," said Chin in a rum-thickened slur.

She spun back to Chin, now dull-eyed with drink, but glaring, nonetheless. Her breast and ribs stinging anew, she thought to apologize to him, but a hollow one it would have been, for if the circumstances were to present themselves again, she would have done the same. She straightened, a strange calm befalling her as she took the bottle from his increasingly limp hand. She met his stare as she poised the bottle over the wound and poured. She took great satisfaction from the resulting bellow. It was cut short, however, by the crack of the knotted rope on the bench at her knee. She started, as if she had been the one struck, and her hard-found will dissolved.

As she picked up the threaded needle, her pulse raced, her mouth gone dry. She had repaired many a man, but never damage done by her own hand. Periodically, she paused to swipe the sweat from her eyes; putting a needle through skin wasn't as easy as one might imagine. Chin's jaw muscles stood rigid with determination to present a stoic front. And yet, no amount of resolve could prevent his flesh from twitching at every stab. The needle slipped often from her blood-slicked fingers.

She worked under the added pressure of being observed not only by the rope-swinging watchdog, but two others, loosely disguised as assistants. One, small and squat, with huge bulging eyes and an inordinately wide mouth, Frog, as she privately christened him, stood poised with a knife—being disinclined to trust her with it—to cut the thread as she knotted off each stitch. The second, tall and thin to the point of almost frail, with a neck and limbs befitting a great bird, Crane ripped bandages in between sprinkling sand under her feet whenever the floor grew too slippery with blood. She resented their lack of trust, flattering herself as one who possessed enough honor not to exact revenge on a wounded man.

With a sigh of relief, she tied off the last stitch. She moved on to the next one injured, and then the next, all the while working under the severe mask of Watchdog and every man she treated. Those who conceded to being treated by her were, for the most part, as stoic as Chin. Unflinching as she sewed their flesh or set their bones, they didn't scruple, however to smirk at her terrified state.

The bastards!

She glanced at the faces of each one and tried to match them with those she had seen during the fight on the *Constancy*. It was impossible that she could have been directly responsible for every injury, but clearly they thought as much. She focused on her task, allowing her bent head to take the brunt of their malice. Now bloody to the wrists, she could smell her own sweat above the press of bodies around her. Her jaw ached from being set. Determination turned inward, some might have called it "fortitude", but her father, brothers and husband had called it "stubbornness."

Be damned if I'm going to be cowed by a bunch of pirates!

At least that was what she told herself until her pace slowed. Mastiff swung his club-rope with a resounding *whack!*, spurring her to work with renewed fervor. Under more ordinary circumstances, she could have worked with confidence; she had staunched a war's worth of wounds. This wasn't the maiming and dismemberment as wrought by cannon fire. Hand-to-hand battle produced more in the way of slashes, fractures and dislocations, dismemberment being limited to knuckles, noses or ears. The blood, however, ran just as red, the agony just as real.

The hatch grates were drawn back and t'ween decks was flooded with daylight. With it came a downdraft of fresh air; she inhaled deeply several times through her nose to clear away the fug of blood, vomit and unwashed male. The lowering to the hold of plunder from the *Constancy* began, bulging net after net. The process involved a great deal of cursing and shouting, often requiring her to shout into the ear of her patient. Those injured in the loading process took their place in the makeshift sick bay's line: a gaffing hook to the foot, a smashed hand, and one who had taken an inopportune step and tumbled through the *Constancy's* hatch.

And then, she was done. Wincing, she slowly straightened and waited. No one stepped forward; no one beckoned. Flushed with exertion, she washed the blood and filth from her hands in a bucket and dried them on her hem. Little could be done for the shift she wore, now smeared red from chest to knees. All told, there had been well over a score to be seen, all now either resting comfortably in their hammocks or back on duty. She wasn't ashamed to admit there was a small part of her that had enjoyed the work. For once, she had felt useful, a sense she had thought to be long dead.

Mastiff, Frog and Crane having disappeared, she stood half-expecting someone to either drag her away to be confined somewhere, or returned to Blackthorne's cabin. Many of the men circled around her as if she carried wharf fever, while others intentionally brushed against her as they passed, murmuring lewd remarks. She retreated to an as out-of-the-way corner as could be found in such tightly-packed quarters: atop a sea chest wedged between the aftmost guns — Yes, she needed to remember that at sea cannons were called "guns" — and waited.

There was a bone-rattling bellow of "Swabbers!" She picked up her feet, crusted with the same slurry of sand and blood that fouled the floor, to allow the pile of reddish-brown crumbles to be swept away by one of the men who appeared armed with brooms, mops and buckets. He worked with a low-voiced grumble of "Damned landsmen what don't know how to mind a deck. Swab. Swab. Swab. And not a moment's rest. T'was like the Glory Almighty was coming to visit."

Mess was called, with all its furor of gathering men. The pirates hunched over tables slung between the guns and gobbled down their meal oblivious to the cargo nets which still passed up and down. The smell of food reached her, but her stomach was closed, the scent leaving her queasy.

A dull ache seemed to have permanently settled behind her eyes. It was a different sort from the pain which thudded where she had hit the back of her head. The sense of fulfillment faded, and cold fingers of fear clawed her gut again. The price of idleness was time to think. Nothing pleasant came to mind, only broken recollections of the ominous warnings heard on the *Constancy.* She looked down at her hands, now resting in her lap, and wondered when the trembling might stop. She buried her head in her hands and covered her ears, in hopes if she was to block it all out, she might wake from this nightmare. A more desperate hope was that she had actually drowned and was dead.

That would make this Purgatory, she thought, scanning the pirates.

And a fitting description it was: a soulless, damned-looking lot they were. There was, however, none of the despondency or misery one would expect in Hell's waiting room. These men laughed and jested, poking good-naturedly at each other as they ate with zeal.

Through the clamor of men and handling of cargo nets, she felt first through the floor, and then heard the footsteps coming toward her, heavy with irritation and the desire to make that displeasure known.

"Ah! So, the lamb couldn't find its way through the wolves back to the flock?" Blackthorne jeered as he drew up before her. "Have to be a dull-witted dawcock not to be able to find your way aft."

"No one said... You never..."

"Tach! Must I bid you to breathe, as well?" he cut in, an annoying habit, she was coming to discover.

Exhaustion and tension had rendered her uncommonly over-sensitive, for his image blurred.

"Bloody hell, not blubbering again," he said at seeing her eyes fill as he handed her down from her perch. "Your bladder lie too close to your eyeballs, does it? Shall I leave you with them, so you might truly have something to wail about?" he asked with a gesture toward the men.

He was back in character, she thought glumly as he shoved her back toward the Great Cabin, a considerably more circuitous path with the tables now set up and hatches opened. The affable, engaging captain seen among his men was gone, the glowering, fractious one returned.

Once in the cabin, she quickly retreated to her previous spot. Standing there, she gazed out the window at the low-slanted sun's rays. The day was almost over and of prodigious proportions it had been. She hoped to never see another like it. There was, however, the niggling possibility that it might be her last. Fixed on that thought, she was deep in observation of the patterns of light and shadows on the water, committing them to everlasting memory, when she was interrupted by Pryce's arrival.

"We've cleared the prize of everythin' need be," he said, pulling up before Blackthorne, now seated at the table. Behind him, she could see the deck still teemed with the shipping of the *Constancy's* plunder. "We've looked from tops to wells. T'weren't no other women yet, exceptin' the cap'n's wife there."

Pryce looked at her with a coldness that reached across the room.

"Guns disabled?" Blackthorne asked.

Folding his hands behind his back, Pryce proudly rocked on his heels. "Aye, sir. Guns spiked and rudder disabled. T'will be the 'morrow earliest 'afore she'll be makin' ready. There be no danger o' her givin' chase, nor makin' port soon."

"Well done. Any of her crew come over?"

The First Mate's stern countenance brightened with pride. "Aye, ten, sir. 'Pears they'd heard of the *Ciara Morganse* and couldn't pass up the opportunity."

"Very well, then. Pass the word for these fine specimens of seamanship, so they might sign the book."

The moment Pryce stepped over the door's coaming, Blackthorne spun around at her. "In there!" he hissed, with a swipe toward a curtained doorway. "And don't come out until you're bid."

Cate slunk along the margins of the room and ducked around the velvet barricade, into what she thought to be an anteroom. She froze at the sight of the bunk in the thin light passing through the porthole. The captain's bed. *His* bed.

It was a less than subtle hint. Cocking an ear, she heard nothing more than Blackthorne rustling about. For the moment, it seemed safe.

She sagged against the wall. Bracing her head in her hands, she drew several shuddering breaths, striving to loosen joints that had constricted into knots. A clearer head was going to be necessary if she was going to survive this. The tightness in her chest and pressure behind her eyes were harbingers of a breakdown of epic proportions bubbling just beneath the surface. Lucid thought was becoming nigh impossible, her mind leaping from one panic-laden thought to the next. She drew down on herself even tighter. Anyone who dealt with animals knew they could sense fear and would feed on it. Now was not the time for any such display, not with him just the other side of the curtain.

Cate sat on the edge of the bunk. This was the moment of privacy and quiet she had longed for, and she strained to think. She eyed the port high on the bulkhead. It was large enough that she could slither through, but beyond waited nothing but ocean, and sharks. The space was considerably larger than her cabin on the *Constancy*, it was still small enough that one glance showed there were no doors or windows. No one would be coming in, but neither would she be getting out.

Voices from the salon broke her thoughts. She rose to peek between the curtain and the wall. A worn leather book now lay open on the table before Blackthorne, quill and silver ink bottle arranged beside it. The *Constancy* converts stood opposite. Viewed from the side, they looked vaguely familiar, some a little more than others. Several pirates filed in and took up positions along the bulkhead, apparent witnesses to the proceedings. Pryce stood at his captain's elbow, a hand poised over the pistol in his belt.

Blackthorne straightened and assumed a grave demeanor. "Can any of you read?"

There was a unified declination and humbled murmurs.

"Very well, then. I'll summarize: this is a pirate ship."

The statement was met with surprised looks and nervous tittering.

"I know, 'tis obvious, mates." Blackthorne's smile was audible. "But I'm obliged to make that known. We abide by the Code of the Coast, as set forth by Morgan and Bartholomew, and our articles are as such: there will be no gaming, for money's sake, nor smoking. As a side note, I might add: spit on me decks and live to regret it. And all marlinspikes shall be eyed and spliced. If you've no eye, then see the armorer directly. No drinking alone below decks and no bottling your tot. No carrying an uncovered light after eight o'clock..."

Blackthorne's graveled voice rang clear as he recited the list. Many of the strictures were common sense, essential for the co-existence of so many men crammed on a single vessel. The newcomers listened, intently nodding.

"...to keep their pistols and cutlass clean and fit for service. He what sees a sail first, shall have the best pistol or small arms taken from said vessel. No man shall withhold information pertinent to the safety and welfare of crew or ship. There will be equal shares in everything taken..."

Cate sagged, the blood draining from her limbs. Blackthorne's voice faded as she stumbled back onto the bunk.

"Took the women, the unlucky ones bein' raped before their family's eyes, 'til there were nothin' left."

"Heaven help any woman taken by those slavering curs."

The words rang all too clearly.

She dug her nails hard into her scalp, hoping the pain might this time wake her from this nightmare.

It didn't.

A quilt lay at the foot of the bunk. She snatched it up and pressed it to her face, to muffle the sobs of desperation and terror that erupted. She prided herself on not being the typical woman, who collapsed into a sniveling wreck at the least provocation, but it seemed she had been doing more than her share these last days. Hopelessness had been visited upon her before, but those had been trivialities compared to this.

"...and stand your watches without dereliction. Do you swear to abide by these?"

Blackthorne's question snapped her back to her surroundings. She shakily returned to the curtain in time to see the Constancies solemnly nod.

"Sorry, mates. I can't hear your heads rattling. Call out like the tars what you are."

Pryce stepped forward and soundly cuffed the nearest one on the back of the head. "'e's yer captain, now. Ye'll be showin' him the respect what he's got comin'."

"Aye, sir!" came a chorus with renewed vigor.

"Very well, make your mark. You've now joined the Brethren of the Coast."

Each of the fledglings bent to scrawl his mark and then give his name. Blackthorne entered it with flourish. It was a solemn but brief ceremony.

"Welcome aboard the *Ciara Morganse*," Blackthorne announced as he capped the ink. "And mind now, I'm your commander. Withholding information will be penalized."

He allowed for the weight of that to settle, and then asked with whip-like sharpness, "Who was the woman?"

Cate's heart leapt at the thought of being so blatantly investigated; he knew full well that she could hear every word. It wasn't so much fear that made her blood pulse; no one on the *Constancy* knew anything damaging of her past. Her annoyance stemmed from someone snooping about in her affairs.

Two Constancies shrugged while the remainder groped for a name.

"Name's Harper, sir," said one, at last.

"That was Captain Harper over there?" Blackthorne countered, with a vague wave toward the *Constancy*.

They were momentarily puzzled, thinking it a trick question. "Nossir. That were Cap'n Chambers."

Blackthorne leaned forward on the table with sharpened interest. "You're sure?"

"Positive, sir." All heads nodded; eager to be in the good graces of their new captain.

"Not Littleton?" asked Blackthorne.

"The Commissioner's wife and daughter? They died weeks ago, sir."

"Aye, commended them to the deep, we did," added the other eagerly. "With proper words, of course."

"Of course," Blackthorne said, head bent in thought. "Very well. Well done, and all that..."

A wave shooed them all out with the exception of Pryce, who lingered expectantly.

"Cast off then and make weigh," he said to Pryce, still distracted. "You've got your course. Go. Go."

"Cap'n, Bullock and his lot are at it again," Pryce said, lowering his voice to barely audible.

Blackthorne stiffened and swore. It wasn't good news, but at the same time didn't seem to come as a great surprise.

"Heard 'em a-tryin' to rouse his mates," Pryce added circumspectly.

"What's that piss-vinegar of a sea lawyer up to now?" came Blackthorne's low-voiced vehemence.

"The usual: too much work, others a-shirkin' their duties, twice-laid cordage—"

"That's the best cordage money can buy."

"Aye, as any man worth his salt knows well. 'Tis a malcontent for sure, but he has the ears of many, too many."

"Very well, an extra ration of grog for all," said Blackthorne after a brief reflection. "Not many complaints can swim through that. And pass the word to the galley 'tis time for duff. That should appease the Furies," he ended with a grandiose swipe.

"There be another matter—" Pryce began with some hesitancy.

"Suffering Jesus on the cross, now what?" Blackthorne grumbled more out of frustration than anger.

"Towers, Smalley and Quinn: they be drunk during the raid... *again*. That makes three in the month."

"Don't I know it," sighed Blackthorne. He made a wry noise. "The Demon Rum calls louder than their hides, eh? Witnesses?"

"Six, what are willing to step forward and claim inconvenience, but there be more what will help make the case, if need be."

"Very well, pass the word we'll muster the Company after we're aweigh. Make it so, Master Pryce."

"Is she the one we seek, Cap'n?" Pryce asked in an even more clandestine tone.

Blackthorne paused to consider. "Dunno, Pryce. Dunno."

He waited until the clump of Pryce's boots had died, before calling, "You can come out now... if you haven't jumped overboard *again*."

Cate stumbled back from the curtain, at first fearing she had been caught eavesdropping. With a hand that shook far more than imagined, she smoothed her hair and made herself as presentable as possible when wearing nothing but a torn and blood-stained shift to go meet her fate. At the last moment, her confidence wavered, and she pulled the quilt from the bunk. Donning it like a cape, she settled the folds over her shoulders, feeling far less vulnerable as she stepped out.

It was early evening, the cabin's saturated colors of the day giving way to the muted, half-tones of impending dark. Blackthorne was in the midst of lighting the candles. One brow lifted under the edge of his headscarf at seeing her swathed in the quilt, but no comment was made. It was another one of his disconcerting habits: ignoring the obvious to pounce on the obscure.

"You're letting the *Constancy* go?" she asked, careful to strip all emotional inflection from her voice.

Blackthorne stopped with the taper suspended over a wick. "Certainly. Why not? We have what we came for, or so it would appear."

His same brow arched, this time with suspicion. "What interest is it to you?"

"Nothing. I was led to believe you... pirates," she struggled with the word. He noticed and smirked. "That you always force captives to join your crew and then destroyed the ship."

He genuinely laughed, a flash of white splitting the black abundance of beard, and blew out the taper's flame. "Aye, that can be the case. Forty more hands can make duties lighter. But," he cautioned, wagging a finger, "twenty souls here under protest can be even more burdensome. So, we take what we can," he went on, tucking the book back into its place on a shelf, "and let them go, assuring of course, that their gratitude doesn't come in the form of shooting us in the arse. With any luck and fair winds, we'll be leagues away before they can make port and report us."

"That's very generous." Cate was afraid to hope the same compassion might be extended when it came to the dispensing of her final fate.

Blackthorne shrugged off the compliment as he flopped down in his chair once more. "Generosity will get you killed, darling. Practicality: now there's a friend you can count on."

Mindful of the quilt, she sat across the table from him. "So, you... pirates... share... everything?"

"Aye," he said affably, amused by the break in her voice at the word "pirate." "We've a plunder book what lists all what's taken; 'tis open for any man to see. The bosun and gunner get a share and a half. The quartermaster gets a share and three-quarter, and Captain—that would be me," he pointed out, with a teasing glint, "receives two. But everyone gets a share of everything, *no* exceptions. 'Tis the Code," he added with an underlining sweep of his hand.

"How..." Cate gulped, the words not being where she had expected. "How many are there aboard?"

Leaning his head back, he closed one eye in calculation. "A hundred and seventy-four, but we're still a bit short-handed."

"That many," she said faintly. Struck by a wave of queasiness, she raised a hand to her head. Seeing it shake, she tucked both underneath her legs.

"Are you well?" He lurched up and came around the table.

"Yes," she stammered, shying. "Why?"

"You just turned the color of spoilt custard. You need rum!"

"No! No! Please...!"

Her protests were too late; he had already seized the bottle and was refilling her glass.

"Can't have you falling out on me deck." He cast a worried eye toward her that suggested said "falling out" might occur before he could finish pouring.

A cold sweat prickled her forehead. It wasn't as if she wasn't under enough of a massive strain without having to keep drinking the vile stuff, she thought moodily as she took the glass. The thought occurred that he aimed to render her insensible, in order to take advantage of her, but she could handle her drink far better than that.

Once confident that she wasn't about to "fall out", he pulled up a chair and sat. Their knees nearly touching, he hunched interestedly forward.

"What did you say your name was?" he asked. A taunting smile grew at her hesitation. "Trying to remember, eh? They do say the less you lie, the less you are required to remember. Let's have a real name this time, luv."

She hung on to the glass as if it were an anchor, needing something solid to hold onto, a weapon, if necessary. He wasn't a large man, but his nearness was disquieting, nonetheless. Clutching the quilt tighter, she inched sideways in her chair.

"Catherine Harper."

"As you said before."

"No, I only said Cate, before. Can't we just accept that and move on? What difference does it make so long as it isn't Littleton?"

He leaned back. Tenting his fingers to his lips, the dark eyes were keen as a predator's. "And does Cate Harper have any family?"

In desperate need of fortification, she drained the last bit of rum from her glass and glared at him over the rim. "Fishing for someone else to ransom, Captain?"

Her bravery held but for a few moments. The urge to flee surged again. She was on her feet before realizing it, only to discover there was no place to run. Trapped, she turned to the window.

"No, Catherine Harper has no one, absolutely no one," she said to the night.

"Any slab-sided dolt can see that you are a lady by speech

and carriage, in spite of your clever disguise," he said dryly, rising behind her.

"Disguise," she cried, spinning around. "You were the ones who —"

"Details," he said with a dismissive flutter of fingers. He circled, regarding her again as if she was prized livestock. "In spite of a sojourn at sea, you've the skin and teeth of a lady as well. Someone has paid dearly for your maintenance."

"There's no one."

"Did your mother not teach you not to lie?"

Cheeks heating, she crossed her arms over her chest. "I'm not lying. There's —"

She was cut short at seeing his gaze drop to her hand.

"You wear a wedding ring," he observed in a cunning tone.

"Please don't take it." She clutched her hand to her chest.

"Why would I do that?" he asked, his face screwing in puzzlement.

"You pirates take everything, don't you?" She didn't scruple uttering the word now, employing every bit of the loathing that boiled to the surface.

"Aye, that we do, but I can assure you one silver ring wouldn't signify," he said amiably, but then his tone hardened. "And I beg that you spare me the stuff-and-nonsense of you being the good Captain Whatever-His-Name's wife."

"I told you, there is *no* one."

Cate bit her lip with the realization that with that succinct declaration, she might well have sealed her fate: by her own admission, she was worthless as a hostage. The list of possibilities of what might be done with her had just narrowed.

She looked into one of the gallery's thick panes. The face looking back from amid a bramble of hair was that of a stranger: blank-eyed and haggard, a hag, no better than the beggars and whores who roamed the streets, someone to be used and abused with little regard. She felt the ship shift under her feet and the sails catch. Their momentum building, she watched the lights of the *Constancy,* and any hope of escape, fade into the twilight. With it, too, went her meager bag of possessions.

Everything was gone.

In spite of the quilt about her, a cold desolation settled over her. It was the final kick in the gut, Providence telling her once again that she was to have nothing... *ever.* Anything she ever managed to gain would be taken.

"What of your husband?" Blackthorne's blurred reflection in the glass moved as he circled behind her.

Cate rolled the silver ring between her fingers. Ornate,

yet simple, with small rosebuds twinning over a latticework background, it was now all that was left. Clutching her hand to her chest, she closed her eyes in benediction of all she had lost.

"He's gone," she said dully.

"Gone? Gone, as in to another island? Or, gone as in...?" asked Blackthorne.

"Gone, as in prison," she cried. Spinning around, the quilt fell from her shoulders. "Gone, as in never to be seen again. Gone, as in I'm totally alone. Gone, as in there is not a single soul to know if I'm alive or dead!"

The weight of the day had taken its toll. Terror, battle, near drowning, and now captivity were all too overwhelming. Rage overcame sensibility. Squealing, she balled a fist and swung. Blackthorn chuckled as he easily fended her off, infuriating her all the more. Fingers curled, she lunged, seeking to claw his throat, face... anything! Artfully dodging her attempts to knee him in the groin, he seized her wrists and pulled her against him. She screamed in anger more than fear.

"Quiet! Belay!" he hissed.

Pressing her face deeper into his shoulder, the pistol at his waist digging her ribs. Cate bucked against his body, lean and hardened by years at sea. Wrestling with her brothers had taught her how to fight; he flinched and grunted when her blows found their target. She felt a tug at the neck of her shift and heard the sound of fabric tearing.

Cate landed a solid kick to his knee and broke free. She leapt for the broad sill of the windows and hooked her fingers on the ledge, clinging to the slim chance of escape. Freedom was just below: a sea glittering in the starlight. The water was farther down than she had imagined, but rational voices didn't prevail. Diving after her, he seized her by the waist, striving to pull her away. Her fingers burned, the joints tearing. She kicked out and knocked Blackthorne's legs out from under him. He sprawled on top of her, one arm trying to pull her back, the other reaching to break her hold. Failing at that, he grabbed her wrist and squeezed, digging his fingers deep between the bones. A searing pain raced up her arm and shot down into her hand. Her fingers went numb, and she lost her grip with a suddenness that sent them both tumbling along the sill.

Blackthorne came up on top of her, his hips grinding hers. His breath hot on her chest, she slapped and gouged, going for his eyes, nose... any point of weakness. He caught one arm in mid-air and wrenched it around under her, while nearly catching the other. As they rolled, one way and then the other, she screamed and he clapped a hand over her mouth. She bit down until she heard the satisfying crunch of flesh. Grunting in pain, he jerked back and tried to shake her off, but she hung on like a terrier on a rat. Finally, he slapped her across the face. The blow sent her reeling backward. She came hard up against a gun with a force that knocked the wind from her.

Taking a few deep breaths, she looked up, Blackthorne had closed in and his face was just a few inches from hers, she got a thunderous look. The blacken eyes gleamed with a brilliance that made him capable of any act of mayhem or madness. She sagged back, the gun's cold brass at her back another scream bubbling in her throat, but he stopped just beyond arm's reach.

"Scream again and you'll do it hanging from me bowsprit," he said in a low, gasping growl.

He twisted his arm around to examine the side of his hand, a curve of red droplets bright in the candlelight. Glaring at her in disgust, plunging his hand into his mouth, he looked around and snatched up a bottle and trickled rum over the bite, swearing as he shook off the pain.

Coming at her with a swiftness that was too quick for her to react. He grabbed her up, half-caring, half-dragging her across the room to the curtain and, with a low animal sound, shoved her through it.

"And come out at your peril!" he snarled.

Cate strained to curb her own hard breathing in order to hear what was happening on the other side of the curtain: stomping about, and a great deal of grumbles and curses, much unkindly toward women in general and her, specifically. She heard a heaving grunt, and the quilt slid under the curtain with enough force for it to land at her feet.

She stood staring into the dark room. There was nothing but a curtain, no way of barricading or locking it. She inched her way forward with a groping hand extended. She stubbed her toe on the bunk and heard a smug snicker in the salon. He was still out there, listening, waiting. Sleeping on the bed seemed ill-advised. When he came in — and surely he would — he would expect her there. Determined not to give him the satisfaction of another sound, she clamped her mouth tight and felt around to the far edge of the small space. At the head of the bed, she found a book tucked in between the bunk and the bulkhead. Its hefty weight promised to make a fair weapon — the only weapon thus far — and she tucked it under her arm. Once reaching the room's corner, she felt for the quilt and curled up with it on the floor.

Exhaustion was an anchor dragging her down. The events of the day flashed through her head like a riffled deck of cards. The speed with which they passed had a hypnotic effect and her joints loosened. Muscles tensed for too long trembled and twitched as they let go. Deeper and deeper she sank.

Cate woke with a start. With no idea what had awakened her, she tried to quiet her pounding heart in order to hear, straining to see through the darkness. She shied at a spectral light glowing at the ceiling and felt quite foolish at seeing it was only the moon through a deck prism. A greenish pool on the floor, the thin ray was the only light in the otherwise stygian void. The curtain moved, and she jumped then gasped with relief at realizing it swayed with the motion of the ship.

There was a noise, the same or different as to what had wakened her she couldn't tell. She held her breath, as if listening might help her to see. She couldn't shake the sense of eyes being on her. Severe disorientation seized her at realizing that she was no longer on the floor. She was somewhere else, but with no recollection of how she had come to be there. Shifting her weight ever so slightly, she felt the lumpiness of a mattress under her and smelt the sharpness of male. A bed, the captain's bed most likely. Her blood pulsed in her ears as she felt with her rear, and then a hand. She was alone, so far.

The feel of eyes on her was unshakeable, however. She wormed farther back against the bulkhead and pulled the quilt higher as she strained to hear what she couldn't see.

Sometime later, Cate heard another sound: an eerie, unearthly cry, which seemed to emanate from the bowels of the ship. Long and querulous, it faded to a slow death. An animal was her first thought, and yet too distorted by distance to be sure. Within a few moments, she heard it again, this time seeming to originate from outside and high above.

She lay awake through the night, jumping and starting at every creak, pop or vibration. At last, when the black of night gave way to the thin grey of dawn, she dozed off, too exhausted to care.

3: THE LIE BEHIND
THE TRUTH

A DISTANT POUNDING JERKED CATE AWAKE. Only her eyes moved as her sleep-muddled mind strove to sort out what had wakened her. The brilliance of morning squeezed around the curtain and through the porthole in glaring shafts which sliced the cabin's gloom.

"Cap'n!" There was no mistaking Pryce's bellow. The Great Cabin's door was knuckled again with increased vigor. "Cap'n!"

Someone stirred in the salon. The rustle of clothing and creak of leather was followed by a groggy, "Eh?"

"Beg pardon, Cap'n, but you're desired—"

"You can come in, Master Pryce." Neither was there mistaking Blackthorne's throaty growl.

She heard the halting clump of boots, and then a hesitant, "Cap'n, if you be of leisure—"

"Bloody hell, Pryce. Come in the damned room and stop caterwauling like a wretched fishwife!"

Even at her distance, Cate jumped at Blackthorne's roar.

The footsteps sidled farther.

"Beg pardon, sir. T'wasn't wishin' to intrude." Pryce's insinuation wasn't lost: a woman in the captain's cabin was apparently a familiar scenario.

"There's no intrusion to be made, Master Pryce." Blackthorne's reply came around a huge yawn.

"Some o' the hands represent as they heard screamin' last night, of the womanly sort."

The comment came not in the way of accusation, but advisably, a delicate suggestion that a bit more discretion might be exercised the next time.

"Did they now?" said Blackthorne coldly. The scrape of a chair was followed by the stomp of a foot and labored scuffle of walking with one leg asleep. "And pray what did the remainder hear?"

"Nuthin,'" came dully after a brief pause.

"Uh-huh. I thought as much. She's in there, if you desire to inspect for damages. 'Course, that would be to risk stirring her up *again*. You fancy caterwauling, do you, Master Pryce?"

Pryce sputtered and humphed.

"Was there an initiating purpose to this visit?" Blackthorne prompted.

"Huh? Oh, aye, sir! The bosun sends his compliments and, if yer of yer leisure, desires ye to attend. He says the larboard lift blocks an' crosstrees on the fore gallant won't answer. And the Company muster will be a-waitin' yer leisure at eight bells."

"Very well, lead on, Master Pryce," said Blackthorne through another yawn and the two left.

The salon now quiet, Cate took the opportunity to wake further.

Through a dull headache, she sought again to come to terms with where she was. A part of her concussed mind clung to the familiarity of her surroundings — the watch bells still pealed, the boatswain still bellowed, the holystones still scraped, and the caulking mallets still rapped — and insisted if she was to close her eyes, she could still be on the *Constancy*.

"This isn't the *Constancy*, it's the *Sara Morgan* or *Carry Morgans*, or whatever," she said aloud. She had been aware of Pryce calling the ship by a different name, but was at a loss as to what it had been.

Cate opened her eyes and blew a long sigh. Yesterday, she had prepared to never see the sun rise again. Seeing the morning rays cut the cabin's gloom had to be taken as a victory. The bone-rattling terror had given way to mere gut-knotting dread. Her hands no longer shook, the quaking reduced to no more than sporadic tremors, and her heart had slowed to a rate which promised it wouldn't leap out of her chest after all.

Awaking in Blackthorne's bunk, with no idea of how she had come to be there, was unsettling. Even more worrisome was to think she had slept through being moved and wrapped in the quilt. With all the fitful waking, she didn't think to have slept so soundly. Wondering what else she might have slept through, she ducked her head under the blanket to delicately sniff and took a meticulous inventory of her body. There was no stickiness or soreness, nor any trace of the aftermath of sex or violation. It was another befuddlement: a visitor in the night had been expected, and yet none had come... or had he?

The smell of a man rose from the sweat-stained mattress

and pillow. Musty and sharp, it was mingled with hints of rum, cinnamon, tar and orange oil. It wasn't objectionable. If anything, it made her realize how much she missed the smell of a man in the morning. It had been a long time, a very long time.

As Cate lay there, she heard the scamper of feet. At sea or land, the sound of rats never changed. She reflexively checked her toes, fingers, lips and nose to assure there had been no nibbling, as she watched the rolling red back — and a sleek, healthy beast it was — lumber along the wall. The surprise came with a brindled face poked out from under the curtain. First impressions were of a fox, but it was considerably smaller, longer of body and shorter of leg. The creature darted forward and pounced. The rat gave a startled squeal, a feeble kick and was dead. Holding its prey by the neck, the brindled beast regarded Cate with beady, vertically-slitted eyes. Seemingly a bit surprised by her presence, it pranced off with its treasure to be devoured in privacy.

The call of nature forced Cate to rise sooner than she would have preferred. She rose stiffly, taking several steps before her legs became reliable. She listened carefully to verify the salon was still empty before making her quilt-swathed entrance. The privy closet was in the far corner. She was excessively grateful for that tradition of the sea: the captain having his own convenience. Groping her way to the forecastle or asking for a chamber pot was unthinkable. If she was at sea a hundred years, however, she would never become accustomed to the feel of the wind and spray on her bared bottom.

After, she took in her surroundings. The Great Cabin was a man's room; make no mistake, an eclectic collection from every corner of sea and continent. The *Constancy's* walls — bulkheads, at sea — had been pristinely whitewashed. These were walnut, dark and rich with the patina of time, smelling of oil and wax. The mizzenmast marked the forward third of the room, the remaining space dominated by a carved mahogany table centered over a Turkish rug. The sidechairs were equally elaborate, with brass studded seats, their tooled leather worn to a dull sheen.

Opulence and riches were expected — these were pirates, after all — but only luxuriant pragmatism was found, luxuriant at least by any standards in which she had lived of recent. Every object was unique, but at the same time functional, selected for utility rather than to impress: a velvet chair, because one might wish to sit. Before it sat an ottoman, fashioned from some kind of drum-looking something, in case one needed to rest his feet. A water-stained locker sat next to the chair, because one needed a place to set something, such as the thick book there now, a

French classic. A candelabra hung next to it, because one needed light to read.

By the side-lighted, double doors sat a massive Oriental porcelain urn, its inglorious task being to hold a lethality of swords, cutlasses and sabers. Charts bulged from similar gilt-trimmed urns scattered about. Silver and gold cups sat next to ones of leather or wood; after all, one needed to drink. Battered horn lanterns perched next to silver *epergnes*; one needed light. The two cannons, their brass glowing in the morning light, were a cold reality against the warmth of human occupancy, and yet, were quite fitting.

Perhaps the most intriguing of the room's features were the books, a rare luxury and one which had been fully indulged. Cases, with moveable arms that locked or unlocked with a single flip, sat everywhere. Gilded and richly bound, under closer scrutiny, many of the volumes proved to be collections of classics, and in several languages.

Amid the live sounds of a ship under sail, she hitched the quilt higher about her shoulders and perched on the arm of a chair to stare out the windows at the rich hues of sky and wave. According to Chambers and the Constancies, she had committed a mortal mistake: she had allowed herself to be captured. She smiled faintly. Now she could be the one to tell the pirate tales and several fallacies she could correct. She felt frayed and worn, stained and bruised, humbled, but not beaten, not yet. Now, there was nothing except what she had always done: survive. She was a captive, but hadn't been thrown overboard, lips cut off, or innards nailed to a tree... yet.

Things were looking up.

From the corner of her eyes, she saw something move. She looked, but found nothing. With a second glance, she found a small lizard sitting on the window sill. With bulging orbs for eyes, the thing's tiny throat pulsated with each breath. It darted first one way, then another. At one point it fixed a pale, reptilian eye on her, considered her to be neither edible nor threatening, and flashed out of sight through a space in the boards. Another appeared clinging upside down at the top of the window. It scampered about and then disappeared outside.

She gradually became aware of voices on deck, their agitation increasing by the moment. She was startled to see what had to have been all hundred and twenty-odd, the entire ship's complement, gathered. With the mizzenmast as a shield, she watched as a resounding cheer erupted. In the glare of sunlight, the milling throng faced the bow, like metal filings toward a magnet. They gave a rousing shout, their arms raised in much the same fashion as spectators at a hanging. Then there was a great stirring, like someone being brought forward.

A fearful shriek, a high thin cry of pain rode the air. The crowd cheered, their agitation shifting to approval. A few moments later, came another cry, lower and filled with resentment. There was a scuffle, and then a man broke from the crowd and dove for the foremast ratlines. He scrambled up the rope ladders as gangs of pirates gave chase, racing up both sides, eventually going so high she could no longer see them. Their path up and across the yards could be tracked by the gazes and brandished fists of those on deck. From high above came another, and then the blur of a falling body. It caught in the rigging, spun, hit the rail, and then disappeared into the crowd with an odd thud, like a sack of wet meal.

A slightly puzzled hush fell over the pirates, a few grumbling with disappointment or disgust.

Stunned, Cate stumbled back, eventually coming up against the table. She was still standing there when Blackthorne stepped out of the crowd and sauntered into the cabin, the bellow of "Swabbers!" coming from behind him. He was barely through the door when he drew up short at the sight of her, his mouth curling in displeasure.

"You look like you've just seen a ghost," he said, pitching his coat aside.

"I'm not sure what I just saw," she said shakily.

He followed her line of sight to the milling crowd outside, now dissolving. "Oh, that. Company business. Justice desired serving."

"Throwing a man from the yards?"

He turned to give her a queer look. "He wasn't thrown. The stupid sod fell. Never was much in the tops," he said more to himself. "'Tis an unfortunate mess, now."

He cast a thoughtful glance toward the deck. Hoses had been rigged, the swabbers setting to work.

"T'was a disciplinary action," he said, turning back. "Those three—or two now—were drunk whilst on yesterday's raid. Their own mates came forward to claim their drunkenness was cause for injury or inconvenience. 'Tis a direct violation of the Articles. They were judged by their peers; leaves the Captain completely out of it, praise God!" he added under his breath with a roll of his eyes. "The sentence was lopping of an ear... err, last ear in Towers' case. A bit slow on the pick-up, that one is."

"You cut off their ears?" The pained cries still ringing in Cate's head, a wave of queasiness took her. She had witnessed any number of punishments—stocks, ear-pinning, pillory, ducking—many cruel and sometimes bloody, but this seemed uncommonly so, especially when done to one of their own, this so-called Brotherhood.

He smiled tolerantly. "Flog a man and he's not worth his salt for days. Caning and drubbing is no different. Put him in irons or bilboes, and he's on his arse, at his leisure. Keel-hauling renders him as useless as flogging, and then what with all the rigging him up, throwing him overboard, dragging him the length of the ship, not to mention the mess after..."

Blackthorne shuddered dramatically. "Most instances, a man's forced to cut his own off, but strikes me as damned barbaric. No, a quick snick and Bob's your uncle, the fuddling mump learns his lesson, hopefully. 'Tis not torture they seek," he said, looking outside once more, "only justice. And those scuts will be a constant reminder to every man what lays eyes on him. Feeling better today, are we?" he asked, swiveling around to her.

It took her a moment to follow his abrupt shift, and managed an uneven, "Yes, thank you, Captain."

All things considered, she felt much better.

"Nathan." He dropped his battered leather tricorn on the table. "I'd fancied you'd call me Nathan... Cate?" The graveled voice held the question.

She nodded, managing a smile. From amid his glossy beard broke a gold-studded smile that lit the room.

There was an awkward moment. For a man who seemed to have a response to everything the day before, he was markedly ill at ease, searching the rug at his feet as if he might find the words there. The scratch marks, livid on his chest amidst the heavy growth of hair, brought a sense of satisfaction. Hopefully, he would think twice before trying her again. She saw the hand she had bitten was wrapped in a doubtful-looking strip of rag. In the spirit of atonement, and perhaps a bit of endearment, she considered offering to put a bit of salve on it. Never being one to dodge the unpleasant, she took the first step. Anything was better than this insufferable throat clearing.

"Shall I—?" she began.

"A pact," he declared. His habit of interrupting hadn't improved.

She looked to see if he was jesting.

He wasn't.

"I beg pardon?"

"A pact would answer: I stay on this side of the room," he said with a sweep of his arm in a general direction of where he stood. "And you won't attack me again. Agreed?"

"Attack! I never—" Her cheek heated, feeling once again the sting of where he had hit her.

"Tell that one to the fishes. A fine state of affairs and thank-yous for showing a little kindness—"

"Kindness," she sputtered. "But you—"

"What?"

"And then, you—"

"What? Any signs of ill-handling are your own bloody fault. Not a hand was laid, until provoked."

"Provoked!"

"Nasty habit that, repeating everything you hear. Have you suffered this affliction long?" he asked, peering with affected interest down the long line of his nose.

Cate eyed him, trying to decide what he was playing at. Madness and flaws of character had been mentioned in the pirate tales. First, there had been the bullying brute, then cajoling and compassionate with his injured crew. And now, here was another manifestation which smacked of intentional disarming. If so, he was a crafty one, indeed.

She rubbed her brow in frustration. "I surrender."

"Ah, a sane voice at last. A truce it 'tis."

"Then by your leave," she fumed, retreating to the corner she had been sent to the day before.

"Sit. Sit." He waved her back. "We'll call... it... here," he said, toeing an inconspicuous board. Visually following the plank's seam, it ran from under the table, across the room, to the middle of the double-wide doors.

"Hungry?" he blurted. "Tea?" The query came more as a declaration than offer.

At first she thought she hadn't heard correctly. His changes of subject were dizzying.

"Yes, tea would be lovely." An offer of coffee—of which she was in desperate need—would have been met with even greater relish, but she would take anything.

He purposefully strode to a narrow companionway leading below. "Mr. Kirkland!"

Nerves already on edge, she jumped at his bellow.

Quick footsteps could be heard below, followed by a querulous, "Aye, sir?"

"We require tea."

"Beg pardon, sir?" The invisible man's dismay was palpable.

"Tea, Mr. Kirkland. We require tea, *if* you please."

There was a long pause and a befuddled "Aye, sir" and fading footsteps.

Nathan turned back with an elaborate sweep of the hand. "Tea, directly."

Frowning with a bit more concentration than might have been necessary, he busied with charts and logbook. The dark eyes crept up at one point to linger with open avidity on her bare calf. The look was gone with a quickness that made her think perhaps it had been imagined, a mask of inscrutability now in place. Nonetheless, she drew her legs under the chair and rearranged the quilt more closely.

Cate had noticed blessed little about him earlier. In the light of a new day, he wasn't nearly as ominous. He was slightly above average height. She had expected a larger, a more formidable figure for someone who had been accredited with such deeds as he. Shot thirteen times? Beyond an aristocratic nose, the high cheekbones and forehead, not much more could be discerned, for his features were lost in the abundant beard.

There was no getting past the hair: a voluminous, mop-like snarl that reached well below his shoulders. Bound by the omnipresent headscarf, which showed signs of once having been blue, the raven-colored mass was a tangle of braids. Some were made up of only a few strands, while others were nearly the thickness of a finger, many of those haphazardly worked together into larger braids. All were secured by random bits of colorful bits of yarn or thread, twine, or strips of cloth. A delicate metallic jingle accompanied his every move. At one point, he turned the back of his head to her and the light caught near a score of what she first thought to be silver beads. She then realized they were actually tiny bells, barely the size of the tip of her pinky.

"*...one for every virgin...*"

The mind reeled.

Aside from his hair, a few rings on his fingers and a tattered sash at his waist, there was nothing peacockish about him. Compared to the ornate swords in the urn, the one at his side was a workman's model. His baldric, its hand-sized buckle and pistol, were equally plain.

He felt her staring, and so she diverted her attention to anything: the great guns poised at the stern windows. Their muzzles jutting under the gallery sill, they lurked like two pugnacious brass watchdogs. Blackthorne followed her line of attention and smiled.

"A ship's only as good as her stern chasers," he said with a loving gaze.

Said affection was borne out by the names roughly inscribed in the wooden carriages: *Widower* and *Merdering Mary*.

"How many do you have?" Cate asked.

He flopped in his chair and propped his feet on the table, but then yanked them down.

"Thirty-six." The announcement came with no small amount of pride. It was considerably less than the count given on the *Constancy*; one more bit of gross misinformation.

"And we can serve up a minute-fifty barrage for hours, thanks to Pryce and Master Gunner MacQuarrie. They do know how to drill a crew," he said, eyes rounding in admiration.

She cringed at the mention of the First Mate's name. The walnut-colored eyes didn't miss a thing, the dark dash of brows narrowing.

"I can't say I entirely trust the man. He sought to have my clothes cut off," she said, suppressing a shudder.

He chuckled. "Can't say as I blame him. I'd wager not a man aboard hasn't fancied that."

The man she assumed to be the earlier-beckoned Kirkland came up the steps from below, bearing a tray. The apparent cook was a round man with an even rounder face. Like many others, he wore a kerchief around his head, this one being so small it clung precariously to his bald, sun-scaled crown.

"Would the lady care for a bit o' toast?" Mr. Kirkland asked, hovering anxiously.

"Bread?" The closest to bread she had seen on the *Constancy* had been ship's biscuit, appropriately called hardtack, since only lengthy soaking rendered it edible.

Blackthorne chuckled at her awe. "Aye, soft tack. Ovens were installed a bit ago. Not large ones, mind, but enough to allow for a bit of variety. Pirates are a heartless and scurrilous lot, but our bellies still appreciate a fair meal."

The last time Cate had eaten was breakfast past, under Grogan's watchful eye, and meager it had been. Vomiting and the terrors of the day before had left her quite sharp set, and her stomach growled loudly at the suggestion of such a feast. Blackthorne was quick to clear his throat loudly enough to cover the sound.

"No worries, luv," he grinned. "Let it never be said someone went hungry under me watch."

"That would be lovely, Mr. Kirkland," she said at last.

"And perhaps a bit of fruit?" the cook suggested.

She nodded, and he scurried away, obviously pleased by his insightfulness.

Blackthorne rose and made the host. The ritual of serving — the murmured inquires of "Milk?", "Sugar?" and "Honey?", the clatter of porcelain and tinkling of the spoon — eased the tension.

As he bent, she noticed there were bells in his mustache, as well. Similar to those in his hair, they hung asymmetrically: one at the corner of his mouth, the other high over the opposite lip.

"*...one for every virgin...*"

Then what do those two mean?

Tar-stained, but long-fingered and finely-boned, his hands moved with surprising gracefulness. The porcelain's delicacy was a sharp contrast to the lacework of fine scars across the backs and knuckles as he passed her cup.

He poured his own, sipped with exaggerated delicacy and nearly gagged. Struggling against the urge to spit it out, he rolled it from side to side in his mouth. He managed a hard swallow at last, his lip curling in disgust.

"Vile stuff," came out in a half-strangled rasp.

She took a sip and closed her eyes in pleasure. These being pirates, something in the "gunpowder" variety had been expected, but this was aromatic and slightly spicy, one never tasted before. Setting down the blue-flowered cup, she looked up to find him staring, round-eyed.

"What?" Hitching the quilt higher, she glanced to see if she was more indecent than thought.

"Your eyes. They changed color."

"Oh, that," she said, averting them to the table. "I've been told as much before. I'm sorry, I can't help it. It depends on—"

"No, no, 'tis all well... it's just... if you might warn a soul. Yesterday they looked like—"

"An idol that cursed you, I think you said."

"Aye. Now, they're the color of Gordos Bay."

Cate had heard any number of references through her life, most people being at a loss to assign a name to the color, but never anything quite that impassioned.

"Almost green, then," he said pensively. He ducked his head to see once more. "And now, almost blue... but not quite. Odd... indescriptably odd."

He shook his head, his bells jingling with the movement, and then darted another look to see if they had changed again. Seizing upon the distraction, she cleared her throat, in essence calling the meeting to order. She gave her hair another cursory smoothing. Half-drowned and sleep-mussed, wearing a blood-smeared and torn shift, she knew she must have presented a sorry sight.

"May I ask again, Captain," she began levelly, "what do you plan to do with me?"

His expression sobered. His features were carefully arranged, a skill at which she was discovering he was very accomplished. "Why were you on the *Constancy*?"

"I had to leave England, rather quickly," Cate said after some deliberation. "The *Constancy* was the first ship away for a price I could afford."

He cocked a suspicious eyebrow. "Wanted to leave or *had* to leave?"

She pensively chewed the inside of her mouth as she traced the scalloped edge of the saucer. Hours of sleeplessness had provided hours to think. There might be no family willing to pay for her return, but there was another who would, no questions asked. As she was given to understand, Kingston, and hence the authorities, was very near, meaning her sojourn with the pirates could be very brief.

It all depended on the whim of a very pragmatic, yet unsettling pirate.

"Captain, I'll make it easy for you. You and your men pulled me out of the water and saved my life. The least I can do is return the favor."

She took a deep breath. She was a captive on a pirate ship. What could be worse? Revealing herself, however, didn't come easy. After years of secretiveness, false names, lies and being suspicious of every person met, confession to a stranger was now necessary, one known for treachery in pursuit of a prize. And yet, it was that very trait upon which she depended.

"There is a price on my head. None so large as the ransom of a commissioner's daughter," she conceded, smiling briefly, "but His Majesty's authorities will pay at least enough for rum to last you and your men for several days."

One brow twitched, but his face remained carefully impassive. "What...?" He stopped to clear his throat. "What could you possibly have done to draw such attention from His Royalness?"

"Ever heard of Bonnie Prince Charlie?" She watched him carefully from under her brows for his first reaction. For many Englishman, it was a very sensitive issue, raw feelings often very near the surface. If he was one who fiercely resented Charles Stuart's campaign, her future could be very bleak.

His face screwed in confusion. "Certainly. Who hasn't? What the bloody hell has a Catholic upstart seeking to overthrow the Crown, whose only outcome was the destruction of every fool crazed enough to follow, have to do with anything?"

"My husband and I were two of those crazed fools," she said without rancor. "Reluctantly, but that's another story. Brian, my husband, was an officer in the Stuart army. Since I always rode with him, I was considered to be 'aiding and abetting the enemy.'" She chuckled, shaking her head in disbelief. "At one point, there were even handbills for my arrest."

He absent-mindedly scratched his beard, jerking his hand down when he thought her looking.

"Last night, you said you had no one. What of your family?" he asked.

"All very far away and probably dead; I haven't seen or heard from any of them in a very long time."

"And his family?"

Cate took another sip of tea. "If they were caught harboring, or even so much as associating with a criminal such as me in any way, they could be arrested. Their lands would be confiscated, they would lose everything."

"You don't sound Scots, that's for bloody sure." Blackthorne leaned back, hooking his thumbs into a belt buckle nearly twice the size of his hand. "Can't smoke that accent of yours, but it is most certainly *not* Scots."

"Oh, I'm not; Brian was a Highlander, though. Clan Mackenzie," she said with a spark of pride. She sobered as she toyed with her wedding ring. "The day before he was captured, he told me to forget him, consider him dead. God, as if I could!"

She braced her elbows on the table and dropped her head in her hands. Grinding her palms against her forehead, she was grateful for the protective curtain of hair that fell around her as another emotional outbreak dashed to the surface. The fall into the sea must have washed away every bit of fortitude she possessed, leaving her inordinately fragile.

"Does he know where you are?" he asked.

"If only," she said, choking back the tears. She heaved a quivering sigh. "He was captured almost five years ago. I haven't heard from him since. I was told he had been transported, but I have no idea where."

"Did you not make inquiries?"

"And pray enlighten me as to just how was I supposed to do that?" she bristled, looking up. "'Excuse me, Your Lordship, might you overlook the warrant for my arrest for the moment, and pray tell where you took my husband?'" She made an unladylike noise in the back of her throat.

"So, you've been living alone?"

Living alone.

It sounded so simple. And yet, there was a note of appreciation in his question; he wasn't altogether unfeeling of the magnitude of what that entailed: wandering, living in rat-infested hovels, existing on scraps, always alone. Alone, cold, hungry... and above all, afraid.

Cate smiled, apologetic for having flared. "I moved to London; large cities are ever so much easier to disappear into. I'm a fair hand with a needle; I can do fancywork no one else can. At one point, a family took me in as a tutor, because I could read and write, but I had to be careful. The most casual association with me could mean imprisonment."

Blackthorne leaned back in his chair, intently grave. "But then, you had to leave?"

She sipped her tea and nodded. "The authorities were closing in. After a few close calls, I decided it was time to leave. I went to the docks in Bristol with every shilling I had and bought passage on the first ship away."

"You were headed for Kingston. Do you know anyone in Kingston?"

"Hardly," she scoffed. "Mrs. Littleton would have been my only acquaintance. It would have been of great advantage to have a recommendation, even a place to go, but it doesn't matter now."

Cate finished her tea, the cup clinking softly on the saucer as she set it down.

"So, Captain, you have your prize before you. Report to the nearest garrison you have Catherine Mackenzie, and you'll be the richer man for it."

"You said Harper, before."

She winced at her ruse being exposed. In fact, he was smiling, as if he expected the duplicity and was proud of her for it.

"Yes, well, it's actually Mackenzie; Harper was my maiden name."

Blackthorne leaned forward. "Why are you telling me this? It could mean the hangman's noose—"

"Drawing and quartering."

He sat back, duly impressed. "The Crown prides itself on doing no bodily harm to women, officially at any rate."

"It was made eloquently clear that they were willing to make an exception in my case," Cate said with a grim smile.

Heavy footsteps, amid a goodly amount of labored breathing and florid cursing, interrupted them. Crane and Toad, her two guard-assistants from the sick bay, came through the doors lugging a massive dome-topped chest. The smashed lock dangling from the hasp, its contents foamed out from under the lid. Toad now wore a bandage about his head, the ends flopping from his crown like rabbit ears. He was comical-looking, until the bloom of red over where his ear had been, and the streaks of dried blood down his neck and shirt came into view. Close behind them came two more men to deposit smaller trunks. Knuckling their foreheads, all took their leave.

"I passed the word for the... err... um... well, I know how women are about their... things..." Blackthorne, or rather Nathan, frowned in the puzzlement as to what could be so valuable.

"Pray tell them 'Thank you'." She looked to her lap to hide a smile. "It's a lovely thought, but there's only one small problem: those aren't mine."

His smile faltered into a displeased curl. "Blundering, cod-handed dolts! They claimed 'twas all —"

"There wasn't much to be found." She looked away, for it was embarrassing to have to admit of being so near destitution. She winced at the stab of loss. She blinked to clear her blurring vision as she looked out the windows, to where the *Constancy* had vanished. She felt Blackthorne watching, but elaborated no further.

"Might I suggest that you find something, unless you desire to go about like that," he said, rising.

Seeing him abruptly side-step from the imaginary line in the floor reminded her to keep to her side as she followed him to the trunks.

"I have nothing," she said evenly.

He flipped open the lid of the largest, its ransacked contents — silk, satin, lace, ribbons, ruffles and linens — spilling out. She recognized the churned snarl of whites, pinks, blues, greens and yellows as having been Mrs. Littleton's.

With a pang of remorse, she ran her fingers along the silver crest which adorned the front of the largest, an oval, full of flourish and detail, it bore a scripted "L". She was familiar with the exact contents of all three trunks, for she had been the one to pack them. Being the only other woman aboard, she been the one to care for the ill women. She had sponged their fever-wracked bodies, day and night melding into a blur. She had overheard a crewman mumble something about "a couple of days"; she had no alternative but to accept that as fact.

Their death had been a blow. In the short time, she had become close to Mrs. Littleton, but most particularly Lucy. There had even been suggestions that, once arrived in Kingston, she might find a position in the Commissioner's household. Those hopes disappeared over the rail as the bodies were sent to the deep.

"These are women's things, aren't they?" Blackthorne asked.

"Yes, but Mrs. Littleton was a good twelve inches shorter — and at least double at the waist — and Lucy was a girl of fifteen, barely half my size."

The smaller trunk had belonged to the younger. A sleeve stuck out, lilac-flowered, with the same silk flowers at the elbow. She touched the flowers, smiling inwardly as she recalled Lucy in that very dress as she strolled the *Constancy's* decks.

Blackthorne frowned, clearly unfamiliar with the feminine complexities. "Can't you just fix up something? I thought you said you were fair with a needle."

Cate looked down, fingering a pink satin sleeve, heavily ruched with lace. "Certainly, in a couple of days, but I'm not sure how practical any of this is going to be. These are ladies' things: silks and satins, and fine laces."

"You're a lady."

"Hardly." She made an unladylike noise. "It's not usually the first word to come to mind when describing me. Regardless, I don't think any of these would be appropriate for a ship of this... nature."

"You mean a pirate ship?"

She met his dark gaze squarely. "Yes, a pirate ship."

"No worries, luv." A flash of ivory split the beard as he grinned. "'Tis many a far stronger man what shrinks at the word. Hell, some days I struggle with it meself."

The humor faded, suddenly becoming very distant. And then he shook his head as if to rid himself of a thought.

"Aye, these are very fine things," he murmured, fingering an azure brocade sleeve.

"All in good time, but in the meantime, I'll be in need of something."

Mr. Kirkland's arrival brought them back to the table. A plate of toast awaited, with a small dollop of jam, a sliced orange and a battered silver knife. The honey jar had been slid from the teapot next to the plate.

Blackthorne sat only to rise abruptly and head for the door.

"Is there anything else that I... err, we can get you?" he called over his shoulder.

The offer held the tone of being meant only in jest, and yet a strain of sincerity.

"Some hot water," Cate said on a surge of unadulterated self-indulgence.

That stopped him in his tracks. "Eh?"

"A basin and some water... to wash with." Her heart quickened at the prospect. A trans-Atlantic voyage demanded severe conservation of fresh water, and hence no allowance for a luxury such as washing. She had no soap, but the thought of hot water alone sent a thrill through her. His puzzled look gave her a sinking sensation that she might have presumed too much.

He saw as much and his gaze softened. "Treasure is in the eye of the beholder, is it not?"

Mirth lit his eyes as he bent an elaborate bow, touching his fingers to his heart, and then lips. "Your wish is but me command, m'lady."

❧

Hovering fretfully at the top of the companionway, Mr. Kirkland indulged Cate in four more pieces of toast, another orange and enough tea — Alas, not coffee — to float the ship. Now anchored by food, she felt considerably steadier. Kirkland then brought a steaming ewer, a porcelain basin, ringed with images of frolicking cherubs, and a sponge.

"Picked and cleaned it, myself," he beamed.

From a chest of drawers, he produced a length of cloth intended as a towel. Face burning with embarrassment, he then scampered away.

She moved her toilet to the sleeping area. The curtain posed a flimsy barricade, but it provided the impression of privacy. Modesty demanded she keep the quilt about her — prying eyes and all — but pragmatism pointed out the impossibility. She poured a measure of water into the chipped basin and shed both quilt and shift.

It was her first opportunity to inspect the damage from Chin's knife. Lying just above the full of her breast, the length-of-a-finger cut was now lightly crusted with dried blood. The nicks on her ribs and midriff were bright with newness in comparison to the white lacework of old scars. Those, which ran from the curve of her ribs to the flat of her belly, had been long forgotten. It had taken the threat of another blade to call them back to mind. In consideration of all the damage from so long ago, it was a puzzle how Chin's knife could have prompted her to react as if she had been nearly eviscerated.

Troubling, but she shook the thought away.

Later, all very much for later.

A basin and a sponge wasn't a real bath, but it was luxurious compared to the wooden bucket of seawater and the hem of her shift, the sum total of her ablutions for the last two months. The water was dank but fresh, not salt. It was glorious. In spite of its initial warmth, it cooled her skin and sent goose flesh creeping up her arms.

She closed her eyes and allowed her mind to ponder Captain Nathanael Blackthorne.

It hadn't gone unnoticed that he had effectively eluded

answering her questions regarding his intentions. In fact, he seemed to ricochet between not wanting to say and not knowing. Neither thought was comforting. It still remained to be seen if he would rise to the bait and turn her in for the reward. Initial impressions had been his interest was only mildly piqued, but if she had learned anything about the good Captain it was that he was a master at keeping his council.

As Blackthorne sat sipping tea, he had appeared benign enough, but even a lion could look peaceful when sleeping. She had eyed him at the table, wishing she had paid more careful attention to what the Constancies had told of him. So much had been said, it was nigh impossible to separate the horrors and misdeeds credited to Blackthorne from the other names bandied about. She fancied herself a good judge of character, but Blackthorne was difficult to fathom, partly because his features were so buried and partly because he was rarely still. He shifted roles like an actor. Was the real Blackthorne the bully she had met in the cabin or the compassionate one met kneeling next to the wounded Chin? Or was it the disarming charmer who had just taken his leave, the inscrutable temporarily tilted aside? Or was it all an act, with the single intention of getting her to drop her defenses?

No, only the foolhardy would be sucked into believing any of the façades. The malignancy, which most assuredly lurked behind the curtain, rendered him doubly treacherous. Besides, even if the Captain indeed proved to be benevolent, there were still a hundred and twenty-some pirates aboard who were not.

As Cate dried off with the scrap of towel, she glanced about the dim room, curious for an insight as to Blackthorne, the man. It was, however, more austere than the salon. Aside from the quilt, the narrow bunk sported a worn canvas-covered mattress and a faded checked pillow. At its foot sat a sea chest, with intricately knotted rope handles. A small stand was next to the bed, a sconce over it. Atop the stand was a stack of books: *Catullus*, something in French which she couldn't read, and *Moll Flanders*. Eclectic taste, to say the least. A dull gleam in the bunk's corner caught her eye, a bottle wedged there. Uncorking it, she sniffed: Madeira. A washstand in the corner, a low stool, a row of empty pegs on the wall, and a hanging locker containing a disreputable rain tarpaulin completed the room.

No extra clothing, no luxuries, no hints of the person or his past; contrary to his colorfulness of character, Nathan Blackthorne, famed pirate and scalawag, was a man of simple needs and tastes.

Suddenly guilty for having invaded his privacy, Cate turned

to a more pressing problem: clothes. Donning the soiled and crumpled shift once more, she went through the now empty salon to the trunks. She held little hope of finding another shift. Several had been soiled during the women's illness, and in the spirit of decency, she had dressed each in a clean one before burial.

She hesitated at the side of the largest, chewing at the inside of her mouth. The owner of this trunk had once been alive, breathing and talking, loving and being loved. Now, Mrs. Littleton was gone, leaving nothing but a few possessions to mark her passing. Gathering her resolve, she lifted the lid and groped through the tangled mass. She held a hope, though a desperate one, that the pirates had been through enough in their pillaging of the *Constancy* to have found her little bag, the one she had so carefully hidden, so that it wouldn't be found. For her to find it there would have meant Providence had smiled upon her, a rare occasion indeed. The backs of her eyes began to prick at the thought of what had been lost. She shook it off and set to digging with more intent.

Just as her hand hit something hard—a hairbrush, it felt like—the clump of boots announced Nathan's arrival. She rose and bobbed a curtsy. Slightly flushed with exertion, his arms were laden.

"I come bearing gifts," he declared.

He reached as if over an invisible barricade and dropped the cloth bundle he bore into her arms. She shook it out to find a man's shirt and breeches.

"They'll answer fine. I can't recall the last time I wore breeches; it's certainly better than a quilt," she said.

"The hold's full o' swag, but nothing seemed..." He struggled for a word, and finally landed on "Appropriate," but winced, not happy with that one either. "We'll be putting in on the 'morrow, the next day the latest; perhaps we can find something better then."

The breeches were sky blue velvet, the shirt a fine lawn, with deep-laced cuffs and collar. As she held the shirt up for inspection, it was difficult to overlook the elegant fabric's transparency. Suitable for a man, under a waistcoat and jacket, it was otherwise quite revealing.

"Oh! I brought this, too." From his sleeve, Nathan pulled a long strip of cloth, its ragged edges evidence of having been torn from a larger piece.

"It's for... well, you know... it's..." He cleared his throat meaningfully and crisscrossed his chest. "It's to help with... things."

Agitation radiated from him like heat from a brewing pot, his displeasure seeming to stem from the very items he had just given her.

"You're not one of those men who think women shouldn't have legs," she asked?

His discomfort gave way to indignation. "The last woman I knew to wear breeches tried to kill me."

"And somehow, it was the breeches fault?"

"What else?"

She thought him to be jesting until she saw his deadpan expression.

"I'm sorry," Cate sputtered, holding up what was meant as an apologetic hand. "I'll try to give warning, if I'm taken by the urge."

"I would appreciate that," he said coldly.

The smell of dankness, wet wood, stale body odor and old vomit met her nose, strong enough to be smelt at arm's length.

Her stomach rolled, and she blurted, "I'll need to wash these."

"Excuse me?"

"Wash. They need washing." Even if it meant using seawater, the smell of that would be far preferable. Standing in nothing but an oversized shift was hardly the time to be particular, but on some things she was unwilling to compromise.

His lip lifted, wrinkling his nose. "Why?"

"Because they smell."

"Like what?"

"Any manner of things. Sniff."

She shoved the offensiveness under his nose. He obligingly bent, audibly sniffed and straightened. "Not bad. I've certainly smelled worse."

It was all too clear that it could have smelled like a dead horse and he would have said the same.

"Not on me." Tension was making her more sensitive and truculent than what was customary.

"Have you any concept what it took to find those for you?" he demanded, propping his hands on his hips.

"No," she said, somewhat chastened. "But I'm not wearing anything that smells like... that."

"I don't give a bloody damn if you lie naked in the bunk for the next fortnight."

With a disgusted growl and an angry swipe, he turned and made for the doors, veering at the last to the rail at galley companionway.

"Mr. Kirkland! The *lady* desires to wash."

He made a great show of walking the boundary line. Just

short of the door, however, he trounced his foot down on her side, making a defiant gesture behind him. He skidded to a halt before a mass of gape-mouthed crewmen gathered at the door.

"What are you looking at, you bunch o' knot-headed laggards?" he shouted, scattering them like chickens from the garden gate.

⌒⌒⌒⌒⌒

Cate's face heated with embarrassment as she stood next to the bunk and ran her hands over her rear and down her thighs. There was no looking glass. Only self-consciousness was her guide. It was awkward to be wearing britches. She had worn them as a child and into her later years of youth, but rarely since. Inordinately large, the shirt and breeches barely touched her body. Even with the shirt's voluminous tails tucked in and the ties at the back drawn tight, the waistband still hung precariously at her hips. A belt might have answered, but there was none.

With an experimental shift of her shoulders, she tested the bindings around her chest. She smiled privately at Blackthorne's fretfulness but was grateful for his thoughtfulness. Modesty had never been her burden. She didn't consider herself large-breasted, but in view of the lawn's sheerness, precautions were necessary. She checked the binding's knot a second time. Short of walking about with her arms crossed, she was still unsure as to what to do about the neck opening. With one of the ties missing, it gapped nearly to her navel. The binding prevented exposure, but the draft was disconcerting.

What I wouldn't give for some stays just now.

Mrs. Littleton and Young Lucy's were in the trunks, but either would have required extensive alterations before they could have been serviceable.

The shirt was for the most part dry and clean, or rather *cleaner*, there being a limit as to how much could be attained with cold seawater. The breeches were still damp and quite crumpled; the velvet unappreciative of being washed in a bucket. The state of undry, however, wasn't unpleasant. She was not yet accustomed to the tropical heat and the breeze through the damp cloth was quite refreshing.

Cate tentatively pushed aside the curtain and went out into the salon. Its empty state was a reprieve of having to face anyone. In spite of the stern's expanse of open windows and the breeze through the cabin's double doors, she was in desperate need of fresh air. With no wall or encumbrance other than a forbidding seam in the planks, she still felt trapped. Careful to stay on her side of that demarcation, she paced and wondered if she was to be allowed out of the cabin. No mention had been made one way or the other. No guards were in sight, although she could feel eyes on her.

The boundary line imposed by Blackthorne ended perpendicular to the coaming, a raised barrier at the bottom of the door to prevent water from pouring in. Whether the coaming was part of her limit was unclear and Blackthorne... err, Nathan was nowhere to be seen. His voice could be heard now and again, broken by wind and ship.

She paced in circles, each pass a bit closer to the door. Nothing was said. No one seemed to notice. Steeling her nerve, she stepped over the coaming and waited in the shadow of the afterdeck's overhang.

Nothing.

She inched farther. A few of the hands nodded as they passed, casual and noncommittal. A few inches further brought notice in the way of raised eyebrows and elbowing each other to exchange significant looks. Pirates they might be, but they were still sufficient creatures of tradition to stare at the scandalous sight of a woman in breeches. It made her even more aware of her bare calves, the visible division of her legs and her rear for all to see.

This is going to be more difficult than I thought.

She was instantly struck by a difference in atmosphere. Captain Chambers' deck had been a quiet deck, "Silence fore and aft!" a common cry. The *Constancy* hadn't been a tyrannical vessel, although more than once she had seen a man started with the same bludgeon Mastiff had brandished at her. Compared to *Constancy's* guarded reserve, this was cheerier, a chatty ship. For such a barbarous rabble, to find slovenly disorder on the verge of mayhem would have been no surprise. Instead, the decks were scrubbed to whiteness, the smell of fresh paint wafting in the air. Brass, or any other surface which could be induced to shine, gleamed. The sheets hung on their pins or kevels in close-ordered ranks.

Alert for any sight or sound of Scarface, who had attacked her yesterday, she glanced about, hoping to see Nathan. From overhead came Nathan's voice, ragged and torn, like someone just awakened from a deep sleep. Inching farther took her into the blaze and warmth of the sun. She shaded her eyes and saw him on the quarterdeck. In essence the roof of the Great Cabin, the afterdeck was bracketed by a pair of elegantly curved stairs with scrolled rails and balustrades. With as much dignity as could be gathered, all the while expecting to be sent back like a recalcitrant pup, she mounted the steps.

At the top, Cate's step slowed. A twitch of Nathan's brow and quirk of his mustache acknowledged her presence, but he left her to stand for some moments, his version of a reprimand. The space was populated with several more crewmen, going about their duties. At her arrival most either left or moved farther aft, leaving her and Nathan alone, or as much so as could be managed on a ship.

"Do... you... mind...?" she asked.

One eye narrowed as she sidled closer. "Do... you... plan... to... take the ship?" he asked, mimicking her halting query.

"Hardly. I was unsure if I was to be allowed... out."

"If you weren't, you would have known," he said with a severe look. "Shackles are blessedly difficult to overlook."

Something had been bothering her about him from the moment she had topped the steps. It finally struck her.

"You shaved!"

The abundant beard was gone, a swatch of newly exposed and shockingly pale jaw in its place. The only remnants were a spade-shaped beard over a strong chin and a mustache, its silver bells still in place. With a long sweep of bold jaw and high cheekbones, under all that hair had lurked a very comely face.

"Did I?" He feigned astonishment as he passed a hand along his now-smooth jaw. "Ah, yes, I recall now: Navy Sunday."

"It isn't Sunday, is it?" If so, being captured had disoriented her worse than previously suspected.

He scowled. "Of course not; Navy Sunday is on Wednesday."

"So, today's Wednesday?"

"No, goose. 'Tis Tuesday."

Cate pressed her fingers to the bridge of her nose.

"...a day of washing hammocks, bathing and laundry and such," he was saying. "A high holy day for you, to be sure," he added with a dramatic roll of the eyes. "Navy Sunday; you'll love it."

"But you said today is Tuesday."

"Is it?" Touching a finger to his chin, he struck a thoughtful pose. "Oh, aye. So, it 'tis. Just setting an example: cleanliness is next to holiness—"

"Godliness."

"Eh? Oh, whatever." He ended with a broad sweep of his hand and then added with a suffering air. "Leadership is an ever-pressing burden."

Between his grimed shirt, tattered collar and cuffs, worn breeks missing buttons at the knees and tar-stained fingers, she had a strong sense his personal grooming was far from burdensome.

He again took his eyes from the horizon to regard her shrewdly. "With all due respect, you make a better woman than you do lad."

"Thank you... I think."

Still staring at his transformation, it was easier to see that he was jesting. His smile was broad, brilliant and quite charming.

"T'would appear a belt might be in order," he said, eyeing her judiciously.

Cate tugged self-consciously at the sagging waistband. "I hesitated to ask for one. I was afraid you might use it on me first."

A corner of his mouth twitched, but he was otherwise unresponsive.

"I thought I might ask leave to see to the injured?" she asked hesitantly.

"And what, pray tell, do you seek to gain from that?" His query was more in the way of wonderment than suspicion.

"To see how they do."

He made a derisive noise in the back of his throat. "You were the one to attend them, ergo you above all should know. They've not been added to the Butcher's Bill, so one will assume they *do* well enough."

She flinched at his sarcasm. Just because a man hadn't been listed as dead didn't necessarily mean he was in the pink. Seeing her reaction, he relented to explain.

"Chin's confined to his hammock on pain of being lashed in if he shows a leg. Three other names are on the binnacle list: one pukes every time he rises, another stove his ribs in—No need to risk putting one through a lung, eh?—and the last still can't raise his arms, so he's a worthless scug. The balance are to their duties on pain of being accused of malingering."

Shouting on the forecastle distracted him. As he craned his head, the wind lifted the hair from his neck and she nearly gasped aloud. God knew she was familiar with scars, but this one was particularly grisly. Running just under the bold line of his jaw, it wasn't the location so much as the nature of it: thick, curving gnarls of white against tender skin of his throat. It was a wonder what horror could have inflicted such a thing. In morbid curiosity, she waited for his head to turn, to see if it continued to the other side.

It did.

In the absence of a beard, another tattoo was now visible, curving like a collar at the base of his neck. It was an interwoven, chain-like design, strongly suggestive of Highland designs. The woad-colored pattern was muted by his tan. Under the protection of shirt and hair, the blue was brilliant against the pale ivory of his skin.

Cate had stood on the Constancy's quarterdeck many a time, but never did she experience what she did then. The difference between the two ships had been felt while lying in her cot, but there on the quarterdeck, it was even more pronounced. The *Morganse* sailed with an ardent zeal, a fine thoroughbred straining to run. Her heart quickened and her breath came short with the same thrill as if she was riding that same horse, too spirited to be controlled and yet racing too fast to jump off.

Chambers had spoken affectionately of his ship, but never had she seen him at the wheel, a point she made to Nathan.

"Ordinarily 'tis not the captain's charge, but I can't bear to be away from her for long," he said, lovingly stroking the wheel. "We belong together, she and I, I and she. Besides, it does the crew well to see the captain standing his watch, same as the rest."

"It looks as if you've done this for ages."

"Sailing, you mean? Went to sea at twelve."

"No, I mean at the helm, with the *Morganse*."

He gave her a tight-lipped smile. "All told, only a few years of late; lost her there for a bit, I did."

"What happened?" she asked, bracing a hand on the binnacle against the roll of the swell.

"Mutiny."

The word was uttered no differently than if it had been "ague" or "storm."

Her face heated with embarrassment. "I'm sorry, I didn't mean to—"

"No worries, luv." There was a reassuring flash of a gold and white smile. "A minor setback there just for a bit, but she's mine now." He stroked the wheel again, his fingertips tracing the curve of the worn-to-a-polish wood.

"*Ciara Morganse*," she said, careful to pronounce it as closely as Pryce had on the *Constancy*, a far cry from *Sara Morgan*. "It's a bit of an odd name."

"Aye, *Ciara Morganse*," he corrected. With a lilt reminiscent of the Highlands, it came out '*kee*-h-rah'. "It's Celt. It means 'black gift from the sea,' roughly."

"Was she a gift?"

Nathan looked away, sobering. "Some would call her that."

Cate took his abrupt change in demeanor as an indication of having reached the limit of what he was willing to discuss. As they talked, she noticed curious looks on the part of the crew. At first, she thought it was the shocking sight of her in breeches, but gradually came to realize the gapes were aimed at their newly barbered captain.

"I'm ashamed to confess, this isn't quite what I had expected," she said looking down to the main deck.

"You were expecting what: debauchery, rampant drunkenness, chests of gold, piked heads and disemboweled bodies?"

"Not the bodies." Such a juvenile concept left her feeling quite foolish, the condition worsened by having to admit to it.

"Not the bodies," he muttered, both mystified and amused. He closed his eyes and gave his head a sharp shake. "For all our renown, a pirate ship is first and foremost a ship, and must be run as such."

"You're saying there is no difference between this and... say, the *Constancy*?"

He waggled an admonishing finger. "Nay. We are a ship, but we run things considerable different. Captains are elected, as are quartermaster, bosun and such."

"I thought pirates were free spirits, freedom of the seas, where the wind blows and such."

"Oh, aye, we're that to be sure, but one must have rules. Otherwise, 'tis all a-hoo, from the f'c'stlemen to the boomtricers, or from the bracemen to captain of the crosstrees. Foredeck crew wouldn't know what the afterguard is up to. Gun crews would be firing all willy-nilly without a master..." A flutter of hands and rings flashing in the sunlight embellished the chaotic picture he painted. "Nay, a chain of command is necessary, which Morgan and Bartholomew discovered directly."

"I've heard of them," she said slowly, struggling to recall the details from the conversations overheard on the *Constancy*.

"Code of the Brethren. The Pirate's Code. Code of the Coast. As I said, without rules there's havoc and in that they did abound. So, the two old walruses called a truce, sat down across from each other and wrote it out, a pistol in one hand and a bottle o' rum in the other."

"Rather civilized."

He laughed grudgingly. "For an uncivilized lot, eh? Bear in mind, many of these men have lived under tyranny in the Royal Navy; they've seen the hell of the wrong person being the only one under God, and have assured it shan't be suffered again. Matters of piracy — raids, ambushes, boardings and such — are a company decision. Piracy, however, requires stealth, and stealth requires a plan. The execution of said plan requires discipline on the part of everyone."

"Other than electing the captain, what else does it include?"

"Bunch o' things. You've heard most of it."

She winced at recalling the induction of the Constancies overheard the day before. "I was distracted." An understatement, to say the least; terrified was more the word.

Her excuse was met with skepticism, but he didn't press. "Each ship has its own terms; a man's mark is his pledge to abide. I shipped on one what—other than the milk goat and a couple of chickens—no animals were allowed. The captain had a morbid fear of anything furred or feathered; thought they would suck the life from him as he slept."

"And if they don't abide?"

"On some ships, discipline is the quartermaster or bosun's concern. As you just saw, we call a ship's Company, the unfortunates meeting a court of their peers, and not the most forgiving lot they are."

"Then where do the stories come from of the captain flogging and keelhauling?"

"Oh, aye, 'tis reserved for the merchants and Navy." He chuckled dryly. "You'll find no ropes, nor three sisters starting a man. Any pirate captain what orders such things on his own accord would stand a good chance of facing the same himself or worse."

"There's worse?"

"There's no such thing as an ex-captain on board." He paused, allowing the implications of that to sink in. "There's but two choices: death or marooning."

"Marooning?"

He nodded grimly, looking away. "Cast adrift or left on an island to die. In the spirit of human kindness, the soul is customarily given a water gourd and a pistol." He held up a beringed index finger. "One shot."

"One shot," she echoed dully. She gulped at the implications of that: a slow death, suffering from heat, starvation, thirst, exposure and loneliness, or use the pistol and end the misery. Mercy was provided, but only by one's own hand. "You've... seen... this...?"

His mouth pressed in a grave line. "First hand."

Cate braced against the binnacle. The move would have appeared to the idle bystander as a reaction to the pitching deck. The reality was her knees threatened to give way.

"What other rules are there?" she asked, desperate for a change of subject.

"In the Code or the Articles?"

"Articles, I suppose. I shouldn't desire to inadvertently violate something." Of greater importance, she thought, was the existence of rules regarding hostages.

Idly scratching an arm, he recited a list, many of what she had heard the day before. Most rules were based in common sense and efficiency. She found it difficult to concentrate on his words, distracted as she was at the sight of him handling his ship. With an unexpected pang of envy, she watched the long fingers skimming the wheel's spokes. They were the hands of a man holding his beloved, pausing to caress a soft curve, seeking her needs, guiding her at his pleasure.

"Most pirates came by way of the Royal Navy, press-ganged during the war," he was saying. "The war ended and His Majesty was no longer in need of 'em. Having been gone for years, many had no family to which to return, so they went back to what they knew: the sea, excepting pirating was the only ready employment."

Cate closed one eye to regard him. "I can't imagine you in the Navy."

He made a derogatory noise. "And justifiably so, since I wasn't. I always loved the sea; got it from me sire, I suppose."

"And always desired to become a pirate?" she declared, heartened by her ability to announce it before him.

His countenance darkened. "No!" He checked himself, quickly assuming a more benign attitude. "I came by that by an entirely different course."

Another sensitive territory blundered into—and so many there seemed to be—she sought another subject.

"So, what are you doing out here? I mean, have you a destination?" The question was rooted in more than idle curiosity. It was safe to say the ship's destination would have a direct impact on her future.

Devilment lit his eyes. "Prowling, luv; cat after the mouse. A bit o' pirating, looking for anyone unsuspecting what may cross our hawse."

That statement was borne out by a lookout posted on every masthead.

"And then what?"

He peered at her as if she was a bit dim. "Cut 'em out."

"That's stealing."

He chuckled dryly. "That, my dear, you'll find 'tis a matter of perspective. Enemies are contrived any number of ways: wrong race, wrong religion, wrong king or just wrong words. A privateer steals in the name of the one what finances him, often finding himself on the wrong side of the very law he thought to honor. Just ask ol' William Kidd. He had the blessings of the Crown itself. He took ship upon ship, all for the glory of King and Country. Only by the time he returned home to deliver said prize, he had been declared a pirate and was hung for his efforts."

"First Holland was our friend and Spain our enemy. A flick of the pen and Spain was our ally, France and Holland our enemy. Then France was our friend, and Holland and Spain..." He gave a shrug. "'Tis easier to assume them all as foes. Piracy is honest: we take it because we want it."

"But, if you take it—?"

"Ah, but what if it had been stolen in the first place? Thievery comes in many forms."

"So, you see yourself as some kind of a Robin Hood?"

A laugh erupted from him loud enough to cause men at the ship's waist to look up from their work.

"Hardly. Nothing so grand. 'Tis every man for himself." He cut a sharp gesture toward those same ones looking up. "Every one of those blighters would take it all and be damned the rest, would that he could."

"On deck there. Sail ho!" came a cry came from high above. "Four points to larboard. Rounding the point, sir. A sloop: twenty-two... make that a twenty-four. Flying the Company flag."

Wheeling around, Cate saw the oncoming ship's flag. The Cross of St. George showed prominently in the canton, but the field was blue and white-striped, not the infamous red and white of the East India Tea Company.

"The Royal West Indies Mercantile Company," Nathan said with thinly veiled contempt. "Rarely are colors flown to be believed, but 'tis every reason to believe this one. The treacherous blighter wants us to know who he is."

"Orders?" Pryce bound up the steps and pulled up short at the sight of his freshly-shaven captain. His grey eyes cut accusingly at her.

"How do you make her?" Nathan demanded.

"She's the *Nightingale*, or the *Faithful*, for anyone what cares to see the difference, painted up like a tart on the Sabbath. Privateer. More like a wolf in sheep's clothing."

Cate recalled hearing on the *Constancy* of sleights of hand: ships being taken and then disguised for the purpose of evil-doing.

Pryce spit contemptuously over the rail and then fixed a reproachful eye on his skipper. "It were a risk to come here. They been a-layin' fer us."

"A risk known and well worth," Nathan said with a significant look. "Damn. I fancied she'd had enough of our fire and thunder off Barra Terre. Very well, let's give the sod what he seeks."

"She runs better, and she has the wind. We've land in our lee to boot," Pryce said, indicating the nearby island with a cautionary nod.

"That she does, but we have the greater will, have we not?" said Nathan with a fleeting smile.

"She's brailing up her courses, sir," came a call from overhead.

"Well, there's your answer, if anyone fancied she meant to hail us for tea, eh?" Nathan grumbled.

Cate understood precious little of the exchange, but none of it sounded good, she thought as she watched the lower corners of the *Nightingale's* mainsails draw up. Even a landsman as herself could see the two-masted ship was smaller and sleeker, her sails triangular as opposed to the *Morganse's* square, and ran her length rather than across. A long, dove-tailed streamer broke from the *Nightingale's* peak and the pirates gave a jeering roar.

"What is that?" she asked.

"He's declaring his superiority, like he's the goddamned Commodore hisself. We're expected to hove to," said Nathan.

"'Tis usually reserved for ships sailing under the King's papers," Pryce explained with equal contempt.

Nathan glared across the water. "Not bloody likely, the split-tongued, master rogue. She might be smaller and handier, but she's outnumbered and out-gunned. Action stations. Hoist the colors."

A heavy flap, of a different timbre than canvas, drew her attention upward. There Cate saw the black and white banner as it was unfurled from a backstay, and a cheering roar went up from the crew. When seen from directly overhead, the haloed skull leering down, it was even more massive and imposing. Cate burst in a half-laugh, half-sob, seized by a thrill of fear, and at the same time, an inexplicable surge of empowerment and pride.

"On deck, there. Sail ho!" came from above again.

"You've gone feeble, mate. We've made her," Nathan called up.

"Nossir, 'tis another. Larboard astern."

Nathan cast an eye in that direction and swore. "It would appear an escort had been sent for the good ship *Constancy*."

Guilt heated Cate's face, as if she was somehow responsible for this. It was possible the two ships had intercepted the *Constancy* and Chambers had told them of her being taken. Judging by Nathan and Pryce's reaction, this was a continuing rivalry, which made her presence no more than coincidence.

"She's the *Eclipse*, sir," came from overhead shortly after.

"Captain Eldridge Simmons, commanding," sighed Nathan with a scornful smirk.

"Harte's minion," said Pryce.

"More like sacrificial lamb," Nathan shot back, grudgingly. "One would have liked to assume His Pompousness Commodore Harte would have sent one with a stomach for the smell of powder."

"Which means?" Cate asked, more testy than intended.

Nathan smiled tolerantly. "The Royal Navy puts a great store in its gunpowder. A ship is set out with an allotment and not a grain more. Anything beyond said allotment is the captain's expense. Yon Captain Simmons is ambitious, but he's also cheap."

"Which means?" she pressed.

"Which means our fair foe will do everything in his power to avoid using the one thing what could gain what he desires: a prize, and a fat prize we would be."

"Thrice a'fore he's cut 'n run," Pryce put in.

"And more than likely to now. Pass the word to Mr. MacQuarrie: bar and chain shot. Dismast them before they splinter ours," Nathan told Pryce as he handed off the helm. "Clear the decks. Blood is what these bastards came for, so let's show them theirs."

Pryce thundered down the gangway, the men scattering to their posts ahead of him. They raced either to the guns, and the ship's defense, or the rigging, and the ship proper. None of the dread seen on the *Constancy* was here. These men knew full well what was about to come, and like a glutton dove in without regard for indigestion.

In the face of the burst of activity, Cate's first urge was to do something, yet had no notion of what. She discovered again that it was possible to be bathed in a cold sweat in the tropics, an icy stream of it trailing between her shoulder blades. Seeing the pirate ship bear down on the *Constancy* had been a nightmare. Now she stood on that very ship as another enemy bore down. It was like a revisiting bad dream: scary yet familiar. The waiting, however, was the same, time being ticked off by each wave cut by the *Nightingale* and *Eclipse's* bows.

"Mates," Nathan called down to the main deck. "Yon ships desire our heads. Let's hand them their arses instead. Blow these bastards back to the festering hell from which they came. A fourth of me share to the gun crew what takes out their helm."

A rallying cheer went up. The ship vibrated as the port lids slammed open. Shirts cast off, backs glistening with sweat, the crews manned their guns, ramming home wadding and charges.

Bellowing "Heave!" they hauled on the side-tackles, the guns rumbling home into their ports.

The *Nightingale* was the first to fire: a shot across the *Morganse's* forefoot.

"Manners, if you please, Mr. MacQuarrie! Pray send that sodding bastard a reply to his invitation."

The Master of the Guns glared down the long barrel of the gun nearest the bow, intent on the swell. "Fire!"

The gun barked, MacQuarrie arching his body away from the recoil. A tongue of flame licked out from a cloud of smoke and a ball shot out, hurtling across the *Nightingale's* bow. The deck still vibrated under Cate's feet from it when Nathan pulled her around to him.

"You need to get to the hold," he said. "They will seek to rake us by the stern, so go as far to the forepeak as you can. And for God's sake, keep your head down. Mr. Pryce, a pistol, if you please."

The requested weapon was delivered. Nathan took it and matter-of-factly set to checking the load and priming. When finished, he touched a finger to her chin, his gaze fixing hers.

"Listen to me, luv. Take this. Save it for yourself. If we're boarded, use it. Even in breeches, with those curves you'd never pass for a man. *Do not* allow yourself to be taken. *Sabe*?"

Cate's gut knotted at what that meant. She looked to the ships looming closer. Was the enemy of the pirates automatically her salvation, or was the *Nightingale* a menace to all in her path? Where did the Devil lie? Either ship could be her deliverance, rescuing her from a fate worse than death — until her identity was discovered. Imprisonment and the executioner's block waited after that.

There were no answers, only instincts. She looked into Nathan's steady gaze, solemn and intent. Was he to be her captor or protector? Savior or curse?

"Very well," she said and took the weapon.

"What?" he mused at her surprise. "Shocked to be armed? 'Tis one against over a hundred. We'd have to be a bunch of cod-handed, dutch-built dolts if we were to be shot by a lone woman. And to what point or purpose would it serve?"

Nathan paused to regard her anew. "But then, perhaps I presume too much. If you prefer to be with them, then say the word and allow us to save the powder. You'll be adrift within half a glass and aboard that fair ship before the sun is below the gun'nel."

Her silence was his answer.

"No worries." Grinning at her dismay, Nathan winked. "'Tis

old hat. I've suffered far better and survived far worse. Now, do *not* come out, no matter what you hear."

He leaned to kiss her lightly on the top of the head. "I swear I'll fight for you. Now go."

She was too numb to be startled by his gesture or words. She felt herself being urged toward the steps. By the time the shock had worn off, he was gone, deep among his men. She woodenly made her way to the forward companionway through the throngs of scrambling men. She saw their mouths move, but their voices were muted, as if heard under water. At the top of the steps, she stopped to look back at Nathan, shouting orders from the quarterdeck break.

Damn him! He was enjoying this.

He caught sight of her and smiled.

With a smile like that, how could she not have faith?

Winking, he waved her on.

"Lively, now. Bear a hand, there. Puddening chains, if you please, Mr. Hodder" was the last she heard of him as she went below.

The scene t'ween deck was chaos, but an organized one. Muskets and cutlasses were dispersed, while strips of cloth were secured around heads, arms or waists, to differentiate themselves from the enemy. Tubs of slow-match and baskets of cartridges were brought up from the hold, while wet sand was spread against slippage in the inevitable blood. Over the din could be heard the rap of the carpenter and his mates' hammers, for "Clear the decks" meant not only stowing every object which might pose a hazard, but knocking down the cabin walls.

Cate took Nathan's instructions to mean she was to go to the lowest point possible, and so continued downward. She hung onto the manrope to keep from being bowled over by the hands racing up and down with laden arms. At the bottom of the steps, she balked. The hold was dark and airless, smelling of things gone too wet for too long. What checkered light that managed to squeeze through the grates lost its battle against the void and died within a few paces.

She turned away from the stream of men, toward the bow. Clutching the pistol, sliding one foot in front of the other, she groped her way past casks, hogsheads, bales and crates. Each step took her further from the furor of preparation and the comfort of human voices faded. She thought a few times she had reached her destination, only to discover it was a barrel or some other obstacle. She pressed ahead, Nathan's final words still ringing in her ears.

If I'm not to worry for him, then why did he tell me to shoot myself?

At last, a blind hand verified a solid wall before her. The ship veered and lurched. She skidded on the wet boards and came down hard on one knee. Swearing away the pain, she crawled to the wall and planted her back against it, ignoring the wet coming up through the planks and soaking her breeches.

"Don't let yourself be taken."

Where had she heard that before? she thought grimly. The advice came readily enough, but she had yet to be advised as to how she was to accomplish it. Such advice carried even more weight coming from a pirate, the very one she had been warned against. Unlike the *Constancy*, she felt a kinship with Nathan and his men, for their hatred of the *Nightingale* had been as instant and visceral as Highlanders sighting British patrols.

"Save this for yourself."

She looked down, but in the blackness could only feel the pistol. It was a chilling prospect: to kill herself in the face of being taken prisoner. Or, she thought fondling the cool metal, had Providence provided her another way, a means to escape it all?

One shot and be eternally free.

It was the first time since everything had been lost that she held a weapon. True, a blade had always been to hand, but a pistol promised an efficient end to the misery, starvation, and worst of all, loneliness.

Click.

And then what? She contemplated at what point she would hear no more: the metallic working of the hammer, the gunpowder's hiss or the discharge itself? Or would she be aware long enough to hear the retort in the hold, fading as her life did?

All further thoughts were blotted out by the first great gun blast, the next only seconds after, followed by a rolling sequence from fore to aft. The reverberations clashed into each other and settled in her bones. Cannon—guns, on a ship—was nothing new to her. Those experienced before, however, had been with land under her feet and a husband at her side. Now, she was surrounded by nothing but sea and strangers. She knew little of sea battles and didn't share Nathan's confidence: two ships against one seemed impossible. The piercing of twelve inches of oak wasn't unthinkable, dooming them all to a watery death. She tried to convince herself that she should find courage in those guns: they were the *Morganse's* defense, their safety in every bone-rattling burst.

The splintering crash of the *Morganse* taking her first hit dissolved all resolution. Cate felt the ship shudder through the wood at her back. The *Morganse* sagged, but then came up on the swell, rising above the pain, and fired. The voices of *Widower* and *Merdering Mary* joined in from the captain's cabin, confirming that Nathan's prediction: the *Eclipse* had crossed the *Morganse's* stern. The deadly duo aft fell mute, and the starboard guns spoke as the *Eclipse* crossed. The *Morganse* was now in a crossfire.

The ship's timbers creaked under the strain of firing, flinching at every hit. It became a hypnotic din: the guns' roar, the crash as they leapt back against their tackles, the bellow of men and rumble of carriages being hauled back into place.

Roar. Bellow. Rumble. Roar. Bellow. Rumble...

It was a three-beat tempo from a thirty-six-piece orchestra.

The crossfire was short-lived, the guns firing on the *Eclipse* going quiet. The retort of the *Nightingale's* guns, however, grew louder, which meant she was pressing nearer.

Fingers of fear crawled up like the wetness at Cate's bottom. The water seemed to jet higher between the planks with every roll. The waves rushing past the hull sounded too much like water over a falls, pouring in, the ship becoming nothing more than a coffin. The acrid smell of gunpowder overpowered the hold's dankness. On the smoke rode the shrieks of the wounded and dying and the smell of blood. It seemed impossible that anyone could remain alive in the face of all the gunfire.

Not Nathan, please, not now.

The deck pitched as the ship carved another turn. The thud of the great guns gave way to the staccato crackle of small arms: muskets and pistols. The barrages were a pummeling assault, one lethal wave overlapping the next. The ship slowed, and then came the grind, and scrape of wood against wood, like two gigantic tubs, the wood at Cate's back reverberating with the collision. All sense of motion ended. The musket fire intensified. Deafened by the guns, she could barely make out what sounded almost like an infantry charge: the cries of men, the clash of swords and sporadic pop of pistols.

And then, it was quiet.

The quiet brought no sense of peace. If she had been scared before, she was terrified now. She wished she had paid more heed to the stories on the *Constancy* and knew more of what constituted victory at sea. On land, it was often a matter of which side took the fewer casualties or gained the most ground. Was it a simple matter of which ship was still afloat, which captain still stood, or were there other deciding factors?

She clutched the pistol and waited. Joints aching, hand cramping, time became interminable, marked off by her shuddering gasps from holding her breath while striving to listen. Smoke rendered the muggish air nigh unbreathable. She vibrated with the desire to go help with the wounded, Nathan's final demands the only thing holding her back.

No, not "final demands."

"Final" was a word which put him too near the grave. "Parting wish" sounded ever so much bearable.

Having wished for the sight for so long, when the lantern appeared, she thought the glow through the gloom and smoke to be a dream. Unsure if it was friend or foe, she cowered against the bulkhead, clasping a hand to her mouth lest the rasp of her breathing reveal her location. There was nothing to be done for her heart; hammering so loudly, it was sure to give her away.

"Hoy! Missus?" came a voice through the dark. "Cap'n begs you leave."

And then, the light disappeared.

Rising stiffly, Cate groped a return path, the fogged light through the grates and the cries of agony her beacon. Finding the steps at last, she came up to the gun deck into an ethereal world. The sun streamed through the ports in glaring shafts through whorls of grey smoke, the men moving like dark ghosts. From the swirling clouds came voices, thickened and muffled, orders colliding with pleas. She came upon a wounded man leaned against a gun carriage. As she knelt, she was touched on the arm.

"He's gone," the pirate shouted, semi-deafened by gunfire. His smoke-blackened face pinched with grief as he looked down at his fallen mate.

Her ears still ringing, it took a moment to fully understand what he had said. Her first impulse was to argue, but then saw his meaning. The man sat clutching his abdomen and the shard of wood which had speared him, nearly the thickness of his arm. His life oozing between his fingers, he wore the shocked look of one knowing he was about to die and naught to be done about it. Another, sprawled nearby, had been taken by a more merciful means, half of his head cleanly swept away.

The drive to find Nathan strengthened. Seeing him safe would allow her the peace of mind to tend the rest. Wiping her eyes, now burning from the smoke, she climbed to the main deck, the dread of what she might find weighting every step.

The last rays of afternoon slanted on damage that was far worse. The breeze, which now barely stirred, failed to clear away the stench of death. She had seen the havoc wrought by a cannonball on an open battlefield. It was nothing compared to what sixteen pounds of hurtled iron could do, smashing through everything—and everyone—in its path: shredded canvas, splintered wood, and snarled rope, the shattered bodies resembling half-butchered hogs. Hanging shoulder-high, the smoke shrouded anyone standing, giving them a ghastly headless appearance.

Cate's bare toes curled as she picked her way through the destruction, cautious of the treacherously slippery blood, which streamed toward the scuppers, the surrounding sea taking on a brackish pink cast. She closed her ears to the gurgling coughs and death rattles which she passed. It was too late for them. Pryce hunched over a man propped against the bulwark; Kirkland was not far away with another casualty. Tiptoeing through offal and vomit, she felt something round and slightly giving underfoot. She looked down to see a fingertip sticking out. More could be seen lying about, single knuckles to entire digits, with the occasional pinkish curve of an ear.

The silence in the aftermath of battle was always the most deafening, the elation of victory doused by destruction. These mariners bore the added pain the damage suffered upon their ship, a lady who had fought as valiantly as they. Their efforts were divided between tending their mates and her. As before the battle, it was a scene of chaos, but again with purpose. The powerful voices of the captains of the tops, forecastle, waist, and the like, rallied their men. The mariners busied with tending each other, tying rags about bloodied limbs and heads. Some sat stoically as his mate fished into his flesh with a knife for whatever battle had inserted. The more seriously injured laid waiting, either to die or for help, whichever came first.

The price of victory.

The wreckage of rigging and spars was already being cut away and tossed overboard, along with the bodies of those past identification or Nightingales. No one here would mourn the latter.

Her heart lightened at finding Nathan. He stood amidship, sword clutched in his fist. He whirled around at her approach, eyes still wild with the exaltation of battle. His bloodied blade raised and then lowered at seeing it was her. His cuffs and sleeves were crimson. A fine spray of blood, like paint flung from a brush, flecked his face and chest hair, kept brilliant by his sweated skin. A trail of scarlet ran down several braids from a dark blot on his headscarf, near his crown.

Nathan swiped the blood from his smoke-blackened face. His

breath coming in ragged bursts, he lurched unsteadily toward her, but stopped when his foot hit something: an arm, severed near the elbow.

He kicked at it in frustration and fury. "Goddammit to fucking hell! Is this what you expected, woman?"

A nearly decapitated body lay at his feet. A vicious swipe of his blade finished the job, and he bent to snatch the head up by the hair. She stumbled back several steps when he charged at her shaking it, the dead eyes rounded and frozen.

"Pirates! Heartless, soulless, ravaging, barbarians, without a shred of decency or humanity," he shouted, the cords in his neck rigid.

Nathan grunted with the effort of tossing the thing over the rail. "Goddammit, I didn't want this," he extolled to the sky.

Chest heaving, he stood staring across the water. "We had them: three against one, at the least. They boarded in the smoke, but we pushed them back. The sharpshooters mowed them down like pigeons. Then we boarded..."

Rubbing an arm with a hand that shook with weariness, he looked toward the *Nightingale*, and said in a hoarse whisper, "It's worse over there."

He blinked, like a sleepwalker awakened, and turned as if seeing her for the first time. "Are you all right?"

In view of the carnage all around, she choked a mirthless laugh, sounding almost maniacal in her own ears. She managed a nod. The small gesture gave him ease. Dashing at his face with his sleeve, he swayed. He took a step, staggered and his knees buckled. Cate caught him with a shoulder under his. A crewman lent a hand, and they guided him to the quarterdeck steps.

Kneeling before Nathanm, she tried to take his sword, but he wouldn't—or couldn't—let go, and she had to pry it free. Now she could see that a good portion of the blood on him was his, pouring from near his crown.

"Are you all right?" he asked, focusing on her this time.

She bit back a smile. "You look bloody awful."

He swiped at the blood on his face and flicked it away. "Can't say as I disagree. Seems I didn't duck fast enough."

Nathan lurched to his feet and leaned over the rail to retch. Several more spasms took him before he shakily sat. His ill-focused gaze steadied on her.

"Planning on putting me out of me misery?" he asked dully.

Cate looked down to find the pistol was still in her hand. "Give me a good reason and I'll use it."

She dropped the weapon on the step and bent to help him to his feet. "C'mon, you need to lie down."

Mumbling in protest, he rose, nonetheless. He swayed precariously, and she braced a shoulder under his.

"Cap'n, orders?" Pryce shouted, drawing up before them. His face was soot-blackened, as well. Rivulets of sweat had carved flesh-colored lines, which gave him an odd striped appearance.

"Where be the captain of that fair vessel?" Nathan asked.

Pryce dabbed the sweat from his face with his sleeve. "Which piece o' him would ye care to address?"

"Burn that fucking flag," Nathan said, glaring at the other ship.

"He'll take it personal."

"Good, because it is. Pray set that hulk aweigh as soon as possible."

"She looks helpless," said Cate, noticing the *Nightingale* for the first time. The two ships sat virtually yard to yard, bound by lines and boarding planks. Ravaged and listing badly, the *Nightingale* was a sorry sight. Main mast splintered, yards tangled, shredded canvas draped from her waist to nearly her bow. Wallowing on the swell, she slumped in the water, her spirit as shattered as her rigging. The *Eclipse's* sails, in the meantime, were no more than a blot of white at the line where sky and water met.

"And that concern would be mine, how?" Nathan's brown eyes glared ghoulishly through the glistening red. "A pirate with fewer scruples would have torched her, and then listened to them scream, until the magazine caught and they all went to the depths."

"You're to be commended for killing a captain, but not destroying his ship?" she said in disbelief.

"No, I'm to be commended for being alive and he's not."

"The *Nightingale* has able hands and land in her lee," Pryce said, dispassionately. "They'll do."

Nathan wobbled. His legs buckled and his weight sent Cate staggering. Pryce dipped a shoulder to take the load and half-carried, half-drug him into the cabin.

"Put him on the bunk," she called from behind. "And take off those boots."

Pryce did so, pitching them into a corner. He passed Kirkland at the door, bearing hot water and cloths.

The cook hovered as she filled the basin, critically eying his captain, now splayed on the bunk like a rag doll. "He should be bled."

She suppressed a reflexive shudder. "I think we've had quite enough blood let for one day. After all, the body does require at least a little upon which to carry on, don't you think?"

Kirkland clearly didn't "think", but forbore pressing the point, and scurried out to go tend the casualties.

"Can't abide bleeding." She hadn't realized she had spoken aloud until she heard Nathan grunt in agreement.

Nathan made a flailing attempt to rise. Failing, he fell back on the bed, gasping. "I shouldn't be here," he said and gathered up for another try.

"I have yet to witness bullheadedness to stop bleeding," she said, pushing him back down.

Cate sat on the bunk to deter him from another escape attempt. She carefully pulled away his headscarf and dropped it to the floor with a sodden *splat*. His high forehead was divided by a sharp line of deep bronze below pale ivory. Head wounds tended to bleed profusely, and this one was no different. Taking a rag, she swiped away the blood in order to see more clearly.

"You've quite a head of hair," she said quietly, hoping to distract him as she probed.

Underneath his scarf, there were several inches of loose hair before being woven into the multitude of braids. One ended abruptly at his shoulder, sliced away by a blade. Blooming in their newfound freedom, the hair ends sparked in the candlelight with a multitude of colors: sable, umber, sienna, the occasional sorrel and even bronze. Feeling through the heavy silk, she finally located the wound: a nearly finger-length gouge, running along the curve of his skull. Seizing the candle from the sconce, she held it higher for better light.

"Hmm, it looks like if it wasn't for that scarf, a good piece of your scalp would be gone."

Nestling the basin on the mattress between them, Cate cleaned the abrasion and the area around it, picking away bits of hair, cloth and wood. The water swirled redder with each squeeze of the cloth. The feel of his flesh made him so very real, no longer the personification of a legend, but a man, warm and breathing—a bit raggedly at the moment, but still doing so. At first, he twitched at her every move. Gradually, his shoulders eased and his body uncoiled, the hand curled in his lap falling open. She looked down at one point to find he was observing her just as closely.

"You have double eyelashes," she said in quiet astonishment.

The thick dark frame around his eyes was composed of two rows, one a hair's breadth above the other. In the candlelight, it was difficult to see, but she was sure a blush rose from his collar.

"You have a chipped tooth, just there," he said, tapping a gold one of his in illustration.

"Could use some soap," Cate said, looking away. Soap, at

least the kind not made with lye and ash, and didn't burn the skin, was a rare and expensive commodity.

"Sorry, luv. 'Tis a pirate ship."

She smiled wryly. "No mind. It's been years since I've owned any. Here, push."

Cate directed his hand to the bit of cloth over the wound. He did so, shaky but gamely, while she set to washing his face and neck. More damage was revealed. Many of his knuckles were sliced and scraped. A thread razor-like line of blood marked his neck, a wider one across his wrist. She felt a slight queasiness. Had any of those ` that bit deeper, and it would have been his fingers, arm or head lying on the deck.

She was struck with a shocking wave of relief. He was barely more than an acquaintance; it was inexplicable that his welfare would be such a concern. He had wormed his way into her heart already.

Charmer.

He brought the word a whole new meaning.

Veering from a path of thought she didn't want to take, she asked, "When you told Pryce to burn the flag, he said '*He'll* take it personal.'"

Nathan was quiet for so long she thought he might not answer. Glancing down, she found him staring off with a remote expression. She had thought it a safe question, but his personal boundaries were an elusive fence. Having stumbled upon several of those limits that day, it was clear he possessed more than average.

"R-W-I-M-C." He spoke each letter with firm distinction. "Royal West Indies Mercantile Company. You have heard of it?"

"Only mention and none of it flattering."

"Justifiably so, darling." His lips pressed into a firm line. "The *Nightingale* was a privateer, a licensed hunter to dispatch anyone who might be 'inconvenient' to the Company."

"That's nothing more than a hired assassin."

Nathan smiled grimly. "That would be in the eyes of the one holding the gun. A privateer doesn't have the balls to rob on his own; he needs someone to cover his arse by paying his way, promising to hold his hand when he fails. If he succeeds, he wraps death and destruction up in a tidy package with a bow, and calls his murder and thieving 'for the greater good.' Pirates are the only ones honest enough to call it what it is and die in the process, to the dismay of no one."

"And the 'he' would be..."

"The current lord-on-high in these waters, one Lord Breaston

Creswicke," he said, posing as pompously as could be lying in bed with one hand pressed to his head.

Cate twitched at the name.

"You're familiar with him?" he asked, sharply.

"Only in name. Pryce was probably correct: *he* won't appreciate his flag being burned, would he?"

Nathan puffed with the satisfaction of a task achieved. "Nay. I can only hope it's the first thing he sees when the *Nightingale* finally makes port."

"Why didn't you sink it, if you detest him so much?"

He shifted, suddenly restless and defensive. "Have to have been a bit daft to give them quarter, didn't I? By rights, I should have taken them all hostage, strip them of *everything,* including their dignity, and send that wreck to the depths. That's what any good pirate would have done. But then, why not send that pitiful mess back, let him see he'll have to do better than that to take the *Ciara Morganse,* allow those men to report how the *Morganse* raked their decks with musket fire, until no one had the courage to take the wheel, and then, let them wonder what lengths it will require the next time?"

Nathan snorted in disgust, looking a bit silly with an arm up over his head. "Sir Spineless Simmons hauled his wind at the second volley, tucked his tail and ran, leaving his consort to take the brunt. With some able handling and a bit o' backbone, they could have had us.

"Full broadside was how the *Nightingale* wanted it, even in the face of our sixteens to his twelves. We had the size advantage too; we ran close so as to keep him from firing up into our rigging while we had free run at his. Musket fire finished off what was left; a rain of hell with sixty firing at will."

Pausing to switch hands, his shoulders twitched with indignation.

"The bastard wouldn't hove to, even when he knew he'd been bested. His men and ship were nothing more than a means to him. Aye well, we sent him off to a world where he shan't be annoyed with such trifles. He's in Jones' hands now."

"What would push a captain to be so fool-hardy?" Cate asked, squeezing out the rag, the water now brackish with blood and grime.

Nathan glanced up briefly. "There are two great motivators in this world, darling: ambition and fear, and not necessarily in that order."

"I understand ambition, but what would make him so afraid?"

"Not what? *Who?*"

"Creswicke? He has that kind of power?" She had heard

as much on the *Constancy*, but had taken it more in the way of exaggeration.

"He has a way of making examples what leaves lasting impressions," he said with a cold finality.

Nathan fell quiet as Cate worked. When she finished washing, she removed the basin to the washstand. He took that as his cue and attempted to rise. Hindered by her hand firmly on his chest, a dueling match ensued: he determined to rise and she, not.

"You should be lying quiet," she said, pushing him down.

"Bloody hell, woman. I've no time to be cosseted," he said, batting her away. "I should be tending me ship."

"You should be—"

Nathan lurched to his feet in spite of her insistence. In the process of struggling, his hand had come away from his head. The blood welled with renewed force and tracked down his forehead. Head high in defiance, he took two steps, wobbled, and then staggered to the basin, just in time to be sick. She caught him as he reeled sideways and wrestled him once more to the pillow. Scooping the cloth from the floor, she clapped it back in place—not sorry to see him wince—and redirected his hand to it. Knocking back her hair, she stood over him.

"If I thought taking your breeches would keep you here, that is exactly what I would do."

"Can't wait to see me in me altogether, eh?" The tease was short-lived. Darkening with determination, he attempted to rise again. "I need to tend me ship."

"You're as white as that pillow."

The pillow in question was actually a dirty, off-white, but the parallel held, nonetheless.

"I need—"

"Am I to assume you prefer being seen wobbly like a colt and vomiting over the rail like a landlubber?" she demanded.

Chastened but not beaten, he laid back on the pillow, glaring up. "I'll not lie here, whilst me ship—"

"Shall I call Mr. Pryce, then?" Huffing with aggravation, she wrung the cloth in the bowl and set to cleaning the blood from his face... again!

"Torturing me, you are," he huffed indignantly. "If you were so damned concerned regarding me miseries, you'd at least allow me a spot of rum."

Having been married to a Scot for a number of years, she was well-versed in stubbornness, and in the process, fancied herself as having cultivated a similar streak of her own. In dealing with said Scot, she had learned a frontal attack was too often ineffective; a feint to the flank often proved best.

"There is still bandaging to be done," she said with a suggestive lilt. "I'll wager you've a fair good headache."

"Hurts like the dickens," he said, anticipation heightening.

"Well, in that case," she began judiciously, "a bit might be allowed, for medicinal purposes only."

"Of course!" Sobering, he lowered his voice. "Of course."

"Very well, then, a bargain?"

"Negotiating is it?" He brightened at the prospect. Batting his eyelids affectedly, he settled in for the challenge. "A parlay it is. Your terms?"

Mindful of the delicate nature of such proceedings, she paused, taunting him with a prolonged consideration. "You stay in that bunk... and I'll fetch the rum."

"This bunk, for that rum," he reiterated, gesturing toward the salon. "Agreed!"

The village idiot could have seen his wheels of deception turning. She would have done no differently if positions were reversed, she thought as she fetched the bottle. His face fell in predictable proportions at seeing her pour a dollop into a cup.

"You said, the rum. Those were the terms," he said in stunned betrayal.

"I didn't specify how much, did I?" It was her turn to affectedly bat her lashes. "You were planning to jump up the instant I turned my back."

"They say power corrupts," he muttered, darkly.

"*All* the rum..." She held out the bottle in evidence of her good faith. He made a furtive grab for it and fell back into the pillows, clutching his head.

"All the rum," she said loudly enough to be heard over his cursing in pain, "for *all* the night."

Nathan glared from under his arm. "Think you're some strategic genius, eh? Very well, we have an accord."

Face screwed with discomfort, he took the bottle and a long pull.

His dignity ruffled, he pointedly ignored her, at least as well as one might while having his head bandaged, grunting noncommittally to any remarks she made. Gradually his agitation eased and his responses grew more disjointed. Little by little, the bottle became too heavy. She handily caught it as it rolled from his lap and set it within easy reach, in case he was to wake.

Nathan's eye was beginning to swell; it would be black by morning. Lying with his bare feet askew, the bandage a white slash against the darkness of hair and tan, he looked pale and fragile. Beaten, but not conquered, he would rise again, just... a little... later. Between the blood-matted hair and sullied shirt, he was a mess, but it would have to wait; there were more injured waiting to be attended.

"Sleep well, Captain," she said as she picked up to leave.

He stirred and asked groggily, "Where are you to sleep?"

"I doubt if there will be much of that tonight," she said, stopping at the curtain. "Worry not; I'll find someplace. Good night, Captain."

"Nathan." came a drowsy voice. "I've asked you to call me Nathan."

As forecast, it was a long night. The moon had nearly completed its journey across the sky when Cate finished with the casualties. Tiredly rubbing the back of her neck, she strolled the main deck. She drew in deep draughts of the night air into her lungs to clear them of the fug of sweat, vomit and blood she had been breathing for the last several hours. It had been a night of extractions, removing from bodies what musket and cannonball had inserted. She had been in blood most of the night, either washing it away, probing in it, squeezing it off with stitches, or staving it with bandages. The soles of her feet were raw from the sand spread on the blood-slicked boards. Over a score required attending, some Nightingales. Bleeding on the *Nightingale's* deck, they had pled to join the *Ciara Morganse*. Already short-handed, and with not knowing what the butcher's bill might be, they had been taken on. Between herself, Pryce and Kirkland, all had been seen to, and now all rested comfortably, thank you, Demon Rum.

It had been enlightening to watch Pryce. A man of passions he was. As fiery as he was commanding his men, his compassion had been limitless, either holding their hand while they suffered, or whispering comfort in their ear as they died.

Away from the makeshift sickbay t'ween decks, the scene was quite different. The *Nightingale's* plunder of rum, wine and beer had been consumed, as testified by the numerous dark shapes of bodies sprawled and slumped, several of which she nearly tripped over. Those still upright huddled in the glow of the lamps, proclaiming on this victory and reliving those of the past.

The combination of darkness and drink made her uneasy. It was known to prompt many a man to mischief he mightn't have committed else. She moved nearer to the Great Cabin, and the deterrence provided by a captain, sleeping though he was. Leaning against the rail, she tipped her face into the breeze.

She was coming to relish the soft tropical nights. Granted, the air lacked the bracing freshness of the Highlands and the stars weren't the icy pinpricks of the northern skies. The Caribbean air wrapped one like a mother's blanket, the stars glowing with the warmth of a hearth's light through a window.

Exhaustion drove her inside. The low-angled moonlight banding through the gallery windows showed her way to the sleeping quarters. She drew the curtain aside carefully, lest the rings rattle. Once her eyes adjusted to the dim, she could make out Nathan on the bunk. His outline was limned by the blue-green of the moon through the deck prism, one arm flung in slumbering abandon. She listened to his even breathing, its raspiness echoing his graveled voice. It was a fetching sound; resting her head against the doorframe, she lingered.

It had been more than a little annoying to learn that both Pryce and Kirkland possessed a credible skill at sewing the flesh, and with something far more fitting than the sailmaker's needle she had been handed to mend Chin's leg. It seemed they had been having a bit of a go at her. Their captain had to have been in on it, she thought unkindly. She felt quite put upon, but seeing the innocence with which he slept dissolved her annoyance.

At length, Cate moved to the table. There she slouched in a chair and tried to think of a single place in her body which didn't ache. Every joint felt as if it had been ground into the next. She sat staring out the stern gallery, shaking with fatigue, covered in vomit, blood and filth, pulsing with a sense of fulfillment.

She had been needed.

Every bone ached, but at the same time, she was exhilarated. The true reward had come in the grateful faces. She was very familiar with the way men away from home yearned for a woman's touch, a kind word and a smile often doing more than bandages or salve. What she had forgotten was how taxing the process could be, as if each man had taken with him a small piece, until there was nothing but an exhausted body and a drained spirit.

With an exhausted groan, she fell across the table, pillowing her head on her arms.

Another day done. How many more to go?

4: CAPTIVATED

CATE WOKE TO THE PUZZLING sensation of being tugged by the hair and a strange smell, curiously reminiscent of hay and barns.

Not knowing where she was only added to her disorientation. Not in bed, certainly, but where? She cracked one eye open to a sideways view of a room. A cabin... a hard surface against her cheek... sitting rather than lying... And then the night before came tumbling back.

Her hair was pulled again. Not painfully, but more out of impatience. She pried her cheek from where it stuck to the table, turned her head, and was met by two vertically-slitted golden eyes, a startled bleat and a blast of goat breath.

"Ah, you've met!"

She sat up at the sound of Nathan's voice. He stood braced in the doorway of the sleeping quarters, hair matted, blood-streaked shirt rumpled and askew. Both eyes had blackened in the night, one swollen considerably more than the other. It left him looking quite cockeyed.

"We haven't exactly met," she said, eyeing the goat. The beast ducked its head to snatch her hair again, bleating in protest when Cate reflexively jerked away.

"Hermione, mind your manners, you ruddy beast. You needn't be afraid of her," he directed to Cate.

He balefully regarded the goat as he crept across the room. He moved with the utmost care of one suffering the severe aftermath of a night of overindulgence. Careful not to cross the line of demarcation, his path veered to snatch up the rum bottle as he passed. "She bites, but only when in drink."

"I'm not afraid. It's... She's... I wasn't expecting—"

"No goats?" He mused on the thought as he slouched in his chair. "Can't imagine why not. Come to think on it, there's been one on nearly every ship I've served. Good milk, not to mention fresh meat on the hoof. Gives the men a bit of the sense of home, too. Never could abide pigs aboard," he added as an afterthought. "They don't fancy the sea. Nothing more unsightly than a seasick pig."

"Where's your bandage?" Pulling her attention from the goat, she saw that Nathan's headscarf was back in place. A dark circle, looking suspiciously like blood, bloomed in the neighborhood of where he had been wounded.

"Can't be seen as infirmed," he said with a flap of the hand. He took a drink from the bottle. "Besides, 'tis fine," he said with his eyes closed, waiting for the rum's restorative effects.

"I rather doubt that. A wound like that doesn't disappear overnight."

His eyes popped open to give her a dark look from under his brow. "I had one mum and shan't be in need of another, if you please."

While she slept, cups and a pot had been left on the table. The pot was still hot, surprisingly so. Pouring, she was pleased to find it was coffee. She gestured to Nathan in silent query as to whether he desired any. A shudder and a lift of the mouth was her answer.

She took a drink.

Tea was fine for afternoon parlors, but nothing started the day like a good cup of coffee. This particular cup, however, tasted like musty socks and had a thick gritty texture which left a coating on her tongue and an edge on her teeth. She wondered how much delicacy would be required to convince Mr. Kirkland to change his brewing methods.

Sensing she was being stared at, she looked up into an intent gold-eyed gaze at her elbow. Hermione's narrow nostrils flared interestedly in the direction of her cup.

"She fancies tea," said Nathan.

"This is coffee," she pointed out to the goat as it persistently nudged her arm.

"Aye, well, she's only a goat. Mr. Kirkland!" The bellow directed toward the galley companionway was but a shadow of its former self. The effort evoked a pained grunt. "It would appear Hermione has been left wanting... *again!*"

"Aye, sir," came a querulous reply from below.

"Mind your meal as well," Nathan said to Cate, with a narrow look toward Hermione. "She's no manners a'tall. Away with you, you wretched, cloven-hoofed spawn of the Devil."

Name calling having no apparent effect on her goat feelings, Hermione blithely turned away to browse the room.

Kirkland appeared directly with what could only be assumed to be a dish of tea.

"Is it hot enough?" Nathan demanded, following Kirkland with dull eyes. "You know how she gets, if it isn't hot enough."

"Aye, sir," the red-faced cook replied tolerantly, setting the steaming dish with care at the animal's cloven feet. "'Twas near jumping out o' the kettle."

Nursing the kind of headache earned through exhaustion, Cate sipped her coffee against the back drop of the goat's indelicate slurps.

Pryce came in to interrupt their domestic scene. Quite slumped with exhaustion, he reported, idly scratching Hermione's ears, while she mouthed his sleeve. Bracing his head with a delicacy befitting a crystal bowl, Nathan listened to the list of damage, a litany far too technical for a landsman such as Cate to comprehend. Nathan scowled with the effort of listening, the corners of his eyes tightening with the throb in his head. From the seaman-like discussion, she was able to glean that the *Ciara Morganse* had inflicted nearly lethal damages, but had not escaped damage herself. In spite of it all, the ship was still able to make weigh, but was in dire need of a place in which to lick her wounds.

"*Isla de las Aguas de los Santos Sedientos,*" Nathan announced in Pryce's wake.

"Water of the Thirsty Saints Island?" she asked.

"*Muy bien. Habla español.*"

"Almost exclusively, my early years."

"Could explain that accent of yours," he mused with an air that suggested he was still of two minds regarding her truthfulness of her identity.

"Rather a lofty title for a very diminutive spot of land," he said, returning to the subject at hand. "Supposed to be some magical springs, or some such nonsense somewhere or another."

Nathan plucked a piece of fruit from a plate in the center of the table. He peered at it, sniffed, curled his nose and put it back. He grabbed up the honey jar instead, swirled his finger inside and popped a golden glob into his mouth.

"We go in with them thinking we aim to raid," he went on, licking the stickiness away. "We give them the opportunity to ask for quarter, and then agree, if they bring us water and wood, and a bit of beef, if they're so inclined. Why do all the work when you can get someone else to do it? I call it winning all 'round!"

"How do you figure that?" There were so many things wrong in that argument, she didn't know where to begin, the most troubling being he thoroughly believed it to be flawless.

"We get what we desire and they don't get their fair town rampaged, which is exactly what they want. It's genius. Hostages, torture, pillaging, mayhem: 'tis nasty business. All that blood and wailing 'tis bad for one's humours. This is ever so much more better and pleasanter for everyone involved."

He lifted the bottle in a toast to the grandness of his scheme.

"Why am I confident 'genius' isn't the first word which comes to their minds?" she said under her breath.

"A town so far off the trade routes they mightn't have seen a ship in months, perhaps years. 'Tis perfect."

Nathan rose carefully, wincing at the movement. He critically surveyed her and the ruin wrought by a night of tending the wounded. She was smeared to her feet with dried blood, vomit and filth.

"We may even find you some clothes. Those seem a bit... soiled?" he said dryly.

He frowned, considered, and then began tentatively. "There is the chance—a very remote one, mind—that I might have not represented meself in the most flattering aspect."

Humble clearly was not a natural state for him.

"There are times when one becomes..." He paused to clear his throat several times. "One becomes, oh, caught up... Still, I might... stipulate that our pact... might still prevail..."

She checked for the line on the floor, thinking she might have inadvertently crossed it and was about to be admonished.

"...you yet agree... not to... attack?" The lilt in his voice held the question.

She ruffled at the implication it had all been of her doing, but desisted, knowing it would prove little. She might have been the one to throw the first punch, but she had been taunted beyond endurance. From a certain point of view, if she leaned ever so carefully to the proper angle, it was an apology.

It hurt not to smile, but she remained straight-faced, nonetheless. "Agreed."

His relief was evident in the way of a broad grin and a drop of his shoulders.

"Very well. Agreed," he said, more to himself. He dashed at the floor with his boot as if to scuff the line away. Gingerly placing the battered tricorn hat leather on his head, he squared his shoulders.

"On with it, then." He made a zigzagging path, from one side of the erased line to the other, until he was out the door.

To the rhythmic thump of the pumps and gush of hoses washing the decks, Cate went to check on the wounded, whose name Pryce was entering on the binnacle list. Grooves and Harrison were warm with fever; they would bear closer watching. To those in pain, more rum was administered, water laced with port or honey for the rest.

She came on deck to the sight of Nathan and several others standing before the hose. Arms extended, he turned slowly, allowing the rush of water to wash the blood and filth from his clothes. He stepped to the scuttlebutt, a reservoir for rainwater. He scooped a bucketful and doused it over his head, more or less rinsing the salt water away. After, he shook off like a great dog, water spraying in all directions. His shirt was still streaked with dried blood, but the worst was gone.

Cate smiled privately at seeing a mattress—hers, no doubt, for odds were it was the only one aboard—dragged out given the same ablutions, and then left on the grates to air.

The ship's people moved with nowhere near the same vigor, but were far more vigorous than she had expected after taking such a beating. This was far from the first battle, and God willing, far from the last. She had seen troops so shocked by battle they were barely able to rouse from their blankets. These men showed no such symptoms. They were bound by blood and faith in each other, faith in their ship and her heart and strength, a stronger faith in their captain, who didn't take their lives lightly.

Once the ship was well under way, her people went on to the next order of business: services for the dead.

Tradition held that a seaman's hammock was his shroud. With two round shot at their feet, six such bundles were laid out at the rail: four killed outright in battle and two succumbing to their wounds in the night. One was a man by the name of Croftsford; she had held his hand in his final hour of delirium.

He died with a smile and calling her "Mary."

All hands able turned out. As captain, Nathan presided over the ceremony. His shirt still dark with wetness, one eye ticking with pain, he took a pen and symbolically struck their names from the muster book. It was a solemn scene with a reverence one might have thought these ruffians incapable. Watching from a discrete distance, she was struck by the camaraderie and brotherhood which bound them, a connection no less deep than the blood of a Highland clan. Pirates they may have been, but at that moment they were men grieving the loss of a shipmate.

By their very nature, funerals brought one to recall personal losses. The presence of those gone before could be felt as if called to gather and receive the newcomer. As she looked at the bundles laid out, she couldn't recall their faces. Time hadn't allowed for such familiarity. And so, her mind replaced them with those of her own loss. Grief seized her anew, tightening her throat and pinching her heart.

One face in particular rose and parted from the rest: a good-humored one, framed by a shock of auburn hair and level blue eyes, ever-sparked by mirth. He was there. All she need do was turn and he would be standing, waiting... always waiting. He would give her that smile, the one which could warm her heart from across a room, and the intent blue look that could melt all resolve and tighten her belly. All she need do was turn and step into his arms, and she could know again what it was to be held, and most of all, loved.

"Amen."

The sound of Nathan's voice jerked her back.

Cate closed her eyes and put a hand to her ear. The sound of a body being commended to the sea was one which she would never become accustomed. The splash was more cold and final than the thud of dirt on a casket. Determined not to become a sniveling wreck, she was brusquely swiping away the tears when Nathan turned.

"Are ye well, luv?" The dark slashes of his brows drew down with concern.

"I'm fine." Her eyes filling again, she spun around, putting her back to him. Once sufficiently recomposed, she turned back with a wobbling smile. "Give me something to do."

Grim-faced, Nathan seemed to perceive the motivation behind her request. While he and Pryce debated as to what she was capable — tarring being too dangerous, not strong enough for the pumps, not to be trusted in the rigging — versus what was most pressing, she gravitated toward a man sitting down amid a snow bank of canvas. The three-sided needle he wielded was gargantuan compared to anything she had ever worked with, but a needle was a needle, and she was intrigued to watch the deft movements as he mended sails.

"Billings here is one of the best canvasmen ever t' set sail," Pryce declared coming up beside her. He clapped the man on the shoulder and gave him a brotherly shake. "He kin sew more wind into a sail than the Great Zephyr hisself."

Pryce began to ease away from Billings, craning his head skyward with a side-long glance at his captain, "What be in yer head this fine day, sir? 'Tis a might calm, it is not? But we'll kiss the iron and sew in the rest, aye?"

Weathered to the same butternut brown as every mariner, at first glance Billings possessed no defining features other than a luxuriant, curving mustache. His response, however, came in a nearly unintelligible garble, Pryce nodding intently.

"Very well, then. T'yer duties," Pryce said with a joviality she would have thought impossible, and then directed to her from the corner of his mouth, "Don't mind if he's a bit wantin' on the conversation aspect. He's put but a score o' words together over a year's time. He's a bit o' the idiot about him, but who's to know? He's blessed with magic in those hands."

Cate glanced candidly in Billings's direction. If he had heard—and no reason to believe he hadn't—no offense had been taken. When he looked up to respond, she saw that under the mustache his mouth was severely disfigured, natural-born rather than by accident, by the look of it.

"The Royal Navy don't fly no better canvas than the *Morganse*." Pryce pointed with pride toward the sail in Billings's lap. "See them leeches? Only the Navy and the *Morganse* has corded leeches. And that twine he's a-usin' is waxed, not that tar-dipped stuff; only the Royal Navy uses that."

She forbore questioning how the *Morganse* came to have stores which only the Royal Navy should possess.

"What about the red?" she asked, looking down at a rubricated stretch of canvas.

Pryce's face lit. "Funny that. I t'weren't with the Cap'n then, but he represents he raided a Spanish corvette a'tween Cuba and Cayo Hueso full o' *pastillas* of cochineal. Through a certain series o' mishaps, it got spilt on the canvas stores. Sometimes looks a might pink," he said, judiciously eyeing the sail, "but the effect is still the same. A comin' out o' the sun, she 'pears to be a-breathin' blood."

Cate hid a smile. That hadn't been quite her first impression, but it was close enough.

Amid the turmoil, she became aware of voices rising above all else. They came from a sizeable collection of men at the forecastle. One stood at the rail faced down to the remainder gathered below.

"What are they doing?"

Nathan looked up as if noticing them for the first time, and then regarded her as if she might be a bit dense. "It's an auction," he said around something tucked in the corner of his mouth. It looked to be a tobacco quid that he half-sucked and half-chewed on.

"I can see that. Now?" With all that needed to be done, it seemed an odd time for such distractions.

A closer look revealed whatever it was in his mouth wasn't

tobacco, but something between leather and a stick. "What is that?"

Apparently he had forgotten it was there, for it took him a moment to take her meaning.

"This?" he asked, holding it up. "*Charqui*. Some of the islands around these parts still keep the *boucan* ways of curing meat. 'Tis done on racks over a slow fire, smoked."

Nathan regarded the woodish-looking strip and made a face. "'Tis far better than salt horse."

Cate couldn't help but smile. He was referring to the mariner's beef or pork, which went to sea packed in salt and three hundred-pound casks. The meat was soaked in harness caskets and then boiled in order to render it edible.

"Bite?" Nathan asked, thrusting the brown strip toward her.

Cate felt like a dog gnawing on a bone—not to mention a bit ungraceful—as she took off a small bit of the other end. The texture being much like that piece of leather, she shifted it to the corner of her mouth.

"Just hold it there and let it soften," he said, smiling at seeing her struggle with it.

The meat—beef, goat or pig, she couldn't tell—was pungent with spices, the smoky taste reminiscent of ham or bacon.

He smiled tolerantly, something he seemed to be doing with frequency, and returned to the subject at hand. "'Tis bad luck to have a dead man's dunnage about. The sooner it no longer exists, the better. They've already drawn for their numbers... where they sleep and their mess number," he clarified to her deepening confusion. "Empty spaces, sleeping or at table, might invite the dead to linger."

"But if it's such bad luck, why don't you just throw it overboard?" The whole thing struck her as ghoulish. The bodies barely had time to reach the bottom of the sea.

"And waste perfectly good goods?" Nathan asked around his impromptu meal. His eyes rounded in shocked indignation. "T'would be a sad commentary, indeed. That rigging knife of Wiggins's was the envy of the ship. I'll give eight," he shouted to the auctioneer. "And that pistol. T'was Croftsford's reward for spotting a prize first. And there's a perfectly good rain tarp. Twelve," he called louder.

"'Tis all for a good cause," Nathan said cheerfully in the face of her distress. "The money is collected and sent to the family, if there is any," he added with a dubious frown. Then he brightened. "If not, 'tis kept until the next time ashore and pays for drinks all around. Seventeen! Is there anything you desire?" he asked, gesturing toward the forecastle.

"No," was all she could manage. The chunk of meat was now malleable, but still chewy.

"Sold!" came from the forecastle.

"Ah, well," Nathan sighed. "Be that as it may, the sooner the better all around. Much to do. Bear a hand there," he shouted as he strolled down the deck.

The ship became a beehive, a place where every soul was occupied in one of three roles: sail, repair or prepare. The boatswain and his mates labored at swaying up new spars, setting a jibbom, bending sails, and knotting and splicing a spider's web of new rigging. Over and around them, the carpenter and his mates worked to reconstruct a section of mangled rail, shape a spar, topmast and wheels for a gun carriage, plug cannonball holes with great cone-shaped plugs, and rebuild two gun ports which had been blown into one. All the while, they were required to keep the two bilge pumps in working order to keep up with the rising water, over twenty inches in the well, at last report.

In the way of preparation, Mr. MacQuarrie, the master gunner, and his mates cleaned their respective instruments, swabbed, reamed touchholes and chipped round shot. Shot garlands were filled, slow-match and wadding set at the ready. Cartouche boxes and shot bags were refilled. The armorer distributed weapons to the infirmed. Too well to be in their hammocks, but too injured to perform their regular duties, they were able to oil and clean pistols and muskets, and brighten blades.

"I thought you said the town was going to greet you with open arms," she said as she and Nathan watched the rearmament.

"An over-confident pirate is a dead pirate."

Desperation was the ultimate determining factor in the selection of which task she was assigned. It would seem a ship had two constants: leaks and miles of aging rope. Mariners being pragmatic creatures, they found a way that one could serve the other. And so, she was sat on a low bench and introduced to the picking of oakum.

Nathan was both irritated and apologetic. "Any other day of the week, 'tis considered punishment. Just ask Mr. Ogden: near a fortnight ago he failed to report for his watch and was sentenced to a pound of the stuff for every man on his watch obliged to work extra whilst his lazy arse was lying in a hammock."

"Punishment?"

"Of the highest order: time in the brig or bilboes is but time to be on one's arse, at one's leisure, making more work for everyone. Men will go to great lengths to avoid picking junk until their fingers bleed."

"I don't mind a little hard work."

"You will," he said, with a significant roll of the eyes. "You will."

On the surface, picking oakum was a simple proposition: tear apart old rope, until it was down to its most basic fiber, something similar to raw wool, which would in turn be rolled into long strands of caulk. It was easier said, than done, however. The rope—sometimes the thickness of her leg—was made up of uncountable strands, one upon the other, and was encased in layer upon layer of tar and varnish. Twisting, tearing, pounding, rolling or fraying on a hook were all required. It meant working in a smelly cloud of pitch and a fine, prickling brown dust that clung to everything. The work was hard, the coarse hemp fibers abrading her hands and tearing at her fingers. Between the shock of firing her own guns and taking shots in return, the *Morganse* had taken a pounding in the last battle, both bilge pumps working to capacity. A lot of oakum was going to be needed, and soon.

Picking oakum was nasty and tedious, but it provided the workers with time for conversation. They regaled her with tales, going off on tangents so laden with mariner's lingo the meaning was lost. At one point, the clop of hooves marked Hermione handily clamoring up the steps from below. She pricked her ears interestedly, the pile of frayed rope far too appetizing to be ignored. And so, they were obliged to work on the one hand, while shooing Hermione away with the other.

"'Tis a rare sight to see long-jawed cordage or stretched rag aboard the Cap'n's ship," said one proudly, eyeing the growing pile of junk before them. A spare man with walnut-like knobs for knuckles, he had introduced himself as "Potts". One eye nearly milky, and the other tending to rove, he had the habit of canting his head like a great bird at whatever he wished to see.

"And it's not as if he's afraid o' the canvas," put in another, busily unparceling, removing the canvas protection sewn over some ropes. "Spits in the wind's eye, he does, and laughs when it tries to catch 'im."

"Carried away the st'd's'l and the mizzen course back a couple months ago," added another judiciously.

"Bull!" burst out Potts. "T'were a maelstrom the likes of which no man seed a-comin'! Glass it were that day," he directed toward her. "Ye could o' shaved in yer reflection, if ye were of a mind. The wind come straight down." He slammed his hands together in emphasis, startling Hermione into a bleating protest. "Jest like that! Not a ripple for the warnin'. Any less seaman woulda sheared every stick."

"Cursed he is," came a grumble from behind.

"Blessed he is," put in another. "By Calypso herself."

A guttural squawk and a heavy flap of wings overhead caused Cate to duck. Looking up she found a huge parrot perched on a cask at Potts' elbow. A vibrant hyacinth blue, bright yellow marked its eyes and beak. It ruffled its feathers and smoothed, only to raise its hackles and squawk in protest at spotting Cate.

"Go toss yourself!" it croaked with remarkable clarity and clapped its beak threateningly.

"Beatrice! Mind yer tongue, ye scurvy-ridden bag o' feathers," Potts scolded. "We've a guest aboard, ye rude beast!"

"Fuck off!"

Amid embarrassed titters and clearing of throats, the men shifted uneasily.

"She's a mite suspicious of strangers," Pryce directed to Cate as he stepped down from the forecastle. He then growled at the bird, "And a sorry excuse fer a beast ye are."

"Well, grease me stick!"

"'Tis likely her master spent a fair amount o' time in the less reputable realms a'fore she come here," Pryce explained to Cate, his bronze reddening at his collar.

"Buggering trollop!"

"Sounds as though he was a colorful sort," Cate said. It was nothing she hadn't heard many times over on the streets of East London. If anything, it was a bit endearing that the men were embarrassed.

"Who does...?" She was cut short by a contrary sounding parrot shriek. "Who does she belong to?"

"Eh...?" Pryce closed one eye in puzzlement. He looked from man to man for guidance, defensively hunched shoulders his only response. "Interestin' question, that."

Cate waited for further explanation. None came.

"How do you know it's a she?" Cate asked, eyeing the bird. A huge one it was. From head to tail tip, it was well over the length of a man's arm. Her avian experience was limited mostly to the barnyard and sporting varieties, most of which had defining features to separate the sexes.

The men raised their heads to view Beatrice with a more discerning eye.

"Complains like one," was Pryce's eventual response.

Cate worked for several more hours. At one point, while waiting for more rope to be brought, she stiffly rose and went to get a drink from the scuttlebutt. Filled with rainwater, its contents still took on the taste of wood gone wet far too long or the canvas used to collect it, but it was still far less foul than the water casks. As she moved about, she kept a sharp eye for Scarface, the one who had accosted her within moments of her being aboard. He was nowhere in sight, but she couldn't help but think she heard snatches of his voice now and again. For all she knew, one of his accomplices could be standing at her elbow, for she had little recollection of their faces.

Dabbing her mouth on the back of her hand, she turned to find two men stand there. Doffing their caps, they knuckled their forelocks.

"Beggin' yer pardon, mum. A word?"

Thin, almost to the point of gaunt, his frizzled gray hair showed evidence of once being red. At his side was a younger, squarer one, with a heavy shock of blond hair tar-bound in the forecastlemen's way.

"You're Highlanders, aren't you?" she asked, polite but cautious. Their accented voices had drifted on the wind, their rolled "r's" and clipped consonants haunting her with echoes of her past.

"Aye, mum. Cameron, by name, but Grant by birth. He's Hughes," he added, indicating his partner. He stammered, painfully nervous. "Yer man was a Mackenzie, wasn't he?"

The water she had just drunk turned to lead. Recognition in England would have meant death. Among the pirates of the *Ciara Morganse,* she had thought to be safe. After being singled out, there was nothing to be gained in denying it and so she squared her shoulders and lifted her chin.

"Yes, he was."

They grinned with delight.

"Aye, we thought so. We dinna wish to be forward, Mum, but we kent ye as soon as we laid eyes on ye. May I shake yer hand, Mistress Mackenzie? He was a fine man, mum. I... we wish to honor his memory."

He seized her hand and was pumping it before he realized himself. His eyes bulged and jerked away, flushing. "Pray, beggin' yer pardon, Mistress Mackenzie."

Twisting his hat unmercifully in his hands, he exchanged glances with his companion, who silently encouraged him on.

"We served under him, ye ken, from Prestopans to... well, and after," he ended awkwardly, his countenance darkening. Then he brightened, picking up his purpose again. "He was a fine man, Mum, the finest we'd ever seen. Best officer in the whole cursed affair. Courage of a lion."

"Yes, he had that," she said, wilting under the increasing weight of several of the mariners looking on.

"And when I saw ye stitchin' yon Chin, I said to meself: 'That's Red Brian's leddy.'" His face split into a smile again, studded by a total of four teeth. Then he waxed very solemn. "We just wanted to say as how proud we wuz to serve under yer man, m'm."

With a strained smile, she mutely nodded.

God! Was there no way to quiet them?

"We followed 'im to Hell and back. A natural leader he was. We wuz fair sorry when we learnt o' him so terrible hurt."

"I'm sure he would have appreciated your enthusiasm." She cringed, her gut knotting. *Would he ever stop?*

"And we was right sorry to hear he'd been captured. Bloody *sassenachs!*" He flinched at the blunder. In many circles, such an epithet would have launched a fight. Apparently, pirates overlooked slurs.

More of the crew was now watching. A few inched closer, poised but curious. Noticing the gathering audience, the two Scots bobbed a bow in unison.

"We wished to honor his memory, Mistress Mackenzie G' day, mum."

She sagged against the rail in relief. She didn't look up; she didn't need to. She could feel the men's eyes boring into her back.

No secrets on a ship, she thought ruefully, as she ran a shaking hand over her face.

It had been as much of a public announcement that could possibly be made. She might as well have stood on the capstan and shouted who she was.

She was touched on the arm. She jumped and shrieked. Whirling, she found it was Nathan.

"Beg pardon," he said, falling back. "I didn't mean to—"

"No, no!" One hand pressing to her middle as she caught her breath, she raised the other in apology. "I just didn't hear you."

"Did those crewmen—?"

"No, no!" Ducking her head, she scurried off.

❦

Isla de las Aguas de los Santos Sedientos.

It seemed a lofty title for such an inconsequential looking piece of land.

As the ship paralleled the shore, Cate watched the massive black banner unfurl once more. Seeing the bold image of the haloed skull framed by the angel's wings, she felt the same thrill and tug of pride as when the *Nightingale* had been bearing down, a sense of belonging; sudden and unfounded, but there it was.

"I would have thought you would desire the element of surprise," she said, looking up at the flag.

Nathan smiled tolerantly. "Surprise them, and their first instinct is to fight and fight hard, in defense of hearth, family and all that is dear. But," he said, with an exclamatory finger and a knowing wink, "give them time and they commence to thinking. With that luxury, the mind sets to imagining how much they stand to lose and how much pain — possible death — might be required in the process of defending said valuables."

"Which means?"

"Which means given enough time, they'll meet you at the dock, with the keys to the treasury, their most virginal maids, and desire to know what took you so long in coming. Don't care for that second bit, eh?" he laughed at seeing her wince.

"Isn't there some way to circumvent that?"

"Not really," he teased.

Cate didn't know him fully, but Nathan didn't strike her as a man who would refuse a maid if handed one. The fact of the matter was she considered it safe to say he was a man who had welcomed the company of many women. With his charm and dash, few could resist when targeted by that.

"Brilliant," Pryce murmured in wonderment over his shoulder, once his captain had strolled away. "Treasure given over volunteer-like 'tis just as shiny as that what come with spilt blood. The men appreciate that."

"All of them?" She looked warily across the myriad of faces, Scarface and her earliest moments aboard still fresh in her mind.

He shot a loathing over his shoulder. "No, but those be the ones what tend to seek a Cap'n what thirsts for blood n' mayhem. Now mind, the Cap'n can be treacherous when he's of a mind. I've seen 'im slit a man's gullet and leave the poor bastard with his guts draped over his arm. The Cap'n keeps the rum plentiful, their bellies full, 'n' the swag piles high, a-knowin' a man's dedication takes but two paths: his pocket and his stomach."

"The men seem to love him."

"Or respect," Pryce was quick to qualify. "Don't be a-confusin' the two; there be a fair difference a'tween 'em. Them what don't is long gone, either by choice, or otherwise."

Pryce was gone before she could ask for clarification on the "otherwise". On second thought, perhaps she was better off not knowing.

The thought of being a part of pillaging and destruction, maybe even killing, was wholly distasteful and disturbing.

Death wasn't new to her; she had witnessed a war firsthand, but that had been in the spirit of King and country, not a quest for plunder and riches. But realistically, what else was she to do? These men were pirates before she had been brought aboard— No one could accuse her of being there by choice—and they would be pirates long after she was gone. But be damned if she would idly stand by and watch them bleed. If that was aiding and abetting, complicit by virtue of association, then piracy would be added to her charge sheet, and there was blessed little to be done about it.

When the ship opened the bay, a great gun firing—a quarter charge and without the benefit of a ball—announced them, just in case the townspeople hadn't noticed a thirty-six-gunned black ship, with blood dripping from its sails and decks, flying a prodigious skull-emblazoned banner, was in their harbor. There was a good deal of shouting, the rattle of chain, a splash, and the *Ciara Morganse* was at anchor. The decks which had been so alive under Cate's feet went motionless for the first time in months. It was a novelty and a quite disquieting sensation.

Cate strained to see the little town nestled between the island's mountainous backbone and the sea. It was the closest land since leaving England. Not having pondered it earlier, she now longed for the solidness of land under her feet, to walk on a surface that didn't pitch and roll at every step.

"When are we going ashore?" she asked Nathan, close on his heels.

"As soon as the boats are away, but *you're* not going," he said, wheeling around on her.

Cate rocked back on her bare feet as if she had been struck. She gaped at him, wondering how she could have been so radically mistaken. Her anxiousness had allowed her to forget her tenuous status. She bristled. Worthless as a hostage, now she was simply his possession to do with as he chose, kept in reserve for the best opportunity to turn a coin.

"Why not?" she asked. Even if she was to be shackled, to touch land again would have been worth it.

Nathan's hesitancy gave brief hope of second thoughts. "It's not safe." And then he spun away.

"So, I *am* a hostage then?"

"No," he said with maddening evenness over his shoulder. "A hostage implies there would be someone to pay for you. And since, by your own admission there is no one, then you're not said hostage."

"Then I'm a prisoner."

"No, prisoner implies punishment. You've committed no crime, so there would be no punishment."

"Then I'm being held against my will."

"No, protective custody."

Skidding to a halt, she balled her fists. "Protected from what?"

Nathan stopped. His back still to her, he looked to the sky, and then the deck. Heaving a patience-seeking sigh, he said, "As I said, it's not safe," and set off once again.

"Safe! What's safe have to do with it?"

He drew up, again without turning. A number of responses being disposed of, he ultimately opted for "Everything."

And then, he was gone.

Cate stood at the rail while the longboats were roused over the side, still prickling at Nathan's denial. She wasn't bound or confined, but she was imprisoned, just the same. The ship was a floating gaol, with over a hundred keepers. She looked longingly across the water to the little town. The yearning became a driving need now that she could smell greenery and dirt. With eyes accustomed to the deep hues of the ocean, the vivid mosaic of aquamarine, azure, lapis and cobalt of the island's waters had made her squint, the sight of green, absent for so long, almost painful. It struck her with an impact that rendered her near breathless: she was in the West Indies, the tropics, with palm trees, warm water, sun-dazzled skies, with new wonders at every turn.

So near, and yet so far sat the fairyland, within her reach, but unattainable, all because of one capricious pirate.

Cate's senses had been sharpened by weeks at sea. Along with earth and greenery came other smells of civilization, ones conveniently forgotten: animal dung, cooking smoke, privies, tobacco and the sharper fugue of squalor. Wrinkling her nose, she considered the possibility that she had developed a new appreciation for the sea.

Whether in the Highlands or elsewhere, isolated towns possessed the same sleepy air, resting with the placidity of a cow chewing its cud. This one was bracketed by two lone, brick buildings, representing the opposing powers which controlled its life: the spiritual marked by a cathedral's bell tower, and the secular, with the flag of Spain. The skeletal remains of a garrison peeked through the trees, along with the rudimentary beginnings of a defensive wall around the town, both long since abandoned.

A not-much-better-tended wharf lined the water's edge, bearing out Nathan's conjectures regarding the infrequency of visitors.

Before the anchor was set, Nathan stood surveying the town. Now squatted over a piece of canvas, a chunk of charcoal in hand, he drew it out for the men circled around.

"We'll assume the flag marks where we'll find whoever the power-on-high might be. Bear off for there first, and then fan out. With any luck, whomever is in charge will..."

"Hoy! Cap'n! Lookit!" came a cry from the rail.

Nathan rose, following the look-out's point. "What the bloody hell...?"

A small flotilla of barges, catamarans and boats had embarked from the ramshackle wharf and bore toward the ship. Flags of truce, mostly in the way of tattered handkerchiefs and meal sacks, were in vigorous display at the bow of each craft.

The pirates stood in speechlessness awe. Nathan was the first to regain himself and sent marksmen aloft with a sharp gesture. More were posted on the ratlines and rails. Seeing the swivel guns fore and aft brought to bear, the white flags were waved with increased vigor, amid friendly although tentative hails in Spanish.

The largest barge hooked on, its occupants beckoned aboard. As the first visitor clambered over the gunwale, Nathan seized Cate by the arm.

"No sense in advertising you're here, eh?" he said as he propelled her toward the cabin.

"But I—"

"Shh!" He pressed her inside and away from the door gently, but firmly enough to indicate he would brook no argument. "Discretion is a virtue often overlooked and highly underrated."

Once aboard, the townspeople quailed at being encircled by a hundred-odd armed pirates, now presenting their most heathenish faces. They clung to the rail, making it increasingly difficult for later arrivals to find room. It was difficult to separate one aghast face from another. Mostly men, a few skirts were visible through the press of bodies. Most predominant was a priest, his black cassock stark against the drab of his flock. The sun glinted on the cross at his neck like an overseeing eye, his presence clearly meant to give the pirates pause.

A spokesman stepped forward. Wringing a handkerchief without mercy, he cleared his throat loudly several times.

"*Me llamo Don Rafael Fredrico Suarez de la Corretja.*" The declaration came with the air of one expecting all present to be impressed. He ducked a formal bow, embellished with the sweep of a plumed hat. "*Yo soy el alcalde de este pueblo humilde.*"

"El Acalde" was built like a hogshead atop a cask. His radically askew wig revealed a thin straggle of salt-and-pepper hair.

The exchange in Spanish between El Alcalde Corretja and Nathan came to Cate in bits and pieces, their voices broken by the breeze, or lost amid the shrieks of sea gulls or random cough. Still, the gist of the conversation was easy enough to follow, Corretja's fawning impossible to misinterpret.

"I come on behalf of the citizens of this insignificant, humble village to welcome such a magnificent ship such as this and it's beneficent captain..."

The obsequence drug on. Nathan endured as patiently as his general nature would allow, finally cutting it to an end with an abrupt wave.

"Si, si. I'm sure," he said in fluid Spanish. "And a grand 'good afternoon' to one and all."

Nervousness prompted Corretja into a frantic tumble of words. "As a token of our appreciation, and as your humble hosts..."

That was the fourth time the word "humble" was heard in as many minutes, many more possibly adrift somewhere on the wind.

From the moment El Alcalde and his party had stepped aboard, wealth was gathered at the pirates' feet: cages of chickens and ducks, baskets of fresh fish, oysters and clams atop dripping beds of seaweed, pots of honey, bundles of tobacco, baskets of vegetables and fruit, and two shoats: a treasure trove for such a small place. As the offerings piled up, Corretja's oiliness wasn't lost on Nathan, as indicated by a periodic snarl. It was an expression; however, a stranger might have taken as a sneer.

At length, a small chest—very small—came forth and with great drama was opened to display its contents of coins and jewelry. Atop it all sat a religious icon and cross, none so subtle reminders of the town's moral fiber, and an even less subtle appeal to the pirates'. Nathan disinterestedly observed the contents. Having failed to impress with that, Señor Corretja grabbed a woman—more like young girl—and shoved her forward, a shriek of dismay erupting from the surrounding women. The girl shrank before the strange men.

There was a heated exchange between Corretja and Nathan. Abruptly breaking off, Nathan spun around and stormed into the cabin. There in the protective shadows, he snatched up the rum bottle and took a badly needed drink. He swore in fluent and foul Spanish—nodding a vague deferential apology to where she stood in her protective cove—and then swore again, more colorfully than the first.

"May I introduce Isabella Corretja. The lousy bastard is offering his daughter!" He took another drink. He whirled around to her, the blackened eyes going blacker still. "What kind of man hides behind a girl's skirts? I'd wager she's barely fifteen, if she's a day."

He started to pace, but his fermentation was too great for even that.

"Look at him," he snarled. "A fop in beggar's clothing. He thinks we're so daft we can't see through that pitiful charade."

Cate looked out through the door's sidelight once more. Upon closer scrutiny, she saw his point. With the exception of an older woman, who might have been the girl's *dueña*, those around Corretja were *campesinos*, commoners and working folk. Corretja's thread-bare, ill-fitting coat was a poor camouflage over the gold embroidered waistcoat, a ruffled jabot and shirt of quality beneath. The natty wig and humble shoes were incongruous with the silk hose and silver-buttoned calf breeches. More to the point, was the general suspicious nature of the man: the inability to look anyone in the eye. Such reticence could have stemmed from fear, but deception was more fertile ground.

Eloquent in virginal mortification, the head-hanging Isabella had suffered no such diminutions. If anything, she had been enhanced: cheeks pinked, lips rouged and a row of lace hastily tucked, to make her breasts appear fuller. Round-faced with the soft plumpness of youth, where nature had been generous to her at the waist and hips, she had not yet been blessed elsewhere.

Nathan threw a combustive glare at the *alcalde*. "I should take her right there in front of the sodding worm, just to teach him a lesson."

"But you won't, right?"

"No, I won't," he agreed grudgingly. Gaze still fixed on the girl, he snorted in disgust. "Never taken a woman unwilling in me life. Besides," he said, as an afterthought, making a poor attempt at levity, "the young ones are always so much work. He's gambling we'd think her too young or too plain. Ignorant lobcock!"

In Nathan's absence, Corretja directed his minions to spread the ever-increasing offerings in a more advantageous display. By no means a king's ransom, from all appearances it was, however, the settlement's every possession.

Nathan snorted, shaking his head in wonderment. "If they're willing to present all that, imagine what they wish not to be seen."

"You think there's more?"

"Indisputably! The best proof being His Pompousness'

anxiousness to give up his daughter, a grand gesture to keep something much more valuable—to his estimation at any rate—*very* safe."

"But you came only for wood and water."

"And would have been very content to leave with that, and a crew ecstatic at it being achieved through someone else's sweat. Now..." He blew a tired sigh. A tick in one eye betrayed his pounding head. "Now, I've nay choice: every jack on that deck knows 'tis more to be had. If we leave without, or at least give it a jolly good try, there will be hell to pay."

"You mean...?" She couldn't bring herself to utter the word.

Mutiny.

He made a wry noise at her innocence. "In a heartbeat. If one of those bilge rats were to take over, there will be no saving anyone from anything."

His eyes drifted in her direction, and then he shook his head. "If I'm still in charge, I can strive to keep the damage to a minimum."

He stared without seeing at the kegs of rum, now being lifted onboard by way of a derrick yard.

"Still, a prize is a prize." He gave a low, guttural growl and took an angry swipe at the air. "The cold-gutted, old skipjack is about to get his just deserves."

He flashed a rakish smile and took another drink. Blackened eyes, blood – stiffened hair and scruff of a sprouting beard, he looked a right tartar, the pirate she had expected to meet. He strode back out with renewed determination.

To stunned Spanish gasps and lecherous pirate rumblings, Nathan hooked an arm around Isabella's waist and drew her against him. She shrieked in maidenly shrillness. Struggling against him, she pummeled his chest, landing the occasional blow to his face and—Alas!—head. In the process of resisting, her arm was wrenched, and she yelped, more in protest than pain. The priest and several others lunged to her rescue, but fell back at the sight of pirate pistols and cutlasses that were brandished.

"Release that innocent child, you scurrilous beast!" The priest's protests only served to spur Nathan, now nuzzling the girl's neck.

Nathan bared his teeth in a smile, the flash of gold adding to his menace. From Cate's perspective, he seemed inclined toward handing the girl off to his men, just to be rid of her. It was difficult to be dignified with a squirming, screeching girl in one's arms. Instead, he held her, a sharp jerk and a firm shake bidding her quiet.

"Young, and so *very* sweet. A fresh rose what begs for

plucking." He inhaled in heady appreciation, and then swiveled his attention to her father. "We require more!"

Corretja's up-until-then red face blenched. He wiped it with a handkerchief—and such delicate soft hands they were—which sported a monogram large enough to be seen at Cate's distance. Nathan continued to smile admiringly, fondling the girl's hair, her ribbon having come loose in her struggles. The drama continued to unfold. The pirates demanded. The mayor pleaded. Nathan's irritation grew with each round.

Finally, Nathan gave Isabella a sharp squeeze, eliciting a yelp of protest.

"What are ye thinkin', mates?" Nathan called to his rogues. "Hang our fair mayor by his thumbs or his balls? Shall it be sweating, *carbonado*, fuses 'twixt the fingers or the rosary?"

He canted his head, harkening to the raucous cheering, a myriad of grisly suggestions shouted, a cackling, half-maniacal laugh like that of a chicken rising above the crowd.

"Very well. By the balls it 'tis," he declared grandly.

Corretja was seized, flushing to the point of near apoplexy. A sword pressed to his throat elicited a startled "Eep!" giving the impression the man had just soiled himself. Sweat poured off him in a profusion which led one to wonder how his captors maintained their grip. Blood trickled from under the blade at his throat. Cate felt sympathy, reminded of her own pirate introduction. She hadn't realized it then, but now, with the luxury of calm and distance, she saw the theater unfold and seamlessly executed it was: the leering looks, the brandished weapons, the knife at a throat. A well-practiced performance. It was riling to think she had been so easily duped.

"Silver," Corretja shrieked, his voice cracking.

"Papa, no!" cried Isabella, in eye-stretching horror.

Corretja recoiled at his inadvertent disclosure. Nathan's brows arched interestedly. Eyes rounded and fixed on the gleaming blade, Corretja's mouth moved like a fish. Once finding his tongue, he babbled in a nonsensical tirade, until Nathan lost all patience and bellowed, "Your silver, if you please, sir."

"But there is—"

"*Silver!*" Nathan's guttural voice ripped the air, startling all to silence. "And unless your lovely wife and daughter, or any other sacrificial lambs you have at your disposal are encased in it, there shall be no further discussion, *sabe?*"

A cowering, mute nod was his response. Nathan jerked a satisfied nod. "Mr. Smalley, the glass, if you please."

The directive was aimed toward the quarterdeck where the ship's hourglasses were kept. The ship's timekeepers, there were four such glasses aboard, each measuring anywhere from a half-minute to four hours.

"One hour," Nathan announced. "And don't bother coming to us. We'll come to you, torching what comes before us, so I shan't advise secrecy. Mind, this bit o' sweet loveliness will be staying here." Nathan gave Isabella an emphatic squeeze, eliciting another squeak. "Whilst you... you... and you..." he said, pointing to the *dueña* and two others, "will remain as well."

"You, Friar." Nathan beckoned the priest with an irreverent hook of the finger. He waved them off toward the forecastle, pushing Isabella among them. "Stow yourself, the maid and your little flock over there. Mr. Pryce," he called, shifting to English. "Guards, if you please. No one is to go near and no one is to step away."

He shot a glare at his crew in final warning.

There was a tearful departing on the part of Isabella and the other hostages as they were torn from the departing townspeople. Her father offered nothing more than a perfunctory pat on the arm before taking his leave, moving with the wooden stiffness of the doomed to the entry port.

Nathan came into the cabin with Pryce on his heels. He curtly waved Cate back from the door while instructing the First Mate in short bursts.

"We may be required to weigh fast. Set the kedges, t'gallants and jibs, and lay 'er in irons. Prepare a landing party to depart within the hour. I'll be leading this one."

"It turns out that our fair mayor is also a distant relative to the Royal Family," Nathan explained after Pryce's departure. "Some cousin on his wife's side, six or seven times removed, or some such nonsense. He holds enough esteem to have been entrusted with a sizeable sum of silver for safekeeping. An admirable decision, given he was willing to forfeit a wife and two daughters in its defense."

Nathan made a caustic noise. "If the good mayor was canny, he could have given us a token portion, and we would have put this blot on the chart to our stern in grand spirits. As it is, he's about to lose it all."

He paused to take a long pull from the rum bottle. "Stay inside. No sense in advertising you're here, eh? They're only Spanish, but intrigues abound in these waters."

Nathan glanced out the aft windows, the evening shadows beginning to form dark pools at the foot of the palms.

Cate peeked through door's sidelights toward the forecastle where the hostages were encircled by guards, shoulders rigid with the importance of their duty. Against the wall in the back, Isabella cowered in the protective arms of her matronly *dueña*.

"That poor girl is scared out of her wits," she said.

"And whose fault is that? I came here looking for water and wood, not... daughters!"

"They don't know that, do they? Instead, the poor girl could be ruined for life."

"Why do you think I took all those other hostages, including the bloody, goddamned priest? Would you prefer I bring her in here, so the imaginations might truly abound?"

"Don't you dare touch her!" She didn't think he would attack the girl, but didn't know him well enough to be sure. His performance on deck just then had been quite convincing.

A deep crimson rose from his collar and the warm eyes went cold.

"If I were so damned worried, as you so generously suggest, I'd have her in here in three seconds and on the table in four. Nothing enhances a pirate's fame than a good ravishing."

She gave a small, mirthless laugh. "Are you more worried about her reputation or your own?"

"Who made you master and commander, eh? You think I'm so vile and depraved I can't resist violating the first—belay that, *every*—woman what comes before me, no matter how ill-favored? Can't fathom how you've managed to bear the presence of someone so scurrilous as meself!" The fringe of the scarf at his waist jounced at his knees. "I do prefer a softer ride, but the young ones are such a bother. Too tight, all that crying, and then just lie there like a frozen cod."

"It's not necessary to impress me with your vast experience."

"Then I'll save meself the breath of asking if you desire to watch." His swollen eyes rounded in a final emphasis.

Stung, Cate jerked a chair around to the stern window and threw herself into it. His combustion grew as he stormed about the room, his bells jangling wildly with each step. She flinched at the crash of something being thrown, solid as opposed to glass or pottery.

"Damnation seize my soul! I could torture them for the sheer joy of hearing them scream, place bets on how long it takes to die, but I didn't. I could slit their guts and make them dance, whilst I torch the town, out of pure cussedness, but I won't. I could take the lot of them, hell, the whole goddamned town and sell them, but I won't. Scurrilous, vile, blood-thirsty, barbarous, brutal or base: pick a word and that would be me, with naught but a shred of virtue or decency to be had."

If shock had been his goal, he had failed, for none of his

threats were far from what she had heard of him. He seemed to be almost baiting her, daring her to argue with him. On the other hand, his scorn seemed aimed at himself, rather than her. Either way, for all she cared, he could rot in hell and not a moment's sleep would she lose over it.

In an icy silence, Nathan seethed about the room, the clump of boots and slosh of the rum bottle marking his path. The chill in the air was palatable, as proven when Kirkland come up the steps, immediately swiveled and crept back down. As Nathan continued to drink, her uneasiness grew. She hadn't seen him in drink — not this much, at any rate — and hadn't the slightest notion of what to expect.

As she watched the blur of his reflection in the window, more rational thoughts slowly came to prevail. There was the chance he drank due to a throbbing head. Kinder thoughts suggested a state of semi-drunkenness might be a necessary for what he was about to embark upon: engaging in the very violence and mayhem he had sought to avoid. His threats — which in the glare of honesty she knew to be hollow — wasn't the most vexing. What stung was the tongue-lashing.

Nathan eventually stormed out of the cabin. She assumed him gone ashore, and so was surprised when he returned. Still with her back to the room, she listened to him stomp about. Amid heavy exhalations, chairs were jerked, and a bottle was set down with far more force than necessary. It was growing late, the sun too weak to push through the after gallery's thick panes. She heard the scrape of a flint struck and the glow of a candle grew on the glass.

He scuffed to a halt and heaved a resigned sigh. "So what passage must I pay to escape this Purgatory?"

She glared over her shoulder. "I'm no pirate. At least I know right from wrong."

"As do I," he conceded readily. "However, I *am* a pirate, which renders the latter entirely superfluous."

There was the agitated rustle as he set to pacing once again. "Worrying about right and wrong can get a soul killed," he grumbled half under his breath. "And I can't very well conduct what need be conducted, if I have to live in mystery of what's to greet me upon me return to me own bloody damned ship."

"In that case, I'll strive to keep myself and my opinions out of your business."

He scuffed to a halt behind her. "How's about if we negotiate, opting, of course, to overlook said opinions?" His testiness gave way to his more familiar tease. "Truth be told, I rather fancy having you in me business."

She peeked over her shoulder and was met with a smile, one meant to charm. Her face heating, she nodded.

"Capitol," he declared. "Now, how's about I call Kirkland? The man's near apoplectic worrying you might go hungry."

It was that half-time of neither day nor night, when the light grew so thin the world became like a child's drawing: a place of two dimensions, flat people moving against a paper backdrop, shore, trees and mountains all existing on the same plane.

Nathan lingered at the cabin door. He drew a breath as if to say something, but didn't. This repeated several times gave her hope—vague, but hope nonetheless—that he might change his mind and allow her ashore. Settling his hat carefully on his head and his faded to near colorless burgundy coat on his shoulders, he stepped over the coaming and was gone.

From where Cate sat, she couldn't see the boats pull ashore, and perhaps it was best. Seeing him head off to the uncertainty of battle or accident was an unpleasant prospect. Not to be melodramatic, but she knew first-hand how capriciously Providence could strike, how easily one's life could be turned into something unrecognizable. It wasn't beyond reason to think she might never see him again.

She shook away the thought and set to delicately thumbing through one of the volumes stacked next to the chair. Sticky with pitch and tar, her hands were a mess from picking oakum. They were covered with fuzz, which no amount of wiping could remove. The book was in French, a language with which she had but passing familiarity, and so she picked out what words she knew and guessed the rest. It was a thoroughly inefficient way to read, but it passed the time, the ultimate goal. Kirkland brought her a plate shortly. Having little appetite, she picked bits from the soft tack, chewing without tasting. He took away the virtually untouched meal with a suffering eye, leaving a mug of broth in its place. She drank out of obligation.

Cate peeked through the sidelight once more at the hostages, barely visible where they huddled against the forecastle. She felt as much a captive as they. Her future might well be more tenuous than theirs. She wished she could advise them not to worry; she was reasonably confident no harm would befall them. These were pirates, but not the rapacious, plundering barbarians they were purported to be. There was a good chance, however, that point being advertised could be detrimental to their—and therefore her—success.

The grog dispensed, the men gathered amidships instead of the forecastle. The wealth laid at their feet and more to come put them in soaring spirits. They indulged in vast speculations of the prize to come and what the kingly sums might purchase. The lure of piracy was of little wonder: fortunes exceeding a lifetime of labor could be had in a day, squandered the next and regained the next. The bell clanged. A bellowed "Pipe down!" sent them to their hammocks, although many opted to sleep on deck.

Cate roamed the cabin, looking for something that wasn't there. Being alone for five years had taught her much in the way of loneliness, but the emptiness she suffered now was a wholly unfamiliar sort: a void that had been filled suddenly gone wanting, a blanket yanked away on a cold night. She thought to go to bed — sleep could be an excellent way to pass large spans of unpleasantness — but balked at the dark cavern of where her cot awaited. She knew all too well the hazards which came with empty hours in the darkness. They provided a blank canvas upon which the mind could paint an endless number of torturous scenarios of what might be happening ashore. The shrill of female laughter and music echoing across the harbor brought those imaginings in full color. She heaved open the gallery windows and sat on the sill. There, with the sentries' call of "All's well" after every bell, she watched the moonlight's silver dance amid the golden flicker of town's lights on the water.

She had stared for so long, when she finally saw the light, she thought it to be imagined: the flames of a torch swinging a low arc, one, two, three times. A looping circle at the end and it was doused.

Cate sat up at the increased pitch of voices and footsteps on deck. She sped out, in spite of Nathan's directive, meeting Pryce as he trundled down the afterdeck companionway.

"Was that him?" she asked in a low voice.

"Aye. T'were his signal."

She stood at the mizzen shrouds. The longboats' silhouettes were but dark blots against the harbor's oily satin. As they drew nearer, she could hear the jocular murmur of conversation, Nathan's graveled voice among them. She hadn't realized she had been holding her breath until it came out in an explosive burst of relief at seeing him spring up over the gunwale. The moonlight flashed on his smile at seeing her. He then turned to the matters at hand.

Two strapped and padlocked chests were lifted aboard. Neither of remarkable size, they were of considerable weight, requiring a goodly amount of sweating and cursing before they came to rest on the deck. Stirred from their sleep, the torches shone on the greedy anticipation on the men's faces as they gathered around. With not a little drama, Nathan unlocked the great latches, threw open the lids and stood back.

"The good mayor claims over ten thousand pieces." His dubiousness as to the veracity of that was drowned in the joyousness. "A considerable overstatement, by my estimation, but still not a bad day's work, eh mates?"

A rollicking cheer went up, with a great amount of hearty backslapping.

Pryce, being quartermaster, and therefore keeper of both the Prize Book and the prize itself, named a counting detail. Cate was more than a little stunned by the overt trust.

"Honor among thieves," Nathan declared grandly. "Part of the Code, remember: anyone suspected of thievery shall face a court of his equals?" He cast a jaded eye toward the surrounding men. "Not an altogether forgiving lot, to be sure."

"What happened to your face?" she exclaimed when he turned into the light.

His hand flew up to his cheek, wincing when he touched the streaks there, bright and angry.

"Oh, nothing," he said, evading her advances as she sought to inspect more closely. "It's nothing, really. I ran into—"

"Someone with fingernails. I see. No, it's quite all right," she said over his denials. "I'm not shocked at what men do ashore. Although it would appear you might consider exercising a little more discretion in your choices."

"I wasn't doing *anything* except trying to procure a bit of treasure for this wretched lot."

"If that were the case, then where did those come from?" she demanded, pointing to the claw marks. "You should wash that, you know."

"Must you wash everything? I got it seeking these."

He shoved the bundle into her arms, and then stood back. Shaking the bundle out, she found a red-checked skirt, a shift and jump-style stays made of homespun. There was a pair of peasant-like clogs, as well, which at first glance appeared a bit small, large feet the price of being tall.

"Clothes? You brought me clothes?" Cate cried.

"I thought perhaps those might be more fitting, what with your standards being so high and all. I had in mind they were more to your size than those... others." Nathan finished with a disdainful flourish of bejeweled fingers.

She brought the clothing closer to her nose and frowned. They smelled heavily of the previous owner—and quite recent—a strange combination of perspiration, orange water and fried fish.

"You'll no doubt want to wash those." He wore the forced smile of a man already resigned to his doom.

"You took these off someone. You stole these?"

He back-pedaled, grimacing. "Not exactly."

"Is that how you got those scratches? What did you do, knock her down and take them, or, did you get her undressed, and then sneaked off?"

"You don't paint a very flattering picture, either way."

"Then paint a better one."

Nathan sputtered, with several false starts. "There's no pleasing you, is there? A man risks life and limb—"

"Which limb were you risking?" She was in high color and in no mood to be placated. It was mortifying to think someone had lost their clothing—their only ones, by the looks of it—for her benefit.

Cate stalked into the cabin to fume in private, struggling with emotions she didn't understand. The wait had played on her nerves more than she cared to admit. Through the night, she had fought against envisioning what he might have been doing. There had been no orange glow of flames over the town. It was safe to say no buildings had been torched, but by all appearances, other flames had been lit. The wondering had been trying enough; knowing now that he had been pursuing his pleasures the while was far more disturbing than anticipated.

The knowledge stung worse than his cross words. Worse, she didn't understand why. Well, if she were honest, she did know, the question being more a matter of who she was angry with: Nathan, for being a man, doing what men do, or herself, for acting like a naïve maid. Neither was flattering.

Boots and the soft jingle of bells announced Nathan's arrival. He stopped near the table and cleared his throat several times.

"I'm sorry," she finally blurted. "I didn't mean to appear an ingrate."

"Soiled goods from a pirate, is it?" he asked, not a little accusing, and then laughed, a lot derisive. "No worries, luv. Your secret 'tis between us."

As she laid the clothes on the table, he seized her by the wrists.

"What the bloody hell happened to your hands! Belay that. I've eyes for meself," he said, when she jerked away and tucked them behind her back. "I would have thought between all hundred-odd sorry, thick-pated sprats on this blessed hulk, they could find enough brains among them to stop you, before you've gone bloody."

Cate couldn't argue; her hands were nearly that in several places. Her nails felt as if they had been torn from their beds, her fingers so covered in brown fuzz they resembled monkey hands. Those same fibers and grit had worked through her to the binder around her chest, prickling and itching to the point of near raw.

"Mr. Kirkland, oil and ash, if you please." He shouted, relying on his volume to carry the order down to the galley.

"And vinegar... for your face," she added at his questioning glare.

"We'll be in need of hot water directly," he told Kirkland as the stone bottle and saucer of ash were delivered. "And a bit of wool."

Pitching his hat and coat aside, he retrieved the basin from its stand. While she worked the oil and ash into her hands as directed, he filled the basin, bidding her to rinse next. The hot water burned the tortured skin at first, but soon had a balming effect. As she massaged the luxurious heat into the aching joints, a skim of oil and brown fuzz formed on the water's surface.

Critically eyeing her shirt and breeks, in the absence of a towel, Nathan extended his arm. "Here, use me sleeve. You'll be naught but covered in the stuff again if you touch yourself."

Something nagged her the while, something different about him from when he had left. As she dried her hands on his sleeve, she discovered what it was: his shirt was clean, the blood stains gone. She nearly inquired, but to do so would have meant exploring territory best left alone. After all, it was no great stretch of the imagination to figure what he had been doing ashore.

"Rub into this now." His directive broke her from an inexplicable surge of jealousy. Picking a piece of wool cloth, he started to do so for her. His fingers lingered, tracing hers, then he jerked away, retreating several steps. "Carry on for a bit and you'll feel right as rain again."

Living in the Highlands had taught her the palliative effects of wool. Its natural oils soon brought her hands to feel as if they might not fall off at the wrists after all. It was a relief to be able to touch her hair, or anything else for that matter, without sticking to it.

Turnabout was fair play. For form, he objected, but in the end, submitted to having his face tended. There were three parallel streaks, each deep enough to be crusted with dried blood. They curved from his cheekbone down to the line of his beard, also caked. She washed the scratch marks first with hot water — God knew what had been under the unknown woman's nails. She had seen far more minor scratches go foul. His sprouting beard was a soft plush under her fingers, left over-sensitive by the oakum. The dark sable sparked with random bits of russet, copper and gold in the candlelight.

The scenario was becoming a familiar one: standing close, tending his wounds.

"Twice in as many days," he said, divining her thoughts. "If I keep this up, you'll think me a dull-witted oaf."

Many words came to mind, but those would be a long time in coming.

"Mark me," he said, mirth touching the coffee-colored eyes, "if I fall and break me leg on the morrow, you shan't learn of it."

As she stood over him, she delicately sniffed, but detected only rum, wood smoke, a hint of tobacco and him, the same warm spiciness which clung in the mattress upon which she slept. She was near enough to see the blood had been washed from his headscarf, too. There were whitish smudges on the faded blue, which looked too much like face powder for her comfort.

His lids hooded, the heavy veil of lashes fanned darkly across his cheeks. With his head tipped back to allow easier access to his cheek, the scar at his throat was in stark evidence. A scalp-peeling blow to the head and clawed by a whore: a pirate's life was a dangerous one.

Unable to bear the silence, she groped for another topic.

"How long before the repairs are complete?"

Nathan stirred, his brow furrowing. "Day or two, but we'll make weigh as soon as the wood and watering is complete. His Honor, the lofty Señor Corretja shan't bother us whilst we've hostages, but best not tempt temptation. What remains can be accomplished under way."

He shifted in the chair, his agitation rising. "The bastard started having memory problems as soon as we caught up with him. Even his wife crying at pistol's point didn't answer."

"I thought you were going to avoid all that."

"Aye, well, best laid plans, and all that." Nathan smiled faintly. "T'was remarkable the clarity of memory he possessed when we put him on the altar: the chests were hidden in the cellar. Helluva man what uses the church to protect his most precious possessions. I'll wager he didn't tithe his fair share either," he huffed. "Had half a mind to inquire if he desired we take his wife and daughters—there was another, by the way— seeing as how they seemed so burdensome."

He sucked in sharply when Cate pressed into a deeper scrape with the vinegar.

"I'm sorry my hands are so rough," she said, wiping them self-consciously on her breeches. "I should have warned you."

His eyes met and held hers then dodged away. "I'd be a damned ungrateful scrub were I to complain, when it's me own ship what roughened them."

She became acutely aware of his nearness. Feeling her tense, he shifted to a more comfortable distance.

"There," she said softly, giving the scratches a final dab. "All done. You should rest."

Her hand came to rest on his shoulder, sagging with weariness. Other than a piece of dried meat, she had not seen him eat that day, nor the one before. A lesser man would have been bedridden for the day after such a blow to the head. Her presence seemed to have upset his lifestyle in several ways.

Nathan smiled, nonetheless. "I've plenty of time to sleep when I'm in me grave."

He rose and went around the table to retrieve his hat.

"You've a gentle touch, Cate Mackenzie" he said with somber intent. "Pryce represents you've been quite able-handed. You've done this before, the healing and sewing of bodies."

"I'm no physikan or healer, but yes." She sighed, her limb suddenly feeling filled with sand.

"You've done it a lot." It was more an observation than accusation.

Cate nodded, grimacing. "More than I care to think." It wasn't a matter to brag about; one did what one must and could.

Nathan turned his head toward the window, his gaze going distant. "The other day, you spoke of war."

She closed her eyes and nodded.

He fell quiet. His brow furrowed as his mouth worked under his mustache.

"I've seen the hell what can be wrought when two ships — a hundred guns each — haul up to hammer away at each other at a cable's length, throwing four or five hundred-weight of iron at every round, until either the guns explode from overheating, or one at last goes up in a blaze of glory, or sinks in the same. I've seen bodies fly no different than the splinters around them," he said so very softly. He turned his head to regard her with open admiration. "Providence has spared me from a legion of cannon opening fire on men afoot."

Nathan shook off his dark mood and raised the rum bottle in salute. "Lest you think me a cod-handed scrub, and I be forever haunted by me conscience, on behalf of the entire company of the *Ciara Morganse* and meself, I give you joy of your success, and in all sincerity, thank you."

He swept an elegant bow, wincing at the pain brought on by lowering his head.

Nathan seemed to have something more to say, but dismissed it. He carefully settled his hat on his head, the bells in his hair swishing with the movement. He gave a wry smile.

"You'd best change; I don't want it on me conscience that you'd contracted some morbid disease from being required to walk about in sullied clothes. I'll advise Mr. Kirkland you'll be looking to wash, *again*."

He headed for the door, but then drew to a halt.

"You're safe now," he said softly over his shoulder.

And then, he left.

⁂

Cate stood at the rail and watched the anchor and its thick-as-a-leg cable rise. The anchor's great hooks, enshrouded in green seaweed, brought with them the smell of muck and mud. On topsails and jibs, the ship curved out of the bay, and the first land she had seen in almost three months faded.

There was a grand celebration on the forecastle the next night. The men were in high spirits. Tales flowed in a stream as steady as the grog, a number of toasts drank to Captain Nathanael Blackthorne. One couldn't help but notice the flamboyance and credulity of the stories told about him expanded in direct proportion to the amount of drink consumed. It was difficult to imagine one person capable of everything credited to him.

5: LIFE'S ROUTINES

CATE SETTLED INTO THE DAILY routine of a pirate ship, if "routine" and "pirate" might be used in the same sentence: rise with the sun, work, a bit of grog and relaxation on the forecastle after dark, and then sleep.

Trying to learn the names of over a hundred and twenty rogues was a daunting task. With faces weathered to a uniform butternut tan, sun-creased and seamed, separation on that sole basis was nigh impossible.

Mr. Hodder she was familiar with, if not by face, then certainly by voice. As the ship's boatswain, pronounced "BO-sun," his charge was the workings of the ship proper, and hence, its crew. Either by necessity or natural trait, he possessed a voice which could carry from bowsprit to taffrail in a high gale, and all around a fist-sized quid of tobacco in his cheek. A single "Turn to!" could rouse a crewman from the depths of sleep, up and out of his hammock and on deck, before the wind could carry it away.

In spite of his voice, massive gnarled hands and inordinately long arms, Hodder's most outstanding feature was the intricately carved and scrimshawed ivory rings which studded every nook of his body. He stalked the decks, the waist-long eel-skinned and tarred pigtail swinging at his back, rings clattering, and woe unto the wretched, unsuspecting cove who failed to attend his approach.

Millbridge was another easily recognized. Being the oldest, and therefore, most experienced, put him in the revered position of having the last word on any mystery or vagary of nature, or the world: strongest wind, strangest sky, biggest shark or worst doldrum. He was the final authority and touchstone regarding superstition and omens, boils, cuts, dislocations and fevers. Even Nathan and Mr. Pryce yielded to his authority. If Millbridge said, then it must be so. He was the one who appeared while she prepared to sew Chin's leg her first day aboard, with the declaration of "I've seen worse."

Who could argue with that?

As part of his position, Millbridge was spared hardship, either physical or weather. Generous rations of rum and additional shares of plunder all revealed the level of his esteem.

"I thought everyone objected to the privileges in the Royal Navy," Cate said, still a bit unclear.

"There privilege is imposed. Here, 'tis granted," Nathan explained, patiently, "and can be revoked at the drop of a hat—highly unlikely, but a possibility."

He scanned the ship's people, all at their duties. "Millbridge is everyone's goal: to live that long. Bloody unlikely prospect, but 'tis the hope what lingers in every seaman's heart." He grinned a bit wistfully. "All of us fancy a bit of ease in our silver years. Providence must be smiling upon someone what's managed to make it that long. Who be we to tangle with that?"

As a single face among the masses, each man adorned or outfitted himself to be unique against a hundred others, who were also striving for the same. It was a contest with no end. As a result, it was difficult not to stare, and yet they took pride at her doing so, interpreting it as a declaration of their success. Through the days, she found the uniqueness of each and privately assigned temporary names.

The easiest were those who, by virtue of certain physical aspects, resembled animals. Toad and Crane, the two she had met her first day aboard, were the first to receive such titles, until later learning they were Mr. Towers and Mr. Smalley.

Hog, called so because of rounded nostrils and snubbed appearance because of the missing end of his nose, turned out to have the name of Seymour.

Mole, because of his way of squinting when spoken to and a pair of horrifically bucked teeth, was actually Mr. Hallchurch, a pleasant sort that tended to spit with every "s" or "th" uttered.

Chicken, known only by his semi-maniacal cackling laugh that was audible throughout the ship, turned out to be a long-necked man with inordinately small, round eyes named Sombers.

Snake didn't look like one. A tattoo wound his torso, up the side of his face and coiled around his bald head, the slitted eyes of the creature staring down from his forehead squarely into the face of anyone who spoke to him. Not only was Ogden, as she learned his name to be, bald, he was completely void of any hair anywhere on his body.

Ass wasn't meant to be derogatory. It referred to the jawbone the mulatto wore on a leather thong around his neck. In retrospect, it probably wasn't the jawbone of an ass, since it bore three gold teeth. Mr. Squidge, as he preferred to be called, wore the remnants of several of his foes. Hanging from a loop around his neck, the withered segments turned out to be fingers.

There was confusion on Cate's part, because of another man who carried a similar collection. The issue was cleared up when Nathan pointed out that unlike Squidge's, Mr. Pickford's collection was not of fingers, but ears, each bearing a gold earring.

How could she have been so unobservant?

She didn't inquire if some of the fresher-looking bits were souvenirs of the *Constancy* or *Nightingale*.

Nathan and Mr. Pryce were more than patient in quietly coaching her on the names, even going so far as to point out how to remember each:

Similar to Hodder, Mr. Damerell sported gold rings on every part of his body.

"A ring in one's ear improves the sight," Nathan informed her. He failed to explain the powers of those in Damerell's lips, nose and nipple. She couldn't help but wonder where else he might have one.

"Oh, yes indeed," Nathan said, with a delicate clearing of his throat, somehow divining her thoughts. "Even there."

Mr. Scripps was appropriately named. Bare-chested in even the most inclement weather, barely an inch of his body wasn't occupied by multi-colored tattoos.

Pattison had scarified tattoos arching across both cheeks and encircling his eyes.

Rowett, at one point referred by her as Snake the Second, wore a snake skin nearly as wide as his back, fashioned into something akin to a vest, the tails dangling at the back.

"Ate his best friend," she was told.

Mr. White was black. Mr. Towers was short. Mr. Harrier was bald. Mr. Pidgeon resembled a cat. Mr. Broadstreet was pencil-thin to the point of causing one to wonder how he kept from being blown away, and Mr. French wasn't.

Mute Maori was just that.

"Doesn't he have a name?" she asked, eyeing Mastiff, so named when she sewed Chin's leg.

Nathan propped his hands on his hips. "And how were we to know that? He's a mute," he pointed out, apparently not caring that the man, who stood nearby, still had his hearing. "Unless you read Maori?"

Cate wasn't sure if there even was such a language, let alone if a written one.

"No cabin boys?" As she understood, taking young boys to sea was a well-steeped tradition.

"Certainly," Nathan replied. "Have to be a dundering oysterhead to aweigh without. Millbridge there is one." A hand waved in the direction of the ship's patriarch.

"But... he's...?"

"Too old to do aught else," Nathan finished bluntly, but with a certain affection. "The men — and me, of course — desire to keep him about, but those old bones won't stand much abuse, so he's the easiest job aboard."

"Easy" wasn't ordinarily the first word which came to mind when referring to cabin boy. To be one meant to live at the beck and call of every hand aboard. A combination messenger, servant, and valet, they were required to perform any and all menial tasks. It hardly seemed the role for a person verging on antiquity.

"But, I've never seen him in the —" she began.

"Not likely to either," Nathan cut in. "He can't abide women. Some long, lost love doing him wrong, or some such stuff and nonsense, but it stuck with him all these years. Never known him to so much as lift a brow to a whore, let alone be in the same room with one, willingly at any rate. No offense," he added as a rather late-coming after thought.

"None taken, I think," she said, still trying to sort out the image of Millbridge being anyone's lackey.

"Jensen was taken on initially to serve as Kirkland's lad, but he's never allowed the boy over the galley coaming."

Jensen was the youngest in years, but held seniority over many. That edge didn't save him from being the brunt of practical jokes and ribbings. Bright-faced and good-natured, he eagerly faced every menial and dirty task which came with being the youngest aboard. His ability to accept it all in the spirit intended, often laughing the hardest, had endeared him to everyone. Now the tender age of seventeen and at sea for a few years, it was painfully clear that Jensen wasn't a natural seaman. It was suggested, often and none so gently, that perhaps his talents laid in farming, with dirt under his nails as opposed to tar.

"Reminds me of meself," Nathan sighed wistfully one day. "Of course, I wasn't so cod-handed." He winced, indicating perhaps that wasn't quite the entire truth.

"But no regular cabin boys?" Cate asked.

Nathan smiled tolerantly. "Best not have the men see the captain waited upon: sets a bad image. Besides, the lads can be a bit... without defenses," he finished with a strained tone.

It was another arrival upon dangerous grounds, and many of those there were. She was coming to wish for a chart by which to track such hazards.

Life, however, was far from idyllic. A few souls made it eloquently clear they desired no part of her, her presence an affront. She felt their thinly-veiled malignant looks, their comments always uttered loudly enough for her benefit alone. Scarface, or Bullock as his name turned out to be, was always among them, his voice as recognizable as Nathan's. A ringleader, if ever she had seen one. His presence was as pressing as the trade winds. She took careful note of him and his cohorts at all times.

Besides the uncertainty of her fate—Nathan being still slippery on the matter—the issue of quartering was a growing concern. Upon her unceremonious arrival, she had been deposited in the captain's berth. After the first several nights, she had anticipated being relocated to one of the cabins below, but Nathan had insisted she remain where she was, "seeing as how it was finally clean to *your* exacting standards."

He was, of course, referring to a rather unfortunate incident one morning, when... Well, the mattress needed airing *desperately*! There had been cross words and perhaps some hurt feelings—not that ingratitude for his hospitality had been her intention—but her goal had ultimately been met: the oakum-stuffed mattress spending the day on the hatch grates in the sun and smelling much the better for it.

The issue of sleeping arrangements was precipitated not quite a week of her arrival, when she found Nathan one night at the table, the logbook his pillow.

She came in the next morning to find him as clear-eyed and insufferably perky as ever—and yes, perky was indeed the correct word, for the man positively bubbled. She, on the other hand, met the day with considerably less gleeful aplomb. He took an unseemly joy, by her estimation, in making example of that not-so-small contrast. He met the sun like it was an elixir whereas it did no more than deliver her a dull headache.

Mr. Kirkland—Bless him!—was the only sympathetic soul aboard. Every morning a pot of coffee waited upon her on the table, hot enough to scald the unsuspecting. It was a wonder of the ages as to how he managed the miracle, but miraculous it was.

"Let me go elsewhere," she insisted after sufficient amounts of coffee made lucid thought possible. Her voice was raised not in anger, but to be heard over a thunderstorm, the rain hammering overhead. "It's not right. You're the captain; you deserve your own bed."

In point of fact, she had no idea where he slept.

His indifference bordered on annoying. "Inconsequential encumbrances, luv."

She caught sight again of the brindle-coated, fox-faced creature she had seen in the sleeping quarters her first day. The half-cat, half-weasel-looking thing appeared now and again. Most times, it slunk along the wall, head down, industriously sniffing like a hound on a scent. This time, however, it came directly for the table, with a look of complete expectation.

"Come here, me lovely!" Nathan crooned. As he bent to scoop it up, the thing sat up in greeting, braced on a bushy tail nearly as long as its body.

"What is it?" Cate asked watching it slouch into Nathan's grasp like a pet cat, and then inquisitively stretch its muzzle toward her. She wasn't afraid, just unsure what it was.

"His Lordship, Georgie, named after our fair regent. Fitting for a rat-eater, don't you think?" he asked, setting the beast back on the floor.

"It's a mongoose," he said at last, dismayed by her ignorance, "one of the best varmint killers about. Granted, snakes are ever so much more better, but I can't abide the things, always slithering about, dropping down from god knows where." He shuddered dramatically. "His Lordship can make a fair meal of a goodly number of rats per week. Even if he doesn't catch 'em, the damned things will stay in the bilges just to be shut of him."

Oddly, as the animal sat up on its haunches next to her chair, it did possess a certain imperial air.

"Begging?" she asked, looking down.

"Be gone with you, you little blighter! Have a care," he directed to Cate. "He'll have your meal in a blink."

Nathan swiveled a sharp eye toward His Lordship. "Someday Kirkland will catch you and there'll be hell to pay. To the sharks it shall be and I shan't raise a finger to save your hairy arse. 'Twill be an occasion. We'll place wagers on whether a mongoose can swim."

With a mongoose version of an indifferent "hmph!" His Lordship ambled about the room.

"And those things?"

He followed her point, taking a moment to realize what she was looking at, and then swiveled around in disbelief. "The geckos?"

Nathan took a drink of coffee and set to breaking off bits of the mango to feed His Lordship, now sitting up at his chairside.

"Not quite sure how the little bastards got on board," he sniffed disinterestedly. "I can't say I was altogether pleased at the way they multiplied worse than rabbits. God knows what must have been going on behind our backs," he huffed under his breath, and threw a malignant glare at the lizard scampering along the sill.

The lizards were plentiful. Catching glimpses from the corner of her eye, most times Cate would look to find nothing there, and left to wonder if she was imagining things.

"Hodder and Pryce put a bounty on them, but the men damned near beat each other to death with the nets trying to catch the little blighters. They raced them, too—more abiding than the rats on that count—until we began to notice the cockchafer population diminishing by a grand mark, along with other pestilences of a crawly nature."

"Some of the hands tamed 'em, put 'em on little leashes and carried them about on their shoulders. Had a topsman what wouldn't go aloft without one on each. They're abiding beasts, once you get past them looking at you upside down with one eye whilst the other goes off," he said, licking the fruit juice from his fingers.

"Let me move to one of the cabins below," she said, picking up their earlier discussion. She spoke in a considerably lower voice, now that the rain had stopped. "Believe me, I've slept rougher." She ruffled at the possibility that his concerns were based on her inability to weather hardship.

The bantering went on for several more rounds, in considerably higher voice now that the rain had stopped.

"I'll not have you..." His voice faded as he was distracted by something out the stern window. His eyes narrowed, and then sharpened, his attention zeroing in like a hawk on a mouse.

"Here in me quarters: I can keep you safe," he said backing toward the door, his gaze fixed over her shoulder. With reluctance, he swiveled his attention to her. "Below, even with direct orders, there would be no guarantees."

At the door, he paused long enough to sternly point and say, "You'll sleep here," and then stepped over the coaming.

The subject was closed.

Much to her chagrin, there was strong logic in his point. Captain he might be, but human nature—men's nature—was what it was. True enough, the punishment for disregarding a direct order would be severe, but the damage would already be done. There would be no reversing an attack in the night.

"On deck there. Sail ho! A point windward astern," came the hail down through the skylight.

Turning to the window, she saw sails: bright barbs of white against the steel-grey of the departing storm.

Heart racing, she ran to the quarterdeck where Nathan and Pryce stood shoulder-to-shoulder gazing intently over the leeward taffrail.

"Do you see what I see, Mr. Pryce?" Nathan's back was to her, but his smile could be heard, plump with anticipation. "Has she made us?"

"Aye. Wore 'round and straight as a needle she bears."

"It's the *Terpsichore*, Woodbridge commanding," Pryce said after several moments. He spit over the rail. "Creswicke's minion: privateer."

"Another one?" Her voice pitched high at the thought of being pursued yet again.

The two men turned, neither having noticed her there.

"Aye, the waters seem to abound these days," Pryce said with significance directed toward his Captain. Nathan only shrugged.

Nathan cast an eye skyward and then considered the oncoming ship. "Straight at him, Mr. Pryce. We're the faster. We should be able to win the weather gauge. You know what to do."

"Prepare about!" Pryce's cry was instantly picked up by Hodder and then echoed down the chain of command. From there it scattered into a half-dozen crew captains, amid the slapping of scores of bare feet as the hands scurried to their posts.

The water raced down the *Morganse's* sides as she sped toward her foe. Cate shifted her position in order to maintain her view of the distant ship as the *Morganse* pirouetted. Amid mutterings of "Beg pardon, miss," "By your leave, mum," "Have a care," "Mind yer step," and "Over here, if you please," she was bumped and jostled until she found a neutral spot, just aft and slightly leeward of the mizzen mast. Once again, she was left to wonder if the *Terpsichore* might be her salvation or damnation. Communication being what it was it seemed unlikely that word of her wanted status could have passed so quickly from England to every naval vessel in the West Indies. Judging by the zeal with which they readied to fight, Nathan and his men saw the *Terpsichore's* presence as a personal matter, and had nothing to do with her.

"Clear the decks!"

Cate jumped at Hodder's bone-penetrating bellow.

The distance between the ships closed at a shocking rate, their prows slicing the deep blue water. At one point, there was a mass cry of elation: the *Morganse* had gained the precious weather gauge. The intricacies of it still evaded Cate, but its importance was readily grasped.

A puff of smoke and the splash of a ball well ahead of the *Morganse's* forefoot signaled the battle had begun.

Nathan grabbed Cate by the arm. "Get below."

"No!"

"Get—" He was cut off by a ball which skipped off the water and whirred overhead near enough to nick a backstay. "Goddammit, get below! I'll not stand here and watch you be sheared in half."

Nathan jerked the pistol from his waist, checked it, and then shoved in her waistband. "You know what to do, as do I."

He winked and sent her on her way, dragging foot, but going nonetheless.

"Fire as they bear!" Nathan shouted, as she made her way down the aft steps.

Cate's foot had barely touched 'tween deck when the first gun spoke. So, intensified by the confined space, the sound was a physical blow to the chest. Ahead a gun fired, hurtling back against its tackles with shocking violence. The smoke wafted in greyish-white whorls about her skirts as she made her way forward to the passage below. An arm shot out to stop her, while the next gun captain glared down the barrel, waited for the roll and sparked the touchhole, arching his body away from the recoil.

Cate snatched a lamp from its peg and lit it from a slow-match before going lower. The hold was no less forbidding than her first visit. This time, however, she had the light as company, to keep the dank murk at bay. Once more at the furthest point possible, she ensconced herself atop a puncheon, the lamp at her elbow.

She was accustomed to the sound of a small war breaking out every afternoon, before the dog watches and evening grog. Nathan was a firm believer in the price of a hundred weight of powder a cheap investment for gun crews which could hit a floating barrel at will, in any weather conditions, and continue to do so in less than two-minute increments, or marksmen who could hit that same barrel thrice in barely more than one. In that process, she had learned the importance of quickness and even timing, and the hazard of great guns going off simultaneously, putting a huge strain on the ship, to the point of possibly causing her damage.

Hearing the thump of the *Terpsichore's* guns and feeling the *Morganse* shudder when she took a hit, Cate was reminded that this was no practice. She grasped the rim of the cask, her knuckles whitening, the rough oak gouging her fingertips, as she worried for Nathan. Chanting that he had been doing this for years, she tried not to count the incoming shots. To do so seemed to paint a target on his chest. The blessed man had swelled to twice his size at the prospect of a fight. Her presence dampening those spirits, he had wished her away. And so, she was left with doing what she had done for months aboard the *Constancy*: nothing. She would have far preferred being in the thick of it, rather than sitting in the moldering dark waiting to hear a scream, dreading what might await when she at last returned to the world of sun.

Cate braced as the ship veered, took an uncommon lee lurch, and then swept through her pivot. In the dark void of the hold, the maneuver had a dizzying effect. The grind and scrape of the planks working under the strain vibrated into her chest.

And then, almost as quickly as it had begun, it was over. Unlike the last time, there was no musket fire. The fight never grew that close.

By the time the first victorious cheer had erupted, Cate was already at the bottom of the steps. She reached the main deck in time to the rail lined with men, their trousers down around their knees, slapping their bared arses toward the retreating *Terpsichore*. She found Nathan on the quarterdeck. Fixing his breeches, his somewhat guilty look dissolved into a brighter one at seeing her. He winked and nodded, and then set to heartily clapping his men on the back and giving them joy of their win.

The *Morganse* was bruised, but nowhere near as damaged as her engagement with the *Nightingale*. Her people were already putting her to rights: cutting away tangled rigging and pitching the useless debris overboard. Nathan's cheerfulness as her backdrop, Cate bent to the task of tending the injured. Compared to the last time, they were minor and few. She set up her makeshift sick-berth below with what she had: a table, a bucket of hot water, some bandages recently gathered and a jar of salve from Mr. Kirkland.

Mr. French was regaling Cate of how his gun, *Bloody Bess*, "took the *Tersipchore* foretop, whilst *Lucifer* did for the bastard's mizzen," while she worked to extract a sliver longer than her finger from his thigh, when Pryce and young Jensen appeared bearing a box, which they presented to her. Similar to a portmanteau, it was leather-covered, with straps and a handle on top. The inside was filled with rudimentary weapons for the warfare against sickness and injury. Amid the jars, bottles, gauze bags and folded waxed envelopes, sat a shining pair of scissors and tweezers, crafted by Petrov, the ship's smith.

"We've scavenged every prize fer medicines and such, but the pickings have been blessedly thin," Pryce told her, dolefully shaking his head over the box. "Not a one possessed more than vitriol, dead leeches, purges, squill pills, and a rare bit o' poppy syrup. 'Course, 'tis no countin' the things what we had no idea. Needed a Latin master for that. The Cap'n can cipher a bit o' that Popish falderal, but bloody little sense could be made o' it."

His claim was born out by the Latin lettering on many of the labels. Rough translations had been scrawled next to it, most now smeared and water-spotted.

"We woulda taken the first chirurgeon we come upon, clapped 'im in irons, if come the need, but blessed few in these waters," said Pryce.

"There was that one—" began Jensen.

"Ah, yes! I mind him. What was the cove's name? Died of a fever a'fore we learnt if he was worth his salt."

"Tach," cried Jensen, shuddering. "All he could think was to bleed everyone."

"Aye. And cursed ghoulish about it he was. 'Peared to me he just wuz a-wantin' blood to lure his blessed sharks. The man appreciated his shark steaks the likes o' which I ain't never see'd."

And so, armed with her new line of defense, Cate set to work on the powder burns, splinters large and small, broken bones, busted guts and bashed heads.

She was tying off the splint on Mr. Church's arm, broken when he failed to outdistance a recoiling gun, when she became dimly aware of someone behind her, close enough to nudge her in the back. Living on a ship with over a hundred and twenty others, it was common to be jostled, and so thought nothing of it.

"Women are good but for two things and both are with their legs apart," came from so near behind she could feel his breath hot on her back.

Her gut lurched. She knew the voice without looking: Bullock, the one who had accosted her when first arrived. She looked up into Church's insolent grin. She tried to move, but found she was now trapped between Church's legs with Bullock behind her. A quick glance revealed that Bullock had timed his comment well: no one was near, no one to hear, no one to witness.

Setting her jaw, Cate gave the binding a final jerk on the knot hard enough to elicit a pained yelp from Church. She jabbed an elbow into Bullock's as she pushed herself clear, and then climbed to the main deck to their jeering chuckles.

Cate retreated to the safe shadows of the Great Cabin for the remainder of the day. Bullock's comments had put her at ill-ease. They were a stark reminder of how tenuous her status aboard was. It was only through Nathan's protection that kept her safe. If anything was to happen to him...

She shied from finishing that thought.

As much as Nathan denied it, she knew her presence caused problems. Bullock was one symptom. The two crewmen, Hughes and Cameron, revealing her involvement with the Stuart Uprising was another problem. The knowledge hadn't gone without comment, if not incident. The Uprising was seen by many English as a direct threat to their King: England's soil had been invaded, English lives lost. Any participants in such an insurrection were seen as traitors; animosity ran high throughout the realm, including a pirate ship. She hadn't been deaf to the crosswords and epithets uttered by some of the men.

Again, she wondered why Nathan kept her aboard, what he planned to do with her.

He had assured her she was not to be turned over for the reward, declaring, "Never in all me days have I been that desperate."

She was being kept, but for what? Hostage or prisoner? Slave, mascot or pet? Insurance seemed more fertile ground: a bargaining chip in reserve, with either the Royal Navy or the Royal West Indies Mercantile Company.

It was wholly confusing. For months on the *Constancy,* she had listened to railing against women aboard and the bad luck which they apparently carried in their skirt folds. Surely pirates would be of the same mind, if not more so. That night, she made her case to Nathan. A shrug and a dismissive flap of the hand was her answer. Mr. Pryce had exhibited a proclivity for superstition, so she pressed her case with him. His mouth compressed as if a great mystery of the ancients had just been posed. "Aye, ye've a point there."

A Company Council was called. The exact logic was lost to her somewhere in the debate. The final outcome, however, punctuated by a cheer, was from that point on she was to be addressed as "Mr. Cate."

Lolling atop a cask looking on, Nathan raised a bottle in salute. "I'm good with it!"

The subject was closed.

❧

The *Morganse* found a cove in which to hide and lick her wounds inflicted by the *Terpsichore,* and those which lingered from the *Nightingale.* It was an open but protected place, the ship's masts merging with the ratcheted spine of the island curving around her.

All hands set to their duties with a gleeful eagerness. Battle had disrupted the Morgansers orderly world, and they were anxious to set it back to rights. They set to knotting and splicing, conversation requiring a raised voice in order to be heard over the woodpeckerish rap of caulker's mallets, and Chips and his mates, looking harried but happy. Wood and watering parties were sent ashore as well as hunting parties for fresh meat. Foragers were sent to gather fodder for Hermione and anything else which might be had. In the West Indies, apparently all one need do was put their arm out and food was to hand. After years of eking out an existence on scraps, such a state of plenty seemed edenic to Cate, if only she could see it.

"Let's give 'er a new set o' boots and tops," declared Nathan, and then jabbed an elbow at Cate's side. "It's cleaning. You'll love it."

It would seem the sea was of the opinion that the bottom of a ship was solely intended for weed, barnacles, shells and any number of other things to grow, including the insidious *teredo*. The shipworm was described to her as nothing more than a mass of sawblade-like jaws set on devouring the ship from under their feet. Able to make holes the size of Cate's thumb, the creature itself nearly as long as her arm, with such voraciousness that surely, if she bore an ear, she could hear them munching away.

Anything wooden and afloat in seawater required careening, the regularity rising with the temperature of the water in which she plied. It meant literally running the ship on shore and divesting her of everything, including guns and rigging. It was an arduous and monumental undertaking, rendering the ship as vulnerable as a beached whale for the best part of a month.

A good amount of the *Morganse's* bottom was copper-sheathed, denying worms and barnacles access. Another portion was studded with copper nails, a massive expense, but one her captain willingly paid to keep her bottom sweet. A space between copper and waterline still existed, and so boot-topping it was, as Nathan had so colorfully ordered. It was an intermediary measure: shifting guns, rigging and cargo to roll the ship on her side—a parliamentary heel—baring the space below her waterline to be breamed.

"Only a strake or two," Cate was told. The strakes, the planking seams in the ship's hull, could be seen if she stretched far out over the rail. While out there, in the clear water underneath the ship, she could catch glimpses of the green skirt of weed wisping with the currents.

She was pulled back by the skirt, like a parent jerking a child from a precipice. Turning around, she came directly into Nathan standing there.

"Going somewhere, are we?" he asked in a low voice, with a mixture of suspicion and dare, but daring her to what?

Startled, she could only sputter. He spun away, apparently losing patience in waiting for her to find an answer.

The workload required all hands. No parties made the pull ashore for the mere sake of fun. And so, once again, Cate was tempted by the nearness of land. She gazed longingly at the long gleam of white sand between the azure and emerald of water and trees, so near and yet so far.

With no skill at carpentry, useless at knotting or splicing, lacking the strength to move guns or do heavy-lifting, and Millbridge barring her from helping to stow the cabin, Cate was sat down to making besom brushes: bundling and tying twigs onto the ends of branches. Dipped in tar, the brushes were set afire to heat the graving, the hull's coating. The heat and fumes poisoning the worms, the fires softened the graving enough for the irons and scrapers to remove the weed, barnacles and other filth.

Cate moved about careful not to trip over the tackles rigged for the network of lines over the side from which the men dangled. "One or two strakes" put the decks at an acute angle. In truth, the incline was not much more than when the ship was heeled over sailing, but her motionlessness — baring the cove's minor swell — made it seem far more precarious. Not unlike when on that same tack, the topsmen scampered about in the rigging with the agility of monkeys and the industriousness of squirrels.

There was a good deal of convivial shouting and swearing. It must possess an energizing effect on men, for it seemed they could rarely accomplish a task without. The deck grew hazy with curls of smoke rising from the sides, acrid with an odd mix of burning weed, sulfur, tar and perhaps a tinge of cooking worm. The smoke wafted low across the water and ashore, hanging among the trees like tobacco smoke wreathing a man's head. Bits of canvas were rigged at the ports and hatches to funnel air below where the noxious smoke tended to collect. Fire and ships were mortal enemies, a ship being barely more than a pile of aged wood saturated with tar and paint, and so lookouts stood at the ready, with hoses and filled buckets.

Both sides complete, the *Morganse* righted for good, Nathan yielded to Hodder, chafing to the point of near apoplexy over the ruin of his precious paintwork. The swarms of besom-brush-bearing ants were replaced by paint-brush-bearing ones, the sharp smell of fresh paint joining the heady fug of breaming.

Declaring "idle hands and all that," and disinclined toward revealing the ship's fixed whereabouts with the daily great gun practice, Nathan ordered small arms practice instead: knives, pikes, boarding axes, sabers, cutlasses and the like. A series of chalk circles were drawn on deck and the smell of the sweat of exercise mingled in the air as the pirates honed their hand-to-hand skills. Stripped to their breeks, their chests shone with sweat as they sparred and parried with uncommon intensity, the classrooms taking on an air of competition. Under the watchful eyes of their mates, the combatants were cheered on by a large audience lining the ratlines, yards and yet-to-be-painted rails. Beatrice shouted a bawdy repartee from amid the men peering down from their roost.

Cate stood by with her blood box—so named by Nathan, since it appeared every time there was blood—for injury was frequent. She smiled faintly as she watched, thinking it wasn't unlike when Brian's men had trained in preparation for raids, clan wars or during the Uprising. There was, however, one difference: a blood-lust abandon.

"They look like they are trying to hack each other to pieces," she said, wincing at the sight of a vicious swipe by Mr. Rowett, his snakeskin vest tossed aside.

"Pirate." Nathan offered the single word as an all-encompassing explanation. He sat next to her atop a cask, watching with a sports-like avidness.

"Which means kill a'fore gettin' killed," Pryce added from Nathan's other side. He stood leaning against the rail, arms crossed loosely on his chest.

Distracted, she didn't see what happened to cause a cheer to go up, proclaiming Rowett the victor. Those two were barely away, before two more stepped into the circle, squared up and the fight commenced again.

"Y' know Cap'n," Pryce began thoughtfully, eyes tracking the fight. "If'n she's to be here, she should be able to protect herself."

"Right you are." Nathan pulled his eyes from the match. "Should things happen, you could be need of defending yourself. Can you fight?"

"You mean, as in fists?" she asked warily. The "should things happen" comment was casually made, but his meaning was clear and not to be taken lightly.

"No. You're feisty, but no match." Nathan paused to shout encouragement to one of the combatants. "What about swords? I hear tell on the *Constancy* you were quite admirable."

"You're too kind," she said tartly.

"No, I mean it. Isn't that how you saw it?" he said, thumping Pryce on the shoulder.

"Aye, verily sir. A fair hand, to be sure."

"For a woman," she said, peering around Nathan to Pryce.

"Well, to be sure," Nathan equivocated as did Pryce. Alighting from the barrel, he took her by the arm. "C'mon, let's see what you've got."

The crew gathered around and a lengthy group conversation ensued revolving around the finer points of weapon selection, size and weight, the grip being of greatest significance. A more serious debate followed as to who was to be her opponent. Jensen was the first option, by virtue of their similarity in size and his need for practice. Pryce dismissed that out-of-hand, pointing out the lad's lack of skill could mean her accidental injury. Through the process of elimination, Nathan was finally urged forward, the tacit agreement being if anyone was to cause her harm, let it be the captain.

The next thing she knew, she had been shoved into the circle, armed and facing him. Wiping her palm on her skirt, she clasped the sword, the grip biting her flesh. A cutlass, actually, curved and wicked, meant for close-quarter fighting, as on the deck of a ship. Much lighter than the long swords of the Highlands, it came alive in her hand; "blooded" as Brian had called it, "a blade that knows its purpose."

"Loosen your grip a bit, luv," Nathan instructed calmly. He stood with his arms relaxed at his sides. Circling catlike, sword in hand, he became the pirate, barbaric and deadly, the one she had expected to meet.

"Don't allow your enemy to see fear," he said. "Stare him in the eye; make him wonder…"

Cate lunged, catching him off guard. It brought a cheer from the crowd and a short outburst of bemusement from Nathan. The surprise lasted less than the time it took for his arm to come up in almost playful defense. Irritated that he dared to take her so lightly, her attack grew more focused with each stroke. Amid the scrape and clang of metal against metal, a small smile gradually tucked one corner of his mouth, pleased and even a bit admiring.

"Keep your elbow down, lass," Pryce shouted. "That's it. No, no, keep it down!"

Calling a halt, Nathan seized her elbow. "Keep it down here," he said firmly. "Let it come up too high and you're leaving yourself open." He poked her sharply in the ribs with his finger, eliciting a startled squeak. "Next time, that could be a blade."

They squared off, Nathan's dark eyes fixed on her. Without out a flicker of warning, he attacked, pressing her back. Not possessing the strength or skill for a prolonged offensive, she was obliged to rely on defense. Arms and legs burning, she was envious of his freedom of skirts to tangle his legs when he lunged or reposted. Too soon, a flick of his blade and her sword was wrenched from her hand, clattering to the deck. The hands cheered anyway, shouting words of encouragement, many impressed that she could bear a sword at all.

Nathan clapped her on the shoulder as she worked the sting from her fingers and shook out her arm. "Not bad, luv. With a little practice, you could be fair. The problem is strength."

His words inflated and then bruised.

Damn him! He wasn't even breathing hard.

"Don't look so wounded," Nathan laughed, slapping her jovially on the back. "Bloody awkward for a woman to be as strong as a man; doesn't sound appealing a'tall. What of it, Pryce?"

"Well, she could buy herself a bit o' time. But strikes me she'd get herself hurt a-carryin' a sword. We can get 'er practiced up, but she'll be a-needin' somethin' more. How's about a knife?"

Pryce pulled his from at his back and handed it off to Nathan.

"Think you could handle that?" as Nathan asked as he handed it to her.

Cate balanced the weapon in her hand, feeling its weight. The steel shone coldly in the sun. "It was a long time ago, but I used to have one," she said quietly.

Nathan caught her tone and sobered. "Your husband?"

Nodding, she swallowed an unexpected lump. "He thought I should be able to protect myself." The irony in the repetition of that theme brought a faint smile. "He and his men taught me how to use one, how to kill."

Nathan hesitated, the men circled around staring.

Forcing a smile, she griped the handle overt confidence. "So, what would you like me to do with this?"

The awkward moment past, Nathan's graveness deepened. "You'll need to be able to protect yourself and be ready to kill, if you must. Could you do that?"

Her throat tightened. A cold ball formed in the pit of her stomach. "I've done it before," she said, meeting Nathan's gaze.

It wasn't meant as to be cavalier nor bold, but facts were facts.

"Fair enough." Nathan clapped her on the shoulder in assurance.

With little hesitation, Mr. Pryce was voted best knife-bearer and, therefore, Cate's new master.

Pryce's knife was returned to him. Nathan pulled a dagger from his boot and handed it to her. "Go ahead, luv, show us what you have."

She rolled the scrimshawed weapon in her hand, its ivory

patina glowing. Well-balanced and compact, it was considerably larger than the one lost in her bag of belongings on the *Constancy*. It had been a *sgian dhu,* a tiny Highlander's stocking knife. Switching hands, she wiped her palm again, and then re-gripped it several times, until the comfort spot was found.

"'Pears like she knows what she's doing already," observed Hughes as she and Pryce circled each other.

"That's right, Mr. Cate," called Towers. "'Under hand is always better than over'and."

"If you're as short as you are," jibed Smalley. "Overhand is a much better kill if you're tall."

Their arguments faded from consciousness as she focused on Pryce. Slightly crouched, his grey eyes held hers, measuring and waiting. The corner of an eye barely twitched and he dove for her arm, seeking to grab and twist. It was the same move her brothers had used. She slid away and came around to knee him in the backside. He shot forward, the pirates cheering. He stumbled and then whirled back around.

At first skeptical, Pryce now settled in for a true contest. In one flowing move, he seized her arm and jerked her around to poise his blade at her neck.

"That's a kill," declared the by-standers and cheered for more.

They skirmished time and again, taking up various scenarios of possible assaults: from behind, the front or ambushed. Nathan and the others shouted suggestions and encouragements, intermixed with jeers when either was bested. A few times, Nathan or Pryce called a halt, in order to give pointers on stance or angle. By virtue of his strength and reach, Pryce prevailed most of the time, but Cate was able to win enough to prove capable.

Both perspiring heavily now, Pryce posed as an assailant and grabbed Cate from behind. The momentum sent them tumbling to the deck, Pryce coming down on top of her. He cuffed both her wrists in one hand and forced her arms up over her head. She struggled to wrench free, but his hips held her tight. His weight brought her breath short and her anguish rose. The cheering faded, and she heard only his heavy breathing as he grunted and wriggled on top of her. Drops of sweat pattered her skin. She looked up into eyes no longer familiar, predatory and lusting, on a face she no longer knew.

Panic surged. She screamed and thrashed, berserk to escape. The weight on top of her went away. More hands came at her, groping and tugging. Shrieking, she batted at them, pleading for them to leave her be.

And they did. She sat up into a blur of faces, slack-jawed and goggle-eyed. Movement... A person... knelt next to her,

Pryce poised behind him wearing a mask of bewildered guilt. She blinked several times before sorting out the face before her was Nathan's. His mouth moved, but it was like he spoke a foreign tongue. He reached out. She jerked away and lurched to her feet. Warding off more hands, she raced down the deck to the forecastle rail, stopping only because she could run no further. Splaying her hands across her stomach, she looked down. No blades this time. No blood, no agony, nothing, not this time, but...?

They're gone. You know it. They're gone!

Cate collapsed against the rail and dug her nails into a kevel, seeking an anchor against being dragged back to the nightmare.

Something touched her shoulder. She shrieked and whirled, blindly swinging out with the knife she still clutched. A man stood there, his face obscured by the glare of the sun at his back. He shifted, and she saw it was Nathan again.

"I'm sorry." It came out in a thin gasp. Shrinking back tighter against the rail, she looked down at the knife, suddenly strange in her hand, and dropped it.

"Are you well?" His inquiry was carefully measured.

She mutely nodded, starting again when he brushed her arm. Recoiling as if seared, he spread his hands before him in a display of good faith.

"I'm sorry." The words came out in a quavering wheeze. Taking a deep breath, she tried again. "I didn't mean to —"

"You're shaking."

"I'm all right." Cate put up a hand to assure Nathan, but buried it in the folds of her apron at seeing how violently it trembled. "I'm fine."

He wasn't convinced. "Allow me to take you to the cabin. You're scaring the hands."

Senses congealing, she became aware of the men clustered at the waist. They bore the quizzical look reserved for the deranged, and wasn't she: fighting hands that weren't there, screaming at faces that didn't exist? Nathan tentatively took her by the elbow and eased her down the forecastle steps. Numbness gave way to mortification. She walked woodenly next to him toward the cabin, drawn by its promise of refuge. She thought to apologize, but couldn't bear to see their revulsion and pity. Instead, she ducked her head to hide behind the protective curtain of hair that fell down around her face.

Once inside, she paced before the stern gallery.

When does the nightmare of reality become just a nightmare?

Or is one doomed for them to always be as one? Is the reality bent by the dream into something worse than it really was? Everyone claims time heals everything, but when? How long? How much of one's life must be devoured, before it finally goes away?

She was seized with the urge to tear at herself, rip away skin and muscle, down to the bone, if she must, to be rid of the terrors that lay within.

"Don't tell me it's only a dream," she seethed, making short paths like a caged cat. "It was real. I've lived it. I'll carry the scars to my grave. All I have to do is look and I know it was no dream. It was a nightmare, but it's in the past... except it's still here..."

Cate drew up, realizing she had just said far more than intended, far more than she had ever admitted to herself let alone to anyone else. Panting like a half-maddened dog, she turned to find Nathan had withdrawn to the far side of the room. He stood uncommonly still, as if fearing any movement might precipitate something worse. Surely he thought her crazed by now. There was none of the accusation or disgust expected; only the intent gravity which came with seeking to understand.

"Would you be greatly fraught if I were to beg you to come away from the window?"

The unexpected direction of his comment stopped her in her tracks. She looked at the window, and then him.

"You think I'm so hysterical I might jump?" she asked coldly. Wild-eyed and hair probably resembling oakum by then, she had to have appeared quite the madwoman. In the spirit of easing the demonic resemblance, she made a furtive attempt to smooth her hair.

"You did before," he said evenly. "And again, or tried, at any rate, from just there." He gestured to the sill between the two guns.

It took her a moment to follow his meaning: her first night aboard, she had attempted to jump, overlooking of course, that the act had been prompted by him attacking her.

"That was different. I was scared... then," she said with a vague gesture and resumed her agitated path.

Nathan regarded her narrowly. "And you're not now?"

"No! I mean yes... But no... not... Damn it!" she shrieked with a vehemence which startled them both.

She took a deep breath and exhaled slowly in an effort to recompose. "No, it's not pirates... this time."

He forbore pressing the point. He ventured close enough to shepherd her to a chair. Grabbing up the rum bottle, he poured her a small dose. "Drink."

Cate fumbled for the glass, nearly spilling it. Nathan dared to come near enough to guide her unresponsive fingers around it, and then to her mouth, retreating as she drank. The resulting shudder pulled her back into her body. Her heart slowed, and the humiliation settled deeper. She felt him circling, as if observing a lunatic, afraid to go near and yet more fearful to leave her alone.

"Thank you," she said hoarsely, her throat tightened by drink and embarrassment.

"Might you allow a hint as to what that was all about? Did you really imagine Pryce aimed to attack you?" His query was carefully posed, gleaned of all accusation.

"No, I mean, yes, I know… but no…" She dug her nails into her scalp, hoping the pain might help bring a cohesive thought. "I know! I mean… I know he didn't mean anything."

"Then what—?"

"Nothing!" She slammed her hand on the table hard enough to cause the glass to jump. She drew in another deep breath and shakily blew it out. "It's nothing; I'll be fine. Just leave me be."

She felt rather than saw him stiffen. Falling back a step, he curtly nodded. "Very well, then, by your leave."

Regret for being so short with him added the crush of guilt she already harbored. She rummaged through her mental morass to find the proper words, ones that didn't sound hollow or trite, to make amends. She squirmed around in the chair to find that he hadn't left, but only retreated to the cabin's shadowy perimeter. Boots thudding hollowly on the planks, he muttered as he paced. On one pass, he darted near enough to snag the bottle from the table and drank through his agitated orbits.

Head braced in her hands, a part of her wished he would leave her to her misery. And yet another—a very large part— was so very grateful that he was there. To have someone who cared, to catch her if she fell, meant so much, and yet she had no words to tell him.

Slowly, the rum did its part. The world coalesced further: her blood no longer hammered in her ears, her breath slowed to something less than near-hysterical gasps. She could hear the *Morganse's* song of wind and canvas, and felt the ship's motion with the swell. The sky was still blue, the sea was still as deep, and the world was still there, right where she had left it.

Nathan scuffed to a halt somewhere near. He made several false starts before settling on, "You're rather good with a knife, for a woman, that is."

"For a woman, I've had plenty of practice," Cate retorted, bitterly.

"You failed to mention you've a skill at wrestling."

She looked up, glaring. "For a woman?"

"For a woman."

His tentative boyish smile touched a cord, and she reluctantly did so, as well.

Damn him for being able to make me smile on command!

"As I said, I had five brothers," she said.

Sensing it safe, he ventured nearer. Propping his hip against a chair, he loosely crossed his arms. "What you lack in strength, you gain in wile."

She made an unladylike noise in the back of her throat. "I suppose that could be the story of my life."

She emptied her glass.

"Aye, there's a ring o' truth in that," he said, refilling it.

Closing her eyes, she leaned back and sighed. "I'm sorry; I didn't intend to..."

What? Make a complete spectacle of yourself?

He rolled his eyes toward the slap of bare feet passing overhead. "Some of the hands think you devil-possessed. What with those eyes, and now this... Poor bastard, Pryce only figures you wish to cut his throat."

"I suppose he would," she said, grimly rubbing her face. "I'll apologize."

"Don't be surprised if he runs at seeing you coming."

"Is it that bad?" She peered up from under her hands.

He contained a smile. "That bad."

Groaning, she buried her face in her hands. "I don't know what comes over me sometimes!"

In a moment of bald honesty, this wasn't the first time, nor second nor even third. The spells came from nowhere, dissolving as quickly as they erupted. Perhaps Bedlam was where she belonged, somewhere that she could be prevented from hurting not only herself, but everyone around.

Nathan took another drink and pensively rolled the bottle between his palms. "Darling, we all have our dunnage to lug about. 'Tis not necessarily the weight of it, but where we choose to stow it."

Cate looked up into a gaze that allowed her a glimpse of the burdens which dwelt behind his curtain, not to equivocate, but to assure that she wasn't alone. The heavily-fringed lids lowered; the curtain closed once again.

"Thank you, Nathan, I'll remember that. Sometimes, you are a very wise man."

He broke a square-toothed, gold-laced flash. "Scary, isn't it?"

Chuckling to himself, he swaggered toward the door. He paused at the table to pluck a mango from the plate of fruit, kept there by Mr. Kirkland, in hopes of tempting his Captain into eating. He sniffed it, and with a curl of his lip, put it back. He gestured toward the skylight, and the quarterdeck overhead, as he ambled out.

"I'll be just there, if you find you've need of me."

Once alone, she buried her head in her hands and gasped, self-loathing only adding to the dejection and embarrassment. On the brink of a breakdown, she grabbed the glass and quaffed it down. Balling her fists, she closed her eyes once more, and inhaled deeply. When she opened them, the world was still there? The terrors were gone... like a dream.

❧⁂☙

Dark was soon to fall. A thunderstorm had rumbled through earlier in the day. It had been Cate's excuse for her self-imposed seclusion in the cabin. Too embarrassed to be seen after her breakdown, she had spent the remainder of the day there. Frustration had come in many forms during that time. She tried to read, but the words wouldn't stay in focus. She tried to embroider, but couldn't concentrate.

Cate had gleaned what embroidery supplies she could from the Littleton's belongings and made up a small piece to work on. Needlework had been a lifelong love. It had also been her salvation over the last several years. Many a night had been spent hunched next to a sewing lamp, in order to meet a customer's last minute demands. Now she had the joy of doing it at her leisure, the pleasure dampened only by the desperate limit of thread, only a precise amount being allowed each day.

The storm still hung in distant flat-bottomed billows. The rays of the surrendering day streaked from behind it in plums of orange and lilac. The bell ending the second Dog Watch was just rung, one of the abbreviated two-hour periods allowing for the evening meal. It meant most of the hands would be on the forecastle, including the afterguard. There was a good chance she would catch Pryce on the afterdeck. It was rare to find Pryce alone; perpetual motion, he was, but he often lingered there.

It was dark enough for her to use the shadowy margins of the deck without notice, hence avoiding having to face the men or feel their stares. She hung about feigning interest in water and sky. Cocking her head, she didn't hear Pryce's voice among those forward, and so looked aft.

Her intent to apologize was bracketed with trepidation. She was of two minds regarding Pryce. His bearing and ability to verbally pin anyone who provoked his wrath to the bulwarks still scared her. And yet, he could laugh as readily as shake the hands' bones. Once past the ferocity, he was a kindly sort: pleasant, responsive, and courteous. An endless font of tales and superstitions, he was ever-willing to share his repertoire. His authority unquestioned, and would suffer no laggardness or shirking, but he was meticulously fair.

It was that fairness upon which she relied now.

In the dusk, she could see his shape on the afterdeck with someone else. The last ray of daylight flashed on ivory rings: Hodder. Facing the water, she waited for Hodder and his telltale clatter to pass, and then mounted the curved steps. She regretted having to virtually stalk Pryce, but things needed saying. She sincerely regretted her actions; the man didn't deserve having to spend the night wondering."

A peace offering?" Cate held up the mug of grog, procured from Kirkland.

At the sight of her, Pryce had ducked around the wheel. He was making for the steps when she displayed the drink. He stopped, his head coming up like a hound on a scent. Seeing his reluctance to reach for it, she set it on the binnacle between them and slid it across. Beatrice, blithely preening there, was obliged to pull her tail feathers out of the way and made a rude comment. Pryce waited until Cate had retracted her hand fully before seizing upon the mug. He took a long, badly-needed draught, wiping his mouth on the back of his hand.

"Mr. Pryce," she began. He twitched at the sound of her voice, his fists tightened around the leather mug. "Please, I beg, Pryce, I desire to make amends."

His jaw set, determined to see this through credibly. "I'm sorry, sir, if I—I never intended to make ye think I wuz tryin' any kind of foolishness."

"I know that." She bit back her vehemence. Collecting herself, she tried again, calmer. "I know that very well."

Pryce shot her a stony look, the grizzled brows meeting. "'Tis not the impression t'was given."

"I know that as well," Cate said more evenly.

Her apology was an honest one. Honesty, however, was at its purest at its birth. Any attempts to expand or enhance only weakened it. She stood mutely patient as he regarded her with suspicion, waiting for the look capable of cutting her in half or turn her to stone, at his pleasure. This was her atonement and she bore it as unflinching as could be managed.

At the same time, Beatrice cocked her head to regard Cate, too, and her resolve wavered. Being judged by a bird was more disconcerting than she cared to admit. At length, Pryce saw what he needed. A quirk of the mouth and a raise of the mug marked the matter settled. He then drank to it.

Voices in song drifted aft from the forecastle. She heard Nathan, too, and followed the path of his voice the foretop crosstrees. Feet swinging over the edge, he was a dark blot against a dimming sky.

"You don't like me, do you, Pryce?" she heard herself say. It wasn't an accusation, just observation.

Pryce shied, wearing the look of a child caught with his hand in the honey jar. "You'll give me leave to say you're uncommon forward."

"Some people appreciate me for it," she said in a flush of defensiveness. Well, maybe only one: her husband. It would be a lie to say that she had never been told that before. "I can't help it. I was raised far from the niceties of civility and with five brothers. If I didn't speak up, I was forgotten. Don't change the subject, Pryce. You don't like me."

"Not sayin' as 'tis disagreeable. It's just... well... There be eyes that color on a statue in Vera Cruz."

She turned her head, hiding a smile. "Yes, I believe Nathan — the Captain that is, mentioned as much." Indeed, Nathan had, her first day aboard, vowing she meant to curse him.

"I don't mean to reproach you, but why?" she went on. "Did I say or do to put you off? And the Captain, for that matter. Sometimes he looks at me like I'm a two-headed kitten."

Pryce waffled, making up his mind, changing it, again and again. She was on the verge of letting him off the hook upon which he squirmed, when he finally burst out: "With all due respect, sir, to tell ye plain: you look like her."

"Her?" she echoed dumbly.

"And in more ways than one might bear, in a manner o' speakin'."

Cate felt a cold, sinking sensation which she didn't care to put a name to. She braced against the weight of impending doom. Several bricks were about to fall into place in her construction of Nathanael Blackthorne: he was either married or had an eternal love somewhere.

"So, who is... her?" she asked in grave dread.

Wife? Sweetheart? Which would be worse?

"He hasn't told you? Nay, I s'pose not. He's disinclined toward the tellin'," he said, staring down into his drink. The grey eyes swiveled up at her and sharpened. "Ye've seen the Cap'n with his shirt off?"

It was posed more assumption than question.

"Umm... nooo... no, I haven't."

Her cheeks flamed. Having to admit Nathan hadn't found her attractive enough didn't come easily. As the days had turned to weeks, she had flirted with thoughts of something blooming between her and Nathan. The charming smile, flashing eyes and engaging ways were not wasted. At times, he didn't seem to realize their effect. But then at times, it was clear he knew exactly and applied them with purpose.

In many circles, Nathan would have been considered the consummate gentleman. He never bowed, rose from a chair, nor tipped his hat. He discretely excused himself, or conveniently avoided the cabin altogether, when he thought it necessary. That didn't rule out the ribald remarks and colorful turn of phrase, but that was just Nathan being Nathan. Slowly, however, the cold realization had settled in: he wasn't interested in her. There were no overtures, not even the slightest insinuation or the most fleeting of dalliances. Nothing.

Cate felt like a stone among the diamonds. So many women had gone before — his conquests were legend — but why not her? She had longed to ask why, but in the grand scheme of things, what difference did it make? If it was because her voice was too deep, her eyes too green, if she was too tall, her bottom too round or not round enough, or if she was too dull-witted? Which would she rather hear? Which one would ease her best through the nights of lying in that same bunk, staring and wondering?

"Aye, well..." Pryce's mouth compressed in disapproval, clearly thinking her to be either lying or had deemed his captain unsuitable. Either was an affront to his sense of honor.

"All rotated around a woman. What else?" What little light was left caught the spark in his eye of a storyteller settling in. "Cap'n met up with one. A beauty, she were, in her own way," he was quick to qualify.

Pryce regarded her more narrowly. "As I represented, ye put me in mind o' her... tall, well, mebbe not quite so much," he said with a second look. "She had a go-to-hell way o' lookin' at ye — square in the eye, she did — and not a by-yer-leave in 'er. She was a pirate at heart; took to it like a fish t' water. Get her blood riled and she could be ruthless as any man, more so. Could pass fer one too, given a big hat, that is. Not as strong as a man and that vexed her considerable. Got herself into trouble on that score more than the once."

A faint smile came at an unspoken thought. He shook it away before going on.

"As it chances, Hattie had 'er own ship. At first, she and the Cap'n sailed in consort, scourge of the Caribbean. Hell, the whole world was at their disposal," he said with an enthusiastic swipe of his hand. "Then her ship took a ball to the magazine. Blew 'er to smitherines, but Hattie lived to tell of it. By that time, she and the Cap'n were, well, let's just say no woman can resist his charms and she had her own charmin' ways. So, bein' the good-hearted soul that he is, he took 'er in, she 'n what was left o' her crew, havin' in his mind the next prize would be hers."

He glanced to assure Nathan was still in the tops. A raucous chanty had broken out on the forecastle, involving a lonely sailor and bow-legged whores. Nathan's graveled tenor rang from above, enthusiastic, if not a good bit off-key. It was rare to hear his ravaged voice raised in song. He must have been in high spirits, indeed.

"T'was a fiery mix: they fought like cats and dogs, and made love like rabbits... Hmph!"

He made a half-strangled noise and buried his nose in his drink. "Beggin' yer pardon, sir. I think she fancied treasure and prizes, but d'ye see, the Cap'n's not in it for the plunder. He's in it fer his ship. Piratin' is just a means."

The last carried an air of warning. She bristled at the assumption she only sought fortunes, but to deny it would only serve to strengthen his point.

"You were on the *Morganse* then?" she asked.

"Nay. We'd had a partin' o' the ways a bit a'fore. I tried to warn 'im to go to windward o' Maubrick, his First Mate, but the Cap'n wasn't of a mind to be a listenin'," he said wincing.

"Do you think they loved each other?" It was a question that screamed to be asked, but an answer she didn't desire to hear. She was suddenly cold and tucked her hands under her arms.

"Love? Hmm...?" An uncomfortable notion, he leaned heavily on the binnacle to ponder. "Ehh, admiration, fer sure. Common goals, lust, aye. But no, 'twas not my notion Hattie had it in 'er."

"Well," he said, resuming his tale, "the first ship didn't suit 'er. The second was too slab-sided and the third too slow in stays." He shook his head. "She had 'er claws in 'im deep, by then. A women can lead a man 'round, if'n she knows how."

Pryce arched a brow, the sharp grey eyes measuring the cut of her jib, as to whether she was of the same breed.

"Hattie musta tired o' waitin', 'cuz she threw in with Maubrick. Belike, he filled her full o' ideas, a-promisin' the moon. Some say the Cap'n shoulda knowed. Others say she 'n' Maubrick were too smooth, but the day finally come..."

He let the suggestion in his voice finish the thought. He glanced once more to the foretop. He was telling far more than Nathan would have desired and no small wonder. No one appreciated dirty laundry—misfortune and mishap—to be bandied about. But then, he was Nathanael Blackthorne, a legend in his time. Fame had its price.

"And?" Cate prompted.

"Shot 'im."

The words cracked the air. Beatrice ruffled and croaked, *"Flog the bastard!"*

"The Cap'n has two holes in 'im: one in the front..." he said, pointing to just below his right breast. "And one in the back."

"Which one—?"

"Which one looked him in the eye and pulled the trigger, whilst the other spineless scut shot 'im in the back?"

Pryce took another long drink and smacked his lips. "There be only three souls a'knowin' that, and the Cap'n ain't a-sayin'. Cast him off, they did. 'Ceptin' they figgered 'im to be dead straight away, so the mutinous dogs didn't even oblige him the honor of a pistol."

Nathan had alluded to something having happened before, another subject he preferred not to broach.

Cate gulped, sickened. Betrayal was never a pretty thing, but this one was particularly ugly. "But how...? I mean, obviously he lived, so how...?"

"No one knows, but 'im, and he ain't sayin'. He claims he died, if yer inclined to believe that sorta of thing. There be a pouch at his belt with two shots, one flattened, kinda like when it hits bone. The other is all scratched, like it was dug out. Carries 'em with 'im, he does, at all times, just a'waitin' for the day when he can give 'em back, if ye get me meanin'."

"But, he has the ship, so he must have—?"

"They both still breathe, if that be yer meanin'. But aye, that be the interestin' part of it. With the Cap'n gone, the *Morganse* was broken-hearted and would sail for no other man." He lovingly stroked the surface before him. "First chance, threw herself on the rocks she did, impaled on a spire, right through the heart. She sank to the bottom to join her true love."

Now she felt the one being played. Although, she had heard Nathan speak of the ship as if she drew breath, and had seen him engage in what was tantamount to one-sided conversations with her.

Attachment? Connection? Affection? Yes, they all applied.

"Obviously he got her back somehow."

"Aye," Pryce nodded agreeably, looking skyward, as a mariner often did. "'Tis a matter o' speculation. He's the only one what knows and he ain't sayin'. I've heard tell he made a deal with the Devil o' the Deep."

"That's ridiculous," she snorted, feeling extremely tried on again.

One brow arched. "Is it? Take a look, if yer of a mind to doubt it. He carries two holes what no man should have survived. I've seen him walk through hellfire 'n' brimstone and laugh, not a sleeve singed. And I've seen 'im run through by a blade such that no man should live to tell. He's a man what can't be kilt on a ship what can't be sunk. It don't make 'im crazy—no more than bein' dead would," he added in an odd rationalization, "just a mite careless."

"Where's Hattie now?" Uttering the name didn't come easily. "Has there been any word?"

Pryce shrugged disinterestedly as he swirled the mug's contents. "Heard she's dead and heard she's piratin' the spice routes. The Cap'n's still on the prowl, a-lookin' fer either one, and heaven help 'em when that day comes."

He stared off toward the foretop. "Sometime after it all, I seen him in Tortuga. T'was a good thing I knew him from a'fore, cuz I barely recognized him. No one, includin' him could say as how he came to be there. He was a scarecrow, nothin' but the rags on his back a-holdin' his bones together and not near enough o' those to keep 'im decent. He was livin' on rum and whatever scraps throwed his way. He still can pick a pocket better than anyone I ever see'd," he said with a faint smile of admiration.

"An old whore had taken him in, allowed 'im t' live in the goat shed. He smelled like a dead one, too. He couldn't take three steps without a-coughin' up blood. Everyone treated him like he were a leper or had the fever, but he claimed it was bein' shot what gave him the lungsickness. It was his eyes what near killed me: lifeless as a shark, cold and dead."

Pryce shook his head as if to rid himself of a bad dream.

"Bought 'im a decent meal, I did, but he didn't possess the strength t' chew. He could still swallow, so I got 'im drunked up, followed him until he fell out in an alley. Piled him up in a cart and carried him off to a fishin' village, t'other side o' the island. The people were poor there—poorer than most—but decent folk. I left 'em enough money so's they could see to him and theyselves. I went back a few months later, but he was gone. No one seemed to know where, he just up and disappeared, leavin' behind a couple o' lasses with sad eyes and swellin' bellies. It were a year or so before I saw 'im again; I thought he was a ghost what come to haunt me fer my sins."

He smiled faintly at the recollection. "He was the ol' Nathan then... sorta. The burn was back in his gut, a-wantin' nothin' more than his ship and those two black-hearted mutineers, in that order. He was damned single-minded on the matter, but I reckon that were what kept him alive."

Cate held herself in tight check from the quarterdeck to her berth, although her rigidity and stomp gave cause for guarded looks from those in her route. Once past the curtain, she emitted a frustrated growl and flung herself across the bunk. She counted the seconds, hoping her anger would subside. Barely to three, she punched the mattress, grunting with each blow.

So that was it! Now, she knew why Nathan wasn't interested, why he was pleasant, and yet so impeccably distant. It was simple enough. The good news was it wasn't a matter of anything she had said or done. Quite to the contrary, it was entirely out of her hands. Which led to the bad news: it was entirely out of her hands.

She flopped onto her back and stared, the blackened beams overhead shimmering through tears. One leg hung over the side, her heel rapped an agitated tempo against the wood, while a fist pounded a similar rhythm on the bulkhead.

She reminded him of someone else. How simple could it be? It was the one reason she never thought of, the one scenario which never came to mind. Just by simple coincidence, misfortune, circumstance or fate, she reminded him of someone... his precious Hattie.

And what, exactly, do you think you're going to do about it?

Not much, came back the answer. Nothing you can do.

She blindly hurled the pillow across the room.

It wasn't fair!

It was one more stab from Providence: she was to be forever denied anything which might smack of happiness.

A few weeks ago, you were desperate for someone to notice if you lived or died. Where's your gratitude in that?

Rational thoughts wedged their way in. To begrudge Nathan his true love would be to begrudge herself of having Brian.

"That was different," she grumbled moodily. Brian was gone.

One was obliged to question Nathan's judgment. He had never shown the impulsiveness that would be necessary for one to give his heart so readily to someone so treacherous.

Yes, but the heart is often blind.

On a gentler note, it had to have been hellish for Nathan to be constantly reminded of such betrayal and cold-heartedness. More was the question why he was so determined to keep her aboard? Why he didn't turn her over for the reward straightway, or put her off at St. Agua and be shut of her?

Only the ancient sages could fathom what went through that convoluted mind.

"Ooohhh!" Cate growled.

A rap on the doorjamb startled her.

"Are you well?" came Nathan's voice through the curtain.

"I'm fine," she said, more sharply than was warranted.

Cate rolled over on her elbows. Ducking her head between her arm and her side, she sniffed, hoping he wouldn't hear.

There was a grave pause. "You don't sound it."

"I'm fine."

There was a low grumble, another considering pause, and then a shifting of feet. "Shall I pass the word to fetch you something? Rum?" A grunt instantly negated that. "Coffee? Brandy!" His voice brightened with the victory.

"No, I'm fine," she insisted, dashing the wetness from her face.

"You don't sound it."

She choked a smile at hearing his concern. She drew a quivering breath and expelled it slowly.

"I'll be fine," she said with great effort. "As I always am," she added under her breath at the sound of his retreating steps. "Just... fine."

∿⤬∿

Gleaming and freshly breamed, with Mr. Hodder's repetitive call of "Mind the paintwork" in the air, the *Morganse* won her anchors and cleared the cove, a proud lady in her newly applied cosmetics.

Rich in that same pride, Pryce stood at the leeward rail, rocking on his heels. "She'll run through the water now as slick as an old whore's—"

Hodder's sharp elbow to Pryce's ribs and a not-so clandestine thumb jerked in Cate's direction, on Hodder's other side, cut him short.

"She'll be considerable faster," Pryce mumbled into his chest, his face suffused with a unique shade of mahogany.

158

6: WITCH O' THE MOORS

A FEW NIGHTS LATER, CATE CAME out of the Great Cabin. She came out frustrated and feeling wholly a failure. It was a matter of ropes, or that is to say, knots and her incompetence with them.

The Morgansers were tolerant of Cate's lack of seaworthiness. After all she was a woman. When her level of ineptitude with knots was discovered, however, that was intolerable. One's knotsmanship was one's status among his peers, promotions often being based on his skill with not only functional but decorative work as well. Her education was taken as a personal mission, dooming her to endless hours of coaching. She was an accomplished needleworker, but dealing with threads and ribbons had not prepared her for rope which turned into recalcitrant snakes in her hands.

"The Cap'n stocks only the finest cordage," Pryce said severely, the implication being it was she and not the rope which was at fault.

Single diamond, double diamond, clove or bowline up the bight — not to be confused with the bowline bend — sheet, carrick, and not to be forgotten, the cat's paw: and that was considered the "absolutely essential to every able hand" list.

A square knot and a basic slip knot any fool could manage, and the double half-hitch was familiar from her youth.

"Hell, even a half-witted, cack-handed cabin boy can do those," Nathan declared.

Stubbs, the *Morganse's* knotsman extraordinaire was named her "sea daddy": a mentor, someone to teach and pass on every aspect of ship's life. Stubbs' was relieved of all responsibilities except one: to teach her the way of a rope. Grizzled and weathered, Stubbs was ageless, except for a pair of kind blue eyes, pinched by years and wisdom. The Morgansers openly bragged of commandeering Stubbs from a ship they had raided.

An extra portion of shares to him showed their appreciation and insured Stubbs' faithfulness to the *Ciara Morganse.*

"Had 'em line up on deck, we did," Pryce declared, recalling that fortuitous day. "We was a-hopin' for swag and rum, or mebbe a few to sign the roster. Then I spotted that there fob a danglin'."

With a gesture of his chin, he indicated Stubbs's waistband and the knife handle protruding there. From it hung a rope handle, of sorts, intricately knotted and textured to the point of almost being lace.

"Never seen nothin' like it, not a'fore nor since," Pryce said, shaking his head in wonderment. "T'were the best treasure ever."

Aside from his knotsmanship, what separated Stubbs from the rest of the crew was that he was a mute.

"Or nearly so," Pryce qualified. "Blade caught him in the throat, best as we can tell, crushed his voice box like a nutshell. Poor bastard hasn't put two words together since."

The hideous scar at Stubbs's throat and wet rattle with each breath was sufficient testimony. As it turned out, Stubbs was mute by choice. His speech being such a garbled slur, he chose to spare himself the embarrassment and resorted to a unique sign language.

The greatest surprise, however, was when she discovered he missed three fingers, as well as the joints of several others. Missing digits was not an uncommon feature among sailors or men who lived by the sword, but it was a wonderment to watch him maneuver the ropes. The irony of the name was almost too much to bear, but she forbore inquiring if it was really his name or just an appellation.

Even under Stubbs' tutelage, Cate's progress was slow, her fingers growing sore. Squealing in frustration, she would pitch the offending rope across the deck. Stubbs lifted a brow, more reproving than any words. Shame and obstinacy compelled her to retrieve the length and try again. She was maddened further by Stubbs' ability to do it minus three fingers. Upon reflection, perhaps she had too many, hence getting in her way.

As the degree of difficulty increased, her success pitched. Nathan's distress at her ineptitude soaring, he often stood over her during her lessons, unable to curtail his groans of disappointment and frustration. She practiced, driven not by others, but by an inner need to overcome any shortcoming. Some would call it stubbornness.

Earlier that afternoon, she had surrendered from yet another practice, still a failure. In the face of that, she had found solace in the friendlier and more familiar realms of thread. It was a limited pleasure, however, and so she decided to take a stroll.

She had learned if she desired to walk the decks at night, it was best done before the hands had been sent to their hammocks. Hodder's bellow of "Pipe down!" was a relative term, for many of the men preferred to sleep on deck rather than below, where the heat of the day would still be trapped, especially if wind or seas disallowed the port-lids to be opened. It was a hazardous venture to pick one's way in the dark through the amorphous mounds littering the deck. Tripping over one meant to be soundly cursed.

She could feel the change in the ship. The topsails reefed, the fly-by-nights set, the *Morganse* had settled in for the night. The grog dispensed, their voices and music drifting from the forecastle, the men were enjoying their nightly merriment. Aware her presence often tended to curtail their spirits, she crept down the deck until she reached her favorite place at the larboard rail. There she sat between the two gun carriages, a small island of seclusion.

Caribbean nights were unique. A blessed refuge from the day's heat and glare, the night brought velvet air so fresh it made one want to grasp onto something to keep from floating away. The days vibrated with brilliant hues of sky and water. The nights were a palette of blacks, warm and cool: blue, purple, violet and gunmetal. Leaning against the cool iron of the gun, she tipped back her head to allow the breeze against her throat and lift the hair from her neck.

As the *Constancy's* Barnstable had been, Pryce was the reigning king as storyteller on the *Ciara Morganse*. With his orator's baritone voice, he could break into a tale, instantly enrapturing his audience, whether one or several score. Judging by the voices on the forecastle, Pryce was off on ship's business, and others had taken his place, and quite credibly. She closed her eyes and visualized the fantastic tales of raucous conquests, demonic ghosts and improbable feats. She slowly slipped off into her own fantasies.

So, immersed in her reverie, she lost track of time. She stirred as she grew aware of the story being told.

"Aye, Falkirk t'was. Cumberland and his troops had caught up with the armies of Bonnie Prince Charlie..."

She groaned aloud. One could tell by the brogue: it was Cameron. Voice low and steady, building with drama, there was no mistaking a Highlander caught up in weaving his own fantastic version of the truth.

"Surrounded they were, and so Murdoch MacKenzie rallied

his men, chargin' into the gaping maws o' the redcoat artillery. There was screamin' and dyin', and heathers ran red w' the blood. Murdoch led his men to the flank, whilst Red Brian veered to the right and caught the enemy in a fearsome crossfire. But Cumberland's power was too great and they pressed forward, until Murdoch and Red Brian were in peril o' their lives. And then like a banshee, the Witch o' the Moors swept down across the plains. She flew to Red Brian, thinkin' him to be her love, Murdoch MacKenzie and struck down four of the British. Then, realizin' her mistake, leapt over the British cannons to Murdoch's side o' the battle, and struck down four more with her staff, burnin' their bodies to instant ashes with her cursed eyes..."

Frustration and rage jolted through her.

Why can't the stories ever stop? Why can't they leave it alone?

For more than a decade she had run from the truth, but for once it was going to be known.

Cate was up and standing at the group's fringe before she realized it, shaking with fury. "It wasn't eight men I killed. It was three."

Unnerved by her unexpected appearance, the men gaped. Hunched like scolded schoolboys, they exchanged furtive glances.

"We had been marching north for weeks, the entire Stuart Army" she began, stepping into the margin of the lamplight. "Hawley's troops were hard on our trail, close enough for small skirmishes now and again, scouts encountering pickets mostly. It was only a matter of time before there was a major engagement. It was January. It was cold and had been raining or snowing for days. We were in ice and mud to our knees. The horses were tired and half-starved, as were we all. For weeks we lived on nothing but drammoch — cold water and oats."

She paused, batting her hair from her face. The light of the ship's lanterns blurred into the flicker of campfires. Those before her merged with another time, when she had lived amid other men: kilted, haggard and grim, marching under cloud-scudded skies. She felt the sharp stab of starvation once more, and began to shiver from the bone-soaking dampness and cold.

"Murdoch, my husband's uncle, and the other officers decided it would be best to choose the ground, instead of the enemy choosing it for us."

Cate stopped again, straining to sort out the tumble of memories As if straining to listen, the *Morganse's* chorus of rigging, canvas and water had gone still.

"It wasn't Falkirk. To be honest, I don't remember exactly where it was. It had been a matter of just putting one foot in front of the other for so long, it was just another godforsaken stretch of land. It might have been near Bannonchbroch, but I can't be sure. We came to an open plain of sorts and decided we would make our stand there. There was a bit of a hill to one side. The camp followers—women and children, laundresses, servants and whores—were sent up there, to be out of danger and to watch."

She heard a jingle and thud of boots. Nathan was somewhere behind her, but she paid no heed. She shook now, either from cold or emotion she couldn't say. The hair on her arms prickled as the wind in the *Morganse*'s rigging became the sleet-laden wind across the open moor. She saw the dark streaks of rain in Brian's hair as he had kissed her good-bye as they had done so many times before. It was war. It had been months of sending him off to another skirmish or battle, knowing that to wish to never have to do it again might mean to wish he wouldn't return. She clutched her arms tightly about her middle, once again seized by the helplessness and terror of that day.

"The dragoons formed their lines at the far end. Brian and some of the other officers dismounted, preferring to fight afoot, as their men did. They lined up just below the hill, facing the cannons. At the first barrage, they charged."

The recollections tumbled faster: the acrid sharpness of powder smoke, the icy cut of the wind, and the explosions of cannon.

"We took the advantage; the dragoons fell back. I could make out Brian on the right. He was tall and red-haired; I would have known him amid a thousand. He was doing well, as he always did in battle. He claimed it was luck and Providence. Murdoch was well to the other side; he was nearly the same size and coloring as Brian, but I knew the difference."

Cate took a quivering breath, gathering the courage to relive it.

"It all happened so quickly, and yet it all seemed in slow-motion. I watched the dragoons advance, pushing closer and closer toward Brian. It was only a matter of time before they would be on top of him. Someone had to do something... someone... me... I had to do something... anything! I screamed to warn him, again and again, but..."

She swallowed, her hand trembling worse as she brushed away the tears tracking her cheeks.

"I couldn't just watch. I don't know what happened," she said, her voice going thin from the rawness of screaming. "All I remember is running down the hill to jump on the first horse, Murdoch's black gelding. I rode as hard as I could. Somewhere, I picked up a sword. It must have been sticking in the ground;

how else could I have come by it? I rode as hard as I could toward Brian. The soldiers were on him by then. I ran one over with the horse. I heard his skull crunch under the hooves. That was the first."

Her hands closed, once again feeling the bite of the leather reins. The horse was battle-hardened and eager to join the fray. Slogging through the icy mud, it strove to gain speed with every stride.

"It was nearly the other side of the fighting before I could turn the brute. As I came 'round, another was trampled. That was the second."

Her fingers twitched and two rose. Her breathing was coming faster now, as she felt the heave of the horse's sides between her legs. The clash of metal — bayonets, sabers and swords — and the screams of the wounded came from all around. The field was a slippery quagmire of churned grass, vomit and blood. She squinted through the smoke and rain, straining to see.

"I rode hard back to Brian. A dismounted dragoon was charging toward him, his sword raised, ready to hack him in half. I remember seeing the light reflect on the blade and wondering where it came from because there was no sun. I swung down with the sword as hard as I could..."

As if on its own volition, her arm raised to vaguely mimic a chopping motion.

"I felt the blade hit bone. My arm was twisted and I lost my grip. That was the third."

Three fingers rose.

Her breath quickened, in tempo with the horse's wet rattle. Her voice cracked as the words came in halting, broken tumbles.

"It was all so much a blur: I tried to get back to Brian. Someone grabbed the reins and the horse reared. I went off backwards and landed face down in the mud. I pushed up, but all I could see was boots in front of me. I looked up to a dragoon standing over me. His face was spattered with blood; he was half-crazed and blinded by the battle. His sword came down... and..."

She sucked in at the steel's cold through her flesh and the pain of her bone shattering underneath. Swaying, she braced against the lurch of her stomach. Forcing her eyes opened, the lantern light flickered on the faces before her.

"I don't remember anything... much, until I woke up in a house... somewhere. I thought for sure my arm had been cut off," she said, looking down at the limb as if it belonged to a stranger. "I should have been cleaved in half. His sword must have slipped from the blood on his hands. It hurt. God, it hurt!

There was nothing to help. No whiskey. Nothing. I could hear men screaming; they suffered so much more…"

Fists curled, nails gouging her palms, she closed her eyes against the agonized wails. The smell of blood and sickness filled her nostrils, of destroyed bodies and broken spirits.

"They held me down and sewed my back. I tried not to scream, not with so many others so much worse off. I was broken up inside, but there was little to be done for it. I was told Brian was out in the yard. He was badly slashed, but he was alive… still… so far…"

She felt once more the pluck of the needle through her skin by the very men for whom she had done the same. There was no describing the hot throb of the ensuing fever, the burning thirst an entire loch couldn't slake, or lying in the smell of putrefying flesh and wondering through a fever-hazed mind, if it was hers or Brian's.

Where was the glory of war then?

What she couldn't tell them was the days of agony during the jolting ride home in the back of a pony cart, of slogging down semi-frozen mud, mountain lanes with nothing more than a bit of straw as a cushion and only Brian's bloodied plaid to cover them. She lay half-propped in the corner with his head pillowed on her lap, his body even hotter with fever than hers. And all the while, there had been the burden of guilt for rejoicing in his suffering, for it meant he was going home.

Clamping her eyes tighter, she quaked with the effort to rise above the quagmire of memories that threatened to engulf her, drag her down to where she might drown. When she finally reopened them, Cameron and Hughes images wavered in the tears which flowed freely now. Ashamed, they ducked their noses into their drinks and fixed their gazes on the deck or off into the distance.

Her voice now steadied with conviction. "I knew exactly who I was trying to save. It wasn't Murdoch MacKenzie, believe me. I certainly knew the difference between him and my own husband. And I was no 'witch o' the moors'." She choked laugh at the absurdity. "I was just trying to save my husband."

Then Cate blinked and was delivered back to the *Morganse's* deck, the tropical breeze now drying her damp cheeks. Bewildered, the realization of what she had just done congealed: years of hiding wasted. She had drawn them a map, herself the treasure.

"So, there it is, gentlemen, the grand adventure. And I'll save you the trouble of wondering: yes, there is a reward to the hero who turns me in. His Majesty would be very pleased to have Catherine Mackenzie, the wife of Red Brian." Tears now rolled freely. "I am at your pleasure."

She turned to find Nathan directly behind her, wide-eyed and solemn. He raised a hand to her, meaning to say something, but she brushed past and ran to the cabin.

Nathan drew up before his men amid nervous coughs and throat-clearing. They were mute, most fixing their eyes on the deck. He watched and waited, alert for the first sign of how it was to be, what course they were going to choose in light of what they had just heard, a confession, for all intents and purposes. No sense in tipping his hand just yet. If at all possible, this needed to be their decision, or them thinking as much. If he were too mutton-fisted, it could all go pear-shaped, and quickly. Sometimes it was like trying to drag a dead ox to drink, but as always, pulling was ever so much easier than pushing. If he had his way, he'd rig the grates and let the lot of them taste the nines, but this wasn't his decision to make. The matter hung in a fine balance; one wrong word could tip the scales, setting a course that could never be reversed. Even if it were to go right, there would always be the chance of betrayal. The coin's call was ever so much louder than a pledge. Brotherhood could purchase precious little on the streets of Tortuga.

It was Pryce who stepped into their midst, Hodder at his side. *Good men!*

"Be there one of you motherless whoresons what fancies the King's coin might weigh more agreeable in his pockets?" Pryce waited, providing each the benefit of a gimlet eye, one that could dissect a liver without one's knowing. "Anyone?"

Pryce waited, daring anyone to speak. At length, he nodded in satisfaction. "Very well, then, so be it. And if any of you blessed plagues o' the sea decide those pounds are a-callin' a bit too loud, see me and I'll double it." He gave that a moment to sink in. "Now, who's with me?"

A hearty "Aye!" went up.

Pryce turned to Nathan with a reassuring smile. "She's safe with us, Cap'n."

Cate flung herself across her bunk and sobbed. She kicked her feet and pounded the bulkhead at the unfairness of being forced to drag up and bare what she had strove so valiantly to suppress for so long. She kept the memories locked away, for once loosened, like a pillaging horde of Teutonic ogres, they could seize her and pull her toward the pit from which they rose.

It was her fear of those demons which had always prevented her from seeking the pleasant memories and the benefits found there: the comfort of a familiar face or the reassurance of a smile. Now she cried until exhaustion weakened the demons to the point of losing their grip and were washed away. She was free then to pick through her memories, in search of what she needed: human contact.

Through all the deprivation and squalor of the last years, the lack of the touch of another person—other than in anger or in passing—was what left her the most bereft. Starvation of the belly is nothing compared to the spirit hungering with the need to be touched. She knew the inexorable yearning for warmth, to feel the spring of skin and the pulse of life throbbing just below the surface: to be held. Not necessarily of a sexual nature—God knew she missed that, too—but just... held. Finding such an embrace, one of consolation and tenderness, in her memories, she gave herself over, wrapping herself in it like a cloak.

Sometime later, Cate found herself sitting on the stern gallery. How she came to be there she wasn't quite sure. She felt drained, empty and hollow, like a glass bubble, and curled deeper those imagined arms for protection.

Her confession before the Morgansers had put a massive "C" for "criminal" on her chest, or perhaps "W" for "wanted," or more significantly, "R" for reward. Stripped of her anonymity, she felt exposed and naked.

"As if Nathan would notice," she said ruefully to the night.

The running was over, a five-year cat-and-mouse chase finished. It wasn't an unpleasant thought. From a certain point of view, it was what she had wished for: no more hiding, no more fear. Imprisonment and death were no longer an amorphous hazard; they were now a fixed feature on the horizon. Her trial would be a brief interlude, and then death. Drawing and quartering was traditionally reserved for men, but the Crown had vowed to make an exception for her. Such executions were carefully orchestrated. She would be hung just enough to fulfill the obligation, then laid out and eviscerated, her still-beating heart displayed before her. Beheading would be next, a welcomed end by then. Her body would be burned, the ashes scattered. The lack of a grave would be of little consequence, however, for there would be no one seeking it in order to grieve.

The first impulse was to wish for more time, but that would mean going back to running. Time suddenly seemed a commodity, each ring of the watch bell slicing away another thirty minutes.

Cate rested her arms on her bent knees and allowed the breeze to cool her face, still hot from tears. The crying was long ended, but her head still felt heavy and tight. Nathan's step was overhead; his absence from the cabin was glaring. He had no more to say to her either.

She wondered what his response would be to her deception. It couldn't in truth be called that, for she had been straightforward about her criminal status from the first. It had been revealed with purpose, in the hopes the prospect of a reward would bring her out of the pirates' clutches. She had always had the impression that Nathan had been suspicious of her truthfulness, but he was yet to press her on it. The question rose again as to why he kept her aboard. She groaned aloud, too tired and too emotionally spent to explore that, yet *again*. After such a confession, she held little doubt that he would be forced to either tip his hand or just give her over.

Head propped against the window's frame, she gazed at the silver-lit sea stretching behind the ship, and allowed herself to slip away to another night, a world, an age away.

So, lost in thought, she didn't notice Nathan until he was standing near the mizzenmast, gaping a yawn. With the cabin dark, he would have assumed she had retired and didn't look for her. He seized his chair and dragged it toward the sill. He pulled up short, startled to find her there.

Recovering quickly, he leaned against *Merdering Mary's* carriage. "I thought you to be abed."

"No." Her voice was scratchy and thickened from crying.

"So now we know," he said lightly crossing one ankle over the other. "There are no secrets on a ship. We'd seen your shoulder and the... other bit." He winced at that admission.

"Have a jolly good gawk did you, ogling the freak?" Cate asked bitterly.

Most of her first minutes aboard were blurred. There were flashes of being mauled, and the mortification of being exposed, her clothes being torn away. Half-drowned and terrorized, she hadn't been aware of anything other than escaping.

"That's not how it was," Nathan said evenly, "for the most part, at any rate. We saw one who had suffered greatly and lived to tell of it. We saw a comrade, a mate, one christened by the same blade as we."

"I show them to no one," she said, balling her fist. She had never seen the scar on her back—could never bear to—but it was described in the broadsheets. It might as well have been a brand, for it labeled her, and doomed her if ever caught. She pressed her hand to her stomach, some of the scars there thick enough to be felt through the fabric.

As for those, she couldn't think about it.

Nathan's levity faded. "There's no shame in it, darling. We all bear our marks. Take pride. You can spit in the world's face, because you've lived to tell of them."

"You think I'm lying, don't you?"

How could he not? How could anyone believe such a tale: a single woman riding foolishly into battle to save her husband? To her own mind, the entire ordeal possessed a dream-like quality, as if she had watched someone else.

The corner of his mouth quirked. "And what of it, if you were? The effect is the same: the marks would still be there. You suffered no less, regardless the cause. Any fool can see there's more to it and only a fool would inquire. Hell, no one tells everything," he said with a mirthless laugh. "Couldn't get a bloody word in edgewise, what with everyone jabbering."

He wasn't being cavalier, nor taking her story lightly. With a body more battered by far, he spoke with the eloquence and weight of experience. He spoke not down to her, but as equals, joining her into a brotherhood of those christened by battle, either on the decks of a ship or fields of war.

She rested her chin on her arms and turned her attention to the night once more. Clouds swathed the moon's hips, its three-quarter brilliance illuminating the night in silver and the purplish-black hunched shapes of islands, which dotted the horizon. The stern lamps gilded the *Morganse's* wake. Beyond the glow of the lamps, the ship's path streamed away in a phosphorescent V-shape.

"It's beautiful, isn't it?" she sighed.

"Aye, 'tis beautiful."

She turned to find his gaze fixed on her, his profile frosted by the moon.

The space between them was filled with the sounds of the ship and low-voiced hands. Sails reefed, her wings clipped for the night, the *Morganse's* voice was but a whisper of her daytime chorus, the water barely rustling as she slipped past.

Stillness, however, was not Nathan's natural state. He soon began to shift, the creak of his belts and tinkle of bells seeming to shatter the silence. He hazarded further movement only enough to resituate and then settled. Soon, however, came the drumming of fingers on his belt. He was clearly troubled by something.

Little wonder what, she thought ruefully. He would be glad to be shut of her. Then he could have back his cabin, his bed and what answered for a peaceful world in a pirate's way of life.

After clearing his throat several times, he said, "You jumped on a horse?"

It took her a moment to smoke his meaning. Her shoulders moved in a half-shrug.

"I grew up on a farm with five brothers."

"Five brothers." He gave a low whistle. "Your father must have been proud."

"Would have been prouder with six, but settled for five." She was disinclined to elaborate; it hardly seemed worth the effort, at that point.

"So, Witch o' the Moors is it?" he asked.

She twitched at the raw nerve touched.

"Scary, isn't it?" She heaved a sigh and ruffled her hair in frustration. "How can they make up such outlandish drabble from something so horrible? Do they think it was some kind of a game?"

He nodded knowingly. "Happens all the time, darling; a fascination with the macabre and the grisly."

"You never inquired much regarding my past." He had been keenly interested in her identity when she first arrived, and then seemed to have lost interest, never pressing for further details.

Nathan shrugged. "We all have a past. Backgrounds—where we came from, who we are 'tis many times best left unsaid. If a man desires you to know, he'll tell you. You might find yourself learning far more than intended, and then you're obliged to carry that secret, share his burden. Not many shoulders are wide enough to carry all that."

"How much are you carrying?"

Nathan's gaze dropped quickly to the sill between them. "Enough."

He paused considering, the space between his brows furrowing. "All I care is that the men know a sheet from a shroud and live by the ship's articles. From there..." A shifting of his shoulders finished the thought.

A wide smile flashed in the moonlight, as he said, "Most believe their former lives were drowned when they crossed the Tropic of Cancer."

"Drowned?" It was an intriguing thought. If only His Majesty's Courts would see it the same way.

"'Tis the superstition at any rate," he said, the grin widening.

Cate made a low growling sound as she rubbed her forehead on her arm. "I never wanted to be famous."

He pursed his lips, his sprouting beard making a soft rasping sound as he rubbed his jaw. "Fame's not so bad. It can bring you free rum and your choice of the best whores."

"Can't say as I ever pined for either one."

"People recognize you. They know your name."

"I've rather been striving to avoid that," she said tartly.

He ran a thoughtful hand along the curve of his mustache. "You can control it... mostly. Sometimes it takes on a life of its own, begins to grow with or without you."

Suddenly she felt so very tired. "All I wanted was Brian alive. The rest was only what was necessary to that end."

"People who do what they must to get what they want are to be admired."

"Including killing?" She shot him a doubtful look. "Do you find that an admirable trait?"

"Admiration comes in many forms, luv, under many masks," he said evenly.

Nathan's eyes found hers and held them. Glittering in the moonlight, the umber depths were laden with wisdom far too advanced for his years, the fruits of hard-earned lessons.

"When you came in, I was thinking about the night before Brian was supposed to be captured," she said, looking to the night once more.

He looked up, scowling. "*Supposed* to be captured?"

She nodded, ruefully smiling. "Arrangements had been made for one of the tenants to turn him in the next day. We were all starving. It was a way for his family to receive the reward rather than risk a stranger reporting him."

"What about you?"

"I left that morning, before he was to be taken. The authorities were too interested in him to notice me."

"Lord deliver us from noble men," he grumbled, with a tolerant roll of the eyes. "You got nothing?"

Cate smiled weakly. There had been a reward for both she and Brian. Dreading a life without him, she had been willing to sacrifice herself as well. The arguments had been passionate, Brian intransigent, claiming to see her safe away would allow him peace of mind to face what was to come. Her name was stricken from the family Bible; she no longer existed. And then she was spirited away to a series of clansmen and sympathizers, escorting her under the cover of darkness, night after night, until she was far enough south and no longer readily recognized.

"His family sent me a little when they dared through connections. The mail or couriers were too risky," she said.

She looked up at the moon once more, lop-sided and waxen. "Our last night was a night like this, except cold. It was Brian's last opportunity to see stars and breathe fresh air, so we slept outside. We took quilts and found a quiet spot."

There were no tors or lochs, and the stars didn't sparkle with the same brilliance as in the crisp mountain air, but she saw that night just the same. She couldn't tell Nathan everything of that night. There had been no tears; those had been used up. They barely spoke, for there was little more to be said. His was going to be the easiest: imprisonment, trial, and then death, probably all within a moon's cycle. Hers was the worst: to keep living, alone, half of a whole. She watched the dawn rise from over his bare shoulder as they made love for the last time.

Nathan looked off to the phosphorescent glow of the ship's wake.

"Your husband was a wise man." His graveled voice was a tight rasp. "I know what it 'tis to lie in some stinking cell waiting for me final dawn, whilst trying to decide which I fancied more: to see the sky or draw a clean breath. The sword or a noose is preferable to entombment."

She had managed to delay matters for a bit, but there was no way around it, the inevitable always being exactly that. "So," she said softly. "How's it to be: the nearest garrison or all the way to Port Royal?"

"For what?"

"Turn me in." She leaned back against the window frame, drinking in the heady mix of freshness and salt. "I want to enjoy every last moment of freedom I can. In a way, I'm ready to be done with it. It will be a relief to not live in constant fear."

"'Tis painful to deflate your hopes," he began carefully, "but you shan't be turned in anytime soon, not if this lot of oysterheads have anything to do with it."

She swiveled around, curious to see what he was playing at. "How can that be?"

"They voted." He jerked a thumb toward the cabin door and then held up his hands in defense. "Upon me word, I had nothing to do with it."

"But there's a reward." Pulse racing, she curbed her soaring hopes, afraid to believe.

"There's barely a man on this ship what doesn't carry some kind of a price on his head," he said, rising to his feet. "Turn in one, and I would be obliged to do them all. Bloody inconvenient that. I'd have to press a whole new crew."

Nathan paused at her elbow and bent to peer at her. "You'll be well tonight, then?"

"I think so," she said unsteadily, bracing her head in her

hands. Protection. Safety. Caring. Haven. Home. She now had it all.

He hesitated near the mizzenmast, inclined toward leaving, and yet reticent to do so.

"So, let's see..." he said, coming back. Rolling his eyes in affected consideration, he sat amid the creak of leather, his knee brushing hers. "We've treason—that's to be admired; I've never managed that one—Murder. Conspiracy..." he said, ticking off the charges on his fingers.

"Defamation against the Crown," she put in. "Mayhem—there was a war, after all. Espionage—an assumption on their part, but it's impressive on the broadsheets. Lewd conduct—a woman traveling with an army of men couldn't possibly do otherwise, could she? Sorcery and witchcraft—I suppose my eyes had something to do with that."

They laughed quietly. He had alluded to the evil-natured color of her eyes many a time.

"You've a charge sheet to be proud of," he declared, with a flash of ivory and gold between his lips.

"And now, I can add piracy, I suppose."

Her intent had been light, but his expression darkened. "Not if I have aught to do with it. We'll claim you were a hostage, and if necessary, was used most egregiously."

"That won't help the reputation, but then I suppose I have none to defend."

"It will keep you from the noose," Nathan said with conviction.

To what end if you're gone? The bitter thought swept in without warning. She quickly batted it down. Besides a home, Nathan was offering a future. He and his ship was a godsend and she would take it, be damned the cost.

He leaned to touch her arm and she was suffused with a flush of warmth. Cate looked up into a walnut-colored gaze, intent with concern.

"You'll be well, tonight?" he asked again.

"Yes." Her throat tightened, touched by his sincerity. Now she would be, better than ever. "I still think I'll stay here for a while; I'm enjoying the night too much."

He laid a hand to her shoulder and frowned. "You're shivering."

"Am I? I hadn't noticed."

In nearly a single motion, he tossed the baldric from his shoulder, slid off his coat and whirled it over her.

"Better?" he asked, tucking it in.

"Mm, thank you." She snuggled deeper, the place on her arm where he had touched her still glowing. The burgundy-colored folds might have been worn, but they were strong with his warmth and scent. She felt a bit voyeuristic for using him thus, but was eager for anything which brought him that bit closer. "Seems impossible for someone to be cold in the Caribbean."

"I learned long ago, nothing is impossible; improbable, maybe, but never impossible."

⁂

The next morning, Nathan stood at the weather mizzen chains. Heeled nearly four strakes, the *Morganse* raced through the water, the waves curling in a high arc over her nose, soaking the deck in rain-shower thoroughness.

The *Morganse* was always testy about setting a starboard tack, griping, threatening to fall away. Like any woman, there was more than one way to make her sigh.

Aye, me darling. As you wish.

There was but one soul between them, and she took the share. Justifiably so; she possessed the greater heart, the courage to face the sea every day and the will to make it her own. He was but a means to her ends: to give her enough canvas, a light hand at the wheel and a fair course.

An imprudent vessel she was, always asking for that bit more canvas than she could carry, not like other ships what cranked and shuddered, with spars that creaked and popped like an old tar's bones at the adding of so much as a staysail. Her spirits ran high, extending past ration as she fought to kick up her heels like a high-blooded horse, willing to run until her heart burst. He found it best to entice her with what she desired most: a full complement of jibs and staysails, shaking out the reefs in the mizzen top to keep her true. Give her, her head, and then creep in the braces, when she wasn't looking. Let her royals and courses fly, and she was as happy as a fat whore with a full purse.

The chains buried in the foam, he swayed with her motion as she ate the waves, shaking off one while reaching for the next. He closed his eyes and grasped the shroud. Some claimed the wheel was the way to a ship's heart. Her shrouds were her pulse, a direct line to her lifeblood: the wind. He bent his head to listen to her song, her tempo of water and wind, sough and whistle, thrum and roil.

No need for log lines. She was making eleven knots if she made a fathom; and the wind a bare four points off her nose.

Damn! How she loved to point!

If it weren't for that skirt of weeds she carried — Gotta careen her soon — it would be twelve for sure. Still, eleven was sufficient to overrun any vessel to suffer the misfortune of putting across her bow.

She continued to gripe—No need for a hand on the wheel to know it—reminding him the stowage required a bit of a shift aft; she preferred not so heavy on the peak. Nothing to be done until at anchor. With a full day of the hands sweating it out in the hold, a night of revelry ashore would be the only balm.

Once she hummed, the helm steady, he could relax and attend to other matters, ones which had pressed since before the Midwatch.

Nathan checked over his shoulder toward the quarterdeck. Too wet to sit at the bow where she preferred, Cate perched in the lee of the afterdeck, working. The woman didn't know the meaning of rest. A working fool she was, going until she fell over, if saner heads weren't brought to bear. A few days prior, her scissors had needed sharpening, and a skill for the honing of edges was discovered. When asked how that came to be, she answered: "I had five brothers."

Knives, swords, broad axes, hatchets, and harpoons—the *Morganse* bristled with a host of sharp-edged objects. Consequently, she spent a portion of most every day, sharpening. Hone stone, oil, leather and rags became her constant companions, all stowed in a small basket. This day was no exception; she busied with several rigging knives the men brought, anxious for a few minutes of conversation, while she worked.

Pryce slipped aft to the quarterdeck as Nathan made his way forward. The odd wave caught him now and again, but he knew the feel of his ship well enough to know when to duck. To his mind, a man who couldn't bear being wet had no business at sea, but by the same token, it was a wretched fool who didn't have the sense to avoid a wave square to the face.

Mr. Fox, master of the larbolin f'c'stlemen, hovered at seeing his Captain approach. The man tended toward being as fastidious as an old schoolmaster about his realm. He waved Fox off, just to set the poor man's mind to rest. This was not a matter that reflected on his crew, reeving new foretackle blocks, at the moment. Keeping his distance, but with a canny eye, Fox touched his forelock and returned to his duty.

"You, sailor," Nathan called, tapping one on the shoulder. "Name's Cameron, am I right?"

"Aye, Cap'n!" The man knuckled a hasty salute, disconcerted to find his commander so unexpectedly close, and being addressed directly, at that.

"Pray a word with you and your... mate." Nathan urged the

man aside, beckoning his comrade to follow. "To your duties, mates," he barked, to the remainder who stood gaping.

Snapped from their torpor, they bent to their tasks with exaggerated fervor.

"You spoke of the Rising last night?" he asked of Cameron once out of earshot of the others.

What the bloody hell was the other's name?

Cate's scene on deck the night since had been grist for the rumor mills as it was. The Captain in private conference with these two would only fan the fires, but the need to know outweighed all caution. Stiff orders could be given, but that would only serve to drive the talk further underground.

"Aye, sir," came the response, still cautious of where this audience might lead.

"Then you knew of Mr. Cate's man?" Nathan asked, lowering his voice.

"Captain Mackenzie?" Relieved, Cameron grinned, bobbing his head enthusiastically. "Aye, sir! Me 'n' Hughes, we served under 'im."

Hughes! Why couldn't I remember the blighter's name?

"Can you tell me of him? What sort of man he was?"

It wasn't a comfortable matter to broach, but his curiosity vexed him all night. Any dullard could tell by the look in her eyes when she spoke of him that the woman was still thoroughly in love with the man. But it did defy all reason what manner of man would drag her through a war and then leave her alone. To his mind, a kiss o' the gunner's daughter would be too good.

"The best, sir," Hughes replied adamantly. "A man among men he was."

"Aye, sir, we'd follow him anywhere, to Hell and back."

"And Culloden was Hell, sir."

Both nodded gravely.

"Brave?" Nathan was keenly alert for those first unguarded reactions.

A slight hesitance in the ship's forward motion was all the warning need. They ducked as another wave broke over them.

"To a fault, sir," Cameron answered eagerly, water dripping from his chin. "Never led a charge mounted; always afoot as the rest of us. And never left a wounded man on the field; retrieved every one hisself, if the need arose."

"Aye, I saw him carry many a man off the field," Hughes put in, sputtering seawater.

"Fought like the Dev'l possessed him himself," Cameron said. "Saw 'im near cleave a man in half, once't."

"Aye, could swing a claymore like a child swings its rattle," Hughes went on, both nodding earnestly.

"Then, he was a big man?" Nathan asked, frowning slightly.

Cameron closed one eye in estimation. "A good head taller than yerself, sir. Had to duck his head at near every door he passed."

"And near twenty stone, with hands near twice as wide as most," Hughes said, fanning his fingers out in example.

Nathan looked to the deck. This wasn't going as he had expected, at all. He had been thoroughly prepared to despise the man.

How the hell could such a bastard suddenly become a bloody hero?

"And handsome, too," Cameron continued, clearly eager to please, dodging the tails of another wave. "T'weren't narry a lass what didn't swoon at his passing."

Sobering, Cameron paused, carefully choosing his words. "And he loved the leddy, sir. They loved each other; any fool could see it."

"Yes, you'd have to be a doddering fool not to see it," Nathan echoed under his breath.

Yes, a blind man could see it, indeed! Any fool could hear it in her voice, or see it in those cursed blue... green... whatever eyes!

"Took her everywhere w' him; they were inseparable. Heaven help the man whatever gave her an off look!" Cameron finished, shaking his head dolefully.

Having heard enough accolades for one day, he waved them off, back to their duties and their mates. He stood absent-mindedly thumping the rail with his fist. So, lost in thought, he was grateful for the occasional wave in the face to bring him into focus.

Smite and burn me!

She'd had a good man, and loved him well. No man could ask for more.

His worst fears had been proven correct. He had been ready to despise this Mackenzie, and deserving of it he was, judging by what he had heard... until then. How the hell did he go from shiftless bastard to saint? It was unimaginable that Cate would give herself over to anything less than a paragon, but then he knew well enough that ration and judgment were rarely matters for the heart. He'd seen many a great woman put her hearts in lesser men.

Pirate, soldier, peon, king or otherwise, to his mind there was an order to the world: women bore children and men protected them both. It was a simple axiom, and there would be a damned sight less troubles in the world if there were more to honor it.

He bore little tolerance for a man — a bloody goddamned hero or no — who failed to do so. It was only a shiftless lout what would put a woman through a war just to leave her alone to starve.

On that basis alone, he was ready to skewer the bastard on first sight… if and when he was ever found… and he *would* find him. God strike him blind, by all that was holy on this earth and sea, he would find him!

7: WEE BIT O' PRIATING

A S THE DAYS GREW INTO a fortnight, Cate gradually became inured to the pirate ways and their "wee bit o' pirating," as Pryce called it. "Cap'n's on the prowl!" the hands declared, with an anticipatory gleam in the eye and knowing nods.

The *Morganse* stalked like a large black cat. Once the unwitting prey was spotted, a small cat-and-mouse would ensue, probing to discern who and what the prey might be. The meeting was usually a quiet affair, anticipation and preparation — making ready the guns, hauling up cartridges, wads and shot, clearing the decks, laying the splinter netting, dispersing weapons, wetting the sails and sanding the decks — requiring more than the taking itself. If the sight of the blood-dripped sails weren't sufficient, the sight of the massive black and white banner bearing the haloed skull framed with wings caused the hapless prey to douse its topsails. When she did give chase, it rarely lasted more than a watch. On rare occasion, a shot from the bow-chasers was necessary, with great caution lest the hull be breached, the precious prize destroyed. Within hours the ship was stripped of everything deemed valuable, and the *Morganse* was again on the hunt.

Cate sat on the forecastle — or "f'c'stle" as a true mariner would say — one afternoon. She loved it there. The wind whipping her hair, the spindrift touching her face, whatever sailing was, it was that much more on the forecastle. The deck and ship were more alive; the rush and power of wind and water that much more stirring; the sails overhead that much more immediate. Up there, if she was to close her eyes, it was the nearest thing to being free of the Earth as any human could wish. Noticing her joy, the jacks had made an arrangement of boxes and crates into a seat which she used whenever conditions allowed.

There were drawbacks. It meant she was obliged to discretely look away when any of the hands were on the head, for the bow was their only convenience, just as she did whenever someone stepped up to a pissdale. Having had brothers and a husband, the call of nature was unremarkable. It was of mortal consequence to the men, however, and so she made a great show of pretending not to notice.

From the corner of her eye she saw the lad Jensen sidling near. When she was first arrived, he had been painfully shy. Then he stumbled into a loggerhead, a heated iron used to melt tar. Stinking of slushing from the masts—an odious job of lubricating with galley fat—he stood like a deer ready to bolt while she treated the burn.

Now blushing brilliant, he knuckled his forehead. "G'day, mistress... sir!" he corrected quickly.

His hand shot out to present her with a small box. Barely the length of her little finger and only slightly larger in circumference, it bore an intricate knotted rope detail carved at each end.

"It's a needle case," he beamed. He took it from her to demonstrate how the top pivoted to reveal a hollowed out groove. Going near purple with embarrassment, he gave it back and clutched his hands behind his back.

"It's beautiful, Jensen." And it was. The polished surface glowed, its grain a deep reddish color. "Is it mahogany?"

The joy from Jensen's face faded. "No, 'tis salt horse, m'am."

"Beef?"

She gaped at the box. She had heard the men laughingly allude to carving it, but had thought it as jest.

Jensen's young brow furrowed with the intensity of a craftsman discussing his trade. "I picked through a week's ration just to find the right piece."

Cate bit her lip. How does one ever go about giving a proper "Thank you" for something so thoughtful as that?

"Wanna come help?"

She looked up at Nathan's voice. He stood poised at the top of the forward companionway, lantern in one hand and ring of keys in the other, looking expectant.

Cate glanced around. Sailing free with the wind two points aft, this according to Pryce. A cloud of snowy sail was on display overhead. Practicality must have prevailed, for the ivory of those flying off the forestays was unadulterated red. The expanse of sail was fashioned to catch the wind, for precious little was to be had. The *Morganse* moved at a crawl. Only with generosity did the log lines read four knots. It was making for a long day. Tucking Jensen's gift in her pocket, she rose to follow.

Nathan trundled down the steps, pausing there to snag a horn lamp from a post. Once lit, he handed it off to Cate and, with the same lightness of foot, ascended to the hold. It was a marvel how his feet never seemed to touch the wood. Years of living on a ship bore its rewards.

She groped her way down, lurching with jarring effect at the bottom when she expected another step, but there was none. Nathan forged ahead, the darkness immediately swallowing him. She had been in the hold twice before. It was no less foreboding now.

The lanterns were a weak defense against the pressing gloom. Fearing to lose sight of Nathan meant to be doomed to an eternity of roaming in the dank netherworld, Cate doggedly kept on his heels. Struggling to maintain her footing on the treacherously slippery boards, she followed Nathan's bobbing glow, appearing and disappearing as he wound through the cargo. Through the creak and rumble of the ship's working came the scuttle and scamper of tiny feet. She preferred to believe it was His Lordship hunting. The lantern cast grotesquely distorted shadows, and she scolded herself for allowing her imagination to run too freely. Still, she couldn't shake the feeling of eyes on her. Fearful of something jumping out to grab her by the leg, she kept tight in Nathan's wake.

She felt it before she saw it, a whoosh of air overhead, something—a shadow—coming straight at her. A part of her knew it was only a shadow, and yet there was no denying the press of flapping wings. She shrieked and dove, throwing her hands over her head. Looking up, she found Nathan wearing a look somewhere between perturbed and amused.

"What was that?" She risked a peek upward, afraid to see her imaginings hadn't strayed far.

Nathan stood there smiling, *the bastard*!

"Our dear Artemis." He raised his lantern higher and gestured with his head.

Cate cautiously straightened. It was her worst fears: two eyes stared back. Her vision finally adjusting, she could make out the low hunched shape of...

"An owl?"

"Artemis." The lamp flashed on his widening grin. "Goddess of hunting, wild things and the moon. Appropriate, don't you think?"

Biting back a few rude remarks, Cate peered closer. Perched atop a platform wedged between the ship's knees, the bird was not unlike those she had seen before: moon-faced with a buff-colored body.

"A barn owl?"

Nathan shrugged, regarding the creature with pride. "I suppose so. No one's asked and to my knowledge, she's not said."

"She?" Her suspicion grew as to why every animal on board — and a menagerie it was growing to be — was always female.

"She just appeared one day, off Portland Point... Jamaica; blown in on a storm, more than like. She sat in the ratlines for the day, and then — after a bit of a commotion on the part of several men — we found her t'ween decks. Hung about there for a while she did and then came down here. She moves about, especially at night, but seems to fancy here best."

He grinned again at that. "Shortly after she arrived, we noticed a marked drop in the rat population, no reflection on His Lordship, of course."

"Of course," she muttered, still not fully recovered.

"Earns her salt, does our dear Artemis," he said almost lovingly. Cate felt a pang of jealousy for anything which could elicit just pride and admiration. "But don't go trying to pet her. She's a bit ill-mannered when it comes to that. Beatrice's influence, I expect."

It would figure that Nathan would blame Beatrice. Other than His Lordship, he didn't seem inclined toward an amenable relationship with any of the animals, but apparently an owl had won him over.

"You'll have heard the ship is haunted?" he asked with an odd combination of shyness and pride, pleased when she nodded. "That would be our dear Artemis. Makes quite the mournful noise when she's of a mind."

The back of Cate's neck prickled. She had been wakened her first night aboard by just such a sound. The ship being haunted seemed quite possible at that point.

"So, she just... stays?" she asked.

"Aye, well, unless we're in port," he said judiciously. "More often than not, she goes skulking about. Out cutting about I suspect," he said with a scolding glower at the bird. "Floozie!"

Artemis returned an unblinking, broken-necked glower.

"But, she always comes back, catches up if we've weighed without her. We put in for careening once. Gone for a couple of weeks, she was; we began to think she'd found a better home. But then, she came back with a mate just as we cleared the reef. Set up housekeeping. You know how women are when they have that nesting urge," he said as an aside, suggestively rolling his eyes. "Been a wretched nursery down here ever since."

Now that he mentioned it, she could see bits of twig, straw and feathers sticking from underneath the owl. Artemis seemed to know that she was the object of conversation, striking several noble poses.

"I don't see any little ones," she said.

"Oh, once they've grown, she runs them off. Sort of the natural way of things, don't you think?" There was an odd glint in his eye and he chuckled. "Thoughtful she is, always making sure land is near."

"Where's her mate now?" Cate asked, peering cautiously around.

"Open-minded sort, she is. He goes gallivanting off, but she always takes him back."

"Lucky man."

He caught the lilt in her voice, but opted to ignore it. He gestured toward the floor directly below the roost and the pile of small, dark, pellet-like things.

"There are three or four rats apiece in those. Not bad, eh?" he said, proudly. "The men sell them and the feathers for charms and such, mostly to the conjure women in these parts. One hand feeding the other, or whatever."

Artemis' attention swung around, her head making circular movements like the speeding hands of a clock.

"Ah, see there. She's on to something, now," cried Nathan.

Cate looked warily over her shoulder into the darkness, wondering what the owl saw.

"Just mind your hair." He straightened with a meaningful look. "Don't want any unfortunate incidents and have to cut Artemis free."

Cate's reflexively hand went up to smooth it, just in case. "What about His Lordship? I thought he was for the rats."

"Oh, aye," Nathan said, unfazed. "Had a bit of a falling out there at first. There were a couple of nasty rows in the middle of the night."

He frowned at the memory and then waved it away as he did with so many other things. "Beatrice had a few things to say on the matter, but an accord was met. Parrots don't cotton to hunting rats and Artemis didn't care about the masthead, during the day, at any rate, so..." He shrugged. "There's enough for everyone, and each unto his... or her territory."

The bobbing light signaled he had moved on.

"Don't owls eat lizards, too?" she asked, thinking of the ship's geckos as she followed close behind.

Nathan's chuckle came from out of the darkness ahead of her. "That's why only the fast 'tis aboard. Once in a while, snakes and the like stumble their way aboard, what with the cargo and all.

Between dear Artemis down here and His Lordship up there, the little slimmers don't stand a chance," he said without sympathy.

Her mind reeled at the staggering amounts of philosophies and commentaries in that and so much categorically askew, she had no way of knowing where to begin to respond. What went on in that mind of his was a marvel.

"A few men complained — bad luck and all that — but once they found the rats no longer were chewing their digits, they were agreeable."

Sometimes his pragmatism could be staggering, she thought as they pressed on.

Over the slosh of water and ship's rumbling, she heard the rattle of keys, and then the raspy squeak of hinges on a heavy door. Nathan stood aside to beckon her through. The door slammed shut behind them with a crypt-like thud that felt as if she had just been entombed. Judging by the duller echoes, it was a smaller room which Nathan now picked his way through, lantern on high. Then he stopped and turned.

"Here we are," he announced, the lamplight flashing on his grin.

Cate gaped as the light fell on a long pile, well over shoulder high. "What is all that?"

"Swag."

Nathan was already making his way around the perimeter and disappeared behind it. Cate stood awestruck. Gleaming bright in the lamp light, she had heard of piles of pirate treasure, but seeing it was entirely different. It was a dazzling array of everything anyone, in the wildest corner of their imagination, could consider valuable. If it had ever been made of gold or silver, it was there. If it had ever been used in any way, shape, form or fashion by those of privilege, it was there.

In any circle, it would have been considered a king's treasure trove. One could have easily set up housekeeping from what spilled from the cargo nets, crates and hogsheads, and an elegant place it would have been: chairs, paintings, fire screens, porcelain, and clocks. A sequined, silk lizard with jeweled eyes stared out from a knot of plumes and brocades. Next to it was a statue of a naked woman reclined in a chaise, flung against a crate of what looked to be champagne bottles, amid a tumble of royal-looking staffs, orbs and chalices.

She moved the lamp, its light catching additional stacks along the bulkhead of the more mundane: bags of rice, tea chests, sugar, salt, cocoa, coffee, spices, bolts of fabric and bricks of indigo.

"Where did all this come from?" It was a fairly stupid question, but the only one she could conjure.

Nathan popped up beside her, waggling his eyebrows. "Pirate!"

He pushed past and ducked out of sight.

"What are you looking for?" she asked when astonishment finally gave way to curiosity.

"A looking glass; I thought I saw one down here. Thought you might fancy one."

Coming from the far side of the pile, his voice was somewhat muffled. She followed his progress by the glow of his lantern, a warm pool of light amid the darkness, reflecting off the pile.

"I thought those were bad luck."

He straightened to peer at her over the pile. "Whatever put that in your head?"

"I don't know. It seems like everything else is."

He grunted and muttered something which sounded like one of his favorite oaths, including a vaguely derogatory reference to women. There was a loud rattle, and then a cascading, metallic crash, resembling a tinker's cart overturning.

"Damn!"

Holding the lantern higher, she squinted into the surrounding tomb-like darkness. "Are you all right?"

"Fine. Pinched me finger, is all." His voice echoed dully over the clatter of his rummaging.

The bone-soaking blackness aside, she was struck by something far more overpowering than the muggishness of things gone wet far too long, a revolting odor that assaulted her nose to eye-watering effect.

"What's that smell?"

The racket stopped and Nathan's head appeared. Tilting it, he sniffed and frowned. "Bilges, I expect." He disappeared once more.

"Haven't you ever considered cleaning them?" she asked through her hand pressed over her mouth and nose.

Nathan stood with a barely tolerant look. "Darling, not everything in this bloody world has to be cleaned." Shaking his head in dismayed wonderment, he bent back to his quest.

"It smells like someone died down here."

Halting again, he looked around, considering. "I think someone did." Eyes rolling in thought, he gave a definitive nod. "Aye! About twelve years ago."

Nearly gagging, she cleared her throat, trying not to cough lest she stir the thickened air further. "It smells like he's still down here."

"Only those froggish French bury their dead in the ballasts.

Although it has been a while since the sweet cocks were opened," he said as an afterthought. "Damned lot o' pumping, what with all that water pouring in, but if it will abate your delicate sensibilities..." A lift of the shoulders finished his thought.

He returned to his search, his chuckling drowned by the noise of his rootling about. Blinking her watering eyes, Cate surveyed the chaotic collection.

"Has anyone ever considered organizing all this?" she asked, idly kicking at a silver epergne with her toe.

"Organize?"

"Yes, pile things up; put things away. Put the silver with the silver, the crystal with the crystal... At the least then, you would know what you have down here. Some of this is going to be ruined," she warned, eyeing the water splashing up between the planks with each roll of the ship.

"Plenty more of where it came from," he said through a suppressed amusement. "We've a book. We know everything what's here."

"Why haven't you taken more of this for yourself?" Lantern on high, she surveyed trunks of every size, boiling over with velvets, tapestries and silks. She had thought Nathan's quarters to be modest in its appointments, but now in light of all this lavishness so near to hand, it was positively Spartan. Velvets, brocades and silks spilled from silver-studded trunks, and yet he wore the most basic of basics. The light reflected off the shiny surfaces, shooting apparition-like glows on the walls.

"With all this, you could be living like a king."

"Naa!" It was a throaty sound from somewhere in the gloom. "I've the clothes on me back and me ship." He popped up next to her, startling her. "There's nothing I lack of."

And then he moved away.

"What are you going to do with all this?"

"Sell it," he replied, barely audible above the clamor.

"And then what?"

"Spend it." He straightened again, now far down the pile and scowled. "What else would I do with it?"

"Save it?"

He gave her a wary look, as if strongly suspecting a trick question was involved somewhere. "And to what purpose would that be?"

Cate shrugged, scanning the pile. She was beginning to get the feel of this rummaging. "I don't know; your old age?"

Nathan's hearty laugh echoed dully, a skeptical snort ending it. "Blessed little sense to be found in that: I'll be long dead."

It gave her a bit of a chill to think about the possibilities of such a prediction. "How can you be so sure?"

"Because I've been a pirate long enough to know that pirating will be the death of me, luv," he said, still fizzing. "Damn!"

"Now what?" she called, squinting toward the glow of his lantern.

"Nothing. Stubbed me toe."

"You've never considered the possibility of growing old?"

"Got it!" came a victorious cry.

With a metallic crescendo, he came around with a gold-filigree mirror so large it barely fitted under his arm.

"You mean grow old and gray on the porch rocking, with me grandchildren on me knee? No, never considered it, because it's never going to happen."

He cast a loving look toward the beams and bulkheads. "There'll come a day when time will be up for me and this ol' girl, and we'll go down together. Did you find anything you fancy? If there's something you like, 'tis at your pleasure."

Cate stood back, hesitant. "Is it all yours?"

"Strike me buttons, no. Shares, remember?"

Even once divided among the eight score of men, there was still enough in any single share to provide one to live out their days in more-than-modest comfort. And yet few did; not even the ancient Millbridge or the impaired Billings or Stubbs.

"No worries, luv. You're part of the crew now. You've a share coming."

Bent looking, Cate abruptly straightened. "Since when am I a part of the crew?"

"Since the night you told your story on deck." He hunched one shoulder. "They voted; it's settled."

A share of all of that was overwhelming. Jewelry, silks, china and lace were hardly the stuff of her existence. She balked at the prospect of selecting something. Possessions had been limited for so long to the small meal bag, lost on the *Constancy*. And before that, she had never been one to indulge in privilege, let alone such riches.

"I could use a footstool, for while I'm stitching." Picking up the search, she swung the lantern about trying to cast a broader light.

"Wouldn't you like something else?" he said, following at her elbow. "Something a little more... nice? I just thought maybe you might desire... Well, it just strikes me you should have something nice, that's all."

Cate looked back at him through the dim and smiled. "No, it's very well, Nathan. I already have what I want."

She did indeed, standing right there before her and all around, for that matter: being needed and belonging, a home. All that, plus a knight in shining armor, albeit slightly tarnished.

Her foot struck something, and she looked down to a small trunk half-buried in the riches.

"Here it is." She tugged the trunk free and tipped it into the light to inspect more closely. Ornate but simple, it had tooled leather straps and detailed silver corner pieces. "Perfect."

Nathan came around to take a closer look. "Doesn't look like much."

"It's perfect," she beamed in the face of his patent disapproval. "It's just the right height for my feet, and has space to store my threads and such."

His eyes ran once again over the pile. Ultimately he came back around to the trunk and gave it a scornful glare.

"Very well," he grumbled in barely contained disappointment.

Stalking off toward the door, he muttered another oath, this one definitely involving females and several other creatures.

⌒⌒⊚⌒⌒

Cate stood before the new looking glass, admiring it. The addition was an improvement, its reflection already brightening the cabin.

With the gilt-frame under his arm, Nathan had carried it with purpose up to the Great Cabin, but had shied just short of the curtain.

"I'll pass the word for Chips," he declared and ducked away.

With a few raps from the carpenter's mate's hammer, the new glass was affixed on the wall above the washstand. The old one, dim and crackled, had been barely the size of a dinner plate. This one was considerably larger, but still only reached to mid-chest. To see herself entirely would have meant to shove the curtain aside and back out into the salon.

She was touched by Nathan's thoughtfulness, although at the same time was a bit befuddled. He had dismissed her thanks with a casual wave, but she was sure she had seen a deepening of color about his collar. To see the reflection of another being made her feel not so alone, but at the same time, it gave her the disconcerting sensation of being watched.

It had been a long time since she had seen herself to such an extent. Among her possessions had been a piece of glass, so small no more than one feature at a time could be seen. It, along with everything else in that small bag, had been lost when the

Constancy had sailed away. It took her a few moments to garner the courage to take an honest look.

The last time she had seen herself—in the mantua-maker's shop where she had worked in London—she had looked like something for the knacker's. She had gained enough weight that her collarbone no longer jutted under her skin and the hollows under her eyes were gone. With the added weight, a bit of softness had returned to her face, but her jaw was still bold, too much so by her mother's judgment. Her mother had often bemoaned her shoulders, as well, too wide and square to be considered either feminine or fashionable. The corners of her mouth still curved on their own volition. The trait had been often assumed to be impertinence and had brought many a rebuke from her seniors. Her father's brows and nose were still there, the brow was softer, her nose not quite so turned up at the end.

Her skin was now tanned, not as deeply as Nathan's and ruddier than his bronze. She was accustomed to the color of her eyes, but they were a bit of a shock then. Her darkened skin intensified them, the jade—their current color—almost glowing. Nathan's reference to an idol which had sought to curse him was understandable. Her eyes could change, as he and many before him had noted. With no rhyme or reason that she could discern, they shift into colors similar to those seen in the local shallows and reefs.

It was a surprise to see how much her natural mahogany had lightened. She had been able to see the ends enough to know that they had gone almost tawny. But now she could see she looked as if she wore a copper crown.

Cate picked her brush from the top of the stand and began brushing the "maddening tangle" as Nathan referred to it. A lifetime of wrestling with it had been fruitless: braids, tails, pins and ribbons were flung off with equality. While living in the Highlands, a haven to the concept of proper, she had been urged to wear a cap, as did all gentlewomen. After failing time and again to keep it in place, Brian had ceremoniously flung it out the window. On the *Constancy*, she had tried a headscarf which seemed to serve everyone else well. After several furtive tries, securing it so tightly as to cause her head to ache, the cloth had been last seen floating in the ship's wake.

She had come to envy the pigtails of Hodder, Heap and many of the crew, most particularly the forecastlemen. Their hair had been secured in the time-honored mariner's way of a pigtail—most well down the length of the backs—and then tarred, head, tail and all. There had been one day, as she had eyed one such seaman, when Nathan had divined her thoughts.

"Wretched waste of tar." He cast a skeptical look at her billowing mass and scowled. "Not sure there's enough aboard."

A few steps away, he paused at a slush bucket. Tugging the paddle free, he considered the tallow-based, malodorous ooze used to lubricate the masts, and then directed a speculative look toward her hair. For the briefest of moments, she had harbored a sinking sensation he mightn't be jesting.

Shaking his head in a jangle of bells, he had shoved the paddle back in place. "It would appear mankind has not yet made the discovery."

Given sufficient attention, her hair could be coaxed into orderliness, hanging in smooth coils about her shoulders. The first touch of breeze, however, and it would be back to the "maddening tangle."

Sighing — for there was little to be gained — she put the brush away and left.

Cate had become enough of a mariner to notice the moment she stepped outside that the wind had shifted. More astern now, it meant the *Morganse* was "running free," moving with the wind. It rendered the decks quite airless. The forecastle would be the only hope of any relief. Cate arrived there to find Hermione had taken up residence on her seat. It required being more stubborn than the goat, but eventually Cate shooed her away, Hermione casting a complaining bleat over her shoulder as she clopped down the steps.

She was barely situated before the cry of "On deck there!" came from the lookout straight overhead on the foremast.

Pryce and Nathan, glasses in hand, met at Cate's either side.

"Where away?" Nathan threw to the foretop.

"Hull up 'n one point free to larboard."

The men peered with great interest at the speck of white pricking the horizon, dead ahead, visible only on the rise of the swell.

"Do you see what I see, Mr. Pryce?" asked Nathan over her head. A piece of jerked meat was tucked into the corner of his mouth.

"Aye! A fowl fittin' to be plucked."

"Something about this one not to my liking," Nathan said after some moments.

He arranged Cate at a kevel and handed her the spyglass. "Hold this and watch that."

"What should I watch it do?"

The corner of his mouth quivered. "Just watch."

Several rounds of bell, changing of the watch and aching

arms later, Nathan come up behind her. He peered interestedly over her shoulder, the ship now hull up regardless of the swell.

"Well?"

"Nothing," Cate sighed. Her hopes had soared at the prospect of having something of significance to report, so that she might appear seaworthy just once.

"Nothing, eh?" Nathan said with something between surprise and doubt.

"Nothing except a bunch of men saluting each other on that deck back there."

"Poop deck, darling," he said taking the glass and gazing through it. "That is a poop deck and a glorious one, indeed."

Pryce came alongside, pulled out a pocket glass, and together the men considered the not-so-distant ship, coming on like a charging ram.

"Nothing more entrancing than the shine of midshipmen's buttons, unless it's the captain's, eh Mr. Pryce? And pray look at all those shining brass buttons," Nathan said.

"Shining and glorious indeed," Pryce said, grinning. "Looks like she's usin' yer trick o' paintin' canvas so as to conceal her guns."

"Aye, well, they do claim imitation is the sincerest form of flattery."

Nathan lowered the glass and glared at the triple fleur-de-lis flying from the mizzen stay. He made a skeptical, throaty noise. "French my aged aunt's arse. Well done," he declared, patting Cate on the shoulder.

She beamed under his praise, in spite of not having the faintest idea as to what she had done.

"A wolf in sheep's clothing 'tis what we have here," he explained to her confusion. "A Royal Navy frigate she is, looking to entertain us with her innocence."

"'Pears to be the *Valor*," Pryce said after further examination. "A sixth rate twenty-four and none so grand as our sixteens."

Cate nodded, trying to appear to take the meaning of that bit of information—the *Valor* carried twenty-four guns, none larger than what the *Morganse* sported — with the significance intended.

"Commanded by Captain Eldridge Prichard, and a worthy foe he is, when he's sober enough to find the poop. A slave to the Demon Gin he is," Nathan added.

"The waters are fair stirred up these days," Pryce said with significance.

Nathan batted his lashes affectedly. "Can't begin to put me mind as to why."

Pryce seemed inclined to make further comment but resisted.

Redirecting his attention to the *Valor* again, Nathan made a sarcastic noise. "Anyone with half o' brain would wear 'round, and tear off like smoke and oakum at the sight of our sails. He desires us to believe he doesn't know who we are and that we are too cod-headed to have smoked who he is."

He scanned the water and cast an eye skyward. "On to it then."

Nathan stepped to the break of the forecastle to shout, "Mr. Hodder. Mr. MacQuarrie. Pass the word to your men. You know what's to be done."

⁓⌇⊙⌇⁓

It was a fascination to witness the next while: a delicate operation executed with the precision and ease gained only through practice. MacQuarrie readied his crews and guns, the port lids still closed, as did the *Valor*, as observed and reported by the eagle-eyed Damerell at the crosstrees. In the meantime, Hodder readied men and ship.

Closer... Closer... The vessels bore down on each other.

The *Valor* was now close enough that her individual faces could be made out, peering over her rail. The next bit happened so fast, Cate wasn't sure if she had imagined it. The painted canvas fell away from the *Valor's* side and her foremost guns fired, but too soon for effect. The *Morganse's* port lids flew open, the guns rammed home and the bow-chaser fired. The smoke had yet to clear the forecastle, before the *Morganse* had pirouetted — with a great deal of bellowing by those hauling on the braces, tacks and sheets — and sped away into her own wake. The Union Jack and a commodore's streamer broke out from the *Valor's* peak, and the race was on.

The *Morganse* settled in like a steeplechaser, the water rushing past her sides at an ever-increasing rate. Leaning far out over the windward rail, Cate could see the *Valor's* new press of sails and the increase of white foam at her cutwater.

"You have something in mind?" she asked Nathan.

He stood leaning against the binnacle, his arms casually crossed. His cheeks rounded with a square-toothed grin. "A man without a plan is a man what plans to fail, or die as the case would likely be. We got their attention; now let's see what Ol' Prichard is made of. All I require is a few hours of staying ahead — not too far, mind — the night's new moon and a steady glass, which shows every sign of being so."

It was a steady glass, but the seas cut up rough, with a heavy swell. The *Morganse* leaned into the waves — "close-hauled on a

192

larboard tack, 'n the wind five points off 'er nose" — flinging a steady curl of water to leeward. She ducked her head to take an occasional wave over her bow, the spindrift flying nearly to the afterdeck.

No log line was necessary. That the *Morganse* outdistanced the *Valor* was clear enough, so much so an old jib was rigged over the side — to leeward, hence out of the *Valor's* sight — as a sea anchor, intentionally slowing her. It meant it would appear to the *Valor* that the *Morganse* was sailing her heart out to escape. Cate wondered what Nathan was playing at, but he seemed disinclined to elaborate. The hands exchanged knowing looks and nods. They knew, and so would she, in time.

Their course led down a near mile-wide channel between two strings of islands. Those to leeward varied, from steep-sided and sizeable, to barely more than a dry spot in the water. Those to windward, considerably farther away, were no more than monotonous low strips of white beach, fringed with palms.

A joyous whoop drew Cate's attention to the bow. The decks were at a shocking pitch. In spite of the manropes rigged from fore to aft, every step needed to be planned. A couple of times, she was snagged by the nearest seaman to keep from taking a hazardous tumble. Reaching the forecastle finally, she looked farther forward to see Nathan nearly to the tip of the jib-boom, nearly half the ship's length out over the water, standing as casually as he had next to the binnacle. He braced an arm against a stay as he rode the rise and fall of the boom like a Roman rider. He threw his head back and let out another whoop, similar to what that same rider might have given.

"Won't he fall?" she heard herself say.

Mr. Fox, the captain of the forecastle jacks, looked from supervising his men to Nathan with mild interest. "Nay, the *Morganse* would never allow it. Wet as Neptune he'll be and never notice."

He shook his head in wonderment. "'Tis the likes ain't never seen."

"Him standing out there?"

"Nay. Him 'n this ship. 'Tis but one soul a'tween them. Best step aft, sir, or you'll be as wet as a whale yerself."

A wave breaking high just then, its plums sheeting across the deck, made his point.

The ship's people went about their routine as they would any other day. There was no worry, no furtive glances aft to see what the *Valor* was doing. That task was all reserved for Cate and she performed it admirably. She paced, until the day faded and the *Valor* was reduced to no more than a ghostly blur of sails and lamp glows. The sea suddenly seemed overcrowded. She could still feel the ship's presence, like someone breathing over her shoulder, pressing, looming, so very... there.

Unable to bear it, Cate went into the cabin, hoping to find something to occupy her mind. She found Hermione meticulously flicking the last bits with her tongue from Cate's dinner plate, left by Mr. Kirkland. It was just as well; her stomach was closed. She was too distracted to read, and couldn't concentrate sufficiently to stitch. She gravitated to the length of cord lying on the gallery sill. Eager for the opportunity to practice her knotting without prying eyes, she sat and began, and began... and began, swearing under her breath each time. Somehow, somewhere, she was making the same mistake time and again.

Nathan came into the cabin and her heart sank. It would be an understatement to say he was distressed by her ineptitude so far as knotting was concerned. He seemed to have taken it as his personal mission and a dogged instructor he was.

His eyes lit at seeing the rope in her hand. "No, the shank's too long," he said, perching next to her. "Start again."

They sat heads bent, shoulder-to-shoulder. It wasn't a complete accident when she shifted for a better view when Nathan demonstrated, bringing the length of her thigh against his. His fingers moving like moth-wings over hers, she frequently became lost in watching his hands, the bones and tendons flexing under the bronzed skin, burnished to golden in the light. The fine web of scars across his knuckles was a constant reminder of how closely he had come to being no different than Stubbs.

A clearing of his throat and "Mind your task, lass," set her back to the lesson.

"Now, this is the tree," he said grasping the section of cord. "The loop is the hole. And this other end is the rabbit."

Cate checked her urge to roll her eyes. Instead, she fixed them with affected interest. The chant of a rabbit capering about, rounding trees, and popping in and out it of holes was not novel. Stubbs had repeated it seemingly time-out-of-mind. And yet, in Nathan's throaty rasp, his breath warm on her arm, it sent a tingling rush through her. His sleeve brushed her arm, and her fingers went thick and clubbish. At one point, he paused, his attention veering to her. "You're worried."

She flushed, not realizing she had been staring over her shoulder at the *Valor*. Nathan's observation came with a slight quivering at the corner of his mouth, as if he was holding back from laughing at her.

"I'm not made for cat-and-mouse." Truth be told, she had

been in desperate need of a distraction, the practicing but a means to keep her hands busy.

"I see you—everyone, for that matter—go into this, like you already know you're going to prevail," she said, her frustration bubbling to the surface.

"No, the shank's too long. Start again." He smiled faintly. "I'm still alive, aren't I? Aye, there is an advantage to be reaped from being the most feared ship in the Caribbean."

"Blood dripping from the sails and deck have to help," she said, working the rope.

"Aye, that and thirty-six guns, deadly accurate, and sharpshooters what can lay nigh on to three barrages a minute. We out-gun and out-man most and the rest are too near pissing their britches at the thought of confrontation."

"Even the Royal Navy?" she asked.

He gave a tight-lipped smile. "They attack only when ordered and with great trepidation at that. The loop goes this way. Start again."

"Ordered by their commander?"

"One Commodore Roger Harte," he announced grandly. Then he cut a sharp look, noticing her twitching reaction. "You're familiar with him?"

"Only by mention on the *Constancy*, and here a few times."

She felt his gaze on her for some time, as one might look for deception or hidden meanings. His lashes, copper-tipped by the sun, were almost golden in the candlelight.

"I get the impression there is a history between the two of you," she prompted.

"Hmm? Oh, aye. History could be a word," he mused. Rubbing the side of his nose, his smile grew more lopsided as he considered. "Running spurt. Difference of opinion..."

"Rivalry?"

Nathan sobered and shrugged. "That too. One does have to admire a dedicated enemy."

"Can he do the same?"

A deep calm befell him and his lids lowered. "Oh, aye."

She looked back over her shoulder. The *Valor's* lights were like a pestilent hovering of fireflies. The *Morganse's* stern lamps illuminated her own wake with a molten golden glow.

"It's not you they seek," he said evenly.

She glanced at him, and then away. "Are you sure?"

He smiled with the patience of a parent with a child afraid of thunder. "As sure as the tides."

Cate shifted, toying with the cord. Nathan frowned at seeing that she wasn't convinced. "Darling, there's no worry. You shan't ever be turned over to him."

She had spent nearly a fortnight formulating a list of possibilities of what his plans might be for her, but so far, nothing. If she wasn't to be turned over for the reward, then what?

He saw her doubt and winced. "In the midst of all this barbarity, luv, a pirate has but one thing upon which to rely: his word. And I give you mine: you shall never be handed over to Harte, nor anyone else. You can mark me on that."

So, touched by his sincerity, she reached for his hand where it rested on his leg next to hers. He jerked away as if seared and launched to his feet. He was nearly to the mizzenmast when Somers, the boatswain's third mate, appeared at the door.

"Mr. Hodder's compliments and duty, sir. We're standing by."

"On to it then," Nathan declared and darted away.

She sat staring in his wake, confused and doubly defeated. It wasn't the first time she had seen him recoil and scamper away for no more reason than her nearness. She might be a widow, but she preferred to think she might still have a little allure left.

"Don't flatter yourself, my dear," she muttered.

No, it wasn't the first time she had seen him race away, but would it be the last, at least with reference to anything she had to do with.

Cate settled to the knot once more, but the cord blurred. Squealing, she pitched it into a dark corner. In pure honesty, her frustration had nothing to do with the rope. Discontent gave way to curiosity at voices coming outside, low and urgent. She went out to find a sizeable cluster of men around a number of empty beef barrels lashed together. Two staffs had been rigged at one end, a lantern swinging from each.

"Silence fore and aft!" It was a wonder how commanding Hodder's voice could be even in no more than a loud whisper.

The makeshift barge was lowered in the ship's lee. A line was fed out, until the breeze caught and it drifted away.

"Douse the lamps," murmured Nathan.

The *Morganse* veered from the barge's path. The sea anchor at her side was cut free, and she shot off on her new course, like a horse given its head.

"Won't they figure out that was just a bunch of barrels?" she asked of Hodder, watching the *Valor* follow what must have looked like the *Morganse's* stern lights.

Hodder smiled faintly, his multitude of ivory rings glinting in the starlight. "Oh, aye. Even if 'tis but an hour, t'will be too late."

He directed her attention to the topsails and jibs, now charcoaled to obscurity. On the moonless night, the black ship would be nothing more than a dark blot on the water's oily satin.

Cate stood amidships. Venus, a diamond low in the sky, was soon blotted out by the jagged edge of land looming near. Uneasiness prickled between her shoulder blades as the islands, the ones they had paralleled all day, came closer. Obviously, Nathan had something in mind, but it was still a worry.

The watch bells were reduced to no more than the rap of Hodder's knuckles on the binnacle. The lead lines were flung, the depths passed aft to the afterdeck by word of mouth. Men stood at the ready at the tacks and braces, should a change be necessary in a moment's notice. A complex system of flashes and waves of watch lamps were employed to direct the helm as the ship tiptoed her way through.

The black spine of land before them eventually split, a passage between two islands showing itself. The land on both sides closed in as they slipped through, the air becoming heavy with the smell of damp earth and rotting vegetation. The breeze brought the howls and cries of night creatures. A hunch-shouldered blur swept overhead, Artemis, taking her leave. The land eventually fell away and the smell of jungle gave way to salt air. The lead lines were stowed as the *Morganse* came hard about and flashed out her sails, their ivory glowing in the starlight.

Cate might not have been much of a seaman, but she had sense of direction enough to know that they had made a U-turn and were now backtracking. The *Morganse* was heading north, judging by Polaris over the forestays, while the *Valor* was assumed to be still on her southerly heading, the string of islands now between the two vessels.

Time. It wasn't always one's friend. Late into the night, Cate laid across the bunk. She didn't bother to undress, for sleep was an unlikely prospect. An ever-so-slight disturbance in the ship's easy motion brought her up from her bed. On deck, she was met with the sight of sentinels of rock on either side. Jagged with palm trees, they towered over the masts. She glanced up to see Artemis roosted on a foreyard.

"Barely a biscuit toss," murmured Mr. Pickford in awed admiration as land slid past. "The Cap'n knows his waters."

"Calypso's hand is in this," said Ogden over his shoulder. The snake tattooed on his head glared down as he canted it toward the bow. "There she is now, a-leadin' us."

Cate looked forward. Indeed, there was a flash of silver, but it appeared more like a cavorting sea hog.

There was another hesitation in the *Morganse's* motion, as her keel brushed the sandy bottom. A bit later, there was a vibration, felt only through a hand on the rail, as she skimmed a reef. Then she shot out into open waters.

"The wind holds," Nathan declared lifting his face. "Master Pryce, let's fly all she will bear."

"Now what?" Cate asked, feeling quite bleary-eyed. Impending dawn was a lavender blush at the line where water and sky met. She had no idea when Nathan had last slept, but his spirits and voice were buoyant.

"The good Captain Prichard awakes to his Officer of the Watch bidding him joy of the morning and informing him of a ship larboard astern. There will be no doubts as to the who," he said with a smug glance toward the red-crowned sails overhead.

"After a certain amount of arguing over coffee as to how we managed to achieve such a commanding advantage, he'll commence to maneuvering for the weather gauge — to windward, to put us in his lee," he explained to her confused scowl. "Toward those islands over there," he added with significance.

Islands had a staggering tendency to all look the same, but those to windward were easily recognized, for they were the same strand she had stared at all day. In the pre-dawn, when the world became one-dimensional, only the gleam of white sand defined their shape. The *Morganse* was where she had been earlier that day, except the *Valor* was now ahead of them.

The mouse had just become the cat.

He rocked on his heels in expectation of her next query. "And then?" she finally asked.

The first rays of the sun broke on his face as he waggled his brows. "All good things come to he what waits."

The *Morganse* flattened and ran like a horse with the bit in its teeth. The song of canvas and rigging was lost in the rush of the water down her sides, her cutwater slicing the deep blue. Her decks took a severe pitch once more. Readings from the log lines were called out from the leeward chains. Ten. Ten and two fathoms. Eleven. Eleven and four. Twelve and three.

Nathan laid aloft on a topgallant yard and there remained. To Cate's mind, there was a grand difference between chase and being chased. Nathan's half-smile and gleeful spark suggested he took a greater joy in the latter, outwitting his enemy as opposed to besting. Some hours later, he slid down a backstay, landing as a fairy might on a toadstool, and said "Sail ho!" with a beaming flash of gold and ivory.

Cate felt pity—only a modicum, but pity nonetheless—for the faceless, hapless Prichard. The *Valor* had to be suffering a certain amount of confusion, if not outright concern, as to how she had kept pace with the *Morganse* earlier, but now was being so handily outpaced. Eventually the *Morganse* was obliged to spill her sails, ever so slightly so that never a shiver nor flogging sail was seen, sure signs of a ship deliberately slowing. Cate was put to mind of that cat having now caught the mouse desired to play with it.

Nathan was in the mizzentop. His attention fixed well ahead of the *Valor*, he called directions down to the helm. The *Morganse* pressed the vessel like a shepherd dog goading an unwitting sheep, the *Valor* slipping farther and farther to windward, in order to gain the favored position.

By then, the *Valor* was near enough that the faces of her people could be seen as they scrambled, her port lids opening. The *Morganse* was astir, too: her boarding party making ready, dispensing weapons, affixing strips of red cloth around heads or arms to mark them as Morgansers, and preparing the boats—which had been stowed aboard at the first sighting of the frigate—to be roused over the side the instant word was given.

Nathan shot down a backstay. "Bow-chasers, if you please, Mr. MacQuarrie. Let's kick 'er in the arse and see if she might be encouraged a little faster."

He stood with his eyes fixed on the chase with a half-smile of anticipation. Something was about to happen and soon. Cate had no sooner stepped up next to him than she saw the *Valor* stop with a suddenness that sent her wake roiling up her sides nearly to her bow. The breeze brought the grind and howl of wood against a hard surface, and then the crackle of shattered rigging. Her topmasts came down on the heads of her people, draping her bow in canvas. One is never aware of the constant motion of a ship until one is seen entirely motionless. An unnatural and eerie sight it was. The *Valor* was hard aground, up by the bow, her deck slightly angled toward the *Morganse*.

In the midst the hands rollicking cheer, Nathan was already down the steps and at the waist, shouting orders along the way.

From behind, Cate heard Pryce make a caustic noise. "Ain't no chart on the earth what shows that shallows, I kin warrant ye that."

The *Morganse* luffed up near enough for an easy pull across to her prey. The *Valor* had no topsail to douse, but a white flag—more like a tablecloth—showed at the aft cabin.

"Away all boats," called Nathan. A resulting splash could be heard from all four corners.

The deck was a mob of men, wild-eyed for battle, surging for the rail. Cate gaped in horror at seeing Nathan tuck a pair of extra pistols into his belt and a wicked-looking knife in his boot. He meant to go with the boarding party!

"You're the captain. You don't need — " she pleaded, grabbing him by the arm.

"Aye, but I do." And he was gone.

In the melee of men pouring over the side and down the nets, Cate didn't see which boat Nathan was in. As they rowed toward the *Valor*, She strained to find him in the scores of heads. And then, she saw him, *the bastard!* He stood like a damned figurehead at the bow of the lead boat, urging his men on.

The boats drew up at the *Valor's* side and were nearly hooked on, when the Valor's muskets opened fire on the unsuspecting pirates. It was a gross violation of a white flag. At the same time, the Valor muskets opened fire on the *Morganse*. Someone knocked Cate to the deck and flung himself over her as musket balls and wood splinters shot past.

After the first barrage, the Morgansers raised their heads to glare over the rail. A roar of protests and obscenities dissolved into the furor of response. MacQuarrie and his gun crews stood in red-faced fury. They didn't dare employ his great guns, not with their mates in the line of fire. They were handcuffed and livid for it. Muskets, already to hand from arming the boarding party, were snatched up, the sharpshooters scurrying aloft.

Cate wound up half-crouched behind the bulwark, wedged between Squidge and *Wido Makr*, as etched near her shoulder on the carriage. Squidge paused in his firing to toss her a cartridge box and kicked a musket to her, for her to begin reloading. She fell quickly into the rhythm of tearing the cartridge's paper with her teeth, pouring the contents down the hot barrel, ramming, priming and cocking. Squidge held out the empty weapon, ready to grab the next, grumbling "Bear a hand! Bear a hand!" when she fumbled. With the steady resupply of cartridges and powder delivered, the barrels soon became so hot, she had to use her apron.

There were none of the rolling gun barrages. This was a battle of marksmen, meticulous picking off, a cry of victory going up at seeing a target fall. The air grew thick and acrid with smoke. Balls whirred overhead like a swarm of enraged bees. Spent balls bounced and rolled about the deck. Amid the continuous splat and crack of lead hitting wood, Cate felt splinters brush her body and tug at her clothing.

Underneath the gunfire, she could hear the clash of hand-to-hand fighting on the *Valor*. Through the disembodied voices bouncing between ships and the cries of the wounded, she strained to hear the one in particular: Nathan's. She felt herself slip back into another time, during the Uprising. It had been Brian she had worried for then. The anguish, smoke, sweat and blood, however, were all the same.

"Hold fire!" It was Hodder, from somewhere farther amidships.

And then, it was quiet, eerily so. A cheer went up at seeing that the Valors had surrendered, their raised hands visible as Cate stood.

The breeze stirred, and the deck cleared. The smoke still hung in grey whorls in protected nooks. The jubilation of victory was brief. The Morgansers set immediately to seeing about their ship and mates. Cate set to seeking the injured and tending the worst. Only a few had been hit, most just grazed. Mute Maori had dug a ball out of the flesh of his massive leg with his rigging knife before she could reach him. Scripps bemoaned the disfigurement of one of his precious tattoos. Several of his fellow topsmen had already offered good-natured suggestions as to how the scar might be incorporated in a new one.

Overall, the mood was relaxed victory. A job done and done well.

Sombers glared at the *Valor* as Cate wrapped his arm. "Praise God that goddamned hulk was straked. The sodding bastard woulda opened his guns else."

Cate glanced toward the *Valor*. Running up on the reef had left the ship leaning at least a strake, nearer to two. The gun ports allowed only a few degrees of variation in their elevation, which meant, if the *Valor* had fired, the result would have only been a great deal of dead fish.

"The spineless fucker was willing to kill himself and take every jack with him, all for the glory of King and Country," came Hodder's voice from somewhere behind her.

"Or endear 'imself," put in Pryce grimly. "Aye, a-coming back dead could be a damn sight better n' comin' back empty-handed, where the Commodore is concerned."

Cate worked to treat the wounded, but her mind was with Nathan. She snatched glimpses over the rail toward the *Valor*, but saw nothing of what was happening over there. She cursed herself for over-reacting. She had sent Brian off to battle with far more aplomb, and he had always come back unscathed... for the most part.

At length, she paused in her labors at seeing the *Valor's* boats being loaded. Piles of plundered clothing, she judged, including flashes of the unmistakable Marine red. Once loaded to the point of near swamping, instead of being brought across, each boat was cast adrift, a torch tossed atop when the wind caught. They trailed away like a column of Viking funerals, their progress marked by curls of smoke.

Another lick of flame appeared, the *Valor's* Union Jack and commodore's banner set afire. The Morgansers jeered and hooted, baring their arses over the rail. The blazing fabric dropped from the *Valor's* poopdeck and floated down, a small hiss marking the flames' death in the water.

Still no sign of Nathan.

Cate snatched a glass from the binnacle and focused on the *Valor's* decks. Its downward angle allowed her a full view. It took her a moment to realize what she was seeing: an entire frigate of men all naked as Adam. Standing so closely packed together, their white bodies looked like maggots wriggling in the sun. She thought she should look away, but their eloquence in indignation was too delicious. Some were almost purple with outrage; they had to be the officers.

Cate scanned the wreck and ruin. It was rather shocking the damage that could be wrought by no more than musket and blade. The dead scattered about was testimony enough. A thin crimson stream poured from a scupper amidships, several triangular fins thrashing in the water directly below.

She flinched.

There it was again, that same stab, like an onset of the gripes. It was like a great fist seizing her gut and twisting.

The great hand of guilt.

It struck after every engagement, at realizing what she was a part of.

Pirates.

Cate couldn't reproach the Morgansers. To blame them would be to blame the hound for howling. She could see them on the *Valor* — easily, for they were the only ones clothed — and their familiar faces, the ones she lived among, the ones she laughed with and mended their bodies, now taunting the defenseless and naked Valors. The bitter taste of revulsion rose in her mouth at seeing the injured and dead had been stripped. The sight called to mind the aftermath of several battlefields. The scavengers picked through the bodies, going so far as to cut off fingers for rings and bashing out teeth for the gold.

And so, regret for what? At what point do you think you could have caused a different outcome?

"What a cold-hearted bitch you've become," she said under her breath.

Too late, my dear. That happened the day Brian left.

There had been no massacre, nor atrocities here, and there

well could have been after such a gross deception. She was no neophyte; she knew what was done in the heat of battle, in war or when fighting for one's life. And fighting for their lives was exactly what the pirates were doing; their blood smeared her apron and crusted her nails. If anything, the pirates had been the ones to fight by the rules.

It was kill or be killed... wasn't it?

The glass grew slippery. She wiped her palms and peered again.

Still no Nathan.

She choked down the fear that tightened her throat at the thought of him lying somewhere, that it was his blood draining to the sea.

Cate cursed Nathan for this damned feud of his. In a moment of honesty, she knew what troubled her: all of this destruction was because of it. This drive to best Harte and Creswicke went far beyond anything she had witnessed, including the Highlander clan wars, which could span generations over a mere patch of land.

Nathan's was a blood vengeance, to be sure. Over what would probably never be hers to know.

"Tut, tut. Oogling are we? What would your mother say?"

Cate spun around to find Nathan standing behind her, grinning, still flushed with the exultancy of battle. Blood spattered his sleeves, and he had a scrape on his chest, but he was whole... blessedly whole. Her heart warmed at the sight of him. She was caught between throwing her arms around his neck with joy and giving him a piece of her mind.

"Where did you...? How did...?" she cried. Then anger won out. "Damn you, you bastard. How dare you go running off like that. You could have been shot... or killed... or..." Her mouth moved like a fish for air searched for words.

Nathan shook his head, jangling his bells, and flipped a braid. "Charmed."

This exchange was made while he spun her about and patted her down, seeking to assure that she was well. He held up the side of her skirt to exhibit a hole, much like that which might have been made by a musket ball. The corner of his mouth tucked up, and he gave her a paternal glare. His displeasure at her failure to find safety deepened at finding another.

"What happened?" she asked, interrupting the berating that was in the offing.

He shrugged and dabbed the sweat from the side of his face. "Everything and nothing. Opened fire on our heads, the dung-souled maggot. Sharks what had been following the ship got those what fell in the water." A bit shaken at that recollection, a disgusted noise related the pursuant carnage.

"I can't believe they fired on you, not after a white flag."

"Pirate." Under his mustache, his mouth took a grim curve. "Nothing so low should reap the benefits of anything so gentlemanly."

"But you…"

Nathan waved her away. "We did no different than every pirate from Bartholomew to Teach: took every shred of clothing. Clothes, tarpaulins, blankets, right down to the hammocks, the table napkins and the cook's apron: we took anything and everything what could be possibly shifted to cover one's arse."

He looked judiciously to the *Valor's* shattered rigging. "'Course the sails remain, but that Number One duck will be blessedly rough on one's bum."

Cate recalled seeing the boats being loaded. "But you —?"

"Burned every stitch." He proudly rocked on his heels. "Allowing the men their pick, of course."

"Of course," she muttered to herself.

"Unlike the aforementioned sea rogues, we left them a boat, dinghy, truth be told. They shan't die of hunger or thirst, although sunburn will be a definite hazard," he said, curbing a smile.

"Won't they wash that off?"

Nathan looked with little remorse at the haloed skull and wings which had been painted on the *Valor's* side, shockingly white against the deep blue hull. "I pity the poor sod what will have to hang his bare arse between the Devil and the deep blue sea to do so."

He shrugged as he turned away. "A week or so, and someone will come looking."

"And Commodore Harte?"

He stopped and turned, his smile broadening. "Will be oh, so very annoyed."

Whoops and hoots of celebration broke out as more men topped the gunwale, returning from the raid.

The celebration was on.

The *Ciara Morganse* was on the prowl again.

8: HAVENS

IF SAILS WERE A SHIP'S heart, then the tar was the *Morganse's* lifeblood. The black goo coated every inch of the standing rigging, the sun's heat often causing it to drip in glob-like rain. In combination with oakum, it was tediously packed between every plank, literally keeping the ship afloat. Tarring consequently was a never-ending task, the smell of tar stoves, hot pitch and loggerheads as prevalent as the sea itself. That same lifeblood, however, in swinging bucketfuls on lurching decks was a hazardous combination. Burns were commonplace.

On tarring days, Cate came to keep the stoneware jar of burn ointment and bandages in a basket at the ready. She knew the high-pitched scream unique to burns. Of all the injuries, she found the burns to be the most difficult to face. Pirates were a stoic lot, but burns often pushed them beyond the pale. Her patient often gone white with pain, herself feeling a peculiar shade of green, she swallowed down the rising bile as she tweezed the raw, seeping flesh clean, applied salve, and then the wrapping.

One such day she heard the familiar scream. Rising instantly, she grabbed the basket at her feet and followed the commotion to her next patient. He sat on the forecastle steps, hunched over his arm, rocking in silent agony. The offending tar had been yanked away, leaving an open oozing blister nearly the size of her palm. With eyes only for the injury, she knelt to inspect, setting the basket next to her.

"I knew eventually I'd have you serving' me on yer knees."

She froze at the voice and looked up into Bullock's scarred face. He saw her surprise and grinned insolently. She ducked her head, intensifying her focus, but could still feel his brooding glare. Resting his arm on his thigh, he didn't extend it as much as he might, forcing her farther between his knees. He groaned and swore, making a large show of his suffering, all the while leaning back, obliging her to come nearer yet. His breath blew hot on her neck. She inched away, but not far enough for comfort's sake — at the taffrail would have been too close. From the corner of her eye, she saw the grimed fingers pluck a lock of her hair from on his leg.

"Hmm! Be yer quim the same color, darlin'?"

She tried to rise, but was stopped by his foot on her skirt. He made no attempt to move it.

Bullock's comment had been uttered loudly enough so that there was no mistake, yet low enough for her ears alone. Glancing around, she saw that he had timed the comment well. A burn was nothing new, this one too minor to draw comment. On a deck filled with men, they were alone.

Cate jerked her hair free of his grasp. Biting back several retorts, she prayed her hands to be steady, determined not to let the bastard think she was afraid of him. Still, she couldn't meet his gaze and he knew it. Over the smell of tar and burned flesh was his reek, a combination of sweat and animal lust.

He bent, his lips brushing the top of her head. "The Cap'n thinks we're over here a-exchangin' love notes."

She shook with the effort to not flinch, carefully measuring what it would take to land an elbow squarely in his crotch. Loath to cause a scene, she refused to play into his game, although she fancied an accidental slip of the tweezers, gouging the raw flesh.

Keeping her eyes fixed on her work, Cate strained to recall where she had last seen Nathan: on the quarterdeck, virtually the length of the ship away. Of course. Bullock wouldn't have had the courage, else. It was a small blessing: Bullock was dangerous in more ways than one. A "goddamned, swivel-tongued, son-of-a-double-eyed Dutch whore" as Pryce had called him, the man was the contagious type. His agitations could spread through a ship faster than wharf fever. Causing a scene, obligating Nathan to take action, could only fan the fires of dissention.

Giving the burn only a perfunctory cleaning — his arm could fester and fall off, for all she cared, the longer and more agonizing the process the better — she fumbled with the jar's cork. She scooped out the mixture of tallow, wax and sweet oil, and took great satisfaction at seeing him flinch when she touched the raw flesh, admittedly rougher than might have been required.

He gave a lewd smirk. "A man can't help but wonder what it would be for those hands to be a-greasin' his cock."

Cate lurched backward, ignoring the sound of her skirt giving way as she stumbled to her feet. The jar crashed to the deck. The hands nearest paused, looking interestedly on as she backed away, rigid. She kicked the cork from the shattered crockery and splattered ointment, hitting Bullock in the shin. Smiling, he regarded her with the cold-eyes of a shark, his leering chuckle echoing behind her as she stalked away.

Her path aft intersected Nathan's as he came forward. She sought to brush past him, but he seized her by the arm, his countenance dark with concern.

"Did he…?" Nathan eyed her skirt and the section of torn waistband.

"No." She jerked away, continuing to the cabin.

"But I saw —" Nathan said, close on her heels.

"No!" she shot back over her shoulder.

"But you look —"

She whirled around, balling her fists. "No!!"

Spinning away, Cate headed for the cabin. Nathan gave chase, but pulled up short when she ducked through the curtain. The shadow underneath the velvet's hem revealed that he lingered. He exhaled loudly enough to make his displeasure evident. In her sliver of privacy, she gave way to a mute tantrum, grunting with the effort of pitching the pillow at the bulkhead again and again.

"Are you well?" came Nathan's voice through the curtain.

"I'm fine," she said between ragged gasps.

There was a fair pause. "It doesn't sound like it."

"I'm fine," she said with far more anger than intended. She took a deep breath, collected herself, and said in careful measure, "I'm… fine."

She heard him draw breath to say something, and then thought better. Grumbling darkly under his breath, she heard him stalk away. Hodder bellowing "Swabbers!" blanketed his footsteps.

Once she was alone, she resumed her fit, swearing to herself colorfully enough to make a sailor proud and her mother appalled. Seething, she paced the tiny space. A part of her screamed she should tell Nathan. An appealing thought, pictures of flogging and keel-hauling coming to mind. Her pride argued it would be too much like running to someone else to solve her problems.

She watched Bullock for several days after, unscathed and as brash as ever. With "No secrets on a ship" echoing in her head, she vacillated between hoping Nathan knew of Bullock's comments and dreading that he did. If Nathan knew, then he might feel compelled to retaliate. That could lead to refueling the mutinous fires, stirring the burning pot called Bullock.

And so, she kept her counsel and lived more cautiously, conscious of not allowing herself in compromising situations: never in the company of just one crewman, never going below or to isolated corners of the ship alone. On a ship with nearly two hundred men, it wasn't difficult. Living in such close quarters suddenly didn't seem such a burden after all.

Besides care-giving, another responsibility was thrust upon Cate one day.

When the *Valor's* stubbed masts had still pricked the line between water and sky, Mr. Cameron, hat in hand, had sidled closer.

He repeatedly cleared his throat. "'Cuse me, mum... sir!" The blunder prompted a more vigorous twisting of his hat.

Clearing his throat again, a tortuous sound. "Compliments, to ye, mum... sir! A word w' ye?"

"Certainly, Mr. Cameron," she said, mildly curious and a lot wary.

"Well, mum... sir!" Eyes downcast, his mouth moved in search of words. "I was recallin', from before, when we wuz marchin' to Stirling."

"...*marchin' to Stirling*..." Caught unawares, the memories those few words brought was like a punch in the gut: freezing weather, hundreds of Highlanders, hungry, trudging toward a battle.

Cate could only manage a wheezing "Yes?"

"Ye can write, sir." The simple observation was tinged with awe.

She blinked at the unexpected turn of subject. "Well, yes, I both read and write." Aside from landed gentry, few women could. She had been taught only through her mother's intransigence.

"I knew it!" He beamed then sobered. "Well, mum... *sir*, I recollected seein' ye at the fires, writin'... for yer husband's men."

"Yes, I remember," she said faintly. She wrapped her arms about herself against a sudden chill. Scores of men, facing battle, fearing it to be their last, had desired to send final words to loved ones. Unable to write, they had come to her. Through the night, she had furiously scratched words of love, last wills and tearful farewells.

"Might ye consider the same... now... perhaps?" Worrying the hat, he looked up with hope and dread.

"You, Mr. Cameron?"

"Aye." Nodding, his assault on the hat's brim intensified. "'Tis been... well, you'll know how long, since... everything..." He left the thought to complete itself. "I've not sent word home since the day we marched."

"Never? Your family hasn't heard from you at all?"

"Wife, mum," he corrected politely. "I had a wife and bairns."

"And you've never sent them word." She gleaned as much accusation from that as possible. After all, it had been nearly two decades since she had heard from her own family or vice-versa.

"No, mum, I kent it was terrible bad of me, but I never..." He shrugged and looked to his feet.

There was little basis to rebuke the man. Given distances, the scattering effect of war, the scarcity of paper, and the cost of postage, not to mention the not so small detail of illiteracy, communication was difficult verging on impossible for most.

"I understand, Mr. Cameron." Now she was the one to look to her feet, in hopes of relieving him of his embarrassment. "Life does have a way of sweeping one off in directions not always anticipated. Will there be someone on the other end that might read?"

Cate politely overlooked the small detail of the cost of receiving a letter. When she had left the Highlands, the widespread poverty had made a spare copper a rare find.

"I'd be pleased to write for you. I'll ask the Captain if he has paper." She hoped inwardly the coffers of the *Ciara Morganse* were rich enough to provide for that.

In Cameron's wake, Cate braced against the scuttlebutt to compose herself. What Cameron hadn't seen during the war were the wounded and the dying for whom she had written. Day and night, crouched in the dirt, she wrote the words dictated through parched lips. Sometimes, the lips ceased moving, and she completed their last thoughts, closing as tenderly as possible, sometimes adding small addendums to inform the family of their loved one's last moments. She had been the final bridge, a solace not only to the helpless, but the distant families, as well. It had been exhausting work and she wouldn't have surrendered a single moment. When weariness burned her eyes and stabbed her shoulders, she drove herself with the single thought that, if the tables had been turned, if it had been Brian dying on a nameless battlefield, what a treasure a last letter would have been.

It was with that frame of reference which propelled her through hours of writing for the Morgansers. An eyebrow twitching with suspicion, Nathan provided paper without comment and presented her a small silver traveling case, which contained a tiny inkwell and a place for quills.

Word passed quickly. Over the next many days, the pirates came to her one by one, sometimes in the light of day, sometimes in the confessional dark of 'tween decks. They dictated, facing her square on, wide-eyed and earnest, or with their backs turned, embarrassed by the sentiments they desired to be put to paper. The words were often the same: reasons and excuses for long absences, exhortations of remorse, longings and well-wishing. Hunched over a crate or puncheon, lantern at her elbow, she wrote — in small tight lines for some, brief singular words for others — to daughters, mothers and wives, sweethearts and sisters, grandmothers and aunts, with a heavy smattering of fathers, brothers, uncles and sons.

One night, after one particularly draining session, Cate returned to the cabin, exhausted. She slumped in a chair and fell into a trance-like stare at the table as she rubbed a hand gone clubbish from gripping a pen for so long. The watch bell had just rung — possibly five times, she thought.

Nathan was at the table already, the golden lamplight crowning his head as he bent over chart and logbook. Drawing his knife from his boot, he sharpened the quill, scrutinizing it several times before it was to his liking. At length, he uncorked the ink, dipped the quill and set to writing against a backdrop of water, wind and the ship's people. The scratch of the quill, the periodic tinkle of silver or scuff of leather when he shifted his feet: such interludes weren't uncommon, the two of them in the same space sharing nothing more than each other's company.

Companionship.

A concept too readily dismissed. It wasn't necessarily a bad word, unless one was to desire more, so very much more. Still, to a soul drowning in desolation, it was a floating bit of flotsam upon which to cleave. She basked in it. In spite of his preoccupation with matters of his ship, it was near enough to having him to herself.

For Nathan, sailing was as compelling as religion. To interrupt his rituals felt a violation of its sanctity. It was a chance to see him in his most natural state, no facades, no pretense. He was pensive and methodical with his log and charts, making entries, checking and rechecking courses. With delicate surety, he walked the brass dividers over the chart in their measured increments. His mouth sometimes screwed aside in deep thought, or moved as if in private conversation as he calculated, his fingers mathematically tapping the surface.

During one such inner dialogue, he looked up from under his brows. They drew together at seeing her flex her hand. Final notes were scratched in the log, sanded and brushed. Closing it, he rose and pulled his chair around so that they sat knee-to-knee.

Nathan took Cate's hand and, cradling it as if it was made of glass, began massaging. She twitched at the uncommon breach of the meticulously maintained margin between them. He ducked his head in apology, thinking he had been too rough. They lived in close proximity like a married couple, and yet without the remotest hint of intimacy. Broaching that perimeter happened, but rarely: when they both reached for the coffee pot, pointing to a spot on a chart or during her knot tying lessons. She tended to start when that happened, drawing back as if burned. While he shied and often bolted, she was left with a tingling sensation as if touched by St. Elmo's fire. All in all, it was doubly surprising for him to be so attentive just then.

"What the hell were you doing?" he finally asked, without looking up.

"Writing letters," she said, wincing.

He made a cross-sounding noise. "You led me to believe t'was only for one or two, not the whole damned complement."

"As I thought... at first."

He rose. With a few adroit flicks, he undid the strip of rag at his wrist which secured the leather palm and tossed both aside. From her blood box, he took the Roman-numerated Number 37 jar of salve and a stoppered bottle of oil. He scooped a bit of salve, added a few droplets of oil, and then dribbled molten wax from a candle into his palm.

"You're not the only one with a few cures," Nathan said to Cate's curious look.

Working the concoction between his hands as he sat, he took her hand once more. Her fingers clawed inward, except the middle one which stuck out at an odd angle. The sweet, earthy scent of beeswax and sharp, resinous of camphor rising between them, he cradled her hand in his and with gentle deftness worked, divining with surprising sensitivity where the soreness lurked in every knuckle and joint.

Nathan's hands were always a fascination, her fatigue rendering them that much more spellbinding. The warm moisture of his breath brushing her forearm suffused her with sensations stirred from a long, deep sleep. It had been years since a man had touched her other than in violence. She flushed with longing and allowed herself to imagine what else those nimble hands might do.

"Let the cack-handed clods write their own," he grumbled.

Caught so far afield, it took Cate a moment to find her tongue. It wasn't worth a reply, anyway. He knew full well the men didn't because they couldn't. This sudden flush of protectiveness was both surprising and touching.

"Why didn't they come to me or Pryce?" he said moodily.

"Because you're men," she said, with the strained patience which came with exhaustion.

"What's that have to do with it?"

Too tired to argue, Cate shook her head, rubbing her temple with a free hand. "They desire privacy."

"You know."

"Because I'm a woman." She looked up to find him grinning. "What?"

The smug grin broadened. "It would appear you've arrived."

She shook a head too fogged by weariness to follow. "Do you ever make any sense?"

Busily massaging, he lifted an unapologetic shoulder and let it fall. "Don't always have to. Sometimes, 'tis easier not, but I am now. Do you not see? The men, they've accepted you; they trust you more than I or Pryce. Bravo, luv. Bravo!"

Blinking, she slogged through senses muddied by long emotional hours: she was no longer a visitor—she belonged. Looking down at the raven crown of his bent head, she wondered in what scheming she had been unwittingly involved, if this turn of events was by plan or hazard.

"You need rum." He rose, leaving her to stare at the wooden surface before her.

"I need something," she said, over him clattering about in the cabinet, "but I don't think it's rum."

"This is a particularly fine brandy." He presented to the squat green bottle as if it was royalty. "If this doesn't fix what ails, then there's no fixin'."

She reached for the glass, only to have a spasm seize her, the glass skittering away. With a pained yelp, she clutched her hand, frantically trying to rub the cramp away. Clucking his tongue as if she were a child, Nathan took it and sat again.

"You're good at this," she said, wincing.

"Years of practice, luv." Intent on his task, his lashes fanned darkly across his cheeks, the sun-bleached tips bright copper in the candlelight. "After hours of sword practice, there were times I couldn't move me fingers to let go. Always had to make me water before, because I couldn't hold me cock to do it after."

She sputtered a laugh. "Well, I suppose that would be a problem, wouldn't it?"

The corner of his mouth took a wry tuck. "You've no idea. Bloody difficult to attend your business with the wrong hand."

Her gaze fixed on his right hand and the fine lacework of scars which webbed it. The last two fingers were unnaturally flat, as if severed, and at an angle acute enough to nick off the outer nail corners. The two middle fingers bore tattoos of small birds, facing each other in flight.

"Are those sparrows?" she asked.

"Nay, swallows. See the tails?" Intent on his ministrations, it was several moments before he added, "'Tis a seafarer's tradition, a larger one after his first ten thousand miles."

A jerk of his arm flipped his sleeve back to display exactly that on his forearm. This one, however, clasped a string in its beak. A heart dangled from the string, impaled by a dagger, the droplets of blood trailing down his arm.

"One gets another for every five thousand miles after," he said, flipping the sleeve back.

"That's a lot of miles," she said faintly, mentally adding up the distances in evidence.

"Lifetime at sea, darling. They're a mariner's symbol for safe travel, of sorts."

She drained the glass, and he refilled it. The brandy was indeed a very good one, deep and mellow, with a tart berry-like undertone. The skeptical side of her wondered why it had taken him so long to bring it out. It was making its presence known, a fortifying ember blooming in her stomach, burning the fog from her head.

Her gaze settled on a braid at his shoulder. It was adorned with a silver bell, one of the score which decorated his hair and mustache. She heard them at his every step and yet had never seen one close. Barely the size of the tip of her little finger, it wasn't a bell in the classical sense, but a clamshell, a tiny pearl the clapper. The surface was tooled with inscriptions far too fine to decipher.

"What?" he asked.

"Hmm? Oh, your bells." Flustered at being caught, she forged on before caution stopped her. "I was once told there was one for each virgin."

"Did you now?" he mused, hooding his eyes. He snorted and shook his head. "Virgins are highly overrated. The ones with a bit more experience are ever so much more agreeable."

Checking himself, he sobered, and resettled to his task.

Dragging her thoughts away from paths that shouldn't be followed, Cate focused on the swallows and strained to recall lore regarding the little birds. Facing each other, as his fingers moved, their beaks periodically touched, as if kissing.

"Don't swallows mate for life?" Cate asked.

Nathan stiffened. His grip tightened, but quickly returned to its soothing ways. Without looking up, he said quietly, "Something like that. Most prefer to think of them as a sign of good luck. To spot one at sea means land is near. Some say when the bearer dies, they swoop down and lift his soul to heaven."

"In the Highlands, they thought swallows carried the souls of dead children back to their mothers."

They both fell quiet, a territory neither wished to explore. Her mother had passed when she was twelve. Nathan had mentioned his only in passing, but judging by his sudden inwardness, he had lost his at a young age as well.

Watching his fingers continue to work their magic to a mesmerizing effect, the birds on his knuckles seeming to flutter, her gaze traveled up his wrists. A woad tattoo ringed both, an intricate chain identical to the one at his throat. His pulse was visible, a surge of life throbbing just under the surface. Hers quickened at the thought, the warm rush in her belly from more than the brandy.

So near and yet so very far.

Sometimes it was almost physically painful.

Cate fought against the urge to close her fingers around his and hold Nathan's hand… just once —

Instead she focused on the rhythmic circular strokes of his thumbs over the sore joints and spaces between. Toughened by years of handling ropes, a captain's life had softened the calluses, leaving them pleasingly abrasive. Her lull was interrupted by an unusually rough spot near the base of his hand, pressing now and again into hers. She watched with mild interest to see what it was…

"You've been branded," she blurted at seeing the raised "S".

"Aye," Nathan said, half-amused by her shock. "What did you think it was?"

"I don't know: a scar or… something." She almost said, "You have so many already," but managed, "May I see?" instead.

"Not much to look at," he said, but extended his hand, nonetheless.

The back of his hand cradled in her palm, Cate lightly traced the "S". Old and well-healed, it stood out, pale and sharp. The leather palm protector had covered it enough for her to think it was no more than another scar. Blockish in design, its head sat at the brawn of his thumb. Most notable was the size. It was more akin to what would befit livestock, reaching well down onto his palm. It was a gruesome sight, her hand reflexively curling closed at the thought of the hot iron touching the delicate skin.

"It's so barbaric," she murmured on a surge of brandy-induced boldness.

"Ancient history."

She gave him a level look. "Ancient history is what they lock away in books. You carry that with you every day. I've seen brandings; they're horrible."

He lifted one shoulder and let it drop. "Not the worst."

"Did you mind?"

"I minded like hell when it was done," he quipped. Brow furrowing, he sobered. "Smelling me own flesh cooking, hearing it sizzle, 'twas the most bothersome."

Shuddering, Cate braced to allow a wave of nausea pass.

"It only lasted a few seconds," he said, unmindful of her reaction. He frowned in vague concentration, slightly surprised by his own recollections. "I don't remember anything after that."

"And now?"

Nathan forced a smile. "Don't think about it much."

"I've seen you rubbing it."

He stiffened. "No, I don't. Aye, well, perhaps a bit, now and again," he added, relenting under her steady gaze.

"How did you come to be branded?" Cate asked, sitting back. In a sense, it was a silly question. Brandings were common for a number of offenses. She mentally ran through the alphabet. A, B, D, F, M, R, T and V: adulterer, blasphemer, deserter, fraymaker, murderer or malefactor, rogue, thief and vagabond. It was a puzzle: "S" was usually reserved for slaves and applied to the cheek, not the hand. Two African members of the crew were proof of that.

Nathan took another drink, closing one eye against the brandy, then stared off to the point she thought that he might decline to answer. They sat with their knees touching, and yet he was so very distant. The candlelight gilded the sharp line of his profile and sparked on the beads in his mustache. From outside came the soft rumble of thunder. A press of freshened wind leaned the ship, and it began to rain.

"I was arrested," he said with great measure. "I broke the law. There was a trial, and they did this."

"Somehow, I don't think it was quite that simple."

The sable-framed eyes widened with discovery. "Can't get much past you, can I?"

Shaking his head and blowing out a long sigh. "I was a merchantman at the time. I'd worked me way up the ranks quickly; I was the youngest to make captain in the Company's history," he added with a bit of boast. "One day me employer took a dislike to me; must have irritated him somehow or another."

He glanced up, and then away. "I was accused of falsifying manifests and smuggling slaves."

"You're the last person I would think would deal in slaves." There were a lot of things she didn't know about him, but of that she was sure. Someone, who treasured his freedom as greatly as he couldn't possibly rob another person of theirs, even if that person wasn't considered a person in many circles.

Nathan snorted. "Not bloody likely. I'd have shot any

bastard I caught at it. The thought of being sold, treated like no more than a piece of livestock, shackled and confined..."

His voice shook with sudden vehemence. The knuckles around the bottle whitened, the cords in his wrist popping out. Realizing himself, he glanced up shyly.

"It was all very neatly arranged. There were bills of sale, paid witnesses and a magistrate whose mind was already made up. A man's word, glowing recommendations from his superiors and years of stellar service were brushed aside. I was found guilty and given this."

Curling his hand closed. The corners of his eyes pinched and his mouth tightened in recollection. Luckily, the body doesn't recall the pain itself, only the memory that it had hurt.

He finally opened his hand to look dispassionately down at it. "Smuggler. I was banished from ever sailing legitimate again. No one would ever trust me with a ship or a cargo, or anything else. I'd be lucky if a captain would take me on as a hand, let alone able-bodied. I had to choose which hell I desired to live: pirate or never sail."

Nathan tipped the bottle for another drink, the ragged scar at his throat a reminder of the perils with which he lived. His shirt gapped, allowing her a glimpse of the banner and "Freedom" etched over his heart and the odd-shaped patch of corroded skin there. It was a vast understatement. For Nathan, freedom was a credo, a way of life no different than the swallows.

Head bent, he pensively gazed at the bottle as he rolled it in his hands. The creak of his belts and the rain pattering on the boards overhead were the only sounds. His shoulders shifted under his shirt, hunched with humiliation.

Shaking himself, as if to rid him of the memory, he looked up with a smile that was but a shadow of its usual brilliance. "Captain Nathanael Blackthorne was born that day and I've been celebrating his life since. That was nigh on to twenty years ago; a ripe old age for a pirate. Captain Nathanael Jonathan Edward Blackthorne," he repeated, as if being formally presented at Court.

"Almost sounds like royalty," Cate mused in an effort to lighten his mood.

He snorted. "King of the Gutters, I was."

Gazing impassively down at his opened palm. "I thought of cutting the thing away. A snick of the knife and I could have had me life back, except..."

"Except that would have made your employer the victor."

Cate's mind shied from the gruesome image, the cold calculation required to take a knife to the tender skin and peel it away. To do so, however, could have meant losing the use of it, rendering him a partial cripple.

Nathan titled his head to regard her. "Sometimes I think you have a touch of the witch in you," he said in wonderment. "You've the sight, to be sure. It's those cursed eyes. There's no hiding from you."

She gently squeezed his arm. "I'm no one to hide from."

"So, it would seem," he said, smiling faintly. "So, it would seem."

A delicate cough drew their attention to the door and Mr. Hallchurch. "Cap'n, Mr. Prythe's compliments and duty," he said, knuckling his forehead. "He begth a word with you on the f'c'stle, at yer pleasthure, sir."

He nodded half-heartedly. "Me compliments to Mr. Pryce. I'll be there directly."

Cate demonstrably flexed her hand as he rose. "It feels much better. Thank you." And in all earnestness, it did, the camphor glowing in every joint.

Taking her hand, he bent to kiss her knuckles, his mustache a soft bristle on her skin. He smiled, one genuine with warmth and charm, and gave a hint of a wink. "Anytime, luv. Anytime."

Cate gazed in Nathan's wake. She was touched that he had lowered the curtain behind which he lived enough to allow her to see his vulnerability. The emotion had been genuine, the story not. It had been told with the ease of the oft-told lie, and yet the anguish and pain had been of a caliber which only reality could spawn. He had allowed her the story, but not the truth. That he couldn't allow.

Not yet.

Once again, the more she learned, the less she knew about the enigmatic pirate captain.

9: THE CURSE O' FRIENDS

IT WAS SEVERAL DAYS LATER that, shoulders aching and fingers cramped, Cate rose from practicing her knots, a failure yet again. Hitches had been added to her expected *repertoire*. The clove came easily enough, but the rolling and backhanded still gave her fits. The function of a hitch being to secure a line to a fixed object, Nathan had provided her a piece of handle from a broken gaffing hook. That now suspended on the arms of a chair, she had worked through one set of bells to the next, through the smoke and roar of gun practice and Hodder's call to mess. Somewhere or another, she was making the same mistake time and again. Squealing in frustration and pitching it across the room had provided no insight as to her error. She told herself the fading light was why she quit, knowing full well it was no excuse by Nathan's measure.

"Should be able to manage any knot in the dark," was his evaluation.

Cate went to find a particular hush had befallen the deck. It was unusual for an hour usually filled with merriment. Like putting a child to bed, the *Morganse* had been made ready for the night: courses and royals gull-winged, mizzen tops and topsails reefed, course posted on the traversing board and grog dispensed. She looked to the forecastle where the men usually gathered, but it was empty.

Instead of gathering on the forecastle, as was the custom, the men were clustered before the capstan. Seated, crouched and sprawled, their upturned faces were transfixed on the single figure atop it. Legs dangling, a lantern to one side and a bottle on the other, Nathan sat on the hub with a book in his lap. His roughened gravel voice was lowered into the rounded tones of an orator as he read aloud, adding his own subtle inflections to the prose. Hermione looked on as a benignly interested bystander, or rather, a sea lawyer, comfortably ensconced on Cate's forecastle seat.

The lamp's molten halo gilded the line of his profile and glinted on his rings as he reverently turned each page. The contrast of two worlds colliding in this one man was startling: an educated barbarian, cerebral and complex cocooned in ruthlessness and mayhem, a legend as a means to survive. He caught sight of her from the corner of his eye and stumbled over a word. Clearing his throat, he bent his head with renewed focus.

The end of the session was punctuated with a muffled thump of the book closing and scattered groans of disappointment. Cate hung in the shadows until all had dispersed.

"So," she said quietly, leaning against the capstan at Nathan's knee, "the insensate, scurrilous pirate reads...?"

"Defoe." Nathan held up the volume in exhibition and loudly cleared his throat. "*Robinson Caruso.* 'Tis a favorite."

Cate took the book and thumbed through the pages. "A man snatched away, marooned, yanked from one world to be rudely thrust into another." She looked up, arching an inquisitive brow. "Any parallels?"

"It's a good story," he said, examining his hands in his lap.

"Survival under adverse conditions, rising to overcome all odds, mastering of a world, is always a good story."

He considered as she turned the pages. "One you have heard often?"

"Only on rare occasions," she said with a level look. "Usually, it's of someone of remarkable instincts and a sharp mind. A person of those traits is to be admired."

The umber eyes searched hers carefully for hidden meaning or innuendo. Finding none, Nathan snatched up the bottle at his elbow and took a drink. "Hardly. All I have done is gotten by, with a little help now and then. What of you? You've been abandoned, marooned in the middle of London, surviving the unsurvivable."

"That was London," Cate said, declining the proffered bottle. She had been no more than one more maggot in the festering carcass known as London. It had been Hell, but nothing compared to what he must have lived, the scar at his throat and the brand on his arm testimony enough.

"'Tis easy to be alone in the middle of a crowd," he countered. "You've been taken from what you know, thrown into what you don't. You've adapted, made a life."

"I had brothers; it was easy to fit in here." Uncomfortable with the subject being on her, she waved him away, a gesture alarmingly similar to one she had seen him use a score of times.

"I was speaking of you, Nathan. Somewhere you lost your world, didn't you?"

Now he was the one uncomfortable. Leaning on his hands, he watched his swinging feet with exaggerated interest. "There are no secrets with you about, is there?"

Cate bent nearer, waiting until several hands passed before continuing. "You've lived elbow to elbow with people you're whole life, and yet you've kept yourself so hidden you don't even recognize yourself sometimes."

The corner of Nathan's mouth tucked up wryly. A shoulder lifted and fell in a half-shrug. "There are times I am required to pause and recall how I came to be... like this. 'Tis a shorter trip than you might imagine," he added judiciously.

"Do you like being a pirate?"

"I've learned to," he said examining his tar-stained fingers.

"That wasn't my question."

He looked up and smiled widely — a little too much so — and swept a grand hand. "Why wouldn't I? Freedom. Me ship. The sea..."

The breeze tugged at the opening of his shirt to reveal the tattoo over his heart: "Freedom", soaring swallows on his arms and fingers, symbols for the thousands of miles traversed and bare knuckles reserved for milestones to come. Those, plus the intensity which filled his eyes, left little else to be said.

"You could have all that as a merchant," she said.

Nathan sobered quickly. "That would be to exist at someone else's pleasure."

"And you aren't at their bidding?"

Cate inclined her head to indicate the men now gathered on the forecastle, tuning their fiddles. Hermione regarded them balefully from her adopted perch. Apparently preferring solitude to serenade, she rose, paused at the steps to file a verbal complaint, and then clopped down.

He winced, conceding her point. "Allow them a bit of plunder and blood, and they'll follow nigh anywhere."

"And you prefer that?"

"I can live with it. I *have* lived with it," he added with a note of victory.

"What if someone was to come along and tell you it could be another way?"

"What if someone came along and said you could have your life back?" he shot back with equal evenness.

Now she was the one to wince. "I'm not sure I'm that same person anymore," she said, brushing at a non-existent spot on her skirt. There was no advantage in pondering such nonsense, for it was never to come to pass.

"No more than I," he said complacently.

"Would it be so long of a jump to go back to what you were? I mean, pray don't misunderstand. I'm not saying there's anything wrong with what you are—"

"A pirate?" he asked, dryly.

"It's not necessarily a bad word," she was quick to add. "It's more a matter of how you see yourself. Do you want to be something else?"

"Would I?" His legs kicked faster while he considered. "The question is more: could I?"

Alighting to the deck, he strolled to the weather main chains. Bracing his elbows on the rail, he lifted his face into the breeze. An updraft lifted the tails of his headscarf and strands of hair, and wafted them about his shoulders. Cate leaned against *Wido Makr* beside him, the iron cool through her skirt. He stared sightlessly into the night, the wind pressing his shirt to his chest.

"I've been at sea a long time." Nathan's graveled voice bore the agedness of Millbridge. "It's a rough world out here; I've seen things and done more. It changes a man."

Strolling aft, Hermione paused to eye Nathan, and then came to nudge his hand.

"See Mr. Hodder, you seed of Satan," he said without rancor to the goat. "You'll not have your tobacco or grog until the First Watch is rung, and you know it well."

With what might be called a goat's version of a dirty look, Hermione turned and left in eloquent disappointment.

"Always have a care with that ruddy beast," Nathan said to the goat's receding backside. "She takes advantage at every turn. Indulge her too soon, and then she dupes someone else into another. Before you know it, you've a drunken goat staggering about. Gives the men cause to think they can take the same advantages."

"You're ignoring my point," Cate said evenly.

The corner of one eye twitched with discovery. He twisted one ring, his brows knitting. "Some say every man is a barbarian, only civilization and the fear of God what keeps it caged. Others claim we're all good in the beginning, evil being but the result of bad choices."

Nathan looked up, the dark eyes troubled. "But can one see that bad choice and then go back?"

He reached into his pocket and pulled out a length of cord. She inwardly groaned. It had become a custom—and a very annoying one, by her reckoning—for him at odd times to produce such a piece, announce "You need practice" and dropped it into her lap. He could be as tenacious as a terrier. To her relief, he began to work the piece himself. A good portion of it had already been worked into something like an intricate chain in a pattern very similar to the tattoo which collared his neck. His fingers moved with a sureness which rarely required him to look down, the show-off.

"Some claim atonement, an 'I'm sorry' in some form or fashion is sufficient to return one's purity," he said. "But does that erase the barbarian or just slap him in irons, until next he escapes? And what of the deeds he's done: the lives taken, the wreck and ruin? Are those undone? Do the dead live? Does a hacked limb return?"

Nathan made a derisive noise. The bells in his hair rustled as he manipulated the cord faster, the swallows on his knuckles fluttering almost to the point of taking flight.

"One would have to be a rather calloused lout to think an 'I'm sorry' is going to set any of that aright. It strikes me 'tis a matter for the powers what be, or whose god you die under," he said.

"You think there's more than one?"

"I think everyone believes theirs is the only one. Beyond that, we don't know and no one is sayin'. A well-kept secret, to be sure. I've seen more religions than there are lands to count. Hell, there's probably a score represented right here on this deck. And they all have one thing in common: they think their god is the right and only one."

He fell broodingly quiet. A fiddle and hornpipe broke into a jig on the forecastle, while others clapped and whirled, their feet pounding the boards in great glee. "

A man draws his sword and sees the Devil within, and the horror what can be wrought by his own hand." Intent on his hands, he didn't look up. "The smell of the kill does things, hardens you, makes you unfit for the company of no one other than those who have smelt the same."

Such soul-searching rarely came easy for anyone. Brian battled much the same. Like Nathan, intelligent and educated, he had been compelled by circumstances to commit violence and mayhem. For Brian, it had been clan wars and French kings, but the effect had been the same: a blooded sword and haunted by the eyes of the dead staring back.

She recalled well Nathan's rant in St. Agua, flaring at her for suggesting he might violate the virginal daughter of the town's mayor. She understood now that his anger at St. Agua had not been aimed at her, as she had thought, but at himself.

"So, you don't think you can put the genie back in the bottle?" she asked.

Nathan's head came up at that. The gold of his smile glinted in the lamplight. "Oh, so you've heard those tales as well."

"A few, when I was a child," Cate said, determined not to be diverted. "There is more *civilized* in you than you think."

He brought his face to the wind. Closing his eyes, he inhaled deeply. "I've killed men, many men; more than I care to list. I've hacked and bludgeoned, and shot and beaten…"

He bit his lip, shying from completing the thought.

"There is a Hell, you know," he said conversationally. He glanced from the corner of his eye. "Have you ever thought about what it is?"

The question was posed as one not intended to be answered. Nathan tapped his chest over his heart. "It's right here. It's a Hell of one's own making and there is no Hell like the one you can provide for yourself. Dante's Inferno held nothing compared to the tortures a man's own soul can provide. There were no flames, unless of course, burning is what you fear most."

"You don't think of Heaven?"

He smiled grimly. "I've seen nothing to prove it to be no more than a pipe dream. Pirate, darling," he said gesturing toward their general surroundings. "St. Peter has no place for the likes of us. One such as yourself need not worry about Hell, for such a place would never befall one as pure as you."

"I'm hardly pure," she scoffed under the singing on the foredeck. "I've slashed, killed, shot-"

"Aye, and all for the purest of reasons."

He gazed at her with startling gentleness. "There is no horror in you, darling. You're not capable. One is not a monster if driven by monstrous deeds. That's survival and 'tis what we are put on this ol' Earth for."

"And you?"

"I've a list of wickedness a dozen times over and all for the worst of reasons: I exist because I must. A better man would have found another way."

"And die in the process?" She pointedly looked toward his hand and the "S" branded there. "You had few choices."

"Aye, but choices nonetheless." He looked dispassionately down at his hand. "I could have cut the thing away and be done with it."

"But you said that would have been a victory for the man who put it there. That kind of resentment and hatred turned inward can be an ugly thing. I've seen it," she added to his skeptical look. "As you said, all that doesn't make you a beast;

it makes you a survivor. How much of that was done because if you didn't, they were going to do it to you?" she pressed in the face of him attempting to wave her off.

The corner of Nathans mouth tucked up grimly. "Most of it."

"And how much of it did you do because you enjoyed it?"

He snorted, looking away. "None of it."

Cate shifted closer, ducking her head to catch his eye. "The savage can't recall a single face of his victims; the decent is haunted by them all. The truly wicked man wouldn't give any act a second thought. That you worry is proof you're not."

He was a man who could hide every thought, and yet a series of thoughts could be seen crossing his features. There was the flicker of discomfort at having a well-kept secret discovered, and then the wonderment of how she could have known. Next came awe of her insight. And finally, acceptance, with a bit of redemption, in knowing he wasn't alone.

"Pipe down!"

Cate jumped at Hodder's bellow, calling the men to their hammocks. There was no pipe *per se*, but the effect was the same. Those on the forecastle gathered their instruments and filed past. The men on watch were about, but occupied elsewhere. The two of them were alone as could be on a ship of nearly two hundred.

Nathan stirred from the thoughts into which he had retreated. "Are you saying I should go back...to the *real world*?" he asked, with a mocking roll of his eyes toward the distant civilized world.

"No," she said evenly. "In many ways, it's more treacherous there than here. I've seen lying, cheating, betrayal, blackmail, rape, stealing and treason, and all by *civilized people*, often with titles. Pirates are more civilized than many back there in their salons and parlors. All I am saying is: if you're unhappy, there are choices."

The knotting paused as he leaned an arm on the rail and gazed at the night. At one point, he glanced toward his hand, where the brand laid unseen. His gaze shifted to fingers curved around the knotwork and the images of the swallows across his knuckles, all the while glancing from time to time at her from the corner of his eye. The corner of his mouth tucked wryly, and he straightened, decision made.

"If I have to face Hell itself and twice a day to have what I have now," he said, his gaze intent on her face, "then I'll keep it the way it is and say, 'Thank you, very much.'"

He held up the cord between his hands, the lantern light bright on his smile. "There."

The cord had been converted into a delicate necklace. A

pendant-like knot anchored the center, the looping sides almost lacy. An identical, but smaller knot made the closure.

"It's exquisite. Where did you ever learn to do that?" Cate cried.

"Years on a ship, luv, several of which were spent on the spice routes. Here, turn 'round."

"It's for me?" Flattered and baffled to near speechlessness, she did so, lifting her hair out of the way.

Passing it around her neck, he worked with the closure for some moments. Finished, his hand lingered at the curve of neck.

"Let's see how it answers." He turned her back to face him and re-arranged the center decoration. "It looks fine. This is a Chinese knot for good luck."

"I notice you're not wearing one."

"No need." He gave his head a quick shake to jangle his bells and then touched the tattoo at his neck. "I've plenty of me own charms."

"I love it." She anxiously felt for the pendant. It hung just below the notch of her collarbone.

"Wet it a few times to tighten the knot and it will never come off—unless you desire it, of course," he quickly added.

"Never!" It was her first gift in years.

She kissed him on the cheek, the impulsiveness embarrassing them both.

"Thank you, Nathan. You're a true friend," she said, her cheeks heating.

Nathan's smile faltered and then faded. His reply went forgotten as he stiffened. His head came up like a hound on a scent. His hand went to his sword as he stepped before her, pushing her back against the bulwark. The space between the gun carriages was now a small fortress, Nathan poised at its entry.

Cate strained to listen, trying to fathom what it was he had heard. Nothing. Wind, water, block and canvas: only the *Morganse* spoke. Her humanity, however, had fallen uncommonly mum.

Pryce loomed out of the darkness. "D'ye hear it?" he asked in a hoarse, urgent whisper.

He nodded, his head still canted. Waving Pryce aft with his sword, a mouthful spoken in a single gesture. Pryce nodded gravely and faded away. Nathan turned for the bow, but stopped, of two minds whether to leave her there or take her with him. Decision made, he took her by the arm, a twitch of his mustache bidding her quiet.

Up to the forecastle and down, then working his way aft, he cruised the deck without so much as a footfall or bell tinkle. She pressed her skirt against her legs, the mere rustle of the fabric seeming to shatter the stillness. The people they passed hooded their eyes, fixing their attention on whatever they were doing. They had heard it too—whatever it had been—and made every effort to appear otherwise.

Aft of the capstan, they met up with Pryce. Hodder was now with him, a bludgeon in his fist, his multitude of rings as silent as Nathan's bells. Nathan angled his head ever so slightly in question, the pair's almost imperceptible shake of the head his answer.

Nothing.

Cate ventured to whisper to Nathan "What was it?"

The corner of his eye drew down at her ignorance.

"Round shot." Spoken so lowly, it was more a matter of reading his lips than hearing.

She did recall hearing the hollow rumble of a cannonball rolling.

"'Tis the message of conspiracy," Nathan added.

"The goddamned, yellow, lurking, lump o' roguery. A scug of a beast o' the two-legged, back-biting kind what doesn't have the balls to show his face." The starlight caught the hatred which glittered in Pryce's eyes.

"'Tis meant either as warning or announcement that something's afoot," Nathan said with considerably more reserve.

"Something?"

Her puzzlement brought a sharp look from the corner of his eye. Of course, how could she be so dense?

Mutiny.

The shot garlands lining the bulwark between the guns were always full, ready to hand for battle, but also for someone who, under the cover of darkness, wished to set one on its way. The air on her arms raised and her neck prickled. The so very familiar deck suddenly became a forbidding jungle. Shadows she could have earlier named were now possible lairs for predators, every creak impending assault.

"You've a knife?" Nathan asked.

She nodded, touching the side of her skirt.

"Good. Go find your best," he said to Pryce and Hodder. "Arm and post them. You'll find me in me cabin."

The tone of his voice suggested he wouldn't be lounging about reading, nor playing draughts.

The three exchanged significant looks. None of this had come as unexpected. Pryce and Hodder sketched a salute and set off. Nathan guided her inside.

"Sleep well," he said urging her around the curtain and to her bed. "'Tis naught to be worried about."

It was worth noting his pistol was still in hand. Another,

seized from its hiding place inside the urn at the door, was now stuffed in his belt.

Cate stood staring at the curtain, once again in stunned wonderment of Nathan's ability to understate.

Sleep came... finally, in fitful bursts. Cate jerked awake at every creak of a block or plank, slap of a wave or heavy tread. Daylight came at last by way of the port overhead distinguishing itself from the bulkhead. Its square of light on the floor progressed from a thin grey to lavender, to pink, to coral, and then finally the glow of full day.

Gray and grave, Pryce and Hodder gave their captain their morning reports while she and Nathan were at the table. Nothing notable. Nothing remarkable. Nothing to portend. The round shot, however, had not set itself rolling.

The tension was palpable. The hands smiled, but not as readily, their laughter sounding forced. There were no robust hails from the tops or forecastle. Everyone suffered a tendency to jump at routine noises: a rigging knife or marlinspike dropped, a bucket kicked over, or the scuttlebutt dipper hitting the deck. As Nathan, Hodder and Pryce went about their duties, their voices were louder and more imposing, Hodder's reaching bone-rattling proportion. The trio moved in an ever-shifting triangulation. If one was aft, the other was forward, another amidship. It couldn't be missed that this orchestration included one of them always within a few paces of wherever she happened to be.

Feigning interest in anything, Cate found herself examining each face from the corner of her eye, in search of clues as to who the conspirators might be. It was altogether disquieting to think the ones now smiling and knuckling their foreheads as they passed could have been the perpetrators. The ship suddenly became a very small space.

No accusations were made, but neither were there inquiries, for Nathan knew the effort would be wasted. Behind every carefully blank face could lie the truth, but only a lie would be his answer. Nathan was eloquently familiar with the watch lists and duty rosters. He knew who would have been on deck, who would have had the opportunity. She had the impression he strongly suspected who the conspirators were, but was disinclined to act... yet.

She watched Nathan go through his paces, the Master of Denial on stage once more. There was a secondary discomposure, however, another burden which Nathan carried. It was most evident when she was in close proximity, but it wasn't until that night that she was to discover its nature.

Cate woke with a start.

After Bullock's comments, she was prone toward waking at the least noise. She wasn't sure how long she had been sleeping. It was late enough for the moon to have risen, its icy-blue shaft slicing the cavernous dark.

She heard again what had wakened her: footsteps and rustling in the salon. She rolled on her side to see a thin band of light squeezing underneath the curtain. The noise was perplexing; at that hour, Nathan was usually much more discrete. It could have been Pryce. The Captain's cabin was public domain on a pirate ship, but it was rare for anyone to avail themselves upon the privilege. A swish of bells, nearly obliterated by the commotion, announced it was Nathan, although the cadence of his step was unrecognizable. His boots scuffed to a stop. There was the soft *pop*! of a cork being dislodged from a bottle, followed by the slosh of liquid and an enthusiastic gulp. Whoever it was needed a drink badly.

The pacing resumed. Growing more animated, it spiraled until its orbit centered before the curtain. She wondered if the performance was meant to draw her out or if Nathan was too preoccupied to realize where he was. Finally, the boots stopped, the toes protruding under the velvet.

There was the canvas-like rip of a throat clearing, as if there was a chance she would have slept through the preceding performance.

"Madam, I desire an audience, if you please," called Nathan in uncommon formality.

Her curiosity dampened by trepidation, she rose, shrugged the quilt over her shoulders and went to meet her summons.

Nathan fell back a step, apparently surprised that she had done as he bid. He ducked a rigid bow and beckoned her to the table to sit. With little reason to decline, she did. The fact that he was disturbed by something, and that something had to do with her was eloquently clear. If he had been a cat, his hair would have been standing on end. As it was, it roiled about his shoulders like a tangle of snakes.

He took another drink from the bottle clutched in his fist then, as an afterthought, thrust it toward her. "Drink?"

She eyed the proffered bottle warily. "Am I going to need it?"

"Mebbe." For as expressive as Nathan could be, he also could be maddeningly opaque.

Heeding the less than subtle warning, she took the bottle. Hesitating—God! She hated the stuff—she braced and took a sip.

He took pleasure at her ensuing shudder. Jerking a terse nod, he set to pacing once again.

"Madam, there has been a calculated attack on me character, a scurrilous and grievous affront of which I cannot abide."

She had seen magistrates conduct business with less officiousness. His formality was wholly uncharacteristic and not a little disquieting, but she kept her features carefully arranged as unobtrusive and attentive as possible.

"There have been a number of matters that have come to me attention which demand being addressed. Firstly, there was the unfortunate scene with me bunk."

Now frowning slightly, she strained to follow his train of thought. It finally came to her: a few days after her arrival, he had caught her dragging it outside. In her own defense, it had looked suspect and smelled worse; she had only wished to air it. It hadn't occurred to her at the time, but in retrospect, she could see how he might have taken offense.

Her attempt at an apology was cut off.

"And then, there was the matter of the decks, in me *own* cabin, I might add."

She harbored less guilt for washing the cabin floor. It had looked dirty, her intention to be useful.

"I'll not have you slaving about like some scullery maid!" had been his comment at the time, and with only a small amount of discussion, she had agreed to resist such impulses in the future.

Nathan pivoted to jab an accusing finger so squarely at her nose she ducked. She didn't think he would deliberately hurt her, but given his mood, miscalculations came easily.

"And then there was the matter of the hammocks," he said in a war-like declaration.

"They were stained, and they smelled," she shot back before she could stop herself.

"They are washed *every* Wednesday, each man being responsible for his own."

In a rising heat, she wondered whether he was upset over the disruption of routine or that she had robbed the men of the opportunity to do it themselves.

"Am I being disciplined?" she said, ruffling. "If so, then put me off at the next port. I had no wish to be such a burden."

"Hold your course and speed. You shan't slip from under this so easily... and I've only begun!" Settling his shoulders, he continued. "And now, out of the blue, without provocation or warning..."

His mouth moved wordlessly, unable to utter the words.

Surrendering, he stood over her and glared down his nose. "I demand you explain yourself!"

"Excuse me?"

"Did you mean what you said?"

"I don't know." Baffled, she pressed her fingers to the bridge of her nose. "I didn't... I mean... What are...?"

"You called me a friend. A friend, mind. What the bloody hell did you mean by that?" Vibrating with acrimony, he commenced pacing, the rum geysering from the bottle.

"That was yesterday," she sputtered.

"Ah-ha! Exactly! Thought you could drop that stinkpot and it would go unnoticed?"

Her first reaction was to laugh, but thought that unwise; he didn't seem of a mind to be dallied with. She wished she knew him better, that she might more accurately read his moods and swings.

"If you had called me an ass or a sottish bugger or a dutch-faced princock, I would know how to respond to that. Or even if you'd slapped me face, at least I'd know what I'd done, but this... *this!*" he cried as he stormed about, the scarf jouncing at his knees.

Nathan stalked the room, spewing a black tirade in a rapid succession of languages. Her neck grew stiff with visually following his circuitous path. Married to a Scot and living in the Highlands had given her a thorough education in dealing with tempers. Unless bodily harm was eminent, riding them out as invisibly as possible was usually best. Eyes down, she folded her hands in her lap.

"A stab to the heart, that's what it is, and goddamned uncivil to boot. Friend! *Tach!!*"

He took a drink and then an angry swipe at the air. His shoulders jerked, elbows working at his sides. "I'm not alone on this, be assured. I've conferred with Pryce and he concurs. Blessed unseemly! I'll have you know, madam, I am a pirate and under no circumstances does that allow — nor come with the expectations — of my being a friend to *anyone!*"

She turned her head to cover a smile that couldn't be suppressed. It was endearing — another term she was confident he wouldn't appreciate — that he was so upset. She was beginning to regret what had only been best intentions, but those often went unrewarded.

Pacing Nathan slowed to a few measured strides. Timed to punctuate each word, he ticked his points off on his fingers. "I've been nice. I've been cordial. I've made polite conversation.

Hell, I even gave you me bunk. I haven't shouted or called you names —"

"Well, there was that one time..."

His lip took an ugly curl. "You were cleaning, madam. Cleaning, mind you. You had to be stopped. This is a first you know," he said, narrowing an accusing eye. "I have never had a woman call me anything so vile or the likes of this in me entire life!"

He stopped in mid-stride and rolled his eyes, striving to recall. "Nope. Never!" he said, with a definitive thump of his fist on the table that made her jump. "It defies all logic. Damn perplexing creatures, women. Incomprehensible!"

Nathan continued to storm the room. "If you've a complaint, woman, then out with it. We fancy ourselves as running a civil ship. We might be pirates, but we don't go a-name calling just because it suits our fancy. We've a Ship's Council; file your complaints as any worthy sea rover would."

Throwing himself into his chair, he slouched, his outrage fading to resignation. "I've known a vast number of people in me life," he said, as if that fact was of relevance.

Given his acrimony, it seemed unwise to now attempt to discuss the very thing that had set him off. Not everyone appreciated an examination of something so personal. And yet, he was so bereft she couldn't sit in silence. Sensing it safe, she picked up the chance to possibly defend herself, or at least mollify a bit of his pique.

"How many were friends?" she asked carefully.

He slid down farther to prop his boots on the table. "What is this 'friends,' anyway?" Posing the question as if it were a condition or disease, certainly not something to be sought.

She closed one eye in thought. Her first urge was to mock him: anyone knew what it meant. Considering his life, however, it was possible he had never enjoyed the opportunity. Pirates. Treachery. Bloodshed. Killing. Mutiny. Raid. Kill. Plunder. Hardly fertile ground.

"Umm... trust?" she said.

Making a scorn-laden noise at the back of his throat, Nathan rolled his eyes. "Bloody little o' that... and dwindling each day." He slid a cutting look at her that quelled any doubts as to what he meant.

He fell quiet, the dry rasp of his thumb brushing back and forth across the brown glass the only sound.

"Two, mebbe three," he said at length. He seemed a bit surprised by the revelation, but it was unclear if it was because there were so few or that there were that many.

His boyish innocence was heartbreaking, for someone who had lived elbow-to-elbow virtually his entire life, and yet could count less than a handful as trustworthy.

It was possible that his standard for assigning such status was higher and was affronted by her having assigned it so cavalierly. She had assumed it would be taken in the same way as she had intended. She had been without connection for so long—no husband, no family, no home... no friends. She had found a raft in a sea of loneliness and she clung to it, joyous for that small bit of salvation.

"If you like, I'll take it back," she said.

"What will that accomplish?" he asked, sulking. "Can't unring a bell."

"*Dong!*" she said brightly in a pitiful mimic of a bell. "There, see: undone."

The end of his mustache reluctantly lifted, the familiar humor returning to his eyes. "That easy, eh?"

The storm had passed. Like those of the Caribbean, his anger boiled in, raged and crashed, and then departed with nothing more than a faint rumble.

She rose and lightly laid a hand on his shoulder. "Rest assured, the word has been stricken from my vocabulary. You'll never hear it again. Do we have an accord?"

Nathan smiled with considerable relief and lifted the bottle in salute. "Agreed."

She bent nearer and said in a loud whisper, "Be assured, however, good Captain, this by no means implies that I shall be changing my opinion."

Flourishing the quilt as if it were the royal robes, she strolled back to the sleeping quarters. From behind her came the sound of Nathan taking a drink and a rumbling groan.

"Bloody woman!"

10: MASTER OF ARTS

AS MEMBERS OF THE BRETHREN of the Coast, equality for the men of the *Ciara Morganse* came in many ways: equal voice in affairs of piracy and equal shares in the resulting plunder, as well as equality in choosing who was to lead them through it all. Daily, Cate came to understand the delicate balance Nathan maintained as captain. The volatility of commanding pirates raised its head with startling abruptness one morning.

The day had started with Cate waking from one of those sleeps so deep it took her several moments to collect where she was. She laid snuggled deep under the quilt. Blinking the drowsiness away, she listened to the ship and her people slowly come to life, as would any household.

The *Morganse* stirred from her slumber and shed her nightclothes of reefed sails. She stretched her arms with her fresh wardrobe of canvas and leaned into the wind with renewed intent. The water at her sides slipping faster, she picked up her daily song of wind and rigging. The holystones were next, cleaning Mr. Hodder's sacred deck. Starting at the forecastle, the hollow growl of the great blocks of sandstone gradually increased as their handlers inched their way along on their knees. Directly behind came the thump of the pumps and gush of water. Next, the rhythmic slap of the decks being flogged dry.

Pryce and Hodder could be heard above it all. Pryce's exact words couldn't be made out, but there was no mistaking his thrust: some poor soul found slacking. As boatswain, Hodder required a voice which could carry from bowsprit to taffrail, topmast to bilges. What he might have lacked in Pryce's resonance, he made up admirably for in volume and all around a nearly fist-sized quid of tobacco in his cheek.

From the salon came footsteps, a vehement curse—Kirkland's, by the sound—followed by a heavy stomp and a simultaneous high-pitched squeal of a rat meeting an inglorious demise.

Very soon after, she heard the soft padding and snuffle of His Lordship, considerably more industrious in his task. Whether it was for appearances—lest he appear laggardly in his duties—or spurred by hunger—having been robbed of his most recent meal—Cate couldn't tell.

The bell clanged—eight times, she thought. Hodder bellowed the men to breakfast with sufficient force to spring Cate from her snuggery. She dressed to the slap of bare feet as the hands hurried to their meal.

Artemis, roosted on the back of the captain's chair, looked up from her preening when Cate rounded the curtain. It was an unusual sight, for the hold was customarily the owl's preferred place.

"I suppose this means the rats have all moved up."

Cate automatically checked along the walls and corners. She had lived in places far more infested, where one was awakened by feet tracking atop them. Still, it didn't mean she liked having them about.

Artemis regarded her with a baleful reserve and then lifted a wing to continue preening.

Through the expanse of gallery windows, the Caribbean morning stretched before Cate. It was the picture of perfection, so long as one had a great appreciation for blue skies, billowing white clouds, dazzling sun and vast stretches of indigo water. It was a far cry from the clouds, drizzle and fog of the Highlands. There the only variety was the degree of chill and damp. Far behind her were the round-backed mountains and stretches of pine forests, tumbling burns and sea-like expanses of moors. The smells of peat, heather and pine, always sharp in the air, had been now replaced by tar, canvas and salt.

The ship's wake streamed white against the deep blue sea. Noting clouds on the horizon, impaled by an island's mountaintops and heavy with rain, she checked for the wind: leeward, downwind, and hence no threat.

"Beginning to feel like an old salt," she said, smiling to herself.

As always, coffee waited. It was the mystery of the ages as to how Kirkland foresaw her arrival, for the pot was always steaming, to the point of perilous to the unsuspecting. The porcelain cup and creamer might have been chipped, and the silver spoon a bit tarnished, but they were always there, carefully arranged, waiting. Almost at the same time that she noticed the honey pot and extra plates, the smell of scones baking rose up the galley companionway.

Cate settled in for her next routine: steaming cup of coffee in her hand, leaning back in her chair, and listening to the ship come alive.

At the sound of feathers, Cate cracked one eye open in time to see Beatrice arrive. Alighting on the chair next to Artemis, the parrot set to a raucous outcry of indignation. She considered Nathan's chair her private domain and voiced a piercing shriek of objection. Artemis looked benignly at Beatrice, and then to Cate. Finding no sympathy or reprieve, she flew away in an almost silent beat of feathers. Beatrice assumed the sacred spot and, puffed with satisfaction, struck a noble pose.

Peace restored, Cate closed her eyes once more. The ship hummed with increasing industry. A skeleton afterguard remained on the quarterdeck, for the *Morganse* was a lady of high maintenance, a queen always in need of her attendants. Their voices drifted down through the skylight directly overhead. She smiled faintly, the lowest regions of her belly tightening at the sound of Nathan's voice.

She often wondered what Nathan's voice would have been had it not been so destroyed. Soft, to be sure, for it still held vestiges of that, but never with the richness of Brian's. His had been deep, and yet so very soft, a warm hug on a winter night. As she and he would lie together at night, reviewing the minutia of the day, her cheek resting on his chest, its bass would resonate in her bones. Even at a whisper, Nathan's gravel was like torn velvet, a more-worn woolen blanket on that same winter's night, rough yet holding the promise of more comforts to come. She had never thought another voice would touch her as Brian's had. And yet Nathan's did, but differently, as no other.

"Clap on to that sheet, you ill-begotten son of a double-poxed, Dutch whore! What the fucking hell...?" echoed down through the skylight.

Ah yes, touched her like no other.

"What?"

Startled, she opened her eyes to find said angel-voiced soul standing at the door with a puzzled look.

"Hm? Oh, nothing," she said, sitting up straighter.

His curiosity deepened by worry, Nathan's brows knitted tighter as he came farther in. "You had the look as if you were hearing angels singing. You're not going to lose your mess number on me, are you?"

The question didn't seem intended for an answer, and so she didn't.

A curl of his nose, a scowl and a flutter of fingers deposed Beatrice from her roost. The bird moved to the edge of the table. Cate could feel the single-eyed stare as she peeled an orange and eventually held out a section. Beatrice crab-stepped across the table, took the offering in her claw. She immediately sidled away to eat with as birdly manners as one might expect.

The pursuant absence of conversation wasn't unique. Nathan was often preoccupied with matters of his ship. It was common to see him tapping the glass, pricking a chart, or writing in the log, while balancing his coffee in the other hand. Come to think on it, she had never seen him entering into a personal journal. Many people kept one, especially those seeking a connection. A captain lived elbow-to-elbow with men, and yet was isolated by the position of command. Pryce was probably Nathan's nearest thing to a confidant, but even that was quite limited.

No secrets on a ship.

Indeed, that could well be the case, for nothing put to paper could be guaranteed as secret.

The scones arrived. As Cate ate, she tried to decide what it was that struck her so odd, thinking perhaps she was still deep in her earlier daydream. And then, she realized: Nathan was eating. He had plucked a mango from the plate, diced it into chunks with his knife, and was now using it as a fork.

She often wondered what kept him going, for it was rare to see him eat. Occasionally, he would walk about with a piece of smoked *charqui* tucked in the corner of his mouth, like one might a cheroot. She had seen him at times sipping from a cup of something that smelled similar to the hands' meal, obviously thinned considerably. He had taken the fruit from a plate which had a permanent resident in the middle of the table. Strategically placed out of Hermione's reach, with a dome of stiffened gauze over it and sprigs of sage around as deterrents to vermin, it held an ever-changing variety: fruit, boiled eggs, wedges of cheese, pickles, kippers, soft tack, *charqui*, anything that could be grabbed and eaten. She suspected Kirkland, distressed by his captain's apparent lack of appetite, kept it there in hopes of tempting him.

She watched with guarded pleasure as he plucked up a scone. She smiled privately at seeing him slather it with honey to the point of drooling over the sides.

There was one secret she knew about Captain Nathanael Blackthorne: he had a sweet-tooth. The honey pot, and its accompanying spoon, was a permanent resident on the table. His coffee was always heavily dosed. Many a time, she had seen him stop to either take a spoonful as one would a dose of physik, or swirl his finger inside and pop a golden dollop in his mouth.

Nathan nibbled at the scone's edge, the bells in his mustache flashing in the morning light as he chewed industriously, licking the dripping sweetness from between his fingers, and dashing the crumbs from his mustache and beard.

He flicked a Bombay bomber from his plate as casually as one would an ant at a picnic, sending it on a long arc out the window.

"Damned geckos have been slouching again. Might feed you to Artemis, if you don't bear a hand and show a leg," he directed louder to the general room.

Nathan paused in his chewing to eye Beatrice as she sidled over to Cate for another morsel. "You're going to spoil her appetite."

Cate wondered if he was speaking to her or the bird.

With a squawk of protest and a swirl of feathers, Beatrice soared out the gallery window and curved up toward the quarterdeck.

Mr. Kirkland topped the galley steps and came to a dead stop just as Nathan swallowed carefully, followed by a gulp of coffee. Joyousness flushed his florid face at seeing his captain eat. He eagerly rushed forward uttering an effusive list of other temptations—sausages, bacon, soft-boiled eggs, toasted soft tack, fried fish or an omelet—but was waved away as Pryce came in.

"The crew begs yer leave, Cap'n."

The ominous weight in Pryce's voice brought Nathan instantly to his feet. Cate rose as well without knowing why. Both men stood poised, an entire conversation in one look.

"What's...?" Nathan swallowed, straining to maintain his casualness. "What might this be in regard to?"

Jaws flexing, Pryce's grey eyes narrowed to slits. "They've... grievances, sir."

A sharp rise of voices on deck gave veracity to his statement.

Nathan nodded faintly. "Who?"

"Same as before." Pryce's bass dropped to a bare shadow of itself.

"How many?"

"More than the last," Pryce said, with considerable reticence, and then hissed in a burst of hushed vehemence, "God rot their eternal souls and strike them blind!"

Nathan's throat moved as he gulped. "Very well, I shall attend directly."

He stared in Pryce's wake. He closed his eyes and swayed. Hands working at his sides, he emitted a low growl through clenched teeth. He shook himself like a great dog, and then turned to her, his features now carefully arranged.

"It might be best if you were to remain here." He winced at

the increase of impassioned shouts from outside. "It could be dangerous, what with the crossfire and all."

Crossfire?

Cate stood confused to the point of speechlessness. Nathan came around the table to take her by the arms, his fingers digging her flesh. He threw a loathing glare over his shoulder toward the cabin door and the uproar beyond.

"Things could happen quickly. I might not be able to..." He choked off the thought. "When... *if,*" he emphatically corrected, "anything should... happen, stay close to Pryce. He should be able to protect you. They know you're here, so there's no hiding you. You have your knife?"

Mechanically nodding, she touched the side of her skirt and the reassuring weight there. Assured by that, he went to one of the urns near the door and reached in to almost his armpit to draw out a pistol.

"Keep this with you," he said, checking the primer. He shoved it into her waistband and with a tone that turned her blood to ice said, "Save it for yourself."

She stiffly nodded, her thoughts refusing to move.

"I'm sorry," he said haltingly. "I... I meant to do you better."

Cupping her cheek in his hand, he gazed intently at her, taking in every feature, and then kissed her on the forehead, warm and yet so brief. He turned to survey the room as if committing it to memory. He drew up at the threshold and swayed. Squaring his shoulders, he stepped into the glare of day and tumult with his customary swagger.

Cate stood transfixed, trying to decide which was more startling: Nathan's sudden trepidation or his kiss. She started at the sound of footsteps and whirled to find Mr. Kirkland at the top of the companionway, round-eyed and pale.

"I heard rumblings." He looked toward the increasing mayhem on deck and wrung his hands. "I thought it to be only the usual complaining. I should have warned the Captain."

"What is it? What's happening?"

"Mutiny." Blenching, he barely whispered the word. "I'm not saying for sure, but..." A cringing shrug completed the thought.

Cate strained to assemble fleeting bits Nathan had told her weeks ago.

Mutiny. He had said it, with his usual insouciance.

"*...once... marooned... lost me ship...*" Her embarrassment at having inadvertently broached something so delicate had precluded her from probing any deeper. It had invoked visions of anarchy, violent mobs, pistols and bloodied sabers.

Heart hammering, she looked from Kirkland to the door and the invisible mob. "So, what happens?"

He rolled his eyes doubtfully. "If it goes smoothly, marooned... or cast adrift."

Marooned: left on an island to die.

She glanced toward the windows. It was the West Indies; islands were as constant as clouds. At the moment, any which were visible seemed very inaccessible.

Adrift, then. The same, but worst to her mind: cast off in a boat alone, until heat and thirst ended the misery.

She closed her eyes and swallowed her breakfast for a second time. Not Nathan. Not Nathanael Blackthorne. It couldn't end that way. He had endured before and had lived to tell the tale. It only followed that such would be the case once more.

"And, if not smoothly?" she could barely rasp, her mouth had suddenly gone dry.

"If it's close, the decks will be red."

She was confident he wasn't referring to the paint drizzled over the ship's edges.

Drawn by the rowdiness, she went to the door, but recoiled at the sight of all hundred and seventy-something pirates gathered, dark, weathered, half-dressed and barbaric. Weapons, in the way of firearms and blades were in the armory, under lock and key. A ship, however, possessed a vast number of lethal implements. Snarling like a currish pack, they perched on every surface — capstan, rails, ratlines and yards — brandishing hatchets, poleaxes, harpoons, pikes, hooks, barrel staves or any other possible weapon ready to hand. A flash of hyacinth blue darted overhead, Beatrice settling on the mizzen masthead.

"Things could happen quickly..."

Once more she checked the pistol at her waist.

As Cate looked from face to face, she was stricken by betrayal, much the same as Nathan had to have been feeling, if not more so. These were the very faces which had smiled as she had chatted, treated their wounds, and listened as they told of families and loved ones. Now they were no more than ravaging dogs snapping at the very hand that fed them. To see their violence turned outward on their enemies was one thing; to see it inward itself was far more fearsome.

Nathan stood unflinching before the crowd. Any sniff of weakness would be a cue for this rabble of sea wolves to attack. On any other ship, the captain could have sent the troublemakers scattering with a single bark, but these were pirates, exercising their rights as given by the ship's articles. Liberty suddenly seemed a double-edged sword, the gain of one coming at the expense of another.

The plaintiffs, judging by their belligerent stance, loosely formed around Nathan, Pryce barely an arm's length away. His countenance could be an open book or he could be as inscrutable as the sphinx. His disapproval was eloquent in the stony glare and rigid stance, but it was unclear if it was provoked by the complainants themselves or his captain being challenged.

"Who be spokesman?" Pryce's booming voice brought the proceedings to quick order.

"Y'er Quartermaster," came a sneering shout from the crowd.

"Aye," Pryce said evenly. "But a man's grievances best come from his own damned mouth. If ye've complaints enough to bear arms against yer Cap'n, then ye's can jolly well haul yer arses up and voice them like a man, instead o' cowerin' about like Spaniard-lovin', spineless curs!"

Like a bucket of sea water, he doused the riotous enthusiasm. He pointedly ignored those before him until the leader was singled out by virtue of the others falling back. All attention swiveled to one individual. Cate shied.

Bullock.

Cate fished deep into the pool of names which she had learned over the last weeks, but could only snag a few for his cohorts: Clark—even more sour than Bullock, if that was at all possible—Hibbett—gullibility written all over him—and Reed—his arm still wrapped by the bandage she had put there but a few days ago.

Hanging at the cabin door, she strained to hear.

"Ye've gone soft, Cap'n," Bullock was saying, his companions enthusiastically nodding. It seemed a good sign he still showed Nathan proper respect. "We should o' taken that ship as prize..."

"Which? The *Nightingale*?" Nathan cut in.

"Aye! Instead, ye allowed 'em to pass—"

"With a dead captain, I might point out." Nathan's interjection came in a conversational tone, obliging the crowd to hush further in order to hear him.

"She was listing to near scuppers, masts sheared and hull breached. You were below. How fast was the water rising in the well? Were you and your... cohorts," said Nathan, with a distasteful swipe, "willing to sweat it out on the pumps for the *days* required to put her to rights?"

Bullock blinked a bit dully at his point being so readily dismissed. "Shoulda took the *Valor*, then."

Nathan stood impassively in the face of the inflamed cheers, fists and weapons waving in Bullock's support.

"She was hard aground. How many hours on a capstan and hawse were you and your merry band willing to put in so that we might achieve that glorious goal?"

Nathan crossed his arms and planted his feet. By zeroing his sights on Bullock, he effectively narrowed the confrontation from a small gang to only the two of them.

"We took everything what needed taking, or did you forget something? How long did you fancy we should stood off? Would you have preferred we took her in tow? That would have cut our speed—*and* our escape—by at least half."

Bullock was only slightly set back. "We shoulda took 'er."

"With nigh on to a hundred naked men? Is there something about a hairy arse that appeals to you? Does the sight of gooseflesh give you a cockstand?"

Uproarious laughter broke from all of those around.

"There might o' been women." Bullock said over the crowd.

Nathan nodded agreeably, waiting for the cheering to die down. "Ah, so you do know the difference. Not unheard of for the Navy to carry trollops. What with your fascination with naked men, I hesitated to assume you were familiar with what to do with one?"

"Four ships in a month: they're huntin' us." Bullock's conjecture brought another cheer. His chest swelled, encourage.

"And since when is that a concern?" Nathan demanded, when they finally quieted. "We're pirates. The whole world is *'a-huntin'* us. You fancy that burning them would quench their desire to do the same to us?"

Bullock slid a sullen look toward Cate that turned her cold. She knew the look of a predator, he the pack leader. "By our reckonin' not everything's been divvied."

She was some distance behind Nathan, but he still had a sense of where she stood, and sidestepped to block Bullock's view. His voice fell low and with a menace that caused several to inch away. "She's naught to you and you know it well."

Bullock's jaw thrust out. "She's part o' the prize."

"She's part o' the crew, as does all of you know."

"Not by my vote, nor any of us," Bullock shot back.

His men nodded with a hungry eagerness which propelled Cate back several steps. She was sickened and horrified to think Nathan might lose his ship—his life!—all because of her.

"One over half is all 'tis required," Nathan said with cold evenness. "The matter is settled."

"We should vote..." insisted Bullock, pugnaciously.

"*Again*?" Nathan's brows arched in ridicule. "Do you desire us to keep voting until you get the result what suits you? Strikes me everyone has better things to do than to stand out here in the sun re-deciding what's already been decided."

Cheers shifted to jeers at Bullock's suggestion of such inconvenience.

Nathan waited until it was quiet. "Very well, what else? Put a name to what's on your mind."

His resolve faltering, Bullock looked to his companions, who urged him on with nods and gestures. "We shoulda raided that town."

"St. Agua? Why? Is there a chicken we missed? They brought us everything, whilst you cooled your heels in a cantina, swilling the local fare."

Bullock looked over his shoulder to exchange glances with his cohorts and then back. "We'll be a-wantin' our shares."

"Certainly. Anytime. There's never been a word to the contrary. Might I inquire, however—just on a small point of curiosity, you understand—as to where you fancy to spend it?"

Nathan finished with a grand gesture to the surrounding emptiness of water and sky.

Bullock's brow narrowed. "We want our shares."

Nathan narrowed an eye judiciously. "You've the sound of a man who feels cheated."

Bullock nodded. He bore the look of a bereaved person who was finally having his concerns acknowledged.

"Ergo," Nathan went on, "you believe a cheat among us. Very well, name your man. Mr. Pryce? Mr. Hodder? Mr. MacQuarrie?"

Bullock's face dropped at the unexpected conclusion. The thought of their honesty being questioned didn't settle well with anyone present. A restive, currish growl rose from the crowd.

"Come, come, now. Don't go faint of heart on us now!" Nathan's tone grew more derisive. "You've the courage to speak your mind. Name your cheat. We'll give 'im a fair trial, and he'll be dead before the evening grog."

The gulf between Bullock, his conspirators, and the crew widened. Bullock didn't give the impression of being overly bright, craftiness being more in the line of his strength. Given his due credit, however, he was perceptive enough to realize he'd just been bested. He was, however, exceptional in tenacity—loyalty to his conviction, as some might call it—and he exercised that now, determined to salvage what credibility might be managed.

"We're gonna have to stand extra watches, now." Bullock's point elicited a flare of freshened emotion from all.

Cate's heart pounded so loudly it was difficult to hear. She had crept outside without knowing and now stood at the crowd's fringe. A number of the company stood in reserve, watching and waiting as to which way this would fall. "Had their oars in several boats," as Pryce would say, and none wanted to be caught in the one sinking.

She scanned the grimed and grizzled faces, making a mental list of those who would stand with their captain. Pryce's allegiance was unquestioned.

Two against nearly two hundred; thin odds, at best.

She wondered what Millbridge's aged eyes might see. What direction would he go? His venerable position as the ship's eldest could be a swaying force; many would follow his lead.

Hodder, Hughes, Cameron, Stubbs, Chin, Jensen: it was a heart-sinking blessed few who could be counted on fully.

"Things could happen quickly."

She made a mental note of their whereabouts, just in case.

"Ambitions, Mr. Bullock?" Nathan was saying with measured contempt. "Did you fancy yourself as her master, were the *Nightingale* to sail as consort?"

"Yes" bubbled to Bullock's lips, but discretion prevailed. With the entire company looking on, he knew better than to put himself forward.

"Of course," Nathan went on, "that would mean dividing the crew. Instead of three-watches, we'd be obliged to go watch-on-watch. But pray, I beg your indulgences! When you complained last time of too much work, I wasn't under the impression you sought a second ship to mind for."

Nervous twitters came from several corners. The blood-lust was ebbing; reason and cooler heads were prevailing. Sympathies had swayed, but not entirely. It would take only a small victory on Bullock's part to bring a freshened wave of enthusiasm that could crush Nathan and anyone who stood with him.

"We weren't allowed our say." Sweat gleaming on the bridge of his nose, Bullocks' hands worked at his weapons.

Nathan snorted. "Don't play me, nor anyone the fool. It's not 'your say' you desire, and you damned well know it. Leave us to plan ahead, for just a moment."

A thoughtful finger to his chin, Nathan began circling. At first his path seemed random, stopping before this man or that. Slowly, however, a pattern formed, working like a shepherd dog, picking away at the fringes, until the errant members of the flock were isolated.

"The awkward bit of ridding oneself of one captain is that you're obliged to find another," Nathan was saying. "And right soon by me reckoning, if as you say, the Company is dogging our trail. Who among you are you willing to follow as Captain?"

The question was posed broadly. Heads dropped or looked

away, nervously coughing and shuffling feet. Many eyes swung in the direction of Pryce. As First Mate, he would be the likely choice, yet he gave the impression of a man who was unburdened by ambition. Cate stood afraid to look, afraid any movement on her part might tip the delicate balance. The *Morganse* went quiet, her song of sail and tackle dropping as if she held her breath, her future hanging in the balance, as well.

It was Nathan who finally broke the silence. "Those of you who sailed with Captain Maubrick can shed some light on the perils of the unwise choice."

"Let's see," he began, turning to the crowd. "When was the last time you gent's were required to live on ship's biscuit, sea water and rats? Ah, yes! That would have been when Maubrick was captain."

Nervous twitters and grudging nods of affirmation.

"And then, there was that unfortunate business of the Tenerife crossing: you missed South America. But wait! Let us not forget: that was Maubrick's navigating."

Snickers rippled through the hands. Faces softened, the hackles lowered. Hands didn't hover so readily over weapons and attention began to drift.

"And then," Nathan said, "there was that nasty business of running aground—How many times was that?—But no, wait! That was Maubrick's captaining."

A rumbling murmur rolled across the deck at that unpleasant recollection.

"And then, you were ambushed, the ship raked, until she listed so badly you couldn't pull the guns off the bulkheads. Can't imagine how Ol' Henry managed that," he finished, shaking his head.

"I'll credit, it must have been an easy life with Ol' Henry," Nathan went on. "Wise choice that: no raids, which meant no money for whores, but you gents have suffered before. No work. No worries. No cares. Just at your leisure on a beach... starving, tossing yourselves off, and better yet, no rum."

He paused to thoughtfully tap his chin. "Alas no one took the time; I could have explained how I never allow me crew to go dry."

Nathan continued to circle the insurrectionists.

"Pray, might I point out, just in case the obvious has been overlooked, that the hold is burstin' with swag. Apart from the *Nightingale* affair, not a one for the sailmaker's palm there's been. How many did Maubrick commend to Jones's Locker?"

Heads hanging like scolded pups, Bullock's dwindling flock looked thoroughly wretched.

"A caution to whomever is your newly-appointed: luckily, the swag abounds, because the stores are thin. You'll be needing canvas — that's Leith canvas up there, you know." Nathan ticked off each item on his fingers. "Cordage, nigh every size, at least five hundred yards each by me humble estimation. Add to that tar, pitch, shot, gunpowder, wadding, candles, beef, sugar, salt, flour, pea meal, salt cod, molasses, tea, coffee... and rum, of course, *lots* of rum."

Nathan pulled up before Bullock. "Of course, you can always raid and pilfer for what you need, but you'd best show a leg." He gestured larboard, where there was currently a view of nothing but blue sky and water. "Otherwise, those rats start looking *real* tasty-like. So, who's ready to be captain?"

He finished with a spread of arms in open invitation.

It was as graceful an exit as could be afforded. The neck of Bullock's shirt was a darkened circle with sweat. If there was such a thing as being wretched and at the same time belligerent, Bullock was it, virtually the last man standing.

"Any more complaints?" Nathan called out over the low hum of dispersal.

The entertainment value gone, the need to vote passed, the crowd melted, gone either to their duties or their hammocks. The *Morganse* hummed once again.

Nathan swiveled a glare of unfiltered disgust at Bullock, and said in a menacing low voice, "I thought not."

Pryce slipped between Nathan and Bullock. "To yer duties, mates!"

There are those who claim there is universal pre-determination: nothing ever happens unexpectedly; in everything there is an order and reason. The timing was too perfect to be credited to anything else: there was a squawk, a rustle of feathers, a blur of intense blue and a soft *splop!* of bird droppings landing on Bullock's shoulder.

It was over.

Cate took a long overdue breath. She flexed her hands, working out the ache from being clenched for so long. She waited until Nathan was near enough that no one else would hear before she asked quietly, "So, what happens now?"

"We all go back to our duties," he said with a queer look.

"Just like that?" The men nearby jerked at her incredulous shrillness. "Surely there's some kind of retribution or, or punishment for..." she said, in low urgency.

"Exercising their rights?" he asked blandly. He laughed, amused by the thought. "Not bloody likely. That would be sure grounds for... actions." It was worth noting that he couldn't bring himself to utter the word "mutiny."

"So, everyone goes on as if nothing happened?" The sequence of events was mind-reeling. First, everything seemed calm. The next minute the men were waving weapons, looking to throw Nathan off the ship, and then everyone went back to normal, as if nothing had ever happened. She thoroughly expected to see the malcontents clapped in irons and hauled away, hauled up... something!

Nathan beckoned a passing Pryce. "See to it that the rations are doled out early tonight," he instructed under his breath, and then added, winking, "With extra. And break up Sir Roguery, the sea lawyer, and his band of pewling miscreants."

Stabbing a thumb over his shoulder in the general direction of Bullock, who was now seeking to rally his allies. "Every time a raindrop hits him, he'll swear I arranged it in retribution. Yet, if I treat the bastard with care, he'll swear 'tis because I'm afraid of him." A sly smile grew as he considered. "The former is ever so much more gratifying, don't you think? Make the bastard's life miserable."

Pryce nodded, one beetling brow lifting. "This isn't over."

A look of a different meaning flickered between them, briefly landing on her, and then back.

"One day at a time, Master Pryce," Nathan sighed, tiredly. "One day at a time."

Nathan headed for the cabin, Cate close at his side.

"I thought... you led me to believe my being here wasn't a problem," she hissed.

"It's not," he said, coldly.

"But, if the men don't—"

He whirled around on her at the door. "But they do! You saw when they voted to call you 'Mister.'"

"No, I didn't. I left, remember?" Cate pressed, trailing behind as he went in. "But Bullock and the others—"

"Are a handful of swivel-tongued, gallowsy louts that *will* be dealt with, you can mark me on that."

Nathan snatched the rum bottle from the top of a trunk as he passed and drew up at the table. Dropping his hat, he ran a tired hand down his face.

"But... I never thought..." she began.

One eye peered at her over the edge of his hand. "This is rule by majority, darling. If we were compelled to wait until everyone agreed on everything, we'd never leave port. As it is, there's always going to be the unhappy... with anything."

The rationalization didn't make her feel any better and

considerably less secure. His insistence for her to sleep in his berth took on a new meaning. She was excessively grateful for his stubbornness.

Nathan saw as much and chuckled. "I promise, you will be safe. You've a knife, over half the crew, a First Mate, a Captain..." A bleat came from the galley companionway. "...and a goat on your side. Now what more could any soul ask for?" he finished brightly.

In the face of nearly two hundred, she was hardly assured.

"This one went well," Cate said with careful hesitance. "What about the next? There's always a next, isn't there?"

Conceding reluctantly, Nathan took a drink, thoughtfully rubbing the glass with his thumb. "Most of the time, if you keep their bellies and pockets full, and plenty of rum to ease their aches, there's naught to be concerning."

"But there's always a Bullock."

"Aye." He sighed, shoulders slumping as he set down the glass with delicate precision. "There's always a Bullock."

The sound of footsteps quickly approaching the door caused Nathan to spin around, reaching for his sword and shoving Cate behind him at the same time. He relaxed at seeing it was only Sombers.

The boatswain's mate touched a knuckle to his forehead. "Mr. Hodder's compliments and duty, sir. Sail."

Nathan raced outside and called, "Where away?" up to Hodder, now on the quarterdeck.

The boatswain gestured with his head. "Point 'er so off the starboard bow, sir. Hull up."

Nathan winced at seeing the white of sails and dark dash of a hull bridging the line where sky and water met. "Had we not been so frivolously distracted..." The thought was left to finish itself.

Spyglass slung over his shoulder, he shot up the weather ratlines, spurred not by alarm, but avid interest. Lounging in a stowed staysail, he studied the ship. Several flips of the glass later, he swung down a backstay to alight next to Cate, startling her.

"It's the *Sybilla*. There's no mistaking those red 'n white checks," he announced.

Pryce and the afterguard mouthed oaths in several languages. Low growls rode the air as the word passed forward.

"One of Creswicke's puppets," rumbled Hodder.

"With strings attached tight as no others," added Pryce. "Marauding wolf."

"Slush-handed Samuels, at command," Nathan declared.

"Unless Creswicke finally replaced that double-dutch-handed princock. Highly unlikely," he added as a judicious afterthought. "Worms do tend to knot together."

"Slush-handed?" she asked, looking between the trio.

"Aye, slush: what's used to grease the mast?" Nathan prompted as one would a dull student.

Cate nodded, straining to follow. Slush was the fat produced in cooking. It was collected by the ship's cook to either be sold ashore—for candle or soap-making, and such—or to the ship for greasing the masts, the resulting monies constituting his slush fund.

Nathan threw a scorn-laden glare toward the ship, now closing in at an alarming rate. "A sufficient greasing could prompt the man to sell his own mother, after pulling the gold from her teeth."

"The worm tends to overvalue himself of late," said Pryce.

His gaze still fixed on the ship, Nathan nodded distractedly. "Then our aim will be to render him a mite humbler."

"She's fast," warned Pryce.

"Not so fast, nor more determined than we. She's working for the wind already. Let's get there first."

"And if we don't 'get there first'?" Cate asked after Hodder and Pryce had taken their leave.

Nathan smiled tolerantly. "She'll do everything she can to steal our wind, leave us dead in the water, and then blast the bejeezus out of us with her eighteens, until we're naught but flotsam on the water."

Cate recalled all too well the *Morganse* using that same tactic against the *Constancy*, minus the "blasting the bejeezus" part, of course. The dread of such helplessness visiting again prickled her neck.

The space between the two ships narrowed as they angled for the advantage. Once seen, the *Sybilla* proved to be a smaller ship, with flush decks and more triangular sails. A red flag broke from her mizzenmast, the sight bringing a currish growl from the *Morganse's* afterdeck's complement.

"It means they intend to give no quarter, take no prisoners," said Pryce, glaring.

Cate turned into Nathan's intent gaze at her, his expression pinched by an odd combination of self-recrimination and worry. Before she could inquire as to what concerned him so, he reeled away to the quarterdeck rail.

"Mates," he called below. "That's the *Sybilla* out there."

It was a point needlessly made, for the ship had long been

recognized, judging by their displeasure. Still, a roar of protest and derision was stirred by their captain.

"Yon ship doubts our heart," he shouted. "Leave us serve them theirs on a platter."

A savage cheer worthy of the Roman coliseum went up. The men shed their shirts, bound their heads with sweatbands and spit on their palms, ready to lay into their action stations.

The two ship's paths converged. They veered and swerved, vying for the precious weather gauge, which would be the chaser, and which would be the chased. Running close to the wind, it was a tacking duel, something between a slow dance and a high-speed chess match. It was a race for that small edge which would steal the other's wind. The deck pitched at a treacherous angle as the *Morganse* leaned, her bow as tight into the wind as she could sail, for there lay the advantage. It was a contest of which captain knew his ship best: too much sail could press her down, too taut could spill the wind, not enough sail or too flown loose could cost precious speed. It was a contest between crews; which one could execute hauling the sails, pirouette the most seamless, and bring the wind to their vessel's other shoulder.

The white wakes zigzagged across the indigo sea in perfect unison as the racing vessels reposted and parried. Anytime the *Morganse* prepared for that fateful move, the *Sybilla* countered, ducking and pivoting, denying the opportunity. Pryce's "Ready about!" was warning to brace for another turn. The rigging and blocks shrieked over the bellows of men heaving to bring the *Morganse's* nose around, the decks pitching in the opposite angle as her sails caught the wind on her other side.

The bowlines twanging, the water raced down the *Morganse's* sides, arching like a reversed waterfall at her cutwater. Log lines were unnecessary. Her exact speed was of little consequence, only that she outdistanced her rival. Those conning the helm were alert for a ripple on the water marking a puff of wind, timing the swell for that scant bit more speed, or slithering past a rogue wave which might slap her hull and slow her a fraction.

The decks were a teeming mass with men either manning the sails, preparing the guns, or readying the boarding party. Suddenly over eight score pairs of hands weren't enough for all that needed done. Many doubled and even tripled their duties. Cate delivered baskets of arms from the armory and put final edges on blades, between tending the injured, for sailing with such ferocity came with a price. As Master Gunner, MacQuarrie was torn between preparing the larboard and starboard batteries, and overseeing the bow-chasers. Low brass creatures crouched on the forecastle, they poised at the ready for the first opportunity.

Nathan was everywhere: on the quarterdeck, at the helm, on the forecastle or laying aloft, sometimes idling in the stowed staysails. He was often shouting, but only in the natural way of a mariner: elevated to be heard over the chorus of ship, wind and water. Torn by the wind, his graveled voice could never equal Pryce's or Hodder's in volume. Its weight came through authority. As he worked his way up and down the deck, a nod or an encouraging clap on the shoulder did more in the way of encouragement than any bellow or start.

Nathan's greatest communion, however, was with his ship. More than once she saw him touch a finger to her wheel or backstay, or clasp a shroud—the arm-thick ropes which supported the masts—close his eyes and bend his head, as if in benediction. At one point, Cate saw him standing on the weather chain-plates. Braids streaming behind him, he grasped a shroud and leaned far out over the racing foam, whooping with joy.

An agonized cry drew Cate's attention away. A man shuffled half-bent down the deck clasping his abdomen: another busted gut. After seeing him to his hammock and grog administered— not much else to be done—she found Nathan standing atop *Beelzebub*, the forewardmost gun. The wind pressed his shirt against his body and plucked at his sleeves and tails of his headscarf. Swaying with the rhythmic rise and fall of his ship, he was a creature of the sea, likely to perish if taken from his realm.

"Are we winning?" she asked. At the moment, the tip of the *Morganse's* bowsprit seemed no more than a biscuit toss from the *Sybilla's* stern windows. Keenly aware of her peril, the *Sybilla* swept her stern from side to side like a lady lifting her skirts from a mud puddle.

Nathan smiled, a crooked one of ivory and gold. The spindrift spangled his lashes and mustache. "We're not losing. She hates to lose, especially to that slab-sided, iron-sick hulk," he added, lovingly patting the rail at his knee.

With no idea as to what "iron-sick" meant, Cate took his meaning from his scornful tone. Hardly what she would call a hulk, compared to the *Morganse*, the *Sybilla* was quite gay. A row of red-and-white checks trimmed her sides. The round house, bowsprit and fretwork were gilded, and anything made of metal, which could possibly be induced to shine, did so with a brilliance visible from a good distance.

The glass turned. The bell clanged.

"I weary of this game, Mr. MacQuarrie," Nathan called at length. "Bow-chasers, if you please. Double-shot and on the down roll."

Nathan seized Cate by the arm, and had propelled her to the cabin before MacQuarrie cried, "Fire!"

"The foredecks should take the brunt, so you're to remain here," Nathan said as he drew up just inside the door. "You've your knife?"

She saw then that at some point, Nathan had armed himself the same as before departing for the *Valor*. No strip of cloth bound his arm, but two extra pistols were stuck in his belts and a wicked-looking knife protruded from his boot top. Her heart lurched at the thought of him taking part in another boarding. He had escaped unscathed before; it was too much to hope for such luck to revisit.

Stiff with fear for him, she nodded, touching her pocket.

"Now use this," he said solemnly. He pulled one of the pistols from his belt and stuffed it into her waistband. "*Do not* hesitate: the bigger the smile, the more reason to put a ball between the bastard's eyes. Your word?"

She blinked. It had never occurred to her to be afraid for herself.

Nathan patted Cate's shoulder at seeing her woodenly nod again. "There's a good lass."

"Her rudder's gone!" came a cry from forward. A joyous cheer erupted.

Nathan glanced anxiously over his shoulder.

Cate fought the urge to throw her arms around his neck. "Please don't-"

Her plea was silenced by his finger to her lips. "Hist, now. This is what I do, and child's play it is," he added a bit dryly. "Now hold fast."

He flashed a smile that was presumably intended to reassure her. She wasn't.

And then, he was gone.

As Cate stood there, she noticed Hughes, Cameron, Mute Maori and Chin bracketed the Great Cabin's door like intransigent watchdogs, arms at the ready. The scuff of feet, a cough and low voices at the bottom of the galley steps revealed that access was guarded as well. No one seemed to anticipate they would be boarded, but precautions had been taken, nonetheless.

Over Nathan's shoulder, Cate could see that the *Sybilla's* bow had swung around. There was an advantage, however, in being sideways to the *Morganse's* bow and she took it. She fired. The six-gunned broadside was meant to rake, but had limited effect. Three balls splashed into the sea. Two landed on the deck spent and rolled about like eighteen pound marbles. One dashed from bow to aft, its path marked by a trail of spurting shards of wood.

Nathan spun in round-eyed horror as it streaked for the Great Cabin's door. Cate stood in an odd fascination, as if entranced by the ball as it hurtled toward her. Her mind screamed for her to duck—she thought she heard Nathan shout—but her feet refused to move, as if stuck in tar. She had the impression of it aiming squarely at her nose and felt her eyes wanting to cross. Then the ball careened off the mainmast and shot over the rail with a heavy whirring sound, the splinters tugging at her skirts.

Nathan glared and swiped a gesture bidding her to get down, back... Anything! He wheeled around and cried, "Full aback! Lay 'er in irons!" Pryce and Hodder echoed the command fore and aft.

The *Morganser's* bow-chasers fired again. The guns must have been elevated and on the rise, for this time the *Sybilla's* sails took the worst. The *Sybilla's* own gunsmoke clogged her decks; the *Morganse's* filling the space between the ships. The *Morganse* seized the moment and swept in. A shrieking grind and a lurch, which sent Cate scrambling for a handhold, marked the two hulls meeting. Grapnels were flung, and the Morgansers poured over the bow. Strips of red flapping, brandishing pistols, cutlasses, boarding axes and the like, they shrieked like Tartars as they charged and disappeared onto the *Sybilla's* smoke-choked deck.

The clash of battle drifted from the *Sybilla*: the roar and cry of men, the scrape of metal against metal, the sporadic pop of a pistol. The deeper cough of muskets came from high above, the sharpshooters hanging like murderous monkeys in the rigging of both ships. The breeze pushed away the lingering great gun smoke, leaving only the thinner curls from the small arms remained. Cate stood on tiptoe straining to see forward through the tumult, and by some miracle, onto the *Sybilla's* deck, hoping for a glimpse of Nathan. She thought she caught snatches of his voice. It would have required the force of a great gun if it was to be heard over her heart hammering in her ears.

Damn him! Damn him!

Damn him for putting himself in danger, for being who he was.

"I'll never forgive the bastard, if he gets himself killed." She spoke aloud without meaning to, and apparently louder than she thought, for Chin, Hughes and Cameron gave her a startled look.

She looked down at her shaking hands—When did that start?—and worried that in this condition she might not be able to do what was necessary, if Nathan came back injured. She buried her hands deep in the folds of her apron, not only to stop the shaking but to prevent her nails from digging so deeply into her palms.

And then it was quiet, with no more than the *clank!* and *thunk!* of weapons dropped.

It was over.

She gasped a choking sob of relief at seeing Nathan's head bobbing among his cheering crew. Then he stepped clear of the crowd and into a band of sun breaking through the smoke. Shirt darkened with circles of sweat, sword in one hand, pistol in the other, the whites of his eyes gleamed against his smoke-blackened face. The eyes narrowed as he peered toward her. A flash of white and gold broke the soot when he smiled at seeing that she was well. A tap to his forehead in salute and he disappeared into the jubilant throng of men.

The ships were shifted and secured, the yards triced up lest they tangle. Gangplanks, derrick yards and whips were rigged, so that the prize might be ridded of her valuables. Judging by the net-load after net-load, passed down through the hatches next to where Cate had set up the makeshift sick-berth, most of it was stores: spars, yards, canvas, cordage, blocks, and tar, or victuals.

Tradition held that the defeated captain was to pay his respects to the victor straightaway. After some time and not a captain, word was passed. Still no one showed. Incensed by the slight, Pryce was on the verge of apoplexy, threatening to send a detail to drag the "double-poxed, worm-boweled, ill-beseen prick" aboard.

Cate had finished with the wounded. The maindeck being in such chaos, she returned by way of the 'tween deck to the Great Cabin. Nathan was there at the table. She had seen him safe at the end of the battle, but hadn't seen him since. Seeing him now, unbloodied, was better than any tonic.

His face lit at seeing her top the galley steps. "A butcher's bill?"

She had hoped for a remark a bit more personal, but after all, this was Nathan.

"The Sybillas must be better sailors than warriors," she sighed. "A good number are bashed or broken, but baring something festering, all should survive." She touched wood at the same time. Festering wounds was nothing to take lightly.

The air was pierced by a coxswain's whistle, the *Sibylla's*, for the *Morganse* had none. With the pomp befitting visiting royalty, Captain Samuels was piped aboard. The forewarning still did not forearm Cate for the visage which appeared at the door.

She had assumed pirates to all be of much the same cloth. Roughly the same age and height as Nathan, Samuels was diametrically opposed to him in more ways than he was alike. He was pale of eye and skin, the latter remarkably so for one who presumably spent the bulk of his life out-of-doors. Thick of nose and lips, his skin, no amount of squinting could have rendered him good-looking. He sported the paunch and jowl which came with good living, puffy and soft. He wore a curled wig, brocade coat, gold embroidered weskit, velvet cape and breeches with jeweled buckles at the knee. Gleaming Hessian boots, a massive, ornate silver belt buckle, gilt-and-jeweled sword and a pair of carved, ivory-handled pistols completed his *ensemble*. His crowning glory was a vast-brimmed cocked hat, its purple plume curling nearly to his waist, and a gold-orbed walking staff. Any of those appointments taken individually could have made the man.

Samuels and his contingency filed into the cabin. Hodder, Pryce, MacQuarrie and the *Morganse's* equivalence to officers were present, the impressive figures of Chin and Mute Maori at the forefront. No introductions were made. Judging by the mood, all present were familiar, too familiar. Pryce's glare froze his features. His disapproval must have been contagious, for it had infected all Morgansers present.

With a flare of cape, Samuels posed in his seat as if at court. Nathan slouched in his chair, one leg slung over the arm. The two bristled like two terriers, circling and sniffing, the table between them more a barrier than a formality. The air snapped with a charge. St. Elmo's fire leaping about the room wouldn't have come as a surprise.

"It would appear roguery agrees with you," Samuels said, regarding Nathan imperiously.

"It would appear selling your soul to the Devil agrees with you."

"Few clouds fail to produce silver linings." Samuels wore a fixed smile. If it was meant to assure, it didn't. If it was to ingratiate, it didn't. If it was meant to obfuscate, it didn't.

Nathan angled his head toward the rum and two glasses, squarely before Samuels. "The bottle stands by you."

Samuels winced. Clearly, he would have preferred to have been paid the honor of having someone pour for him. He filled one and shoved the rest across. A lift of the glass and a nod was the only toast offered.

Rolling the drink in his mouth, Samuels nodded in reluctant approval. "Jamaican."

"Only the best for our guests," Nathan said without a hint of hospitality.

"His Lordship begs I inform you that he doesn't appreciate your little escapades: burning his flag, defacing his ships,"

Samuels began. He fondled a lace-edged sleeve. "He takes it personal."

"Good, because it 'tis."

Samuels looked up from under his brow. "You can't escape him. His influence reaches around the world."

"Pray tell him I aim to take that sacred influence, stretch it 'round his little empire and strangle him with it."

They locked stares.

"I'll give him the message," Samuels said in a low tone.

"I know you will," Nathan replied evenly.

Cate wasn't quite sure how Nathan managed it: a barely perceptible slide of his eye propelled her around the table, until she was behind and off to the side of Samuels. It was unclear if it was to move her out of Samuels' sight or where Nathan could see her.

Samuels took another drink. "Do you plan to take my ship?"

"Do you plan to give me cause?" Nathan asked, examining his fingernails.

The corner of the privateer's mouth quirked. "I've always come prepared to barter when you're involved, Nathan."

"Ah, the tar pot calling the loggerhead black. Very well, on the table with it."

Samuels gestured to his men, bidding them outside. Once they had filed out, Nathan drew out a leather pouch and tossed it on the table. It landed with the heavy clank of coins.

"Not entering this on the prize book, I'll wager," Nathan mused.

Samuels' smile was unwavering.

Nathan tilted his head and squinted one eye. "I knew once of a captain found guilty of that: his crew fed him his balls... roasted."

Samuels' smile faltered and then tightened. "My price has gone up."

"How is it that the man with the noose around his neck is always the one to desire to bargain? And now, he demands to be paid."

"Double."

His drink spewed across the table was Nathan's answer.

"Then triple," Samuels' ire rising.

"I could have sworn those were sharks I saw lurking under the counter," Nathan said, with a roll of the eyes.

Samuels' eyes were in constant motion, like a pickpocket darting through a crowd seeking his next victim, taking notice of every aspect of the room, looking for his next means of manipulation, an edge, information to sell next.

Samuels rolled the glass between his hands as he said, "I would have thought you would have had your fill of women aboard."

It was miniscule, but there was a slight crack in Nathan's façade, clearly preferring she hadn't been there. He made a reproving noise and then darkened. "I would have thought you would have a stronger appreciation for your tongue. Another word and I'll cut it out."

"Parlay." Samuels' reminder came as a sneer befitting a play yard.

Nathan was unabashed. "Very well. I'll put it in your lapel and you can take it with you."

Samuels' first impulse was to dismiss the warning. He sobered and eyed Nathan, second thoughts prevailing.

Samuels scoffed. "Empty threats."

Nathan went so very solemn, hardening to a deadly coldness which had been alluded to, but Cate had never witnessed. If it didn't make Samuels nervous, it certainly did her.

"Try me. Name one thing I would have to lose," Nathan said.

Samuels posed with smugness. "What I know."

"Information then is the name of the game," Nathan mused, settling back in his chair.

Samuels winced at having tipped his hand so readily. "Triple."

"Do the words 'hock and heave' carry significance for you?" Nathan fixed him with a stare. "Same as before."

The shoulders under the velvet cape slumped. "Agreed."

Samuels had incrementally sunk lower in his chair with each foray. The exchanges had been a fencing match: lunge, parry, reposte. He now tended to flinch and start at any sudden move on Nathan's part. It hadn't gone unnoticed by Nathan, and he now taunted the man. An overt jerk of his shoulders and Samuels nearly dropped his glass. Cate had the impression that, if Nathan was to go a bit more forceful, the man would launch from the room.

Beads of sweat shone on the bridge of Samuels' nose, when Cate's was met with the sharp smell of fresh paint. A great deal of it would have to have been employed somewhere to account for the strength which wafted through the cabin just then. Merriment of the scheming, mischievous sort could be heard outside, and snickering, like lads tipping privies.

A lizard tongue flicked at a droplet of either rum or sweat on Samuels' upper lip. "This is a parlay. I'm under the flag of truce."

Nathan tented his fingers and shrugged. "Very well. How long do you desire to be aboard under said flag? An hour? A week? I could throw you in the bilges and put you out of mind until the body began to stink."

Another flick of his fingers and Samuels flinched.

"That's against the Code," said Samuels, more dogged.

"So is going back on your word, which is exactly what you plan to do at the first opportunity what presents itself," Nathan said coldly.

A murmur of appreciation came from the heretofore silent audience.

Nathan flashed a smile equal to Samuels' in falseness. "'Tis all a matter of interpretation, and since 'tis my ship, 'tis my pleasure. The same price as before."

Picking up the coin purse, Nathan began to casually toss it from one hand to the other, the coins making a tempting clink at every pass. "On to it then."

Samuels went as alert as a hound on a scent. Nathan's foot came down under the table with a force that brought Samuels an inch or to up from his chair.

"A drink. Information makes me thirsty." Samuels seized the bottle.

Samuels' hand tremored slightly as he poured. He swirled the glass's contents, taking great relish in making Nathan wait. "There's to be a grand celebration," he finally said.

Nathan benignly stared.

"A wedding."

A brow twitched in interest.

"Creswicke's wedding."

Each piece of information came in measured drams.

"To marry Creswicke, a woman would have to be either crazed, soulless or... sold," Nathan said.

Samuels winced. Nathan's acuity was leverage lost.

"Business deal, in the cold light of day," Samuels sniffed disinterestedly. "A rich father, a *very* rich father."

"Where is this virginous saint now?"

"On her way from Boston."

"When?"

Samuels ducked his head defensively. "No one has all the answers." He took another drink. "She's coming and soon; on her way already, for all I know."

A polite clearing of the throat drew everyone's attention to the door and Mr. Towers standing there. He knuckled his forehead in a particularly seaman-like fashion before the visitors.

"Mr. Sombers' compliments and duty, sir. He desires me to tell you..." He rolled his eyes with the effort of recalling the exact words: "All squared away."

"Very well." Nathan sprang up with the eagerness of someone who had just heard long-awaited news.

"C'mon, c'mon! Show a leg there," he said, urging Samuels up. "I desire you to bless me with your opinion of our handiwork."

Nathan pressed Samuels outside and then stood back in anticipation. Samuels hesitated, raced several steps forward, and then slowed as he gaped at his ship. The *Sybilla's* deck and every soul present was now bright pink—red and white did indeed make a very festive color. The paint dripped from her scuppers like frosting on a French confection. The giggling from the Morgansers grew louder, amid the muffled thuds as they elbowed each other into silence.

Samuels whirled around. "You gallowsy, false-tongued bastard. We had a deal."

"Which would have only held water until the next person slushed your palm. Don't play righteous indignation with me. Mr. Towers?"

"Aye, sir! Solvents and paints taken n' tossed, as desired, sir. T'will be hell to pay a-gettin' it off," he added, unable to curtail his smile.

A paint bucket, pink drooling from its lip, and a brush was delivered to Nathan's outstretched hand. A piece of old canvas was used as a doormat for those pink-footed men, giddy as school children, returning from the *Sibylla*. Samuels was guided to it. With great care not to spatter, Nathan smeared the rigid Samuels with pink, from the brim of his cocked hat to his Hessian-booted toes. After a few flourishing strokes across the chest for a finish, Nathan dropped the brush into the bucket with two-fingered delicacy.

Grinning, he tossed the money bag to the sputtering Samuels. "Worth every farthing."

Nathan took a step back, cautious of the wet paint. "I deserve a great thanks for saving your arse. How else are you to return with credibility without some show of defeat? You're the one what declared no quarter; wanted to blow me out of the water and take me head for the reward."

His hands useless, Samuels blinked the paint from his eyes. Cate felt a wave of sympathy—albeit a small one—for it must have stung like hell.

"It's not your head he desires," Samuels sneered. "The prize is triple if you're alive."

Nathan doffed his hat and executed a sweeping bow. "Pray give me regards. Away with you now. Ta, ta!" he called as Samuels stalked back to his ship.

A heavy *thunk!* of the boarding axes and the *Sibylla* was set free of her bonds. Uproarious laughter broke out from up and down the *Morganse's* deck as the ship drifted away.

"You tormented the poor man," Cate said to Nathan under the levity.

Nathan shrugged. "I gave him enough rope to hang himself. T'was not my fault that he took off running, figuratively speaking."

"Setting fire to his britches wouldn't have been your fault either, figuratively, that is."

"Can't help it if the man is oversensitive to heat." Grinning, he strolled off.

Pryce came up next to her at the rail. He peered up at the red "No Quarter" flag at the *Sibylla's* mainmast. "After havin' that flashed in their face, many a captain woulda took their water and boats, an' let 'em die a-drinkin' their own piss. Others woulda unmanned 'em, cut out their tongues, or slit their eyelids and let the sun bake their eyeballs."

Pryce ducked his head between his arms on the rail. The wide back convulsed under his shirt, and for the first time, she saw Pryce openly laugh.

"I'll warrant this is a damned sight better," he wheezed.

11: THE BRETHREN

IT CAME ONE NIGHT THAT the *Morganse's* decks barely pitched, with only the faintest trace of foam streaming from her cutwater, "bearing well on a port tack on a tops'l breeze," as reported by Pryce.

There was a joyous mood aboard. Still in tearing spirits with their victory over the *Sibylla*—pink-tinged feet now a badge of honor—it had been another fortuitous day. The *Morganse* had come upon a sloop, riding low in the water, alone, "beggin' fer the takin'," declared Pryce.

"Flyin' a Spanish flag," Nathan had snorted, peering at it through his glass. "You'd have to be a French fuddler to believe it."

Surrendering at the sight of the famed pirate ship and her blood-crowned sails, the ship proved to be Dutch according to her papers handed over by a profusely sweating master.

"Her guns had been tampioned so long it would have required a bloody beaver to chew them out," Nathan sniffed in disdain afterwards.

"Aye, a pitiful example of seafarin' she were," Pryce said. "Near ancient, with twice-laid rigging and furry-bottomed. The guns were honeycombed and fit to blow up in the face of the first hen-hearted swab stupid enough to touch a match. Held together with nothin' but paint, they wuz."

As it turned out, someone had banked on the ship's innocuous appearance to allow her unencumbered passage, because she had been filled to near foundering with *pastillas*, bricks of cochineal, a dye treasured by royals, merchants, and more importantly, the captain of the *Ciara Morganse*. There had been enough lifted from the hold to keep the crowns of the *Morganse's* sails red for time out of mind and add a retirement-sized sum for every share.

Cate enjoyed the merriment from her box seat, for on the forecastle was the heart of the celebration. Tapping her foot, she joined the singing when able to pick up the words, throwing in the strength of her voice when the starbolins challenged the larbolins in competitive rounds. In the midst of one such competition, a crewman came up beside her. He bent and in a loud whisper, offered his compliments and represented that she was required below: an injury, the exact nature of which she couldn't quite make out. It wasn't an uncommon request. At times, it seemed to come as regularly as the watch bells. She rose and followed, weaving virtually unnoticed through the festive throng to the companionway below.

Barely halfway down, her senses pricked and her step slowed at seeing the deserted t'ween decks. After Bullock's remarks, she had made it a practice not to be alone. As her eyes became more accustomed to the dimness, her qualms were eased by the cocoon-like forms of occupied hammocks, swinging farther aft, and two men nearby hunched over a game of draughts.

Her messenger stood expectantly at the top of the steps leading to the hold and her spirits sank. She loathed the cavernous belly of the ship. She teetered on inquiring if there were some way the injured soul might be brought up, but immediately quashed the thought. If someone was hurt, the least she could do was suffer a little personal discomfort to give help.

She was nearly halfway down the companionway when a movement at the bottom of the steps caught her eye. She looked up to find Bullock standing there, a predator looming out of its lair. Cold fear pricked the back of her neck at hearing footfalls coming down the steps behind her, the two draughts players.

It was her experience that time often stalled in moments of danger, allowing every intricate detail to be observed: the thud of her heart against her ribs, hot breath of the one behind her on her neck, the smell of Bullock's sweat, the clatter of the bones in his pigtail, and the throbbing vein at his temple. The seconds preternaturally ticked as she measured her options.

Run!

She hitched her skirts and spun, directly into a hand clamping over her mouth. She was hit at the back of her head and the world faded. Internal voices screamed as she was half-carried, half-drug away. She flailed and took a neck-snapping cuff to the face. She screamed, but to no effect, the hand at her mouth jamming it back down her throat. The sound of the crew's merriment on deck echoing down the hatchway, the dank void of the hold closed in as she was taken deeper.

Not again! Not again!

Reality merged with nightmares, melding into a new horror, too nightmarish to be real.

Cate was thrown down on a hard surface. Chain, she thought. The cable tier then, near the forepeak. For some reason, knowing where she was held importance. The smell of sweat, bilges and sea bottom rendered the air nearly too thick to breathe. Bodies pressed into the small space and hands snatched at her.

The hand at her mouth blocked her screams, sounding maniacal in her own ears. Panic seized her, blotting out all other thoughts but one: escape. She clawed, bit and gouged, a demon possessed by that single notion. Rank breath blew hot in her ear. She jabbed an elbow in its direction and hit something soft and fleshy. With a strangled yelp, the grip on her mouth loosened enough for her to bite down. She heard a crunch, and tasted blood and grime. An enraged growl filled the small space. A fist clouted her in the face, and then the stomach, driving her breath out in a violent *whoosh!* A droning sound filled her ears.

Frantic, Cate fought, and was beaten harder. Her arm was savagely twisted behind her back, the bones of her wrist grinding to the point she thought it broken. Hands fumbled roughly at her front. The lantern light bobbed wildly. In the erratic light, she saw only a blur of faceless heads on a mass of bodies. A fist rose from that mass; she turned her head, taking the blow in the temple. Fingers gouged her skin as her bodice was ripped open. She kicked. There was an animal growl and her breast was given a cruel twist. Her screams into the palm at her mouth went from panic to pain. A body came down on top of her. She bucked and kicked, but to no avail, her arms and legs pinned. She felt the moist heat of a mouth at her breast. She gave a high thin shriek from the shattering agony of being bitten, so hard she thought her nipple to be gone.

Fingers dug her thighs, seeking to wrench them apart. She fought to curl into a defensive ball. Her arm, twisted under her, felt as if it had been torn from its socket. The grasp at her middle tightened, and she was hit again, in the jaw and stomach. A coppery taste filled her mouth, and she began to choke.

This couldn't be happening. Not on a ship filled with men! Where are they? Where are they!!

The desperation spurred her into a greater frenzy. Better to die than to live through this again.

Not again! Not again!

Cate struck out with her feet. Just one good kick: throat, gut or balls, whatever luck would provide. Something hard, either a fist or a knee, drove into her gut, again and again. She slumped, too dazed to move as her legs were yanked apart. A weight came down on top of her, the thick ropes underneath grinding into her spine. He panted hot and ragged in her ear as his hips worked between her thighs, eagerly thrusting, but to little avail.

An incensed bellow vibrated the small space. The man on top of her lunged to his feet jerking her up with him. Barely clear of the floor, she was dropped, coming down hard. Her gut convulsed, black spots swirled behind her lids. She was snatched up again. Whoever held her was knocked from behind and they shot forward together to land in a tangled heap. Her head slammed the floor again. The ringing in her ears reached a higher pitch. Bursts of red pricked the edges of her vision and her grip on the world began to slip.

The small space became a tumult of heaving bodies, filled with curses and grunts, the meaty slap of fists hitting flesh. She curled on the floor as they fought over her, beyond caring when she was trampled or kicked. A pleasant numbness settled over her. It promised an end to the nightmare; all she need do was surrender to the looming oblivion. She gave over to the spiraling flashes, allowing them to draw her down further and further...

Amid the voices, there was one, graveled and gruff, so familiar and very near.

"Cap'n. Nathan, yer killin' 'im!"

Pryce. It was Pryce!

Arms roughly scooped her up; she shrieked and kicked. The grasp around her tightened, and she heard an urgent shush in her ear, the sound thickened by ragged breathing. She opened her eyes into another pair. Bare inches from hers, they were black and wild with rage. Seeing her look up, Nathan swore in relief and clutched her to his chest with a gasping sob. She surrendered into his haven of warmth and safety, and the turmoil faded behind them.

Nathan's heart hammered against her cheek. She was vaguely aware of shifting patterns of light through her lids as he carried her, and then the jostle of climbing steps. Amid urgent voices and pounding feet, she cracked her eyes to see worried faces trust at her, inquiries and orders colliding. There was another jolt of hastily mounted steps again and they were back in the cabin. The clatter of curtain rings as Nathan barged through told her they were back in the sleeping quarters. There, with exaggerated care, he lowered her to her feet.

"Are you all right?" Still caught up in the rush of combat, he set to frantically patting her over.

"I'm fine." The lie came too easily, and yet she lacked the faculties to say aught else.

That simple acknowledgment, however, appeased him. He backed away, holding his hands out as if he feared she might topple over. Satisfied she would remain upright, he retreated another few steps to snatch what served for a towel from the washstand. Wadding it up, he pressed it under her nose. A wooden arm moved to assume the task, the cloth instantly bright red. Someone was bleeding. From all indications, it was her.

Emotions washed over her, like surf on a rock. There were so many, so fast, she felt as if she might drown. Unable to choose which one first, she responded to none. She should be crying, hysterical, screaming, shaking... laughing... something. Instead, she stood much like that rock, holding the towel to her nose and mouth.

As emotionless as Cate might have been, Nathan pulsed with enough for both of them. His blood still up from fighting, they coursed through him like lightning bolts, looking for a place to strike. He drew back and with several deep breaths in an effort to achieve a façade of calm.

Nathan's sleeve brushed against her; she looked down to see she was exposed nearly to the waist, the full curve of both breasts taught against the tattered edges of her shift. She thought to do something, but her arms refused to move. Seeing as much, with exaggerated daintiness, Nathan tugged the torn edges together to a modicum of decency. The muscles in his jaw, however, where white.

"Thank you." The voice was so foreign she thought perhaps someone else had spoken. It seemed important that be said.

He smiled, a weak attempt, but one necessary for the benefit of both of them. "No worries, luv. T'was naught more than what any gent would do."

"How did you find me?" she asked from under the wadded towel. Her head throbbed horribly, everything still a jumble of disjointed events.

The smile grew, more honest this time, but soon faltered. "Beatrice. The bloody beast set to caterwauling; wouldn't belay until we followed."

A commotion rose from the ship's caverns, the voices and scuffling of one group roughly herding another.

"What will happen... to them...?" She couldn't bring herself to utter a name. The mere hearing of their muffled voices made the ship suddenly feel too small.

"Any number of things," he said distractedly. "Anything short of a slow, agonizing death being too lenient by my estimation."

Clucking his tongue in admonishment, he took the towel from her and dabbed the blood from her chin. "I'll be called up as well." He smiled grimly. "I've drawn blood, killed an unarmed man. On that offense, I'll be meeting me own judgment."

"Because of me?" Panic surged at the thought of another mutiny.

"No," he said with measured patience, "because four miscreants took a crack-brained notion."

Like learning to walk, putting one thought in front of the other, she strove to comprehend. He stood before her, disheveled and blood-smeared. He had killed a man, his own crewman, because of her. The nightmare she thought to be over was just beginning, the hellishness spreading to everyone near. She could lose him, and would have only herself to blame.

"He couldn't have been unarmed. Every one carries a knife," she said.

Nathan smiled tolerantly. "Aye, like coppers to a cook, they are, but that will be a matter for them." He canted his head toward the unseen deck.

Cate felt rather than heard the ship come alive with a rising tide of agitation, the air charged like St. Elmo's fire. The voices of eight score of men rose to a feverish pitch, demands colliding with explanations. Pryce's bass cracked out, and they fell quiet.

"What will they say?" she asked.

"Anything they want and nothing that will stick. Justifiable, plain and simple," he added, more for his own benefit than hers.

Nathan's fist closed around the sponge with a force that whitened his knuckles, the water dribbling on the bed between them. "I killed what needed killing. If only God can take a life, then call me Jehovah, for I'll do it if it needs doing and with a clear conscience on me judgment day."

"Cap'n?"

Startled by the voice at the curtain, Nathan whirled, seizing his pistol with one hand and shoving her behind him with the other. He made a guttural noise of both relief and frustration, and lowered his weapon.

"Aye, Mr. Pryce?"

"A word, sir, if ye please," came a voice through the cloth.

"Come."

Barely stirring the velvet, Pryce slipped in. Cate cringed, the space suddenly too crowded. More aware of her dishabille than she, Nathan moved to block her from Pryce's view. Pryce averted his eyes, nonetheless.

"She's the right to accuse," Pryce said without preamble.

"Do you think that's entirely necessary, Mr. Pryce?" Nathan shot back testily.

"She's a right to declare and witness her justice." The proclamation came evenly, without prejudice.

Nathan barely glanced over his shoulder at her. "The lady

declines. You know me wishes." His voice dropped to a rumbling vehemence. "I want them dead, the worst way possible. If that means a slow-match to their balls, allow me to be the one to light it."

An arch of his brows indicated Pryce didn't disagree. "One didn't live to face his crime."

"A knife to the liver is known to do that," Nathan said laconically. "You be the Quartermaster, Pryce. Dispensing of justice is at your pleasure. You've always proven to be most imaginative."

Pryce's composure faltered. Cate's fogged mind was able to grasp his surprise: Nathan had just absolved him of any hesitancy or guilt, freeing him to deal with Nathan's fate the same as anyone else. If Nathan were to fall under the hammer of ship's justice, Pryce's likelihood of assuming command would hinge on his lack of prejudice or allegiances. He would also be the only barrier between her and the rowdy mass outside.

"Carry on, Master Pryce," Nathan said, cutting off Pryce's attempts to object. "I'll attend directly."

Puffed with displeasure, Pryce touched his forelock and left.

Nathan's braids fell in a curtain about his face as he studied his blood-caked hands. Would the men see hers, or the man he killed? Surely, if they saw the one, they would realize the other, or would pirates only see the blood of a fallen comrade and want more in the name of revenge?

"I'll be fine. Go." It was surprising how effectively she was able to lie again.

He looked up and curved a wry smile. "Do you ever say that and mean it?"

His smile broadened in gratitude. "This shan't take long."

It was unclear if he spoke for his benefit or hers.

She glassily watched him leave, straining to fully appreciate what he was about to face: a court of his peers passing judgment on the slaying of a mate, a member of the Brotherhood. Murder or justifiable? It was reasonable to believe justice would come swiftly and wouldn't be gentle. Beyond that, her concussed mind was unable to fathom.

Icy talons of shock and numbness sunk deeper into her gut. A part of her argued she should move, do something. No decision came, however, the task of standing consuming every shred of will. Her gaze drifted, eventually coming to rest on a corner of the rug upon which she stood. Not necessarily fascinating, but with no motivation to do else, there she remained.

A rap on the door frame stirred her sufficiently to murmur a response. Jensen shyly pushed his way in bearing a ewer of steaming water. His brilliant flush stirred her self-consciousness, and she tugged at the fragments of her bodice to something more decent. Frowning, Jensen's mouth moved as he filled the basin. The words thudded in her ears, as if heard underwater. He turned with an expectant look. She nodded, only because she thought she ought. With that, he left.

Cate was dimly aware of the rising turmoil of the crew assembling on deck. Still muzzy-headed, the words were lost, but the mood was readily judged. Tension? Yes. Blood-thirst? Not yet. Her senses pricked at the sound of Nathan's voice, loud and gruff above the rest. Commanding? Yes. Defensive? Not in the least. She tried to concentrate, wanting to know — needing to know more — but that battle had been lost before it had begun.

Wash.

The directive, simplistic enough to be grasped, came from somewhere within. She fumbled, the ties of skirt and stays' laces being maddeningly elusive. With a shrug of the shoulders, her shift fell away, landing at her feet. With arms that seemed to be someone else's, she wet the sponge and began to mechanically dab. The room was warm, yet her skin was icy to the touch. She looked at the blood-smeared limb. Sickness rose at the back of her throat at wondering whose blood it might be. Slowly turning a hand before her face, she examined the scraped knuckles and broken nails. The sight stirred recollections, but nothing tangible enough to be grasped. The light glinted on the hairs snagged under one nail and revulsion seized her: they weren't hers. Her gaze drifted down to her naked body. She swayed at seeing the patches of blood, oozing scrapes and welling bruises. Her thoughts moved like rusted gears as she strained to piece it back together.

From outside came cheers, raucous and angry. They quieted just as quickly, while one rang out, defensive and heated: Bullock.

Cate quailed and gasped, the sponge landing in a wet splat at her feet. Drawing a shaky breath — Breathing. Yes, breathing was important — she bent to retrieve it. She straightened to look squarely into the glass above the washstand. A wretched creature stared back, battered and bloodied, features swollen to the point of grotesque. The circular pattern of a bite marked her breast, bright red where the dark rose center met the milky pale.

Another inch, and...

She carved a slow spiral and crumpled to the floor. Curling into a ball, she wished for a shell in which to crawl. If she could make herself small enough, it... she might go away.

Cate felt more than heard Nathan's hurried approach.

Cracking an eye open, she searched the planked floor for a hole into which she could dissolve. There were none.

"I know you don't fancy —"

His words died in his throat. Swearing, he set a bottle on the nightstand and snatched the quilt from the bunk as he knelt. He murmured little nothings as he brought her to her feet, discretely snugging the quilt about her as she rose.

"Have to bear an eye on you every minute, don't I?" he gently chided, as if she were a helpless child. A backward kick sent the discarded clothing to the corner as he guided her to sit on the bed.

Frowning worriedly, he uncorked the bottle and, over her feeble objections, pressed it to her lips, not satisfied until she had taken several sips. The sting of the rum on her lacerated mouth brought tears to her eyes. The liquor burned her raw throat — Had she screamed that much? — when she swallowed. It landed in a hot ball in her stomach, sending instant fortifying jolts through her.

Nathan scooped up the sponge, pulled up the stool and sat, the basin now at his feet. He dabbed with the sponge, mopping the blood from her nose and mouth, being particularly cautious of the split lip. She tended to twitch and start at his every move, and so he signaled in advance, extracting one limb, and then another. As he cleansed, the basin's contents became a brackish pink.

The washing stung, but not as badly as the fact that he couldn't bring his gaze to meet hers. Several times he tried but failed. His responses to the few times she spoke were curt. He didn't say as much, but she knew he blamed her for having been so foolish as to fall into such a trap, his ship now in an uproar. She wanted to tell him he needn't be concerned with telling her: she already knew. She stared at the top of his head, listening to him mutter darkly under his breath and slowly came to realize his anger was turned inward. He wasn't blaming her; he was blaming himself and self-flagellation always wielded the sharpest barbs.

"What happened?" she asked stupidly.

"Nothing." It was one of his poorer lies. Still distracted by the shouting outside, he was now markedly calmer. "Justifiable, they said. Bloody too goddamned right," he huffed, jerking his shoulders. "I'd like to see any of those cod-fisted bastards do any different."

The increased pitch of voices forced him to raise his at the end. So stirred and angry they were, so reminiscent of the attempted mutiny.

"What's going on out there?" she asked, shying at the increased shouting.

"The Court's still convened," said he matter-of-factly, and then shot a loathing look over his shoulder. "This shan't go unpunished. The sods are lucky all they did was lay hands on you."

His vehemence came out in his application of the sponge, growing more vigorous by the moment. Seeing her wince, he sat back, idly fondling the sponge.

The near-mob's shouts pitched another octave higher, snarling at the smell of blood. They were shouted down by Pryce, so that two quavering, defensive voices might be heard.

"Punishment will be brought." Nathan spoke ostensibly for her benefit, but he seemed to glean considerable satisfaction from it. "And before all. Every man shall bear witness, lest there be a misunderstanding of how it was and to see what will happen to the next one."

"How...? I mean who decides what...?"

Nathan blinked, surprised by her ignorance. "A jury's selected."

He eagerly seized on the small diversion. Considerably calmer now, he resumed washing in easier strokes. "Half of their own choosing, and half not. If they're found guilty—No time to be wasted there—Pryce can announce punishment or a jury can choose."

"...a court of peers is always more harsh than the captain might..."

Now more than ever, she saw the wisdom in Nathan staying above the proceedings, no matter how badly he wanted to be the one to pass sentence.

In times of extreme hazard, the mind has a way of barring all thoughts other than those required for survival, and thankfully so. Later, once safety was assured, the barriers would drop, as they did now. She was safe. The realization gradually settled over her. The warm water and the gentle friction of the sponge stirred her senses and delivered her back to reality. The tremors started from deep within, building like a tidal wave. When they broke to the surface, she shook with teeth-clattering violence. Alarmed, Nathan seized the bottle and tipped it to her mouth. She coughed and sputtered, only to have it pressed to her lips again, leaving her no option but to swallow or drown.

Earlier, she had wondered where they were, but now the tears arrived. Knotting her already throbbing eyes, they spilled over and she slowly fell apart. Nathan crouched on the edge of the bed and held her. Making little shushing sounds, he clutched her tightly enough to prevent her from hurting herself as she squealed and pounded his chest. At times shaking as hard as she, his strength and solid warmth kept her buoyant above a yawing pit of misery.

With the breakdown came a sharpening of her senses, the world coming back in brutal clarity. She could hear Pryce now, like Caesar before the Romans, listing the possible punishments: *By the board. Hock and heave. Hoisting. Strappado. Rosary. Fuses.*

Cate had no idea of the meaning; the imagination was sufficient. She put her hands over her ears, unable to listen as sentences were handed down, chanting this was Bullock's fault, not hers. But it was impossible to deny that she had put herself into their hands and allowed it to happen.

A bottle of brandy arrived and was liberally applied. Kirkland came with a pot of chamomile tea from a tin found in Mrs. Littleton's trunk.

"For the love of Christ, man," Nathan cried, watching him pour. "She's not just been told the damned cat spilt the milk!"

Elbowing him away, Nathan poured a generous dollop of brandy into the cup, and then demonstrably dumped an even larger amount into the pot, his glower staving any complaints.

High, thin screams of torture carried on the air. Nathan looked to see her reaction, daring her to object. If only the most barbaric could take satisfaction in suffering, then a tartar she was, for a part of her took deep pleasure at justice being served, pirate justice, but justice, nonetheless. Revenge did have its place. She had entertained serious doubts when hearing it said, but it was manna for a starved soul.

As she sat on the edge of the bed, Nathan on the stool at her knee, she realized what an intimate scene it was. Blood, tears and snot: God, she was a wreck! The times she had allowed herself to imagine him coming to her bedside, it had hardly been like this. Out of gentlemanly forbearance or brotherly lack of interest, he appeared not to see as he dabbed her face with the sponge once more and smoothed back her rampaging hair. A jar of salve was brought, sworn to cure everything from palsy to pox. Nathan discretely held up the quilt and averted his eyes, allowing her to apply it to the raked skin and bite on her breast.

Sometime later, Cate heard Nathan outside the curtain giving Hughes and Cameron stern orders loudly enough for her to know the two Highlanders, possibly the most devoted to her, would be on guard. The knife, a permanent resident in the corner of the bed, was checked. A pistol was deposited at the bed's foot, after Nathan made a great show of priming and checking it in front of her. A small bell was set on the nightstand, within easy reach. A second oil lamp was hung, the candles restocked. She wondered how she was to sleep in such brilliance, but the thought of a dark room was even more disquieting.

Tucked well up, a cool cloth on her head, the camphorous vapors of salve curling in her nose, a steadying furnace of rum and brandy in her stomach, sleep loomed.

"The Fates have spoken. You shan't be worried again," Nathan told her solemnly.

And yet, she did.

Waking wasn't necessarily a thing she wanted to do. Oblivion was ever so much more appealing. Still, forces drove her toward that very thing. Foremost was the desire to rejoin the living, a strong second being the need to know she wasn't alone. She cracked open one eye. The feat came with difficulty and regret. The sliver of light stabbed her head. She winced. That small movement proved a grave mistake. She gasped. The battered muscles of her stomach knotted and refused to move for her next breath.

The curtain stirred, followed by the tinkling of bells and creak of leather.

"Hist, now. Hist. Quiet, luv. Be still." Nathan's gruff voice was a mere whisper.

Cate flinched at his touch. The sudden movement set off a series of protests throughout her body. She opened her eyes into a pair staring back, a nose but inches from hers. The corners of the eyes crinkled as he smiled, though a bit forced.

"There you are." Nathan's graveled voice was suede. "Kirkland insisted you weren't in there, but I bet him a guinea to the contrary. Are you in need of anything? Kirkland thought he heard you stir."

She recognized much of that as a lie, but made no comment, touched that he would make such effort. The port was closed. She had no reference as to the time except for the dull glow of the deck prism. The air was heavy with the stillness of hours that neither day nor night would claim. She risked moving her head ever so slightly in negation and then grimaced against the agony which shot through her from that small gesture.

"No." The word came in a bare croak. "I'm fine..." That gross distortion of the truth stopped her. "I... I could... I am thirsty." The taste of blood was still thick in her mouth and cloyed in the back of her throat.

While Nathan filled a cup at the ewer, Cate struggled to sit up, biting back the oaths which came with it. As he pressed the cup to her lips, she heard the groans of tortured men once more. The sounds had rose and fell on the night air, rendering them unearthly and inhuman. Their moaning and pleas for mercy had haunted her in her sleep, leaving her to wonder if it had been theirs or her own which had wakened her. She looked to Nathan, but his expression was unchanged. If anything, he bore an air of satisfaction. Another cry was heard and Nathan's gazed fixed on hers, daring her to object.

Half-sickened by the voices, she nearly choked on the sip of water. Clucking his tongue, he dabbed her mouth. He fell quiet. His brows knotted as he pensively fondled the cup.

"Perhaps you should come see," he suggested delicately. "Witness your justice, know that none of them will ever do you harm again."

"Vengeance doesn't make it go away," she said dully, resettling her head carefully on the pillow. "What happened?"

"Aye, but you'd be knowing you don't suffer alone." Nathan gave Cate a level look. "Now more than ever, you'll be safe. Every man aboard knows the price."

"It doesn't change men."

He winced. "True enough. An aching cock can speak louder than the cat o' nines."

"Thank you." It occurred to her she had said it already — several times — and yet, it seemed important to continue to do so.

"No worries, luv. I should have had Bullock flogged just for the way he looked at you. Crew and mutiny be damned, at least he would have thought again about..." He choked off the thought, clamping his lower lip between his teeth.

Seeing her settled, Nathan made to leave, but stopped at the curtain.

"This isn't the first, is it?" he asked, slowly turning back. His lips whitened under his mustache. The corners of his eyes pinched with the apprehension of what he already knew to be true.

A cold rush took her, a crawling sensation prickling the nape of her neck. She imperceptibly nodded. There was nothing else to be said.

He closed his eyes and swayed. Then he left.

Cate slept fitfully. When sleep could no longer protect her, she could hear moaning of the condemned. If any thoughts of sympathy for them rose, she need only move; the resulting aches and throbs erased them all. Still, hearing them was agonizing. She pulled the quilt higher and buried her head deeper into the pillow.

"Good God, man! Swab those decks!" shouted a graveled

voice from on deck. "She can't be seeing that!" was the last she heard.

The next morning, Cate woke with the elevation of spirit which comes with having survived the night, not unlike when one suffers the ardors of fever, nightmares or terrors, which could only be dissolved by the pink of dawn. She woke, however, when the aforementioned pink was still in its infantile stages of grey.

Awake? Yes. Alive? Yes.

Willing to move? Not quite.

Enduring the discomfort brought on by the simple act of breathing, she took inventory, searching for three things on her body which didn't hurt. Failing at that, she contemplated the prospects of remaining in her snuggery for eternity.

The ship rode easy "on a t'r'gall'nt n' royal breeze," as she had often heard Nathan call it. As daylight animated wind and water, the *Morganse* shook off her nocturnal lethargy, and her song raised several octaves.

Cate listened to the ship stir, awakening no differently than any household. She heard the rumble of Pryce's voice taking several hands to task, his displeasure neither a pretty sight nor sound. The clang of the bell had barely faded before Mr. Hodder's ungracious rousing of the men from their hammocks. Not long after came the grind of the holystones, gush of water and flapping the decks dry. The bell rang, and the hands were called to breakfast, with a clash of mess kits and hurried slap of bare feet.

Amid all that, however, there was a perceptible reserve in the hands' manner: their conversation lacking the customary levity, their step less energetic. Listening to the cries of the tortured couldn't have been pleasant for them either.

Cate was watching two geckos darting about the porthole when the curtain stirred. Presuming it to be Nathan, with something between awe and amusement, she saw Beatrice push her way under the hem. In determined parrot-steps, and with as much dignity as could be managed by a bird afoot, she crossed the room. In a rustle of hyacinth-colored feathers and a flash of black underwing, she rose to the washstand. Taking a moment to disengage her tail feathers from the basin, she settled and regarded Cate with one beady eye.

Poking through the fog of the day before, she recalled Nathan telling her it had been Beatrice who had sounded the alarm and led to her rescue.

How does one go about thanking a parrot?

The presence of another living being was a comfort, even if it was no more than a curmudgeonly bird.

"Flog the bastard," said Beatrice.

Cate carefully smiled. "I can't say as I disagree."

She sighed as contentedly as her aching body would allow. This was home or the closest to it in several years. At times feeling like a barnacle on the keel, she had found the sense of belonging, usefulness and friendship, contrary to Nathan's protests. Nothing could cause her to jeopardize any of it.

Through swollen eyes, she went back to the gecko, now on a beam. Anyone who complained of cockroaches or rats on a ship hadn't lived in infested garrets, where it was necessary to leave precious bits of food as bait. Shoes could be worn while one slept, but it was difficult to protect fingers, lips and noses from being gnawed. The patter of feet in the night was now a comfort, His Lordship on the prowl.

Thinking back to those times brought back several recollections. The hammering head she currently suffered was nothing compared to those which sprung from hunger, the ache of battered stomach muscles nowhere near the sharp pangs of starvation. She had been fed well on the *Constancy*, and even better on the *Ciara Morganse*, but she would have gained weight on ship's biscuit and water. Still a shadow of her former self, she could no longer fit a finger between each rib.

Nathan's tap on the doorjamb startled her. He must have tiptoed, for his appearance came without so much as a tinkle of a bell. He backpedaled at the sight of Beatrice. Her head came up from preening and the two squared off in a territorial stare.

"Must she be here?" he said, regarding the bird dolefully.

"I'll allow you the privilege of explaining," Cate said careful to move her jaw no more than necessary.

Biting back several remarks, he kept an eye on Beatrice as he kicked the pile of her discarded clothing farther into the corner. The smells of bilges, moldy hemp and male sweat stirred. Her gut roiled, and she was beset by a renewed wave of panic and revulsion.

Nathan's nose twitched, his countenance more troubled, as he said, "No need in trying to repair that bit o' business. I brought you these." He produced from under his arm the shirt and velvet breeches he had given her when first arrived.

"We should be putting in anon," he said casually.

Putting into port was news; there had been no prior mention.

It led her to wonder if it was indeed a planned stop or an accommodation on her behalf.

"How do we know she's not a he?" he asked, swiveling to regard Beatrice severely.

Cate frowned, eyeing the parrot as well. "What difference would it make, anyway?"

"Plenty, depending on his motivations." He arched a suspicious brow. "What says *he's* not in here *ogling*?"

Suddenly self-conscious, Cate tugged the quilt a little higher. "Don't be absurd." Admittedly, the bird was showing more interest, verging on affection.

"I'll see to it that something more decent is found," he said, picking up his earlier thoughts.

Nathan hung between the bunk and the curtain. Aside from being in territory into which he didn't ordinarily venture, his uneasiness seemed to stem from something else. With a sinking heart, she realized that he expected her to dress, and judging by the stern set of his jaw, was disinclined to argue the point. The night had been no easier on him: the dark shadow of his beard echoed the circles under his eyes. He repeatedly glanced at her, and then away, making her wonder if her appearance was that disagreeable. A glass hung on the wall, but she couldn't garner the courage to look. The narrowed vision in one eye, thickened lips and an overall hot puffiness were guidance enough.

As she contemplated trying to finesse her way out of dressing, she shifted with another kind of discomfort: she needed to go to the privy. As perceptive as ever—Damn his eyes!—Nathan picked up on the situation.

"I'm sure we can—" he offered, anxiously hovering.

"Not bloody likely," she growled through clenched teeth. Under no circumstances was she going to subject herself to using a chamber pot, even if there was one aboard, which Nathan doubted. He was quick to assure her, however, that other arrangements could be made. She would have to be far closer to death for that. Once again, she was grateful for the time-honored tradition of the captain having his own convenience. Having to traipse all the way to the forecastle head seemed an insurmountable expedition.

Nathan discretely retreated to the salon, although the toes of his boots were still visible beneath the curtain's hem. Cate moved with eloquent care in sitting up to the complaint of every nook of her body. On the edge of the bed, she drew several cautious breaths, allowing the light-headedness to abate before rising to her feet.

In halting increments, she dressed, daring to peek down

at herself. Her neck and chest were a crisscross of angry red nail gouges. The bite on her breast was another story, the tooth indentations now a dark maroon amid a halo of purple fading to yellow. Seeing it made it throb worse. There was fortuitousness in donning the men's clothing: no stays and a waistband which barely touched her tender midriff. The binder secured her breasts, but she still hooked her arm under the left one as she took her first experimental steps into the salon.

Cate crossed the room in mincing steps, the slightest jar of her breast causing her to gasp. Nathan saw as much. He knew. He had seen it first hand, for heaven sakes.

No secrets on a bloody, damned ship!

The thought was more than a little disquieting. At the time, she had been too stunned to care if he saw. Now, it was an awkward truth.

The ship's motion didn't help matters; there was an unexpected lurch. Nathan dove to catch her as she careened sideways and shepherded her the rest of the way. At the privy closet door, he declared an urgent need to check a chart, his loud humming and drumming of his fingers on the table providing her a curtain of privacy.

Beatrice had moved to the galley gangway rail by the time Cate came out. The bird stared back benignly, as if she had been there right along.

"I thought I smelled coffee," Cate said hopefully as she shuffled to the table.

Nathan saw her seated. She looked dubiously at the mug on the table before her, her hopes sinking.

"I thought I smelled coffee," she repeated, dully. That which sat before her was most certainly not.

"Whipped egg and ale," he announced brightly to her questioning look. He sobered and said from the corner of his mouth, "I shan't hold out hopes of aught else forthcoming from Kirkland's brewing den of Satan, until it's drunk. It seemed a small price in lieu of being bled."

He circled and prowled from a distance in thinly veiled disapproval of the shirt and breeches she wore. Gulps of rum required to tamp down the anger he currently masked, he chattered of anything and everything, except the blessed whale in the room. She eventually grew cross and yearned for at least a modicum of directness. To her relief, he was at last called away — some crisis involving the foremast cat-harpins and swifters — and the salon fell quiet, leaving her to cautiously sip her ale.

Sometime in the night, the cries of the tortured men had

ceased. She kept her eyes averted, afraid of what scene might await outside. She wondered how far pirate justice went, if it followed the habits of civilian courts back in England: leaving a criminal's head impaled on a pike or the body rotting in a gibbet. She had looked to Nathan for an indication of what to expect, but none had been forthcoming, and she was loath to ask.

A tug at her sleeve broke her stare. Cate looked into a pair of golden orbs at her elbow. Hermione's gaze shifted in broad suggestion from Cate, to her drink, and back.

"It's... well, I'm not sure what to call it, but it's not tea."

Hermione sniffed interestedly at the proffered mug and bleated in complaint.

"Pray see Kirkland on the matter. I'm a bit incapacitated."

The beast nudged her elbow, demanding to be petted. Cate obligingly scratched behind the silken ears, feeling a bit better for the company. She thought the rustle of feathers she heard was Beatrice taking her leave, but it was Artemis, appearing from below. The owl alighted on the back of Nathan's chair and stared.

A triumvirate of women, she mused.

A dash of movement caught her eye: a gecko, perched on the sill of the stern window, eyeing her as well.

How does one discern the sex of a lizard?

"Well, here we all are, eh? A sisterhood amid the Brethren."

True to Nathan's word, port was made that afternoon. Seen from where Cate sat on the gallery sill, under the sun hanging in a hot orb, the little town appeared barely capable of clothing itself, let alone having any to spare. Nathan waved off the minor detail.

"I have the acquaintance of someone, who knew someone else, who had a connection with someone else, who had access to someone else."

In other words: don't ask.

Cate bit back the observation that the stays, shift and skirt he deposited in her arms smelled markedly of fresh laundering. A small fragment of soap was placed ceremoniously atop the folded clothing. Laden with bits of flower petals and leaves, it was heady with the scent of lavender and roses.

Nathan dismissed her gratitude out-of-hand. "It seemed someone who worshipped cleanliness deserved something to put upon its altar," was all he said.

She impulsively kissed him on the cheek in gratitude, not

only for the clothing but for everything this last day. It was then she discovered that he wasn't above blushing.

"Still need to find something to do with that hair," he muttered gruffly and ambled off.

She smiled. It was an old joke. Her unruly locks were a running point of contention with him, good-natured but determined. There was a certain irony in it, coming from someone who barely contained his own mane.

The days passed. Cate's confidence incrementally grew. She was still subject to jumping at an unexpected noise, the pop of a plank, creak of a shroud, clump of a boot, or slap of a wave sending her cowering. Shying at being left alone, she was given to periodic fits, vacillating wildly from sobbing to vacant stares. The smell of bilges, muck and hungering men cloyed stubbornly in her nose, causing her to snort and snuffle. Nathan hovered over her as if she was an enfeebled aunt. She grew fractious and wanted to rebuke him, but found that she had neither the will nor the wherewithal to do so.

The death of his own crewman was on Nathan's hands. She would have never requested or expected such a deed, but the fact was he had killed in her defense. It was unclear if it had been a simple act of violence, chivalry or if there had been a greater meaning in it. He wasn't saying and it was blessedly difficult to ask.

Men were dead; there was no romance or glory in that.

Cate mentally marked off the small blessings. She had been lucky, she kept telling herself. She was whole, nothing was missing, the bite above her nipple a sharp reminder of how close she had come. Her face was swollen, but there were no broken noses or teeth, not even a finger. Her throat hadn't been cut, and most importantly, albeit sore and bruised thighs, Bullock and his pack had failed at their initial mission.

So, why didn't she feel lucky?

She carefully searched the face of everyone she met, from Squidge to Hodder, Towers to Smalley, Jensen to Millbridge, looking for any signs of recrimination or reproach, accusation or resentment, but saw none. For that matter, she saw nothing. She didn't inquire as to what had befallen Bullock and his cohorts, and no one said. Every trace was gone, no belongings or gear auctioned off, no recollections over a cup of grog, no mention at all. It was a Brotherhood of Silence, in which she was an inadvertent member. What threats had been made to guarantee that silence was an even better kept secret. On that mark, she was an outsider looking in.

In the long run, she had taken no worse beating than a

forecastleman in a minor blow. The matter was over, forgotten. They had moved on, just as she was expected to do.

And so, she did. Nothing more was said—nothing more need be.

END OF PART ONE

12: A PLAN AWRY

CATE CAME OUT OF THE cabin and lifted the hair from her neck to allow what little breeze there was to cool her neck. Her shift was damp with sweat and she wriggled against the stays where the linen stuck to her ribs.

The *Morganse* had been before the wind since the morning sun struggled up through a haze-shrouded horizon. It meant moving with the wind, the effect being as if there was no wind at all, and the air pressed like a hot mask at one's face. Consequently, she had spent much of it in the cabin where what little breeze there was funneled through.

Cate had practiced her knot-tying—in peace, but to no avail—and read. Later, she had embroidered. There was precious little thread remaining; each bit she treasured. She took great joy of watching the images of flower, vine and leaf emerge with the addition of each stitch. Through the weeks hence, Nathan had often observed over her shoulder, fascinated as well.

"I've been around the world, more times than I care to count, and I've not seen work like that," he said in open admiration.

Nathan reached to examine it more closely, but thought better, his hands being so tar-stained. Instead, he tucked them into his belt and peered over her shoulder. He showed a surprising knowledge of design and color. As he bent, his braids fell forward, brushing her shoulders. His breath warm on her neck set her glowing both from his praise and nearness.

But now, eyes too tired and light too poor, she stopped working. Nathan had proclaimed repeatedly he didn't care how many candles she burned.

"Light it up like a wretched lightship, if you wish!"

But such indulgences didn't come easily.

The night threatened to be nearly as warm as the day, the air and sea too heat-stricken to stir. She thought longingly of the Highlands, with its cool lochs and tumbling burns in which one could splash. To dream, however, only served to highlight one's misfortune.

Cate stretching her back and working the stiffness from her fingers, she followed the voices outside. She balked at the mass of men. It had to have been the entire company. The last time she had witnessed such a gathering, it had been incited by Bullock's agitating, but there was a vast difference in the mood now. There was a tension in the air, but more in the way of vested interest rather than dissension.

Gathered under the halo of the lamps, Nathan and Pryce were at roughly the center. Nearby, atop stacked bags of Hermione's dry fodder, Millbridge looked comfortably on from a position of honor. Away from the light of the lanterns, the moon shone on the intent faces. There was no smoking allowed on board, but chewing tobacco was, although lo unto the poor unthinking soul who spat on Hodder's holy deck! Those who chose to indulge did so from the leeward rail, adding an odd, staccato chorus of spitting.

She halted at the outer margins of the gathering to listen.

"Nay, nay," Pryce was saying. "That won't answer. The Royal Navy'll smoke us a'fore we're clear o' the harbor."

"I 'aven't 'eard you come up with anything yet," pouted Smalley.

"Now, now, mates," Nathan intervened. "Squabbling don't pay the purser."

Nathan's face lit at spotting Cate and he beckoned her near. As she picked her way through the crowd, the smell of the night's ration of rum rose amid the stronger ones of unwashed male and sun-baked clothing. Nathan gallantly rose from his seat atop a cask.

"Good evening, luv." Mirth sparked his eye as he bowed deeply. "Our compliments. We wish you joy of this fine evening."

"Good evening. Gentlemen," she said, nodding graciously to those she passed.

With a small amount of shuffling, a seat was arranged for her next to Nathan.

"The problem is: we've no idea of when she's to arrive," he said, resuming the discussion. "If we knew that, the rest would be of minor consequence."

"Yes, but the only one what knows that is Creswicke," argued Squidge, a murmur of agreement coming from the rest. "And I don't fancy him telling us."

"Well," Towers sighed, morosely. "There has to be someone what knows."

A silence fell as each man retreated into his own thoughts.

Looking across the faces, she slowly came to find a semblance of order in the gathering. Larbolins apart from starbolins, the men were loosely clustered according to their duty assignments, generally in the vicinity of their leader: Hughes, Cameron, Diogo, Damerell and the balance of the f'c'stlemen near Fox, Hodder with his mates. The topsmen stood with the topsmen, Chips with his carpenter's mates, Jimmy Bungs and the coopersmates, and so on.

Cate leaned toward Nathan and whispered, "May I inquire what this is about?"

"By all means," Nathan replied, jovially. He bent to pick the bottle of rum from at his feet. He started to take a drink, but paused with the bottle poised at his mouth. "Would you care for a bit?"

Devilment quirked his mouth at offering temptation. It occurred to her that it mightn't have been the first bottle of the evening.

"No, thank you, I don't care much for rum," she said.

Amid the ensuing disgruntled murmurs brought on by that revelation, Nathan regarded her with a narrow look. "So, you keep saying."

"There's a lot you don't know about me, Captain."

"Indeed, there is." His jaw worked sideways as he scrutinized her. "Indeed, there is."

The walnut gaze lingered. Then he straightened and cleared his throat. "A man without a plan is a man who plans to fail. Therefore, we plan, in hopes of a bit of profit."

"At whose expense?" she asked.

"Lord Breaston Creswicke..." began Smalley.

"Of the Royal West Indies Mercantile Company..." continued Towers.

"Is betrothed," Nathan completed, his eyebrows lifting in emphasis.

"Ah, yes," she said, recalling Samuels' revelations during his ill-fated visit. She smiled faintly, wondering if he had yet divested himself of the pink paint.

"And so, you're going to kidnap said fiancé?" she asked.

"Exactly!" Nathan declared, pleased at her ability to grasp.

"Problem is," continued Pryce, less enthusiastic, "with no idea of where, what or when, we're sailin' blind."

The pirates called out a number of suggestions—people, places, options—many of which were shouted down before the presenter could finish.

"'Tis obvious Samuels doesn't know when she's coming, or

he would have held out for more money else." Nathan said in his usual cold pragmatism.

"So, we're left with the who, a possible when, but not the where," sighed Pryce.

"Someone must know," she cut in, picking up their frustration.

"Obviously, Creswicke," sneered someone from the rear.

"He never comes out o' that stronghold of his in Bridgetown, so we'll not be a-squeezin' it out of him," Pryce added with prim disdain.

"You can bet your Aunt Maud's bloomers, he'll have 'er guarded, that's for sure," said Towers, with a lugubrious shake of his head.

"Guarded by whom?" asked Cate.

The men stopped, perplexed by her query.

"Who's to guard her?" she repeated. Looking from face to face, she came around to Nathan.

"Probably the Marines," he said, squinting speculatively. "What have you in that lovely mind?"

"If the Marines are to guard her," she began slowly, picking through her line of logic. "Then wouldn't it follow that the Marines would know when she's to arrive?"

The men exchanged glances, uncertain. Nathan looked thoughtfully at the deck between his feet.

"Just ask the Marines?" he asked, looking up dubiously from the corner of his eye.

She was a bit taken back at their failure to see the strength of her point. "Certainly. Why not? You could learn everything you need."

Pirates weren't shy about expressing their misgivings and did so with verve then.

"But how do we do that?" Chin's voice finally rose over the others.

"Kidnap one," someone shouted from the shadowy reaches, eliciting a laugh.

"Torture 'im until 'e talks," called another from the opposite direction. The prospect of inflicting pain brought an enthusiastic cheer.

Nathan batted an irritated hand, quieting them all. "Nay, that won't answer. Who's to know the one what we take would be the one knowing?"

"Well, we can't very well just walk in and ask 'em," blurted Towers, ruffled by Nathan's dismissal.

"Why not?" Cate asked.

"Because, me darling," Towers said, condescendingly rolling his froggish eyes, "they'll take one look and smoke who we are."

"Serve nothin' but to get us arrested," put in another faceless voice, bringing further murmurs of approval.

"Then send someone who doesn't look like a pirate," she said, a bit testily. She looked from one to the next, waiting for the response that never came. Instead, they stared blank-faced... except Nathan.

"And who pray tell, would that be?" he asked, his gravelly voice dropping to a near purr.

"Me."

Nathan was both stunned and suspicious. "You'd do that for us?"

"Certainly, why not? You've all been so good... about everything... It's the least I can do."

Pryce crossed his arms and swiveled a severe eye. "Put a name to what be on yer mind?"

"Go to wherever the Marines are and talk," she said, suffering to point out the obvious.

"That's it? Talk?" Nathan gave her a queer look.

"Yes." Seeing doubt was rampant, Cate explained in slow, patient terms. "With all due respect, gentlemen, it's not a difficult recipe: put men and drink together, add a little flattery, perhaps a flutter of the lashes, and it's but a matter of time."

Puffed at having their weaknesses so handily dissected, the men reluctantly agreed. In order to execute said plan, there was only one person who could carry it off; she waited patiently until they came to the same conclusion. Nathan's displeasure at the prospect was patently obvious, and he suffered no hesitation in voicing it, but in the face of the final vote — one man, one vote — it was approved, leaving him little choice but to go along.

"Where do we begin?" she asked.

"Eh, well," Nathan said slowly, drawing a pensive hand down the curve of his mustache. "Hopetown is the first landfall between Boston and Bridgetown. 'Tis likely they would put in there for water and victuals, before pressing on to Barbados."

"Then we should start there."

Cate blew out the candle that night. She laid fingering her knotted pendant and staring at the deck prism overhead. Hopetown was but a day's sail, by Nathan's estimation. Reef points shook out and sail packed on, the *Morganse's* eagerness for her new destination could be felt, the decks pitched with a new stiffness.

She was not without conscience. The thought of aiding the

kidnapping of another was wholly uncomfortable, the terrors of her own taking being fresh in her mind. But the cold facts were that she was aboard and therefore a part of it, whether she wished it or no. To argue against it could have put herself, and most importantly, Nathan at risk, the near mutiny still looming near. Bullock was gone, but the seeds of dissention could still be lying, ready to sprout on the not so fallow ground.

The crew had voted, the decision made. Now it was but a matter of the how. Had she not spoken up, someone else—most likely Nathan—would have been obliged to do something. The incident with Bullock had already put Nathan at risk. Guilt weighed heavily, and she was anxious to repay him, everyone for that matter.

Hostage-taking had been very common among the clans in the Highlands. It had often been a contest as to which they valued more: a relative or the cattle. There had been one snatching of a person, however, that had been far more violent...

That was different, far different.

Whoever this unfortunate soul was would have it far better than she had, for there would be someone waiting to comfort and protect. The woman would come to no harm, not aboard the *Ciara Morganse*, not with Captain Nathanael Blackthorne commanding.

How different it could have been, had I known as much then.

It wasn't fear or apprehension which made her heart race. She was just... anxious. Among a hundred plus unwashed and weathered men, a hyacinth-colored parrot, a mongoose, a goat and an enigmatic captain, she had found an anchorage. She had learned to trust these men, and now they were learning to trust her. Her greatest fear was of disappointing them, most particularly Nathan.

This was something which she could do as no other aboard could: entice men to drink and talk.

Child's play!

Somewhere in the cradle of thoughts, darkness and the easy motion of the ship, she slept.

Cate woke sometime later to the horrifying paralysis of someone standing over her, faceless and breathing heavily. Shrieking, she scrambled for the knife hidden at the mattress's corner.

"You awake, luv?" The disembodied voice came out of the inky void.

"Nathan?" She gasped, sagging with relief.

"Did I give you a start?" His usual throatiness was thickened. The words slurred, the smell of rum rode each one.

"What in the world are you doing in here?" Heart still pounding, her own breath came in tight wheezes.

Nathan had been drinking, how much being the question. She had seen him in drink before, but only pleasantly so. The basic nature of a man could change unpredictably when drunk. How much would it require for Nathan to cross from friend to assailant? It had already compelled him to a startling invasion.

"Pray, a word, if you please," he said precisely.

Cate nodded, but then realized the gesture was lost in the darkness. "Yes?"

More at ease, she inched away from the bulkhead and returned the knife to its home. In the darkness, his dark form was limned by a lucent green of the prisms. A boot scraped the floor. The mattress dipped when he collided with the bunk and caught himself. Such clumsiness was disconcerting. Never had she seen him put a foot wrong. He was most certainly *very* drunk.

"Need to know something." Nathan audibly swallowed like the condemned, and then said determinedly, "I need to know… if you're coming back."

"Back?" It took her a moment to realize his meaning, made doubly difficult by having to guess where his face was. "You mean, tomorrow?"

"Aye. Are you… coming… back?"

She gaped into the darkness, thinking surely she had misunderstood. "Why wouldn't I?"

A swishing jingle of silver and creak of leather marked his movement. By the sound of his breathing he was very near. She heard the familiar rasp of the stubble of his beard as he passed a hand along his jaw. There was the intake of air in preparation to say something, but then exhaled heavily and gulped in dread.

"It occurred… maybe… perhaps… I mean… you might be thinking to… to escape."

His face was obscured, but his trepidation couldn't be mistaken. She bit her lip, choking back a rising lump in her throat.

"I hadn't considered myself a captive, of late at any rate. Am I?"

"Are you what?"

"A captive."

"Oh," Nathan said, puzzled.

A hand trailed along the edge of the bed toward the nightstand. With a certain amount of fumbling, the flint box was struck, and she squinted at the glare. The candlelight flared on his profile. Weaving precariously, he blinked, as if noticing where he was for the first time. His sockets blackened pools in the shadows cast by his skull, he struggled to steady unfocused eyes. Swaying once, and then again, he turned to brace his back against the bulkhead. He slid slowly down, a muffled thump and clatter of his sword marking his reaching the floor. Cate inched down on the mattress, in order to be more on his level, and propped her head in her hand.

The candle's amber haloed on his head and shoulders, the rest of him lost to the darkness. One arm resting on a bent knee, the other limp in his lap, his gaze fixed somewhere in the vicinity of the toe of his boot.

The dark dashes of his brows drew together. "'Tis why I feared to allow you ashore," he murmured more to himself.

Nathan's eyes pivoted up to hers, with a heart-stalling mixture of yearning and fear. "I thought you wouldn't come back."

"I hadn't realized I was being held against my will," Cate stammered, playing along, for surely it was another one of Nathan's ploys. He was drunk. No more need be said.

"You're free to go, luv." He gulped again. The near black orbs searched hers, hoping for the answer he wanted to hear, afraid of what remained.

Nathan's mouth worked as his rum-fogged mind searched for words. "Anytime. At your leisure, just say the word."

"Where do you fancy I might go?" Heart pounding, her breath caught, knowing all the while she didn't dare believe this to be true.

"Someplace. Any place, but here." He shook his head, waving his hand toward the beyond. "A ship, the sea's a rough place, especially for a woman."

"I'm comfortable." She nestled deeper under the quilt. "For the first time in years, I have purpose and a place to belong."

She paused, fondling the blanket as it occurred to her that this might not be a moment of truth, but another one of Nathan's elaborate evasions, a long-winded way of desiring her to be gone. The hand draped on his knee flexing, he could swing wildly from maddeningly evasive to stunningly blunt. Which was this? Between the deep shadows and the rum, she had no way of knowing.

"If you don't mind, too much," she began, measuring each word, "I thought I'd return... for a while... at least?"

Nathan tipped his head back against the wall in relief. Shoulders sagging, the hand in his lap clenched into a victorious fist. He glanced up shyly, and then away. She ventured to touch him lightly on the shoulder and his head jerked around.

"Thank you, Nathan."

He scowled with the effort of thinking. "For what?"

"For giving me a home, a place to belong. It's been a long time."

Fumbling, his hand came to rest over hers and squeezed. "Anytime, luv."

His eyes aimlessly traversed the dark room. Like a great tree, he slowly toppled sideways into the darkness, his bells clattering softly on the floor.

"Nathan?"

Rising on her elbow, she strained to see. He lay on his side, only his hips and rear now lit. She slipped off the bunk and picked her way through his out-flung limbs to kneel next to him. Asleep or fallen out, a blissful smile curved under his mustache. She pressed her fingers to her lips to suppress something between laughter and tears. Checking to make sure the salon was clear, she retrieved his coat from atop a trunk and brought it back to spread over his shoulders. Bells jingling faintly, he stirred, and then settled, sighing contentedly.

"Sleep well, luv," she whispered. Smoothing stray hairs from his face, she tucked the coat more snugly around him.

Blowing out the candle, she crawled back into bed and slept as she had never before.

⁂

The island of New Providence proved to possess two roads, which intersected at a given point. Cate stood at said crossroads, feeling like a character in a fable, trying to choose which fork to follow.

After Nathan's midnight appearance at her bunkside, she had wakened the next morning to His Lordship shuffling about an empty bedside; Nathan was already gone. When he finally made his appearance in the salon, he was his usual, insufferable, cheery self, shouting for Mr. Kirkland, coffee and Hermione's tea. She waited for him to say something about the night before, but either through his typical fashion of ignoring the inconvenient, or the convenience of drunken forgetfulness, he gave no sign of recollection. Perhaps it was just as well; morning-after scenes could be awkward. The sentiments expressed were dismissed, as well. Best the whole thing be forgotten.

The *Ciara Morganse* had slipped into New Providence's back bay under the pinking skies of dawn. Nathan had spent the bulk of the day and into the night pacing, haranguing everyone in his path. Beatrice and any topsman who could find sufficient excuse, retreated to the mastheads, much to the admiration of everyone left below.

"You don't have to do this. You've done more than enough to prove yourself," Nathan intoned more than once.

Nathan briefed and debriefed Cate again and again, only to return after each with a finger skyward and a "One more thing", until she finally excused him with a stern finger of her own and an exasperated "Get out!"

The plan was basic, therefore with less room for complications: where there are taverns, there are soldiers. It was a simple axiom. Somewhere in Hopetown was a tavern or alehouse where the garrison's Marines gathered to drink. Cate was to find said tavern, posing as hostage from the *Constancy* and just escaped from pirates. In essence, it was the truth, and so, provable. After, it would be a simple matter of playing damsel-in-distress, drink enough to be sociable, sit, wait and listen. By evening, she was to return to the bay where a boat would be waiting to deliver her back to the *Morganse*.

In the time Cate had known Nathan, he had never seemed the pessimist: his glass—better yet, rum bottle—was always half full. As the plan solidified, however, he came up with an endless list of what-could-go-wrong scenarios, to the point of Mr. Pryce looking strained when Nathan launched into a lengthy and convoluted premise of the entire Royal Navy springing up from nowhere.

Nathan had been adamant about seeing her ashore, as if by some stroke of stupidity, she might not find it, and then wouldn't relent, until he had seen her through the trees to the road. She was glad for his arm, however. For her first steps on solid land, she was rubbery-legged. She had become so accustomed to the liveliness of decks under her feet, the ground was too solid and unyielding, and never where her feet expected it to be. Giggling, she staggered against Nathan as he led her to the road, as if she had emptied Nathan's half-full bottle.

"I don't like this." Nathan glared at the road, no more than a glorified path, and then her. "I don't like it a 'tall."

"Nonsense. How difficult can it be?"

"You're unarmed."

Cate inwardly groaned at what had been another point of contention.

"I can't very well claim to be an escaped captive wearing a pistol, now can I?" she said acerbically, as she had every time. Pryce had thankfully concurred or Nathan would have never relented.

"Allow me to at least walk you to the—"

"And risk being seen together?" She arched a brow, driving home the unfortunate implications of that.

"Sundown," he warned, shaking a finger at her as if she were a wayward child. "I'll be right here — as will you! Now, you have your knife?"

"Yes!" *For no less than the fortieth time,* she thought crossly. He had insisted on sharpening it himself to the point she wondered what kept it from slicing through her pocket.

Unperturbed — as always — Nathan pressed on, continuing to make her feel like that same juvenile being sent off for its first day of school.

"Mind your purse."

"Don't stop for any strangers."

"Don't walk too fast."

"You should have a parasol."

"Mind the heat."

"Nathan, good-by," she said with finality.

"I'll be right here at dark. Can you remember that?"

"I'd have to be a complete dolt not to," she huffed under her breath.

With an encouraging pat on the arm, she gave him a peck on the cheek. She didn't have the heart to look back as she took her leave, unable to bear his forlorn look.

Now ashore, there she stood at the literal and proverbial fork in the road. In all the briefings, no one had mentioned this. With no other option to hand, she followed the time-honored tradition: plucked a piece of grass, closed her eyes and dropped it. The blade fell pointing left, so left she went.

The road was no more than well-pounded wagon ruts dotted with the occasional oxen or horse droppings. Its width could almost be spanned by extending her arms. Privacy and solitude were scarce commodities on a ship, and so she strolled relishing every moment. Her senses were assaulted with sights, smells and sounds, and she eagerly devoured them all. She hadn't felt terra firma under her feet, nor heard anything alive other than a seagull in over three months; St. Agua had been a cruel temptation. As she went deeper into the protection of land and trees, the air grew denser, becoming almost too thick to breathe. Stopping often in open-mouthed awe at the edenic forest, she experienced the same thrill of discovery that the first explorers must have suffered. The verdant lushness, bright jeweled tones of birds, insects and flowers stabbed her eyes after months of naught but saturated blue. The smells alone made her heady: leaves, moss, green — yes, green did have its own scent — and ferns, mixed with the sweet earthy smell of dirt and the pungent animal stench.

It was heavenly!

Amid the raucous calls from bevies of multi-colored birds, chittering and scolding could be heard, small, furry beings alarmed at her passage. Her step slowed at hearing a slithering rustle in the grass at her ankles.

"If it crawls, slinks, scuttles or slithers, don't touch it!" had been Nathan's admonition.

"No danger there!" she said aloud.

All too soon, Cate found herself in the middle of Hopetown. The sun's heat and light glared off near-white of the crushed oyster shells which paved the streets. It muffled the clop of the horse hooves, the wheels of passing carriages and carts grinding softly. A small town by many standards, it seemed a metropolis to her. It wasn't Edinburgh, London or Bristol, but it was the largest—only—town she had been in for months. In many ways it was the same as every town: people scurrying about on their daily business, hawkers with their push-carts and colorful shop signs over the sidewalk, advertising their wares: silversmith, glassblower, tailor, tobacconist or wigmaker. Palm trees notwithstanding, what separated this from the other cities were the multi-colored faces that peeked out from under the hats, bonnets, kerchiefs and parasols: white, black, brown, and yellow, with every hue in between.

It was fascinating!

Cate peeked in the windows of the first few shops she passed. Glares from the proprietors set her on her way. The passing citizens eyed her—a woman unescorted was to be noted—disapproving sniffs the most common reaction. It was no wonder, she thought, looking down at herself. In her worn clothes and tar-stained shoes, she was quite beggarly. She followed the lumbering waggons, handcarts and freight drays, and the smell of the waterfront to the lesser side of town, for that was where she would find the taverns which Marines would frequent. As the surrounding voices grew more boisterous and sharper-tongued, she felt less conspicuous.

Mumbling something about "damned pauper", Nathan had tucked a purse heavy with coins into her pocket. Her stomach rumbled as she passed the street vendors. Breakfast had been marginal. Mr. Kirkland, so distracted by the prospect of her departure, had burned the porridge beyond salvation. She still hadn't acquired a taste for ship's biscuit—Every time she looked, she swore she saw things moving in it—softened in broth. She bought a roll from a lady with a basket on a corner. Filled with diced meats and vegetables, it was so very reminiscent of bridies, the meat pies of Scotland. After an orange on a stick, she tried something called plantains, cooked over a small brazier by a woman in a brightly striped skirt.

She came across two taverns which held promise, but the clientele was too well-dressed, and so she moved on. Down the street a bit nearer the docks were four more taverns, roughly forming a square: *The Rose and Crown, The Pewter Pot, The Admiral's Cabin* and *The Sign of the George*. Finding a shady spot under a fragrantly flower-covered archway, she waited. In this section of town, a woman standing alone drew attention, but for different reasons. She was approached by men offering their coins. The first one took her rejection kindly, the second and third was a bit dim. Some of Nathan's dark oaths, mixed a few learned from her husband sent them scurrying on their way.

Standing and waiting proved not as easy as one might have predicted. When walking all was well, but once still, Cate discovered the consequences of months at sea: everything moved, the world swaying in ghostly memory of waves. A hand anchored to the wall was of little help. A few times she had to catch herself, feeling she was about to topple over. Bracing a hand to her forehead, she closed her eyes, but instantly found that the wrong thing to do, the oscillating only intensifying. The only solution was walking and so she did. Strolling slowly, she bore a sharp eye on the establishments.

Heat and thirst were beginning to take their toll when luck finally came her way in the form of four bright red coats of Marines. Jostling and guffawing, they paid her no heed as they passed within a few feet and barged into *The Rose and Crown*. Four more immediately filed in, followed directly by three more. Apparently, she had found the glory hole! She began to smooth her hair, and then checked herself: if she was supposed to have just escaped, a bit tousled was to be expected. She stepped across and went in.

The taproom was a fairly large, saw-dust floored, low-ceilinged affair, with rough tables and benches. Decades of fire, candle and tobacco smoke had blackened the beams. The air was thick with a combination of ale, burned food, wax and tinges of urine and vomit. A typical tavern. The keeper behind the counter gave her a minatory eye—there was only one reason a woman would enter alone—and then went on about his business, assuming her to do the same. The Marines were scattered among several tables in the room's middle, and so she chose one off to the side. As she sat, she caught the whiff of something else: her own sweat. She hadn't thought to be that nervous.

The servant girl, a waif with brown snakes for braids, appeared wordlessly, setting Cate's tankard in front of her with the same amount of enthusiasm as she had taken the order. The ale was sour, but not bitter, with a slightly sweet aftertaste that made it tolerable. Best of all, it was cool. She tipped her head back to let it slide down her throat and wash away the road dust. It had been a long time since she had been able to enjoy a drink. Heaven knew, rum flowed freely on the *Morganse*. God, how she hated the stuff! It tasted like old socks, but she didn't dare say as much to Nathan—

"Pray, I beg pardon, Madame...?"

Cate snapped from her reverie by a male voice. She looked up into the blue and white of a Royal Navy uniform.

"Commodore Roger Harte, your servant—"

She had the sudden sensation of falling backwards and jerked with a violence that shot her drink out of its mug. With reflexes of a swordsman, he artfully dodged the flying liquid, although a fine spray of ale glittered on the dark blue wool.

"No, mind," he said, waving away her apologies and attempts to wipe the mess with her apron. "Please, leave us shift over here. You!" he called sharply to the sullen serving girl. "Attend this and bring us two drinks. Cider?" he asked of Cate.

Too flustered to think else, she weakly replied "Ale".

Harte's surprise and disapproval of her drinking something so common was evident, but fleeting. He drew a vast handkerchief from his sleeve—deeply-laced and scented—and fastidiously dabbed at his coat.

"Commodore Roger Harte, at your service, Madame," he announced once more. He swept off his hat and made an elegant leg.

Still discomposed, her voice failed. Clearing her throat, she tried anew. "Cate Harper."

He seized her hand and kissed it, flashing a smile of even white teeth meant to charm. "Enchanted. Shall I join you?"

He sat without an answer, the drinks arriving shortly thereafter. It was worth noting that he had ordered nothing specifically for himself, and yet a glass—not a mug—was set before him, with the significance of it being exactly as he would wish.

"It's so enlightening to find someone as charming as yourself, in an establishment such as this." Harte spoke in a carefully cultured accent. His nostrils flared slightly with distaste. "These small settlements can be at times such a tribulation. I couldn't help but notice you were unescorted."

Cate smiled faintly. That pointed observation could have its feet in either chivalry or overtures of a baser sort. In desperate need of time to compose herself, she dipped her nose into her drink and regarded him over the rim.

It was difficult not to stare. Across from her sat the man whose warships had pursued the *Ciara Morganse*, fired with intent to kill. Given the reaction by any Morganser, most especially Nathan, at the mere mention of his name, Harte wasn't the monster she had expected. He was fairly good-looking and relatively young for one of such advanced rank. Verdantly green-eyed and cleanly profiled, the golden hue of his skin—a product of years of living outdoors—had an undertone of blue-blooded sallowness. In spite of its deepness, he had one of those nasal, flat voices which made even the most exhilarating words sound painfully dull. Plumed and powdered, gilded and laced everywhere that could possibly support it, she was gratified to see his linens beginning to wilt from the tropical heat. A longing for Nathan's simplicity seized her...

"Don't you agree, *Madam* Harper?"

Cate blinked to find Harte staring expectantly at her.

"Don't you agree, *Madam* Harper?" he repeated. He pointedly looked down at her hand on the handle of her tankard and her wedding ring gleaming dully.

"Yes, I dare say." She smiled vaguely, straining to recall what he might have said.

She had no experience with His Majesty's Navy, but enough with the Army to know his type: rigid, reserved, ambitious and judgmental. He was doing so that very moment as he drank: openly regarding her over the rim, trying to decide which category in his regimented life she belonged: lady, servant or common whore. The latter seemed the more fertile ground.

"I've not seen you before and I come here frequently." The smile he displayed was a bit forced and suffered a cruel curve. "You've a strange accent, but you've the speech and bearing of a lady, although you drink ale like a monger's wife. You've the skin of a lady, too, although you have been in the sun of late. Tall, although," he added more to himself as his eyes raked her, assessing her as one would a new milch cow.

It was becoming glaringly apparent that he didn't mean to leave until his curiosity was satisfied. With no other apparent choice, she gathered her nerve and began.

Cate displayed her own charming smile, coyly batting her lashes. "I beg you to excuse my awkwardness, Commodore. I've just escaped from a pirate ship. I'm a little discommoded and—"

"Oh, dear! My poor, poor..." Harte's mouth moved wordlessly during this honest display of emotion. "I had no idea. Are you all well? But of course, you aren't! What did those blackguards do to you?"

"No, no, I'm quite well. They were ever so kind."

He leaned forward with startling intensity. "Tell me of it. What unfortunate set of circumstances put someone so delicate in such dreadful harm?"

"I was on a ship from England: the *Constancy*. Do you know her?"

"I certainly do," he said with sudden vehemence. "The Commissioner's family was to have arrived on her, until they were ruthlessly slaughtered by pirates. I'm sure it was only by Providence that you—"

"Slaughtered?" Cate blurted, gaping.

"Ruthlessly cut down as the captain pleaded for their lives," Harte said, through clenched teeth. His fist curled around his glass.

"By who's word?"

He bristled at her disbelief, unaccustomed at being questioned. "The captain; I received his report at Fort Charles. He also represented that a woman had been taken."

She eyed Harte with new suspicion. It seemed highly unlikely Captain Chambers would have manufactured such an outrageous lie, unless of course, he had been coerced. The probability leaned toward the truth-bending had started with the one seated before her. Her stomach clenched at the sudden feeling of a fly lured by a spider. There was only one person who could disprove Harte's claims: her. She bit back any further objections; to do so might not best serve her purposes.

"And yet, the pirates spared you," he said with renewed interest.

"Why, yes," she replied faintly.

"Then I must conclude you've been on the *Ciara Morganse*. You'll be acquainted with Captain Nathanael Blackthorne, then?"

"Blackthorne?" She shifted under the green gaze which had gone slightly reptilian. "Yes, I believe so. An odd chap, with strange hair?"

"Yes, that would be Blackthorne," Harte said, coldly. "I hope he didn't... *harm* you."

"No, not at all," she said as emphatically as she dared, while demurely bowing her head. "He was quite the gentleman."

"So tragic," Harte murmured, quite sympathetic. "The terrors you must have been forced to endure, and yet you faced them with such conviction and bravery."

Cate feigned sudden interest in her mug, swallowing down both ale and a withering retort to his patent presumptuousness.

She didn't appreciate having someone putting words in her mouth, but at the same time realized the hazards of defending Nathan too stridently.

She covertly studied him. On the surface he was courtly of manners, a consummate gentleman, but too much so. Just underneath the surface, however, was falseness and cunning, thinly veiled, waiting to erupt at his first displeasure. Beneath the low hum of conversation in the room, however, she heard a dull tapping. His middle finger rapped the table with the slow, rhythmic regularity of a dripping eave. A nervous tic of some sort, for his fixed expression of civility showed no sign of awareness.

Harte began to say something, but was interrupted by a loud outburst of laughter from a table of Marines. A look immediately blanketed their jocularity.

"Pray tell, madam. How did you manage to escape?" he asked.

"They put in to water and wood." She winced at sounding too much the seaman. Harte didn't seem to have noticed. Hopefully, he would also overlook the obvious flaw: no pirate ship would put in so near a garrison.

"I represented I needed to... well..." She cleared her throat meaningfully.

He had the good graces to look away, his sense of propriety preventing him from inquiring further.

She assumed a more beleaguered-damsel air. "I was able to slip away into the bushes. I found the road and walked into town." That part could be easily verified by the heavy layer of dust on her shoes.

Cate sat back, pleased with presenting her story, his open admiration proof she had done so credibly. His gaze then shifted to her necklace and her newly-acquired confidence sank. It pressed credulity that a hostage would wear such an adornment, possibly a gift. She searched for a response, in case he was to ask.

"You're a very brave woman," Harte said with surprising compassion. Realizing himself, he stiffened. "I have caused you delay in this disreputable place far too long."

He rose abruptly. "It is my duty, as an officer of His Majesty's Royal Navy and as a gentleman, to assist one so delicate and distressed as yourself. I would be pleased and honored, if you would accept my offer of hospitality on behalf of a particular friend. Her lovely and refined home has been my residence whilst I visit this desolate quagmire. I dare to assume that you shall find it quite agreeable."

"No, no! I'm not in need —"

"Oh, but my dear, Madam Harper, you are. A woman, alone? I could not bear the thought, if I were to leave you here, unattended."

Hovering like a hen over a lost chick, no amount of declining or refusing would repel him. She found herself being escorted down the sidewalk, his firm but gentle hand at her elbow. Disoriented, she felt a cold panic. A stranger walked at her side, rigid and reserved, uniformed and gilded, shoes tapping ridiculously lightly on the bricks, the clump of boots and creak of leather replaced by the swish of lace and satin. She missed Nathan's rolling gait...

Nathan! He would be frantic.

She glanced to the sky to judge the time: mid to late afternoon, still time. Her step slowed and the grip on her arm tightened. She needed to return to the tavern and finish what she came for. If she failed to return, the possibility Nathan might think his fears—God, that seemed so long ago!—had been fulfilled, or assume that she had lied. She had to get back, somehow.

But, how? Presently, she was being ushered toward... whose house?

⁓⦿⦿⦿⁓

"Where the bloody hell did she go?"

Squawking in protest at the Cap'n's bellow, Beatrice retreated to the bowsprit.

Pryce observed from a reasonable distance. The Cap'n was amiable enough, in his own unique way, but bore a black temper. Once witnessed, few chose to have visited upon them again. It was a rare thing to see, but an ugly one that bide long on one's mind.

The Cap'n paced before Towers and Smalley—both rigid at attention, and wisely so—swearing. One of the best cursers, land or sea, bar none. He brandished a fist at the pair, and then, thinking for the better of it, stabbed a finger instead.

"I sent you two with one simple duty," he rumbled threateningly. "One lousy task! How goddamnedably difficult can it be to keep after one woman?"

Sweating profusely, a permanent state since their empty-handed return, the two misfortunates cringed. Onlookers skulked at the margins of the scene, lest they draw his attention next.

"Honest, sir," Towers begged. "We had her: she was sitting at the table... at *The Rose and Crown*," he added importantly, as if knowing the name of the establishment might somehow add credence, and hence, dispensation.

"Aye," chimed in Smalley. "She was there and Harte came in and—"

"Harte! Suffering Jesus on the cross, Harte found her?"

The two exchanged glances, nodding eagerly.

"Aye, Cap'n!" Tower's tongue flicked out to lick his lips, eyes rounding with drama. "He cum in and sat directly, as easy as kiss yer hand."

"What the screamin' blazes is Harte doing there?" the Cap'n shrieked.

"Don't know, sir, but the *Resolute* is in," said Smalley.

A fourth rate sixty-four, thought Pryce. A warship. Not good.

"What the hell's fury is the pride of the Royal Navy doing here?" The Cap'n only verbalized the same thing everyone was thinking.

"Same thing as her consorts, I expect, sir: the *Solebay* and *Flamborough*," added Smalley.

Both sixth rate twenty-fours.

"Two ships?" The Cap'n stalled, frowning. "That doesn't make any sense at 'all.

You're sure?"

"I'd know 'em like I'd know me own sister!" Towers rocked on his toes.

"Yes, I suspect everyone has known your sister," grumbled the Cap'n under his breath.

It wasn't unusual to see such ships, especially the twenty-fours, in the same harbor, but only in support of a large garrison, such as at Fort Charles, Port Royal, or Bridgetown, unless...?

The Cap'n was clearly thinking along the same lines.

"Sounds like they're up to somethin'," put in Pryce.

"Aye, Mr. Pryce, so it does," the Cap'n replied, still lost in thought.

"The place wuz swarmin' with Marines, too," Smalley added, anxious to pursue any in-roads of approval. "Looked like a pot o' red paint exploded."

The Cap'n scowled, a good sign the worst of the storm had passed. "Did Harte seem to know her, familiar like?"

The two seamen traded uncertain looks. It was Smalley who answered. "Can't say, for sure, sir. He jest walked up, kissed 'er hand n' pulled up a chair."

The Cap'n's frown deepened. "How the devil's hoof did you manage to lose her?"

"We went to get two more ales..."

"Aye, the girl wouldn't attend, so we fetched it ourselves," Smalley clarified.

"And when we came back, she was gone." Towers held out his hands, as if to show they were, indeed, empty.

The Cap'n shook his head, his mouth in awed disbelief. "It

takes two of you to get a damned ale? Any idea where she went? Did you inquire or look around?"

"We asked the tavern keep," Towers said eagerly, relieved to have at least done one thing right.

The Cap'n waited. "And?"

Looking away, Towers clamped his mouth tightly closed, Smalley dropping his gaze to his feet.

"And!!" The gravelly voice ripped the air. The men quailed, several onlookers retreating as well.

"And," Towers started, with great trepidation, "he said as the Commodore probably took her upstairs to his room, where he takes all 'is whores."

The Cap'n's lip twitched as he digested that. Decades at sea, Pryce had known the look of a storm brewing and there was one building then, fit to erupt. Those who had shipped with the Cap'n for any length of time fell back another step.

"We're to go ashore." With a thunderous glare, the Cap'n pivoted on his heel, and stomped for the accommodation ladder. "Mr. Pryce!" he bellowed over his shoulder. "All boats ashore! Those two miscreants," he hissed, stabbing a finger as if it were a blade, "will be accompanying *me!*"

The Cap'n paused at the top of the ladder. Pryce, who had been striding behind to keep up, skidded to a halt. "Spread everyone out. Find her. And when... *if* you do, get her aboard with all haste. I'll be along, directly."

With Towers and Smalley scampering ahead, the walk to Hopetown was not a long one, but still provided Nathan more than enough time to visualize in grim detail all manner of perversities which might be befalling Cate at that very moment, each involving captivity and bodily harm.

The coincidence of Harte being at the same place, at the same time was too much. Dark thoughts of collusion and betrayal skulked, even though in his few rational moments, he knew it to be impossible. There was the nagging thought that she was part of an elaborate scheme. His first urge was to dismiss that out-of-hand, for he grossly doubted the Commodore's ability, to either conceive or carry off something so fantastic. Still, the doubt was firmly in place and not to be dislodged, until he had seen for himself.

Time would tell. The first matter of business was to find her.

Truth be told, he didn't think the Commodore had the nature for such devious acts, nor Cate the tolerance. He tended to not give Harte much credence, but any man with any amount of power and control, confronted with a beautiful woman, might resort to any amount of coercion necessary to make her more pliable.

If that were the case, he wished he could be there to see it. Cate struck him as one who wouldn't succumb without a blood-laden struggle.

Unless...

Belay that!

Just exactly which case did you fancy: that she had thrown in with Harte, or she's been arrested?

There was the chance it had been as the noisome duo had said: she had been drug up to a room to be used like a common whore.

Not bloody likely! She'd castrate 'im before he could lock the door.

At the moment, Cate being arrested was vastly the lesser of concerns, although it curdled his gut to think of her in chains, lying in one of those stinking cells.

God, the dirt! She'd never abide that.

A flapping overhead broke his concentration. Muttering moodily, he glanced skyward to see Beatrice's bright plumage alighting in a tree just ahead. Ruffling then smoothing, she tipped her head, scrutinized him, and then threw her head back and squawked.

"Oh, put a stopper in your gob!" Nathan jerked an irritable shoulder. "It's not as if there weren't enough pestilences in me life."

Protesting loudly, she took flight and soared ahead.

Once in town, they pressed to the shadows. Smug in the security afforded by virtue of its size, Hopetown took little notice of comings and goings of such as the likes of them. Besides, any pirate worth his salt knew how to get in and out of any spot on the map without notice. Towers and Smalley hastily led him to *The Rose and Crown*, as indicated by a sign over the door.

"Bloody royalists clear out here." he thought, *looking up at the red rose superimposed over a crown. Put it in your pipe and smoke it, mate.*

A quick reconnaissance of the building proved there were no entrances other than the street.

"I wouldn't suggest the front door..." Towers said *in sotto.*

"The place is crawling with red-coats," Smalley finished.

"Did the keep say which room is Harte's?" Nathan asked, peering up toward the second floor. Seeing both shake their heads in negation, he gave a resigned sigh. "Aye well, on to it, then."

Bidding them to stand watch — one didn't dare assume they

would know enough to do so on their own volition—he used Smalley's tall frame as a ladder to reach the edge of a rear balcony. Agility and determination pulled him up and over the rail, landing lightly outside the window.

As luck would have it, the window was open, and he slipped in. Too late he discovered the room was occupied. A man and woman were in bed, sufficiently preoccupied, however, he judged his chances good of going unnoticed. Tiptoeing, he was well past halfway when he heard a deep voiced, "Hey, mate! Wait yer turn. She's on my shilling."

"Sorry." Nathan sidled toward the door, tipping his hat. "Concentration, mate. No lady 'tis flattered to think her charms aren't sufficient to hold a man's attentions... or vice versa. Madame." He flashed a smile meant to charm as he backed out the door. "Please, pray continue. By all means..."

He slammed the door shut behind him and breathed a sigh of relief.

Nathan checked the hall. Rooms were to larboard and starboard. Some doors stood open, instantly eliminating them as possibilities: the good Commodore would definitely desire his privacy.

The first closed door was unlocked, the room empty; same for the second. The third was unlocked, as well, and he pushed it open without pausing to listen.

"Hoy! What the bloody...!"

Occupied.

The next door was unlocked. Leaning to listen, he heard the movement of someone inside and tapped lightly.

"Come in!" It was a female voice.

His heart leapt. The door was open before he could heed the internal voice screaming that it wasn't Cate. He skidded to a halt at the sight of the occupant: female well enough, large, blowzy-haired and naked.

"Oh, you sweet thing!" Her pendulous breasts wobbled as she charged at him with open arms, squealing, "I've always liked the dark ones."

Her embrace drove him back against the door, the force slamming it shut behind him. His objections were cut off by an onslaught of a tongue to a gagging proportion while a hand latched expertly onto his crotch. Floundering to fend her off—a bloody octopus, she was!—he groped for the doorknob at his back. At last, he wrested free of her grasp enough to get the door open. He slipped around and outside, pulling it shut as a barricade. He gripped the knob, his arms nearly jerked from their sockets as she threw her weight into tugging at the door, all the while pleading for his return.

Soon enough, the pounding ceased; inside went quiet. Nathan cautiously released the knob. Safe enough.

"I'm getting too old for this," he muttered, trying to wipe the taste of her off on his sleeve.

Several minutes later, he stood in the hallway, struck with indecision. The other three rooms had been empty. There was no sign of Cate or Harte, leaving him to wonder if they were already done and gone.

Snorting aloud, he instantly negated the idea. He wasn't made of wood. In the process of imagining what sounds Cate might make in the height of passion, several scenarios of his own doing had come to mind, none of which could be completed in anything less than an afternoon. Come to think on it, however, Harte didn't strike him as the sort to possess enough imagination to go much past the knowledge of a virgin whore: ten minutes, and he'd be back to limp as an old sock.

All options exhausted, there was nothing left but to take his leave. Voices echoing up the stairs told him the taproom was still full — No sense in risking that — and no servants' steps were to be had. And so, he backtracked to where he had begun.

Stopping at the door, he listened carefully, and swore under his breath.

This cove has the stamina of a racehorse!

Cautiously turning the knob, he winced at its squeak. Stealthily slipping in, a canny eye for the pair in the bed, he tiptoed through. As he reached the window, one leg over the sill, he felt someone watching. He slid a sideways look to find the woman looking back. Legs wrapped around the panting and thrusting one atop her, she winked, nodding approvingly. He tipped his hat to the whore's disappointed pout and slipped out the window. Slithering over the rail, he dropped to the ground, grunting softly with the impact. Towers and Smalley still hovered against the shed where he had left them.

"Anything?" he demanded, shaking one leg from the sting of landing too heavily.

"Nothin', Cap'n." Towers put a hand to his nose, making a face. "Blimey! What's that smell!" Nathan's first urge was to blame Towers; he announced his arrival well in advance to anyone who had the misfortune of being leeward. This markedly offensive odor was, in fact, coming from himself. He raised an arm and set to coughing from the perfume of his noxious assailant.

"She wasn't there," Nathan growled, after clearing his throat. "Any other thoughts?"

Like some comical clock pendulum, Towers and Smalley shook their heads in unison. Looking skyward, Nathan silently sought tolerance and guidance from any deity that might be watching.

"All right now, mates, bear a hand," he said, drawing them to attention. "There is a tall, copper-headed woman and a commodore, probably together, somewhere in this bloody blot on the map. It shouldn't be a tall challenge to find either one. Spread out and the first one what finds Mr. Cate is to haul his wind back to the *Morganse* with her in tow, toot sweet."

"Aye, sir!" came a chorus.

"What about you, Cap'n?" Smalley asked.

"Never mind, me. I can bloody well mind for meself. I want her on that ship, with all possible haste. Now, shove off!"

Nathan turned just as a blue blur cut through his view.

Blessed Beatrice, again!

Soaring like some kind of a masquerading buzzard, the parrot circled several times, finally landing on a roof peak, and then carried on like she was possessed by Satan himself. He mouthed several oaths, batting a dismissive hand at the beast.

Beatrice swooped past as he strode for the street, so low as to force him to duck, clacking her beak at him as she passed. Alighting on a shed's peak just ahead, she bobbed her head and chattered. Not a dozen strides later, Beatrice dove again, scuffing the crown of his hat, then arced off to perch atop a post.

Slowly stalking toward the pestilence, said pestilence incrementally flitted away. Nathan clenched his teeth. It had been a very bad day, thus far, and he was looking for something to kill or maim. Retreating to his steady advance, Beatrice ultimately turned up an alley, and was sitting atop a stack of casks when he rounded the corner. Stopping, he scowled. "Are you trying to lead me off?"

Arching her wings, Beatrice berated him with several guttural cackles. *"Tea time! Tea time!"* she said, bobbing her head with avian urgency.

"Bugger it!" he sighed. "Don't have any better ideas of me own, might as well follow a bloody bird."

13: SOCIAL SKILLS

"Lady Bartholomew Dunwoody," Roger Harte announced and made an elegant leg.

"Oh, my sweet dear, Lady Bart will do quite famously."

Somewhat dazed, Cate found herself making her curtsy before a regal but stout, elderly woman in the marble foyer of a vast house, murmuring some vague salutation.

Harte frowned, worriedly hovering over Cate. "Madam Harper was taken hostage by pirates and only just escaped."

"Oh!" Lady Bart's hands flew up to her cheeks—a gesture Cate was soon to discover to be habitual—her small mouth rounding in dismay. "It's no small wonder the poor dear is so regrettably disheveled. Scurrilous and reprehensible beasts, the lot of them," she declared breathlessly, a state of being Cate was also to witness with frequency.

"Upon my word, Diggie," the woman huffed, rounding on Harte. "When are you going to rid these waters of those savages, so a lady might pass in safety and freedom of these indignities?"

Not waiting for an answer, she seized Cate by the arm and whisked her up the stairs.

"Come with me, you poor, poor, bereft child," Lady Bart crooned. Her motherly tone was in sharp contrast to her heavy lean on Cate's arm, as if seeking support rather than offering.

"We've a bit before tea; I shall see you to a room, so you may refresh yourself. Oh, dear, that hair. Sally?" she called as they mounted the stairs. "Sally? Where is that girl when you need her? Sally!"

Topping the curved stairs, Lady Bart, her ample bosom heaving under her kertch, swept Cate down the hall on a wave of flourish and endless chatter.

"Yes, Ma'm?"

Lady Bart drew up before someone who was far from a girl: middle-aged, stern-faced and dour-mouthed.

"Sally, there you are! We have a guest—"

"We have several guests," Sally interjected.

"Don't be impertinent," Lady Bart retorted, absent of ire. Fanning herself with one hand, she scurried down the hall with Cate in tow. "Pray, attend Madam Harper. She is in desperate need of all assistance."

Her Ladyship paused in her march to cast another fretful look at Cate, a hand rising to her cheek. "And this hair. Oh, you poor thing, and so tall. Pity," she declared, pressing Cate farther down the hall. "Those vile creatures wouldn't even allow you a brush and a mirror. Oh, and where did you ever come by eyes colored such as that?"

Before she could answer, Cate was standing in a large bedchamber, laced, satined and frilled on every surface which could support it.

"Oh, when I think of the insults you were required to endure," Lady Bart sighed. "Alone, with all those men..."

She stopped. Her shocked expression gave way to morbid curiosity as she whispered, "They didn't... *do* anything, did they?"

She held her breath in anticipation of delicious details.

"No," Cate said. "They were very kind."

Lady Bart's mouth drooped with disappointment, but it faded quickly. "*Mrs.* Harper; you're married then. Where *is* your husband? Oh, how frantic with worry he must be. Perhaps we might send a—"

"I'm widowed."

"Oh, my condolences for your loss," Lady Bart said, without a hint of compassion as she pushed open the windows. "I'm widowed myself, you know: lost my dear Harry eighteen years hence."

Cate considered it possible she had talked the man into his grave.

"He visits most nights," she went on matter-of-factly, fluffing a pillow, re-arranging a vase of flowers on a table, and then swept toward the door. "He always was such a thoughtful dear..."

Lady Bart's voice faded down the hall, leaving Cate to deflate in silence. Her respite was cut short by Sally's arrival, laden with brushes, towels, ribbons and other necessities to wage war against Cate's state of dishevelment. A small chambermaid scurried in her wake bearing a steaming ewer. Emptying her arms on the dressing table, Sally stood back with one hand on her hip to survey Cate with a critical eye.

"Miracles in minutes," Sally sighed in private wonderment. "Gonna require Providence's hand in this one."

Cate raised a self-conscious hand to her tangled mass. Never had she been made to feel so inadequate with efficiency.

"Well," Sally said, filling the basin. "My experience is cleanliness is the best place to start. Let's see what's to be found under all that grime."

The water was hot, the soap finely-milled, impregnated with bits of lavender and rose petals. Once the layers of road grit, salt and sweat were removed, Cate's skin was its softest in months, nay, years.

Once past her austere shell, Sally proved to be a kind-hearted soul. Her business-like air stemmed from coping with a doddering mistress, for whom she nurtured a boundless love and tolerance. Her first suggestion for Cate's hair was a proper cap. Following a brief contretemps in which Cate flatly refused, Sally seized the brush and set to work.

As Cate sat on the stool before the dressing table, it occurred that Nathan would have enjoyed witnessing Sally's exercised attempts to bring her snarled bramble into order. "Oakum is more orderly," was often his comment. Given sufficient attention, her hair could be tamed into long curls about her shoulders without a touch of the iron. Too mindful of the timepiece on the mantle, Sally was disinclined to do so.

"Tea is at three sharp. M'lady sets great store in everyone attending. The miller's cat can expect the hospitality of this house time out of mind, but only if it attends with an open heart and promptly."

Sally ultimately resorted to severely pinning Cate's hair back. Piled high at the crown, it cascaded in semi-orderliness down her back. With a flourish of ribbon, and several flowers from the vase tucked in, victory was declared.

The chambermaid returned with a freshly ironed kerchief, edged with delicate lace. Making no attempt to hide her disapproval at Cate's sun-exposed skin, Sally muttered a soliloquy of "too tall," "nothing decent," "won't answer," as she tucked it into the edge of Cate's bodice. Cate's apron, fashioned from lightweight sailcloth by dear Billings, the ship's sailmaker, was taken. Stained and sullied with blood and all manner of ship's filth, it was carried off with two-fingered disgust, while another was passed around her waist and tied off with a crisp bow.

"Make you at least a little decent."

Feeling somewhat refreshed after the hurried *toilet*, Cate was guided from the bedchamber to downstairs. She felt prepared to face whatever was to come, when she was handed off to the downstairs footman, who led her down the highly-polished hall. Gilt-scrolled double-doors were opened, and there she stood in the drawing room. The drone of conversation stalled as the attention of its dozen or so occupants swiveled around. The men launched to their feet and bowed. An awkward silence hung in the air as the seconds were ticked off by an unseen clock. Clenching her hands in the folds of her skirt, Cate felt like an insect in the yard, the chickens eyeing their next morsel. Smiling nervously, she wondered again how she ever came to be there.

"My sweet dear." Lady Bart's shrill shattered the silence. She pattered across the room on incredibly tiny feet. "Everyone, pray allow me to name... Oh dear, what was it? Oh, yes, how dreadfully silly... This is Madam Catherine Harper, a particular friend to our dear Diggie."

Diggie?

Leaning heavily for support, Lady Bart towed Cate from person to person, while rattling off names, titles and an endless array of staggeringly irrelevant bits of information. Cate strained to connect names to faces, but abandoned all hope after the third person: a woman in bright green watered-satin dress, a towering powdered wig and a voice befitting of a five-year-old.

Introductions blessedly complete, Cate was ushered to a gilt chair — dubious in both size and strength — near the window, teacup in hand. Having seen her seated, Harte took up the chair's twin opposite a low tea table. An elegantly hosed calf extended, cheeks gleaming from a recent shave, he was freshly linened and powdered, a pert bow finishing off his tightly queued wig. He was one of those people who would be regal if dressed in rags.

"Rags" was exactly how Cate felt. She drew her feet under herself, in order to hide the indecent display of unstockinged ankle and sadly worn shoes, barely more than clogs. Her petticoat wouldn't have been considered short had the room been occupied by those who toiled for a living. Aware of her hands, now tar-stained and tanned, she buried them into the folds of her apron as best as could be managed while holding a cup and saucer. Compared to the powered and pink tones of those present, she felt as brown and leathery as Nathan's hat.

"Diggie represented you were taken captive by that vile Captain Blackwater," announced Lady Bart, alighting in a high-backed chair.

"*Blackthorne*. Captain Nathanael Blackthorne," the Commodore said tolerantly through an enduring smile.

"Pardon? Oh, yes, well, of course." Lady Bart shuddered for what appeared to be only for drama's sake. "Dissolute creatures. The civilized world would be *so* improved if we were rid of those despicable beasts. Diggie, I beg, can't you *do* something about those people?"

"Not to worry, my dear Bart," began one of the first gentlemen to be introduced, be-laced and blue-satined. The Honorable... oh, something! "Our Diggie has eradicated virtually every pirate ship in the West Indies. Blessed few remaining now. A dying breed, praise God, thanks to him."

"Hear him! Hear him!" came a restrained murmur.

Coldness pricked between Cate's shoulder blades.

"That Blackthorne chap has managed to give you the slip several times, has he not?" mused a younger man standing near the fireplace.

Henry, no Harry! No, wait, Fordshaw!

His outward demeanor unchanged, the muscles in Harte's jaw flexed.

"Yes, a few." He turned to Cate with intense conviction. "But mark me: that gnat shall be swatted from existence."

Under the conversation of the room, Cate heard a tapping noise. From the corner of her eye, she could see Harte's finger rapping on the black-lacquered surface of the tea table between them, marking a rhythm similar to the clock ticking on the mantle.

Cate looked to her lap, the tea forming an icy knot in her stomach. If someone had asked, she would have said sailing was a noisy business, but not until it was gone did she realize the degree. A seaman's voice was perpetually raised to be heard over plank, block, canvas, wind and water. Well over a hundred men lived elbow-to-elbow, and yet one was required to shout to be heard by his mess neighbor, anger and conversation often at the same volume. Having become accustomed to noise which one could lean against, she was left swaying by soft, reserved voices, the delicate titter of laughter, the clatter of china and rustle of silk. Here, the clearing of a throat was a vile disruption. The once moving air was now still, to the point of near suffocation, heavy with perfume, pomade and pomanders.

A surge of heat rushed from her chest and up her neck. Just as it touched her cheeks, it turned to ice, and gooseflesh shot down her arms. She closed her eyes against the high thin ringing in her ears. The room pitched violently, and she snapped them open once more.

No reprieve there.

"...that horrible slaughter," finished the woman in green. She pivoted her attention to Cate and peered down her nose. "Oh, my dear... Madam. Harper, was it not? Yes, of course. The Commodore informs us you were aboard the *Constancy* when it was set upon by those pirates in such an egregious manner. Such fortune to have escaped with your life from that shocking incident."

"You were there!" exclaimed... Fordshaw—she was sure that was his name. Eyes rounded with anticipation, he hunched forward, teacup forgotten in his hand. "Oh, I beg, pray tell us of it... unless, of course, it was too shocking," he added with a miserable attempt at compassion.

"Well, of course it was shocking," Lady Bart interjected from her chair, with a vigorous flourish of an ivory and silk fan. "The thought of that sweet dear, little Lucy Littleton begging for her life, after those men had..." Her mouth moved fish-like as she groped for an appropriate word. "Well, you know... had their way with her—"

"No!" Cate was surprised by her own vehemence.

There was a unified rattle of teacups falling to their saucers.

"Beg pardon, dear?" It was Lady Bart who ended the stunned silence.

Every eye in the room swiveled on Cate. Literally perched on the edge of their seats, they leaned in for the sordid details.

"No," Cate repeated, more quietly but no less fervent. She drew a shaky breath. "I'm sorry, but no, that is *not* what happened. The Littleton's died of a fever—"

"By what account?" demanded the honorable elder across from her.

Cate met his challenging look. "Mine. I was there."

Sympathy befell every face, with pitying eye-rolls and murmurs of "Poor thing", "Deranged" and "Shocked." Her sense of entombment in lace and satin, hosed legs and slippers deepened.

There was a value, however, in being thought deranged: no one is comfortable in face of it, hence conversation swerved away. Having failed to provide the amusement sought, they moved on, leaving her unobserved. Deflating with relief, she leaned back and closed her eyes, only to be swept by another wave of giddiness. The room spun again, sloshing like the *Morganse*'s bilges. She clutched the arm of the chair and opened her eyes in search of a solid fix.

Cate cast an anxious eye toward the window and then clock. It was nearly four; the walk back to the longboat would require at least an hour and stepping smartly at that. Somehow, some way, she had to extract herself from this horror. She was already sure to be late; Nathan would have to be patient.

She smiled at that thought. Now there was a contradiction in terms: a patient Nathan Blackthorne. Animated, circuitous, funny, imaginative, vociferous; many words could describe Nathan, but patient was not one of them.

As Cate idly sipped her tea, she caught a play of eyes over

Big Wig's fan. The room was quite warm in the late afternoon hour. The ladies' fans were in full employment, but cooling was a secondary function. There was a language of the fans, a silent dialogue of suggestion, flirtation and clarification. She was familiar with this particular tongue, as carefully schooled as was every female present. The target of most of messages was the Commodore. Judging by the hidden eyes, touches to the right cheek or heart, he more or less had his pick of the room.

Cate's train of thought was interrupted by, "I'm given to understand our dear Lord Creswicke is sparing no expense on his upcoming nuptials."

The comment came from the direction of the fireplace. Fordshaw?

"Readily achieved when you're the head of the Royal West India Mercantile Company," snorted His Honorable. "I shouldn't care to imagine how many of our coins have gone toward payment for that."

Snickers and murmurs of agreement passed around the room.

"Marrying well certainly does the pocket no harm, either," sniffed Lady-in-green.

"Poor thing," sighed another dispassionately. "I suspect the girl doesn't comprehend what awaits her."

"No matter, if she does or not," said Elder-in-the-chair. "The arrangements are made, signed and witnessed, as I hear it."

"Mutual advantages," mused Mr. Fireplace. "Her father acquires direct connections to the Company — and a tidy empire our Lord has built — while Lord Creswicke receives thousands of pounds and exclusive access to Boston's markets."

"Fair trade all around," cried someone.

Another wave of knowing laughter rounded the room. Underneath the titter of knowing laughter which came from around the room, the rapping on the table at her elbow grew more emphatic. Too slow for a heartbeat, it was just as unfailing, but weighted with menace.

"It might be said we all benefit. If it wasn't for his privateers and our good Commodore," Elder-in-the-chair said with a deferential bow in his direction, "we'd be at the mercy of those wretched pirates. Heaven only knows what our lives would be, and not a hope of safety or peace."

Approving murmurs were uttered, the Commodore bowing from his place.

Cate sat stiff, hoping no one would notice her white-knuckled grip on her saucer. She meant to take a sip, but the cup rattled, clattering even louder as she set it back down.

"Are you well, Madame?"

She looked up into Harte's intent green gaze. She nodded, but judging by his frown, he wasn't convinced.

"Diggie, I've been given to understand you've been made charge of Lord Creswicke's more, shall we say, delicate arrangements?"

Harte reluctantly shifted his attention to Elder-in-the-Chair. "It would seem Lord Creswicke has found my services indispensable."

"Do tell, Diggie!" Miss Big Wig declared, bouncing with child-like anxiousness. "What is His Lordship's latest folly?" cried another.

Harte sipped his tea, allowing the suspense to build.

"Lord Creswicke's *betrothed*," he said, with disdainful emphasis, "will be under my charge, until her arrival to Bridgetown."

"I thought she was in Boston," Mr. Fireplace said.

"Indeed, until some weeks ago, she was," said Harte, smug with importance. "As we speak, she is bound for the West Indies."

"When is she to arrive in Bridgetown?" asked Miss Big Wig conversationally, nibbling a biscuit.

He cocked a brow in calculation. "Sometime in the next fortnight, but probably less, but she shan't be going—"

Blessing her luck, Cate closed her eyes. It was for only the briefest of moments, but was stricken with another wave of violent dizziness. The room heaved like the deck of a ship. Her hand jerked as she grabbed for the arm of the chair, the cup and saucer crashing to the floor. She lurched to her feet and teetered. Harte caught her by the arm.

"I'm sorry," she murmured, touching a shaky hand to her forehead. "I beg your leave. I must be more tired than... Perhaps I should..."

"By all means, my dear," Lady Bart cooed, rising.

Against a backdrop of mutterings of "Airs", "Thin blood" and "Burned feather,"

Her Ladyship took Cate from Harte's grasp.

"You need your rest. You're positively frayed. Now you shall be seen back to your chamber, where you can lie down..." Lady Bart droned as she took Cate away.

In the shuttered light of the bedchamber, Cate lay on the bed.

The house had long fallen quiet, Lady Bart and her guests having retired through the afternoon heat. The small clock on the mantle chimed six; supper would be rung soon.

Upon returning to the bedchamber, Sally and the nameless chambermaid had stripped her of her clothing and deposited her in bed. Tucked up under a coverlet, wet cloths laced with lavender were applied to her forehead and chamomile tea poured down her throat, all in the spirit of aiding her recovery from the arduous ordeal at the hands of pirates. Once satisfied that she rested comfortably, they left her to her peace... at last!

There would be no sleeping, however. By now, Nathan would be pacing, assuming he had ever stopped since her departure.

The dizziness she suffered was troublesome. It was a wonder how one could feel so landlubberish on land. Reclined even now, she was obliged to keep one foot on the floor to assuage the sensation of being pitched out of bed. She could have been well on her way, else. Instead, there she lay stripped to her shift, feeling more a hostage of Commodore Harte and Lady Bart than ever on a pirate ship.

At first, she had thought the dizzy spell to be a blessing: an opportunity to escape not only the parlor, but the house. Instead, the house had been brought to full attention. In retrospect, the dizziness had been so severe, escape under her own power would have been nigh impossible. All she need do was fall and break a limb, and she would be imprisoned forever.

Feeling as if she was being watched, she looked around the room into a number of faces staring back. Miniatures, figurines and cherubs peered from wallpaper, fabric and frames, scrutinizing her with everything from demanding to outright accusation. The portrait of an old man, no doubt some revered, ancient ancestor judging by the position over the mantle, bore the most penetrating glare.

"This wasn't my plan," she huffed defensively. "All you need do is hang there. We, the still-living, have it a bit rougher."

Adding to her annoyance was an increasing racket coming from outside. Muttering one of Nathan's better oaths, she rose to investigate, feeling carefully for the floor her first few steps. As she pushed open the balcony doors and went out, she recognized the sound just before seeing the brilliant hyacinth-colored flash of a parrot in the trees.

"Beatrice?"

"It certainly is!"

The gravelly voice came from behind. Startled, yelped as she spun around. "Nathan!"

He swung a final leg over the balcony rail and stood before her puffing from the climb.

"What on earth are you doing here? Come in here before you're seen," Cate hissed.

"I played bloody hell trying to find you." Nathan shook an admonishing finger at her as she pulled him inside.

"How did you find me?"

The thought of him looking for her was touching... but...

"Didn't fancy I would find you, did you? Looked all over!" Hooking his thumbs in his belt, he struck a triumphant pose. "Thought you could give me the slip—get away clean—but I found you."

Cate fanned a hand, backing away. "What's that smell?" Even as she asked, she knew: there was no mistaking cheap perfume.

"I had me virtue threatened."

"You couldn't have been in much of a hurry, if you had sufficient time to stop at a whorehouse."

"I was attacked. An innocent, I was!"

Cate pressed a cautionary finger to her lips. She lowered her voice, which obligated her to move closer to both Nathan and the smell. "How did you ever find me?"

"My impeccable instincts—" Her dubious stare brought his boast to an abrupt halt. "And Beatrice," he conceded, crestfallen.

A myriad of questions popped to mind, none of which she desired to pursue. Capture for him meant an appointment with the gallows.

"You have to go, before you're discovered."

"I came to help you escape," he said, resisting her attempts to urge him back to the balcony.

"Escape? I don't need to escape."

"Aren't you under arrest?"

"No," she said, puzzled by such a far-flung assumption.

Nathan prepared a reply, but then noticed she wore only a shift. The soot-colored eyes flicked toward the tousled bed and eyes she had always known to be warm went cold. He stalked to the bed to snatch up the bedclothes and shake them at her.

"Ah, so it would appear the fly didn't mind being caught by the spider after all. A roll at the tavern wasn't enough, eh? Decided to give the sheets a wearing here, as well?"

"What are you talking about?" Cate asked in clipped precision.

Growling in disgust, he pitched the sheets aside. "I know you went to his room. You're a faster worker than I'd credited," he said with grudging admiration.

"You're not making any sense."

"Coy does not suit you, Missy. I had the inseparable duo follow you—"

"You had me followed!" She flinched at her own volume, and hissed lower, "How dare you. You didn't trust me..."

Nathan stalked back, glaring. "I trusted you, *then*. I sent them to assure you were safe. I see now I was grossly misguided in me concerns."

Cate flushed at his accusation. "We don't have time for your childish arguments—"

"Childish!"

She waved away his indignant sputtering. "So far, I know Creswicke's fiancé is definitely en route. She should be here within the week, more or less, but she's not to go to Bridgetown directly. She's to stop off somewhere, but I haven't been able to learn where."

"Did he tell you all that during the first shining-of-the-sheets or the second?" Nathan shot back with a cutting edge. He tilted his head to critically survey her. "Did your hair up for him, too, I see. Sweet-smelling soap; fancied up for him, too," he added, leaning nearer to sniff. "Prettying yourself up, employed all your tricks; bloody fast work for less time than a watch."

"What do you care?"

No longer of a mind to deal with this senseless sparring, she drew a deep breath, and said in measured calmness, "Supper will be rang directly. I hope to know more by the time it's finished. Shall I try to make my way back, or would you prefer I just keep going?"

He exhaled sharply through his nose. "I'll be in that garden, *tonight*." He pointed toward the balcony and then stabbed the finger at her. "*You* be there!"

A baring of teeth punctuated his demand. With a low grumble, he turned on his heel and headed for the balcony.

"How are you to get away?" she asked from close on his heels.

"That would be me own problems, wouldn't it?" Nathan snapped over his shoulder. Checking the grounds below, he threw a leg over the banister, pausing to glare once more. "*You* be there!"

And then he was gone.

Cate watched him disappear into the woods at the garden's edge with a sinking sensation. The look on his face had been quite damning. She was beginning to think this entire venture had been a bad idea. Worse yet, he acted as though it had all been her idea.

She had barely turned when the bell in the hall sounded, announcing it was time to dress for supper, Sally entering on cue. Behind her trailed a small legion of assistants, bearing a dress and all the necessities to render Cate presentable.

By most standards, the gown laid out on the bed was a simple one, but it was the noblest Cate had worn in a very long time: striped dimity, cream and azure, over a floral petticoat.

She stood in the middle of the maids as they buzzed about like skirted bees, tugging, tying and pinning, often with conflicting instructions: "Stand straight," "Bend over," "Put your foot here," or "Don't move." A stomacher pinned, filet lace apron tied, a few plucks at her hair, a black ribbon at her throat, and she was declared ready.

She turned to the mirror and a complete stranger stared back. It only added to the sense of disorientation suffered since Harte had whisked her out of the tavern. She glanced over her shoulder toward the balcony and the long shadows of the garden beyond. Somewhere out there, Nathan was waiting. She wondered if he would approve of what he saw, or if the accusation and mistrust exhibited as he went over the rail would only deepen.

Any further thoughts were cut short by Sally's urging her out the door.

Once again in the downstairs foyer, Cate stalled at hearing voices echo from the drawing room. Gathering her nerve, chanting "Only be a little longer", she made her entrance.

Supper at Lady Bart's was apparently the social height of the region and her guests dressed accordingly. The sight brought instant flashes of being at Court. Not near so grand, the opulence was shocking against anything she had experienced in nigh a decade. Nothing so trivial as a tropical evening had dampened the guests' verve for style. Swirling hooped skirts, ruffles and flounces, flaring coattails and deep cuffs, it was a riot of vibrant colors of satin and silk, brocade, moiré and taffeta. As they craned their necks to see who had entered, their rice-powdered faces looked like a covey of ghosts. Seeing it was only her, they returned to their conversation. Harte materialized at her side to seize her hand.

"I was so distressed that you might be too indisposed to join us," he murmured fervently over her knuckles.

Cate felt a compassion for Harte's valet; the poor man must have been exhausted. The Commodore's linens were fresh, his jacket brushed and uncreased, and the bow at the back of his head as crisp as ever a ribbon could hope.

She forced a smile, while attempting to graciously extricate her hand. Taking no notice of her intent, he tucked it into his elbow. She made her curtsy before Her Ladyship on his hand.

The furniture had been cleared to make room for the grandeur, and so the guests milled about in small clusters while waiting for the dining room doors to open. Even in her new finery, she felt like a brown wren among the peacocks. She shifted first on one foot then the other at Harte's side. As uncomfortable as she found him on a personal level, she was grateful for his presence.

For the first time in her life she felt protected by the Royal Navy. Erect and square-shouldered, in his navy and buff, bullioned epaulets and ornaments of commendations gleaming under the chandeliers, his resplendency deflected the stares.

The crystal cup thrust in her hand contained a punch of some sort, with rum. Ah, well. There seemed to be no way of avoiding it in the West Indies. It was both fruity and spicy, and most particularly, cool. It was delectable. Her tension drained with each sip, the twirling sensation she suffered earlier being replaced by a pleasant lightheadedness.

Her uneasiness abated somewhat. It wasn't as though she was without social skills. Although she was rusty, it wasn't difficult: a smile, a nod, murmur some inconsequential something on the rare occasion when addressed. The problem lay with such parlor skills were not her nature. Standing next to Roger, the cold disapproval from the women was easily managed. Jealousy was rarely a good color on anyone. While she observed the women, however, she looked up several times into an emerald haze of him watching her. She smiled faintly and buried her nose into her drink.

The way the men regarded her was another matter. Distracted by laughter at the far end of the room, she looked back into an expression of raw hunger on the part of young Fordshaw. The same came from Lord Something-or-Another, earlier in blue now in peach moiré. Another mentally undressed her where she stood. Emboldened by her sullied status, their assumption was if she had played the whore to the pirates—Blackthorne specifically, his appetites well-known—she would now do the same for them. She longed for one of the fans the women brandished in grand style, so she might send a few messages of her own, namely a good bash across the face, or somewhere lower and more efficacious.

Cate shifted closer, more grateful still for Harte's presence.

It was the third—no fourth—glass of punch which brought her to see Roger in a much more pleasant light. He wasn't without his charms. Once relaxed, he was witty and quite knowledgeable on many subjects. Clean-profiled, tall and regal, under different circumstances she may have found him attractive, in an aloof, thin-blooded sort of way.

She worked her fingers together, feeling the metal cool of her wedding ring. It was a constant reminder of a past life. After losing Brian, another man in her life was never a consideration. Nathan had been a complete surprise.

Nathan. She shied at recalling his look as he slid off the balcony: betrayal, heavily laced with the satisfaction of suspicions rewarded. He had expected the worst from her and, to his mind, she had fulfilled the prophecy. The warm flush of the punch dissolved under the chill of that reality.

She felt Roger looking attentively down at her. "Have no cares," he said in quiet earnestness. "I'll assure that you are at my side."

It took her a moment to fathom what the devil he was about. Seating arrangements? Good Lord!

Supper was called, a matched pair of footmen opening the doors. Lady Bart took the head of the table, the Commodore opposite. His position of honor spoke loudly to Lady Bart's regard. Cate was whisked into the seat to Harte's right, much to the displeasure of those scrambling for that same spot. The lush-eyed Fordshaw, a heart-shaped *mouche* at the corner of his mouth—declaring himself both kissable and a lover—was to Cate's side, Miss Big-Wig across. As the toasts were given, her stomach rumbled.

The bounty at Lady Bart's table, however, struck Cate almost ill. For the months, she had lived on ship's fare, and before that on what could be begged or scrounged. Now she was faced with over a dozen dishes. More than once, she looked down to find the cold, startled looks of her food staring back: fish, doves, crabs and a suckling pig from its silver-platter repose in the middle of the table.

Her stomach might have been empty—several cups of punch aside—but it was now quite closed. She ate without appetite, much of it becoming a glutinous mass in her mouth. The wines, and excellent they were, however, flowed like the proverbial river, the footman seeming to have taken up a permanent position at her elbow to refill her glass. Roger grew more intent with concern at seeing her poke her food about the plate. Like an obedient child, she tried to eat, but only wound up scattering it, piling it up, and scattering it again.

As the servants moved like wraiths at the table's perimeter, conversation fell into small localized groups. The low hum of one blanketed the next, the titter of female laughter high over the men's deeper. Amid the tinkle of silverware and china, came the rise and fall of Lady Bart's shrill. Conversation at Cate's end of the table was dominated by Big-Wig. Harte her primary focus, Fordshaw a distant second, she piped higher when either man sought to address Cate.

As Big-Wig prattled on, Roger arched a questioning brow at Cate, the significance of which was unclear. Cate returned a vague smile, hoping her discomfiture wasn't too apparent. It had been a long time since she had worn anything so restricting.

The stays were too short, gouging her back and ribs at every breath. The gown was too narrow at the shoulders and too short at the sleeves, the banded cuffs cutting her arms.

"Is everyone a guest?" she asked of Roger during a brief lull in Big-Wig's dialogue. Her head buzzing from the wine, it was a silly question, but conversation of some sort seemed requisite.

"That would depend on one's categorizations," he said under the table's chatter. He scanned the table briefly. "A few are just arrived from Barbuda, here for the season."

Cate nodded knowingly, in spite of not having the foggiest what "the season" might entail. Days? Weeks? Months?

"A few more are somewhat more of a permanent arrangement, having arrived months ago," he said with open disapproval.

From the corner of her eye, Cate saw Mrs. Big-Wig, fork gone forgotten in her hand as she craned an ear. Out of open malice, Cate lowered her voice further, obliging Roger to lean nearer yet.

"Has Her Ladyship not heard of putting a pineapple on the bed?" she asked.

Roger hesitated, and then unsteadily laughed at the tradition of using the celebrated symbol of hospitality as a means to inform a guest of having overstayed their welcome.

Perhaps the thought of being so handily excused struck too closely.

"And pray, how long do you plan to visit?" Her question had been meant as a jest, but a poor one. Her cheeks heated. "I'm sorry; I didn't mean to be forward."

"Not at all." He was so much more handsome when he genuinely smiled as he did then. "The lodgings in Hopetown are insufferably dreary. Lady Bart has been kind enough to indulge me of her hospitality."

For a fraction, she felt sorry for him.

"Have you known Lady Bart long?" she asked.

Momentarily distracted by something said down the table, he seemed surprised by the question. "Yes, I made her acquaintance some years ago, shortly upon my arrival to the West Indies. I met her husband first, of course, but since I have come to consider myself a friend."

Glancing toward his hostess, he smiled with the same regard one would show toward an eccentric aunt. "Bart can be trying, but she is a dear."

Time passed. Dinner dragged. The room became oppressive, in spite of the opened doors and windows, and bank of fans overhead, operated by a doe-eyed slave boy in the corner. Rivulets of moisture trickled from under the wigs, leaving flesh-colored paths on the rice-power. The heat combined with perfume, sweat, and pickled eel brought a prickle between

Cate's shoulder blades. Wondering if her cheeks were as red as they felt, she looked up into Roger's intense green look. Good heavens. Surely, he didn't think her flush was on his account.

Attempts on the part of Lord Whatever-His-Name to catch Cate's eye were easily ignored. Directly at her elbow, however, Fordshaw's efforts were not. Such a dandyish sort, she wondered what he could possibly want with her or any woman, for that matter. At one point, his foot came down on hers, the slippered toe brushing her ankle. The side of his leg came against hers. Soon after, his forearm pressed her, with a meaningful look from the corner of his eye.

Cate was opting between a fork into Fordshaw's hand, a well-aimed spoonful of aspic to the face — or better yet, her entire plate — or a more overt table knife to the ribs, when Roger turned to direct a footman. Fordshaw took the opportunity to lean close enough for his breath to be warm on her neck.

"I wish you joy of your escape." He lifted his wineglass to his mouth, cupping the curve of the glass as if it was a breast, and ran the tip of his tongue suggestively along its rim. "Might I offer you something in the way of further condolences in your hour of need?"

Inwardly seething, she lifted her glass as if in a toast. She batted her lashes with all the charm and innocence she could muster, and said through a frozen smile, "Touch me again, and I'll cut off your cock with this table knife, just as I did that pirate while he slept."

The dainty laugh she added at the end, as if having just heard something witty, drew Roger's attention. He scowled at Fordshaw, now pale under his powder. Fordshaw smiled unsteadily then made a great show of shifting both his chair and attention away.

"I say, Diggie," Lord Peach-Moire called from the far end as the cloth was pulled for dessert. "Where did you say Lord Creswicke's intended is to land?"

"I didn't," Roger said somewhat dryly, pleased when all ears turned his way. "She's destined for her aunt's home."

He rolled a sip of wine in his mouth, ostensibly appreciating its bouquet, but actually allowing the suspense to build.

"Here!" Lady Bart cried, beaming. "She's to come here. The poor child is my niece."

Caught in mid-sip, Cate choked. Sputtering, she flapped her hand, assuring all she was fine. Following insincere murmurs regarding her welfare, a reserved exclamation of surprise made its way around the table.

"Lady Bart, I beg, pray tell how, in good conscience,

can you allow your niece to be married off to that... that...?"
Miss Blue-Dress.

"Upon my word, it wasn't my idea," said Lady Bart in evident
distress. "It was that grasping brother of mine; his foremost
concerns revolve on two things: his connections and his money."

"Does he have any idea of Lord Creswicke's, err... nature?"
asked Eames' judiciously.

"Well, if he doesn't, he should," Lady Bart sniffed. "I've
written him dozens of times, protesting this arrangement most
vehemently, and he has chosen to ignore me on every count. The
best I can do now is offer the poor girl a quiet refuge until the
momentous occasion."

Dessert crept. Cate picked at her apricot tart, seed cake and
comfits. Eventually Lady Bart announced the meal complete. The
ladies rose and retired to the drawing room for sherry, while the
men remained for their port, walnuts and cigars.

Cate barely wetted her lip in sherry. She always found the
stuff excessively sweet. In the absence of male influence, the
women's conversation quickly spiraled down to childbirth,
child rearing and bad husbands, of which she had no frame of
reference, and therefore nothing to add. She squirmed against
her stays, a raw spot now growing under her arm, and dreamed
of the time when she might again draw a full breath. One foot
idly waggling, she half-listened to aimless dribble about people
she didn't know, while glancing repeatedly toward the windows.

Her mind raced with far more important issues. Learning
the fiancé's destination was not good. If Nathan was determined
in his plan, it meant having to pass under the nose of not only
a Commodore, but several Royal Navy ships. It was difficult to
imagine Nathan would be so foolish as to attempt something
so harebrained. And yet, if the stories she had heard on the
Constancy were any measure, he would dare any number of
hazards in order to embarrass Harte.

She strained for ways to talk Nathan out of this plan of his,
but a larger and more immediate problem loomed: escape.

Time was not on her side. Dinner had taken nearly three
hours; it was well after dark. Nathan was waiting; she had to find
a way to slip out. The further she delayed, the further Nathan's
doubts in her would plunge. Between Roger, the guards—no
house of this stature would be without—guests, servants and a
Commodore, escape unnoticed seemed nigh impossible. Nathan
had slipped in and out in broad daylight with alarming ease.
Even with the cover of darkness, attempts on her part promised
to be executed with considerably less aplomb.

Out from under Roger's scrutiny had been a step in the right direction, but she was still faced with a roomful of women. Going to the privy wasn't an option; she had already seen the footman slip a chamber pot under Mrs. Blue-Dress's chair.

Risks be damned, she abruptly rose. Playing the distressed damsel to the fullest, pleading a headache and exhaustion, she backed out of the room. Once in the hallway, she sagged against the wall and closed her eyes.

Alone at last!

Someone touched her on the arm, and she shrieked. Whirling around, she found Lady Bart standing there.

"He's waiting for you," the matron whispered in breathless drama.

"Waiting? Who?"

"Oh, you don't have to play coy, my dear. I saw your impatience, and he is *so* anxious." Lady Bart winked conspiratorially and patted Cate's arm. "I know all about it."

He? Cate gaped. It was outrageous to think Nathan had somehow communicated with Lady Bart. Surely some kind of alarm sounded would have been sounded if a pirate had been discovered in the garden.

"Diggie. He's waiting for you just outside." She squeezed Cate's arm and winked significantly. "Be off, my dear, I assured him there would be no awkward interruptions."

The tiny-footed woman slipped back into the drawing room, leaving Cate in a cold sweat. In the spirit of avoiding "Diggie," she could either stand in the hall for the remainder of the evening, or go to her room. Either scenario placed Nathan and Harte in roughly the same vicinity. Or she could go outside to evade an unwanted suitor, while looking for one who had no intention of being one, suitor, that is.

She shook her head. I've been around Nathan too long. I'm beginning to sound like him.

"I can do this," she chanted under her breath, beating a tattoo on her leg with her fist. She walked with the animation of the condemned. "All I need do is go out, dismiss him, and then I'm away."

It was galling Harte would be so presumptuous. She had given no reason to think she was about to go running off into the night with him. For one of his character, such impulsiveness seemed markedly out of character.

Cate's step slowed with niggling second thoughts. She was well-versed in social behavior and its minutia, and had taken particular care not to send any false signals. She had no fan; no mistakes there. Somewhere in the middle of dinner, there had been a time or two when their gazes had met. Nothing had been meant as flirtatious, but apparently, he thought otherwise. Roger's passionate impulses might have been flattering, was it not for the possibility they were prompted by something other than her charms. He bristled at any mention of Nathanael Blackthorne, which lent credence to his ardent attentions stemming more from rivalry.

No matter. He was about to be set straight, and in short order.

Cate pushed open the doors, and stepped into the garden and its smells of jasmine and damp earth. She stopped to inhale the fresh air as deeply as the stays would allow. Rendered by the moonlight in a palette in hues of silver and indigo, it proved to be a dismaying maze of hedges and shrubbery. Stones grinding softly underfoot, she followed the winding paths. Feeling vaguely like a rat in a maze, she hoped Providence might smile this once, and allow her to find Nathan first.

"Madam Harper?"

It wasn't the graveled voice Cate hoped to hear.

She jumped, and yelped, "Roger! You startled me." Touching a hand to her chest, she wasn't as startled as she posed; it provided the time to recompose.

"You've called me 'Roger', may I call you Catherine?" Not the usual nasal flat, his voice was now deep and husky—so *very* enamored.

Cate laughed, as hollow and false as those heard all evening. "No one has called me Catherine since my father; Cate will suffice."

"Lovely, *Cate*."

She flinched at his breathy joyousness. All powers of concentration absorbed by her worry for Nathan, she stammered badly, then opted for the dense-headed approach. After all, ignorance was claimed to be bliss.

"I thought you to be with the men, having their port and cigars." Bearing a false smile, she fixed her attention on him in order to resist the driving urge to look around for Nathan.

"I was waiting upon you. Did Lady Bart not tell you?"

"Perhaps she did," she said faintly. "I must have forgotten." *So much for ignorance.*

He stepped closer yet. Considerably taller, his nearness forced her tip to her head back in order to see his face.

"I must speak my heart, Cate." He stammered then forged ahead. "I've found I am fascinated by you; you've entranced me and I am compelled to be with you."

Outwardly impassive, she cringed inwardly. He clearly meant to sweep her off her feet. If anything, it was having quite the opposite effect: she was not moved. Well, maybe moved to scurry away, but certainly not attracted, as so obviously hoped. Fawning men she had never found appealing.

Cate fell back a step. "Isn't this somewhat sudden?"

"I know my behavior may seem impulsive and erratic." He turned away to clutch his hands to his chest. "There was someone—someone else so very special—and I hesitated, playing the gentlemen and the fool. Since, I couldn't help but think, if I had been a little more... forthcoming, it might have gone quite differently."

Swiveling back, he pressed closer. His hand hovered at her shoulder and then alit. Not exactly a resounding statement of affection.

"Now, she's gone, but you are here, and I have resolved to seize this opportunity." He hesitated, and then with a choked gasp, clutched her close. "My heart swells at the thought of the bravery and courage you've shown."

Not the only thing swelling.

Cate wriggled, trying to push away. Harte whispered something unintelligible, probably meant to be quite romantic, and then kissed her, so very chaste. Protesting against his mouth, she flailed. He was inexplicably encouraged and his arms around her tightened.

"Let 'er go, mate!"

His grasp firm, Harte straightened as Nathan stepped out of the shrubbery shadows and into the moonlight, pistol in hand. "Well, well, Nathanael Blackthorne."

"Commodore." Nathan sketched a mocking bow. Sobering, the pistol was brought more to bear. "Now, if you please, let 'er go."

Harte's arms still around her, the air between the two snapped with mutual hatred. "And if I refuse, do you propose to shoot me?"

"I might."

The Commodore made a low sound that might have been a taunting laugh. "There are Marines everywhere. All I need do is shout."

Nathan canted his head, considering. "Fair enough, I'll be captured, but she'll be dead." He gestured with the pistol, his voice dropping to a menacing low. "Now, let 'er go."

Harte gave Cate a sharp push, hurtling her at Nathan. Meant as a distraction, instead Nathan caught her smoothly, his eyes never leaving Harte. He swung her around, up against his chest and pressed the pistol to her jaw hard enough for her to yelp in pain.

"You wouldn't dare," Harte sneered. His fists balled

uselessly at his sides; in deference to Lady Bart's hospitality, he wore no weapons.

Nathan chuckled. "Really, now? In that case, watch this next bit."

"Na—" she began.

Nathan cut off her protest with another jab of the pistol, clacking her teeth together. "Shh, quiet. You're coming with me, darling. As I recall it, we've unfinished business."

He nuzzled her neck and nudged his hips against hers. Harte's expression darkened.

"You can have 'er when we're done with 'er, mate. I bid you good e'en."

The pistol firmly in place, Nathan backed away, taking her with him, the foliage closing in around them. Several more steps later, he pulled her around and gave her a solid shove.

"A path, just there. Go!" he hissed in her ear.

Cate hitched her skirts and ran, Nathan close behind. The shadows crisscrossing the path rendered it nigh impossible to see. Within a few strides, a shoe came off; she stumbled, going down hard on her knees. He jerked her back up onto her feet and propelled her forward.

"Marines! Marines!" cried Harte.

Footsteps and heavy crashing of several men could be heard converging on them.

Nathan pulled to a stop and looked back. "Keep going. The fatuous twosome is just ahead. Go."

"But—?"

His fingers dug her shoulders as he spun her around. "Go!"

The urgency in his voice and the sound of oncoming footsteps spurred her away as he braced to meet their pursuers. From behind came the grunts and thuds of fighting. Then all was quiet, except the rasp of her breathing. The urge to go back was strong, but Nathan's last words had been for her to run, and so she did as best as possible with the cumbersome skirts. At length, she broke out onto a road, but had no idea of which way to go. She started at two men popping from the bushes on the opposite side: Towers and Smalley. They motioned her across. She fell in between them as they sped away.

They kept up a rapid pace until at the beach once more. Pryce stood by the longboats, waiting like a protective father. Several more familiar faces loomed out of the night, coming up silently behind him.

"'Bout time ye's got back," he barked without ceremony, then craned his neck to peer behind them. "Where be the Cap'n?"

"He fell behind," Smalley reported.

"He said he would catch up," Cate said, worriedly looking back.

Pryce eyed her in her finery, considerably now worse for wear, and then stared in the direction of town. Decision made, he seized her by the arm and propelled her toward the waiting boats. "Orders is orders, and ours is to clap on and ship ye directly."

"But, Nathan—"

"If he's a-comin', then he'll come. Otherwise... Else he'll come when he might. It's back to—"

"No!" she shrieked and yanked free. "I will not leave him!"

Pryce gave the benefit of a glare known to turn a subordinate to stone. "'Tis not to be a-leavin', 'tis to be followin' orders, just as—"

"I will not! You can't make me."

Brows arched, he said with menacing lowness, "Ah, but Mr. Cate, can and will."

She sank back on her heels. He could and he would. She was a woman alone against a gang of pirates, looking particularly menacing in the dark just then. They could do anything they darn well wanted, and there wasn't a blessed thing she could do about it. Years of dealing with a stubborn-as-a-rock Highlander, however, had taught her the wisdom of alternative approaches.

"Isn't there something in that precious Code or ship's book or whatever, of yours that requires the crew to save their captain?" she asked of all of them.

An unexpected tack it was. The men rocked back, puzzling it out.

"Could... mebbe be." Pryce cast a pensive gaze to where the *Morganse* laid at anchor, and then said under his breath, "Haven't ever read all of it."

"Sounds likely," said Squidge, pondering.

"Not savin' 'im could almost be seen as mutinying." The import of Smalley's point struck them all, and distasteful it was.

"If isn't, it should be." She waited and watched. "I say, we make all efforts to preserve the Code and go get him."

There was a quiet cheer in favor.

"You'll not be a-goin' anywhere," Pryce said, grabbing her by the arm once more. "Yer goin' aboard."

Her victory plummeted to panic, and the tears welled. "Allow me to at least stay—"

"Mr. Cate, by yer leave. The Cap'n desires ye aboard, and direct as direct orders could be."

"I am safe. I have all of you around me," she said, spreading her arms toward the circle of pirates. "If something happens, I promise to swim for the ship. How's that?"

"Well..." Pryce ducked his head and kicked at the sand. "Aye, but if anythin' wuz to happen—"

"I'll make sure he knows it was my doing. He won't shout at me near as much."

Pryce made a hawking noise. "He wouldn't dare."

14: PATHS CROSS

THEY WAITED. THE MOON MADE a steady path, its shadows tracking an arc across the sand, and they waited. Cate paced, Pryce close behind, determined she was not to be out of his sight, and they waited. Several times she tried to persuade him to go find Nathan, but the first mate was staunch in his determination to obey orders.

She grumbled loudly about men and their silly rules. She stalked the beach, kicking away her skirts, with the sounds of Nathan fighting the guards echoing in her head. She couldn't rid herself of the vision of him lying in a pool of blood. She cursed men in general. Then she cursed men who insisted on being noble and trying to save others who could—if given enough time—have managed their escape on their own.

The prick of a pin in her ribs broke her thoughts. The half-hanging stomacher was yanked free and pitched, pins and all into the darkness. She wished a moment's privacy to be rid of the underskirts, and attend a more pressing matter brought on by copious amounts of wine. She veered toward the bushes. A glaring Pryce blocked her within a few steps, arms crossed and as imposing as Goliath.

"'N what be in yer head?"

"I need to… umm…" She made a vague gesture and then gathered her poise. "I desire a bit of privacy which cannot be denied."

She realized too late that he suspected her of sneaking off, which she would have, had she thought of it.

"Yer word on it?"

Pryce saw Cate's hesitation and his mouth tucked up grimly. He put out a hand with the authority of one accustomed to having subordinates always near, and said, "A length, if ye please."

The rope was brought. He knelt at her feet and looked up expectantly. She lifted her hem and watched with a sinking heart as he secured it around her ankle with one of those insufferable knots which she had never mastered and had no hope of undoing.

"I'm not a ruddy dog," she said to the top of his head.

"Fair enough, 'cuz the Cap'n wouldn't give a rat's arse, if 'twas nay but that," he said without looking up.

She pushed through the bushes, now mindful of not tangling the rope. When she was reeled back in, a pair of underpetticoats were strung on the tether, blazing bright in the darkness. As fearsome as the first mate of the famed *Ciara Morganse* was, it was a wonder at how readily Pryce was discommoded by a few women's underthings.

"You left me little choice," she said evenly.

Her regained freedom was limited. Her pacing path was confined to short passes, Pryce never more than a stride or two away. At length, he blocked her path and sternly pointed to the sand at the base of a tree. She sat, reluctantly but without protest. He plopped down next to her, drew his knife from his back and set stropping it on his boot.

"Pryce, what is it between Nathan and Harte?"

Intent on his task, Pryce smiled, not wholly surprised by the question.

"Ah, now there be a history, but 'tis likely a matter the Cap'n should be a'tellin'. 'Tis not my place to be a-sayin'. Can't say as I'm familiar with all the particulars."

"Ezekiel Pryce, you know more particulars than any man on this ship, including quite possibly Nathan himself. Pryce, please? I need to know. Otherwise, I'm left thinking I'm the cause of what's between them."

It was a categorical overstatement—Cate didn't flatter herself that much—but it was her best ploy. Pryce snorted, whether in disbelief or at the outlandishness of her assumption being unclear. With a bit more prodding, he gave way.

"No so sure as t' how it all come to pass. 'Twas afore I was with 'im. It's my notion the Cap'n was captured early on. Harte had 'im in the brig, a-headin' for Fort Charles, when somehow or another the Cap'n contrived to escape. Blew the ship's magazine and then waved g'bye as he floated away on a hatch grate. Aye, he's managed to escape the Commodore's clutches three, mebbe four times."

He fell into a considering quiet.

"Harte chased the Cap'n through a storm the likes of which no man worth his three squares woulda dared. Led the entire Royal Fleet square into a royal disaster. They lost three ships, with a butcher's bill longer than could be counted. Meanwhile, the Cap'n was a-ridin' out the storm in Tortuga, with a bottle o' rum and a whore on each hip... beggin' yer pardon, sir," he added hastily, swiping his hand across his mouth.

"I seen fer my own eyes, when the Cap'n delivered six street whores to the Commodore's big birthday doin's, promisin' a hundred pieces of gold to the first one what could bring 'im off, beggin' yer pardon again, sir," he hastened to add again. Even in the poor light, a dark flush could be seen rising from his collar.

"There was the Commodore with his breeches undone and all his glory right for all to see, all six applyin' every trick they knew!" he said, fizzing with laughter.

"I can tell ye plain—bore a hand, I did—in causin' for a hogshead to be delivered to the Commodore's ship. Just as it swung over, the thing busted open..." His shoulders shook, tears of mirth welling in his eyes. "The Cap'n must o' looked like Saint Patrick o' the West Indies collectin' up them snakes. They spilt out on deck... men runnin' and screamin', clambering up the mast and jumpin' ship whether they could swim or no."

The mirth overtook him. It took several minutes for him to recover sufficiently to continue. "A little piece o' paper floated down congradulatin' the Commodore on his genius on riddin' the ship o' rats, signed by the Cap'n."

Pryce paused to check the knife's edge with his thumb and then resumed honing.

"I'll tell ye plain, to my way o' thinkin'," he began over the rasp of metal against leather, "the bitter end was when the Cap'n got the Commodore so arsey-farcey, he was a'firin' on his own ships—sunk one, in the doin'—a-seekin' to protect a town. Whilst the Commodore and his men were all a-roil, we slipped in, cleaned it out as easy as kiss yer hand, and then cut out the Commodore's barge."

"So, Harte blames Nathan for his setbacks?"

He stopped to regard her through a squinted eye. "Ambition is a merciless master and, as black's the white o' my eye, Harte is its slave. The Cap'n has managed to break many a rung off Harte's ladder to success. The good Commodore wuz set on bein' Admiral-on-High by now, if it weren't for Cap'n Nathanael Blackthorne."

"That explains several things," Cate murmured more to herself. Old rivalries and jealousies were a volatile mix. It went a long way to explain Nathan's sudden touchiness.

"Could be part o' the reason how Harte and Creswicke come to be so tight," he said, looking off across the water. Lamps doused, the *Morganse* sat like a serene dark mistress awaiting the return of her lover.

"Mutual enemy?"

"In a manner o' speakin'. Could be the Fates wuz a-bringin' them together anyways, and the Cap'n just the happy convenience."

He checked the blade once more, and then experimentally scraped a patch of the several-day stubble on his cheek. Satisfied, he slipped the knife back into its place.

"Or, he's managed to make two very devoted enemies," she said, considering.

"Aye." He grinned, rubbing the back of his neck. "There be that too. The Cap'n sure and certain has a way about 'im, in that regard."

It put the kidnapping of Creswicke's fiancé into a new light, going well beyond lust for money or adventure.

"And then I came along, right in the middle of it," she sighed.

"Y'll give me leave to say, sir, 'tis nothing on yer account. It coulda' been that blessed bird over there," he said, gesturing toward Beatrice roosted in a nearby tree, luminescent in the starlight, "and they'd go hammer and tongs at each other just the same."

The moon was past its zenith, dipping behind the treetops at the far side of the bay, when she implored Pryce one more time.

Pryce, the Amiable disappeared; Pryce, the Bullish returned. "If'n he could have been here by now, he woulda."

His failure to argue further she took as a positive. She shied from the nagging image of Nathan lying in the bushes, injured and helpless.

Pryce glanced toward the eastern sky and a low-hanging Venus. "'Twill be light in a bit."

"Then, we're going?" Her hopes skyrocketed as she lurched to her feet.

"*We're* goin'. *Yer* stayin'," he said, rising.

"No, I'm not!" Teeth clenched, her breath came quicker. She tried to hold the fierce pose. Exhaustion and worry weakened her defiance, and she wavered. Face crumbling, her chin began to quiver.

"I beg, Pryce. Please. I can't just wait and wonder. Besides, you need me to show you where I saw him last."

"Oh, very well. But ye'd best not get hurt! And if ye do, jest keep goin', becuz we won't be able to bear ye a hand when the Cap'n goes after ye!"

He had to shout at the finish, because she was already far down the beach.

"It's not a lot," Pryce said, looking down at the glistening blood, kept wet by the night's damp. A disquieting number of footprints converged on the churned spot of dirt.

"It's enough," Cate countered tartly.

"If'n we'd come sooner, he'd still be gone," Pryce said with maddening evenness, divining her thoughts once again.

Cate led the small party of Morgansers to Lady Bart's and where she had last seen Nathan. An internal clock had ticked since she heard him fall. Had he escaped unharmed, he would have met them on the beach. That failing, her best hope was that he was alive and being held. Harte's "gnat squashed" comment haunted her. It hadn't been uttered lightly. On the contrary, there had been great intent in those reptilian eyes.

Unbeknownst to her — Damn his eyes! — Pryce had dispatched men to check the town, goal, thieve's hole and garrison. They had returned to the shore with the pink of dawn breaking on their shoulders and empty-handed. It meant Nathan had been taken somewhere else, somewhere that deeds far too heinous to be witnessed could be carried out.

But where?

The garden was heavily-trampled. With no clear tracks to follow, there was no way of knowing. She tried to take it as an encouraging sign that there was no blood trail, but a thin reassurance it was.

Cate chewed the inside of her mouth. The task of searching each and every of the plantation's buildings loomed larger, and the clock was still ticking.

"Hoy, lookit!"

All heads turned to follow Squidge's point to a nearby tree.

"It's only Beatrice," Towers grumbled, waving a dismissive hand.

Beatrice's head bobbed, markedly agitated. Arching her wings, she squawked, several of the men wincing at her shrillness in the morning's quiet.

"*Cap'n, ahoy!*"

They looked to each other, at the parrot, and back.

"*Cap'n, ahoy!*"

Pryce approached the bird with a narrowed eye. "C'mon, speak up ya useless pile o' feathers, or I'll be a-feednin' yer carcass to the crows."

Beatrice rose with a shriek and soared low through the trees, bright against the sky's pale. Circling back, amid several obscenities, she repeated her cry, and set off. Exchanging puzzled looks, the people shrugged and followed.

The marauding pirates traversed the plantation with

shocking ease. Lady Bart's showed all the signs of having once been a grand place, but it had gone to recent ruin. The distant barking of dogs, startled chicken protests and curious bleats of goats marked their progress, but with no shouts of alarm. Still, with a Commodore and Marines about, extreme caution was required.

Beatrice was their only hope, and a shining one she was. Several times she circled back, seemingly to round them up and hurry them along, repeating her message and coarse remarks. At last, she settled on the rooftree of a squat building. Barrel hoops, wagon wheel rims, anvils, and water vats marked it as the estate's blacksmith. The Morgansers crouched behind the crumbling stone walls of an abandoned byre. If there were any further doubts as to Beatrice's credibility, the scarlet of two Marines posted at the barn's double doors was confirmation enough: such security isn't necessary if inside was only iron and bellows.

"Smitty woulda been a'workin' by this time o' day," Pryce observed, eyeing the bare wisp of smoke curling from the chimney, a forge yet to be stoked.

"Why the blacksmith?" asked Smalley.

Cate answered before she thought. "Shackles and chains."

A bitter bile rose. In cold evaluation, the smithy was a wise choice: close enough to the house for convenience, and yet removed enough for privacy.

A low growl emitted from the others.

"Bastard."

Cate couldn't disagree with Chin's assessment.

"Now, now, gents. Wasted hate is wasted energy. Let's be sure o' what's afoot here." Pryce's calm was betrayed by his knuckles white on the hilt of his sword.

So much now made sense. Cate's suspicions had been correct, but there was little satisfaction to be gleaned. Ambition had its price; someone as advanced in rank as Harte's, at his young age, had to be consumed by it. His hunger, however, was not yet sated. Arresting someone as renown as Nathanael Blackthorne still alive would deny him his personal justice. Bringing Nathan in "accidentally dead," would supply Harte with both his pound of flesh and the prestige of ending the pirate's reign of terror.

"Now what?" sighed Ogden. The snake tattooed on his head peered down with an equally puzzled look.

At that early hour, neither of the Marines struck an imposing figure: one slumped on a barrel, the other on an overturned bucket. Leaned against the barn, both were asleep, judging by the gaping mouths, oblivious to Beatrice's boisterous proclamations from overhead.

"Pride o' the King's Navy," Pryce snorted contemptuously. "You stay." He drilled Cate with one of his most piercing looks. "The rest o' ye's watch her, whilst I go see what's what."

With a final warning glare, Pryce crept away. He made his way to the back of the barn, his path marked by glimpses of him behind a bush or abandoned cart. Quaking with anxiety, Cate contained herself until he had disappeared around the building. She broke away in a hiss of protest from those left in her wake. Following Pryce's darting path, she caught him up. He whirled, reaching for his sword, and then gave her a withering glare. She pressed a finger to her lips, smirking at his displeasure.

The back of the building offered no access; no windows or doors, not even a loose board. They separated to investigate further. Cate discovered a crack in the weathered siding and urgently waved Pryce over. He stood while she squatted, and they put an eye to the split. They jerked back at the sight of red coats inside: five, maybe seven Marines, clustered in irregular groups. Judging by their actions, there were more out of their narrow line of sight. Pryce thumped her on the arm and pointed.

It was Nathan. He sat in the straw, slumped against a post. His arms were held high by shackles on his wrists, suspended to a beam overhead. Head lolled between his arms, his body curved in a defensive inward arc, as if expecting another blow, or God knew what else.

Fury shook her, and she swore under her breath, Pryce nodding in avid agreement. She vibrated with the urge to tear away the boards, Marines be damned! Pryce's hand on her shoulder steadied her. A silent argument ensued, a pantomime of gestures and expressions, offering and negating as to what should be done. The only thing they could agree on was to retreat, where they could argue further.

"He's in there," Pryce reported grimly upon their return. "Bastards 'ave him strung up like a slaughtered pig."

"We have to get him out of there." Cate only uttered what everyone else was thinking. Her hot rush of anger had ebbed, the cold calm of calculation settling in.

The first suggestion was an outright frontal attack; after all they were pirates and eager to do what they did best.

"There has to be nigh a dozen o' them red-bellies in there, plus them what's posted guard," Pryce said. "We can take 'em all, well n' good, but one shot and we'll have the whole mess on us. The Cap'n appears in no condition to show a leg."

"We need a diversion," she said more to herself. A few seconds more and she snapped her fingers. "I've got it."

Their lack of confidence was obvious, but with no option at hand, a decoy was necessary.

"Just wait for the cue," she said, with a sly smile. "I promise, you'll know it."

Cate crept away, leaving Pryce to grumble in protest. The men worked their way to the rear of the smithy, while Cate, wrestling with her gown, dodged among the cribs and coops, until she was directly across the yard from the blacksmith's front doors.

Poised to make her move, she stopped at hearing the rapid approach of hooves and wheels. She dove deeper into the shrubbery and peeked back to see a two-wheeled curate pass, Harte at the reins. The two Marines idling at the door snapped to attention when he pulled up, scurrying to open them for him.

Luck was with her: the doors stood open, the guards attending their commander inside.

Her hair had flung off most of its pins and tumbled free about her shoulders. She ruffled it further and then slapped her cheeks to redden them. Taking a deep breath, she sprung up and raced for the barn. With a siren-like scream, she ran, wildly flapping her arms. Skidding up before the doors, she threw her head back and gave another frenzied howl, circling and flailing in apparent hysterics.

From inside came shouts of alarm and running feet. She flew at the first Marine out the door, and screamed, pounding his chest with her fists. She ran to the next, maniacally babbling. Harte appeared, flanked by more Marines. Pitching to a new stridency, now alternating from hysterics to sobbing, she launched at Harte. He touched her arm, and she jerked away to run terrorized to the next, clawing at the vermillion fabric as if for protection.

"Dear God, Catherine!" Harte exclaimed. He pulled her to him, and she arched her back to yowl squarely into his ear.

"Stop them!" she wailed into Harte's coat. "Stop them! Don't let them take me. Not again!"

"Pray, who? I beg of you?"

"Pirates!" she cried in wild-eyed shrillness and threw a terrified look over her shoulder. "No, no, don't let them take me. Nooo...!"

While she burrowed against him, the Marines were dispatched inside and in a defensive position around them, as if the pirates might materialize directly. Since there were no tears—she wasn't that good of an actress—Cate kept her face deep in the crook of Roger's shoulder as she cried, going louder at the least suggestion that he might move away.

"Commodore," shouted one of the soldiers, running from the building's dim. "Commodore, Blackthorne: he's gone, sir."

"Noo...! Nooo...!" she screeched, scrabbling frantically at Harte's coat, the effort made worthwhile by a satisfying ripping sound. "Don't let him have me, plleeaasseee! Not again"

"Don't just stand there," Harte cried. "Go get him."

The hallmark of a good soldier is calm before battle, but nothing in Harte's training had prepared him for a hysterical woman. Perfect! The longer she could keep him off balance, the better. She thought to throw herself in front of the charging Marines, but Harte's grasp was too firm. They had said Blackthorne was gone; that would have to be enough.

Roger stiffly patted her shoulder as he held her, with words Cate supposed were meant to be comforting. Murmuring more useless nothings, he guided her to the carriage. He leapt in beside her, a pop of the whip and the horse was off on a high trot. She kept her face hidden. Her performance had opened the floodgates, and she now swung wildly from make-believe hysteria to the real thing. The image of Nathan hanging by his arms was there at every closing of her eyes, and she began to shake with a mix of revulsion and fury at the monster that had put him there; the very one she now clung to. Growling like a rabid dog, she hammered him with her fists, one landing at his jaw, another, his ear.

Roger applied the whip to the horse.

Now at a full gallop, the carriage soon slid to a halt in a spray of gravel at Lady Bart's doorstep. Harte eased Cate out of the carriage and bustled her into the house. The servants met them in the foyer, the entire house being thrown into an uproar. Leaning heavily on his arm, ostensibly for support, Cate dug her nails into the flesh of his wrist as she was taken upstairs. Lady Bart appeared at the top, clad in a wrapper and a cap, its flounced edge hanging ridiculously low over her nose.

In a confusion of voices, curious faces peeking from behind chamber doors, Cate was ushered down the hall to her room and deposited on the bed. Red-faced at having entered a lady's chamber, the Commodore quickly exited, leaving Cate to end her performance.

"Oh, you poor dear." Lady Bart circled the room, clapping her hands to her cheeks. "To think, you were abducted right from our very garden, taken by that insidious, vile, disgusting creature and dragged off like some kind of an... an animal. I don't know why Diggie refuses to do something about those perfidious, barbaric creatures! We must be rid of such disreputable criminals, right here in our very midst..."

Sally appeared and Lady Bart's voice faded from Cate's awareness. After a flash of dismay at Cate's ruin, the gown a ghost of its former self, she undressed Cate in her confident manner, and snugged a wrapper about her shoulders.

"Here," Sally said, under Lady Bart's monologue and pressed a glass into Cate's hand. "Drink this. It will give you ease."

It was brandy and a very good one. Cate's eyes watered at the first sip touching her throat, raw from screaming. The liquor set off a pleasant glow in her stomach and she began to sag. It had been a very long night. It seemed impossible it had barely been a day since Nathan had set her off for Hopetown.

"Let's wash you up," said Sally, in a motherly tone as she set down a basin of hot water. Exhaustion turning her limbs to sand, Cate yielded to her competent hands, while Lady Bart rammed about the room like a ranting bee in a bottle.

Under Sally's watchful eye Cate finished the brandy and another was poured. At the senior maid's silent bidding, the chambermaid intercepted Lady Bart, and crooning patiently, steered her out of the room. The door was pulled shut and blessed quiet befell the chamber.

Sally surveyed Cate critically as she sponged her arms. "Will you be well?"

"Yes, I'll be fine," Cate sighed, touched by her sincerity. With some effort, she raised a hand to her head. Surprised to see it quivering, she let it fall back to her lap. "I didn't realize I was so tired."

"That would be the brandy working. Drink up and then take your rest."

Brandy finished, Cate allowed herself to be tucked deep into the quilts. Sally moved in virtual silence across the Turkey rugs to pull the shutters closed, and then left, the latch of the door clicking faintly behind her.

Lying on her side, Cate fingered the knotted pendant at her neck, suffused with the contentment of a goal accomplished. That shining victory was tarnished, however: her plan had only gone as far as providing a distraction for Nathan's rescue. Escape for her wasn't an option, not yet at any rate. To do so would be to risk leading Harte and his Marines to Nathan.

Cate had the sudden sense of being watched. Lifting her head, she met with the glare of intense accusation from the nameless Dunwoody ancestor on the mantle.

"What?" she huffed at the ancient face. "I've done all I might.

Nathan's free. The rest will just have to bide until I can think of something... something... later."

Leaving the town in their wake, Pryce was caught between the need for haste and the burden of a battered and dazed Cap'n. And so, they pushed on as hasty as could be managed.

Confident any pursuit was outdistanced, Pryce called a halt in a quiet glade. With a running stream and good defenses, he figured to bide, until the Cap'n could find his legs.

Pryce wryly smiled. 'Twas a wonder how cooperative a soul could be at gunpoint, and so soon being yanked from his warm bed. Two strokes by the town's sleepy-eyed smith, and the Cap'n was free of the shackles. A few coins smoothed ruffled feathers and bought the smithy's silence, but such loyalty would only endure, until the arrival of someone with a larger coin, and make no mistake.

Watches posted, Pryce hunched down next to where the Cap'n laid, head pillowed on a log, and gave him a critical eyeballing.

"How bad is it?"

The Cap'n's voice was a start, figuring him either asleep or out cold.

"If I may make so bold, I've seen ye worse, but more oftener I've seen ye a damn sight better. 'Pears they had their way with ye," Pryce said judiciously.

"A bit," came with effort and a sigh.

An outright blatant exaggeration on the Skipper's part, it was. It was Pryce's notion a fair job of beating had been done. Eye swollen shut, split lip, scraped cheek, nose bleeding—not busted, just bleeding—he promised a sight by the morrow. The raw wrists told the tale: they'd taken their time. It had been a beating, but a careful one: not to maim or kill, just inflict pain, and a good deal. T'was a sorrow not heeding Mr. Cate's pleas. Might be the Cap'n could have been spared considerable abuse.

The Cap'n grunted as he shifted. "Stand by and allow me to get me head clear." In the spirit of that thought, the one eye which could open did so, squeezing shut in rapid succession. "How the bloody hell did you find me?"

"A little bird told us," Pryce said dryly. He directed the Cap'n's attention toward a feathery flash of blue perched overhead.

"The bugger's been a talkative sort, lately." The Cap'n groaned and closed his eyes.

Pryce rose and searched out a suitable leaf. Folding it into a cup, he made several trips from the stream with water for the

Cap'n. The first few sips were swished and spat, the next drink drunk as if God's milk.

"Mr. Cate gonna be near apoplexy when she sees you," Pryce mused.

The Cap'n's grim smile was checked by a split lip. Probing his face and working his jaw, he said, "Might be well-advised if I were to stand off out here for the while. You'll be obliged to keep her shipped. Otherwise, the bloody woman will track me down. Most determined woman I've ever met."

"'N no bones about it," Pryce agreed heartily.

The Cap'n saw something which didn't serve. "She is aboard, is she not?"

Pryce looked to the ground between his feet. Damn! Now there was what he dreaded most. Eyes like a hawk, the Skipper had, able to see into a man's soul better than a witchy-woman. Failing orders was galling enough; failing the Cap'n like some fond and feckless scrum was worse.

"She made it aboard, did she not?" the Cap'n repeated, the battered face clouding ominously.

"Well, d'ye see—"

"Where is she, Pryce?"

"Well, t'was like this, you know how she can be—"

"Where is she?!"

"We needed a diversion, and so..."

"Where the goddamned hell is she!" Blood set to trickling from the Cap'n's nose.

Pryce drew a deep breath. "Harte's got her." The Cap'n would never hit him, but he braced for the storm in the offing.

"How the...?" He blenched and rolled away to puke.

Pryce winced in sympathy. He'd suffered stove-in ribs, knew the agony what would come with each wretch, and bore a hand at the finish. Alternating between gasping and swearing, the Cap'n clutched his sides, while Pryce fetched more water. Much to his relief, this time it stayed down.

"I'm glad it's you, Pryce," muttered the Cap'n at one point, fondling the makeshift cup. "If it were her, she'd insist on that damned honey water of hers."

"Aye, she would, at that. Sets a great store by it, she does," Pryce heartily agreed. "And sure, as a cock's crow, you'd be drinkin' it, and the Devil take ye."

"No telling her 'No', is there?"

"No, there ain't. Nathan, I beg yer leave. She wouldn't hove to. Hell, you know how she is."

"Don't I, though." The Cap'n sighed, that small movement causing him to wince.

"Ribs broke?"

"Nay, just tender. Me stomach took the worst. I've the impression they weren't quite done with me, yet."

"Aye! Ye wouldn't be a-drawin' breath else."

The Cap'n took on a dogged look. "I can't leave her, mate, not with him."

"Aye." A blind man could have seen that coming. Getting the Cap'n to stay put whilst the rest went to fetch Mr. Cate: now that looked to call for a fair bit of doing. When the Skipper set his mind, one might as well try to turn the tides.

Pryce squinted up from under his brows. "Don't suppose you could mebbe stand off a bit, do ye? Won't do 'er or anyone else much good, if yer laid out in the bushes somewheres."

"Always the pragmatic." The Cap'n grinned as much as he dared. It didn't go unnoticed that the question went unanswered. "Might you spare a bit of that rum you hold so dear?"

"I'm speechless as to what ye be implyin'!" Pryce said, feigning ignorance.

"Buggering hell, man! You've toted that flask, since the day you shipped. You fancy it more than you fancy a fat widow. Now, give over."

In grudging good-humor, Pryce fished the flask from his shirt and they shared, the Cap'n in careful increments. No sense in wasting it, if the Cap'n was just going to puke it. While they awaited the rum's restorative powers, he regaled the Cap'n with Mr. Cate's performance in front of the blacksmith's. He laughed, clutching his sides.

"She's one brave lass," Pryce said admiringly. "I ain't never seed the likes."

Considering the tales, she told, the scars she carried, the woman had endured what would have broken many a man. Instead of slinking—and not a mother's son would blame her and she did—she looked the world square on and told it to "Go to hell!"

"Aye, it's a rare attribute," the Skipper said looking off. "'Tis is likely to get her killed by and by."

"Likely to get *you* killed. She's near as crazed as you."

The Cap'n struggled to his feet and swayed. He took several halting steps, as if unsure of where the ground was. Finally, he folded to his knees at the stream's bank. He dipped a hand, like he was of two minds. Then he crumpled to the ground and rolled to land face-down in the water. Grasping a rock, he floated like a corpse, the water swirling reddish-brown in his wake. In the time a normal soul would have foundered, he rolled over, hair streaming like kelp. Pryce rubbed a tired hand over his face. The man was always half-fish.

Eventually, the Cap'n stood in midstream and shook off like a great dog. The blood and filth gone, he was white as a ship's biscuit, but nearer to decent. The eye once matted shut stood open. He sat next to Pryce and put out a hand for the flask.

"What's in yer head regardin' her?" Pryce asked, smacking his lips in satisfaction after his own pull.

It took the Cap'n so long to reply, Pryce allowed he mightn't.

"I'm on beam ends on this one, mate." The Cap'n lifted a hand then dropped it in surrender. "There's not much I can do. She's married."

Pryce squinted, thinking perhaps the Cap'n had been hit in the head harder than credited.

"Never caused ye to set yer sails aback a'fore."

"I don't know. Scupper and burn me, if I know why, but it does this time."

Cate floated between the delicious netherworld of sleep and the harsh reality of day, knowing it necessary to leave the one, but unwilling to cope with the other. At length, she let go of her desperate grasp and allowed the day to drag her up to join it in all its glory.

She had no idea of the time. The shutters blocked the sun, the room too dim to see the clock. She contemplated the benefits of lying abed, waiting for it to chime. Reprimanding herself for such decadence, she rose. Wrapped in a corner of the quilt, she shuffled to the window and pushed back the shutters. Squinting, she shielded her eyes against the brilliance and checked the sky. Brooding clouds gathered in low behind the trees, but she determined it to be well past midday. As if on cue, the clock chimed a delicate "two".

She groaned aloud. Tea was not far away. Soon Sally would burst in to prepare her for another session with Lady Bart and her guests, including the ever-impressive and omnipresent Commodore Harte. At the moment, she couldn't imagine how she could look the bastard in the face, let alone speak, pleasant being in the realm of impossible. She pinched the bridge of her nose, and measured the prospects of pleading a headache, illness... better yet, insanity. Given her earlier performance, the latter would be readily credited.

Cate looked up into the judgmental stares from the room's faces.

"I beg your leave, but I'm fresh out of answers," she said crossly to the circular curia.

A light scratch at the door was the only warning before Sally burst in, arms loaded. Spreading her burden on the bed, she propped her hands on her hips and regarded Cate with a critical eye. "You appear rested."

"I feel much better, thank you." Physically, sleep had been rejuvenating; emotionally she was spent, thought and conversation coming only with effort.

A gown—and all its accompanying accoutrement—had been brought, another pass-down, no doubt. In a surge of defiance, Cate declined and insisted on wearing her own. If she was to meet Lady Bart's guests, it would be as herself. Sally put up a fair protest, but Cate's doggedness prevailed. There was some turmoil regarding the whereabouts of said clothing, with the off-chance they had been disposed of. At length—and great relief—they were found. Carefully spread out in place of the gown, Cate's skirt and stays were barely recognizable after a transformational laundering and pressing, the apron as pristine as the day Billings had crafted it.

"You don't have to go," Sally said.

The cogs of Cate's mind ground slowly, dimly wondering if perhaps she had voiced that wishful thought without realizing. "Excuse me?"

"Tea." Sally enunciated, as if Cate might be a trifle dim.

"I thought attendance was compulsory."

Sally waved that off. "I could give your compliments, and then your regrets. I'll tell them you're too distraught and not at your leisure."

Cate bit her lip. Sally's directness was both unique and refreshing. The offer was tempting, deliciously so. She could play the overwrought victim, but to do so would run the risk of missing word of Nathan's welfare. If he had been captured or found dead, heaven forbid, it would be the highlight of the afternoon.

No, she would go.

Cate was ushered to a stool before a dressing table. Mesmerized by the rasp of Sally brushing her hair, she closed her eyes. It was a luxury, one life rarely allowed. Sitting on a tufted satin stool, before a table laden with toiletries befitting of a lady of substance, she felt decadent.

The brush abruptly stopped. Cate snapped from her reverie to find Sally solemnly staring at her through the mirror's reflections.

"Did Blackthorne hurt you?" The maid's voice was sharp and abrupt, but rooted in earnest concern.

Cate had given it no mind, but the ruined gown, hysterics and a tear-swollen face would have given the impression she had been ravished, or at the least, used rough.

"No; I appreciate the thought, but no, he didn't hurt me," Cate said, smiling faintly.

"You love him, don't you?"

Cate looked again into Sally's steady gaze, the hairbrush poised in mid-stroke. "Beg pardon?"

"You love him," Sally repeated evenly. Romanticism softened the stern features. "You have been on that ship with him all that time, and now you love him."

She set to brushing once more, muttering under her breath, "Some women have a way of picking the wrong man."

Cate shifted gaze to the weary, turquoise-eyed image before her. Did she? Had she fallen in love with Nathan?

A pang of guilt knotted her gut. Since losing Brian, she had never considered the possibility of another man. For years, it had seemed traitorous to think of another man in her bed. But the cold hard facts were she was ready. It was painful to look into the mirror and admit it: Brian was gone and Nathan was there; he was most definitely there. For the last weeks, her world had been suffused with him.

Did she love Nathan though? Did she feel for him as she had felt for Brian: the stirrings of the heart which came with an unexpected glimpse, or stirrings of the flesh at a smile or coffee-and-cinnamon-colored look... or the emptiness which came when he wasn't about? Was she willing to do all the same things, take the same risks and instill the same trust, in hopes of the same in return?

"Yes, I love him." The admission smacked of the desperate fantasies of a widow, probably past her prime.

"I thought so." Sally brightened with fanciful speculation. "Is he dark? I've heard he's dark, with eyes that can stop a woman's heart and lead her to destruction."

Cheeks heating, Cate bit her lip. "He is that."

"I had me a man once," Sally said after a protracted silence. She applied the brush with renewed industry. "I loved him so much it hurt. Then one day he up and turned pirate; left me with barely more than a by your leave."

The heavy hair was brought up from Cate's neck and pulled a ribbon around her head. Sally gave a wistful sigh. "They're a difficult lot to love. Heaven help the woman that falls in love with a pirate."

Tying the ribbon off with a flourish, Sally bent enough to find Cate's reflection once more. She smiled with a spark that rendered her years younger. "Ah, but they're worth every bit of the pain, aren't they?"

This time, Cate felt better prepared as she went down the stairs to take on Lady Bart and her guest-filled parlor. Sally's prescriptive dose of brandy had stiffened her spine and dulled her senses sufficiently to render the prospect of the afternoon tolerable. After all, what could they do that hadn't already been done? Embarrass? Stare? Ignore? Pity? Whisper behind their hands or, for that matter, behind her back?

In the foyer, Cate's courage faltered—more like shattered— at seeing Roger Harte step out to intercept her path. It took every bit of resolve to keep from recoiling when he pressed her knuckles fiercely to his lips.

"I'm so pleased to see you have regained yourself," he said. The green eyes burned with intensity. "I was so very concerned for your welfare and peace."

In other words, you believed I had gone completely around the bend.

It was a testimonial to her acting ability. His belief that she was a faint-hearted, quailing rabbit, ready to fall in prostration at so much as a coarse word was more than annoying.

Keeping her eyes averted, until her glittering hatred was mastered, Cate murmured a polite, non-committal something. She tried to retrieve her hand, but he clasped it firmly, stroking the back of it with his thumb.

"You have nothing to fear," he said.

She cringed at his big-brother-watching-over-the-defenseless-woman tone.

"Every precaution has been taken: extra guards posted and two Marines at your chamber door. So, you see, my dear, you have nothing to fear," he went on.

Behind a frozen smile, she inwardly groaned. If no one could get in, neither would anyone be going out. A sword now hung at his side, a pistol—so laden with gold and ivory, it looked more ceremonial than practical—was tucked at his waist, presumably all for her protection.

Voices from the drawing room echoed down the hall. Roger cleared his throat loudly, either to warn of their approach, or as a chivalrous but ineffective attempt to cover what was being said.

"It is unfortunate when one must face the outcomes of a weak decision," came a male voice.

"She should have done the honorable thing, to be sure," said another.

Cate knew the remark for what it was: a thinly-veiled reference to the common premise that a woman, caught in such a compromising circumstance as a pirate hostage, should kill herself. She looked up into Roger's sympathy verging on pitying gaze; he was of the same mind. The rationale behind that conclusion always left her wondering: was the woman to do so to save herself from being subjected to the horrors, or to save those around her the social horror of having to face her?

This from people who wouldn't have the courage to do as much themselves, she thought bitterly.

Their entry brought an uncomfortable hush. All would be aware of her earlier performance. Now, as the cowardly hostage, she was not only fallen, but deranged. A wave of unsteadiness swept her. Not as before, when struggling to regain her land legs; this was more like the condemned awaiting their fateful hour. Misinterpreting her unsureness as delicacy, Roger saw her seated, and then took up a shepherd-like position at her elbow.

The cool reception absolved her from the necessity of idle chat. She was avoided as if she was a refugee from Bedlam, apt to launch into hysteria at the least provocation. It was an effective shield, and she augmented the impression with an occasional eye roll or twitch. The men regarded her with more reserve; Fordshaw must have related her threat. At the same time, they were intrigued, challenged as to whom among them possessed the manly fortitude to tame the wildcat, the prospect of losing said manhood if they failed their restraint.

She wasn't without experience in drawing rooms and the higher life; quite the contrary. It wouldn't be an empty boast to announce that she — this pitiable wretch — had been at both the French and Spanish Court. To declare that Brian's clan had been well-connected with both royal houses through business, political and religious avenues would surely be met with cold disbelief. And if she were to let it slip, not overtly, but in a quiet, by-the-by manner, that her maternal grandmother was a Hapsburg, the royal house currently sitting the Spanish throne, she would be thought to be completely around the bend.

To see their shock was a grand temptation, but she kept her counsel.

As Cate scanned the room, there was the chance Sally's brandy dosage might have been a bit of overmedication, for determination was giving way to stubbornness. Lady Bart's hospitality wouldn't be without limits; there were ways of getting oneself literally shown to the door. Her lowly stature was being tolerated only in deference to the good Commodore, but that umbrella would stretch just so far. Given the matron's long-suffering inclination toward charity, however, it would have to be something grandly stunning, an offense of the highest degree to provoke ousting.

So, what was it to be: aspersions at ten paces? Spitting? A belch? One of Nathan's colorful curses? A cry of "Long live Prince Charlie?"

No, that could get you arrested.

A woman sat in the chair opposite the tea table and arranged herself. It took a moment to recognize her as Mrs. Big-Wig — Mrs. Devaynes, that was it! — now wearing a semi-normal sized wig, a pink bird perched ridiculously at the crown. She allowed Cate a hollow smile, and then pointedly diverted her attention to a woman opposite. Cate continued to sip her tea, wishing it were something stronger.

Conversation droned. Roger, the intransigent sphinx, at her side, Cate sat transfixed on the corner of a rug several feet away. A floral, its green leaves recalled the churned ground where Nathan had fallen, its red flowers his blood. Hatred surged. Unwittingly or not, every person in that room was a pawn in Harte's insidious game, including Lady Bart.

At one point, Roger was drawn away — Lady Bart, with some household detail — and Cate heard a polite clearing of a throat from Devayne's direction.

"Tell me dear, if you don't mind — ?"

Cate stirred, startled at being addressed. "Excuse me? I beg pardon?"

Mildly flustered, Devaynes hesitated, and then leaned over the table to say under the conversation, "I pray you don't think me forward, if I were to inquire...?"

Cate nodded, cautious of where on earth this line of questioning might lead.

"Well, I was wondering...? Can you tell me, my dear, what was it like... to be with that pirate... you know, when he...?"

Thinking surely, she had misconstrued, Cate leant nearer. "When he... what?"

"Well, all night..." Devaynes said, dismayed at being obliged to expand. "*All* that time, for that matter. What was he like? I saw him once, you know, in Port Royal. He looked so deliciously barbaric. Was he... different? Did he, well... you know...?"

Cate gaped. The woman looked like a cat being offered a dead mouse.

"I don't believe it's a matter which bears discussion," Cate said coldly. The woman's boldness deserved the embarrassment of a blunt denial.

Devaynes stiffened, the bird in her hair impudently peering down. "Oh, come, come, my dear — "

"Harper. My name is Catherine Harper." Her voice rose as her patience faded.

"Yes, of course... Mrs. Harper. It will be just between us." A wrinkling of the nose was given in affirmation. "Just tell me if—?"

Cate looked to Mrs. Green-Dress-Now-Wearing-Yellow-With-the-Ridiculous-Child's-Voice—Killingsworth—and another woman, heads canted in avid interest. It was too ironic, and not a little repugnant: they thought she should have killed herself, but since she hadn't, the vicarious vultures wished to be entertained, brutal rape to become parlor chat.

"I hate to disappoint, but he didn't do anything," Cate insisted.

Mrs. Killingsworth sniffed, her disapproval mitigated by her childish tenor. "Oh, come now. *Everyone* knows the pirate character."

"What would you like to know?" Cate demanded, now of a volume to end all other conversation. "Would you care to hear how I was bound spread-eagle, and he screwed me again and again until I begged for more? Or would you be more interested in the size of his cock, or his prodigious appetite that required feeding, over and over..."

Her voice quavered as she began to recite:

"*...a maypole of so enormous a standard, that had proportions been observ'd, it must have belong'd to a young giant.*"

There was no shame in having read Cleland's outlawed novel. Judging by the scandalized gasps, several present had read it, as well, to the point of recognizing the passage.

"*Its prodigious size made me shrink again; yet I could not, without pleasure, behold, and even ventur'd to feel, such a length, such a breadth of animated ivory...*"

Somewhere to her left there was a intake of air, Lady Bart on the verge of fainting. Looking from face to face, she saw everything from Roger's shocked rigidity to round-eyed horror, pity, and finally bemusement. Amid nervous throat-clearing, two or three women sat eager for more. Now on her feet, but not sure how she had come to be there, Cate glared.

"I hate to disappoint any of you, but nothing happened, not last night, or last week—not *ever!*"

She gripped the folds of her skirt lest they see her hands shake. "You can think anything you want. But just for the record: I was treated with more civility by a gang of pirates than the likes of you."

Cate raced out, determined none would have the satisfaction of seeing her cry. Once in the hall, she leaned against the wall and closed her eyes. She felt being stared at and looked over her shoulder into a blue-eyed cherub on the wallpaper.

"Well, after all, I did mean to be excused."

The painted gaze grew more accusing.

She thumped the wall with her fist. "I don't know what I'm to do next"

Overcome by the need for fresh air, she ran down the hall and out the garden doors. She followed the path until she came upon an arbor. Bracing against its post, she deeply inhaled the night air, heavy with the smell of greenery and damp earth, hoping to quell the tears brimming so very near the surface.

Dammit! Get hold of yourself!

She straightened at hearing the crunch of approaching footsteps on the gravel pathway. She turned to find Roger coming toward her, wearing a look of severe consternation.

"Catherine," he murmured huskily, clasping her hand. "I'm so sorry. How you must—"

"Please, don't!" She pushed him away, choked by his nearness. "I don't wish to be touched just now."

It was more excuse than lie. He inched away, nonetheless, with hideous understanding. "Yes, just so. Of course, my dear—"

"Don't call me that!"

"Yes, I'm sorry, Cathy—"

"Don't call me that either," she cried, clutching her fists until her nails gouged her palms.

"Yes... Yes... Of course,... How thoughtless. I beg your leave; I should have allowed how you would be feeling."

"How am I feeling?" she flared. "You think Nathan banged me too, don't you?"

He stiffened at her vulgarity. Unable to meet her gaze, he looked to the ground and nodded.

"We all know what corrupt creatures they are, and there is no reason to conclude Blackthorne would behave differently." He kicked at the stones then looked up. "It's common knowledge what happens when a woman is taken by..." He clamped his eyes shut at the thought.

"He didn't do anything!"

"My heart swells to think of the bravery and courage you've shown," he said over her protests. "You're a widow. I can provide for you, protect you. I'll see Blackthorne hanged for what—"

"He didn't do anything!" she shrieked. A little while ago, he thought she should have killed herself. Now, he was professing his affection, whatever the hell that meant.

Disbelief flickered, but he was too much the gentleman to call her a liar. "You only did what Blackthorne forced upon you. You'd never play the whore."

"A desperate person can do desperate things. You know nothing of me." She swiped at the wetness on her cheeks, anguish giving way to anger. She wanted nothing more than to throw all the times Nathan had bested him in his face. To do so, however, might well be to her own detriment. Harte wasn't a man to be trifled with.

His demeanor hardened; the engaging graciousness dissolved. The menace, suspected to have existed just beneath the surface when first they met rose, to the surface like oil on water. "You need not protect him."

"You only want me because I was his. You only seek an excuse to kill him."

He flinched at her insight. The reptilian gaze fixed on her and his mouth took a cruel curve. "What difference is it, so long as he is dead? He's a vile pestilence which should be swiped away."

"Then do it on your own cause, not mine."

Harte inhaled, as one did in preparation of a sudden move, and his hand flexed, either to make a fist or draw a weapon she couldn't tell. Either way, he thought the better and exhaled through his nose, long and slow, as a parent does with an unruly child. His hand settled on the ivory pistol butt at his waist, instead, the middle finger tapping its *lento* rhythm once more.

Harte forced a smile which, through tense lips, was more the baring of teeth. "Clearly, you're distraught," he said coldly. "You're hysterical. You require rest. I'll pass the word for your maid to see you back to your room."

He pivoted on his slippered heel and stalked away. Furious, she picked up a stone and hurled it after him. Missing by a ridiculous margin, Cate snatched up several more, firing them off, squealing at each toss. Whirling around, she looked for something to break, something that would shatter into thousands of satisfying little pieces. Finding nothing, she crumpled next to a bench and wept.

She cried the tears expected with frustration and anger. Along with those came the unexpected ones of anguish, rejection, hopelessness and isolation, all brought on by the pain of being forced to admit to a roomful of despicable people that Captain Nathanael Blackthorne, pirate and rogue, ravager of women extraordinaire, wouldn't have her.

In long wracking sobs, she cried until it hurt too much to do so anymore. Hitching and snuffling, she blew her nose without heed on the hem of her skirt, knowing Sally would have it clean by the morrow. Cradling her head in her arms, she pressed her cheek against the stone of the bench and cooled her heated face.

Cate traced a finger along her arm and thought how long it had been since she had been held. She missed being loved: the sense of belonging, having a reason to wake or draw breath. For the most part, her most treasured memories of Brian were of in bed: long, swirling nights of limbs entwined, or lying quietly together reviewing the minutia of the day. It led her to wonder if it was Brian or the lovemaking which she missed most, holding and being held, looking forward to nights, anxiously awaiting for that heart-stalling moment when he blew out the candle and rolled to her. Who would have thought the corporeal joys of marriage could lead to such despair? The higher the mountain, the deeper the valley and she had toured them all. It had been said memories kept one warm; she could attest with all certainty that was a categorical fallacy.

It was appalling to think she had degenerated into one of those pitiful widows desperate for a man's body and shelter. Over the years, she had taught herself to ignore the yearning, desire's rush that tightened her belly, leaving her full and moist. That was the past. She longed for the warmth of a body next to her when she woke in the desolate void of darkness.

But Nathan didn't want her; she reminded him of someone else. That was wrenchingly evident every time he walked past, every time he turned away when she spoke, every time he scurried from the cabin when she entered. She had seen the don't-make-me-do-this expression, averting his eyes far too many times.

"You remind him of her."

No more chilling or damning words had ever been spoken.

So why does he keep you aboard? Why doesn't he set you ashore and be rid of you?

It was a bafflement, which endless hours of pondering in the dark couldn't solve.

Nathan's precious Hattie was like living with a ghost, haunting from the ship's every nook, often driving her from the bed, obliging her to walk the decks, until weariness cloaked her mind. In those playground-of-loneliness hours of the night, her imagination ran rampant. She couldn't look at the bunk without seeing two writhing bodies, one with snaking black hair. She couldn't help but wonder if he had ever kissed her there, in front of the gallery, or over there, pressing her back against the gun, urgent and needing. Did he ever hold her in his arms here, or in his lap in that chair over there? Did they ever gaze at the stars from the forecastle, or lay together watching the moon through the porthole?

Her mind knew he didn't want her, but her body paid no heed and prepared for him anyway, waking breathless and pulsing. Living unwanted and alone for years had been easy. Unwanted before someone who made her heart race: that was indescribable misery. What shreds of pride she still possessed prevented her from throwing herself at him. Be damned if she was going to become some pitiful wretch groveling for whatever scraps of affection he might fling her way.

But it was no matter: Nathan was gone. Of that she had no doubt. Between his injury and suspicion, her failure to attain any significant information, and the proximity of a Commodore and the Royal Navy, he would be far away by then.

Pirate, as he had often reminded her.

Leave him to his precious Hattie, she thought moodily.

Angrily batting away tears, stubbornness surged. This was the West Indies, the New World, which meant a new life.

She had a feeling Harte was not done with her; he had something more in mind. She needed to distance herself from him and the authorities, and soon. It was a pity, for Hopetown was sizeable enough; she might make a living as a seamstress, as she had done before. The best hope was some place which was not under King Georgie's rule. In Europe, moving from under one flag to the next meant long arduous journeys. Here in the West Indies, it was a simple matter of from one island to the next, a new flag overhead and a new life.

A Spanish possession was most promising. She spoke the language, and was familiar with the way of life. Nathan had unwittingly become a benefactor in her new life, his coins in her pocket her means. Those would have to be saved for passage, however. Food and shelter would have to be found other ways. She had done it for years in the squalid streets of London, she could do it again.

In a convoluted way, she felt she had a plan — in desperate need of further development granted, but a plan, nonetheless. The first step was to get away from Harte.

Flashes of red wool were visible through the greenery and on the paths in every direction.

"...extra guards have been posted..."

Yes, Harte had been quite thorough. There would be no going anywhere today.

Sally stood waiting a discrete distance away. Cate rose and allowed herself to be taken inside and back to her room.

⁓⦿⁓

Feeling drained, Cate sat in a chair staring out the balcony doors. The sun arched its path. The porcelain clock chimed the hours. The hall bell rang: time for everyone to shift their clothes for supper. Almost physically ill at the thought of facing anyone,

Cate sent Sally to deliver her compliments and regrets, pleading a headache. The little chambermaid brought a tray. It was untouched when she returned to retrieve it and light the sconces.

The hour grew late, the house quiet. Cate remained at the window. The eerie, mournful call of a screech owl recalled Artemis's hunched shape in the topgallant yards.

At last, she was alone. Peace.

Voices at the door stirred Cate from her torpor. She groaned aloud.

"...her some dinner. The poor child didn't eat, so I've brought a tray," came Sally's voice. "Pray pull the door? Just so. Thank you," she called over her shoulder to the guards.

Still seated, Cate tracked Sally's path through the room by the clatter of china and silver on the tray.

"I appreciate the thought, but you didn't..." Cate rose stiffly and stopped as Sally set the tray down and press a finger to her lips.

"T'was but a ruse," Sally hissed, creeping closer. "I've come with word: he's waiting for you."

"Who's what?" Cate flared, thinking it was Harte.

"Your pirate, he's outside."

Cate watched dumbfounded as the bed's counterpane was thrown back and, in a few economic jerks, the sheets pulled free.

"I told him you would come directly." The maid dragged sheets toward the window and set to knotting the ends.

"What are you about?"

"Shh!" Sally flinched at her own volume then gave Cate a meaningful glare to remind her — as if she could ever forget — of the guards outside the door. "He desired you to meet him at the same place. Does that answer?"

Cate nodded, though thoroughly confused. This had to be a dream. If this was a jest, it was entirely too cruel.

"I understand now what you see in him. He certainly knows how to please a woman," Sally said with a dreamy roll of the eyes.

"What on earth are you talking about?"

Peering into the darkness to check the garden, Sally went out onto the balcony and knelt to secure the sheet to a spindle. "After you said you loved him, and then when he — well anyway, I couldn't help myself."

She stood, flushed with excitement. "So, on your way!"

Cate gawked from Sally to the garden and back. This had to be Harte's doing, or nothing but a rude jest. In spite of that, the lure of Nathan waiting was too strong.

Sally seized her by the arm and prodded her toward the rail. "Go!"

Heart racing, Cate swung a leg over, pausing to say, "Thank you." It seemed a grossly inadequate, but so very necessary to say.

"Have a care!" Sally's eyes rounded with import. "The guard should be busy for a bit longer, but several more are roaming. Now be away, and take care of that man."

Casting an uncertain eye toward the ground below, Cate worked around until she could grasp the sheet. The last time she had done anything similar, she had been ten years-old, sneaking out of her brother's room. She fell and broke an arm, as she recalled. Working her hands until she felt confident, she started down. Her grip wasn't strong enough, and she plummeted down, the knot affixing the sheets the only thing stopping her. Past that, she plunged to the fabric's end—a good distance above the ground—and landed in an unglamorous heap in the bushes.

Biting back a pained oath, she took quick inventory of her limbs. Finding everything intact, she crouched under the shrubbery. Through the next row of hedge, she caught a flash of red of a Marine's coat, deep in an embrace. Sally had said the guard would be busy. She made a hunched sprint across the path and into the bushes.

The moonlight banded the garden in thin shafts. Engulfed in bushes and darkness, she lost her bearings straight away. She tripped on invisible hazards, and stepped needlessly high over the non-exist. Every rustle of shrubbery or gasp she feared was a broad announcement of her whereabouts.

"Hoy! Who goes there?"

The shouts from behind were cut short by the sound of heavy footsteps running toward her. She dodged at a right angle, meaning to dive under the shrubs. The moonlight flared on a red sleeve as it shot out and caught her by the waist.

"Got 'em!" her captor called out.

"Where?"

"Over 'ere!" called several voices together.

Half-carried, half-dragged away, she struggled, scratching where eyes might be. She kicked at his knees, but her shoes skidded harmlessly off his leggings. He chuckled at her futile attempts, infuriating her all the more.

"You're a feisty one aren't you?" he said. A hand clamped on her breast and squeezed, eliciting a protesting yelp from her. "Oh-ho, and a soft one, too. Got a ripe peach here, gents!"

Against every instinct, she forced herself to fall limp over his arm. As hoped, the grip at her waist loosened, thinking she had fainted. Sagging further, she waited for when her feet touched the ground and his head came directly behind hers. The moment came: she whipped her head back, the sound of smashing nose and teeth indicating she had found her mark.

Bellowing in agony, he clutched his face, blood spurting between his fingers. Now free, she scrambled for cover. More guards converged, with a great deal of swearing and shouting, snapping of branches and trampling boots. A burst of flame stabbed the dark, a musket fired. Under that protective chaos, she slithered away.

The grounds were now on full alert, with voices and running coming from all directions. Now horribly disoriented, wisdom advised she should stop to regain her bearings, but exertion and fear pulsed too high. She inched back, feeling with her foot. It bumped into something: another foot. A hand swept from behind to clamp over her mouth and pulled her away.

"Hist. Quiet, luv."

Hushed and abbreviated as it was, she knew the graveled voice instantly.

Nathan's hand remained, until she nodded in recognition. Arm still at her waist, his chin was at her shoulder as he listened. The shifting eyes slid her way, the corners crinkling with a reassuring smile. Heart racing, she managed only a wobbling one. With a faint nod, he withdrew, taking her with him. His hands, solid on her hips, steered as they ran in a half-stoop through the trees and undergrowth. The commotion was soon left behind. They were left with nothing but the pad of their feet in the soft earth, and the reassuring creak of Nathan's leather and swish of bells.

Hopetown lay directly in their path. Nathan took her darting through its streets and alleys with startling familiarity. The town slept, but its nightwatch was astir. They ducked for cover while two gangs of night charlies raced past in the general direction of Lady Bart's estate. Halfway down another street, heavy footfalls and clatter of musketry of a larger contingent of men came toward them. Nathan dove into the shadowy protection of a doorway, yanking her with him as a cluster of Marines jogged past. Two more gangs passed shortly behind.

His arm flexed at her middle and his mouth came close to her ear. "We'll hold a bit."

A dog barked from somewhere near and a male voice bellowed it quiet. Her heart raced with more than running. Nathan had come for her! He hadn't left with his men. He hadn't thrown his hands up in disgust and left her to Harte. He had come for her! The whys and hows didn't matter just then. He had come back!

His body, heated by exertion, and the thump of his heart

against her back were proof it was no dream. She leaned into his taut strength, pressing her head against his shoulder, his breath stirring her hair. It was the longest she had ever been alone with him. His arm flexed at her waist and his cheek pressed to the side of her head.

He straightened and cleared his throat. "Best away."

By the time the town was behind them, the moon shone bright, painting everything in either flares of silver or swaths of impenetrable black. Nathan spoke only as necessary, but whether it was in the spirit of stealth or that he had nothing to say, a rare occasion indeed, was unclear. His breath came far more ragged than walking would account, his usual cat-like step hitched and uneven. His face was either turned downward or slightly away, unseen at any angle.

They stopped at one point, Nathan claiming perhaps she might desire a rest, although he seemed the tired one. Gesturing her atop a rock, he lowered himself to the ground at her feet, and with a muffled groan, leaned back. They sat quietly, each retreating into his or her thoughts. Near enough for his sleeve to brush her leg, she felt a distance between them, nonetheless, of a far different sort than the physical boundary so carefully maintained.

"What did you do to Sally?" Uttered as a whisper, it was still startling amid the chorus of night creatures. She instantly regretted broaching the subject, the answer quite possibly inviting far more than she desired to know, but the silence was torturous.

He glanced up. "Eh?"

"Sally, the servant woman back there; what did you do to her?"

"Oh, her." He smiled faintly and rubbed his arm, wincing. "Nothing... much."

"You made quite the impression, whatever it was."

"Oh, aye?" The smile grew devilish. "A gentleman never —"

"Gentleman?"

Looking away, he shifted as one does when in search of a comfortable position when one wasn't to be had.

"Did he hurt you much?" Cate curbed her concern, knowing he wouldn't appreciate being smothered with it.

Nathan jerked, and glanced up to discern how much she knew of his capture, the moonlight flashing on the bells in his mustache.

"Not much," he said at length to the ground between his feet. "A good lick to the head brought me down, but no... I've been worse."

He fingered the raw marks at his wrist. The sight of the twisted and torn flesh spurred her disgust for Harte another notch.

"I could have sworn I heard a woman screaming." Nathan looked up at the end, his lilt alluding to her performance outside the smithy.

"You must have been delirious," Cate said, batting her lashes in overt innocence. "Why did he do it?"

"Who? Harte?" His mouth pulled down, weighing that. "Don't rightly know."

"You're lying, Nathan," she said in quiet evenness. "I can tell."

He threw up a look of exasperated irritation over his shoulder. "Seems I vex him, a bit... maybe."

"There's more to it than that. You hate each other enough to want to kill each other?"

He was both surprised and intrigued by the question. "Nah. Could have several times over, if was all that simple. Nothing more admirable than a dedicated enemy, eh?"

Nathan grinned at her puzzlement. "We give each other purpose: if he kills me, the last great pirate ship of the West Indies is gone. Then what ladder would he climb to his success?"

"He needs you?" The line of logic was astounding, and yet in keeping with what Pryce had said.

"Exactly," he said, pleased by her quickness.

"And what do you gain out of this?"

A shrug was cut short by a wince and a pain-laden grunt. "Can't be the greatest pirate without the greatest escapes, now can you?" Nathan said, with a square-toothed grin.

Cate gaped at him. "That's it? To perpetuate your fame?"

"There's worse motivations."

"I suppose that would be in the eye of the beholder. He *will* have you hung, you know."

He looked off into the forest. "He'll try, at any rate."

"You say that as if he's tried already."

Nathan nodded. Two fingers at his knee stirred.

"And you're here to tell of it, so I'm obliged to assume he failed," Cate said, growing annoyed with his coyness.

"Barely, the last time." He winced at the recollection then brightened. "Who knows, maybe third time will be the charm."

"But, if he needs you, why did he try to hang you, twice?" she asked, bracing her head in her hands.

"I'm still alive." It was said as if that simple point explained everything.

"That doesn't make any sense." She buried her head deeper; exhaustion was settling in worse than she thought.

"Doesn't have to. Are you worried for him?"

Cate made a disgusted sound deep in her throat and shuddered. "God, no. The man is unsettling."

Nathan snorted and chuckled dryly. "A categorical dismissal, if ever one was heard. No worries, luv," he said over her protests. If the pat on the leg was meant to be reassuring, it wasn't. "Your secret is safe with me."

He rose, grunting with the effort of straightening, and extended a hand. "C'mon. Pryce will be cataleptic by now, the ol' shellback."

Nathan's taciturnity didn't improve, making a long walk an endless one.

By the few glimpses the moonlight allowed, he had taken a beating, one which would have put many a man to his knees. Cate's eyes brimmed and her heart rung. Bleeding and battered, putting his distrust and disillusionment aside, he had single-handedly braved a commodore and Marines to come for her. And yet, now he would barely look at her.

The man was blessedly confusing.

They had been apart for just a short time, but it seemed more a decade, someone so familiar now a stranger. Conversation which had once come so easily was, now strained, neither able to find something to say. Speaking came with great discomfort for Nathan, but there was a larger discomfort: a tall, blue-uniformed and gilded one who stood between them. There was so much to be said, and yet neither could bring themselves to it.

Pride is the mask of one's own faults. The Old Hebrews had it right. It would seem both of them suffered from a hearty dose of protectiveness of their dignity. In dire need of a distraction from Nathan's bristling silence and her own darkening mood, Cate took the opportunity to relate all she had learned at Lady Bart's table.

"How do you know of all this?" Nathan's surprise quickly melted into suspicion.

"Roger—Commodore Harte—he and Lady Bart said as much. Don't give me that look!" Rounding in front of him, Cate jammed the finger into his chest, not sorry to see him wince.

"What look?" Nathan asked.

"You know exactly: the what-did-you-do-to-learn-that look? I didn't do anything *you* wouldn't have done."

"That's hardly a recommendation," he muttered, rubbing the spot.

Cate propped her hands on her hips. "Would you have bedded him?"

"No!"

"Well, see: neither did I!"

"That hardly proves anything," he grumbled as he brushed past.

"Is this what we have to look forward to for the next... *whatever*," she shouted, striding to catch up. "You're accusing me of bedding everyone in breeches to come along?"

He wheeled around, the moonlight flaring on his thunderous glare. She pulled up in front of him and crossed her arms.

"Mebbe," he mumbled. He pivoted away, picking up his pace.

"Oh!" Vibrating with frustration, Cate followed close on Nathan's heels. "Shouldn't you be more concerned with what you know, rather than what you think you know?"

"You don't know what I know," he barked over his shoulder, bells jangling in the heavy air. "You only know what you think you know, because that's what I want you to know, because you don't need to be knowing any more than what you already know."

She skidded to a halt. "That doesn't make any sense."

"I don't have to make sense."

"Well, it would help those of us around you, if you did," she called to his fading image as he stomped away, puffs of road dust spurting with each step.

Shoulder to shoulder they walked, huffing in silence. The sparkle of the bay was finally visible, the relieved face of Mr. Pryce soon after.

Cate made a point of sitting next to Nathan, but he moved to pose at the bow, his image was a dark blot against the gunmetal of sky and water. He turned once, directed a terse nod to her, and then turned away, his expression lost in the darkness.

As the oarsmen pulled in rhythmic strokes, she looked up at the *Morganse's* yards, spreading overhead like welcoming arms. Whether the welcome was for her, or reserved for the returning lover who stood at the bow was unclear. A dash of azure brilliance marked where Beatrice roosted on the mainyard. A soundless press of air and a dark arrow-shape were the only indications of Artemis swooping past. She arched a steep curve and dove down below deck.

Exhaustion settled in Cate's limbs. It was visible in Nathan as well, his shoulders sagging, his movements sluggish. The joyous relief of stepping back on the *Morganse's* deck was tempered by a heavy feeling, as though wading upriver.

She stumbled past Nathan and Pryce, deep in conversation, to the cabin, where she collapsed into a chair. Eyes closed, she basked in a glorious sensation: home! It was a feeling long absent, one which a soul didn't realize the chasm left in one's heart by its disappearance, until it was filled once more. The walnut walls curved around her like a mother's arms, the creak of the board overhead as soothing. The voices of the ship and her people were as familiar as a family, the smell of pitch, wet wood and salt-soaked canvas more enticing than pies baking in the kitchen.

The brush of leather and a jingle announced Nathan's arrival. Eyes still closed, Cate tracked his progress through the cabin by the changing sounds of his step: a light clump on the wood, muffled thud on the Turkish rug, and finally, a soft scuffing as he stopped somewhere very near. Feeling the weight of his stare, she opened her eyes directly into his, bloodshot and swollen.

"You look bloody awful." she said.

Uttered in jest, it was true. The cabin's light revealed the damages incurred at Harte's hands. The smudge of several days' beard melded with the bruises and dark circles framing swollen eyes. His nose and mouth were puffed. A split spanned the width of his lip, up into his mustache, the bells there crusted in dried blood. One cheekbone, abraded and distended, caused the eye to pull oddly at the corner.

"Thank you," he said grimly, bobbing a mocking bow. "Always look forward to meeting an admirer."

Dropping his hat on the table, he sat with the slow-motion of a person who thought they might never do so again. He gingerly rubbed his face, the stubble of his beard rasping on his hands. He went still then, staring catatonically at a spot on the table.

"When was the last time you slept?" she asked.

Stirring from his torpor, Nathan opened his mouth to reply then stopped, his brows nearly touching in puzzlement. "Day before yesterday," he said slowly. Straining to think, he finally gave up and shrugged. "Mebbe."

Struggling against her own tides of weariness, she grasped for a lucid thought. Exhaustion often led on to cleave onto the smallest of minutia, as if that one last grain of thought might keep one from slipping into oblivion. "That shirt will need washing."

Nathan peered down at the reddish-brown stain that spread over one shoulder and down his chest. He gingerly plucked at it with two fingers, mouth quirking. "Then it would appear your life will have purpose."

He squirmed in the chair in an attempt to find a comfortable position, wincing at every movement. He finally heaved a hitching sigh and toppled forward onto the table. Head cradled in his arms, his braids were a glossy snarl about his shoulders.

Cate pushed up from her chair and fetched her blood box from atop a locker in the corner. Sitting it on the table, she took out a jar, marked Number Thirty-seven in Roman numerals, containing the ointment professed to "cure anything from pox to palsy." A tap on the arm was signal enough for Nathan to extend it. Under the swinging light overhead, the puffed and scabbed knuckles told the tale: he had fought the Marines, until he was down to nothing but his fists. His right wrist had been protected by the strip of cloth securing a palm protector. The left, however, was raw, the skin torn. He had fought against the shackles which had held him, as well.

Cate cupped Nathan's hand in hers, his pulse just under her thumb, and scooped a bit of ointment. Jelly-like at first, the warmth of her hand soon rendered it spreadable, and she dabbed it on the abused skin. An eye ticked, but he remained otherwise immobile against the stuff's sting.

Nathan stirred at the clatter and rumble of the kedge anchor being hauled in. The ship shifted and gained way. He reached for the rum bottle in the middle of the table, took a pull, and then settled his head on his other arm.

Her purpose was twofold: tend his wounds, but more in hopes of a physical connection. It was a desperate bridge and a thin one, but a spoonful of soup was a feast to a starving soul. The deep chasm still yawned; she wondered what steps would be necessary to make amends and regain his trust.

"Thank you, Nathan," she said. A first step.

"For what?" he asked into the folds of his sleeve.

"For coming to get me."

"Twice." Nathan hissed sharply when she touched an especially sore spot. "I had to rescue you twice."

His reference to his deeds as "rescue" brought a smile; a knight in shining armor wasn't quite the image she carried, but the intent had been much the same.

"I enjoyed it so much the first time; I thought we might try it again."

He made a disgusted, guttural sound in his throat. "Bloody woman. Shan't be surprised if you did. Torture me to me dying days you will."

Cate bent to reach the backside of Nathan's wrist and recoiled. "What is that smell?"

It took a moment, but then she recalled where she had smelt

it before, twice: once in the bedchamber at Lady Bart's, and again, while hiding in a doorway in Hopetown.

She pressed her hand to her nose, the ointment's rosemary, camphor and alcohol masking it somewhat. "What is that?"

"I told you, it's from a whore," he said evenly.

An inadvertent turn of the head and gap of his collar revealed the scratches on his neck. There was no mistaking the claw marks left by a woman's fingernails. She stiffened as several images flashed through her mind.

"You shouldn't be going with whores." A flush of embarrassment heated her cheeks at having broached the subject. There were no secrets as to how a sailor filled his time ashore.

A blood-shot eye peeked over his sleeve, a smile curving the split lip. "No better than commodores, eh?"

Face blazing, she dropped his hand. "I didn't—"

"Neither did I," Nathan said evenly, sitting up.

Cate fixed him with a steady gaze, looking for the familiar mirth which usually accompanied his sarcasm. She found none. "You don't believe me."

"Neither do you."

She closed the blood box's lid more forceful than was necessary. "I'm not in the habit of apologizing for something that I didn't—"

"Neither am I," he said rising. She flinched as each barbed word found home.

Nathan could be caustic, but his barbs were usually blunted by a quirk of the mouth and a teasing glint in his eye. His voice too broken by exhaustion to be of any guidance, she searched his face. The ravaged features were those of a stranger, contorted not only by swelling and bruising, but things never seen before: disgust, suspicion, and worst of all, disappointment.

"I had four older brothers; I don't need another—"

"From all appearances, you do," he said with irritating levelness. He pressed closer. Determined not to give way, she fell back a step, nonetheless.

Hot tears pressed behind her eyes as hurt, anger and resentment collided.

"I will not be owned by anyone," she said, balling her fist. She was not about to be used like a piece in one of his circuitous games. He was assuming to set himself up as her lord and master, as if she needed shepherding to prevent her from bedding every man encountered. It was as she had suspected and feared: he wanted no part of her, but neither did he want anyone else to have her, most especially Harte.

The small hopes she had nurtured popped like bubbles in a

boiling pot. The warmth of home dissolved into no more than a foolish whimsy of a desperate mind.

"Payment comes in many forms." His distorted lips curled to reveal a flash of gold.

"How dare you! You presumptuous bast...!" She sputtered, fury striking her speechless. "I keep myself to a higher standard. Rest assured, it is a matter which will *never* be of your concern."

"Never?"

"*Never!*"

Something flickered on the battered face, flinching as if poked in the ribs. He spun away to the window and stood, one hip cocked, an arm braced against its frame. The sea breeze lifted the tails of his headscarf and curled them about his shoulders as he scanned the gunmetal and silver nightscape. He glanced over his shoulder, his gaze settling on her wedding ring, gleaming dully. Looking back to the night, he nodded vaguely, as if concluding a private conversation. He pivoted on his heel and headed for the door. There he paused to give an elaborate, but hitched bow.

"I bid you good e'en, fair lady," he said, baring his teeth. "Have no cares. Your sanctitude is safe."

15: DEVIL'S PATH

ATE WOKE TO THE RUMBLE of thunder. Snuggling deeper under the quilt, she listened to it reverberate across the water, and then intermittent patter of raindrops. Hermione gave a plaintive bleat, taking rain as a personal affront. A freshened gust heeled the ship over. The shower grew to a downpour, drumming the deck overhead. Someone in the salon slammed the windows shut.

Nathan had been puzzled by her preference for them to be open. He pointed out, in barely camouflaged impatience, that the wind which came through the windows was the same as what blew through the door, making one or the other superfluous.

"Is there some tariff on open windows?" she had asked.

Muttering darkly under his breath about females and the parts of various animals, Nathan stalked out, leaving her to her precious air.

A storm-driven puff delivered a fine mist through the port. As Cate considered waiting, the influx increased. Sighing in resignation, she rose to close it. From the corner of her eye, she saw the reddish brown blur of a rat scampering along the wall and under the curtain. She was stepping into her skirt when she heard the padded rustle of His Lordship in hot pursuit: a startled squeal, a furry scuffle, and then silence. As she combed her fingers through her hair, the heady aroma of coffee and baking scones met her nose.

Home!

Rounding the curtain, she caught Jensen setting a steaming pot and cup on the table.

"Joy o' the morning, sir," he beamed. She winced at his enthusiasm and wondered in his wake if that shining face ever met a day with anything less.

Mindful of the peril of the first sip, she bent over the cup to inhale the curls of steam.

"Oh, you've risen, finally." Nathan stood in the doorway

against a pounding backdrop of rain. He shook off like a great dog in a spray of droplets. He slogged across the room with a somewhat stiffened step.

"You're soaking wet," she said.

Nathan stopped in mid-step to peer down at himself and gave her a queer look.

"Aye. You know it's raining out there, don't you?" He jerked a thumb first toward the door and then jabbed a finger at the cup before her. "Or hadn't you had enough of that to be able to notice yet?"

"I'm not that dense of a morning," Cate pouted, hovering over the very same.

"'Tis all in the eye of the beholder, darling," Nathan said with a mirthless laugh.

A soggy squish marked each step as he came round the table. Rain, glistening in the sable chest hair, plastered his shirt to his chest, the tattoo over his heart ghosting through the wet linen.

"Do you desire a towel?" she asked.

"Eh?"

"A towel," she repeated, carefully. "So, you might dry off?"

Water pattered the rug. He shrugged her off with a reproving glance. "If a man can't bear to be as wet as Neptune, he's no business at sea. Besides, bear an eye: 'tis clean." He plucked at the shoulder of his shirt.

Cate eyed the bloodstains, now brown, but faded. "Almost."

"Almost enough."

The downpour outside stopped, the sun breaking free in almost the same instant. A sultry warmth wafted through the cabin, stirring the tails of Nathan's scarf about his shoulders. Sipping her coffee, Cate watched him ruffle through the clutter of papers, logbooks and charts. Like his shirt, Nathan looked only marginally better than yesterday. The bruises were predictably more discolored, but were no larger, the swelling lessened.

A game of eye tag ensued: glancing, looking away only to glance again. Groping for something to break the tension, Cate put down the cup and asked, "How's your head?"

Said body part jerked up. "What?"

Noting that was the second time Nathan had been either hard of hearing or forgetful, she rose and rounded the table.

"Your head," she said. "You do recall being hit in the head yesterday, don't you?" Hard enough to "bring him down", as he had so eloquently put it, there was the possibility he was injured far worse.

"Of course. I'm not daft." He ducked his head and batted her away when she reached to investigate. "I'm fine: rosy-cheeked, right as rain, in the pink, contentedly and serenely, in full feather, fine!"

Conceding — At that point, if Nathan bled to death she didn't care — she returned to her chair. The mood in the room being no better, she tried a different tactic.

"Where are we headed?"

Nathan looked up and there it was again: scorn and suspicion, the same as seen in the bedchamber at Lady Bart's.

"Wondering as to what shall be awaiting upon our arrival?" His inquiry came with far too much edge to be comfortable.

"Are you implying I would start playing you the fool?"

His features were so distorted by swelling, Nathan's smile was nearer a sneer. "No, I don't imagine you that diabolical, but His Courtliness is. There's every possibility he played *you* the fool."

"But he thought I was trying to escape—"

"And you did nothing to change that opinion, did you? Pillow talk can be very persuasive. No matter, luv," he went on, cutting off her incensed sputtering. "Your beloved's plotting is all for naught. *If* as you say, Lord Creswicke's betrothed is on her way, then there's only one course to be had. We will be waiting, but not where Commodore Vangloriousness shall expect. 'Tis a fair anchorage, with a good view."

Cate forbore asking "A view of what?" It didn't go unnoticed that he elaborated no further. He resumed rifling the charts and papers, while she tried to decide if his churlishness was intentional, or if he was just having a bad morning. The former won.

"You're angry with me, aren't you?" she blurted. Her mother had admonished her often for her lack of modesty, but anything was better than this insufferable cat-and-mouse. It was hardly a shot in the dark, however.

The dark eyes came up, measuring. Twisting his jaw sideways, he toyed with a corner of a chart. "Mebbe."

From high above outside came a desperate cry. Cate was instantly to her feet and behind Nathan speeding for the door. She heard the en mass gasp from all hands on deck. She reached the door in time to see a blur of a body fall. She heard the sickening thud of something like a hundred weight of wet meal landing. Nathan was several strides ahead of her. He spun to intercept her as she raced forward, stepping at the same time to block her view. Over his shoulder, she caught a glimpse of skewed limbs and a ragdoll-like form lying in a pool of glistening red. Ashen-faced, all hands converged over the grisly sight. Cate ducked one way and then another to see around Nathan, but was blocked by his body, while at the same time backing her away, until she stumbled over the coaming into the cabin.

She jerked away. "I'm not a child. Who was it?"

Nathan drew a shaky hand down the curve of his mustache and looked to the floor.

"Dammit, Nathan," she said to the top of his head. "I know someone just…"

He looked up, his swollen features pinched with a combination of restrained grief and abject concern. His hand stirred, as if to reach for her, but then thought better.

"Jensen."

It came in a barely recognizable rasp.

Like rusty cogs, Cate's mind ground, trying to absorb what he had just said. "Who? But, how…? I mean… He was just…?"

She abandoned the thought, for both of them knew exactly how it happened, how quickly Fate could strike. Whether on a battlefield or on the deck of a ship, a man could be standing one moment and dead the next. Stray musket balls, lightning, seizures, falling trees… or a fall from the yards, Fate could have its way without notice and without explanation.

She must have stood quite stricken, for Nathan shook her as if waking her from a deep sleep. Chin quivering, she crumpled into his arms and sobbed. He held her, gently swaying and absorbing her feeble blows as she pounded his chest in tear-choked fits. She cried over the death of someone so young. She cried in frustration of the snuffing out of promise and unfulfilled hopes. She cried because, in a world so defined by violence, it was too cruel to see someone's life taken so mundanely, no more than Death's afterthought: "Oh yes, I meant to take him." And yet, Death never made sense. God, the Devil, or whoever was in charge of such matters, worked on a string of logic which no mortal could fathom.

At last drained, she was left sniffling and hiccoughing. An arm still about her shoulders to steady her, Nathan reached for an amber bottle.

"Drink up." The words came gently enough, but bore the edge of a man expecting his commands to be heeded.

Cate ducked away, but finally succumbed under his persistence. He observed closely as she drank.

"I'm sorry," she said in a querulous gasp.

"No worries, luv." His smile was meant to be encouraging, but faltered.

Sniffing loudly, she sputtered in the embarrassment of an abundantly running nose.

"Here, blow." He offered his sleeve.

"No, it will make a mess. Don't you have a handkerchief?"

"Not that I'd find in a timely fashion. Mother Nature's washroom is but through that door. Now, blow."

Need overcoming discretion, she did, laughing unsteadily when he crossed his blackened eyes and missed her nose—first to one side and then the other—before dabbing it.

A preemptive cough broke them apart. Pryce, Hodder and Pickford, captain of the maintop, filled the doorway, solemn and miserable. Nathan hesitated, uncertain as to whether it was wise to leave her. Swiping her eyes, she bid him away. He roughly herded the trio outside to what he deemed most likely out of earshot, a miscalculation, given his level of anger.

"What the goddamned hell was he doing up there?" came Nathan's ragged voice.

Cate flinched at his vehemence, pitying anyone in its path.

"Sweet suffering Jesus! What muddle-headed arse sent a lad, who can barely manage the companionway without stumbling over himself, to the tops?"

"He's a fair eye," said Pickford, defensively.

"He begged leave to prove himself, desirin' to join the topsmen. So, we... I let bid him as lookout," Hodder interjected, even more wretched.

"T'was by my leave, Cap'n," Pryce said in low-voiced solemnity. "I been denyin' 'im for a fortnight. I finally... give in," he added bleakly.

"Out o' me sight, the lot o' ya's. By the tail o' Satan, a sorrier lot I've never laid eyes on. Miserable excuse for command." Nathan growled.

Nathan's lashing out was unfortunate. Her heart broke for all, but Pryce especially. Blame would abound all around, but Pryce cared for his charges as a father for his child. Jensen had held a special place in everyone's heart, but Pryce would take this loss as personal.

"No, wait," Nathan said on the heels of his outburst. There was a tense pause. "Out of line, I am, as you'll all agree, I dare say. You did no different than what's done a dozen times a day, and then some. Go make your peace with your makers, mates, for you'll punish yourselves far longer and draw more blood than I. I beg your leave. We're all a bit...."

His apology died in a flood of effusive deprecations and apologies.

Nathan came back in. His step slowed at seeing her. He grimaced, conceding that no one was above being affected.

"Jen..." Her throat caught, rendering her unable to utter the name. "He'll need to be washed... prepared for..." she said, her mind groping for a solid thought.

Nathan's grip was firm as he corralled her toward the sleeping quarters. "No, you shan't go down there. Allow his mates; they'll be in need of doing something for him."

"Nathan, please, I need to —"

"No." He gave her a gentle admonishing shake as he pressed her back. "Now, you're to go in there and... and... rest," he said, wishing to have found a better word.

"But you can't expect me to just...?"

His brows arched, for that was exactly what he expected. As he pushed her around the curtain, the blunt truth was, other than pacing the salon like a caged cat, there was blessed little else for her to do.

She stood on the canvas rug gazing at the bulkhead when she heard a solid rap on the door frame. She turned to see a beringed hand clutching a brandy bottle by the neck poke around the curtain. The scabbed and tattooed knuckles identified the perpetrator, if there had been any doubt.

"Here!" came a muffled voice. The disembodied fist thrust farther forward. "Finish this, or don't come out."

She took the bottle and a warning finger jabbed at her. "I mean it!"

Clutching it to her chest, Cate leaned against the bulkhead. "Thank you, Nathan."

The scuff of a boot and creak of leather belied his nearness. "You're welcome, luv."

And then the boots moved away.

Cate shook the bottle, testing for fullness, and sighed. "Finished" was probably not to be managed; "more empty" might be attainable. In that spirit, she took another sip.

And so, wait she did, for wait was all she had.

Through Hodder's bellow of "Swabbers!", the thump of pumps and sluice of water as Jensen's blood was washed away, and then the slap of the decks being flogged dry, the watch bells rang... and rang again... and again... and again...

The port was closed, the cabin dark and stuffy. The walls began to press, the space becoming too much like a casket. She threw the port open and drew in several deep draughts, but it didn't erase the bone-chilling loneliness, the likes of which she hadn't suffered in a very long time. The room being more threatening than the prospect of facing Nathan's displeasure at being disobeyed, she left.

Seated at the table, log book and ink before him, Nathan glanced up at her appearance. His brows drew down in disapproval, but he said nothing. She sat while he wrote, his puffed mouth pulled up in a grim tilt. She remained quiet in respect of his task: just as he was obligated to enter the joyful news of marriage or birth, death also had its place in the log.

"Beg pardon, Cap'n?" It was Smalley at the door. Shifting on his stork-like legs, he knuckled his forehead "At you leave, sir."

Newly-shaved cheeks gleaming, Nathan sat motionless then lowered the pen, capped the ink and sanded the page. Closing the volume with a muffled thud, he stared at the leather binding, his fingers pensively fondling the worn edge.

"Are you ready?" Nathan asked, finally looking up. His voice was thickened by lack of use.

Gulping, she nodded.

He donned his coat, settled his hat on his head, and offered his arm. He walked with a firm enough step, but then slowed, stalling just short of the door. Gathered like a congregation awaiting its minister, the men's heads turned at his appearance.

Cate touched him on the arm, and whispered, "Nathan?"

Droplets of sweat glistening in his mustache, his mouth twitched. Moving to block the view of the on-looking crew, she shook him by the arm.

"Nathan? Nathan!" Cate hissed.

He jerked as if woken from a dream and scowled. "Are you all right, luv?"

"I could ask you the same thing. Where were you just now?"

"Must be your imagination, darling, I've been right here." Nathan dismissed her with a wave.

"You were staring as if you were... somewhere else."

He drew back to regard her as if she was deranged. "No, I wasn't."

"Yes, you—"

She was cut off by him abruptly turning to a desk near the door. He scrambled through its contents, until a scrap of paper was found. At the table, he took a long pull from the bottle, then dipped the quill and briefly scratched. Bracing his hands on the table, he contemplated the scrap, and then with a nod, as if concluding a conversation, he tucked it into his coat pocket. Straightening himself, he took another drink and returned to her side.

Worry creased Nathan's bruised features as he looked closely at hers. "Are you ready? Can you do this?"

"I think so," Cate stammered, thoroughly befuddled by the performance.

He took her by the arm, swayed, set his jaw and strode out.

The crew parted to allow them through. Cate sagged at the

sight of the canvas-wrapped bundle laid out on a boarding plank, feet first at the gunwale, and the four reverent men standing with it. A hush fell as Nathan drew up at the head of the still form. Seeming to perceive the gravity of the moment, the *Morganse* quieted.

The entire company was turned out, those on duty stepping away from their post to join the tight gathering. Pryce stood on the quarterdeck, solemnly looking down, Hodder on the helm. Amid nervous coughs, murmurs and shifting, everyone doffed their hats when Nathan cleared his throat.

Standing next to Nathan, Cate didn't know where to look. Certainly not at the canvas-wrapped form directly before her — her mind playing too many tricks — she found a neutral place, between her feet and Squidge's next to her.

Nathan gazed at Jensen's body for several contemplative moments.

"Men, we've an unpleasant business before us," he began. "It strikes one as improbable that something so natural and necessary, so universal as death, should have been labeled by Providence as an evil upon mankind, but there 'tis. Some of us have been visited upon by the ultimate conclusion, caught between here and there, there and here. Bloody unpleasant business. But now, the sands of time have run out for Young Jensen, here."

His gaze still fixed on Jensen, his mouth drew down.

"If, as we've oft been told, the good die young, then we've proof before us. That being said, it bodes ill for those of us still here, who have seen the dawn of more days than we care to contemplate."

A few men nodded, conceding the point. Pirates to the man, "good" was not the first word to mind. Perhaps living was the curse of the bad.

"Ever notice, men, how the graveyard always surrounds the church? One message there, mates: none of us are getting out of here alive."

A titter of nervous chuckle came from the group. The sun crowning their bent heads, their faces hidden, sporadic sniffing could be heard amid a cough or clearing of a throat. Nathan stood solid and square, as a Captain should, his ragged voice uncommonly clear. Cate was so very grateful for his presence; she thought the feeling might be mutual.

"In a dozen different languages, in a dozen different ways, in anticipation and promise of a dozen different heavens, we are told to live our lives as best we can. All things considered, given where we all stand this moment, I think not. Nothing brings that to bear so quickly as the passing of someone so young."

Cate felt the weight of being watched, and looked up into Nathan's eyes, soft and umber through the swollen slits.

"Mother Time will not forever favor us. Let that be a lesson to us all," he ended, his gaze falling away.

He fell quiet, to the point she thought perhaps he had finished.

"Tonight, we will all examine our lives. Can't be helped, all things considered. Dreams, wishes, hopes, ambitions, regrets, remorse, guilt and failure: we all must be prepared to face them, one by one, in our own solitudes, of course, with the pledge to do better. Jensen, however, was too young to be burdened with sins. His life exemplified to all of us what is young and good. Rest assured, his place in his version of heaven is reserved. Thank you, Jensen, for showing us the error of our ways. Let that be his message to us all."

Suddenly so very pale under his bronze, Nathan fished out the piece of paper from his coat and stuffed it into a seam of the canvas bundle. "He's in your hands now, Davy Jones. May it be brief."

Nathan closed his eyes and nodded. The end of the board was lifted and Young Jensen slid away, commended to the sea.

⚜

It was well after dark. Cate had been sitting on the forecastle since the end of the service, lacking the will to move elsewhere.

After the service, an uncommon silence had fallen over the ship. All had witnessed death before; life at sea was harsh and cruel, lives ending abruptly commonplace. To walk away, however, would be a final stamp on Jensen's passing; to linger was to keep his memory alive that bit longer. She cringed at the sound of the auction at the mainmast, though considerably lower-voiced than was usual. The bidding was solemn but intent, everyone striving to gain a memento of the lad.

In her own way, Cate made her farewell, as she had done too many times before. With her head cradled in her arms, she watched the sea, each wave another soul passing. She tried to recall the last time she had celebrated the arrival of life into this world, a dim memory at best. It was odd how death seemed so much more prevalent than birth. How did Man ever continue to prevail with such statistics?

She recognized Nathan's step well before he mounted the forecastle. He drew to a halt beside the stack of boxes, and set a plate of scones and dried apples next to her.

370

Nathan cleared his throat and forced a smile. "You haven't eaten all day. Kirkland is near apoplectic with worry."

"Have you... eaten?"

He shook his head, looking at his feet. "No, lost me appetite somewhere along the way, today. Oh, and here." He fished behind his belt and dropped something in her hand: a small, ebony-handled pocketknife.

"I got it in the auction. It's the one he used to carve your little needle case. I thought you might fancy something of him."

He was, of course, referring to the present Jensen had given her, carved from a piece of salt horse. The backs of her eyes knotted. She had indeed longed to have something of the boy's, but it was too ghoulish to bid for it, and so soon after. She thanked him kindly.

As Nathan shifted on his feet, looking off first one way and then another, it occurred to Cate that the plate, Kirkland or the knife were but excuses. She slid the plate nearer and patted the wood next to her. "Come share, then."

He gingerly sat at the furthest corner. Breaking a scone, she passed him half. Each regarded their portion with the same half-hearted enthusiasm. In the spirit of placating the other, they picked off small bits, chewing without tasting.

They were quiet for a time, distracted by their own thoughts. A few times, Nathan took a breath, preparing to say something, but then lapsed back into his own counsel.

"What was in the note?" she finally asked.

Nathan's head jerked up. "Eh?"

"The note, the piece of paper you put into Jensen's..." Her throat tightened, unable to utter the word "shroud".

"Oh, that." His fingers arced a dismissive dance. "Nothing, just a little something."

"Nathan," she said, sounding far more maternal than she cared.

He flinched. She knew he was being less than truthful, and he knew she knew. Snurling his nose at the morsel in his hand, he dropped it on the plate.

"A word," he said, dusting his fingers off, "to Jones. Jensen was a good man and deserves a good end."

"Jones? Davy Jones? I had heard the legends, but I thought they were just that: legends." Superstition was so deeply interwoven into the lives of mariners, it was blessedly difficult to fray wild imaginings from reality, and yet the least rational seemed the most popular.

"'Tis no legend here, darling," he said tolerantly. "'Tis as real as the lad's body we just commended to him."

He shuddered and looked off, disinclined to elaborate.

"No matter how fervently we like to pretend otherwise, death scares us all," she said at length. She knew it sounded trite and cavalier, but as he had suggested during the service, on such a night, how could they think of anything else?

Nathan grinned. "And the graveyard is always outside the church."

"Brian used to say 'Death begat the believer.' The most pious are often the ones to pray the hardest at the end."

Cocking one eyebrow, he regarded her approvingly. "You've seen it all, haven't you?"

"Enough." It was a simple admission, without the intent to brag; surely he had seen far worse. "Enough to know when your time comes, it comes. There's no stopping it and there's no denying it."

The heel of his boot rapped an idle tattoo against the wooden seat. "Never really thought about it; never really thought me time would ever come."

"Charmed?"

Nathan smiled. His bells tinkled as he lifted one shoulder and let it fall. "Mum claimed as much."

He rose and went to the rail. He toyed with a ring. "For a moment there, I didn't think I was going to be able to send the poor lad off."

"But you did," Cate said, moving next to him.

Nathan reluctantly nodded and looked away. "Aye, the lad deserved his peace. There's nothing for which Jones should punish him."

"And you?"

His head jerked up, looking to the night's sea.

Nathan chuckled, more for Cate's benefit than his own. "No worries, luv. I've made me peace. The rest is in Fate's hands; I can only hope she's a gentle mistress."

They fell quiet again, elbows touching as they watched the black-silk water roll past. Turmoil chewed at her gut. She had made a pledge in Lady Bart's garden and it had dragged at her since. Their heated exchange the night before and Nathan's churlishness that morning rendered it that much more pressing. The matter paled against Jensen's passing, but the death had left her in desperate need of peace. She took a breath. Knowing exactly what she meant to say, her courage still faded. Balling a fist, she plunged ahead.

"Nathan, when this is all over," Cate began, already regretting having started, "with Creswicke's fiancé and all, I was wondering... if it would be at all possible... if, I could... leave?"

Her query was punctuated by an expulsion of air. The worst was over; she had said it. Nathan nodded interestedly at first, but his expression clouded.

"Why?" His intent was to sound casual, but his voice caught. "Is this to do with Jensen?"

"No, it's nothing about him at all. It's something I've been thinking about... for a little while."

Nathan bent and peered into her face. "Did someone bother you?"

Only you, she wanted to say. Only you, because I can't bear to be around anymore, if it's always to be like this.

"No, no," Cate said, with an emphatic shake of her head. "It's just that... that..."

It wasn't going anywhere near the way she had hoped. And yet, it wouldn't have come as a surprise, if Nathan hadn't put up some kind of resistance. Deep down, she didn't believe he would force her to remain. But then, if he saw this as an attempt for her to return to Harte, it could go quite badly.

"It's just, I can't stay on a ship forever. I need a home; I need to start taking care of myself, again... somehow," she said.

"You don't like it here?" Nathan asked dully.

"Oh, I do!" She hoped her earnestness didn't come across as artificial. She ground her palm against the rail. "I was thinking I should start somewhere, to make a life again."

She buried her face in her hands at realizing what a hash she was making of it.

"Certainly," he murmured as he straightened, adding more emphatically, "Of course."

"I need to be not so dependent." *God, that sounded whining!* "I need to be able to make my own way."

"Doing what?"

"I don't know. Sewing, maybe."

Nathan's fist curled at the hilt of his sword. "I will not have you wind up destitute, in some goddamned hell hole somewhere, doing God knows what in order to eat!"

He drew back, visibly collecting himself. "No, you're correct: a ship is no place for a woman."

"I'll buy you a house," he said at last, sounding more like he sought to convince himself. "I've wanted you to have something... anything you desired. You've done a lot for the crew, healing and all; we owe you that much, at least."

"No, Nathan, it can't be like that. That would be trading one dependency for another."

The black dashes of his brows nearly touched. "Dependent! How can you possibly think you're dependent?" He gestured toward the crew and the ship behind him. "You've mended their wounds, sewn their skin, soothed their fevers, set their bones, lanced their boils and heard their confessions. If anything, they've become dependent on you."

Snorting indignantly, he began to pace in short agitated circuits. "They made you a member of this crew. You do your part and contribute your fair share."

"I know, but I've made a promise to myself."

He fought off a smile. "Most promises are made to be broken."

Nathan braced against the rail, his knuckles white against the ebony. Head hanging between his arms, his back rose and fell with each breath. She wouldn't have been surprised if he had just looked up, said "No" and walked away.

"Is it me?" he asked, barely audible. He peered up over his arm, and then back down, kicking a toe at the planks. "I know I can be… grating, sometimes… so I may have been told… maybe… a time or two," he ended awkwardly.

"No, Nathan, it's not —"

"It is, isn't it? I can change." He straightened, his swollen eyes narrowing in determination. "I know I came in on you that night, and I shouldn't have. I promise it shan't happen again."

"That's not it at all. It's just —"

"Go in that cabin." His words came faster, his vehemence building. "You draw a line anywhere on that floor anywhere, and I swear, it shan't be crossed. Better yet, you take the whole cabin. I'll move the charts, the logs, everything, the entire space will be yours, I'll…" he said with an emphatic swipe.

His words came faster and faster, the bruised eyes rounding in desperation. Unable to get a word in edgewise, she finally silenced him with her fingers to his lips.

"It's not you or anything you've done."

"Then stay." Gulping, Nathan's brows tilted hopefully. "The men want you. Hell, even the *Morganse* wants you."

"The *Morganse* has no idea —"

"Yes, she does! I can tell. Anyone can. Look how she sails when you're aboard!" His fingers arced toward the sails.

"It's a charming thought — and I'm flattered — but I don't think so."

His jaw set and he sobered. "Then what will it require?"

Uncertainty wracked her. It would be folly to think this wasn't another of his gambits, toying with her again. In the weeks that she had known him, she had seen him go through a number of personas, but never pleading or humble.

Unnerved by her hesitation, he grew dark and accusing. "You're a hard woman, Cate Mackenzie. They've taken you in, given you a place to belong, brought you into their hearts, and then you walk away. Is that all the gratitude they get? Is this how a friend shows gratitude?" He nearly spit the word.

"Is that what you want?" she asked in a thin rasp, hurt tightening her throat. "Gratitude?"

"I want what you want." He inched closer, his mask of inscrutability now firmly in place. "And, if here is what you want, it would be what I want as well. But if you don't want to be here, then my only advice would be to do as you want."

He stood over her, as tightly wound as the tar-bound rigging behind him. The backs of her eyes knotted, and they filled. Her chest constricted to the point she couldn't speak. He softened as he drew his own conclusions from her silence.

"You belong here." Each word was uttered with singular emphasis, but the quaver in his voice diminished the intended effect. His throat moved as he swallowed. "Nowhere else, just here. Besides," he added, the puffed mouth taking a wry twist, "put your mind to how dirty everything will be in your absence."

He smiled, one of those gold-and-ivory ones, intended to charm... and it did.

Her heart broke.

Independence had been her goal, for she knew the price of dependency: a dangerous commodity that could leave one devastated and bereft. With its burdens and pitfalls, dependence brought love, friendship and camaraderie. Nathan was trying to say, in his own quirky, convoluted way, what she had dreamed of. It came, however, with a price: independence or him, with all the constraints he would impose, inviolate once the choice was made. It meant to be with him, so near and yet, so very far. There was nothing in between.

Here, among eight score of pirates, she had found everything she had longed for: someone to notice, someone to care if she lived or died, a place to belong, purpose... a home. She needed a friend, not a lover, no matter how much it tore at her to admit it. Nathan was all that and more.

If someone earlier had asked "What scared Nathan Blackthorne?" she would have been hard pressed to answer, and yet here he was before her, as mortally afraid as ever witnessed, terrorized by one thing: her answer. He couldn't look up in fear of what he might see, and yet he did so anyway, to allow her a glimpse of his hope.

"Very well, Nathan," Cate heard herself say. "I'll stay."

She quaked as she bid farewell to one dream for another as Nathan made a victorious fist, closed his eyes and mouthed a fervent "Thank you."

The watch bell clanged, drawing his attention aft.

"That will be me watch." A hand drifted toward her shoulder, hovered, and then dropped away. "I'd best be reporting; sets a poor example for the Captain to be derelict in his duties."

Nathan hesitated and then drew a length of cord from his pocket and dropped it in her lap. "You need practice."

Watching as he sauntered away in his hitched gait, Cate thought perhaps a bit more spring could be detected. She smiled.

For all her denials, there was one glaring fact: she loved him, how deeply remained to be seen, but enough to know to walk away would be folly. A one-sided love was better than none at all. She had vowed never to settle for that, until she was faced with losing it. Nothing came without a price: hers was freedom, in order to be with someone who valued his even more. A home, exchanged for a racing heart and unending hope.

A part of her was relieved. Another was sickened, for that part knew all too well that, at any moment, the price of dependence could be visited upon her without so much as a warning whisper.

Could she ever survive it again?

16: WHAT FRIENDS ARE FOR

GIVEN WHAT CATE HAD LEARNED at Lady Bart's, Nathan and Pryce judged it would be a day or two, before the ship bearing Creswicke's betrothed would arrive, and so a course was laid for a place to wait. The men's failure to reference their destination by name in Cate's presence was taken as an indication that she hadn't fully regained Nathan's trust. There was the chance, of course, that he didn't consider such bits of information to be of interest. It was anyone's guess.

The studdingsails—pronounced "stuns'ls"—were set. Sideways extensions of both yard and sail, the vast spread of canvas gave the sense of the *Morganse* spreading her wings, rising from the water to sail like the wind-loving spirit that she was. Their destination was at last pointed out to Cate: a link in a far-flung chain of islands. Emerald against the azure of sky and water, skirted by a frill of white sand, to Cate's eye, it possessed no distinguishing characteristics from the innumerable other razor-backed, hunched shapes they had passed. In the catalogue of islands Nathan carried in his head, however, this one was unique and the *Morganse* made for it with arrow-like sureness.

As they drew nearer, the sails were furled, the ship folding her wings, like a bird circling to land. The topmasts were swung down. Usually executed to reduce overhead weight, in this case it was the ship's version of ducking her head, rendering her almost invisible against the island behind which she now laid.

Impromptu rafts were quickly rigged, some to move all the necessary stores ashore. Cate was beginning to appreciate the concept of "the New World," for that was what lay before her. Her foot tapped an impatient tempo on the floor of the longboat carrying her ashore, anxious for the first opportunity to freely roam land.

From the anchored ship, the island looked exactly as one would expect a pirate safe haven: a broad sparkling bay, with a long stretch of white beach, bracketed by palm trees. Up close, the beach wasn't as pristine as one would have thought. Signs of previous visitors abound: charred stumps of campfires, posts erected in the sand, tree stumps, and piles of discarded coconuts. Still, there was an Eden-like air.

"Damn near every one of these islands harbor wild pigs or goats," Nathan shouted. "Let's have some fresh meat!"

Going ashore called upon an entirely different set of skills, each man assuming a new identity. Those who knew the land or were decent marksmen were sent as foragers. The strongest swimmers were sent with nets and spears. The strongest backs were put to chopping wood or hauling fresh water. The less adept were relegated to propelling the constant flow of craft to shore and back, loading, unloading or setting up camp.

Even with Hodder's colorful expostulations echoing down the beach, rules ashore were considerably more lax; no man was shy in his work, but neither was one shy in taking his ease. If a duty was finished, waiting for the next assignment could well mean lying in the shade with a lavish application of grog.

"Is this what pirates do? Lay around on a beach, drinking?" Cate asked. Years of living in the Highlands had instilled in her the Scots' distaste for anything which resembled laggardliness.

Intrigued by the notion, Nathan paused to look around. "Pretty much. If idle hands are the Devil's playground, best not leave a hand empty, eh?"

He plucked a horn cup from a nearby lounger and downed its contents in a single gulp. Wiping his mouth on the back of his hand, he gave a roguish wind and strolled off.

Eager to see the island, Cate gathered up several baskets in preparation to join one of the foraging parties. Her hopes were dashed by a bejeweled hand on her arm and a "Not bloody likely!"

Cate had brought both her blood box and basket containing honestones, oil and rags. Both proved to be useful. It took both her stones and Petrov's, the armorer, grinding wheel to keep up with the demand for edges on everything from broad axes to skinning knives. She was caught in an odd cycle of sharpening, and then repairing the damage inflicted by the same: a hatchet into a leg, a knife-speared hand and a machete-sliced arm.

The sound of a musket shot broke through the drone of labor. Everyone stopped to swivel their attention to the eastern arm of the bay. A residual puff of gun smoke marked the signal from the lookouts: a ship had been spotted.

...Seven... Eight... Nine...

If it couldn't be heard, the silent counting on the part of every man could be felt.

Ten.

Nothing. One shot, one ship.

"Any vessel bound from Boston would be a-comin' out o' the west," Pryce said, appearing at Nathan's elbow. A clatter of rings marked Hodder's presence. Their gazes fixed to the east, Pryce only put to words what they all appeared to be thinking.

Nathan nodded distractedly. "If they mean ill, they'll pull in for sure; if they're friendly, they'll drop anchor."

Neither scenario sounded pleasing.

Shortly, a runner arrived. Smalley — the longest-legged, and therefore, the fastest — skidded to a halt. "Compliments and duty, sir. Sail!"

"So, I gather," Nathan said dryly. "And?"

"Three-master."

"Ah, well, that narrows it down to roughly two-thirds of the vessels what ply these waters. Report when you can illuminate us more fully."

"Back to work, the lot o' ya's!" Hodder's bellow startled Cate, spurring everyone to their tasks.

Idleness not being Cate's nature, during a lull in the sharpening, she set to packing sand into the freshly Stockholm-tarred, wrist-thick ropes of the boarding nets, and then dragging them into the shade to cool and harden. As she worked, her mind continued to drift to the invisible approaching ship. She was entirely too new to this pirate world and was envious of their ability to go about their duties with such blithe disregard.

Eventually word came from the lookouts on the *Morganse's* mastheads. Cate straightened slowly, wiping the varnish and sand from her hands on a bit of rag as Diogo reported.

"Compliments and duty, sir. It's a three-master, hull up, one o' them French-made, by Damerell's judgment." The news was credible. Multiple vision-enhancing, gold rings notwithstanding, Damerell was the sharpest-eyed of all the ship's people. "Blue-hulled with a yellow-checked boot."

Nathan lifted his head interestedly. "Colors?"

Diogo squinted with the effort of recalling. "Flyin' red and black; looks like a heart with a cutlass through it. He begged me to tell ye of a blue-and-white checked pennant, too."

Nathan's eyes sharpened. "Are you sure about that?"

"Sure, as Damerell can be about anything, if you please, sir."

"Well, rip me jib. I'll be a son-ofa-bitch." Nathan snapped his fingers, grinning. "I think I know who it is."

"Verily, Cap'n?" Pryce asked looking on, Hodder alongside.

Nathan's enthusiasm leveled. "Aye, but discretion 'tis the better part of valor."

"Are they coming here?" Cate's pulse raced in alarm at the prospect.

"No reason to think she would pass a perfectly good anchorage," Nathan said with annoying pragmatism. "She's probably just made the crossing and anxious for anything resembling a solid hook, and in need o' wood and water."

Having crossed the Atlantic, Cate was very familiar with the yearning for dirt.

"What do we do?" she asked.

Nathan and Pryce regarded her, bemused by the "we" reference.

"We make ready for the worst and hope for the best. Sure, as God made French whores, I know who it is, but there is always the Demon Doubt, eh?" It was a thin attempt on Nathan's part to lighten the mood.

"Mr. Pryce, pass the word to Mr. MacQuarrie to gather his crews. They're to be first to ship. Have 'em make ready and clear the decks. I'll attend directly. But if she," Nathan said, with a nod toward the heretofore unseen ship, "plans to take the ship, it will most certainly not be including *you*."

Nathan ended with an emphatic look at Cate.

"Mr. Hodder, whilst Mr. Pryce and I are aboard, you're to be in charge of those remaining ashore… and *her*! Need I review the consequences, if anything should happen?" A not so subtle shift of Nathan's eyes punctuated his meaning.

In a clatter of ivory, Hodder snapped to attention and executed a salute which would have merited the Royal Navy. "No, Cap'n! Rest assured"

"Good man." Nathan wheeled around to Cate. "You will be going on that little forage of which you were so anxious."

"Forage?" she goggled. For a moment, she thought she had misheard. Nathan's sudden change was quite transparent, and she was going to have none of it. With a ship bearing down, next to Nathan was so very much more inviting. "But you said —"

"There's what is commonly referred to among pirates as a dire plight," he said, with an edge of sarcasm. "We do what me might to avoid them, but there's a limit to what Providence allows. Mr. Pickford!"

"Aye, Cap'n?" came the answer in short order.

"You're familiar with these islands?" Nathan's inquiry was superfluous, since Pickford had been made master of the foraging details.

"Aye, sir! Like the back o' me hand." Pickford rocked on his toes with pride, setting the garland of dried ears swinging at his neck.

"Very well, a-foraging you shall go, and you're to take *her* with you," Nathan added with an emphatic jerk of his head.

Pickford blinked in surprise, but made no comment. Cate felt the stab. Once again, Nathan couldn't bring himself to call her by name. She could count the number of times on one hand—a few fingers, in fact—that he had ever done so.

"Roam far, and *do not* come back, no matter what you hear. *Comprendes*?" He spoke to Pickford, but bore her with a look, as if he harbored doubts of her ability to follow orders.

"*...no matter what you hear...*" Cate didn't want to contemplate what that might signify.

Suddenly her knowledge of the pirate world seemed woefully lacking. Did they get on or did they fight like territory-minded dogs? Was the Brotherhood, as Nathan had referred to it, exactly that, or was it an allegiance limited to shipmates? Warring nations or alliances?

Her worry must have been evident; Nathan smiled in the spirit of reassuring her. It didn't. With surprising familiarity, he squeezed her shoulder, and then gave it an encouraging pat.

"No worries, luv. As I said, I know who it is, but you don't live to be an old pirate being careless. I'll come for you as soon as I may. Now go. Go!" Nathan repeated more firmly when Cate didn't move. "I can't pay proper attention to a bloody thing if I have you to worry for. I'll come when I can. Now go."

Again, she understood his cost for having her about. She looked to the circle of grim faces on the awaiting foragers. The jury was in, unanimous.

"The minute it's safe," she insisted to Nathan.

"The. Minute."

He prodded her toward Pickford. "And try not to give the poor man anymore gray hairs than 'tis absolutely necessary," he called after her.

With visions of flashing sabers and roaring great guns, she knew all too well how capricious life could be, how it could take violent turns. She also knew the pain of remorse, the fruitlessness of wishing what one should have done or said. Swept by a wave of panic, she wanted to throw her arms around Nathan and tell him everything in her heart.

Instead, Cate heavy-footed behind Pickford, feeling like an unwanted orphan. She paused at the tree line for a final look, but Nathan was already lost among his men. She could hear his graveled voice drifting down the beach, barking orders no differently than on deck.

She left the white glare of sun and sand, and plunged into the trees' deep shadows. As the undergrowth closed in, the sea breeze died, and the air grew heavy with heat and moisture. The high canopy of trees afforded protection from the sun's full blast, but its sultry presence was still felt. Beatrice's bright blue plumage could be seen soaring overhead. Paralleling their path, she lighted from tree to tree, pausing to indulge in the occasional treat.

Looking up, Pickford paused next to Cate. "She'll call out if there be aught alarming."

Cate looked back toward the now-obscured shore, wondering if "aught alarming" was happening there. She eyed the men surrounding her. Ordinarily made up of clusters of four or six, this detail consisted of over a dozen, each known for his marksmanship. A single musket would have been the standard, and yet an extra, sometimes two, was slung over every shoulder, a minimum of two pistols at their belts, with double powderhorns and shot bags. She determinedly pushed away thoughts of what might be transpiring on shore; silence had to be taken as a blessing. Idleness being anguish's playground, she set to work.

A basket and dibble was shoved into her hands. Ignorant of the West Indies, she was at a loss as to where to start. Under Pickford's and Harrier's tutelage, however, she was soon industriously digging wild onions and ginger. Kneeling in the semi-rotted foliage and sweating, she loved every minute. During her walk on New Providence, she had been able to only observe the lushness. Now she was a participant, in it literally up to her knees. After months afloat, to have soil between her fingers and dirt under her nails... It was heavenly!

As soon as one basket was filled, another was issued. She was shown fruits and nuts—soursop, tree melons, and cashews—as well as those which were to be avoided. In this Garden of Eden, hazards awaited both underfoot and overhead: an inadvertent brush against a branch or sitting under the wrong tree after a rain could mean disaster. Herbs and local cures were shown to her, as well, and she collected them for her blood box: *lis rouge* and plantain, for swelling or sores; physic nut, for poultices and boils; gully root and monkey's hand, for headaches; and fit weed, a cure-all for everything from fainting to convulsions, vomiting to fevers.

So, engulfed in the work, Cate lost track of time. She jerked upright at hearing periodic gunshots, at the same instant knowing they came from inland. Hunters then, doing what hunters did best. The pause to take a drink from the water gourd at her waist allowed her mind to drift back to shore. Her sense of direction told her they hadn't yet moved so far that muskets or cannon wouldn't be heard. That direction was still ominously and blessedly quiet.

Where the trees thinned, she could see the sun make its march across the sky. Several hours had passed, the afternoon heat waning, when the last of the baskets and gunny sacks were filled to overflowing. Pickford and the rest of the party stood in indecision, their captain's strict orders heavy on their minds.

"Do you suppose it's safe?" Cate finally asked. Hands twitching at her sides, she vibrated to be away.

"Cap'n said as the first sign o' trouble, we were to head inland," Pickford said.

"Yes, but there is no 'sign o' trouble', is there?" she said with asperity. "If the Cap'n objects, I'll tell him it was my idea. If we hear anything like trouble, we can always turn around and go back, can't we?"

Pirates they might be; bristling with weaponry, capable of pillage and plunder, sending women and children screaming at the name, they were unprepared to deal with an intransigent woman. They balked sufficiently to claim they did, and then struck back toward shore, laden with their treasures.

Cate's step quickened as the sea breeze freshened. She pushed through the last barricade of greenery, and it met her full in the face, bringing with it the smell of saltwater, burning wood and tobacco. The worst fears had haunted her. As she stepped onto the beach, she expected to see blood and mayhem, cannonball craters and bodies strewn.

Instead, she found two ships on their moorings and the picture of peace. As advertised, the new arrival was royal blue, a brilliant yellow-checked strip banding her hull. The number of men on the beach had nearly doubled, the gently curved sand strip now a festive beehive. A makeshift camp had been set up, with shore galleys and cook fires. Sun dodgers had been rigged: stout branches planted in the sand with a piece of canvas stretched over.

A burst of jocularity came from one such lean-to near the central cook fire. Nathan's laugh was easily identified, although never had she heard him do it so genuinely. As she neared, she could see him and another man lolled in the sand. She turned a quizzical eye to Pryce as their paths intersected.

"Old friend," he offered succinctly. His thick shoulders hunched with disapproval.

Cate looked toward the water and the visiting ship with new interest. "Who is it?"

"The *Griselle*, 'cordin' to the Cap'n." That qualification seemed to hold significance. "Can't be a-sayin' fer sure, but the Cap'n claims she mostly sails the African waters, Arabie n' such."

"And the *Griselle's* Captain?"

Rocking on the balls of his feet, Pryce's skepticism grew. "Don't rightly know, sir. Never met 'im afore, m'self."

Cate studied the First Mate. By the set of his brow and line of his mouth, his mother-hen tendency toward anything which might pose a threat to his precious flock was in full alert. Her thoughts were broken by another burst of laughter.

"Well, at least it sounds friendly," she said.

"Aye, friendly it 'tis." Pryce waggled his heavy eyebrows, and whispered from the corner of his mouth, "I'd be a-steerin' a canny course and bear a weather eye, if 'twere me."

She approached as advised. The two men were leaned back against puncheons or bags in their patch of shade, a bottle of rum at their respective sides.

"You're the one who said we could make it across the street without the guards seeing us," the visitor cried, fizzing with humor.

Nathan pointed an accusing finger. "Aye, well, how was I to know that whore of yours was going to scream her bloody head off?"

"She wasn't my whore; you paid for her. She just fancied me."

They broke into another peal of laughter, the stranger wiping his eye on his sleeve. Their merriment was infectious, Cate smiled without knowing why.

"'Ello, luv!" Nathan called in a slightly slurred voice. His face lit at seeing her. He enthusiastically waved her closer. "I'd like you to meet an old friend—"

"Watch who you're calling old," growled the visitor congenially.

"An *old* friend," Nathan repeated. "This is Thomas."

Thomas' head casually turned, and he lurched upright. A pair of lake blue eyes raked her and he executed a bow from the sand.

"Well, well, Nathan, you old shellback. You never told me you had anything like this aboard."

"Easy, mate," Nathan warned good-naturedly. "Darling, this is Thomas, Captain of yon *Griselle*." He waved a misguided hand over his shoulder.

Cate bobbed a reserved curtsy. "Pleased to make your acquaintance, Captain Thomas."

"Just Thomas will answer." Leaning heavily on one arm, he openly appraised her. "Very nice, Nathan. Very nice, indeed, although you always did have the luck with the women. Always gave me the leftovers," he said to her with a conspiratorial wink.

Nathan cleared his throat sharply. "Come and join us, luv." He hooked a bucket with his foot, dragged it nearer, and invitingly patted the top.

She could feel Thomas' eyes following her as she passed, but was still startled when he reached out to seize her by the hand.

"And what might your name be, lovely?" he crooned, pulling her closer.

"Cate." Nathan uttered it with sufficient sharpness to break Thomas' stare. "Cate Harper."

It was notable that Thomas might have been a friend, but not so much for Nathan to trust him with her real name.

"Charmed," Thomas murmured. He pressed her knuckles to his lips, lingering far longer than would have been proper in most circles. His grasp was strong but gentle as he rolled her fingers between his. "I'll be looking forward to getting to know you so *very* much better."

As politely as could be managed, she extracted her hand from his grip "You said you would come get us when it was safe," she hissed at Nathan as she sat.

Nathan batted his lashes in overt innocence. The bruising now faded to a purplish blue looked like Kohl around his eyes. "Did I? Bloody insensible, that. Although, it might be said no woman is safe with Thomas about."

Punctuated by a shift of the eyes, the comment carried an undercurrent of tension. Ducking her head, she looked up from under her brows to find Nathan, smile gone, one eye narrowed, watching Thomas watching her.

"Pray tell, how did you two come to know each other?" she asked, hoping to break the awkwardness.

Nathan smiled at that. "Thomas and I were mates years ago. About fifteen, were we not?"

"You were. You've always been the older one."

"Not by that much!" Nathan said, puffed in mock indignation. "But, in addition, I also happened to be the wiser."

"Aye, we were on the *Gryphon* —"

"No, no, t'was the *Nautilus* first, then the *Gryphon*," Nathan corrected.

They laughed knowingly, a private joke. She sensed it wasn't a prudent time to inquire further.

She watched the two for the next while, her brothers frequently coming to mind. As they recounted one escapade after another, they ricocheted from something akin to a competition, of who could weave the biggest lie about the other, to mellowed mutual admiration and lauding praises. On rarer moments, they sobered as reminisced about shared hardships and lost friends.

More cautiously, she watched Thomas. She had tried to imagine what Nathan's friends might be like; Thomas was nothing like what she had expected. They were exact opposites: Thomas was tall, broad and fair. The dark blue eyes shining over broad cheekbones and the honey blond hair pulled back into a heavy tail gave him a Viking-like appearance. No woman would have been safe with this dashing pair in port. Possessing the same easy manner and dazzling smile as Nathan, Thomas wore his handsomeness as matter-of-factly as the brace of pistols crisscrossed at his waist, and the massive baldric, its dagger scabbard perched at his shoulder. The mat of golden chest hair at the opening of his shirt was marked by a diagonal scar. It was proof life had battered him as much as Nathan. Like Nathan, too, he talked with his hands, his blunt-tipped fingers punctuating his conversation rather than illustrating.

She looked down at her lap to find her fists clenched—painfully so—her knuckles gone white. She knew why, at the sight of Thomas, her heart had lurched and then sped, and cold prickles raced down her back. She also knew why she had paraded herself just a bit as she walked past him, and why she now sat teetering between cold dread and the urge to throw herself at him.

He looked just like Brian.

The sound of his laugh echoing down the beach had hit her in the chest like a fist. The eyes had been the next shock, the same dark blue to which she had lost her heart. The voice, deep and soft, resonated in her bones. Many similarities ended there. Brian's hair had been the color of bronzed copper, his mouth wider, lips fuller. He had been slimmer built and had spoken with a soft Highlander lilt. Brian would have never leered at a woman the way Thomas just had, nor mentally undressed her as he kissed her hand. But the mannerisms, the smile...

Damn! It was him!

Nathan regarded her, sensing something amiss. She tried to rearrange her expression to something more common, but Nathan's concerns weren't appeased. Saying something could have broken the ice, but the only thing which came to mind was "He looks like my dead husband."

Unable to sit any longer, she lurched to her feet, both men jerking at her abruptness.

"I'm... I... err..." She searched the beach for an excuse, finally landing on a water bucket a short distance away. "I need to wash... Digging!" she declared, displaying her hands. "I've been digging and..."

She spun away, stalling in mid-step to execute a wobbling

curtsy and mumble a barely intelligible nicety to Thomas. Then she scurried off, leaving the two somewhat slack-jawed.

"Wash?" she heard Thomas say in her wake. A disbelieving smirk edged his voice.

Nathan sighed indifferently. "From what we've been able to gather, 'tis a matter of women. Bloody perplexing; strikes without warning. All in all, 'tis best left to lie."

Once at the bucket, she was compelled to do something or look the complete liar. She bent to splash water in her face and found a pleasant surprise. It was filled with island water, sparkling and fresh compared to what she was accustomed to on board. Sluicing it again and again, it washed away not only the day's sweat and grime, but the light-headedness which had seized her since seeing Thomas. As she discretely turned her back to use her hem as a towel, she discovered she was directly downwind from them. Apparently, there were no secrets on a beach either.

"She's stunning," Thomas was saying.

She kept her face to the rough linen of her skirt a little longer lest anyone see her reddening cheeks.

"Is she? I hadn't noticed," Nathan said, offhandedly.

Thomas laughed, a deep and infectious sound. "Either you're blind or a goddamned liar, and a bad one at that."

"She's a... guest."

Cate's cheeks heated further with the sting of Nathan's disinterest.

Thomas gave a derisive snort. "How long have you had her? Any chance of you might be tirin' of her, yet?"

"Hold your tongue, mate," Nathan said, evenly. "She's not that kind."

"Oh, come now, Nathan. This is me, not some shave-tail still on his mama's tit."

"I mean it," Nathan warned, without malice. "She's a good league above us, better than anything either one of us could ever hope for."

"Well, we can always dream, can't we?"

"I wouldn't dare," Nathan said after an interval, so low-voiced she could barely hear. "I wouldn't dare."

As evening threatened, the work details converged to deliver their bounties: basketfuls of crabs, turtles, oysters and shellfish from the bay; nets of fish from the sea and river, and game, two pigs and a goat. With the exception of the last, Kirkland used it all, along with cabbage, pickled vegetables, olives and spices from the ship's stores to make a stew of sorts.

The *Griselle's* cook was a man by the name of Youssef. Black-eyed, solemn, he was as territorially intransigent as Kirkland when it came to his galley. Given the language differences, it required the negotiating skills of both captains and a second cooking fire a designated distance away before armistice could be achieved. At his fire, Youssef jealously oversaw his own version of stew, a more pungently spiced version, enhanced generously with garlic, wine and rice. Hermione blithely grazed while a wild cousin turned on a spit next to a brace of pigs.

As the purple hill shadows replaced the sun's brilliant yellows, pot lids were clanged to beckon one and all. Cate sat against stacks of bagged coconuts, with Nathan barefoot at her knee wielding a small mallet. Several lobsters had been thrown on the coals, and now he sat with a board across his lap cracking shells. Swearing each time, a finger was hit, he doggedly refused suggestions that his rum intake might have influenced his accuracy. Amid the merriment, interjecting his own embellishments to any story being told, he dredged fingerfuls of meat through melted butter and fed them to Cate. Chin dripping, eyes rolled in delight, she insisted several times she couldn't take another bite, but couldn't resist the elegant, slippery fingers stuffing the morsels between her lips.

Hunger sated, the sea rovers fragmented into smaller, more intimate gatherings, their fires dotting the shore like amber jewels. The *Griselle's* crew brought an exotic texture to the gathering, most of her people hailing from African or Asian ports. As their music drifted on the evening breeze, the different strains melded into a multi-cultural, somewhat off-key refrain. Pirates they might have been, but first and foremost they were men, and engaged in what men did best: drink, smoke, tell insufferably unlikely stories of outlandish bygone deeds, recount legends, myths, and folk tales, sing raucous songs and tell ribald jokes, salting it all with a heavy dose of laughter.

Glowing with spiced rum — another of Youssef's specialties — Cate reclined against the bags in pleasant agony. His culinary task complete, Nathan joined Thomas in entertaining everyone around the fire with the chronicles of their adventures. Launching to their feet, they performed recreations, cavorting and pirouetting to the delight of everyone. Nathan was mesmerizing. With an audience at his feet, he was in his glory. Animated hands and exuberant expressions, flashing teeth and devilish eyes, he shamelessly told story after story. The two personalities created a whole, one beginning a sentence, the other finishing. Imitating each other to perfection, they jeered and jested at the other's expense. It was friendship at its purest, and a grand sight it was.

Men filtered from their fire until only Nathan and Thomas remained. Nathan's guard slowly lowered, and became someone Cate thought might be the closest to the real Nathan, the one kept so meticulously enshrouded. He glanced at her frequently, his self-consciousness outweighing his curiosity. It was another aspect rarely revealed: vulnerability, uncertain if she would accept him for what he was rather than what he appeared to be, asking with a faint smile or a twitch of the eye, "Is it too distasteful? Too disappointing? Too ordinary?"

After the initial shock, Cate grew accustomed to Thomas, and was able to focus on the innumerable differences, while striving to convince herself he was nothing like Brian. Thomas' eyebrows were a little heavier, his nose a bit longer, his fingers a little thicker. The bones that stuck out at the sides of his wrists weren't as pronounced, and his two front teeth were squarer. Brian's voice had been softer; Thomas' possessed the deep resonance which came with such a large chest. Still, it was a constant battle not to let down her guard. She was subject to minor shocks: a lurch of the heart triggered by a sound, a glimpse or a word, and the flush of need would surge through her once again. She focused on the ways Thomas was different, but her heart clung to all the similarities.

At one point, they were distracted by a commotion a short distance away, a fight erupting.

"Aren't you going to do something?" Cate asked. She watched over her shoulder with growing concern as the confrontation between the two exploded into a brawl of over a dozen.

Thomas only lifted his head from his reclined position to observe. "Yours, I think."

"Aye, so it would seem," Nathan said disinterestedly. "Hold off. Those two what just jumped in are yours. No," he said, directed to her inquiry. "Pirates."

The single word was offered as an all-encompassing explanation. Still, as uninterested both men posed to be, they suffered that male characteristic of being unable to tear their eyes from a fight.

"If we were aboard, I'd be obliged to put them ashore and settle it there. Saves time all around, I'd say," Nathan explained. He glanced toward Thomas for affirmation, who readily concurred.

"Only a fool would wade into that," Thomas added with conviction and took a drink.

As one would imagine, a pirate fist fight was a nasty, brutal affair and not limited to fists. In point of fact, anything which came within reach was employed, bludgeoning each other with everything from buckets to sticks of blazing firewood. Distance spared Cate the full visual effect of the damage inflicted, but she could still hear the meaty smacks, the crunch of bone and pain-laden grunts.

"Maybe I should go see if anyone needs help," she said.

"Not bloody likely!" Nathan and Thomas said in near unison, with a glare that pinned her in her place.

As predicted, such combat could be sustained for a brief period of time. The fighting stopped with the same suddenness as it had begun. It ended with handshakes, brotherly pats on the back, and toasting each other through broken teeth and spitting blood.

"So, tell me, Nathan," Thomas said from across the fire during a lull. "Just what exactly are you doing here? How did you just happen to be anchored at the Straits?"

"We needed water and firewood and—"

"No, no, no!" Thomas waggled a finger. "Let's cut the bull. This is no water and wood stop. You're up to something. What is it?"

Nathan glanced to Cate and then leaned back on his elbows. Crossing his ankles, the tips of his braids sketched random patterns in the sand behind him.

"Always the nosy one, weren't you?" Nathan said with grudging good humor. "We are awaiting the arrival of a most important newcomer to the Caribbean. But, before arriving, said newcomer shall be visiting her aunt's home in Hopetown."

Thomas sat up with interest and loosely draped his arms on bent knees. "Really?"

"Said newcomer," Nathan went on, situating himself more comfortably, "arriving from Boston, is betrothed to one of the finest and most upstanding members of these waters."

"And since she's coming from Boston, she would just happen to pass through the Straits. And, by some miracle of happenstance, the *Ciara Morganse* will just happen to be there exactly at the same time."

"Exactly!" Nathan declared, jabbing a victorious finger skyward.

The firelight sparked on the amusement in Thomas' eyes. "And to whom, pray tell, is this lovely creature betrothed?"

"Lord Breaston Creswicke."

Thomas' smile fell, the blue eyes sharpening. "Nathan, are you sure you want to do this?"

"Absolutely." Nathan returned a level gaze across the flames.

"Well," Thomas conceded, chuckling softly. "You never were afraid to ram the stick in the hornet's nest."

Thomas' amiability faded as he studied Nathan over the flames. The shadows on his features sharpened, making him more like a marauding Viking. The backdrop of music had diminished by that hour. The low whine of a distant fiddle and the chortle of a hornpipe filled the long silence.

"He destroyed you once. Are you willing to risk that again?" Thomas asked gravely.

"I've been waiting for this opportunity for a very long time; a *very* long time," was Nathan's even response. "Would you care to join us?"

"As what?" Thomas shot back, intrigued.

Nathan tipped his head considering, his bells glinting in the firelight. "We could use a bit o' help. A consort could assure they shan't break to open sea when the *Morganse* makes her move."

"You'll have the entire Royal Navy and every privateer in these waters after you."

"More is the reason two ships be the better." Nathan watched as Thomas considered.

"I'll give you twenty-five percent of me plunder."

A wry lift of a sandy brow came with, "Used to be fifty."

"I've more important needs to consider these days," Nathan said, cryptically.

Thomas laughed loudly to the night sky. "For that small cause, I'll consider it a donation. You'll allow me to consult with my men, but so long as there is a profit at the end, they are babes. Agreed?"

"Agreed."

Nathan rose and faded into the nearby shadows to relieve himself. Weary of sitting, Cate stood, groaning with stiffness. As she shook the sand from her skirts, Thomas appeared at her side with surprising gracefulness for someone of his size and swept an even more graceful bow.

"Pray, would you care to walk?" He displayed a charming smile.

It had been a very long time since she had taken a stroll with a man. Its appeal outweighed the caution of going into the night with a relative stranger. She needed to get a hold on the emotions which had been set churning. It might provide an interim in which she could face down the shock of Thomas without Nathan's hawkish eye on her.

They headed down the beach, side-by-side, but a careful distance between.

Cate kicked off her shoes at the water's edge and waded in the surf. The water lapping her ankles was as warm as the night air. The sand squished between her toes in little jets. Thomas waded beside her, unmindful of the waves washing over his boots. She was growing familiar with the Caribbean's brilliant stellar displays. The moon not yet risen, allowing the night's display to be particularly dazzling. Whoever the ruling goddess of the stars might be was at her finest.

At first, they engaged in the idle chat of strangers, probing to find common grounds. The most obvious was Nathan, and it didn't take long for conversation to work around to him.

"You've known each other a long time?" Cate asked. She remembered Nathan had mentioned an age, but had been too distracted to attend.

"Aye." Thomas nodded amiably, hands folded behind his back. "I've known Ol' Scupperbait for a long time. The hair was barely sproutin' on our chins."

"Scupperbait?"

He laughed with the malicious pleasure which came with revealing an embarrassment from someone's past. "Aye, that's what we called him. The name followed from his first voyage. He was so small and scrawny, he'd get washed across the decks and caught in the scuppers. We were fifteen or sixteen," he said, getting back to her original query. "I saw Nathan make third mate at eighteen."

"At eighteen?" From what she knew of life at sea, it was an impressive accomplishment.

"Nathan always had a way; the men naturally follow him... women, too."

She caught the meaningful lilt and saw the speculative smile which lurked.

"Still do, the men, I mean," she said looking away.

"I'd say the women, too," Thomas mused. "Anyway, we crewed together for years. I was his first mate on his first command."

"You were pirates, then?"

He laughed at her innocence. "No, merchantmen. Nathan didn't tell you of his first command, the *Beneficent*?"

Silence was her answer.

"You've seen his brand?" he asked, wary.

"Blessedly difficult not to," she said tartly. "He told me about when it happened and—"

"He told you that, eh?" Thomas nodded approvingly. They

were still near enough for the light of the scattered campfires to gild his profile. "He must set a great store in you. He doesn't speak of it to anybody, not even me, and I was with him when Creswicke did it."

"Creswicke!" Cate stopped, gaping. "Lord Breaston Creswicke?"

"Aye, didn't he tell you?" His caution returned, alert to having overestimated the extent of Nathan's confidence.

Cate stared into the night, straining to recall what Nathan had told her one stormy night, of manipulation, deception and discovery. "He told me about the brand, but he never said who did it. He said he had riled his employer."

"Aye, well, there's a bit of truth there."

"He was accused of smuggling." The statement was more a seeking of assurance that she wasn't confused.

"Smuggling?" He chuckled humorlessly. "If only it had been that damned simple."

"You mean he lied?" It came as no great shock. She had suspected from the first that Nathan hadn't told her everything.

Thomas looked to his feet. "He wasn't like that at first. Oh, aye, he was always a smooth-talker and could charm the yellow off the sun. To his way of thinking, it's not lying, it's just telling the truth he needs at the time."

Biting his lower lip, he narrowed his eyes, measuring both her and how much more to reveal. Lifting a shoulder and dropping it, his decision was made.

"Nathan had won the *Beneficent* gambling — and they were the other man's dice. He always was the lucky one." he added in wonderment. "Anyway, she was a fair ship. Nathan was a customer's dream: fast delivery, rarely a loss, a master at evading pirates, and all the while undercutting his competitors."

"Creswicke?"

Thomas nodded, pleased by her acuity. "Creswicke had been granted the charter for the Royal West Indies Mercantile Company. It was a favor from the Crown." The edge in his voice suggested further intrigue was involved, but was disinclined to elaborate. "Nathan had Creswicke's eye from the very first."

"Because of his success?"

He glanced sideways at her, and then away. The wide shoulders squirmed under the linen of his shirt. "Ehh... let's just say Creswicke has unique appetites and Nathan made him particularly hungry."

Cate tasted the bile of disgust. Having lived in London for several years, she was familiar with such "tastes": sodomy, bestiality, fetishes, depravities and other deviations yet to be named. She was yet to meet the man, but already possessed a deep hatred.

She ground her feet deeper into the surf's sand, as if it might abrade away the sickening sensation. "And?"

"And, eventually Creswicke made Nathan an offer he couldn't refuse: sail for him or never sail again. It was a credible threat. He'd seen Creswicke destroy others who had dared defy him. Being the pragmatic sort, Nathan agreed. He figured sooner or later he'd find a way out of it. It wasn't an all bad arrangement: he was the youngest captain in the Company and still sailing his own ship."

"It wasn't long after," Thomas went on, "before Creswicke made Nathan another offer, aiming to make Nathan a part of his scheme. Indentured servants come cheap and die by the hundreds in transit. Creswicke was manipulating the books, listing people as dead, and then selling them for the profits. If anyone in London was to question, he'd claim the losses were due to pirates."

Indentured servants.

It was nothing more than a polite term in delicate circles for slavery. Some were prisoners, banished into it. A good many more sold themselves to a benefactor as a means of gaining passage to the Colonies or elsewhere, where they would work off the debt in a given period of years. The reality — often discovered too late — was years could be added at the benefactor's whim for anything from food and shelter, to labor lost due to illness or pregnancy. Many owners preferred indentured servants to Guinea slaves. They were considerably cheaper, came none of the language barriers, and fewer rules governing them.

Brian had been transported as an indentured. Slavery was what it was, which was how she knew he was dead: he would never live that way. She closed her eyes, sickened further to think Brian might have been a victim in Creswicke's insidious scheme.

Suddenly too restless to remain still, Cate started down the beach once more. Thomas easily fell in step beside her. The rhythm of his long strides next to her was disquieting, like a ghost walking at her elbow. They were away from the light of the campfires by then, the brim of his hat casting a shadow by starlight.

"Nathan told him to go to Hell, at least that's the version that can be repeated to a lady. The sniveling worm drug Nathan into it anyway, and gave him a shipload of them," Thomas said grimly.

Her hatred of Creswicke rose exponentially. Even if Brian

hadn't been a victim, the possibility was enough to ignite a deep loathing.

"Nathan tried to refuse, but Creswicke was his boss, his word final. Every man has his limits and Creswicke found Nathan's that day. It's a rare thing to see, but Nathan has a black temper: he came near to killing the man. We wondered why Creswicke didn't have him arrested on the spot. We didn't know that would have disrupted his grander scheme: he didn't want Nathan miserable, he wanted him destroyed."

"Why didn't Nathan just go captain somewhere else?"

There was a flash of white in the darkness as he gave a tolerant smile. "Creswicke's charter gave him the same control of the West Indies as the Company has in the East. To refuse him would mean to never sail as a merchant again. Besides, the *Beneficent* was Nathan's first command; 'tis a special place in a man's heart."

She flinched at seeing Thomas rub the back of his neck under the heavy tail of hair, just as Brian would have done.

"None of us liked it. We sailed for Nathan; we didn't give a goddamn about Creswicke or his company. The manifest looked well enough. We thought it odd when there were Company guards at the gangways, but they represented it was an uncommon bad lot, and we believed them," he said, sounding even more miserable. "We'd barely set the courses, when we began to hear such caterwauling from the hold, t'was like the Sirens themselves. And the smell..."

Thomas coughed and cleared his throat of a sudden unpleasantness.

"With a bit of strong-arming, we overcame the guards and went below. They were children, over two hundred, packed like sheep in a pen. A better price in Charles Town was just Creswicke's excuse to manipulate Nathan. Those poor wretches were nothing more than a blot on a ledger to him."

Thomas clamped his lower lip between his teeth and fell quiet. He took several strides before he spoke again, his voice tightened.

"Some had been sold by their parents, so the rest of the family might eat. Others were from the poor houses and orphanages. The rest: abducted, kidnapped; use whatever word you wish."

The marketing of children wasn't new. After the Rising, the streets of Edinburgh had been rife with rumors of raiding parties, sometimes uniformed, spreading through the night's streets like a plague, sweeping through poor houses or tearing a child from a mother's arms, if old enough to be weaned. The plague hadn't been confined to Scotland. In many seaport towns and even London, gangs roamed stealing children.

Thomas fell quiet so long that she thought perhaps he wouldn't—or couldn't—go on. The mournful cry of a killdeer came from the darkness, scurrying in circuitous patterns ahead of them.

"They were dying before the braces were sheeted home. We couldn't bear it, especially Nathan," Thomas said. "We tried to care for the poor things, but there were so many, sick and starved. Most were walking skeletons and some couldn't even walk. They were dying a dozen a day. The screaming and the crying..." His words choked off, his hands spreading as he relived the helplessness. "The canvas we buried them in weighed more than the poor waif inside."

The lobster and butter, swimming in chowder, took a turn for the worse in Cate's stomach.

"Finally, Nathan had enough. Hell, none of us could bear it. He thought he knew of a place to go and someone to help. All we could think was to get those poor souls to land, food and help."

His countenance grew grimmer. "From Bridgetown to Charles Town was no secret; anyone worth his salt knew what our course would be. A privateer was waiting, one of Creswicke's marauding wolves. There was no offer of quarter or parlay, nothing. They fired on sight."

Thomas closed his eyes, the sandy brows drawing together.

"We were out-gunned from the beginning. They were a twenty-eight to our fourteen and those only eight-pounders to their sixteens. When the balls started finding their target, the screaming only got worse." The last came in a tight whisper.

Cate had repaired what fragments of iron and arm-long shards of wood could do to a full-grown man. The destruction on small bodies, packed tightly together, was too easily envisioned. In such close quarters, the air choked by screams and smoke, below decks would have been a grisly chaos.

"We broke off. The *Beneficent* was fast, and Nathan can beg more speed out of a ship than any man at sea, but she was shot up. Their chasers pounded us in the stern the whole way. Finally, a ball hit the rudder, and when the *Beneficent* swung around, they had us in a broadside."

Thomas made several attempts before he was able to resume. "She broke into flames straight away. Afire, listing hard and no rudder, Nathan managed to keep the crew's wits about them enough to run her aground, but easy like, so's not to bring the rigging down on us," he said, with no small amount of admiration. "What with those bastards still firing on us, we tried to get as many of those poor wretches ashore as possible. Those what could ran while we carried as many as we might, but the ones too sick, the ones we couldn't get to…"

Thomas' voice shook. He blinked several times and roughly swiped his face with his sleeve.

"Nathan sent us into the jungle, told us to keep going. Last I saw, he was on that flaming afterdeck, firing the swivel gun like a demon possessed."

They ran until their burning limbs and lungs would allow no farther. They pressed on through the jungle, confident of being pursued. But it wasn't the two men or the children the enemy was after.

"We went back to get him, but there was nothing but a burned-out hulk and bodies. The only prisoner they took was Nathan."

Thomas fell quiet, meditatively studying his hands as he flexed them.

"From what I heard," he said. "Creswicke met Nathan at Bridgetown with the writ for his arrest in hand: smuggling, falsifying documents, flying under false colors, you name it. There was a trial, if you're inclined toward calling it that. In the middle of it, some poor slave woman was dragged forward—one of Creswicke's own—to swear that Nathan was her son. With that black hair and black eyes…" He faded off and glanced at her. "I've seen mulattos near as light as you. It was no great stretch for Nathan to be one."

"And the son of a slave is a slave," Cate sighed.

Thomas nodded. "And the property of the mother's owner. There were paid witnesses present who swore to anything. Hell, it coulda been Mother Clary's cat and the magistrate's finding would have been the same. Nathan was declared a slave."

Thomas'stopped walking and fell quiet, his eyes narrowed to slits as he recalled.

"Nathan was thrown in the holding pens with the other poor bastards waiting to be sold. Garrick—a mate of ours, and a good one—and me were there when Nathan was brought up on the block. Like the others, they stripped him naked and shaved his head. You could see he'd been beaten to the point of barely able to stand. There was an auction, of sorts. Creswicke made a grand show of bidding for him, and then…"

He drew a deep breath and blew it out. "And then, he was branded."

"But the "S" is usually on the cheek," she said, still mired in disbelief.

The corner of his mouth tucked up grimly. "It would seem

Creswicke couldn't bring himself to ruin the very face he cherished so much."

A dull silver lining in a dark cloud: Creswicke's unseemly appetites had turned out to be Nathan's salvation.

"It wasn't good enough for Creswicke to use the regular iron. Like Nathan was an animal, he used an iron meant for one. The executioner stood on Nathan's hand to hold him still. Every finger was either broken or disjointed from Nathan struggling… and the scream."

Thomas shook his head with disgust. "But Creswicke wasn't done with his little sham. The law was every slave taken in Africa was to be branded by the company shipping him. And so, he had the Company mark put on Nathan."

His hand came to rest high on his chest, above his heart. It was exactly where the odd-shaped scar was on Nathan's chest, just below the banner and the word "Freedom" etched in his skin.

He fell quiet again, carefully recalling.

"Creswicke had this sick smile on his face, his eyes all bright and shining as he declared Nathan was a runaway, claiming it was bounty hunters not privateers that had brought Nathan in. Punishment was fifty lashes."

"That bloody, frigging, swiving bastard."

Cate's blasphemy brought a smile to Thomas. "Aye, that and more. Save yourself the trouble, m'lady. I've called him every name, in every language."

Thomas' face went dark. "Nathan had been flogged before; he knew what was coming. Only hatred kept Nathan on his feet as they tied him to the gibbet. Fifty lashes and the man was silent as a monk to the last."

He peeled a cautious look in her direction. "Do you know what it is to see a man have his back flayed, to hear his skin rip with each stroke?" He shuddered violently. "I've seen it too many times; still can't abide it. I've only let the cat out of the bag once in my command and regretted it since. Nasty business. It's no pleasure to see a man standing in his own pool of blood."

A cold prickle crawled down Cate's back. Yes, she had seen floggings, and no, there was no pleasure. If anything, he had grossly understated the brutality. A man, his limbs bound, his body bared, the torn flesh tense and quivering in anticipation of the next blow. The tang of blood would have replaced the stench of scorched flesh. A man's character was revealed at the first strike; some collapsed and sobbed like a child, others met each stroke with stoicism braced by pride. It went beyond punishment: it a meant to break a man.

Thomas blew a long breath, exorcising the grisly scene.

"Garrick and me found Nathan that night. He'd been flung like the night's slops into a pen not fit for a pig. I think Creswicke was hoping Nathan would crawl off someplace and he could catch him for a runaway again. Only God and the Devil know what he would have done then," he added under his breath.

Cate knew what Thomas couldn't put to words: inhuman cruelty. Confinement, hacked limbs, whippings, blindings, castrations... and worse.

An outcropping of rock blocked their way, and so they perched there, watching the tide purl out. A number of tidal pools formed in the scooped out rock, the diamond-like grains of sand in their bottoms sparkling in the now-rising moon. It was a miniscule world of claws, antennas and spines.

"Me and Garrick tried to care for him," Thomas went on, kicking at a shell with the toe of his boot. "Nathan was out of his head for days. Rum and laudanum didn't answer. I had the knife in my hand, ready to cut the damned 'S' off him," he said, looking down, flexing his hand. "It might have cost him his hand, the use of it at the least, but at least he'd be free."

He shook himself of the thought. "But Garrick stopped me, representing that there was another way."

"Pirate," she heard herself say dully.

Nathan was a marked man. He could either live among the vilest of the vile, where capture meant to be hung, his body tarred and left on display to rot, or his head on a pike, the walnut eyes gone black in death, picked to vacant holes by the crows; or he could risk being caught as a slave, meaning captivity and degradation at the hands of a monster.

"Aye," Thomas sighed solemnly. "Freedom, in another world. There was no escape else. Every bounty hunter in the Seven Seas knows what that "S" meant. But it needed to be Nathan's choice, so we waited."

The strength of friendship. "Two, mebbe three" Nathan had said, when she had asked how many he had had in his life. Two, for sure, for they had held his life in their hands and kept him safe.

"We took him to a conjure woman—at least I think she was a woman. She sent us off, made us leave him there. I paid my last respects, because I figured him to be a dead man."

He stared, but was seeing something far different than the campfires, now directly across, flickering orange-jewels along the shore. The gay voices and music could still be heard, broken and muted by the distance. The *Morganse* and *Griselle* sat like somber queens, adorned in their amber-glow necklaces of lamplight.

Gone in thought, or overwhelmed by the memories, Thomas was quiet for some time. The rattle of crabs scuttling behind her, Cate watched a phosphorescent fish dart about in one of the pools. Feeling as if she were being watched, she turned slightly to find a pair of disembodied eyes on stalks peering interestedly back.

"Never sure what happened," Thomas threw into the silence, his angular features troubled. "If it was that conjure woman, or Creswicke, but Nathan was never the same. I mean, aye, on the outside he was, but inside... When you looked him in the eye, he just wasn't there anymore."

"I wish I could have known him before."

His mouth a firm line, he said with gentle sadness, "No, you don't. That person is gone; it wouldn't answer."

His fist balled where it rested on his thigh. "That was when we all turned pirate: Nathan, Garrick and me. Garrick had been in the Brethren. He had been aiming to go honest, but went back, and took us with him. Neither one of us wanted to leave Nathan alone; we knew he'd go do something crazed, just to get himself killed. He did his best, in spite of us. We mended him from burned to broken, beaten to slashed. We were with him when a blade run him through. Killed that bastard myself," he added in a pride-laden aside. "You've seen his leg?"

"No, I've never seen him —" Cate looked away, industriously brushing at a non-existent spot on her skirt.

"Oh, aye, of course." Thomas demonstrably cleared his throat. "Aye, well... hmm... we almost lost him there. It festered to where we considered takin' it. Then a conjure woman showed up; I swear she stepped out of the night." He frowned, pondering. "She gave him some herbs or potions, or some such, and brought him through. He walked with a crutch for months after; made it bloody difficult for him on board."

"But there isn't a brand on his chest now," she said haltingly.

Looking off into the night, Thomas nodded grimly. "Nathan put up a fair front—he's good at that, you'll have noticed?"

Cate nodded wryly. "Fair front" was a vast understatement.

"He did his best not to let on, but you could see the thing eating at him. The "S" was bad enough, but to have Creswicke's initials on him, marked and owned, it was like Creswicke had his claws around his heart, squeezing the life out of him."

He blew a long sigh. "So, one night, whilst he was lost in drink—a fair regular occurrence—I—" His voice caught. He looked down at the hand resting on his leg. "I cut the damned thing off."

"What did he say?" she asked, horrified. Waking up to a piece of one's chest cut away had to have been a bit of a shock.

He looked off, intrigued by the thought. At length, he shrugged. "He never said... and I never asked."

They rose and headed back. They walked in silence, emotionally drained. Her anger with Nathan for lying about the branding and Creswicke surged anew. She then chastised herself. It was her own fault, for poking her nose into matters which were obviously too sensitive, had she taken a moment to realize. She couldn't begrudge him. She harbored a few of her own secrets for which she would lie or any number of other things to protect. It was hurt she suffered most, Nathan's failure to trust her. She had gained his confidence enough not to be told "No," when she inquired, but no further. He had allowed her only what his pride could allow.

"What made all of you go your own way?" she asked at last.

Thomas' broad shoulders twitched. He looked off into the night and said off-handedly, "Oh, time and tide. Garrick stuck with him for a bit longer, but I... chose to move on," he finally landed on.

"Somehow, I doubt it was that simple." Cate said tartly, peering up at him.

He cocked his head to regard her. "You're a smart woman; tall, but smart. Heaven help the man that gets himself tangled up with a smart woman," he declared with a gesture skyward. "Aye, there was more to it: a woman."

"What else?" she snorted.

"Money and women, only two things worth losin' a good friend over," he said sagely. "We both thought she fancied us; even came to blows over her. She'd filled him full of all manner of notions. When she finally chose me, he disappeared."

She glanced toward his left hand; she didn't recall seeing a wedding ring, but admittedly it wasn't a reliable guide. "What happened?"

"Oh, eventually she ran off with the captain of a packet she fancied more." Thomas rubbed his finger thoughtfully alongside his nose. "I heard later she died in childbed."

Something said he wasn't as unaffected by either the separation or the death as he would like her to believe. Cate felt more than heard the beat of feathers whisking past her head. Jerking aside, she looked up to see a soaring shadow disappear into the darkness of the trees: Artemis, on the prowl.

"I've wondered if, maybe, Nathan had somebody, somewhere, a wife, or family, or... something," she ended lamely.

It was an explanation which had risen more than once, when striving to rationalize Nathan's disinterest in her. As unpleasant as that truth might have been, it would have explained so much.

"Nathan?" he sputtered. "What in all that's holy made you think a thing like that?"

"He wears a ring on his wedding finger." She was flustered by revealing how closely she had observed Nathan. She reflexively twisted at her own ring. Aside from his hair and bells, his pistol and sword unadorned and workmanlike, there was no flash or flourish. The rings seemed quite unfitting.

Thomas burst out laughing, the deep rumble echoing across the water. It startled the killdeer into flight, protesting as it arched off into the night.

"If you'll notice, Nathan wears several rings," he said, dabbing one eye.

He stopped to exhibit a massive fist before her face. "A fist makes a much stronger impression on a man's jaw when it arrives in the company of metal." He jabbed the air to punctuate his point. "Nathan's never been a big man; a little help answers well."

He resumed walking, his hands falling to rest on the heels of his weapons.

"Nathan drop the anchor? Nay, I doubt it," he said, returning to her initial question. "I haven't seen him for a *long* while, but he never was one to pine over a woman half a world away, when a dozen are at his feet. He takes his opportunities as they rise, beggin' your pardon, ma'am." He mockingly tipped his hat.

"I just thought, maybe, since he... never..."

"Never!" Thomas skidded to a halt, gaping. He bent closer as if he might have misheard. "Never?"

Cate shook her head, grateful for the protection of darkness to cover her heated cheeks.

"Never," he repeated to himself. His face screwed in puzzlement. "Now that is a wonder. And a handsome one like you? Nay, it defies all logic. I've never known him to pass up anything in a skirt, sometimes even without. You're sure?" He peered down at her skeptically as if she was confused. "I could have sworn..."

He trailed off in invitation for her to pick up the thought. She was mum.

Head down pensively, hands folded at his back, Thomas walked for a short bit.

"Hark ye," he said, stopping again. "What if we were to have a little fun? Make him think...?"

"No, I'm not playing sophomoric games. I remind him of someone, someone he thoroughly detests." The admission came no easier then than the dozens of times she had repeated it in the privacy of her bed.

"But, you're interested?" Suddenly shy, he kicked the sand, sapphire blue peeking up from under the straw-colored lashes. "I'm just asking, because if it weren't him, I would be willing to step forward."

Thomas flashed a dazzling smile meant to charm. So reminiscent of Brian's, she had to turn her head to keep from either laughing or crying, she wasn't sure which.

"With all due respect, I'm not interested either way," Cate said firmly.

"Hmm... you could have fooled me," he muttered falling into step next to her. He stopped again after only a few steps, fists braced on his hips. "How long did you say since you've shipped?"

"A little over a month."

"And he never... once?"

"We're friends."

"Ouch!!" Clapping a hand to his chest, he dramatically staggered backward. "Colder words were never spoken." He shrugged and waved it away. "Well, if you ever find you're no longer welcome on the *Morganse*, the *Griselle* will always be waiting."

Like one of those feathery-antennaed creatures in the pools sensing every disturbance, she was acutely aware of Thomas beside her. With the creak of leather, the soft rush of his breathing, a mobile mouth that readily smiled, good humored eyes, and a well-honed sense of irony, he was just like...

Cate clamped her lower lip between her teeth. Perhaps the walk had been a mistake; she wasn't ready, not yet. She had thought Brian to be behind her, and yet there he was, right beside her.

"Were you with Nathan when he was shot?" she asked, determinedly taking a new line of thought.

Thomas stiffened, his step slowing. "He's been shot?"

"Twice—at the same time—according to Pryce." The story had haunted her, Pryce's version being long on graphic and short on details.

"No reason to think Pryce would make up such things. Damn!" He swore again more vehemently, thumbing an errant strand of hair behind his ear. "Nathan's had no kind of luck, has he? And yet, I swear he's been charmed his whole life."

"He's alive," she said, in the spirit of finding a positive.

Thomas nodded distractedly, leaving the obvious unspoken: at what price had that survival come?

"His mother was supposed to have been some kind of a seer or some such; maybe she had something to do with that," he said.

"What about his neck?" Cate touched hers in reference to Nathan's gnarled scar.

"His...? Oh, that." Thomas hunched his shoulders and looked to his feet. "No, no, I wouldn't be knowing anything about that."

It was obvious that was the farthest thing from the truth, and that he had no intention of saying otherwise.

They walked and talked of everything and nothing. From the islands interior came the chorus of nightjars and tree frogs. They paused to watch the waxen half-orb of the moon, finally high enough to pull free of the island's jagged outline, and then strolled the now-illuminated shore. It was very late by the time they neared the camp once more, most of the bonfires down to glowing embers. The beach was dotted with low dark humps of sleeping men.

Thomas drew to a halt, doffed his tricorn hat and bowed. "It's been a privilege, madam. It's been a long time since I've had the pleasure of such a lovely lady's company on such a grand night."

She smiled. His flattery was more than a little heart-quickening. It was a wonder why he had saved such charms for taking his leave. He pressed his lips firmly to her hand, his blue eyes intent on hers.

"And I do mean it. If that bloody fool over there ever turns you lose, you just pass the word. No matter where I am on the globe, I'll come for you, and that's a promise." A wink punctuated his pledge. His eyes had a way of looking at someone and holding them, and for a moment, she actually believed him.

Cate watched as Thomas strode away.

Her anger with Nathan surged anew. He had lied about Creswicke and the branding. He had looked her square on and lied.

She chastised herself. Pirate he was, and she needed to remind herself of that smaller than truth fact, trust, perhaps... or not!

Thomas' reaction to her inquiries regarding Nathan's marriage status hadn't been reassuring. More and more, it appeared Nathan's rejection of her was as Pryce had represented: she reminded him of someone. Barring radical disfigurement, her prospects were dim.

Cate picked her way through the sleeping bodies, sprawled

and softly snoring. Her pace slowed at seeing a man's shape separate from the black void of a stack of casks. Fear surged when he moved to intersect her path. Then she gasped with relief at seeing it was Nathan, the rattle of the palms masking the tinkle of his bells.

Her heart warmed, as it did every time she saw him unexpectedly. Filling with a rush of emotions, her first urge was to throw her arms around him, and tell him all would be well. The impulse was cut short at seeing the irregularity in his step and a bottle in his fist. He halted and swayed, the smell of rum reaching well ahead of him. Then she caught a brooding spark in his eye, and her freshly-warmed heart fell cold.

"Have a nice walk?" The biting edge in his voice hit a nerve. It was the same accusing and contemptuous tone she had heard on the road from Lady Bart's and later on the *Morganse*.

"Yes, if you must know, we had a *very* nice walk," she said coldly, brushing past. She didn't appreciate being made to feel like a shepherded lass.

"I suppose you were properly kissed good night," Nathan called to her back.

It was another well-aimed barb: first Harte, and now Thomas.

Annoyance brought her to a halt. Cate wheeled around and braced a hand on her hip. His shirt flared in the pool of moonlight in which he stood. He lifted the bottle with a defiant jerk and took a drink.

"Why would you assume the first time I'm alone with a man, I'd be kissed?" she demanded.

His bells sparked like fireflies as he took several unsteady steps toward her. "That's what I would do. Beautiful night, stars, moon..." A hand lifted in illustration toward the night.

Nathan swayed again. With a bit of effort, he focused on her face, and then fixed on her mouth. "A woman should be kissed. 'Tis what they are suited for."

Cate's heart tripped an odd beat and then resumed as a dull thud in her ears. She wanted to be angry, but her heart prevailed again. For all his brashness, sometimes verging on ribaldry, he had never once made such a flirtatious comment. He had to have done a good deal of drinking in the time she was gone to be so inebriated, more so than ever witnessed, except for one night. Barely a week hence, he had appeared at her bedside, rambling a confusion of concerns and feelings, which had all faded with the effects of drink and daylight.

And now he was in drink again.

The thought of Nathan entertaining such romantic notions made her a bit breathless; the stuff of trite romance novels, to be sure. Any woman knew flirtation when they saw it, but there was an oddness about it, verging on... sincerity or jealousy? Squinting into the moonlight, she tried to see his face—as if Nathan would ever reveal more than intended—but most of it was deep in the shadow of his hat.

He pressed closer as she inched back. She came up against a tree, thankfully, for her knees suddenly gone unreliable.

"You would force yourself on her?" Whether she willed it or no, she was drawn to him, a moth to a flame.

He puffed with indignation. "Categorically not. I've never taken a woman unwilling in me life. Certainly, shan't start now."

She swallowed. "And if, she were willing? What would you do?"

Nathan stood close enough now to smell the rum mingled with his spicy sharpness. His lids hooding his eyes, she felt his gaze travel the line of her shoulder and neck. Surely, he could hear her heart thumping, for it nearly deafened her. Bracing a hand against the tree, he leaned nearer, his braids brushing her chest.

"Persuade her," he purred. The tease in his eyes was countered by a dangerous lilt in his voice.

Her head whirled. She held his eyes with hers, determined not to close them, lest it was a dream—one dreamt a hundred times. She didn't dare think... She didn't dare hope... It was almost as if he had somehow known. Had she cried out in her sleep? Dimly—for lucid thought was becoming nigh impossible—she wondered if he had been watching more closely than credited all these weeks and had known her feelings all along.

Fine tremors coursed through her. Breathing became unnatural, jerky and only with effort. Her heart and body knew what they wanted even if her mind disagreed. Her nails dug into the bark of the tree at her back. That and a fragile thread of doubt the only thing which kept her from flinging herself at him.

"Persuade her, how?" Damn! Her voice shook like she was a mere maiden.

"I'd move close." The graveled voice had gone husky, words of sanded velvet. "And put me hand under her hair and touch her pulse just there."

Cate flinched at the unexpected heat of his hand on her night-cooled flesh. The dark eyes, now mere inches from hers, flickered with uncertainty.

Damn him! He knew he could melt her with a touch. His fingers skimmed her collarbone, her skin glowing in their path. He pressed lightly on the vein just under her jaw. Surely, now he would feel her blood racing, all her best kept-secrets known. His grasp tightened, and she grew dizzy, a faint ringing in her ears.

"Then, I would take her in me arms and put me hand just so." He did so, his hand tracing the curve of her spine. His fingers splayed wide at the small of her back, and her belly tightened. "I'd hold her close, feel her breath come short, so warm."

His eyes still holding hers, Nathan's mouth hovered so very near. The heat of his body radiated through his shirt. A heart drummed in her ears, hers or his?

His fingers brushed her cheek. "And then, I'd turn her face up to mine, touch me lips to hers—" She closed her eyes and parted her lips as his mustache brushed them. "And I'd—"

Nathan stiffened and jerked away as if seared. Blinking, he staggered back like a sleepwalker abruptly awakened. He glared as if she had somehow tricked him.

"That's what I would do, *if* she were willing," he said, with a curt wave.

Cate sagged against the tree, incensed and humiliated. She was no schoolgirl looking for her first kiss! Fury surged, and the stars turned to pricks of red.

"Keep looking, *Captain*." She pushed upright, praying her legs would support her. "Someday, *maybe*, you'll find someone just that willing."

The backs of her eyes stung, and she dashed at the wetness on her cheeks as she stalked away.

Damn him! Damn him!

Seething with mortification, she kicked sand at the glowing coals of their deserted fire. Sparks spiraled into the night's sky. Sensing she was being watched, she whirled. Expecting to find Nathan, she was met with two golden eyes, instead. Roosted in a tree, Artemis's flat owlish face stared back.

"You'll find a nice huge rat just over there!" she snarled, with an angry swipe.

Swearing under her breath, she searched out her quilt from the piles of stores brought ashore. Pausing to dutifully stoke the fire, she threw the wood at it with far more force than was necessary. She knelt to scoop out a makeshift bed, sending the sand in curving spurts behind her, and threw herself into it.

Nathan could be brash and abrasive, but never had he been so cruel, and with pinpoint accuracy, alarmingly so.

The bastard.

She rebelled at the thought of being leashed. His presumption that she would be so wanton as to throw herself into the arms of the first man to come along was vexing. Once again, he sought to control her, watch-dog her every move. When she had agreed to stay, she had known such would be the case, but she hadn't bargained for him asserting himself so soon.

"I managed years on my own—on the worst streets of London, mind—and did very well, thank you very much! I had a damned father and five damn brothers, and I don't need a damned another of either."

She squirmed and huffed.

Yes, but you went into the night with a man you barely met.

Thomas' resemblance to Brian had caused her to throw all caution aside. That little oversight could have been disastrous.

But it wasn't...

But it could have.

As she glared at the flames, cooler thoughts began to prevail and she settled her head more comfortably. There was a chance Nathan's concerns were well-founded. After all, he knew Thomas and what he was capable of far better than she.

"If he was so blessedly concerned, then why didn't he come looking?" she grumbled to the fire.

Perhaps he did, but had gone in the wrong direction, and by the time realized...

"Bull! That was no excuse for being so cruel and taunting..."

Somewhere in that morass of thoughts, she slept.

Sometime later, Cate woke. Eyes rolling, she lay wondering through a sleep-fogged mind what had woken her. Then she heard the soft rumble of male laughter very nearby. Moving her head slightly, she could see Nathan and Thomas through the flames, sitting amiably, a bottle of rum stuck in the sand between them. Their voices were loud enough to be identified, but not so much as to make out their words.

Moving her head, a bit farther, she could see Nathan more fully. His features gilded in a molten glow, his smile was a brilliant slash amid the ebony of mustache and beard. The darkness and distance sanded harsh lines and years from his face, providing a hint of what he might have looked like in his youth. Thomas' presence had taken years off him. Nathan was always quick with a smile, but never had she seen him laugh with such sincerity or seem so at peace.

Still prickling from humiliation, she couldn't help but smile. Their words weren't important. At this hour, they would be speaking of matters which were meant only for the ears of a friend.

Nathan reached for the bottle, and his eyes caught hers.

Uncertainty hung for a moment, and then a corner of his mouth twitched. He winked and turned his attention to Thomas.

Settling deeper in her nest, Cate slept with Nathan's laughter soft in her ears.

⌘

From the corner of his eye, Thomas observed his friend, idly poking a stick at the fire that didn't need tending.

His conversation with Cate had opened Pandora's box. Now, it weighed heavily. It was a matter he kept well-stowed, tucked behind a lifetime of badness. Hell, a full list it was: brutality, violence, shame, regrets, horror, much of which was too vile to revisit. By his years, any man had his share, but living at sea—as a pirate—provided a soul an inordinate supply.

If he had known then what he knew now, he would have physically carried Nathan out of Creswicke's office years ago, kicking and screaming, to be sure. Instead, he had carried Nathan from a stinking pen, naked, beaten, flogged and branded, to a stolen skiff—his first act of piracy—and spirited him away.

He doubted Cate would have believed him, if he had told her a mysterious current had swept the skiff across the waters to an island where none had existed before, and to a strange hovel, with an even stranger woman inside.

At least, he thought it was a woman.

Even now, he shuddered, chilled in spite of the fire. Bordered on evil she did. But she did right by Nathan, hovering over him like a hen over a chick, murmuring all manner of chants and incantations, rattling her cup of bones and bits, anointing him with unspeakable potions. He'd seen many a sorceress in his day, but this one...

He shuddered again. In spite of the woman's spells, Nathan screamed like a tortured man losing his soul, in an agony rooted far deeper than torn flesh. By his judgment, if it hadn't been for the ogress, they would have buried Nathan there.

She sent them away. Several fortnights later, Nathan showed up, big as you please—Never did figure how he knew where we were—with a ship and nearly a full complement of crew. He had only asked once how it came to pass and knew Nathan well enough to know the outlandish tale was the only answer he was going to get.

The first months after, those had been the most difficult for all of them. Nathan was burdened the most, knowing it was his hand which had delivered them to that fate. Garrick had been their savior, showing them the pirate's world. Nathan rose like the proverbial phoenix, and typical Nathan, had thrown himself at the bad situation determined to make it the best. Each day, however, with each piratical deed, Nathan had withered, withdrawing behind beard and hair.

Thomas squinted to the night sky as he tried to recall the last time he had seen Nathan: ten years, at least. He hadn't been prepared for what he saw. He had heard the fantastic tales, believed less than half, but now, was obliged to reconsider. The pirate had devoured him, eaten away the real man, leaving only a façade.

He stared across the fire, in search of the man he remembered. There were glimpses: a look, a turn of phrase, a gesture. But so much was different. The eyes were more haunted. After what Creswicke had done, it didn't seem possible there could be worse, but apparently the Fates had chosen something more for Nathan. Injury, torture, mutiny and death: how much of the tales was one to believe? Miracles of navigation and survival; battle and luck; where did one draw the line?

And now, he was seeing something else, something not seen in decades, but there it was, before his very eyes: Nathan Blackthorne pining over a woman.

Who'd have thought? No one, if they knew only the pirate. Anyone, if they knew the man.

Lounging against a puncheon, Thomas took a swig from the bottle. He looked through the flames to the tousled mahogany head peeking from under the quilt.

"What's in your mind to do with her, Nathan?"

Nathan jerked from his reverie. He followed Thomas's line of sight toward the sleeping form and then cut him a cold look. "Sniffing around, is it?"

Thomas winced. It came as no surprise they would eventually circle around to contentious partings of many years ago.

"That wasn't my idea," Thomas said levelly. "'Twas Camilla's choice."

Nathan snorted. "Tell that to the parrot. Not much I can do," he sighed. "She's married."

Thomas frowned. "That was all by the board before."

Nathan's mouth took a grim twist. "Isn't now."

Fingers drumming on his bent leg, he studied Nathan. Over the years, he had seen Nathan in any number of moods, to all the extremes life could bestow. Broody was a rare trait, defeated unfathomable.

This was strange, very strange.

Aside from the bruises of a recent beating, the fire shadows sharpened Nathan's features, hollowing his eyes and cheeks.

No one ever really knew what was going on in that mind, not anymore. There had been a time, but...

"This one's bad, eh?" he asked.

Nathan nodded, pointedly avoiding Thomas as he took a long pull from the bottle.

"Is this Rebecca bad or Olivia bad?" Thomas pressed further.

Nathan swished the mouthful from side to side, swallowed and croaked, "Worse."

Thomas closed his eyes and dropped his chin to his chest. "Damn, Nathan, I'm sorry. Have you told her? I mean, have you said... anything?"

"Aye," Nathan said, contemplatively tracing patterns in the sand. "Several times."

"And?"

Nathan made a frustrated sound and batted at the sand. "And, she says she wants to be *friends*."

"Ouch! Jesus, Nathan, I'm sorry."

Nathan acknowledged the empathy with a half-lift of one shoulder and a vague nod.

"Is that how you would have it?"

"Hardly me choice," Nathan said sullenly.

Unable to sit still, Nathan rose to fetch several pieces of wood to stoke the fire. He dropped back down on the sand, a shower of sparks spiraling skyward.

He felt Thomas' stare and spread his arms. "What?"

Cate stirred at the sharp sound. Grimacing, Nathan waited. "What would you have me do?" he whispered hoarsely once she had quieted.

"Force the issue."

He shot Thomas a skeptical glare over the flames. "And what if I scare her off? What if she hauls her wind and leaves?"

"She wouldn't."

"Aye, but she would," Nathan said evenly, his shoulders jerking. "Bloody damn near did and but a day since. Damn near jumped ship, too."

"Stop her." He saw the folly in that as soon as he uttered it. With eyes that saw right through a man, Cate didn't strike him as a woman who was readily cowed. Bodily harm would ensue for anyone foolish enough to try to bend her to their will.

Nathan made a disgusted noise and waved the suggestion away. He took a drink and then hunched forward, propping his chin on his knees.

"She still loves him; not much to do about that," Nathan said, staring owlishly into the fire.

"Him?"

"Her husband."

"Oh." Thomas took a drink and wiped his mouth on the back of his hand.

"I swear, if I ever find the bastard, and I will," Nathan emphasized with a stab of his finger, "I'll kill 'im straight away."

Knowing Nathan's bent, it was a credible threat. Conviction or provocation could precipitate such an act, more so of recent, if there was any grain of truth to the stories he'd heard.

Nathan pitched several bits of shell into the fire as his agitation grew. "Any man what takes a woman through war — nigh on to a goddamned hero, as I hear it — and then leaves her to suffer God knows what alone, deserves a blade to the gut. God protect us from noble men," he intoned to the sky.

Thomas frowned but nodded interestedly. It explained a good deal of the woman's hardness — not in the way of coldness, for any man could see an internal fire of spirit and flesh — and wisdom. The woman was a mystery and a wonder.

"And you would never do that, leave her, that is?" Thomas mused.

Nathan twitched. They both knew he had left a good number of women in his wake and not always with a proper taking of his leave.

Nathan swiped away the thought. "That was different... 'cuz she's... she's different."

"Charm her."

Nathan rolled a dubious look from the corner of his eye. "Charm her, how?"

"I don't know, like you always do. Hell, Nathan, I've seen you charm the scales off a fish. Flash her that smile of yours and she'll be clay in your hand."

Nathan's bells — God knew where the hell those things came from! — tinkled when he shook his head in disbelief at Thomas' failure to comprehend the delicacies of the situation. "She's different."

"C'mon, Nathan, if you can't be honest with her or me, at least be honest with yourself for once."

"What's that supposed to mean?"

"I think you know."

"Goddamned taskmaster, aren't you?"

Sputtering like a reprimanded school boy, Nathan pointedly fixed his gaze on the fire. Within seconds, his eyes crept back to find Thomas' still staring. "You know, you remind me of me dear old, aged aunt. You'd best hope your face doesn't freeze like that. Fancy yourself me keeper, eh?"

"Someone needs to; you do a damn poor business of it yourself."

"I've made it this far, haven't I?"

"Aye and how much farther had you been else?"

Nathan held his ire for a moment and then slumped. "Aye, true enough."

Thomas's attention drifted back to Cate's sleeping form once more. The fire sparked gold and orange in the tumble of copper hair. "She's too beautiful to be kept in limbo waiting for no one. If you've designs, fair enough. But if not, you'd oblige me to say as much and step aside."

Jaw working, Nathan's gaze settled on her and lingered with a sudden tenderness. "Sad thing is she hasn't the slightest idea the effect she has on men. All she need do is look at you with those cursed eyes and…"

"And what?"

"And, nothing." Nathan picked up a bit of driftwood and hurled it into the fire. "That's what happens: nothing."

Nathan turned into himself, mired deep in his own murk. Silence fell; the fire's hiss the only sound between them.

"So, I've wore 'round to my original question," Thomas said at length. "Put a name on what you're at with her?"

Snatching up the bottle from at his feet, Nathan meditatively rolled it between his hands. At length, he took a drink then blew a tired exhale. "Only one thing I can do: keep her safe, until I can find her husband."

Now there was a novelty: finding a husband?

Thomas's mouth sagged. "Safe, as on the *Morganse* safe? You think it's safe out here?"

"Well, it's safer than anywhere else. Well, it is," he bristled at Thomas' dubious guffaw.

Thomas burst out a laugh, only to clap a hand over his mouth when Cate stirred.

"Sure, Nathan," he whispered, still fizzing with mirth. "You just keep believing that. What makes you so sure she wants to find her husband?"

Nathan gave him a level look from under his brows. "She. Still. Loves. Him."

"I wouldn't be so sure. I could have sworn I saw something different, but you'd know better than I. You'd best be careful with her, Nathan. That woman could wipe the decks with your carcass."

Nathan snorted. "As well I know!"

Cate woke again much later. The moon had set. The air had the feel of being nearer to day than night. The fire was down to mere coals, glimmering red-hot under their blanket of ash. Aside from the rattle of palm fronds, the rush of surf on the reef, and the snoring of over three hundred celebration-worn men, the beach was still.

Twisting her head around, she was startled to find a dark form laying barely an arm's length away. Peering closer, she saw it was Nathan. Sprawled on his stomach, braids snarled about his shoulders, an arm pillowed his head. Hearing the throaty rasp of his breathing, she resisted the urge to touch him. Instead, she enjoyed the connection that came with seeing him sleep. Like the coals, her anger had burned out. She sought to rekindle it, but found she couldn't. Irritated and annoyed, yes, but angry at him, no. It had been Nathan being Nathan. How could she expect anything more?

As she turned, something caught her eye. Next to her head, her shoes sat neatly arranged. She looked back, half-expecting to see Nathan watching, but he remained asleep. And so, she settled back into her quilt-lined nest and did the same.

17: HOT BATHS

THE NEXT TIME CATE WOKE was not so delicate. She was jerked into the new day by a blaze of sunlight in her eyes, and Mr. Hodder's expostulations—one which would cause many a woman to blush—in her ears. At first thinking she was still aboard, she burrowed deeper under the blanket. At last able to assimilate her whereabouts, she peeked like a turtle from its shell. It was no surprise to find Nathan already gone, a faint depression in the sand his only trace.

The beach was alive with activity. Absent were many of the usual sounds of morning—the grind of holystones, pounding of feet to breakfast, or the hails from the tops as the day sails were bent or reefs shaken out—but enough was present to lend an air of normalcy. Pryce could be heard in full vent, prodding some poor unfortunate deemed too laggardly. A baleful complaint came from Hermione. Beatrice was having a bit of her morning parroty say, her vulgarities blending seamlessly with those from the human's. It led one to wonder what a contended parrot sounded like, or if finding her a companion might sweeten her disposition. In that there was, of course, the risk of two irascible birds.

Cate pushed up and knocked the hair from her face in time to see Nathan striding toward her. Sash jouncing at his knees, his attention was fixed on the steaming mug he bore.

"I give you joy o' the morning, luv," Nathan declared brightly as he folded down to the sand next to her. "I assured Mr. Kirkland I would see you got this the instant you showed a leg. Upon me word, the man takes your thirsts as a personal challenge. He represents to have put cinnamon in it. Have a care. It's hot."

He held out the mug for her to inhale the aromatic brew, and then carefully sip. His warning was needless. Kirkland's pride in the temperature of anything produced in his galley was well-known, his coffee ready to blister the first unsuspecting soul.

"It's wonderful. Have you had yours, yet?" Cate asked as she arranged herself more comfortably and took the cup.

Nathan nodded as he watched her drink. "Oh, aye, before the sun was o'er the gun'n'l. Could use another bit, though; can't seem to hit me stride yet." He blinked widely in example.

She held the cup out in invitation. At first, he refused, but then relented. They spent the next while sitting in companionable silence, sharing and observing the flurry of activity on the beach. As soon as the mug was empty, Nathan passed the word for another. Ordinarily, she would have been reluctant to infringe her needs on others, but somehow on that particular morning, sitting next to Nathan, she was content to be waited upon.

She waited with considerable apprehension for Nathan to say something about the night before, but he blithely ignored it to the point she wondered if he remembered. Perhaps, he had been more in drink than thought, or it was just the Captain of Denial in full command of his realm.

They were nearly to the bottom of the second cup, when she realized they had been carrying on an entire conversation and not a word was spoken, a tip of the head, a gesture, the quirk of a mouth, or the cock of an eyebrow communicating every thought.

It was Thomas who finally interrupted their amiable silence.

"Good morning!" he chimed as he crossed the beach. Barely acknowledging Nathan, his full attention fixed on Cate. "Just as lovely under the morning sun as she is under the light of the moon!"

Shielding a hand to the sun, she looked up smiling. "And just as good a liar in the light as he is in the dark,"

Thomas laughed loudly enough to cause several of the nearby hands to give pause. Nathan's cheerfulness faded as he darted suspicious looks between them.

"I thought we'd linger here for the day, Nathan," Thomas said. "We need to water and wood, as well. Allow us the day, and we'll ride the evening tide to take our position abaft the Straits."

Still casting sharp-eyed looks between them, Nathan nodded distractedly.

"We'll be setting the kedges and making ready," Nathan announced at last and rose. "We've every reason to believe our prey should pass within the day or next."

"Fair enough. Much to do." Thomas removed his hat and swept a bow. "M' lady."

"What's he got to be so cheerful about this morning?" Nathan muttered, watching as Thomas strode away.

"Maybe he has a particular relish for mornings," she suggested lightly, hovering over her drink.

Nathan twisted around to peer suspiciously down the sharp edge of his nose at her. "Maybe he had an extra good night."

She batted her eyes with exaggerated innocence over the mug's rim. "Why Captain Blackthorne, whatever are you implying?"

Narrowing one eye threateningly, a precursor to a retort, he suddenly brightened. "I've a surprise."

"What?" Skepticism seemed the better part of valor, at the moment.

"Have no cares," he replied, with a flip of his hand. "Allow me to attend to a few matters with Pryce, and we'll aweigh."

He scurried off, hailing the First Mate. Coffee finished, Cate rose, wincing. Romantic as it might sound, sleeping on a beach did not provide the best night's repose. Sand was surprisingly hard and had a nasty trait of shifting into shapes unaccommodating to the body.

Cate was rigging a drying rack for the herbs collected the day before—a task slowed by being obliged to pause to scratch Hermione's head every time she was butted on the hip—when Nathan found her next. A haversack over his shoulder, he hooked her by the arm and led her away, snagging up the quilt as they passed. He resolutely declined to offer a hint as to their destination, answering her inquiries with no more than a dramatic roll of the eyes.

Down the shore a short way laid a broad creek which they followed inland. It was early in the day, but the walk was still warm. On New Providence, she had been a distracted observer of the new world before her. And yesterday, she had been too preoccupied. Now, following Nathan, braids swinging with his bobbing gait, she walked in open-mouthed amazement.

Going from the saturated blues of sky and water to the vibrant greens almost hurt the eyes. There were vines as thick as an arm and head-high ferns, and trees whose towering heights dwarfed the *Morganse's* masts. Each step brought the damp, earthy smell of fallen leaves and dying vegetation, which mingled with wafts from the flowers, at times so heady and sweet as to nearly bowl one over. Cate kept close on Nathan's heels; a few paces too far apart, and she feared losing sight of him. The going wasn't rough, but the footing did require constant attention.

Cate wondered what had brought Nathan to this sudden urge to go off into the jungle when there seemed to be so much else to occupy his time and mind. It could have been an innocent desire to show her some local point of interest, or a gesture of atonement for his behavior the night before. The latter seemed highly unlikely; fits of conscious wasn't his burden. Her moonlight walk with Thomas was another possible motivation. Out-of-hand, she ruled that out, outright jealousy an even less natural state.

The terrain took an increasingly upward slope. In spite of the canopy of shade, the atmosphere was heavy and still. Wiping the sweat from her face, Cate kept climbing, accepting Nathan's hand to navigate rock tumbles or steep banks.

"A bit more," was her only hint, as he stood in a nearly knee-deep creek to hoist her from one bank.

A patch of brilliance in the verdant shadows finally came into view: the sun's reflection on the surface of a broad pool. Flat rocks stair-stepped down at random angles to form a natural basin. The pristinely clear water made the depth deceptive; it could have been a few inches, it could have been several feet to the crystalline glitter of the black sand bottom. As she came closer, her nose was met with the sharp smell of sulfur.

"Well," Nathan exclaimed, spreading his arms out. "Here 'tis!"

"It's beautiful. How did you ever find this?"

He gestured with the bearded point of his chin. "Stick your finger in."

Kneeling down, Cate dipped her hand in and jerked back. "It's hot."

"Aye. Hot springs, from the volcanoes."

"Around here?" She looked, half-expecting to see lava flowing through the greenery.

"Oh, aye. The Caribbean is full of them; most every one of these islands is some kind of a volcano, either now or before. These springs abound. I thought you might appreciate the chance at a hot bath." He grinned, his eyes sparkling with anticipation.

"I'd love it."

"Have a care. Go in here and you'll be boiled to the bone." He put out a warning arm and then pointed to a waterfall at one end. Barely waist high, it gurgled over a multi-tiered tumble of the rocks. "Go in over there. The falls cool it a bit; you'll be able to linger."

"Oh, Nathan!" She threw her arms around his neck and kissed him on the cheek. Her cheeks burning with embarrassment, she stepped away. "Thank you," she said considerably subdued.

"No worries," he mumbled, waving a dismissive hand. "God knows why anyone would want a hot bath in this foundering heat, but..."

He shifted on his feet and cleared his throat. "There's a fair stand of fern over there, if you'd wish a bit o' privacy. I'll be... I'll just be over there."

Nathan moved to a respectable distance. Turning his back, he folded his hands behind his back and rocked on his heels, while whistling a nondescript tune. She undressed behind the indicated ferns and slipped into the water.

The water at the hotter end had been clear, but the water tumbling over the falls was tinged brownish-green, making the depth of the ledges deceptive. She crept in, lurching in unexpected shallows and stumbling in surprising depths, until her toes sunk into the sandy bottom. A champagne-like effervescence of tiny bubbles boiled up, giving off minute bursts of sulfur as they broke the surface.

She dived to the bottom and hung like a trout on a hot summer's day, and then pushed up, surfacing with an explosion of air.

"Oh, Nathan, this is heavenly."

"I imagined you'd fancy it," he called from amid the greenery.

"Why don't you come in?"

He chuckled. "Can't pass up the prospect of cleaning the whole world, can you?"

"One must have their dreams," Cate mused. Leaning her head back, she swished her hair from side to side, the heat brushing her temples. "C'mon. It's wonderful."

"No... I think not."

"C'mon," she urged, treading water. "I'll stay here, and you can come in over there. It's plenty deep; no one will see anything."

"You'll look." Now he was being coquettish.

"I had five brothers and was married; I've seen everything and far too many times over."

"I'm shy." Nathan's path could be tracked by glimpses of his headscarf through the leaves as he made his way around to the far side.

"Oh, come now. Modesty from a pirate? How many women have you undressed in front of, Captain? What's one more?"

His mutterings and flashes of movement revealed he was shedding his clothes. "Turn 'round."

"Oh, very well." She sighed and did so, closing her eyes for good measure. "I had no idea you were such a prude."

A splash marked his entry into the pool, a sputter when he broke the surface. Not wishing to injure his pride, she kept her eyes closed while she blissfully floated, shivering with delight as the heat swirled through her joints. Over the years—and yes, it had been years—of dreaming of a hot bath, it had involved visions of endless luxuriant soaking.

Tired but unwilling to leave, Cate found a place where she could sit on the rocks and still be immersed to her neck. Modesty was never her burden, but feeling her breasts bobbing, she was relieved to see her hair fanned out enough to cover her. In the discolored water, the rest of her body was but an amorphous blur.

A surge of water against her calves was a precursor of Nathan's arrival. His head broke the surface sleek as a seal at her knee.

"How is it?" He beamed with boyish anxiousness.

"It's heavenly. The water feels like it's alive." The small stirrings of bubbles had felt like tickling little fingers.

"Aye, that would be the spirit of the spring." He swiped the dripping water from his face. His lean arms braced on the rocky ledge, his braids coiled like water snakes around his shoulders.

"The natives say the bubbles are the breath of the gods of the underworld. Bloody rotten breath, I'd say." He cast a disdainful glare toward the sulfur-laden corner. "Anyway, they believe it's the breath of life."

"How can the gods of death give you life?"

"Trifles, darling," he declared with a flick of his fingers. The bells in his mustache sparked in the sunlight. "Don't argue with the powers, luv, just bide and reap the benefits."

"I hadn't realized how much I missed hot water. Come to think on it, I can't remember the last time I had a hot bath."

"'Tis yours for as long as you desire." Nathan pushed off from the ledge. The tattoos at his neck and chest were distorted by the wavelets as he tread. He gestured with his head toward the path which they had taken. "Mind, I'd rather not navigate yon hill in the dark, but the day is yours, luv."

Arching sideways, he dove out of sight in a flash of brown breeches. Perched on her rock, Cate visually followed his image as he cavorted like an otter, his bells twinkling in the bands of sunlight. He shot off to a corner and then curved back. Spouting to the surface, he swam several passes before submerging again. He circled the bottom and rose once more at her knee.

Nathan grinned, droplets of water diamond-like in the ebony of his lashes and mustache. "I believe I've never seen you smile so grand."

"It doesn't require that much."

"Not *that* much, but rare difficult. You deserve all the fineries what could ever be bestowed."

"I've been fairly happy since I've been on the *Morganse*," Cate said in all earnestness.

Nathan beamed and then sobered. "T'would be better if we could dispense with that *fairly* bit."

"A feast fit for a queen, a romantic fire on the beach, coffee in bed, and now a hot bath; you're going to spoil me."

Nathan's eyes held hers, as deep and luminous as the pool itself. "One can only hope."

He pushed back and disappeared to the depths. Arms sweeping at his sides, he swept off around the rocks. A slosh of water marked his exit.

Reluctant to leave the blissful heat, she slipped off the rock and sank to the bottom, spiraling up only when the need for air required. The heat, however, began to take its toll, her limbs going loose-jointed and heavy.

"C'mon, luv!" Nathan stood on shore, his voice muffled by the quilt held before him. Peering over the top, he shook it in offering. "Let's get you wrapped up before the meat is boiled off."

Cate rose from the pool and her legs buckled. Nathan adroitly caught her in the quilt as she crumpled. Bracing her up, he guided her to a sun-dappled spot amid the ferns and moss. Lowering her in the patch-worked envelope, he knelt in the greenery next to her.

"I'm as wobbly as a new colt," she giggled.

"Stay wrapped or you'll take a chill. Give yourself a few minutes," he said, chafing her legs between his hands. "Get the blood going again and you'll do."

Jelly-limbed and flushed with heat, Cate lay as Nathan fetched her clothing and spread them on the grass nearby. From the haversack, he produced a stoneware bottle, cold roasted meat wrapped in leaves and discs of flat, unleavened bread from the *Griselle's* cook fires. His shirttail haphazardly stuffed into his waistband, he sat cross-legged before her blue-and-yellow cocoon and fed her bits of meat and bread.

With his arms resting on his legs, she noticed there were tattoos encircling his ankles. Their pattern was identical to the woad-colored ones at his wrists and neck, a complicated chain-like interweaving, very reminiscent of Highland designs.

"Where were you born, Nathan?"

He jerked at the unexpected question, but answered amiably. "Dover."

"England?"

A vague nod was his answer.

"Pryce said you were conceived in a tempest and born in a maelstrom."

Nathan grinned crookedly, the asymmetrical bells in his mustache drawing nearly level, as he did whenever he was self-conscious. "Good story, isn't it?"

"And the real story?"

He gave her an amber and cinnamon look as he considered how much to tell.

"Mum was Black Celt, but born in England; some said she had the way of the Ancient Ones about her, as did her mother before her. Her father was a merchant; imports from the Indies and thereabouts. When she was seventeen, he took her on a purchasing trip to see the world. She met me father then."

"He was a pirate?"

"No." Nathan was amused by the thought. He popped a piece of meat in his mouth, licking the juices from between his fingers. "A seaman, though. By the time they returned to England, she was with child and her family disowned her. Me father lingered long enough to see me born and then was aweigh."

"Didn't he ever come back?"

"Oh, aye," he said with a half-smile around the mouthful. "Three visits, three proofs."

"Did they marry?" Cate regretted the question as soon as she asked. The shortcomings of a parent were rarely an easy thing for a child to admit, no matter the age.

"No." Nathan took no such umbrage. "Once—when I did inquire—she just said something about 'finally home' and that was all," he said, resigned to the vagaries of a sailor's lifestyle.

He fed her another bite of meat and bread, wiping his fingers on his pant leg.

"You have brothers and sisters? You've never made mention," she said.

"Aye, two brothers and a sister. Nothing to be gained in making mention; I haven't seen either of the boys for years, and me sister died near twenty years ago."

A shadow crossed his face as he chewed. The shoulders of his shirt were darkened by his wet hair. The neck gapped open to reveal the banner emblazoned with "Freedom" over his heart.

"Father left money the few times he came, but there was never enough and, what with four bastards, Mum's family wouldn't help her..." Nathan fondled a bit of bread, the corner of his mouth tucked up in disgust. At length, he shook himself free of that line of thought.

"Finally, she obtained a position as a chambermaid on an estate in the country. Lord Horatio Sidwell," he announced grandly. "Life was good there: plenty to eat, warm beds and lots of country to play in." He smiled, his distant gaze growing soft. "Mum actually laughed during that time."

Pulling the cork, he helped Cate to a drink from the bottle. It was filled with yesterday's rum punch. Compared to the heat of the day and the pool, it was refreshingly cool. As delicious as before, time had allowed the flavors to mellow further, the fruitiness overshadowing the spices.

"One day, Mum suddenly announced that we were leaving," he said, popping the cork back into place. "I think there was a falling out of some kind, between Mum and Lady Sidwell. I recall a lot of shouting. Indiscretions, as it were. Unfounded poppycock really, but we left, nonetheless. She had enough money to buy us all passage to the Indies, in search of me father."

"I loved it!" Nathan hunched forward, his long toes curling with excitement. "The ship, the sea; something had always called, I just hadn't known what. Mum said the Old Ones told her I was born for it. Rather figured, I thought," he added dryly, "seein's how me sire was a sailor, but she put great store in it."

Cate forbore asking what his mother had meant by "Old Ones." Living in the Highland, a land of isolation and strong superstitions, "old ones" came in spirit and living forms, often a fine line separating the two.

"Oh! Umm... a little... something...!" Nathan rummaged in the bag and brought out a small piece of lightweight canvas. Unfolding it, he drew out a length of knotted cord. Cate inwardly groaned, dreading another knot lesson. Surely not now!

"Wrist, if you please," he said.

He waited as she worked a hand free. Jelly-limbed as she was, finding her hand was almost too much to ask, let alone move it. Ultimately, she produced one, the left, as it turned out. He passed the bracelet around, his fingers brushing the underside's tender skin as he affixed it with an intricate knot. It was identical to her necklace, except the ends were long, and adorned with bits of shell, beads and tiny silver medallions.

"But why...?" She asked, fingering it.

Nathan rubbed his finger thoughtfully along the side of his nose and finally said, "The *Morganse* desired you to have it."

There was no part of that which she believed, and yet couldn't find the words to point that out.

"Somehow, I think Mum thought she would find him, somehow," Nathan said, resuming his story, an obvious effort to change the subject. "What little money we had ran out quickly. She started taking odd jobs, taverns and laundry and such, while I took to fishing or stealing whichever came first to help keep us fed."

He drew his fingers meditatively along the drooping curve of his mustache, his eyes darkening. "Eventually, Mum took to whoring. It paid better than the other work," he said pragmatically, "'though I don't think it was any easier on her. I was left to watch the little ones."

He helped Cate to another drink, took a long one of his own, and then stretched out next to her. Cradling his head in his linked hands, he exhaled deeply several times and rocking in languid contentment. As he gazed up into the trees, his chin was lifted enough to reveal the jagged scar at his throat.

"I was too young to really know what was going on, but I knew enough to know it wasn't right," he said to the branches overhead. "I could see it in Mum's eyes; hear it in her voice when she'd ask me to take the younguns away for a bit. One night, I came back early, caught some drunken bastard beating her. Ran him through the leg with his own sword, I did. Then he started after me."

"Did he beat you?" Cate gaped.

Nathan lifted one shoulder in a dismissive shrug. "Na, he was too drunk; between Mum and me, we chased him off." He sobered. His mouth pressed into a grim line. "Other times, I wasn't there; I'd come home in time to help wash the blood from her face."

Her heart pinched at the desperate picture he painted. "Did she ever find your father?"

"No," he said, with a distant look that revealed his mother hadn't suffered that failure alone. "Heard about him a few times over the years, but she never found him."

"Sometime along about then," Nathan said, brightening, "she met up with a man named Beecher; a customer he was, I think... originally."

A walnut eye peered over his arm and narrowed. "Now there was a pirate. Buggering, old, spawn o' the devil, he was." He swore. "He took a special liking to Mum; took us all in, found us a decent place to live—better than the shack, as I recall, at any rate."

"How old were you then?"

"Umm, eleven or twelve." Nathan shifted, arranging himself more comfortably. "Beecher-treated us like we were his own—and was good to Mum. I should have been more grateful."

"Except?" she asked, picking up the lilt in his voice.

His shoulder twitched as he avoided her gaze. "Except, I took exception to him; thought he was trying to be me father. Since I already had one..." His throat moved as he swallowed. "Then one day, Beecher announced he was taking us all away. Seemed like a great adventure, at the time. I always wanted to go to sea, again; I'd loved the trip from England so much, I couldn't wait for the next time."

"Except?"

A smile quirked a corner of his mouth, pleased by her quickness.

"The bile-laden, old blighter decided to make an example of me. Granted, I was wild and filled with rebellion, by then," he conceded reluctantly. "He tried to bring me some discipline; a few times it caused arguments between him and Mum. The other two boys were too young to remember Father, and took to Beecher, but not me; I was determined that the scabrous bastard wasn't going to replace him. Maybe he thought that seein's how I wanted to go to sea, he'd teach me a lesson, or something, I don't know," he said, shaking his head, as if still baffled. "He made the trip every kind of hell imaginable."

"Did you learn anything?"

A large flock of orange and yellow parrots flying over, chattering and squawking momentarily distracted him.

"About ships and sailing, everything, aye. About Beecher?" Nathan asked, angling his head toward her, pursing his lips. "Just that I didn't want to be around him, the old barracuda. Then, we finally arrived at Matelotage Isle."

"Where?"

"Matelotage Isle," he repeated, each syllable with a hiss of disgust. Too agitated to be still, he sat up, bits of moss and twigs clinging to the damp linen of his shirt. "A delicate sounding name for the damnedest, most godforsaken, wretched place me young eyes had ever seen."

With a derisive snort, he shook his head in dismay. "A place that's on the way to everywhere, but near to nothing. But, ah!" Nathan said displaying a warning finger, "you'll not find it on any map. It's a place where pirates go, when nowhere else will have them."

He reached for the bottle and took a drink.

Cate struggled to imagine the place he described. "A pirate penal colony?"

"Hardly, but of sorts," he said, setting the cork with his palm. "There's the ones what are too tired, but not so tired as to die. And there's the ones what are too lowly and vile to be had anywhere else, including Hell."

"Sounds rather hellish."

"An understatement, to be sure. Such a place would need someone from the right hand of Satan to rule it, and that would be none other than Beecher."

"And that's where he took you?"

"Like he was delivering us to the Garden of Eden," he said grimly.

"I thought I heard once of a place something like that near Africa."

"Madagascar? A pirate haven to be sure. Ranter Bay, Fort Dauphin and Isle Sainte Marie; Baldridge, Welsh, Samuel and Plantain had their share of running it, Ol' Avery and Tew sailed out of it, but that was nigh a half century ago."

A hand clenched a fist on his leg. "I hated that place," he rasped, with a soul-felt vehemence. "Every variety of degradation you could imagine was there, and Hell-hound Beecher was the Master of it all."

Nathan's eyes closed as he fought to quell the memories. When they opened again, he cautiously glanced sideways to see if she were looking. A blush rose from the collar of his shirt as he averted his gaze overhead.

"Shortly after we arrived, Beecher announced he was going on a venture and I was to go with him. I begged Mum to allow me to stay, but she insisted, sayin' as it would be good for me, a chance to meet me calling and go to sea under the guidance of an expert." He heaved a long sigh and added, grimly: "Took me first *and* second flogging on that voyage."

"He flogged you?"

He gave a rueful smile as he stretched out on the grass once again, one knee bent. "Became a bit recalcitrant I did, I expect. He had to make an example of me, and he did. I swear he enjoyed every stroke of it. First time, it was two strokes—just with the lash—and second time, it was five with the cat. Bloody unpleasant on a scrawny, bony back. Taught me I never wanted to be a pirate, that's for bloody damned sure. I hated every one of those men with a passion what penetrated clear to me bones."

"Where's your mother now?"

"Dead." The answer was blunt, but laden with loss. "Shortly after we returned, she died in childbed with Beecher's. I remember crouching in the corner, hiding behind a chair, listening to her scream. There was so much blood." Nathan's eyes clamped shut as he bit his lower lip. "I hated him even the more. Shortly after, I left, stowed away; swearing I'd never go back to that hell hole and never to sink as low," he added vehemently.

An awkward silence fell between them as the irony and tragedy of that twisted in the air. She sought in vain for something to say which wouldn't sound like hollow platitudes.

Unable to witness his pain any further, Cate swallowed hard and asked, "Then what?"

"I stowed away on a merchant, and I've been at sea ever since," Nathan finished lightly, as if announcing the "happily ever after" ending to a child's story.

"Have you ever seen your father?" As contentious as her relationship had been with her father, she still couldn't imagine never having one.

Re-crossing his ankles, he re-situated his head on his hands.

"No, never have. Not bloody likely, either. The sea claims many a soul and no one the wiser. Maybe I'll run into him in the hereafter, whatever that is," he finished on a slightly brighter note.

"And your brothers?"

"Charles and Michael?" His jaw twisted sideways as he considered. "Last time I saw them, they were standing at the end of the wharf at Matelotage, waving goodbye."

Having said more than intended, Nathan withdrew into himself, and faded from the poolside glen to somewhere distant, where he wrestled with awakened ghosts. He possessed the maddening ability to stretch out and be comfortable anywhere, from a beach to the tar-caked deck of a ship. His eyelids grew heavy and drooped, and his breath slowed. An infinitesimal sigh and he was asleep.

Nathan's head lolled toward Cate, his hair a spidery black tangle about his head and shoulders. The furrows between his brows smoothed and his lips parted slightly, blowing out gently with each breath.

The heat of the pool glowing inside like a small furnace, Cate fondled her new bracelet as she studied him, as she so often did. It was a rare opportunity to see him near and so still. There was a time, not that long ago, when she had only seen him as the total man. Now he was the sum of dozens of little oddities and details: the small scar at his temple that ran up into his hairline; the clump of three bright copper hairs in his beard at the corner of his mouth, or the single silver one in his left brow. The hooks at the corner of his mustache, the ones she had seen lift the corners of his mouth into a smile so many times, were not a matter of trimming, but a natural phenomenon. Under his mustache, his mouth tended to curve downward from its sharply-peaked center, giving him a certain somber sadness when at rest. At the moment, however, it drew up at the corners in a faint smile. His right hand rose and fell where it rested on his stomach. She could see again the severed ends of the last two fingertips, the nail corners nicked away.

Cate resisted the urge to touch him, trace the curve of his lip, run her fingers through the ebony mat of hair at the opening of his shirt, or touch the vein throbbing at the base of his neck. She rolled toward him as near as she dared and inhaled. Amid the crushed grass and the pool's sulfur, there was the smell of him, with the ever-present undertone of cinnamon, orange oil and rum.

Dampened shirt clinging to his body, in his own barbaric way, Nathan was beautiful in spite of the lingering effects of the beating he had taken. Barefoot, fine-boned and elegant, he bore a heretofore unseen innocence, as if allowing her to see his truth. He slept, and therefore was saved from facing rejection, if she chose not to accept him. Lying there amid the moss and fern, dappled by the lacy shadows of the leaves, he could have been a creature of the forest, but the sea wouldn't relinquish its grip, as proven by the swallows on his knuckles and tattoo over his heart.

Cate still stung with the mortification and hurt of the night before. The wall between them seemed a brick higher. Looking at the thick fan of lashes — copper-tipped by the sun, long and curving to the point of almost girlish — she wondered what it was which allowed him to be so malicious and cruel one minute, and so boyish and attentive the next.

Numbness was going to have to become a permanent state of being, if she was to be around him. She was learning how to keep her heart locked away, and to desensitize herself against the constant barrage of heart-stopping moments, when her breath caught and pulse raced. She had found a small corner in which to keep her heart, close enough so that, if the occasion should arise, it could be readily retrieved, and yet not so convenient as to be inadvertently exposed. It meant living a half-existence, wooden and cold, the feelings she had thought to be essential, now dangerous liabilities.

She contemplated the risk of throwing herself at him, right there, right now. Only fear of the devastation of being repulsed stopped her. Restraint meant there was always a chance; succumbing could mean all hope would be lost.

The gnarled scar at Nathan's neck called to mind the one on her shoulder blade. She could feel the thickened slab pressing when she thought about it. Time did have its benefits: the pain had long passed, though some days the bone beneath ached. She moved her hand under the quilt to her stomach and lightly traced the network of scars there. Most were but hairlines, though some were nearly the width of her little finger. Older than the one on her back, these were from another time, another place.

So much damage; proof time couldn't heal everything.

Limp of limbs, with no strength or inclination to move, she closed her eyes and dreamed of seals in bathtubs afloat with pirate ships.

It was late afternoon by the time Cate and Nathan returned to the shore, the sun a torrid globe a hand's breadth above the island's jagged backbone.

Much had changed in their absence. The pirates were striking camp.

With the fresh water casks filled, firewood loaded, and the galley beams hanging with fresh game, the two ships collected their crews like mother hens calling back their chicks. It was a slow process, men and provisions incrementally returning in longboats and makeshift barges.

The *Morganse's* decks were astir with stores to be loaded, and with what Nathan explained as exchanging her Number One anchor for kedges, lighter, and therefore, more readily retrieved, a significant advantage for a ship lying in wait. The Griseller's operated under the pressure of time: if they were to keep to their Captain's plan, it was necessary for them to win her anchors, clear the bay, cross the Straits and settle to lie in wait while there was still enough light. Even in Arabic, there was no mistaking the bawl of her boatswain and his mates, urging the men to their tasks.

Cate bore a hand with packing stores and loading boats. In between, she sat on a storm-cut ledge of sand, blotting the sweat from her face. Nathan and Thomas stood at the water's edge, arms crossed, intermittently interrupting their conversation to bark orders. Aided by the breeze, they were near enough that she could hear them detailing their attack plan, spoken in a tongue known only to mariners. It was a fascination how two men could communicate so much with so few words. A nod, a grunt, a shrug, a lift of two fingers, not to be confused with that of three, and volumes were spoken.

Business complete, Nathan dropped cross-legged in the sand next to her.

"We'll hold off until the last boat. I thought you might desire to remain ashore as long as possible."

"Firm ground has felt wonderful." Cate leaned to adding in a lower voice, "But hot water felt even better."

Nathan ducked his head, grinning shyly. "'Tis pleasing to hear."

"You think the ship will pass so soon?"

He surveyed the offing with a one-eyed squint. "Aye. A premonition, but a strong one."

"Then what?"

He pursed his lips and counted off on his long, ring-laden

fingers: "Deliver the ransom note, arrangement for an exchange and hide the hostage, until said exchange."

Cate winced at the word "hostage." She had been—and for all that matter, could still be—a hostage. It was an uncomfortable word, with connotations she was disinclined to explore.

"Will Creswicke pay?" The mere mention of the man's name gave her a sense of creeping evil.

"Oh, aye," Nathan said with emphatic satisfaction. His arms came to rest on his bent knees. "He'll pay, if for no other than the simple reason he can't bear the thought of telling anyone she was taken, let alone taken by me."

"What will he do then? I mean, after he's gotten her back?"

His chuckle was heavily tinged with anticipation. "Everything in his power to catch us... catch me, that is."

Nathan shook his head and smiled crookedly. "I pity anyone around him for the next while. He's going to be insufferably insufferable. And he'll do everything in his power to wreak his revenge."

"On you?"

"Who else?" He spread his arms in a prideful display, more like a boy bragging on toppling the neighbor's privy.

"You don't like each other, do you?"

"Not much," he said indifferently. "One does have to admire a dedicated enemy."

"Thomas told me some of it," Cate said carefully, worried of possibly breaking a confidence.

Nathan twisted around. One brow arched in derision "He did now? Rotting ol' looby never could keep a stopper on his gob. Not as smart as he thinks his is, however."

She waited. The lilt in his voice suggested there was indeed far more.

"There's more?" she eventually prompted.

He squirmed, leaning away. "'Tis nothing. Trifles. Inconsequential indiscretions."

"Apparently not, at least in Creswicke's mind." Cate inclined her head into his line of sight. "What did you do, Nathan?"

He twitched, fingers drumming a tattoo on his leg.

"Nathan, what happened?"

He shifted on his rear. Clearing his throat, he gave a wobbling smile. "Well... I might... just *possibly*," he clarified, holding up a cautionary finger, "may have..." His voice faded; his throat moving as he gulped. "I may have bedded his mother," he finally blurted.

Her mouth fell unbecomingly open. "What?" Cate cried with a force which caused several of the men to turn and look.

"How was I supposed to know?" he said, sounding even more like that privy-tipping schoolboy.

Stricken speechless, her mouth moved like a fish for air. "The name would have been a hint."

"All I knew was Lady Arthur, or Anthony, or one of those 'A' names. Bloody royals and their pompous falderal!"

For all his amatory escapades—which were legion, to be sure—this one seemed particularly insidious, perhaps due only to the severity of its consequences. She had never thought of him capable of being that scheming and insensitive. Inconsequential, indeed.

"Nathan, how could you?"

"Allow me to point out, in me own defense, that she never said. I had no idea who she was, so it didn't count, not really. There *is* something to be said about the older ones," he sighed wistfully.

"Apparently it counted to Creswicke. No wonder he was so angry. Obviously he found out. Did he catch you?"

"Not *that* time."

"There's more?" Her jaws were beginning to ache.

"Very well, if you must." Nathan heaved a long-suffering sigh. "I bedded his sister."

Cate groaned and slapped her forehead.

"Lovely, plump little thing she was, fair of hair and blue-eyed," he said with a blissful lilt. He sobered, his jaw twisting aside. "At least, I think that was her."

"Why am I hoping that you're lying?" she said into her hands.

"As God is me witness," he intoned, extending a palm to the sky.

"Somehow I don't think He would care to witness this. Was this before or after Creswicke's mother?"

"After. Decidedly and most certainly, after."

Cate arched her eyebrows expectantly while Nathan examined his fingernails.

"Fight ensued," he finally relented. "I emerged victorious, of course."

"A fight? A sword fight?" The initial shock waning, she was beginning to follow his train of thought—a convoluted and dizzying ride, to be sure.

"Had to defend me honor."

"*Your* honor. What about the sister's?"

His pride deflated at that. "Turned out she was working her way through the alphabet of Company captains. The perverse wench started at Z; the B's came at the last."

Cate braced her head in her hands and groaned again. "So that's why Creswicke hates you so much."

"Could be… part of it… maybe."

She gave him a narrow look. "There's more?"

He hesitated then a slow smile grew. "During the fight, I may have wounded… nicked him." Illustrating with two barely parted fingers, he wrinkled his nose. "Just a bit."

"*May have?*"

"Certainly, was a lot of blood."

"Where…?" She stopped, afraid to hear the answer, yet driven to ask. "Where was he injured?"

Nathan waggled his eyebrows and grinned. "All I'll say, is it was a hell of a place to be wounded. Ah, they're ready," he said, returning a beckoning wave to the hands standing at a boat.

He rose lightly. Dusting his bottom, he handed her up. "C'mon, luv."

Thomas stood at the water's edge, overseeing the last boatload to the *Griselle*. "You've got a bit of a problem, Nathan," he declared, splashing toward them. "Your last boat barely has room for one. You go on, n' I'll toss Cate in mine, drop 'er off as we pass."

"No, no, it's fine." Nathan already had Cate by the arm and was pushing her toward the *Morganse's* boat. "We've plenty of room."

"Nonsense." Thomas seized Cate by the other arm and pulled her back. "Look, the bloody thing is near to the gun'ls now. Be damned embarrassing to founder right here in the bay. Certainly, you don't mean to take her to the bottom?"

Nathan frowned; Thomas gave him a friendly shove, urging him on.

"Go on. Go on. Don't be such an old grandmother. At the rate your men row, she'll be handing you aboard. Now, go!"

Casting a wary look over his shoulder, Nathan waded to the boat and adroitly stepped in. Thomas and his men heaved heartily to set the craft on its way. Nathan stood at the prow, waving a two-fingered farewell, eloquent with trepidation.

"Stretch out! Stretch out, there, I say!" in Nathan's gruff-voice carried easily on the breeze.

Shielding her eyes against the lowering sun, Cate watched the boat pulled across to the *Morganse*, squinting in order to see the men clamor up the black hull. Nathan was easy to spot, hand-over-handing it up a manrope. Once aboard, he stood amidships and waved. She waved back.

"Have they stowed the boats yet?" Thomas asked, coming

up next to her. He didn't wait for an answer, seeing for himself they still laid alongside. "Very well. Call out when they have."

He walked away, leaving Cate to stare curiously after him.

The *Morganse's* boats — longboats, gigs, dinghy's and such — were commonly left afloat. If stowed aboard, they tended to dry out in the tropical sun, causing them to leak, or leak worse, that is. Cate was yet to see one with a dry floor. And so, the boats were rigged to trail like ducklings on a string at the *Morganse's* stern. As the last was being secured, Thomas came from behind and scooped Cate up with startling swiftness. Carrying her in his arms, he splashed through the surf to set her down in the *Griselle's* boat.

"C'mon, lovely," he declared, stepping in beside her. "Let's get you home."

Pushing off, the oarsmen settled to their task, pulling in strong even strokes. His leg snug against hers, Thomas sat hunched forward, elbows on his thighs.

He chuckled in eager anticipation. "You watch Ol' Nathan. He's going to have kittens."

She was about to inquire, but his plan suddenly became obvious: they were not heading for the *Morganse*, but the *Griselle*, instead. Thomas's laugh grew in direct proportion to her alarm.

"What are you doing?" she demanded.

"We're getting his attention. Don't worry, lovely, you're safe. It's just that *he* won't know that will he?"

"You lied."

"Being 'round Nathan this long, I expect you are accustomed to that," he said, grinning.

"I told you I didn't want to play juvenile games," Cate hissed.

His laugh boomed across the water. "He needs a little wake up call, that's all. Nathan has never been canny about what he wants. We'll just give him a little shove. I feel like a bloody, goddamned Cupid!"

Thomas gave her knee a fatherly pat. "Stick with me, lovely."

"Stop calling me that," she snapped, attempting to squirm clear of his reach.

"Yes, ma'm," he said, spewing with mirth. "Yell a bit louder, so he can hear you."

"Go to bloody hell!"

He drew away in mock fear. "Ho-ho! Outspoken lass, aren't you? I'm beginning to understand what Nathan sees in you." Elbow on the gunwale, he looked away across the bay, thoroughly pleased with himself.

18: HOSTAGE

THE BOAT LATCHED ONTO THE *Griselle's* blue hull. Cate rose and tucked her skirt hem into her waistband. The bay's one or two foot swell meant a difference of between two and three feet in locating her first step. As she reached for it—"timing it with the swell" as she had heard seemingly time out of mind—she privately cursed the nameless fool who decided women should wear skirts. Clearly, it had been a man, because no woman would ever make a decision so markedly impractical. Halfway up the side, a pair of strong arms came over the side and lifted her the rest of the way.

The *Griselle's* decks swarmed with activity. The jibs and mizzen filling, the larboard anchor was already on its cathead. Understanding that she was about to go on an unexpected trip, she whirled around on Thomas.

"Where are you taking me?" Cate demanded.

"Stand easy. The point is you're not with him."

"And the point of that?"

"The point of *that* is Nathan will be half out of his wits wondering what's happening to you over here. That little walk on the beach last night was just the beginning." His grin—seemingly having taken permanent residence on his face—grew even further.

"So, I'm just a piece in your little game?"

"No, no. You're the prize, my dear. You're the prize."

Nathan's enraged shouts reached them. Cate drew a breath to reply, but was cut off by Thomas's hand over her mouth.

"She's fine, Nathan. See you in a couple days."

The deck shifted under Cate's feet as the ship gained headway. Over the shouts of the crew, she could hear Nathan's vehement oaths as they slid past.

"That's Nathan for you," Thomas mused, leaning on the rail

next to her. "Always did have the vocabulary and the imagination to be one of the best cursers ever heard."

Cate wrapped her arms around herself and hunched her shoulders. "I don't think I can bear to listen."

She cast a wary eye up at Thomas and considered she might have misjudged him. His jovial manner, his friendship with Nathan and, most of all, his resemblance to Brian had caused her to throw caution aside. She fancied herself a keen judge of men's character and their motivations, and yet with Thomas, had dropped her defenses. Such carelessness could have dire consequences.

"Then don't, or go below. It's no matter. We'll be out of hearing directly," said Thomas.

Chuckling, Thomas strolled away. She felt the stares and the press of the unfamiliar men surrounding her. It hadn't been that long ago that she had stood on the deck of another pirate ship, as much a stranger and captive then as she was now. At least, English had been spoken there. That the *Griselle* had spent most of her time on the other side of the world was revealed in the foreign tongues now heard. The afterdeck there was as crowded as the *Morganse's*: afterguard, watchmen, helmsmen, and the like. It was because of Thomas's presence—as incensed as she was with him—and the safety his nearness provided, that she remained.

Cate stood at the lee rail as the *Griselle* made weigh. There she could keep an eye fixed on the *Morganse*, and therefore, Nathan. At first, the *Morganse's* red-dripped hull was in full view. When the *Griselle* rounded the headland, her view was reduced to only the *Morganse's* spars and rigging. And then, as the *Griselle* plowed across the heavy swell of the Straits, nothing. The *Morganse's* topmasts would have been visible, had they been swayed up, but those were on deck, her head still bowed.

The oddments of her bracelet clattering softly as Cate touched the decorative knot of her necklace. Nathan was with her; she wasn't alone after all.

Crossing the Straits turned out to be the minor issue. Faced with the hazards of coral, rock and sand, and a treacherous current, impending darkness lent urgency to the *Griselle*, her captain, and her crew in finding an anchorage where to lie in wait. Once his ship was secure, however, and the watch lamps were being lit, Thomas fetched Cate and escorted her to his cabin. Beneath the quarterdeck, the *Griselle's* Great Cabin was smaller, but still spacious. It was cozier, with Turkish rugs jig-sawed on the floor, soft elbow chairs, pillows and hassocks. Stacks of books nestled against chair legs, on the gallery sill, chart table and a corner desk. The room spoke of a man who enjoyed his comforts, but not his excesses.

"Plan on sleeping over there," Thomas said, waving a vague hand toward a curtained corner. "You'll find the bunk and necessaries. If there is something you lack, pass the word for either me or the cabin boy. Where has that little snip skulked off to now?" he muttered, looking about. "Anyway, he'll be around. Vittles should be directly. I hope you like Spanish and Moroccan; the cook's from there, so that's what we eat," he finished, with a half-apologetic shrug.

Cate nodded vaguely. Spanish food was familiar; Moroccan was quite another thing.

They stood in the middle of the room, looking anywhere but at each other.

"I think a drink would answer," Thomas said finally and strode purposefully to a leaded glass cabinet. Returning with bottle in hand, he saw her seated.

As he poured, she could see his hands were as battered as Nathan's. Some knuckles were slightly misshapen from bits being severed away. Like Nathan's, several of his fingertips ended at odd angles. The backs of his hands and forearms bore a fine lattice-work of scars, light against his deep bronze. Judging by the scar on his right hand—starting between the second and third fingers and going up—it had been nearly cleaved in half. A miracle that he had its use, it bothered him, for he often flexed it.

The wine proved to be a heady one, a deep burgundy, complex with layers of oak, moss, and berry, and a spicy bouquet. The complaint against red wine was that it didn't ship well, but this one had managed quite nicely. Cate closed her eyes with each swallow; it had been a very long time since she had enjoyed something so good.

They talked one bottle dry, and then another. The third disappeared somewhere during supper: a seafood stew, served over rice, and warm flatbread. After came dessert: a caramelized custard.

"I think they call it flan," Thomas explained over his shoulder as he rummaged through the cabinet anew. "And, if I can find that port... Hah!" he exclaimed, holding up a bottle in triumph. "Now the evening can begin."

The meal finished, they reclined in the elbow chairs, with cups of Arabic coffee, thick and dark, and port. Cate couldn't decide which she enjoyed more. Coffee was always a favorite, but the port was exquisite. Thomas lounged with his legs extended and ankles crossed on a hassock. Once more she was reminded of Brian and their nights before a fire.

Settling her head against the chair's back, Cate lifted her glass. "Where did you say you got this?"

"Card game. The poor dumb bugger was so drunk he didn't know a king from a trey. I could have taken his whole damn ship. I decided I desired the port more."

Conversation came easy, and they talked, the hour candle burning down through its rings, the omnipresent watch bells pealing. At one point, the demands of command called Thomas away. He reluctantly rose and excused himself.

Deep in the chair, with her feet propped up, Cate felt a pang of guilt for being so content in such luxury. It was only a small one, fleeting, barely more. Truth be told, she enjoyed the freedom from Nathan's watch doggedness. Thomas was proving to be a fascinating delight, sweeping her away with his exuding charm and infectious laughter. His openness was refreshing and the lake blue eyes held promise of...

"Another refill?"

Startled, Cate jerked, the port sloshing onto her hand. She looked up to find Thomas at her knee, looking down with a lopsided grin.

She sat up to recompose. "I didn't hear you come in."

Thomas took her glass, eyeing her as he filled it. "Daydreaming?"

"What would I be daydreaming about?" The room had suddenly gone warm.

He drew up the hassock and sat, his knees bumping hers. His elbows resting on the long line of his thighs, he meditatively rolled the bottle between his hands. Finally, he looked up and cocked his head slightly. "You don't know very much about men, do you?"

"Excuse me? I had five brothers."

"And I had four sisters. What bearing does that have on anything?" Thomas countered without malice. He fell quiet, the broad forehead furrowing.

"Years ago, I watched Nathan throw away happiness with both hands. Did he ever tell you about that? Maybe not. It's not my place to say; you'll have to hear that from him, *if* he wants you to know," he added with a warning eye.

Cate stared, confused by this sudden cryptic manner. "And if he doesn't?"

"Then, 'tis of little matter," he said, with a dismissive shift of his shoulders. "It was a very, very long time ago, and there has been a fair bit of water over the decks since. The fact is, as clever as Nathan might be, he's never been particularly sharp on knowing what he wants. Most times, it takes someone else to show him. Sometimes, it requires a sharp blow to the head," he added, with a distant smile.

Cate idly traced the rim of her glass. Cryptic as he was, Thomas's aims were quite transparent, and she was reluctant to be led down a path she had strictly not allowed herself to follow.

"But how do you know —?" she began with great trepidation.

"Haven't you taken a good look at the man? He's smitten. He's like a love-sick puppy —"

"Nathan doesn't —"

"As you said already," Thomas interrupted, impatiently flapping a hand. "And as *I* said, he doesn't always know what he wants."

He hunched forward and peered into her face. "What do *you* want?"

She risked a peek from the corner of her eye. The candlelight played across the sharp ridge of his nose, flaring across his cheekbones, sparking in eyes that searched hers.

"Are you trying to bait me into saying something outrageously foolish, so you can go running to Nathan with it?"

The wide mouth curled at the corners and he coquettishly batted the thick fringe of lashes. "Now, why would I go and do a thing like that?"

"Because you're friends," Cate said meeting his teasing look with a level one. "And you want to protect him from a scheming woman."

"If I thought that, I would have left you back there on that island. Is that what you think you are?"

She gave a tight smile. "What I think hardly matters."

Sobering, Thomas propped his chin in his palm. He pensively stroked the scar which angled across his chest. "To my way of thinking, there's only two involved in this venture: you and Nathan. From that perspective, what you have to say figures an even share. We know Nathan is on beam ends as to what he wants. I'm asking about you."

"Maybe I'm just looking for adventure and fortune."

"With Nathan?" Grasping his knees, Thomas leaned back and laughed. "That's a good one!" he wheezed.

Dabbing one eye, he reached for his drink. "I'll wager he still lives like a monk."

Cate couldn't prevent smiling at Thomas' accuracy.

"If you claim to be looking for fortune, I'd call you a damned fool, because anyone what's been around Nathan for more than a day would know he doesn't give a damn for fortune," Thomas went on. "Aye, he talks about it, but only to keep his ship and crew. Next, I'd call you a liar, and a bad one at that, because one look and any slab-sided dolt would see you don't care two licks about fortune, either."

Cate stiffened at the insult. A large hand came to rest on her arm.

"No, no, no, please," Thomas said earnestly. "That's not what I meant. You're a beautiful woman, even in near tatters and a rope necklace. No money-grabber would settle for that. Nathan is generous to a fault. He'd give a swag pile, if a woman was to demand it, but it's clear you haven't."

One eye narrowed as he regarded her. "I figure there's only one reason you're still on the *Morganse*, one reason you're willing to endure that hardship."

She dodged his all-knowing eyes, her grip tightening onto the glass.

"Nathan said there was nowhere safe enough to leave me," she said in a small voice.

Thomas snorted. "And I'll wake up the King of England tomorrow."

"We're friends."

With the tip of his finger, he brought her by the chin back to him.

"Cate," he began, with the measured patience. "There's only one reason Nathan has you with him. You know it, and I know it, and every damned jack tar on that ship knows it, except Nathan."

His finger moved to stroke her cheek, the blue look softening. "Now tell me, lovely, what do *you* want?"

Heart racing like a cornered rabbit, she took a barely-tasted gulp of port, in a futile search for courage. To engage in wild fantasies about what could or might be, was to pick at old wounds and served little purpose.

"What importance is it to you, anyway?" she asked, pulling away from his touch.

Thomas drew a breath to say something then thought better. Blowing out a tired-sounding sigh, he took a drink. Rolling it in his mouth, he pensively studied the glass.

"Nathan's a friend," he began, carefully measuring each word. "He's the best friend I've ever had or hope to. I haven't seen him in years, but I know I can trust him and I think he trusts me." He looked up, his eyes darkened with solemn earnestness. "It would do my heart good to see the man have a little dose of happiness. Now, correct me if I'm wrong, but I could have sworn you were just as taken with him as he is with you."

Cate stared at her fingers as they twisted the fabric of her skirt. She slid a nervous look from the corner of her eye, deep blue intently meeting hers. She still felt the sting of mortification after Nathan's cruel taunt the night before. Nathan didn't want her. It had been made eloquently clear time and again.

Pressing her fingers to the bridge of her nose, she said, "I don't know if—"

"God's teeth," he exclaimed, rocking back. "You don't know what you want either?"

Dropping his chin to his chest, he heaved an exasperated gasp. "'Pears as though you two were made for each other. Heaven help you both," he finished, raising his hands in benediction.

Slapping his thigh, he rose. Emptying his glass in one gulp, he set it on the table with an empathic thump.

"Well, as I said, the bunk is over there. Don't be shy, but if as you say, you've five brothers then you'll know how a man lives and shan't be shocked. I've the watch, so if you need me, just call out," he said, waving vaguely toward the open skylight overhead. "Sleep well."

Pryce rolled his eyes starward while the Cap'n paced the quarterdeck. The Cap'n took an enraged swipe at the darkness, and in the general direction of where the *Griselle* laid, and demanded for the hundredth time, "What the fucking hell is she doing over there?"

He slammed his hand on the rail and wheeled around. "Did he take her or was this her idea?"

"Don't rightly know, Cap'n." Pryce dared to glance about the decks for anyone or anything that might serve as a diversion or distraction, but the hands had scattered like the weak-livered cowards they were.

"What am I supposed to do?" the Cap'n demanded. A rhetorical question, Pryce considered. "I can't just sail over there and get her."

"You represented as he was a friend."

"He is, but what the goddamned, bloody hell does that have to do with it?"

Growling in disgust, the Cap'n jerked an irritated hand and stomped abaft. Pryce slumped with relief leaning against the rail. The reprieve, however, was too short-lived. He inwardly groaned at the sound of the Cap'n's approach. He knew the sound of that footstep, and the storm and thunder which it promised.

"What am I to do?" Oddly, the Cap'n sounded almost desperate.

"Well," Pryce began delicately. "D'ye trust her?"

"Trust? Her?" Puzzled—as if the word was altogether

foreign — the Cap'n paused to consider. "Of course,... but, not around him."

The Cap'n absentmindedly rapped a tattoo on the rail, staring off into the night. "It's just... I'm not sure she is aware trust is expected... here... now... exactly."

His troubled scowl deepened. "She wanted to leave — said as much — and I thought I'd steered her clear, what with the way the men felt about her, and all, of course."

"Of course," Pryce said circumspectly. His mum raised no fools; he knew better than to argue the finer points of that convolution of the truth.

"'Pears to me yer facing the pirate conundrum: once ye've got yer treasure, then what's to do?" Pryce ventured, once the Cap'n calmed sufficient.

Failing to grasp the point, the Cap'n frowned expectantly.

"Consider, Cap'n. What have we, and every member of the Brethren, spent our lives doin', eh? Lookin' for another man's treasure. Think on it! We search and scrabble, raid, pillage and plunder, lookin' for the gold or silver what some other poor slob found and hid to keep it safe from the next pirate what seeks that same treasure. And as soon as *he* finds it, *he's* trying to hide it from the next."

The Cap'n's mouth took a sharp downward curve. "So, you're saying, immediately upon finding said treasure," he began slowly, "you're invariably and inevitably cursed to a life of maintaining and securing its safety?"

"Aye. And, so long as it be treasure, yer forever to be lookin' over yer shoulder, a-worryin' about who is comin' to take it."

"But, she's not a chest of Spanish coins, she's... Oh, I see..."

Leaning on the rail, the Cap'n buried his face in his hands. He rubbed hard and groaned. "Seems I'm doomed before I begin. So where might I put said treasure?" he asked tiredly, peering through his fingers.

"Dunno, Cap'n," Pryce sighed. "Some treasures be more difficult to hide than t'others."

⌒⌒⌒⌒⌒

"Is that the ship?" asked Cate the next morning.

"Good chance." Thomas lifted the spyglass to his eye. "She's the look of a merchant and flying Company colors."

The next day had broken brightly, Cate waking shortly after first light.

Thomas's bunk had proven to be far more pleasant than anticipated. His appreciation for finer things extended to sheets, and feather mattress and pillows, as opposed to the canvas, oakum-stuffed one on the *Morganse*. It had smelled of him: a male mixture of musty and sharpness. It wasn't offensive, in fact quite the contrary. Sleep hadn't been long a stranger.

Worried for what the day might bring, Cate had bound out of bed. She paced under Thomas's mocking eye as the watch bell marked off the hours. Just past mid-afternoon, legs aching and back burning from being on her feet for so long, she heard the lookouts hail.

Thomas stood watching then closed the glass. "Mr. Al-Nejem!"

An Arabic man large enough to dwarf Thomas in both height and breadth loomed forward. "Aye, sir?"

Thomas lifted his face to the wind and then gave the surrounding water a final look. "Prepare to make way. Hands to the t'gall'nts n' royals. And hoist the colors. Let's make sure they can't miss us."

Touching his fingers to his chest, and then lips, the First Mate bowed and left. In a burst of what might have been Arabic, the *Griselle* flashed out her canvas. The sails bellied, and the deck became alive under Cate's feet. A rousing cheer erupted. The flap of something other than canvas drew Cate's attention to the *Griselle's* tops, where a black banner had been unfurled. This one bore a scarlet heart speared by a cutlass held by an unseen hand. Perhaps it was the infectiousness of the enthusiastic joy of the Grisellers, but the sight of it sent a surge of pride through her which tightened her throat and quickened her heart.

Shielding her eyes against the afternoon sun, Cate could see the approaching ship, running with the wind, by the look of her staysails and studdingsails — Yes, Nathan was a thorough master. She was learning, slower than he would have preferred, but learning. The flag at its mainmast was the same as she had seen her first day aboard the *Morganse*, on the privateer *Nightingale*. Nathan had ordered it to be burned. Seeing the Royal West Indies Mercantile Company's blue and white stripes, with the Union Jack for a canton, now carried a whole new meaning.

As the race of the water at the *Griselle's* sides increased, Cate looked again across the Straits, and the island where the *Morganse* laid. She longed to know what was happening there, but the headland blocked any view.

"Well, they made us," Thomas announced, the glass to his eye. "They just fell off." He gave a satisfied smile as he lowered his arms. "Luckily, these Straits are wide enough; they can pass without raking us, which means we won't have to fire, either."

"So, they think the *Griselle* is after them?"

Thomas nodded. "For now. That's why they're hugging the far shore, which puts them right in line with the spider."

He swung the spy glass toward the island's hidden bay. "Aye, I see 'er; the *Morganse*'s startin' to make her move, t'gallants and royals a-flyin'. Nathan always was a flash with the canvas."

Cate chewed the inside of her mouth. "He's done this before?"

"Oh, aye. More times than one would care to think. For Ol' Scupperbait, the challenge 'tis more the prize. How he loves to best somebody."

"She's opening her port lids, sir!" came the call from the masthead.

"Aye, a bluff; we're out of range." A smug smile was directed at Cate. "He's so busy looking at us, by the time he spots the *Morganse*, it will be too late."

"Alert the gun crews, sir?" inquired Al-Nejem from the other side of the helm.

"Nay. We don't desire a fight, just to entertain them. Pass the word to open the ports and stand by. That'll keep her eyes on us," Thomas said, with a devious chuckle.

Thomas went forward to attend his ship, leaving Cate alone to worry. The targeted ship pressed onward, her bow plowing the Straits' heavy swell. She stood unable to watch, yet unable to move away. Cat-and-mouse was definitely not her game.

Eventually, the *Morganse* poked her masts above the tree line, her ivory-and-red sails stark against the green and blue of land, sky and sea. A huntress rising, she rounded the point and cleared the reef as easily as a lady might sweep her skirts around a table. Then she tore on, a mustache of white water arching at her dark bow. The pursued ship seemed to cringe at the sight of the *Morganse* bearing down; Cate felt a touch of the same cold dread as on the *Constancy*, at seeing the black-hulled ship and massive banner, with its leering skull framed by wings.

The Angel of Death.

"*Ciara Morganse*; it's Celt for black gift from the sea," Nathan had told her. And a gift she was, a black and red phoenix rising from the sea, spreading her wings to swoop down on her prey. She was an even more fearsome sight in the afternoon sun. The late sun deepened the sails' crimson crowns, "...dripping with the blood of her victims..."

"She is a sight to behold," Thomas said, coming up beside Cate once more. "I'd heard about those sails, but I wouldn't believe it, until I saw it. Leave it to Nathan, eh?"

Thomas stood in quiet admiration, as only a mariner would. "A bit of an antique she is, but she sails like she's fresh off the blocks. A lot of things may have changed, but Nathan still keeps his ship shinin' like a diamond in a goat's arse... tail," he corrected quickly and tipped his hat. "Beg pardon, ma'dam. 'Pears as I've away from the genteel company of a lady for too long."

Bronzed profile sharp against the azure sky, his gaze settled on the prey's blue and white flag. A narrowing of an eye and a twitch of a jaw muscle were the only indication of what lurked inside. The sight of it had to have carried a unique meaning for him and Nathan.

Feeling her watching, he smiled self-consciously. "Nathan has a way of sailing a ship that bears no mistaking. Whether he knows it or not, that poor bastard doesn't stand a nun's chance in a whorehouse — beggin' your pardon again, ma'm."

Now almost abreast of the pursued ship, Cate could see her decks. She knew enough of ships to know panic when she saw it: scrambling in the rigging, sails flogging, filling, and then luffing. The ship was downwind of the *Griselle*, which meant the shouting couldn't be heard, but the waving arms spoke volumes.

The *Griselle* ran parallel to the chase and the black ship, but in essence, it was a race between the latter pair. The cold truth was the race was over before it began, the *Ciara Morganse* outdistancing her victim with shocking ease. The only unknown factor was when the slower captain would realize his disadvantage and heave to.

Puffs of blue-black smoke rose from the *Morganse*: her bow-chasers fired. Quailing, the prey veered and bolted, putting her course across the *Griselle's*.

"Son of a bitch!" Thomas cried, more in surprise than anger. "She's making a break for it."

"But, I thought —" Cate began.

"Aye, well, the good captain has chosen to dance with the devil he doesn't know. Mr. Al-Nejem! Give the Gunnery Master my compliments and beg him to put two across the rabbit's bow."

There was a guttural bark and a burst of flame-sparked smoke. The Grisellers paused to track the ball's arc and splash off the fleeing ship's forefoot. Almost simultaneously, a second shot went off with identical results. The ship fired back, the volley whirring harmlessly overhead.

Thomas's eyes rounded in surprise. "You cocky bastard! One through her course, Mr. Nadir, if you please," he shouted to the waist.

And so, it was, with deadly accuracy: a ball through the foresail, the mizzen pierced next. Two more, the rabbit's foretop yard was sheared, and her roundhouse creased, marked by a burst of splinters.

With either nerves of steel or a failure to comprehend her peril, the ship returned fire. The shots came with an irregularity and inaccuracy which robbed them of threat. The peril of the "lucky shot" became more real, when a ball flew near enough over the quarterdeck for everyone to duck.

"Get below," Thomas cried at Cate over the roar of guns.

"No!"

"Get below."

Cate balled her fists and braced as he stormed toward her. "I will not," she shouted up at him. Truth be told, Nathan would have never allowed her to remain on deck, but she had no intention of skulking below, amid the butts and hogsheads, left to wonder what was happening.

"Nathan would hang me by the balls, if something was to happen to you."

"Then tell him it was my fault."

The blue eyes narrowed to dangerous slits. "Small help coming from the grave. Damnation! How in the hell does he manage you?"

Rumbling oaths under his breath, Thomas spun away.

Backs glistening with sweat, the gun crews labored, driven by the indignation of being fired upon by a vessel deemed barely worthy: swabbing, ramming, loading and then, with a rumble of wheels, hauling home the carriages. The space between the ships was thick with grey clouds of smoke, the lick of flame harbingers of another incoming round.

The *Griselle* dealt her damage, but took it as well: a foreyard was sheared, another shot snarling the forestays. There was the pained cry, and then two more. Sections of rail amidships burst into a shower of splinters. A jet of water shot skyward when the scuttlebutt was hit.

"Sharp shooters aloft! An extra ration to the one to take out that captain," Thomas cried.

The ratlines went dark with men bearing muskets scampering skyward. Lethal barrages erupted in overlapping waves, the smoke and smell of gunpowder curling down to merge with what already swirled about the deck.

Shying under the *Griselle's* accuracy, the ship veered on a larboard tack, putting her course directly across the *Morganse's* forefoot once more. The turn brought her stern into view, "*Capricorn*" emblazoned on the sternplate. In a brazen move, she attempted to rake the *Morganse* with a sputter of guns as she crossed, but lacked both accuracy and angle to be effective. Squinting to see through the acrid-smelling smoke, Cate could see the *Morganse*'s damage: holes in the sails and the occasional spout of splinters.

The two pirate ships crisscrossed each other's path with drill-like precision, the *Capricorn* always in the middle. The maneuver allowed each to maintain their speed, the gun crews smoothly shifting from side to side as they carved their turns. The *Capricorn* found herself in the dubious position of having to maintain a two-sided barrage. The pounding from both sides would render her decks a hellish scene. Canvas and wood was no match for twelve to eighteen pounds of hurtled iron. The *Capricorn* wasn't without teeth, however. A volley carried away two of the *Morganse's* jibs and rigging, another hitting her foreroyal.

The *Capricorn* finally swerved away from the *Morganse*. This time, she carried too much sail, too high. The wind heeled her over until her chains plowed the water. Her crew scrambled to compensate, but not before canvas and yards were carried away. The *Morganse* took advantage of the resulting lull in the *Capricorn's* headway to put her sails between the *Capricorn* and the wind.

"Well, he's got 'er!" Thomas came up alongside Cate, and shouted to the helmsman, "Lay 'er in irons. Let's see what this rabbit is going to do."

The *Griselle's* bow nosed to the wind and slid to a halt.

"Now what?" Unable to tear her eyes from the two ships, Cate could barely breathe the question.

His hands coming to rest on the weaponry at his waist, Thomas lifted one shoulder in a casual gesture. "Nathan sends a boarding party, finds what he seeks and takes it."

"Sounds easy enough."

"It is, if the good captain there chooses to abide. If he opts to resist..." He paused, pursing his lips. "Aye, it could be a mite nasty."

"Nasty?" Cate turned to glare up at him. "Nasty!"

"Hand-to-hand combat, blood on the decks; 'tis always nasty business." He looked down at her with teasing glint and a wide grin. "Don't worry! One wrong move and we'll be on that ship like sharks on a carcass. Nathan knows what he's doing."

"People could be getting killed over there," she called as he walked away.

"Then don't watch."

"Damned pirates," she muttered under her breath.

Thomas took his leave, his laugh carrying back to Cate as she pushed the hair from her face. The *Morganse's* momentum had carried her slightly past her prey. Sails luffing, her bow came into the wind, and she drew to a halt. The Capricorn, for the most part, blocked Cate's view of the *Morganse*. She saw the longboats pulled alongside, but little else.

"At the ready, mates, just in case she decides to do something else crack-brained," Thomas called from somewhere behind her.

The ship's being downwind, listening for gunfire wouldn't serve. Arms clutched about her middle, Cate fondled the oddments on her bracelet like a rosary as she watched for the dreaded puff of smoke from a musket or pistol being fired.

Cate squinted to make out the *Capricorn's* deck. Unable to see, she snatched the spyglass from the binnacle and snapped it open. Her sails now luffing, the *Griselle* pitched wildly, requiring Cate to brace against the rail before she could bring it into focus. At last, she found the Morgansers first by their strips of red: weapons brandished, as barbarous and wild-looking as that day on the *Constancy's* deck. She held her breath and progressed incrementally along the line of familiar sea rogues until she arrived at Pryce. Pistol and sword at the ready, his pose brought a chilling recollection of the first day she had met him.

Wherever Pryce stood, Nathan would be near. She moved the glass ever so slightly and found him, squarely before what appeared to be the *Capricorn's* Captain. She felt an odd pang of jealousy. Her own abduction hadn't prompted such personal attention.

"Have they found what they seek, yet?"

She looked up from the glass to find Thomas peering down at her, the late sun gleaming on the stubble of his cheeks.

"I don't think so." She put the glass to her eye once more. "It's difficult to say. No, wait. I think I see a woman."

A small frisson passed through her. She watched with a surge of sympathy at the misfortunate being snatched away. The terror and isolation she had suffered that day crawled like fingers into her chest and constricted.

Lifting the spyglass from her hands, Thomas looked for himself. "Aye, so it would seem."

It was an all too familiar sight: the lick of flames and curl of smoke, as the Royal West Indies Mercantile Company flag was dropped over the side. It floated on the water for the barest of instants and then sank.

"Nathan's always loved to ram that stick into the hornet's nest," Thomas said, more for his own benefit. "Damn his soul, he hasn't learned yet, has he? One of these days, his luck is going to run out."

Cate rubbed her arms to press down the gooseflesh. She couldn't disagree.

"We'll be making weigh soon. Mr. Al-Nejem," Thomas called, turning away.

The entire affair seemed to have taken forever in the coming, and then was over so quickly, it almost seemed a figment of the imagination. Within what felt like barely the flip of the glass, the *Morganse*'s longboats had pushed off, and the chastened and battered *Capricorn* filled her sails. The *Morganse* stood, until the *Capricorn* was well away, then pirouetted and spread her wings to go back through the Straits.

"Bring 'er about!" Thomas bellowed.

The *Griselle* turned, found her wind, and fell in behind the *Morganse*.

"Just stay in her wake," was Thomas's only directive to the helmsman. "When she's hauling wind, there's no catching her. We'll be a spot astern in no time."

Through the day, the *Morganse*'s course paralleled a sharply-peaked strand of islands. The *Griselle*, her decks a furor with the activity of putting her to rights, followed her ever-diminishing pyramid of sails. It was late afternoon when the *Morganse* made her turn, now no more than a white patch pricking the line where sky and water met. By the time the *Griselle* cleared the reef and stood into the small bay, her shadow was long and distorted on the water. The *Morganse* was settled on her moorings, wings folded, roosted for the night. In need of room to swing on her anchors, the *Griselle* tucked into the opposite corner and settled.

The deck lamps were being lit when Thomas appeared to invite Cate to his cabin.

"Cook says he's got a bit o' supper for us," he said, a light hand at her waist. "I don't desire you to go back to the *Morganse* hungry."

Cate stopped short. "The *Morganse*?"

Thomas laughed while urging her onward. "Nathan will be here within the hour, you mark my words. I wish you a decent meal before you're obliged to face his ranting, because, if I know Nathan, he'll be spouting all night."

She sagged in the doorway. "Thomas!"

He grinned boyishly over her shoulder. "You like it?"

The room was awash in the waxen glow of candlelight. Candelabras and sconces sat on every surface that might support one. So many setting about would have been considered a hazard, if not at anchor; it was a vast extravagance. The focal point was the table, bracketed by a pair of candelabras, towering nearly as high as Thomas's head, with multiple tiers and arms.

"Madam," he said softly. The candle's sparked the tease in the lake blue eyes as he offered a chair.

Still grinning with pleasure, he made a dramatic show of pouring her a glass of wine. He filled his own and sat. The candlelight shone on his freshly shaven cheeks. Dark streaks of wetness ran through the blond hair, smoothed and tied in its leather thong.

"If you liked last night's meal, you're going to love this one." He lifted his glass, his eyes holding hers. "To lovely ladies, who don't know their own strength."

The candles shot orange scintillas through the wine as she sipped. The previous night's meal had been a simple affair, with worn china and serviceable silver. Now, the glass from which she drank was delicate stemmed crystal, etched with motifs of cherubs and vines. The silver was ornate and had been brought to a brilliance which was achieved only through hours of polishing with chalk. The plates were porcelain and, like the glass, gold-rimmed. All was formally arranged on a white damask cloth. The air was heavy, but not with the usual smell of tallow candles, nor oil or fat lamps. It was sweet with the scent of beeswax and bayberry, another grand extravagance.

"How did you come by all of this?" she asked, marveling not only at the miraculous transformation, but the finery itself.

"Pirate!" He offered the word with the same insouciant air as Nathan.

"What's the occasion?" she asked, raising a suspicious brow.

The question was met with wide-eyed, innocence over the rim of his glass.

Against the backdrop of rapping carpenter's mallets, adzes and chisels outside, the meal was served by a doe-eyed and solemn cabin boy named Maram and Youssef. Each removal was brought with seamless grace befitting a formal dining room. The first course was a red fish fried to delicate crispness. The second was a dish consisting of chicken and lemons, pungent with spices. The first bottle of wine was soon gone, the level of the second severely diminished. Dessert was a compote of fruits, fresh and dried, steeped in brandy and fragrant with more spices.

"You don't eat like this all the time, do you?" Cate leaned back from the table in glorious agony.

"No, this is just for *special* guests." The candelabras framing the table mantled Thomas's head and shoulders in a gloriole of molten gold. He sighed, resigned. "Tomorrow I'll be back on rice, bread and lentils."

He produced another port from the cabinet. Different from the night before, this one was more robust, with a smoky chocolate aftertaste.

"Oh!" he exclaimed and rose once more. "I have something."

He rummaged briefly in a corner locker and returned with a small bundle of blue silk, the corners knotted at the center.

"Open it," he said, eagerly placing it before her. Unable to contain his enthusiasm, he pushed her hands away to loosen the knot. "Go ahead — now," he said and slid it back.

The slippery silk almost undid itself. It fell away to reveal a pair of hair combs. These were particularly large, with teeth almost as long as her fingers, putting her to mind of the Spanish *mantillas*. Buffed to a low sheen, they were a swirl of translucent layers of every shade of brown from sable, to cinnamon, to gold.

"Thomas, they're beautiful," she exclaimed, tracing the intricate curves and cutwork.

"One of the crew is fair handy with a carving knife and knows the way of working with shell. I had them made for my sister, but it could be years before I ever see her again. It's a hornbill; they're lousy eating, but the shells are worth it." Leaning over her shoulder, he ran an admiring finger along one edge. "Nice, aren't they?"

Nathan's necklace and bracelet, and the sliver of soap were the only gifts she had received in a very, very long time. Such generosity, coupled with the evening, touched her to the point of speechlessness.

"I don't think I've ever seen anything like them. They're too lovely for me." It was difficult to believe anything so beautiful could have come from something so innocuous an animal.

"Nonsense! I've watched you struggle with that hair. Nobody needs these more than you do."

She raised a self-conscious hand, the room suddenly warm. The swim with Nathan had been glorious, the closest to washing her hair in months. The hot water had removed the grime and salt, and now it bloomed into a riotous bramble.

"Here, allow me," he said, too anxious to wait. He fanned his fingers like giant combs and swept them through the unruly tresses. The large, blunt-tipped fingers worked away the tangles and snarls with surprising adroitness. Her pulse quickened at the unexpected warmth of his fingers following the curve of her skull, brushing her neck and temple.

"You've done this before," she teased. "Most men wouldn't be caught dead attempting to arrange a woman's hair."

"As I said, I had four sisters; it was either do it or be thrashed." There was a smile in his voice.

Once worked out to his satisfaction, he gave the heavy locks a deft upward twist, and pressed a comb into place.

"Goes perfect with your color," he declared, standing back to admire his work. "Hand me the other one and I'll get this side."

He preceded in much the same manner, but stopped in mid-motion. Puzzled, Cate looked up to find his gaze fixed on the door behind her. Twisting around, she saw Nathan standing there. He stood uncommonly still, the walnut eyes gone to coal-colored pits.

"Nathan!" She tried to come full around, but was prevented by Thomas' grip in her hair. "Why didn't you say something? You could scare a soul lurking about like a bloody ghoul."

"I didn't desire to intrude. Unexpected company can be such a wretched inconvenience, don't you think?" Nathan said coldly.

"Nonsense," Thomas declared jovially. "Pray join us. We were just having supper. Hungry?"

It was a bit of an empty offer, as Nathan probably saw. The cloth had long been pulled. It was unthinkable that friend or guest would go wanting, if Nathan was so inclined, which by all appearances, was not.

At last Nathan moved. With a cat-like smoothness, not a bell disturbed, he strolled around the table, each dip of his hip a stabbing accusation. "Nay, I seem to have left me appetite somewhere."

With dramatic precision, he inspected the wine bottles, tipping up each to exhibit their emptiness. He reached across Cate to pluck up her glass with two fingers. Sniffing, he arched a brow.

"Very nice," Nathan murmured, coldly. "How much of *this* have you had?"

"What do you care?" She bit her lip, instantly aware of how defensive it sounded.

Nathan threw back his head and drained it in a single gulp, then set back with the same two-fingered care. She had seen him in many moods, but this was different, as dark and dangerous as his precious sea. "Nathan can have a black-temper," Thomas had said. An eruption seemed imminent.

Thomas's hand was now a searing weight on her neck, his thumb repeatedly tracing the curve of her ear. The gesture might have gone unnoticed, but Nathan was in a keen-eyed mood and fixed on it like Artemis on a rat.

"Thomas has just given me these combs—" Cate began.

"A little present," Thomas put in.

"...and he was putting them in for me."

"I dare say." Nathan tipped his head and narrowed one eye to a cutting slit. "Both arm's broken, so he had to do it, eh?"

"Oh, don't be ridiculous." She shifted uneasily, nonetheless. "You should know better than anybody how wild this hair can be."

"Sure," Thomas said lightly. "You'll recall those sisters of mine."

Thomas resumed his task, pointedly ignoring Nathan, who stood with his hands propped on his hips. It was noticeable that, amid all the tension, Thomas was the most placid. If anything, he exuded contentment.

Cate could think of nothing to say which didn't sound defensive. The lavish lighting, elegant table, drinks and gifts: if seen from Nathan's viewpoint, it was an intimate scene.

This is ridiculous. It's like something out of a farce!

"How did everything go with Creswicke's fiancé," Cate asked finally.

Nathan broke his glare at Thomas to direct a tight-lipped smile at her. "Hmm? Oh, fine. Predictably inevitable, as always, fine."

"Everything went according to plan?" Thomas said, concentrating on a deeply entrenched snarl.

"Aye, perfect," Nathan said distractedly. Folding his hands behind his back, he rocked on his feet, and then cleared his throat loudly. "Well, it would seem I've arrived at an inopportune moment, so..."

The thought hung incomplete as he strode toward the door.

"Nathan? Nathan!" she called, but futilely. With a disgusted growl, she sprang up and rounded on Thomas. "You planned this."

She was met with wide grin. "Aye, I did. And it worked. You've got his attention, now," he called as she scurried around the table and out the door.

Nathan was nearly to the capstan, by the time Cate caught him up. She grabbed him by the arm and pulled him to a stop. "Will you wait a minute?"

He whirled and ducked a mocking bow. "A thousand pardons, *Madam*. Forgive me for disturbing—"

"You didn't disturb anything, and you damned well know it!"

"My mistake." Baring his teeth in something between a smile and a sneer, he turned and marched away.

"Nathan, damn it, come back here!"

He spun back in a clatter of bells. He reared back his head to glare at her down the long line of his nose. "Yes?"

She rocked back on her heels. "Yes, what?"

"I had the distinct impression you had something in the way of an obligatory explanation. Well, get on with it," he said, crossing his arms. "Enlighten me."

"There's nothing to explain."

"You're here, aren't you?"

"You think this was my doing?"

"I didn't hear any objections." He spread his arms and craned his head, as if such things might be found lying about.

"He had his hand over my mouth."

"And where else?"

"You bastard—!"

His face dissolved. She made a fist and swung. Nathan easily fielded her punch in mid-air.

"Take better aim before you fire, darling," he growled. His fingers dug her flesh as he twisted her arm aside.

She jerked free and rubbed her wrist, trying to erase the burn of his grip. "Do you think that little of me?"

"No! I think far more of you. However, I think far less of *him*," he said, with a jerk of his head toward the cabin. "You never struck me as the game-playing sort."

"This wasn't my doing."

"Yes, I can see the signs of struggle everywhere." Nathan spun on his heel and stalked toward the accommodation ladder.

"You don't own me," she seethed in his wake. "You can't keep me locked up like some feeble aunt to be let out at your pleasure. I can do as I want."

He pivoted back so suddenly, she almost collided with him.

"By all evidence, I'd wager that's *exactly* what you were doing. By the way, the combs suit you," he said as a begrudging afterthought.

His countenance softened, and he sighed. "True enough. As you have so eloquently and succinctly pointed out, I have no claim on you a 'tall. I only came to take you away from this rabble, because I thought the *Morganse* was where you wanted to be. My mistake." His cutting edge returned. He ducked another mocking bow. "I bid you good e'en."

She followed him, hoping that he would stop again, her fears reaching panic proportions when he didn't.

"Nathan!"

He whirled with an unexpected quickness that made her flinch. He recoiled, thinking she was going to take another swing. She held up her hands as a peace offering, but they still stood a distance apart.

"So... are you saying you don't want me back?" she finally asked.

With a long-suffering air, Nathan crossed his arms. His boot tapped a rapid tattoo on the planks. "Do you want to go back?"

She could see Thomas over Nathan's shoulder. Leaned against the cabin door's frame, arms crossed, one foot cocked over the other, he was a dark blot against the blaze of candles behind him. The white of his smug smile, however, gleamed. She searched Nathan's face for any sign of the familiar warmth or humor, but his features were either lost to the shadows, or obscured by a several day scruff of beard. He was as near a stranger then as he had been their first meeting.

"*Can* I go back?" she asked.

"Do you *want* to go back?"

God, I wish he would stop answering her question with another question.

Biting her lip, she looked to her feet, and braced for the possibility of rejection.

What do I do then?

So, seized by dread, she could barely squeeze out, "If I can."

He leaned nearer and lowered his voice. "You can do whatever you want to do, luv."

Bare inches away, his eyes held hers, and then wavered, uncertainty tugging their corners. The inked pools held the same fear then, as the night of Jensen's death, when she had asked to leave. He had, in essence, pleaded for her to stay. Betrayal was there now, whether by her or Thomas, she couldn't tell. There was something else, a subterranean rumbling of something, so deep and restrained it couldn't be named.

Cate wished she had a deeper understanding of what it was between these two men. It might have shown a light on what transgressions she may have unwittingly committed; what breach of faith may have violated. She needed a Ship's Articles, or something in writing that clearly described her confines. The strain of tiptoeing around, lest she inadvertently trample another of Nathan's secret boundaries, of the come-hither only to be pushed away, was becoming wearisome.

And yet, the thought of not being with him was even worse.

"Yes." She meant to sound confident, but her voice quaked.

"You're sure?" He threw a hard look over his shoulder at Thomas and then tilted his head at her. "Are you absolutely sure?"

"Yes." She gulped, and ventured to ask, "Are you sure?"

He broke into a dazzling smile. "Darling, I've been sure since the day you were dropped on me deck. C'mon."

"A minute, please. I'll be right back." She ran back to Thomas, in spite of Nathan's scowl.

"Didn't I say he'd be coming?" Thomas said, his grin broadening.

"You love it when you're right, don't you?"

He laughed, loud and hearty. "There's no denying it does allow the day to go better."

She rose on her toes to kiss him lightly on the cheek. "Thank you, I think."

"Don't thank me yet!" he called after her, as she scurried back to Nathan. "You've got him hooked, but you still have to reel him in!"

"I'm not looking to catch anything," she called back.

"God help you's both!" he shouted and disappeared inside.

Nathan cast a suspicious look over his shoulder as he handed her down the side. "What did he mean by that?"

"Nothing," she sighed, hitching her skirts. "Can we just take our leave?"

She half-expected Nathan to sit next to her on the thwart. Instead, he sat facing her as they pushed off the *Griselle*.

"Stretch out and row dry," Nathan demanded of the oarsman.

Their knees touched, and he drew back. The small gesture speared any hopes which had dared to soar of things between them might be different. Thinking perhaps he was still annoyed, she thought to say something, but silence seemed the better option. Perhaps enough had been said already.

The peacefulness of the bay was broken only by the low grunts of the oarsmen and the rustle of the water at each dip of the oar. The light of the bow lantern sparked like fireflies on the ripples. She took the opportunity to assimilate what had just happened. Just as Thomas had predicted, Nathan had come for her. It had been a surprising show, but of what? Jealousy? Protection? Male territoriality? Or, had it been another case of Nathan not wanting her, and yet not wanting anyone else—at least, not Thomas—to have her?

Pawn or prize? Would she ever know which one she was?

As they neared the *Morganse*, singing could be heard, inordinately loud for the hour. It was also markedly lacking in merriment, sounding more akin to the heavy-labor chants reserved for manning the capstan or hauling sheets.

"What are they singing about?" she asked.

"'Tis no celebration," said Nathan glumly, and threw a dark look over his shoulder. "I suppose fair warning is in order."

She stiffened. "About what?"

"Our guest—our dear Lord Creswicke's intended betrothed."

"What's wrong? Nathan, what did you do to her?"

He stiffened with indignation. "Nothing! Wretchedly insulting you think I would. It's just...well, it's just..."

19: BELOVED BETROTHED

Tucking the hem of her skirt into her waistband, Cate struggled up the *Morganse's* side. The black hull absorbed any ambient light, making it insufferably difficult to see. She groped overhead in the dark for the next step—no more than a ledge only half-large enough for a foot—while striving to not slip from the dew-slickened step upon which she stood. Two strong arms eventually came over the gunwale to seize her by her arms and lift her up. As she alighted on deck—right foot always touching first—she was met by the sound of female crying and a beleaguered look on every man.

"How is it, man?" Nathan asked, after scampering up the side by the manrope like a squirrel up a tree, show off!

"Not stopped since ye left, sir," Pryce replied with a grim roll of his eyes.

Cate whirled around on Nathan. "What did you do to her?" she shouted over the din.

Eyes rounding, Nathan sputtered indignantly. "Ravaged her! Six, no, seven times, myself, plus every man having a turn! What the bloody hell else do you think we'd have time...?"

His protests faded as Cate ran into the cabin. The lamps were lit, but the sleeping area, from whence the shrieking came, was unlit.

"You left her in the dark!" Cate shouted.

Nathan and Pryce skidded to a halt behind her.

"We thought to put a light, but not a man would pass. Besides," Nathan pleaded, wincing at the sound of demolition emanating from behind the curtain, "we feared for the welfare of herself and the ship were we to leave her alone with a flame."

"We intended as to stow 'er below, but she sheared off in there, 'n stuck tighter than a barnacle on an oyster," put in Pryce, retreating a step at Cate's glare.

Cate pushed the curtain aside and held it. A band of light fell into the room, but not enough to see.

"Noo! Please don't kill me," came a cry out of the darkness.

The crying increased to a siren-like pitch. The curtain falling closed behind her, Cate groped her way forward, using the shrieks as a beacon. Her eyes became accustomed to the dim enough to make out a figure cowering in the floor. Arms over her head, her shoes skidded on the planks as she tried to scrabble deeper into the corner.

"No! Please! I beg...! No!"

"Don't be afraid. I won't hurt you," Cate said as she inched forward.

The woman thrashed and kicked, and caught Cate in the legs, hard enough to take her to the floor. She landed heavily on top of the woman. A struggle ensued: the woman fighting as if being attacked. Cate was dimly aware of a growing light and approaching footsteps as she grappled to extricate herself. Finally, she managed to seize the woman by the arms and gave her a hard shake.

"You're all right! I won't hurt you!"

Cate's pleas seemed at first to have fallen on deaf ears, but then resistance eased. In quavering moans, the woman slumped, perhaps more from exhaustion than terror. As steps came up behind her — Nathan's Cate now knew — and a growing light, Cate struggled to pry the soul free of the corner, a task akin to moving a dead sheep. Once able to grasp her chin, Cate brought the woman's face around into the light and brushed the sweat-dampen hair from her face.

"You're just a child!" She whirled around on Nathan. "She's just a child."

Enormous blue eyes focused on Cate and then settled on Nathan. "Pirates! No!"

Cate's opposition was smaller, but fought with the fury of the frenzied. Cate took the brunt as the woman scratched, kicked and clawed. After a shot square to the chin and an elbow to the stomach, Cate's well-meaning intentions grew more determined. Still, it was no worse than wrestling with her younger brother... until she was bitten. She screeched and struck out, sending the girl tumbling back into the corner. Cate felt herself then being lifted from the floor. She somehow wound up at the door, Nathan between her and the cowering heap on the floor.

"Belay that caterwauling, you shrieking strumpet!"

"Nathan...?"

"Out!" he barked, whirling around on Cate.

"But...?"

"Out!" Nathan shouted, with a swipe. He spun back around toward the woman. "Stay on the floor or stay in the bunk, but stay you shall! C'mon!"

Nathan seized Cate by the arm and propelled her into the salon, not stopping until she was seated at the table.

"Blood box, Mr. Millbridge," he called as he pulled up a chair at her knee.

Nathan took the arm that until then Cate hadn't realized she had been cradling. She made to look at it, but he determinedly brushed her aside. Crescent-shaped and bright red, blood welling from a few places, the bite was on the inside of her forearm, just above her wrist. It stung horribly, throbbing in unison with her heart, still racing from the struggle. It had been a long time since she had been bitten: a foul-tempered Highland pony. This one was no worse, but Nathan was taking the offense as serious, muttering dark comments under his breath as he inspected. He looked up apologetically when Cate winced. As his long, tar-grimed fingers probed, an identical mark could be seen on his wrist.

"You, too, hmm?" she said under the sobbing coming from behind the curtain.

A corner of Nathan's mouth twitched. "Not the first and most probably not the last. I'm obliged to admit; however, it has been a time. Tea, Mr. Millbridge, if you please" he said without looking up as the blood box was delivered.

Dabbing the sweat from her temples, Cate was about to insist she wasn't of a mood for tea. Hospitality, however, was the last thing on Nathan's mind. Fetching the brandy bottle, he poured a bit into the pot when it came. He dipped in a bit of cloth and proceeded to clean the wound.

Biting her lip against the sting, Cate stared at her blood box and mentally sorted through its inventory. Chamomile? Valerian? Lavender? She was reasonably prepared for ship-related emergencies, but woefully lacking in preparations for hysterical women.

"We can't just leave her in there," she said to the top of Nathan's head.

He shot her a look from under his brows. "Why not? I'm not compelled to be nice. Pirate." The last word was offered up as a multi-faceted explanation.

"She's your responsibility."

"No," he said with slow emphasis. "She's a hostage."

"Little difference. Ouch!"

"Sorry. Here, hold this." Nathan directed her hand to the compress. He rose an began rummaging through her box. "You'll not be going back in there with yon she-devil," he warned darkly, pausing to glare over the lid.

He grunted in satisfaction at finding the jar of salve. "It cures everything else, let's hope it works against rabid animals."

Cate sucked in at the sting of the salve, and again when the bandage was tied off with a little more force than might have been intended. The incessant crying was beginning to make her head pound. She prided herself on having faced many an emergency—dare she say, disaster?—with strength and grace. Fire, war, destruction, disease, horror: she had endured them all. Hysterics was quite another thing. Knowing how disturbed most men were in the face of a crying woman, her sympathy for the Morgansers deepened. It was harrowing, and they had endured it most of the day.

Cate frowned, straining to think of what might help. "She might need..."

"To be left lying as any vicious beast should."

"We can't just leave her. We have to do... Something."

With a glare daring her to object, Nathan grabbed the bottle and poured an additional dollop into the pot. "Serve the wench, if you must," he said and shoved the pot across the table toward her.

"Shh! She'll hear you."

"Much more the better. Then she'll know if she doesn't drink this, it will be bilge water and sea biscuit for the next fortnight! And if she does you harm again, I'll slap her in irons until we're rid of her cursed carcass!" He raised his voice incrementally until he was shouting at the end, and all aimed at the curtain.

Balancing pot, cup and light, Cate went back around the curtain to find the hostage had indeed overheard. She sat chastely on the bunk, her large blue eyes meeting Cate as she set everything on the bedstand.

"Who are you?" she asked querulously in a voice torn by tears and screaming.

"I'm Cate. Who are you?"

"Prudence." She sniffed hugely. "Prudence Collingwood." Sniffing again, her fingers flexed at the folds of her skirt in suggestion of a curtsey. Glancing toward the curtain, she leaned to whisper, "Are you a prisoner, too?"

"Umm, not really." Cate said, posing an encouraging smile.

"Were you stolen? Did he take you from a ship? Are you a prisoner? Are you his slave?"

"Slave?" Cate's smile wavered. The child certainly had a vivid imagination. "I think not."

"They're pirates!" Prudence wailed into her hands. "They're going to kill me!"

Melting into a new crescendo of crying, Prudence launched at Cate and threw her arms around her neck. The force drove them both to the mattress. Grappling to escape the death grip, Cate managed to sit up and gather the girl in her arms. Rocking and murmuring little nothings, Cate strove to console the child. It was difficult to admonish the girl too stridently. Her fears were real, as evidenced by the trembling body. Cate recalled suffering many of those same terrors, although she preferred to think she had faced them with a little more alacrity.

Prudence's sobbing eventually subsided, leaving her sniffling and hiccupping.

Hot water! The idea came to Cate as a desperate inspiration. Any woman feels better after washing.

Freeing herself from Prudence's clutches, Cate poked her head out around the curtain. Nathan and Pryce milled about the salon, Kirkland and Millbridge lurking in the margins, all looking thoroughly anxious.

"Hot water?" she asked.

In less time than she thought it possible to reach the galley and return, an arm came around the curtain—No mistaking Nathan's—to hand off a ewer of steaming water. Murmuring vague nothings to Prudence, Cate sponged the tear-reddened face, while praying for the water's palliative effects. Seen more clearly, Prudence proved to be a lovely girl. Glossy, dark brown curls surrounded an oval face with piercingly clear blue eyes, a bow-shaped mouth, and...

"How old are you?"

Prudence looked to her lap and toyed with the silk of her skirt. "Sixteen."

"And you're to marry Lord Creswicke?"

The level of disbelief in Cate's outburst jolted the poor girl. Tears welled and her chin began to wobble dangerously. Prudence's "Yes," came out in a wheezing squeak.

She possessed the rounded, doll-like features which rendered her much younger than her years. Still, sixteen was excessively young, by Cate's standards. True enough, she had witnessed marriages at far younger ages while growing up, and in the Highlands. She had disapproved of those, too. In the face of another hysterical onslaught, Cate swabbed the wetness from Prudence's face and helped her blow her nose on the towel.

"How about some tea?" Cate asked brightly.

Tea certainly had its curative qualities, but Cate was putting her money—and her sanity—on the brandy.

Seeing Prudence propped up, tea was served. The small, bow-shaped mouth drew up in disappointment at the cup. "I usually take mine with lemon and milk."

Once assured there was neither, she balked when met by the brandy. The loud, admonishing sound of a male throat clearing came from behind the curtain spurred her to drink. Within moments, her stomach gurgled, and she blushed. Lest she cause further embarrassment, Cate went about straightening the room for a bit longer, before inquiring when Prudence had last eaten.

"Not since breakfast. I was too scared, what with the pirates chasing us," she said, shooting an accusing look toward the curtain.

Cate was sympathetic, but there was a glaring flaw: it would have been late afternoon before the *Capricorn* would have sighted the *Griselle*. Youth and terror, however, had a way of clouding one's perceptions.

"Aye, food is always the best means to tame the savage beast," came a disembodied, graveled voice.

At length, a tray was brought. Millbridge — judging by the footsteps — stopped short of the curtain and refused any farther. Finally, it was slid under the curtain. The ever-reliable Kirkland had produced toast, a couple boiled eggs and slices of cold meat, which Prudence ate with the enthusiasm of the young. A full stomach, combined with tea, kidnapping, crying and brandy took its toll, and she soon drooped. Chanting assurances of her safety, Cate tucked her up. She promptly fell to sleep, curled up like the little girl she was.

Somewhat haggard and tear-sodden, Cate tiptoed out. Nathan sat quill in hand at the table, Pryce standing across. They looked up with anxious trepidation, Nathan arching a brow.

"She's sleeping," Cate whispered.

"Praise God!" Pryce sighed in a hush. He slumped in relief. "A true worker of miracles, ye are, sir. The woman is relentless. Never knowed a soul what could caterwaul like that."

"She's no woman," Cate hissed and leaned closer to whisper lower yet, "Did you see her? She's a child. She's only sixteen-years-old."

One was compelled to wonder how the men hadn't taken notice.

Nathan sat back and scowled. "I knew our Lord Creswicke had appetites, but I had no idea he had *that* one."

"He must be almost twice her age," Cate said.

Nathan snorted. "And near half again."

"What kind of a man would marry a girl...?"

"A man looking for connections and money," Nathan finished, coldly. "And our dear Lord Creswicke seeks both."

"My God, doesn't the man have enough already?"

Nathan snorted again, more derisively. "The word 'enough' doesn't exist in his vocabulary."

"Aye, pirate he 'tis!" Pryce put in, with his own level of disdain. "No matter how much there be in the hold, yer still mauradin' for more."

Nathan grew contemplatively distant. He jerked and shook himself. "Other than the watch, the men have gone ashore. Do you wish to remain or go?"

The thought of an evening ashore was appealing. On an inexplicable surge of motherly instincts, Cate declined with great regret. "I think it best to stay aboard, tonight."

Nathan nodded, surprisingly without comment. "Very well, I'll remain. Mr. Pryce, you're to go ashore and tend the men."

Nodding a brief salute, Pryce left.

Nathan looked up from under his brow, one lifted wryly. "Slave?"

"No secrets on a ship, hmm? Your reputation precedes you."

His mouth curled in distaste as he glanced toward the curtain. "Most decidedly and certainly not with mere children."

Cate sank into a chair. Until she sat, she hadn't realized the ache in her back. Standing on deck waiting, and the argument with Nathan had taken its toll. The bite on her arm throbbed, and her head pounded, as if she had been the one crying. The quietude of Thomas' candlelight supper seemed a lifetime ago.

Resting her head on the back, she watched Nathan. He took great pride in his charts, each one a piece of artwork in and of itself. She had spent many an hour watching him pour over them, assessing positions or plotting a new course. But, they were currently at anchor.

"What are you doing?" she asked at length.

"Adding a reef; hadn't spotted it until today." He frowned in concentration, an ink-blotched finger tracing the outlines on the parchment. "This island here is actually two. There's a small pass here. A storm could have taken it out recently, but it's there, nonetheless."

"What time is it?" she asked, rubbing her temples while he sketched.

"Middle watch was just rung. 'Tis midnight," he added, knowing her inability to follow ship's time. He paused to look up, the candlelight catching the cinnamon in his eyes. "You've had a full night."

"It would appear I've next to find a place to sleep," she said, fatigue dragging her voice.

"I'll pass the word to ready one of the cabins below," he said, standing.

A rapid sequence of images flashed through her head: dark, dank holds, snoring men swinging elbow to elbow in hammocks, the smell of pitch and gunpowder.

She halted him with a raised hand, still rubbing her temple with the other. "Don't bother. I don't think I could sleep down there."

"Why not? We'll make sure it's nice and clean." Tease touched the graveled voice.

"No windows, no air, no thank you."

"Then how about the deck? Weather glass says fair, and the sky agrees."

Too tired to resist, she allowed Nathan to guide her outside, her arm in one hand and the bottle in the other. Two of the anchor watch stood on the forecastle, so they sat, side by side, with the foremast to their back.

The moon was a bare sliver hanging just above the island's crown. Its thin light allowed the stars to shine like fairy dust, their tiny rays colliding. As he and Cate shared the bottle, Nathan pointed out the constellations and told Greek fables, Nathan Blackthorne-style, in his gravel-gruff voice, and with his own quirky mix of Roman, Greek, pagan, Norse, Hindu, and the mythologies of a world travelled, all heavily dosed with love and lust. She had never realized stars could be so bawdy. They sat shoulders touching. His voice vibrated through her, the soft rumble of his laugh echoing in her bones. The lamps gilding his profile, hands illustrating and punctuating every tale, there was an elegance about him. If she closed her eyes — no challenge there, for she could barely keep them open — she tried to imagine him not as a pirate, but before life had taken its toll.

At some point, the fables faded, and they talked of everything and nothing, dreams and hopes, regrets, fears, ambitions and grand plans, Nathan painting verbal pictures of things real and things imagined, things he had seen and things no one would ever see. Chilled by the night air, Cate snuggled closer, a head suddenly too heavy coming to rest on his shoulder. Drowsy, she was vaguely aware of his arm slipping around her shoulders and her head brought down to pillow on his chest.

"Welcome back."

Shrouded in the gauzy margins of sleep, it was murmured so faintly, she wasn't entirely sure if she had heard it or dreamt it. And yet, the stirring of her hair and the rumble of his voice under her ear seemed proof it had been real.

Together, they slept.

Cate woke curled on the deck with Nathan's sash folded for a pillow and his faded, burgundy coat her blanket. A bit muzzy-headed, it took her a few moments to recollect how she had come to be there. She sat up to an uncommonly empty deck, a mere handful of mariners milling about. Then she remembered that most of the hands had gone ashore, only the anchor watch remained. Stiff and rubbing feeling into one shoulder, she made her way to the cabin.

The salon was empty. Not what one would call a messy person, Nathan still had a way of leaving a trail of evidence everywhere he went. It was a surprise to find no sign of him having been there: no half-drank cup, no crumbs, no fruit peels, navigational tools nor charts.

More striking, there was no sign of Prudence, either.

Cate cautiously poked her head around the curtain and found Prudence lying on her back staring at the ceiling.

"I give you joy of the morning. I hope I find you well?" Cate asked.

"Very well... I suppose."

Judging by the stiffness with which the child laid, Cate suspected quite to the contrary. "Is there something the matter?"

Prudence looked from the ceiling to Cate and back, worry etched on every rounded feature. "I was unsure if I should rise."

Biting her lip, Cate pressed her fingers to the bridge of her nose. "And why shouldn't you?"

"Because... because... I was afraid... and I..."

An annoying inner voice suggested the possibility the child had taken Nathan's directives the night before a little too seriously. She then considered how to go about explaining most of his threats came with little bite and, for all his gruffness, there was a gentleness underneath. On the other hand, such insights might be best left unspoken.

"I heard talk on the *Capricorn*," Prudence whispered urgently. "I heard stories... at night... about the *Ciara Morganse*. They eat their victims and drink their blood. They kill their mothers for the gold in their teeth. The ship is made of caskets... and it's cursed!"

Cate turned her head to hide a smile. She had heard many of those same tales on the *Constancy*. They had been very convincing.

"Those were but sea tales." She patted the girl's arm encouragingly. "It's all well. You'll not be harmed."

"He's a pirate," she moaned, burying her face in her hands.

"Yes, he is," Cate said, pulling Prudence's hands down. "That's Captain Blackthorne."

"He's so scary! He looks mean."

"Well, he's neither scary nor mean." The chance of said captain being just the other side of the curtain, hence hearing every word, curtailed any further remarks. He did, after all, have a reputation to uphold.

"Did he? I mean, has he...? Have they *done* terrible things to you?" Eyes rolling with terror, Prudence left little doubt as to her meaning.

Cate smiled semi-sympathetically at recalling her first night aboard the *Morganse*, waking in the same bunk, suffering the visions of the same horrors. She couldn't help but wonder how much easier things would have gone if there had been a friendly face for her.

At least Prudence has the benefit of her own clothing, she thought ruefully. "No, they haven't *done* anything, and nor will—"

"Are you a pirate's woman?"

The absurdity caught Cate unawares. Her cheeks inexplicably heated. "Prudence, you must be famished."

The girl predictably brightened. "Yes, I am... a bit," she said eagerly. Then her knuckles whitened on the blanket. "Oh, but, *he's* out there. I know he is!"

"Prudence, pray listen. There is no reason for you to fear N... Captain Blackthorne. I know he's a bit... bizarre, but upon my word, you are in no danger."

"I simply can't." Prudence plucked disdainfully at her sleep wadded clothing. "I'm too mussed."

"Mussed?" It took Cate a moment to process the concept. "It's a pirate ship!"

The outburst and blunt reminder was regrettable. Tears welled instantly. Concessions would need to be made soon or a replay of the scene from the night before was imminent, and it would be on Cate's head. Several suggestions were made, but Prudence was intransigent as the aforementioned barnacle. Progress was finally achieved at the suggestion that Prudence undress, wash, and then redress.

"The ewer's there," Cate said, turning to leave, the prospect of coffee weighing heavily on her mind.

"The water's cold."

The tone of voice struck several chords, none of which were

kindly. The urge to once more remind Prudence that it was a pirate ship bubbled to Cate's lips.

"Very well," Cate said through clenched teeth and snatched up the pitcher. "I'll return directly."

Cate returned to find Prudence standing exactly as she had been left.

"I was waiting for help," was the girl's excuse.

Cate propped her hands on her hips. "It's undressing. How difficult can it be?"

"Nanna always helped," Prudence moaned, flapping her arms.

"Nanna?" Cate echoed dully. "Dare I inquire?"

"She's my nanny. The pirates left her behind. We cried and begged, but they refused to bring her. So, I'm all alone." Eyes brimming, Prudence gave a great display of a lower lip.

"Well, not quite," Cate murmured under her breath, and then said louder, "Turn 'round."

Hooks, buttons, ties and laces, shifts, petticoats, stays, stockings, bodices and kertches: as Cate excavated through the layers, she had forgotten how much work "properly dressed" was, Prudence, being of no more help than a common dressmaker's manikin.

"You'll have to make do with the ewer and basin," Cate said, once Prudence was down to her shift. "You'll find a towel next to it."

"What about soap?" Prudence asked eyeing the stand.

Inwardly groaning, Cate pulled out her little bar of French-milled soap Nathan had brought her. Besides her sewing kit and hairbrush, it was her most precious possession. She set it lovingly next to the basin, her nails digging into her palms as she stalked to the curtain.

"There now, satisfied? Wash. I'll return straight away," Cate said.

Squeaking with alarm, Prudence clutched her arm. "You said you wouldn't leave me alone."

"I said, I wouldn't leave you alone with Na... the captain," Cate countered testily. She pulled free and steered Prudence to the washstand. "I'm only going to pass the word for breakfast. I'll return directly."

Cate barged out to the salon, gasping with relief to see that Mr. Kirkland had not failed her: coffee awaited. She grasped the cup with tremulous hands; closing her eyes in blessed relief with the first drink.

Nathan came in. He drew to a halt at the sight of her, his customary morning high-spirits fading. "You look bloody awful."

"Always pleased to meet an admirer," she said edgily, hovering over the cup.

Maintaining a careful margin, he reached behind her chair for his own cup, eyeing her critically over the rim as he drank. "Not the best of mornings, eh?"

"It started well enough," she sighed, then lowered her voice. "A fall from the tops'l yard would have been shorter."

"Not good?" he whispered.

"Not remotely."

A blood-curdling shriek came from behind the curtain. Cate sprung up, but was urged back down by Nathan.

"Sounds like our guest has just met His Lordship." A muscle ticked at the corner of his mouth, a smile denied.

"I should go —" she began.

"Best not. I'm thinking these are introductions best made on their own."

There was a spark of mischievous glee in his eye. His pleasure at Prudence's distress wasn't flattering, but if Cate was completely honest, she found pleasure, too.

Nathan regarded her further and retreated a step. "Perhaps I should take my leave."

"Perhaps you should, but don't be surprised if you return to find a body," she said moodily.

Executing a bow, he circled around her chair, and then tiptoed out of the room. His exaggerated steps and arcing arms caused him to resemble a sword-bearing stork. Closing her eyes, she shook away the vision. She drained her cup, took a deep breath and returned to the battle at hand.

Sometime later, the women emerged, Cate somewhat worn, but victorious. Gently, but not nearly as might have been an hour earlier, Cate prodded a Prudence around the curtain and into the salon. Once again, she gave thanks for Mr. Kirkland and his intuitions, the smell of hot chocolate drawing Prudence to the table far more readily than threats could have achieved.

Prudence sat with the grace of a lady, but frowned unbecomingly at the cup before her. "I take mine with whipped cream."

"The galley is fresh out just now," Cate said and dived with desperation into her second cup of coffee.

Following a brief display of lower lip, Prudence sipped primly.

A plate of still-steaming scones sat on the table. Honey, butter and wedges of mango completed the presentation. The less chipped, more presentable china was in service, the silverware given an extra buff. It would seem the presence of a lady, even one so young, had an effect on everyone.

No one would ever mistake you for a lady, Cate thought ruefully.

Prudence sniffed delicately at a scone, split it open, and then, with the glee of youth, spread honey until it drooled. Nibbling an edge, she poked at the mango with her fork, making a poor task of concealing her disappointment.

Cate heard familiar steps; Nathan's arrival was eminent. She eyed Prudence, judging whether to give warning or just throw caution to the wind. In spite of Cate's annoyance, the child stirred her maternal instincts: the driving desire to protect and aid.

"Prudence," she began lightly. "Would you desire to meet Captain Blackthorne? After all, he is your host and does deserve a show of gratitude." The last was uttered with the weighted tone a mother — or nanny — might employ.

Prudence jerked, her knife clattering to her plate. Puffing in panic, she looked wildly around, as if expecting Nathan to materialize from the bulkheads.

"You'll be fine," Cate said, soothing. "You're safe —"

"Safe from what?"

Prudence lurched back in her chair at the sound of Nathan's voice, Cate's hand on her shoulder the only thing preventing her from taking flight.

"Safe from what?" Nathan said from the doorway, frowning.

"Umm, you," Cate said.

"Me? What did I do?"

"Nothing... yet" Cate added under her breath.

Nathan stopped several paces from the table and stiffened with wariness. "What?"

Clearing her throat, Cate rose. "Captain Blackthorne, allow me to name Miss Prudence Collingwood, of Boston, I believe."

Nathan gave Cate a severe look, his brows high in question. She inclined her head toward the cringing girl and gave her brows a prompting jerk. With the trepidation of one approaching a coiled snake, Nathan inched closer.

"Your servant, Miss." Striking a gracious pose, he swept off his battered leather tricorn and bowed with amazing graciousness. "It is both a pleasure and an honor to have someone so refined and lovely grace this humble ship."

Straightening, Nathan gave Cate an 'Are you satisfied?' look as he strolled the long way around to his chair. He poured a coffee and sat, alert over it.

A strained silence befell the tableau. Nathan sat twitching at Prudence's every intake of breath, fearing an outbreak of tears.

Prudence was rigid, scared to the point of speechlessness—not necessarily an objectionable condition. Cate quaffed her second cup and watched Nathan, wondering what he would do next.

"Soo..." Cate burst out just as Nathan prepared to speak. "How long do you plan for us to linger?" She finished with a significant look for Nathan's benefit.

"The terms were two days," he said slowly, staring back in confusion, "but we'll linger here, until 'tis time for their arrival."

"Arrival of whom?"

Their heads turned together, surprised by the sound of Prudence's voice.

"Arrival of the people who are going to pay good money for your return, darling," he said in a measured tempo.

Prudence brightened and openly smiled. "Then, I'm not a prisoner?"

"You're not a prisoner, *technically*," said Nathan. "Perhaps we shall go ashore today," he declared, looking to Cate for approval.

"Perhaps not," Cate countered with a significant lilt.

Straining to decipher the silent message, Nathan scowled and said slowly, "I thought it would be nice to—"

"No, I think not," Cate said even slower.

"Pray, might you excuse us?" Launching to his feet, Nathan bobbed Prudence a bow, seized Cate's arm and propelled her outside.

"What the bloody hell was all that about?" he cried whirling around on her.

"I don't think taking her ashore is wise."

He cocked one hip, crossed his arms, and patted one foot expectantly. Cate echoed the pose.

"Do you really think we should take a sixteen-year-old girl ashore with over three hundred men?" she asked at last.

"Three hundred?"

"The *Griselle* has gone ashore, too, have they not?"

His mouth rounded in a comprehending but silent "O" as Cate went on. "She's barely gotten used to you—"

"Me! What's wrong with me?"

"For a sixteen-year-old girl, away from home for the first time, everything. Now, imagine her ashore with three hundred more."

Cate pressed her fingers to the bridge of her nose. It was a strain to recall ever being as indulged at Prudence's age, or any age, for that matter; stunningly helpless, at even the most basic levels.

"I can't believe anyone would expect a girl like her to marry—" she found herself saying.

"A bastard," Nathan finished. "'Tis what he is."

"Yes, I get that impression," she said, resigned.

"What's on your mind to pass the day? This island has glorious falls; I had it planned," he said.

Cate heaved a long sigh. It was difficult to ignore the hopeful lilt in Nathan's voice. The allure of cool breezes and shadowed pools made it that much more difficult to decline.

"I'm thinking she and I will do what young ladies do. Oh, don't look so blank," she said testily. "You brush each other's hair and talk about young men."

At least, that was what she recalled. It had been a very, very long time for such things on her part. On a more recent level, it was how Brian's nieces preferred to idle away the time.

He made a face. "Sounds wholly unappealing. Surely, you aren't expecting me to...?"

"Not in life! Perhaps later we might go," she added, in hopes of allaying his disappointment. "But in the meantime, could you please remember she's only sixteen."

He hunched his shoulders and grumbled, "Aye, I'm not decrepit."

"Well, then could you please just be... more... careful," she said in a strained whisper.

"What the bloody hell does that mean?" he cried. "You think I'm some bloody, cock-headed dolt what doesn't know his arse from—"

"Shh!"

"Shh, yourself! I don't give a tinker's damn—" He sputtered to an end, made several false starts, and then started anew. "At that age, I already made able-bodied seaman, crossed four seas, the equator double that, and rounded both horns."

"And I was living halfway across a continent and hadn't seen my family in years. She, however, has seen the inside of her parent's home and a few blocks of Boston."

He drew a surrendering hand down his face. "Very well. Pray, I beg you enlighten me with your wishes."

"Be nice."

"Goddammit, I've been nice. See!" He bared his teeth in something which started out a smile, but quickly grew more befitting of a rabid dog. "I'm a pirate!"

"A little louder and she'll be crying again, and it will be *your* fault."

"And also, it would seem, an embarrassment," he said, crestfallen.

"That's not what I meant either," she said, painfully aware of how hollow that sounded. "It's just—"

"Aye, fair enough." He waved a hand, cutting her off. "Pious and prim as the damnable Mother Superior I'll be. But she can bet her laces, I'll have her thrown in irons if she..." he shouted toward the door.

"Shh! She doesn't know you're jesting."

"Much more better, because I'm not!" Stiffening, he smartly clicked his heels together and struck a sharp but mocking salute. "Permission to breathe, sir?"

She heard the bark, but saw the mirth and bit back a smile. "Only once per glass and with prior approval."

With grave misgivings, Cate watched Nathan go astern. He had agreed and done it with a smile, more or less. But there had been an unfamiliar edge in his voice, and something even more worrisome in his eyes: she had hurt his feelings. She thought to go after him, but Prudence was waiting. She paused to watch the cargo nets being lowered into the hatches, envying the men sweating it out in the hold. As she stepped over the coaming into the cabin, she considered the possibility Nathan was having his revenge after all.

She stopped dead next the mizzenmast at seeing Prudence at the gallery sill. Cate's sewing box opened before her, she held a piece of embroidery, the piece Cate had been working on, the one to which increments of precious time was allotted each day. Resentment surged. Never, either the *Constancy* or the *Morganse*, had she felt so invaded. Biting back several unkind remarks, her first urge was to snatch it away.

"This is beautiful!" breathed Prudence. "Is this yours?"

"Why, yes, it is." On a wry note, on a ship full of men, who else's it might have been? "I only work in little bits."

"It's... it's... I've never seen anything like it." Prudence's finger traced the entwined lines of stitching. "These roses are exquisite! You should have these on your bodice and around the neck of your shift and..."

She surveyed Cate with a sidelong, askance look. "Your clothes are so plain. And your skin is so..." She bit back further comment, good breeding prevailing.

"I well might have done all that, except the thread can't be spared," Cate said, busy with arranging the boxes ivory bobbins.

Prudence's smooth brow furrowed. "Why don't you have any thread?"

"I need to make it last. Most of it — the greens and browns, at least — I put in my physik box, for the men."

"Why would men need thread?"

The girl's complete lack of comprehension of the world she presently stood in left Cate momentarily speechless.

"Because when they are injured, they often need to be sewn," Cate said levelly. There was no sorrow in seeing the girl go ill-looking. She assumed Prudence's disinclination to suffer descriptions of saber slashes, splinters, or damages wrought by a gaffing hook. Taking advantage of the suddenly still hand, she plucked the stitching away and reverently put it back, a satisfactory click of the latch marking it safe away.

"Shall we finish breakfast?" Cate said lightly.

⌘

Prudence was visibly more relaxed in Nathan's absence: she finished one scone, and then a second, along with two more hot chocolates.

"I suppose I should mind about my figure," Prudence said as she drained the porcelain cup. Blushing came readily for her China-doll complexion, and she did so then.

"I shouldn't be too worried," Cate said.

Cate smiled at the vagaries of youth while buttering a scone. She had been spared such concerns. Brian had admired her curves of bust, and most particularly, hips. After years of near starvation, she weighed nearly a stone less than when in her prime, but was gaining weight at last. She touched her waist and wondered on Nathan's opinion. She preferred not to be thought of as "a fat widow," to which many a man aspired to in their old age. On the other hand, her first day aboard Nathan had called her "scrawny." She had never heard him express any preferences one way or the other until his wistful reference to Creswicke's sister as "a plump little thing."

"There are plenty of young lads who will be looking at far more than your figure," Cate said, regarding the scone she held with a new eye.

"Do you think so?" The girl's large cornflower-blue eyes—so blue they tended to look artificial—gave her a perpetually surprised or startled expression, as they did then.

"Of course. You are aware that you're a very lovely girl," Cate said in all earnestness.

Prudence possessed all the aspects of "perfection"—oval face, rounded nose, sloping shoulders, the plumpness of privilege and modest demeanor—all the things Cate never possessed, as her mother had bemoaned with painful regularity.

Prudence cast her eyes downward. "Not really. Nanna always said as much, but she's paid for such things. Mama said

473

so, but she's... well, she's Mama. And Papa never said anything, except worry on what he was to do with me."

Cate was struck with a wave of sympathy as the words of another disapproving father echoed in her mind: incapable of being pleased or satisfied, inflicting a constant pain of rejection and criticism. It was one more connection she felt with the girl.

"You've never had any beaus?" asked Cate. It boggled the mind to think there hadn't been dozens of young men calling.

Prudence smiled dreamily, the blue eyes softening. "There was one. We meet in secret in the neighbor's garden. Papa said I had to be pure, in order to gain a proper marriage."

Mouthing a silent oath regarding ignorant, selfish men — most particularly Father Collingwood — Cate slid her chair closer and took Prudence's hand.

"You're a very pretty young lady," Cate said in all sincerity. "A young man's attentiveness is no crime. Any man concerned on account of another suitor isn't worth having."

Prudence beamed under the praise, but soon wilted. "You speak as if I have a choice. I've been betrothed to Lord Creswicke. What if he refuses me?"

He won't; there's too much money at stake, Cate thought, bitterly. Creswicke's rebuff could be the hand of Providence. Patting the soft hand, she instead said diplomatically, "If I was you, I shan't be concerned on that point."

Prudence accepted the opinion without comment. Appetite suddenly gone — no thanks to Creswicke — Cate broke bits from her scone and nibbled.

"Why didn't your mother or father accompany you?" asked Cate. It was curious why such shielding parents weren't more invested in personally seeing their daughter off to her new future.

Cate suffered greatly from the worry that, as Nathan had implied, Harte had intentionally misinformed her. To do so would have required an intricate conspiracy involving not only the Commodore, but Lady Bart and all her guests. Outlandish and improbable, the suggestion still found fertile ground. Parents showing up unexpectedly could complicate Nathan's plans.

"No, Papa said I needed to learn to be independent. It's my first time away from Boston... ever. Do you think you might show me those roses of yours?" Prudence asked.

"By all means." Cate inwardly groaned at the prospect of using up more precious thread. But, there seemed little choice.

⁘

"Be patient," Cate instructed Prudence sometime later. "It's all in the tension. Let go and you'll be required to start anew."

They sat heads bent close together as Prudence practiced the new stitch on the hem of her shift. It was a joy to have someone with which to share, the chance to discuss color and line of design, different applications of stitches, the advantages of wool to silk, or goldwork as opposed to tambour. They swapped pointers and showed off what they knew. Cate was struck by the delight of having a woman—albeit young—with which to chat and even giggle. It put her in mind of her school days, so very long ago.

During a lull while Prudence worked, Cate fetched her brush. Seated on the gallery sill, she pulled the combs free and shook out her hair. Prudence put down her work to pick up one.

"These are lovely." Prudence turned it in her hands, running her fingers over the intricate carving. "Wherever did you come by them?"

"They were a gift from the captain on the other ship. He's a particular friend to Captain Blackthorne," Cate said, working the brush through her hair. She smiled, recalling Thomas's boyish enthusiasm. "Thomas is very dear."

Prudence looked up with a conspiratorial smile. "Do you fancy him?"

Annoyance spurred Cate to brush harder. "Why would you say that?"

Prudence sighed with exaggerated innocence. "Oh, just something in your voice, I suppose. Captain Blackthorne is so... scary! Those eyes and that hair! He's—" She shuddered dramatically.

Shoving the last comb in place, Cate rose abruptly. "Let's have a hand at those roses."

The stitch in question was one Cate had initially learned in France, she and Brian being there on business, on behalf of his uncles. She had since adapted the stitch by adding several flourishes, the result being both unique and impressive.

At one point, Cate reached to correct a mistake Prudence had made. Prudence seized it and gasped, her eyes rounded in shock. "You're married!"

"I *was*." Cate tried unsuccessfully to retrieve her hand.

Prudence bounced with the excitement. "Does he know where you are? Is he coming to find you? Is he going to rescue you? Is he going to fight the pirates for you? Is he going to kill Captain Blackthorne?"

Caught up in a romantic furor, Prudence fired questions so quickly, Cate couldn't have answered them even if she was inclined, which she was not. The girl had been reading far too many novellas.

"No," was Cate's all-encompassing answer, when Prudence

paused to draw a breath. Freeing her hand at last, Cate protectively covered it with the other. "He's gone."

"Gone? You mean he deserted you?"

"No, gone, as in he's dead," Cate replied flatly. A sudden tightness seized her chest.

The plump mouth rounded in a sympathetic "O." "I'm sorry. My intention wasn't to pry—"

"No, it's quite well." The forced smile Cate had worn all morning returned. "He's been gone for... for some time now."

They bent their heads once more, the conversation limited to only an occasional word regarding the embroidery. Prudence, however, became increasingly distracted and clumsy. Cate waited in wary caution. Something was on the child's mind and there was every reason to believe whatever it was would come soon enough.

"If you've been married..." Prudence began in measured deliberation. The fair complexion flashed brilliant. "You would know what... what it is... to be with... with a man?" Her wide-eyed, China-doll gaze added to her innocence.

Cate stiffened, but kept her expression carefully arranged. The bedding was the first thing which came to mind, especially for the young and lustful, but there was ever so much more to marriage. And yes, at Prudence's age, if anyone had tried to tell her the same, she would have laughed. Admittedly, a few pointers on she and Brian's wedding night might have been advantageous, but then, the exploration and discovery had been so very rewarding. They had been virgins, but by no means virginal.

"A bit, yes," Cate said guardedly.

Prudence's smooth brow furrowed. "Mama wouldn't tell me anything except you must lay back, close your eyes and it would be over soon enough."

Cate smiled and ducked her head. To smile in the face of that stilted analysis could be quite hurtful.

Prudence pressed on. "Molly, the chambermaid, was the only other one who would tell me anything. I don't believe she's actually been with a man, but she posed as if she knew everything. She said you must..." She squeezed her eyes shut, her hands working in the fabric she held. "She said you must spread your legs and let the man put his... thing in, until he... I don't know, *does* something!"

"It hurts, that's what Molly said," Prudence was quick to add, her hands clenched in her lap. She looked up, beseeching. "Must it be just... that... quick and... scary?"

Cate suddenly felt old, like some ancient soothsayer giving

wizened advice to the lovelorn. It couldn't be said that Mother Collingwood's succinct summation was erroneous, but there was so very much more to it.

"For some, perhaps... maybe. After all, how should I know?" Cate said, growing a bit testy.

Being married did not make her an expert. Other than witnessing first-hand, no one knew exactly what went on in a marriage bed. She was reasonably sure hers had been the exception and not the rule, that conclusion being based on other wives' conversation. Their suffering air, rolled eyes, bemoaning "one's wifely duty," and relief when the husband found another "outlet" were all indicators that they did not meet nights with the same relish as she.

"No, not always, if the man is gentle and attentive," Cate said carefully.

Prudence's lower-lip protruded, as if she meant to argue. Regrettably, if pressed, Cate would be obliged to admit that no matter how well-meaning the man might be, the first time was always — had been — painful.

What was it like to be in bed with a man?

Running a hand along her arm, Cate recalled in vivid detail what couldn't be shared with a young girl who, in all probability, had never been kissed: snowy, Highland winter nights under quilts, with a man who wanted nothing more than to bed his wife. How could she describe the long arms and warm hands which held and caressed, the murmurings and exploring, lying languid and flushed, pleasures and pleasing —

"You loved him, didn't you?"

Cate jerked at the sound of Prudence's voice.

"My husband? Of course," Cate said unsteadily. She dashed the wetness from her cheek with a trembling hand. "When you're with the man you love, you'll look forward to doing those things."

Cate couldn't help but smile at that. Ah, yes! All of them, again... and again... and...

Prudence's expression hardened into that of one accustomed to being told anything but the truth. "And if you don't, love him that is?"

Given what Cate knew of Creswicke, she felt as if she was tossing a lamb to the lion. Rubbing at a sudden pang in her temple, she tried desperately to think of a way to not dash the girl's hopes, while not building unrealistic expectations.

Damn you, Father Collingwood, wherever you are!

"Well, sometimes love takes its time," said Cate, lamely.

God, as if the child had any.

Whether satisfied, disappointed, confused, or embarrassed, Prudence allowed the subject to perish. She bent over her stitching with renewed purpose. Cate sat on the sill, ostensibly supervising. She stared at her hand clenched in her lap, her ring gleaming dully, and battled the memories now unleashed. She had learned long ago that once the floodgates were opened, blessed little would stop them. Thomas's resemblance had brought Brian so very near.

Brian's face rose up, his lake blue eyes glowing with need. She looked up to see him leaned against the fire mantle, the flames gilded hip and thigh, and shone like a copper helmet on his hair. She blinked, and he was in bed, head pillowed on his arm watching her undress. He lifted the blanket, inviting her in. She closed her eyes, and they were under the stars, making love their last night together, his mouth and hands memorizing her every surface and curve.

Cate's breath caught in a half-choked sob. Tears welling, she lurched to her feet, stammered a vague excuse and ran from the cabin. Solitude was what she sought, but it was a ship; there was no privacy. She ran to the forecastle and pressed her forehead hard against the rail, in hopes the pain might erase the anguish. The swirling visions only came faster, crushing and devastating, threatening to drive her to knees.

"Are you well, luv?"

She whirled around at being touched. Too shaken to speak, she stared at Nathan through a shimmering blur of tears.

"You look like you've seen a ghost," he said, softly. The vertical lines of his face deepened with concern.

Nathan shook her gently by the shoulders and called her. She dimly thought how rarely he used her formal name. The fact he did so now showed the level of his alarm.

Her mouth moved, but no words came. She began to quake. Emanating from deep within, the tremors jolted through her, until her bones seemed to rattle against each other. She swayed then crumpled against him and sobbed. She clung to him, fearful of the great pit which yawed at her feet, where demons named Isolation, Heartbreak, Loss and Hopelessness waited. She cried for things she hadn't cried for in years, things thought forgotten, and then from the pain of having done so. There were the things she had, and those which she never would. She pounded at his chest at the unfairness of it all.

Time was lost; she had no idea of how long Nathan held her. Slowly she quieted, the floodgates closed, and the ghosts retreated. Still, she clung to him. His shoulder under her cheek, so solid and warm, he promised the safety and protection she hadn't known for so very long. Defender? Provider? Confident? He was so many things, and yet no knight in shining armor.

"I'm sorry," she sniffed. "It's not..."

"Hist, now" he murmured against her cheek. "'Tis all well. Ol' Nathan is here. You're safe."

She sank against him, molding her to his body as he swayed with her. Gradually the tension drained, her muscles twitching and jerking as they released. Her face hot and swollen, eyes throbbing knots, she sniffed again. He offered his sleeve, encouraging her to blow. Embarrassed, and with little choice, she did. Murmuring nothings, he dried her face with his other sleeve then brushed away the strands of her hair stuck in the tear tracks.

"God! I'm a mess!" she choked, dashing at her eyes with the back of her hand. "I'm sorry; I didn't mean to make such a fool out of myself. I just... all of a sudden... I..."

"No worries, darling. You were crying for him." He thumbed away a few straggling tears. The corner of his mustache lifted in a smile that failed.

"How did you know?"

Nathan gave a tight-lipped smile, the corners of his eyes pinched with resignation. "The only time you cry thus is for him. You love him; 'tis no crime that you grieve for him."

"But you shouldn't have to put up with a sniveling woman," she said, toying with a braid at his shoulder. "It's not fair."

He flipped a hand, making a poor attempt at levity. "Ah, trifles, mere trifles. If I minded, I wouldn't be here, eh?"

Putting a finger under her chin, he brought her face up to meet his. "I promise, I'll find him. If he is anywhere on this earth, I will find him."

"He's dead, Nathan." Her voice quavered, threatening to break again.

"So, you keep saying," he said tolerantly and drew her close once more.

It felt so good to be held; it had been years. Until then, she hadn't realized how desperate in need she was for the touch of another human. Other than being snatched, grabbed or accosted. It had been years since she had been held by a man for the mere sake of it. His shoulder solid beneath her head, she could smell the tear-dampened linen of his shirt.

His body stiffened, and he pushed her back to hold her at arms' length.

"You need off this ship, and I shan't take 'no' for an answer, nor do I want to hear or care about Princess What's-Her-Name."

Cate's hopes soared at the prospect. Leaving the ship could mean escaping the ghosts currently haunting.

"It sounds wonderful! I'll go tell Prudence."

Nathan made a guttural sound of disgust. "Do we *have* to take the Princess of Darkness? I know! We'll lock her up!" he declared, with an inspired finger to the air. "We'll put her in the hold; the bilge rats deserve her. No, that won't due. Hermione doesn't deserve that. We shan't have milk for a week. Why can't we just leave her to annoy the anchor watch for the day?"

"We can't just leave her."

"Why not? Why does she have to follow us like some wharf cur?"

"Because you brought that wharf cur aboard, and now it's... *she's*, your responsibility. You made an agreement: Creswicke gives you the money and you give her back safe. How is it to look if you arrive with an injured or damaged hostage?"

The dark slash of brows shot up to the edge of his headscarf. "Damaged? First of all," he began, ticking his points off on his fingers, "*damaged* is exactly what they are expecting. She's on a pirate ship, ergo she's assumed *damaged*. Secondly, I don't give a buggering damn what they think, as long as they pay. And thirdly, how did I wind up arguing when all I wanted was to do something nice. How the bloody hell did that happen!"

"You keep saying you want me to relax, but how can I, if I'm worried about her?"

Agitation growing, he began to pace, hands spiraling skyward. "Hell, and death, there's no telling what the little petticoat might do next. She's constantly ordering you about like you're her damned chambermaid. In less than a day, she's taken over me cabin, has you sleeping on the deck, in an utterly reproachful mood, I might add. You're crying, and you've begun talking to yourself."

"I do not."

"Aye, but you do."

She bit her lip. He wasn't entirely incorrect. "Perhaps to her I am the chambermaid. Do you remember an older woman with her?"

"Aye," he said after a pause to recall. "Caterwauled enough to raise the dead, she did. We were in no need of a grannie."

"Well, in retrospect, bringing *the grannie* would have made things ever so much easier. That was her nanny."

"I'll remember that the next time I kidnap a sixteen-year-old, *if* I ever grow *that* desperate again!" he said, with a suffering roll of his eyes. "You should be subservient to no one. If I hear her bark one more order—"

"She doesn't bark—"

"If I hear her bark one more order at you," he repeated evenly, narrowing a malevolent eye, "I'll... well, I'll... I'll do something, and it shan't be pleasant."

Muttering several unrepeatable oaths, Nathan surrendered by throwing his hands in the air. "Fair enough! Anchor watch didn't do anything to deserve her anyway. To leave her, I'd be losing men overboard hither and yon, like rats off a fire ship. Probably have to shanghai me next crew, since no one what knows a bowline from a ratline would board this ship else."

20: FALLS OF OUR EXISTENCE

"This is wonderful, Nathan." Her head pillowed on the folded quilt, Cate stretched out on the luxurious carpet of moss.

Nathan plopped down next to her, grinning. The sunlight filtered through the dense greenery in broad bands of yellow. The fine mist from the nearby waterfall glistened like fairy dust on his braids and lashes. "I give you joy of your pleasure."

They had come ashore earlier that afternoon. Unshipping Prudence, however, had been quite the ordeal.

"This is'na going to be easy," said Mr. Cameron, standing next to Cate at the rail. Realizing he'd been overheard, he explained in his Scot's brogue. "T'was a fair wrestle t' bring her aboard." He sighed, woefully shaking his head. "T'will be no better achievin' the reverse."

Cate leaned closer to Cameron to ask from the corner of her mouth, "How did you get her aboard in the first place?"

He mouthed the words "Admiral's chair," with reserved contempt.

It was a contraption beneath the dignity of every able-bodied seaman, reserved for the incapable and the inept. No more than a wooden slat looped in a rope dangling from a yardarm, it resembled a swing rigged in a play yard. At the whim of ship, wave and wind, it could be a precarious ride.

"I'm impressed anyone was able to get her in one of those," Cate said, more to herself.

"Alone, nay... exactly." He smiled slyly as, in typical Highlander style, he allowed the suspense to build. "In the Captain's lap."

Sputtering a laugh, Cate tried to visualize that, but found it unnecessary, since it was being played out before her.

Situated deep in a seat, Nathan hooked an arm around Prudence's middle tightly enough to elicit a squeak of protest.

With the grunt and sweat of those manning the halyard, the sling rose. Eyes round as shillings, Prudence squealed and kicked. It was difficult to be sure if it was an inopportune pitch of the ship, or a bit of tomfoolery on the part of those controlling the line, but the chair took a wild arch out over Cate's head as she clamored down the accommodation ladder. She looked up to a grim-faced Nathan, half-submerged in a billowing cloud of yellow skirts. With a grunt of satisfaction, he released his burden into the awaiting launch several inches premature. Prudence landed in an inelegant heap in the bottom amid several inches of bilge water.

Nathan gave every hand in the longboat the benefit of a glare which forestalled further comments. As they pushed away from the *Morganse's* side, Cate retreated to the furthest point of the bow, where she could hide the smile which couldn't be suppressed. The palpable tension transformed the short journey ashore into something akin to Purgatory, everyone present obliged to listen to Prudence, striving futilely to keep her skirts clear of the water, bemoan the destruction of her shoes and lack of a hat.

"A true lady simply never goes out in the sun without one," the child sniffed.

Prudence's third, or perhaps it was the fourth, repetition of said guideline was cut short by Nathan's arm snaking out to snatch a hat—a thoroughly disreputable, sweat-stained affair— from an oarsmen and plunking it on her head. Its flop brim sagged nearly to her nose, but delivered silence.

Once ashore, Nathan made a final, valiant attempt to leave Prudence behind, citing her dress and patent-leather slippers as unfit for traversing rough terrain. He was no match for either woman's stubbornness. Shaking his head as he muttered darkly, he struck off with his female entourage in tow, with a rucksack under his arm and the blue-and-yellow quilt from the bunk over his shoulder.

Nathan led them down the sugar-white shore to where a stream met the bay. There he turned inland, his battered leather tricorn a compass needle pointing the way. Once again, Cate plunged from a world of saturated blues, into a verdant tapestry of color. The shrill cries of gulls gave way to the chattering of brightly-plumed flocks of small, parrot-like birds. Her venture inland a few days before had been through a claustrophobic press of green. Here they walked under a park-like canopy of palms, her neck aching with trying to see their crowns.

Nathan regaled them with one story after another. Cate only half-listened, smiling to herself at the not so subtle variations from versions she had heard many times over. She wondered how historians centuries later would reconcile the inconsistencies: was it a monster or a monstrous wave which had sank the ship; plague or marauding natives who wiped out the marooned crew; a ghost or a precocious sea goddess which had stalked the decks; had the heroic captain been shot five times or stabbed four?

It was an unspeakable joy to have Nathan alone—well, almost. It was easy enough to pretend the child wasn't there. She closed her eyes and listened to the timbre of his voice, ragged, yet mellow, like well-worn flannel. She oft wondered what his voice might have been before it had been so shattered. That there had been violence was evident in the scar at his throat, as to what it had been she dared not venture to inquire.

Prudence was torn between her fear of Nathan and her horror of the unknown. Every flutter, buzz of wing, or snap of twig presented eminent peril. Her base instincts of a man as protection, especially one bearing a pistol, knife and cutlass, ultimately prevailed, and she hung at his elbow. The proximity had caused her fear to give way to something between fascination and morbid curiosity.

At length, Prudence whined of being hot and tired, and they stopped for a rest. Cate sat on the ground with Nathan spread-eagle on his back beside her. Representing that a lady never sat on the ground, Prudence perched atop a rock, near enough for safety's sake, but far enough to be out of hearing.

"It would seem she has overcome her fear of you," Cate observed.

Nathan raised his head to peer down the length of his body to where Prudence sat.

"Can't understand what she's afraid of." He dropped his head back down and said to the trees, "Never hurt a woman in me life."

"You'll have to admit, for someone from Boston, you *are* a bit of a sight."

He lifted his head to glare down his nose. "What do you mean by that?"

Cate twisted around in order to see him better. "You have no idea, do you? To the unsuspecting, you are positively… Let's see, what word I am looking for?"

"Fearsome? Villainous? Rapacious? Scalawag?" His eyebrows waggled in hopeful anticipation.

"No… eccentric."

"Eccentric?" His mustache drooped as he dropped his head back down. "Eccentric." He mouthed the word with visible distaste. "Doesn't sound very impressive."

"Very well, exotic. How's that?"

"Barely better," he grumbled, his dignity ruffled. "Might as well be a bloody schoolmaster."

His indignation struck a chord. Laughter exploded from her. She put a hand over her mouth, her eyes bulging as it fizzed out between her fingers. Nathan rose up on one elbow and glowered.

"I'm sorry," she said, eyes streaming. Only the barest hint of remorse could be managed. "I'm sorry. I didn't mean to hurt—"

Another peal erupted. She clamped her hand over her mouth once more, only to have it explode out her nose.

"Think you're funny, don't you?" he huffed over her giggling, now beyond all control. He was obliged to raise his voice in order to be heard. "So, pleased you're able to find such humor at my expense. Always glad to be of service."

He flopped back down and glared at the trees. "Bloody woman!"

They soon pressed on, Nathan being quite anxious. The trail became steeper, but he assured them their destination was but a short distance more. The increasing sound of rushing water gave credence of something being ahead. The sound had grown to a roar, by the time they rounded an out-cropping of rocks. The foliage fell away to reveal a waterfall curving along one side of a sun-drenched clearing. Nearly as wide as the *Morganse* was long, the falls were an accumulation of a number of smaller ones, anchored periodically by pillars of rock. The water sheeted down in streaks of emerald green and lime, disappearing into a roiling froth of white at the base.

The roar of the cascades made speech impossible, and so Nathan mutely waved them on. He helped them scramble up an incline, and then duck through a stand of flowering bushes, the cerise-colored petals showering their heads and shoulders. They broke out into what struck Cate as almost a room: the walls a tapestry of greens, the carpet made of moss, and a vaulted ceiling of branches. The centerpiece was a large pool, formed by a series of stair-step falls, from knee-high to the height of a man. It was considerably quieter there, the water sheeting over the tiers in a rustling gurgle. The glen's air was thick with moisture, but pleasantly cool.

Nathan spread the quilt for Cate, while Prudence perched on a nearby log. From his sack he produced a half-round of bread, cheese and a stone bottle of cider. While they ate their luncheon, Nathan launched into another tale of island natives and Spanish conquistadors, one out-manipulating the other in some kind of *coup de grace*.

When finished, Prudence's youthful exuberance wouldn't allow her to sit, so fascinated she was with every detail. The flora, that was; anything alive still sent her squealing. After saving Prudence from eminent peril — an inquisitive beetle on her shoe — Nathan drew up before Cate. Rocking on his heels, he looked far too much like a boy anxiously waiting to show his mother the frog in his pocket.

"I was thinking... I mean, if you like... Since it's been a bit... What with everything and all..."

Cate squinted with one eye up at him. "Nathan, are you trying to say something?"

He sucked in a deep breath. "I just thought you might fancy a swim," came out in an explosion. He waved toward the pool. "It's fair deep enough, around the other side, at any rate. I just thought...Well, that you'd like —"

"Nathan, will you just come out with it."

"I meant for you to enjoy today, without all the disruptions and distractions of yon witchy-girl," he finished, with a loathing glare over his shoulder.

Looking back at Cate, he sobered. "You look like you've fouled your hawse. What's amiss, luv?"

"Nothing. I'm fine," she said, busily brushing breadcrumbs from her skirt.

"As you always insist," he said tolerantly. He crouched down to reach and stop her hand. His coffee-colored eyes held hers. "Credit Ol' Nathan a bit, eh? From the first, you stood with your shoulders square and your head up, ready to tell anyone, including me, to go to hell. Now today, you slump along with your head down..."

His words faded as he followed her gaze to Prudence.

"Ah, so I see," he said quietly and sat back on his heels. "In all the flurry and hubbub, I'd forgotten one very salient point: you're a woman."

"You make it sound like a sentence."

He snorted. "Hardly, darling. Without, the world would be a considerably less appealing place: nothing but hairy chests and aching balls. It never occurred you would be one to be longing for that."

His head inclined in the general direction of Prudence, and more importantly, what she symbolized.

"Not *long for*," Cate qualified moodily, toying with the fabric of her skirt.

A finger to her chin brought her head up. "Then what?"

His intuition was alarming. While she had been piecing together the puzzle of Nathan Blackthorne, he had been doing the same. It was uncomfortable to have him poking about in her thoughts. She had struggled with the sensation since she had seen Prudence cowering on the floor. She had preferred to think she was above it, but there it was: jealousy. It was an unbecoming color on anyone and was even less flattering on her.

"It's just," Cate began. "Well, it's just... I mean, look at her. Everyone can see it, sense it. Everyone is different: the men talk different, Mr. Kirkland brings out the best dishes, chairs are pulled out, doors are opened, the men bow... Hell, you even bowed."

"Because I thought you desired it. I could have just as easily spit on her. I'll go do it now, if you like."

"It wouldn't matter," she sighed. He gave the impression of being more than willing to do so, if she was but to nod. "She'd still be the lady, and I'd still be the —"

"That's what's bothering you? A bloody title?"

Nathan regarded her through a narrowed eye. His realization bloomed, and he slumped. "I've only seen you in near rags. It didn't answer you'd be one to fancy dresses and fine things."

She hunched her shoulders defensively and looked away. "I don't."

"Ah, but you do, luv." He scrubbed a frustrated hand at the back of his neck. "For the love of... You've trunk-loads in the hold and more in the cabin, yours for the taking. There's not a tar aboard what would begrudge you a stitch of it."

"It's not that. Besides, it's a ship. I couldn't wear any of it anyway."

Dark with concern, the coffee-and-cinnamon eyes searched hers. "This is what I've done to you, isn't it? Living at sea like a Portuguese fishwife when you could have been living in finery."

She snorted and rolled her eyes. "Living where? I have no place."

His steady gaze prodded her to continue. The memories were all so much more manageable when she kept them stashed away. Once freed, it was like Pandora's box, the pain and regrets devouring her. Each time they were released, they were doubly difficult to pack them away.

"I'm not some poor wastrel who doesn't know what she's missing. I had all that. Maybe not as fine as Lady Bart's, but I know what I lost. My family owned thousands of acres; my mother's mother was third cousin to the Spanish Royal House, a Hapsburg. Brian's uncle was The Mackenzie, the head of the biggest clan in Scotland. We lived on an estate, with dozens of tenants; Brian was laird of it all. I know what I've lost. I just don't appreciate having my nose rubbed in it."

There it was: the stab high up under her ribs which always came with remembering. She rubbed her forehead, cheeks heating in frustration at how horribly desperate she sounded.

"Perhaps I should have ransomed you after all."

She heard the tease in Nathan's voice and looked up, the sight of his gold and ivory grin eliciting a reluctant one from her.

"Save your energy; it's all so very, very gone," she said tartly.

His smile faded, and he sobered. "And I'll wager you mourned when it was gone."

"I mourned for *who* I lost, not what." She would have traded it all to have Brian back, but Fate had chosen not to leave her even that bargaining chip. In a single day — in a matter of a few hours — she had gone from a lady of substance to a nameless fugitive, with nothing more to her name than what could be stuffed in a saddle bag.

"It's just around her, I feel — I feel the same as when I was at Lady Bart's, with Harte and all those others looking at me... like I didn't fit in. Which, yes, I know I don't," she said peevishly. "Never have — not fully — but it's just that —"

He batted his lids in disbelief. "Yet again, with the 'don't fit in'? I saw you wade into the midst of strange men — pirates, I might add — half-naked, and proceed to sew a man's flesh. You've lived on a ship among a hundred-odd and have earned the respect of every one of them, a feat not to be dismissed," he added, wagging his finger at her. "You lived alone in London for years, survived a war and shed enough blood to gain the attention of the Crown."

"And yet put me in a room with silk and lace, and all I can think of is to crawl into the corner. No one will ever mistake me for a lady."

Her throat tightened at the echo of her mother's words. Time and again, she had endured her mother's bemoaning of her lack of grace and modesty, all as impossible to attain as more sloping shoulders and a jaw less bold.

"You're far too much woman to be wasted on fop and frippery," he said coldly.

Cheeks burning with embarrassment, she tried to look away, but he took her by the chin and firmly pulled her back. A tremor ran through his fingertips as he locked her eyes with his.

"And any bastard — man or woman — what fails to see that doesn't warrant being in your presence. The corner is never where you belong. You should be front and center."

He rose and began pacing, his hands carving the air. "Tell

me—hell, tell the entire crew what you desire, luv. If it's a fine house, jewels, servants, then so it shall be. If you want, I'll get you an entire goddamned island, and you can have your personal empire. You can hold court over them all, and they'll be obliged to kiss your skirts and beg your leave."

Checking himself, he drew up before her and smiled. "Just tell me what you want and Ol' Nathan will get it for you."

"None of that." Touched by his resolve, her throat tightened. "I'm not ashamed, nor have I minded—"

"But now she has you looking around, seeing what you don't have," he put in knowingly.

"I know what I *do* have." She looked up and said earnestly, "Thank you, Nathan. Have I ever said that?"

"For what?"

"Everything: my life, a place to belong, food, shelter, purpose... a friend."

He smiled, both recalling his adamant objections when she first bestowed the title. Modesty flowed abundant, the heavy lashes lowering. "No worries, luv. A decent man would do no else."

"And you are decent, aren't you?"

He grimaced and leaned down to say "I'd prefer it if you didn't broadcast that last bit about" in low-voiced confidence.

She smiled. "Consider it done; my lips are sealed."

Tease lurked once more in the cinnamon highlights of his eyes. "I knew you were quality, the moment I laid eyes on you."

"Quality doesn't pay the butcher, nor feed the dormouse," she said tartly.

"Aye, but 'tis an admirable trait what doesn't necessarily come with title or position."

He slid his eyes sideways toward the pool. "Then how's about a nice bath? The Queen of Persia never had one as grand. Better than any *lady* could ever dream of."

He gave her one of those smiles that was meant to charm and it did. The hot bath a few days before had been wonderful, but there had been no opportunity to wash since. The hike had left her hot and sticky, her shift stuck to her ribs under her stays. Filled with regret and embarrassment and touched by his concern, she hoped he didn't notice her eyes were beginning to brim as she nodded. But, of course, he did. He missed blessed little.

With his usual elegant grace and a gesture reminiscent of Mr. Al-Nejem, touching his fingertips to his lips and heart, he bent and swept a hand toward the pool. "M' lady."

Nathan moved to a discrete distance. Cate went behind a fern, its massive fiddle-heads nearly head-high. She struggled out of her laces and peeled away the sweat-dampened layers of clothing. Wary of the slippery rocks, she probed the water's shallows with a cautious foot, until the drop-off was found, and slipped in.

The hot spring had been glorious, alive with fine bubbles. The water here was coolly refreshing, the swirl like caressing arms, massaging her body and limbs. With glee bordering on childishness, she rolled again and again. She dove to lie at the bottom like a trout on a summer's day and then broke the surface in a sputtering explosion of air. Floating on her back, she allowed the eddies to take her under the falls and back around. On one pass, she caught a glimpse of Nathan through the greenery. She heard the scratch of his voice, but the water's rush drowned the words, and so she floated.

Nathan took up a post at the pool's edge, near enough to bear an eye, yet far enough to allow Cate privacy. Well, aye, it meant close enough to catch an occasional glimpse through the ferns. Blessed eternity it was between the sightings of the ivory blur of her body.

He had lost track of Princess Pain-in-the-Arse. Could fall off a bloody cliff, for all he cared.

Might could just prop up the body and collect the ransom. T'would be that much more delightful for Lord-on-Highness Creswicke pay for what was already dead.

By a certain way of thinking, he could be doing the wretched wench a favor: putting her out of her misery, before the suffering began. And suffering she most certainly would, wed to His Haughtiness. Plaques might be issued in his honor for the magnanimity of his humanity for saving the soul from such tortures.

On the other hand, no one deserved misery more than the one who inflicted it. Suffering came in many forms, and she had managed to exploit a heretofore untold number. As the sages are known to say, turnabout is fair play, or misery enjoys company, or some such rot.

His hand brushed his cheek.

The Devil burn me! I forgot to shave.

Cate preferred when he did so, the green eyes going to blue, a sure sign of pleasure. Those eyes were a port to what went on inside that maddening tangle of mahogany. Cross her and risk waking the jaguar. Hard and green they would go, fit to separate a man's gullet from his craw. Please her, and they would go the color of the reefs. Bloody rare sight it was, hence, a judgment based on brief observation.

He moved to the pool's edge, near enough to see Cate, and yet not to be seen. There he knelt over his reflection, drew his knife, and set to scraping the growth from his jaw.

A flash of yellow caught his eye. He looked up in time to see Princess Pain-in-the-Arse skulking about the bank. Swearing under his breath, he allowed a brief fancy of the blade in his fist pressing at her throat.

Belay that! Cate would never abide it I'd never hear the end of it.

It was no great deed to catch up said wench, clap a hand over her mouth, and drag her away from the water, and more importantly, Cate's hearing.

"Where the bloody hell do you think you're going?" he demanded in a hoarse whisper after depositing the noisome wench neatly on a rock.

She gave a prominent display of lip. "I was just going to—"

"I don't care if your skirts are on fire, you'll not disturb her."

Prudence sprang back up. "I just need her to—"

"Nothing! You have had her at the beckoning crook of your finger since last night."

She primly batted her lashes, as if he hadn't seen that one before! "I can't imagine what you're talking about."

"No imagination necessary, darling. Do not try me on. Bother her, and I'll turn up those skirts and give you the spanking you so justly deserve. Now sit!"

A rigid arm pointed, and Prudence did so, stiff as the rock ledge beneath her. He considered returning to the poolside to shave, but on second thought, sat squarely next to her. To his pleasure, she shifted sideways, tucking her skirts away lest they touch the dirty pirate. Crossing his arms, he settled for the duration.

Between the noise of the falls and a flock of parrots overhead in full-voice, it was a bit of a strain, but he could still hear Cate splashing about, cavorting like a mermaid. The mind could be as barren as a desert, but at the moment, his was as fertile as Eden with imaginings of what awaited just the other side of those bushes.

"Can't we—?" Prudence began.

"Shh!"

"Then, couldn't—?"

"Shh! Shh!"

Huffing in protest, she bent her head under the broad hat brim. Her feet soon picked up her restlessness and began rapping rhythmically against the rock.

"Didn't your mother teach you not to fidget?" he asked over the tempo.

"She tried," came from under the hat. Pushing back the brim, she peered up from under it like a hermit crab. "You make me nervous. I can't control myself when I'm nervous" The brim flopped back down.

"Me? What did I do?" he asked, inching away.

"Nothing... exactly." Her voice suddenly went to a pitch which would warrant a mouse. The tempo of her feet increased, her head now bobbing in unison. "You're so... strange."

"Strange?" He frowned. "That's a rather uninstructive observation."

Hunching her shoulders, Prudence withdrew under the brim like said crab. He eyed her and considered the merits of pulling the thing clean to her chin, if he thought it would serve. Instead, he re-crossed his arms and settled back to his vigil. He discovered, if he leaned ever so slightly to port, it brought him to an advantageous hole in the greenery, through which he could see where the sun illuminated the pool and Cate when she passed. It was pleasing to do at least this much for her. The woman was blessedly difficult to please; like pulling shipworms from a hull to learn what she desired. Concern for her drug at him. It was wholly disquieting to see her —

"Have you been a pirate long?"

His head snapped around. "What?"

"Have you been a pirate long?" she repeated more forcefully.

"Long enough," he said with some hesitation as to where this line of questioning might lead.

She nodded distractedly and looked off. There was a brief — and altogether uncomfortable, by his measure — silence. A viper can be ever so quiet before it strikes.

"Have you ever killed anyone? Pirates are always killing. Have you ever killed anyone?"

"Eh?"

"Do you really drink the blood of your victims? Why is your hair so strange? Did you know Blackbeard? Don't the cannons scare...?"

Fired them off like a battery, she did. Like crossing the doldrums, she finally ran out of wind.

"She's afraid of you, you know."

His head jerked up. "What?"

"She's afraid of you." Prudence enunciated, as if he were simple.

Slack-jawed as said simpleton, he stared. "She's never —"

"I'm sure she's never said," Prudence put in, primly. "But how can you expect someone who's afraid of you to tell you so?"

His head was beginning to buzz; he shook it to clear it.

I need rum... bad!

"Why did you made her cry today?" she asked, with far more scold than he cared for.

"I never —"

"She was perfectly fine when *we* were talking." The wench took on an entirely unpleasant imperiousness. "And then, she went out, and you said horrible things. When she came back in, she'd been crying. Anyone could see it."

"Well, aye, she had, but —"

"She was telling me *all* about him."

"Him?"

"Yes, *him!*" Her eyes rounded with significance. "You know, the captain of the other ship. She fancies him," she said, importantly.

Like the dry gripes, a pain clutched his gut. He swallowed hard, his mouth suddenly gone dry.

Suffering Jesus on the cross!

"You could see it in her eyes and in her voice when she spoke of him," Prudence sighed dreamily. Her head bobbed faster, the rhythm of her feet quickening. "Isn't it romantic? It's like a storybook: on the high seas, a woman captive, the handsome pirate rescues her, and they fall in love to sail away."

"Sounds like a goddamned nightmare," he groaned, rubbing his face in his hands.

She reddened and said in high-toned virtuousness, "Blasphemers go to hell."

"Been there, darling, and the goddamnedest place it 'tis," he said evenly.

Her face deepened color, but then she pressed on. "Cate is lovely already, but if she had something more suitable, she could allure him *so* much more readily."

"Not necessarily me first and foremost desire," he said through his fingers.

A rational voice was able to finally break through the fog of irrationality. "Clap a stopper on it!"

Seized by the icy fear that Cate might have heard, he lowered his voice to a level known to make able-bodied f'c'stlemen quake. "I don't know your game, Your Meddlesomeness, but I'll offer you fair warning just the same."

Prudence sat back, lids fluttering in disbelief. "Whatever do you mean, Captain?" Her face started to crumple, chin quivering. "My only intention was to help. Cate's been so kind and..."

Panic overcame frustration at seeing her prime up for another deluge. Panic gave way to horror at the thought of Cate finding the snot crying again.

"Hist, now. Belay," he said in his most soothing manner, as soothing as possible when every fiber of his being wanted to wring the life from the malignant pestilence.

Desperation led him to the cider bottle, and he offered it eagerly. Observing carefully while she sipped, he saw her eyes were brimming, but thankfully her cheeks were dry. He glanced toward the pool and closed his eyes in relief.

Sweet merciful heaven! The gods are on me side! She still swims.

⌘

Cate had knelt in the shallows of the pool. Scooping up handfuls of sand, she had scoured away months of grime and emerged from the water like a nymph, new of body and life. Now, glowing and pink, she had thanked Nathan effusively. For all his denials, he beamed with pleasure.

Prudence cavorted about the glen, marveling at butterflies and picking wildflowers. Tossing the latter on the water, she watched in fascination as they swirled on the pool's eddies and eventually swept out of sight downstream. Mirthlessly pointing out that his daisy-picking days were long over, Nathan had shed his hat and weapons—still at arm's reach—and flopped down on the quilt spread on a luxuriant patch of moss then patted the space next to him for Cate to join him.

Nathan reclined, his hands laced behind his head and ankles crossed. Sitting companionably together as they did, so near and yet never touching, they were almost as brother and sister. Brother and sister, that is, who had been separated at birth and just recently rejoined, for siblings raised together possessed an intimate knowledge of each other. She knew relatively little of him, and he of her.

Eyes closed, he dozed, his chest slowly rising and falling. It must have been a man's trait, she thought as she ruffled her fingers through her hair to dry it. Brian had possessed the same talent: dirt, rock, or deck, he could make himself comfortable. With his shirt pulled taut, the filtered sun spangled in the mist which collected on his hair and lashes, and curved lacy patterns over his body. Now minus his belts and weapons, his hips were considerably slimmer, his shoulders seeming so much wider.

Away from his ship, Nathan was a different man. When with his crew, he was one of a greater whole, the leader, but still reliant on their acquiescence. Command never seemed a burden,

494

but he was always preoccupied, as if half-expecting to be called away for some minutia regarding his ship. He was connected to the *Morganse*, the heart to his body, his ear always cocked to every creak and groan of canvas, plank or rigging. He would never be whole without his ship, but for this small bit, Cate could pretend and was content to have him for her own.

To see Nathan thus provided a glimpse of what he might have been before... everything: genial, without the edge; humorous, without the bite; more like Thomas, in many ways. She closed one eye and tried to imagine him as what could have been: close-shaven, his hair sleeked back and bound with a bow—blue, to show off the silken black and color of his eyes—an elegant waistcoat, silk shirt with a laced neckcloth, hosed and slippered, just like those in Lady Bart's salon.

The image refused to form, for it was never meant to be. Regardless of whatever Fate delivered him, Nathan would always be a man of the sea, "free", just as it was written on his chest.

"Do you remember that age?" Cate asked idly sometime later.

Nathan stirred and opened his eyes. He raised up to crane his head around her in order to see Prudence. He snorted as he lay back and closed his eyes.

"Aye, well enough. Thomas and I was able seaman, by then. Couldn't keep our minds on our duties for the aching balls and stiff cocks."

Cate lifted a brow, considering. "A fair description; my brothers weren't much different."

He lifted his head again to peer down the long line of his nose at her. "And you?"

"Umm..." She closed one eye as she recalled. "I was serving the second year of my sentence at Mrs. Peachwood's Academy for Young Ladies of Virginia."

"Oh, dear. I never saw you for that sort," he said, regarding her anew.

"The operative word was 'sentence,' with two more years to serve, or so I thought at the time."

"Reprieve?"

"Of a sorts."

Sensing a story, Nathan rose to his elbows. "What was your crime?"

"Being a product of the world in which I was raised."

He snorted again. "So, shall we all be punished. And pray tell, how did the young ladies at Mrs. Peachwood's occupy their young active minds?" By the licentious lilt in his voice, the minds were the last thing he was thinking.

"Young men, to be sure. Much more romanticized versions than you're thinking, however."

"Always the way of it," he grumbled good-naturedly. He resettled with his hands behind his head and re-crossed his ankles. "'Tis Providence you women have us men about to show you the way of things, or mankind would have died out ages ago."

She ducked a mocking bow from her seat. "Allow me on behalf of all women of the ages to offer our eternal gratitude."

"No thanks to my brothers, I'm afraid I wasn't near so uninformed," she went on. "I was called before the headmistress, more times than I care to think, for dispelling a number of misconceptions, when it came to all that."

He sat up to consider her through a slitted eye. Only one side of his face had been shaven and only a small patch, at that. It gave him an odd, half-cocked appearance.

"I can see where you might have been quite the adventuress. The lads must have been pounding at your door," he said.

"They tried," she laughed mirthlessly. "Thanks to my brothers, I also knew how to defend myself."

Nathan clapped a dramatic hand on his chest. "A heartbreak for all!"

He sobered to ask, "And how does the granddaughter of the third cousin to the Spanish Crown come to be in Virginia?"

He was of course referring to her outburst earlier, and a regrettable one it was.

"A circuitous route, to be sure," she finally said.

"Pray tell," he said, his interest growing. "You say you lived in the Highlands, yet you sound like no Scot I've ever heard. You say you grew up in the Colonies, and yet you speak Spanish like a native. I've heard you with Ferrero and Novello," he added as an aside.

It was a bit startling to learn that he had been observing her so closely. She was unaccustomed to anyone taking such notice.

"I was born in Nueva España. Tejas, the far northern region." she said finally. "What with prejudices and suspicions as they are, I learned it was easier to just say I was from the Colonies."

"I knew I'd never heard that accent before. So, from Tejas to Virginia." It came more as a conclusion than question.

"Not quite. My mother passed when I was fourteen."

A shadow crossed his face, revealing that he too had known the hollow feeling of a world suddenly gone empty. As a child, he too had stood at the edge of a grave, straining to understand the words spoken about a benevolent and forgiving god, who would answer prayers, and yet not possessing the strength to pray hard enough, or apparently so, for they were never answered. It was a dark path of recollection that she thought neither of them desired to follow.

"It was but a few weeks after Father announced he had no means to raise a daughter. So, I was sent to Charles Town to live with an aunt and uncle," she said grimly.

His continued silence pressed her to go on. "They sent me to be schooled in Virginia."

"And the lads of Virginia were forever grateful."

Her cheeks heated at the hidden compliment. It was a small one, but rarely had he alluded to her looks or appeal.

"Have you ever been to either, Virginia or Charles Town?" she asked, hopeful for a capricious bit of irony, the small thrill of having almost crossed paths years ago.

Nathan pressed his lips, one foot waggling in thought. "Virginia? Nay. The Chesapeake 'tis waters reserved for those who know her. Charles Town, aye, regular-like for a bit, until everything..."

He faded off, realizing that his point was taking him where he didn't wish.

He waved away the thought and cleared his throat. "Prime pirating waters thereabouts."

Uncomfortable with talking about herself, Cate turned her attention to Prudence once more. At no portion in her life could she recall having been so pampered or indulged.

Nathan sat up and peered intently at her. "Married at eighteen for several years—" he began tentatively.

"Four."

"Very well, so it shall be. Alone for five..." he mused, tapping his finger on his chin.

"Why don't you just come out and ask how old I am?"

He smiled, abashed but unapologetic. "Me mum taught me 'tis a wise man what never asks."

"And an even wiser man never risks guessing."

His smile widened. "Wise words."

She allowed him to wait a bit longer. It was disconcerting, for it was the most personal inquiry he had ever made. "Last year was the twenty-seventh time I celebrated a birthday."

A brow lifted ever so slightly and his mouth twitched. "I had thought you to be a bit younger," he said carefully.

"Is that wishful thinking or a heavy-handed attempt at politeness?" she asked lightly.

"Which answer will gain me the most dispensation for having dared such hazardous waters?"

She waited, and finally threw into the silence, "Turnabout is fair play."

His arms resting on bent-up knees, he rolled his eyes skyward in calculation. The answer surprised him. "There was a time I never thought to live to see it. T'was thirty-two years ago Mum laid in childbed with me," he said, looking down between his legs.

She was careful to keep her features immobile. All things considered, with everything which had happened to him, she would have thought him to be bit older.

He fell quiet again at the mention of his mother, the dark brows drawing together. She looked away, to allow him his solitude.

"We have to do something for her, Nathan."

He looked up, following her gaze toward Prudence. A dubious curl lifted his lip. "Why?"

"She's but a child. We can't send her off to be married to some—"

"Bastard," he put in bluntly. "Why not? Arranged marriages happen all the time."

She watched Prudence, hat brim flopping as she flitted from flower to flower like a yellow-flounced butterfly. "I can't imagine being in a loveless marriage."

She turned toward Nathan, one eye closed against the sun. "Can you?"

He shook his head resolutely, the clatter of his bells muted by the moist heavy air. "Me? Not in life."

"Not even for money and position?"

He straightened. "Are you suggesting something?"

"No, no, just inquiring: if there was money or position, or whatever it was you had always sought, would you marry just for that, no love, not even attraction?"

Nathan barely took time to consider. "Nay. 'Twouldn't be worth it."

It was a great relief to hear. Nathan was a pirate, living in a world in which treasure and prize were everything. She didn't think him capable of being so cold or calculating. Thomas had said riches held no interest for Nathan, and she had witnessed nothing to the contrary. But still, she harbored a niggling seed of doubt.

Chin resting on his arms, he fell quiet for some time. Thoughtfully touching his tongue to his lip, he peered cautiously at her from the corner of his eye. "Was your marriage arranged?"

She hesitated. Aside from her earliest hours aboard, it was the first time Nathan had ever inquired or even alluded to either her marriage or her earlier life. Whether it was because he was uncomfortable with her having had one, preferring not to hear about Brian, if he thought it too distressing for her to discuss it, or if it was just general lack of interest on his part she couldn't tell. It occurred to her then that perhaps he thought her objections to Prudence's arranged marriage reflected on her own. In any case, the question was posed so shyly, she couldn't in good conscience refuse him.

She shifted. "In a way. We were already in love. Neither one of us could have been forced into it else. We didn't dare hope to be allowed to marry. Brian had been promised some twenty years before he was born to a girl in another clan. It was part of a peace treaty that his uncle, the head of the clan, decided he wanted out of. If it was broken outright, there would have been war. So, he broke it indirectly, by having Brian marry someone else."

"You?"

"If I had been a member of any other clan, our marriage would have started another war. Since I wasn't even Scots..." She lifted her shoulders, allowing him to complete the thought.

"Violent politics."

"You have no idea," she said with an emphatic roll of the eyes. "More violent and treacherous than any pirate ship."

Pyramiding his fingertips, he examined them thoughtfully. "I would think marriage is not an easy thing: always waking to the same person, week after week...?" He lifted one brow in subtle inquiry.

"But, that's the point. Marriage is the desire to wake to no one else."

"And when the wanting wears off?" He posed the question with the air of one who already knew the answer.

"Never does."

He scoffed, but she pressed on. "You may be angry all day, with all of life's little irritations, but at night..." She sighed dreamily. "At night, you can't think of anyone else."

He stared with an odd mix of caution, skepticism, and curiosity. "Don't you tire of...?" His fingers swirled the air in suggestion.

"The same person doing the same things?" she asked.

His implications were clear enough, the concept not lost on her: a man and a woman married but no longer husband and wife, existing in concentric circles of coexistence, never physically touching. For her, such marital malaise was unimaginable. Her first night with Brian had been as passion-laden as the last. But their union had existed only a little over four years. What if Providence had allowed them ten or fifteen? What then?

Would she have grown weary of bands of moonlight floating across muted shapes under a quilt? Would the fire's glow on bared arms or the candlelight on a chest become wearisome? Would the absence of sighs and muffled moans into pillows be a welcomed relief?

The ragged sound of Nathan clearing his throat snapped her back.

"Sometimes you might... maybe...," she stammered, cheeks flaming. "But mostly, you look forward to it. Anticipation has its place; 'tis sweet nectar. A lot of times, it's not necessarily what they can do for you; it's what you can do for them."

He smiled, the high cheekbones rounding. "Laying on of the hands, eh?"

"Exactly. And when you need said laying on, they will know exactly what to do."

"And if they don't?"

Typical Nathan, he had found the hole in her argument with the same precision as a musket shot.

"Well," she began slowly. "Either you haven't been married long enough, or you're married to the wrong person."

"Exactly my point," he exclaimed, stabbing an emphatic finger skyward. "How do you know who's right or who's wrong?"

She shifted irritably. "There's no checklist. I don't know, you just know. There's a little voice — at least for me — that said, 'This one'. Of course, there is always the Demon of Self-doubt."

He leaned back on his elbows and rocked. "I don't have demons," he said glibly.

"I think you have more demons than you care to admit," she said, and then added in the face of his dubiousness, "You have to be honest with yourself: is it love, or is it lust?"

The walnut eyes narrowed. "Is there a difference?"

"I think so, yes, a vast difference. Don't you?"

He squirmed, looking in every direction but hers.

"C'mon, Nathan. Surely you've thought about it." She nudged him encouragingly on the shoulder. "Come on."

"Oh, very well. Bloody parlor games." He blew the long breath of a one about to exert a great effort. "Lust is..."

His voice lowered as he sank deeper in thought. "Hungers of the flesh: looking forward to the next whore, before you've finished with the first. It's the having, nothing more, which is not to be dismissed," he added, wagging a finger. "It's served me well for many a year."

"As I can well imagine." She looked away, fearing he might feel compelled to elaborate. Knowing of Nathan's escapades was one thing; having them described would be quite another.

His mouth compressed into a grim line. "There are other manifestations." He glanced at her, and then away. The hand on his leg curled into a fist until the tendons stood out. "Lust can be wanting, wanting so badly you shake with it, knowing it's within your grasp, but you can't have it. You can't touch it, and yet you know if you don't have it soon, you'll likely perish."

Unprepared for his ferocity, she was stricken momentarily speechless. "And love?" she asked in a hoarse rasp.

Nathan sat unnaturally quiet. The leafy shadows laced over the line of his nose and high cheekbones. A lifetime flickered across his features, the corners of his mouth sagging with disappointment, disillusion and doubt.

"I think I've only known lust." He sounded moderately surprised by the revelation and then looked embarrassed. "Infatuation, a few times... maybe. Probably more than a few, truth be told."

She ducked her head into the line of his sight. "Never been really, truly in love?"

He lifted one shoulder and dropped it. "Thought I was; certainly, felt like it, at the time, at any rate. If anyone had asked, I probably would have said 'Aye'."

"What happened?"

"It ended," he said without remorse. "Sometimes, it was them; most of the time, it was me."

Stretching his legs, he crossed his ankles and waggled one foot. "It didn't last; few weeks, few months, maybe a year, and then it was over."

"Leaves a vast hole, doesn't it?"

The dark crest of his lashes lowered, veiling his thoughts as she had seen him do so many times. He went inward, where she, nor anyone else, would ever be allowed to go. The answer was so long in coming she thought perhaps there wouldn't be one.

Finally, it came, his graveled voice a rough whisper. "Aye."

They fell quiet, each immersed in settling the dust of disturbed ashes. Combing her fingers through her hair—now dry enough to begin to bloom about her head—Cate tried to imagine what it would be to bear such losses, supposed loves which either faded or soured. Comparatively speaking, her life had been simple: one love, one loss.

Nathan reached to seize the cheese and bottle. Experimentally sloshing the latter, he uncorked it and offered it to her. She took a drink; the cider was sweet while at the same time carried the tang of having begun to ferment. It made her slightly lightheaded and a lot lazy. He cut a piece of cheese, but she declined, not wanting to spoil the cider's pleasantness.

Taking a bite, he slowly chewed while examining the remaining bit in his fingers. "Never found anyone what made me want to take that final oath."

"Final oath? You make it sound like a death sentence."

"Well, you have to admit, 'tis the end of a lot of things," he said judiciously.

"And the beginning of so much more."

Cate bit her lip as she measured her next words. "All those times, before," she began delicately, "maybe those were just flings, infatuations. You haven't found the right person, yet, that's all."

Mouth working pensively under his mustache, he leaned back on his elbows once more. "What if you find them, but you can't have them?"

The lilt in his voice brought a stab of sympathy. Rejection: it was a torture no less than flogging, a daily ripping of the flesh. She had been learning to live with the agony, dealing with it on a day-to-day basis. There was an instant surge of contempt for the thoughtless monster who had inflicted such agonies on him.

"You mean, if they don't want you?" she asked, tactfully.

He looked away. "Or, they're already taken."

Cate winced. "That could be a problem. I didn't say it was all roses."

Shifting restlessly, he muttered something cross under his breath. "Seems to be more thorns than roses."

"You have to be willing to risk the thorns."

Nathan sat up abruptly, his bells jangling. "I've had enough blood drawn." Startled by his own outburst, he forced a smile. "Perhaps I'll fancy the daisies; easier to pick and there's a lot more of them."

His metaphors made her smile.

"Daisies can fade quickly." She chuckled, with less humor than intended. "Keep looking, Nathan. Perhaps, one day, you'll find your rose."

"Thorns be damned?"

It was his turn to smile, one of those gold and white marvels crafted to charm. It worked. She felt it tug in several places.

Nathan gave Cate a piece of cheese. She chewed without tasting as she regarded him anew. His forearm was covered by his sleeve, but the image tattooed there was clear in her mind: a swallow carrying a heart, pierced and bleeding. She wondered what heartbreak had been so devastating as to drive him to mark it into his body, to be worn for an eternity. Had it been self-flagellation, for having been so foolish, or a reminder, never to open himself to such anguish again?

"You have a lot of fine qualities, Nathan," she heard herself say. "You have a lot to offer a woman."

As a series of expressions crossed his face: accusation, suspicion, and finally, grudging acceptance. He bent up his knees and hung his head between his arms, the sable braids curtaining his face. The sun crowned his head in a raven-like sheen, catching on the random hairs of copper, sienna and brunette. His rings glinted in the sun as his fingers worked, setting the swallows on his knuckles to fluttering. Milestones of his life, thousands of miles of seas and hardship, reduced to a few dashes of ink.

"Whores aside, too many times I have been brought to a woman's bed but for one purpose. Once served, they had little need of me." He straightened, raising a warning finger. "Mind you, not that it was all bad."

"Oh, no, never!" To not smile was painful.

"They wanted Captain Nathanael Blackthorne, the pirate, the scalawag, not me."

Toying with his rings, he looked up with a wide-eyed sincerity, which bordered on wonderment. "You're not like that."

"Perhaps I had the benefit of knowing you, before I met Captain Blackthorne," she stammered. Was it her imagination, or had the afternoon suddenly become warm? "Captain Blackthorne is a nice sort, don't get me wrong."

"Scary and eccentric." He grinned, the devilment returning. "That's what I've been told, at any rate."

He drew his knife from his boot and cut another chunk of cheese, lifting an eyebrow as an offering. Distracted, she declined, and he settled back with his own morsel.

Prudence skipped about the pool's banks, squeaking at a toad hopping under a mossy rock. The saffron-colored frock was a travelling dress — reduced skirts and sturdy cloth, its color selected to compliment the dark hair and blooming complexion — but was still not up to the rigors of a pirate ship, nor island exploration. But then, what difference would it make? It was very probable her appearance held very little relevance.

Prudence's captivity was a sharp reminder of her own uncertain status. At one time, she had thought herself to be a hostage, and yet Nathan had assured her to the contrary. That he ducked the issue anytime she pressed regarding his intentions was puzzling. He desired her aboard; that much was clear. The "why" of it remained the question:

Friendship? A long reach there, the proof being his acrimony when she had called him that.

Protectorate? Hardly. She reminded him of someone else, someone for whom he harbored a morbid dislike.

Investment? One niggling point screamed louder than all else: he was a pirate. Deception would be his bread and butter. She strove to prepare herself for when the time came that he would either ransom or sell her.

"Prudence is about to marry a complete stranger, who has no reason, nor motivation to love her," Cate said without realizing it.

"How do you know? Maybe he's dying to have that special woman in his life."

She twisted around to him. "Do I look that silly?"

"No." His grin took on an impish nature, the bells in his mustache taking a rakish angle. "But 'tis worth the try. I sense a purpose in this line of dialogue. Pray enlighten me as to what you desire us to do?"

"I don't know. There has to be something."

Chewing on the inside of her mouth, she watched Prudence pluck petals from a flower.

"You need to tell her she's pretty."

"What!" His gravel voice pitched to a girlish shrill. His mouth hanging open sufficiently to show the bite of cheese in one corner, she was witnessing Nathanael Blackthorne stricken speechless. "I have to what?"

"You have to tell her she's pretty. She needs to hear it; every woman does. No one has ever told her that." It didn't seem that tall of an order. Once past the petulance, Prudence was a very lovely girl. Surely Nathan's standards weren't that high.

"You tell her."

"It won't serve coming from me. She needs to hear it from a man."

"Well, then... let Creswicke tell her."

Cate slapped her palm against her forehead and groaned. "Did you actually hear what you just said?"

His shoulders jerked as he drummed his fingers on his legs. "Why do I have to do it? There's nigh on to three hundred-odd men on that shore. Why can't one of them do it? Get Thomas to do it."

"Believe me, I plan to. Oh, come on Nathan." She nudged him lightly on the shoulder again. "How many women have you told were beautiful and didn't really mean it?"

Cate ignored the fact that he had never made a comment regarding her appearance, one way or the other.

He ducked his head. Under his deep tan, his neck reddened. "Aye, well, quite a few, but I was —"

"Yes, I know the 'but'," she interjected tartly. "This time, it's to be nice simply for the sake of being nice."

She watched him stare at the ground, his mouth working. Dipping her head lower, she caught his eyes. "Please? For me?"

It was a card never before played. It was distasteful to use their friendship against him, but there seemed little other choice.

"Oh, very well, since you put it that way," he grumbled. "I'll do it, sometime or another, but I shan't like it."

"Bear up, Nathan," she laughed. "I know it's a trial being a gift to the ladies, but bear up."

The sound of the waterfalls filled the silence between them. A shriek drew their attention toward Prudence, relaxing when they saw it was only in because of a small bird flitting too closely.

"By the by," Nathan began pensively. "What's this I hear about you wanting a dress?"

"What are you about?"

"Princess Pain-in-the-Arse told me you were desiring dresses. Why didn't you tell me?"

Now she was the one to fluster. "Because I didn't, or don't."

"That's not what she said," he countered with a vague wave. "She said you wished something newer."

"Did she say I said that, or did she say that's what she thinks I should have said?"

Nathan made to respond then paused, closing one eye with the effort of recalling. "Might have been the latter," he muttered. "Don't exactly recall, now. Bloody little wench never stops talking; chatters worse than Beatrice."

Sensitive to his ruffled feelings, Cate turned her head until her urge to laugh was contained. She came back to a narrow look, drumming his fingers on his leg, formulating his next ploy.

"I hear—through sources that I shall not name—that you are in need of thread."

He was plump with smugness. It had been a game of wills between them, he in search of what she was in need and she reluctant to say. Needs and desires: she had long ago surrendered, nay, abandoned those. Besides, frugal practicality had always been her nature.

There was only one way he could have known: he overheard.

"No secrets on a ship, hm?" she said, narrowly.

Nathan had the good grace to be at least a bit abashed at being discovered.

"Well, yes, I could use some," Cate finally admitted.

God, she despised this! A lifetime of attempting to assert her independence wiped away with a simple admission. She felt as if she had just been catapulted twenty-five years back, and now stood at her father's knee.

"Goddamn it to buggering hell, woman," he extorted to the

sky. He yanked at a piece of fern at his foot and angrily pitched it. "Hell, and death, why didn't you say something?"

"It's so frivolous. You have other matters far more important than thread."

Dropping his head to his chest, he let out an exasperated growl that sounded like ripping canvas.

"I've sought to get you anything, everything you could want." His hand on his knee flexed in cadence. "You insist on representing there was nothing you required. What the goddamned blooming hell good is it to be a pirate, if there's nothing I can get you?" His eyes were bulging by the time he finished.

Cate shied like a scolded child. "I don't know. It felt odd to ask. I already feel like an imposition. You've given me so much, it didn't seem right to ask for anything more."

In one fluid move, Nathan was on his knees before her. He took her by the chin and lifted her face. Eyes gone dark as his ship intently searched hers.

"You are not an imposition." Each word was uttered with singular emphasis. "You have as much right to be on me ship as anyone, and I'll shoot the bastard what says different, *sabe*?"

He sat back, more composed. "Now, if there is anything you ever, ever desire, you just say, agreed?" He punctuated it with a final, intimidating glare.

Chastened, her voice caught. "Agreed."

"And the next port, by the horns o' Satan, you'll have enough thread to founder the flaming ship!" His shoulders shifted irritably under his shirt. "Be damned if it'll be said I can't provide a woman some bloody thread!"

21: GHOSTS

NATHAN AND HIS FEMININE ENTOURAGE were still a good distance from returning to shore when they were met by wafts of smoke and the smell of roasting meat.

He stopped to inhale in blissful anticipation. "Going to be fine eats tonight."

They broke free of the trees to see the sun announce its impending departure, the sky slashed with streaks of violet, indigo and orange in a grand farewell. The sugar-white sand, now lilac-tinged in the lengthening shadows, was dotted with the molten glow of bonfires, and the flicker of faggots and torches.

"Bacchanal" seemed a lofty description for a beach writhing with pirates, and yet it applied. Men who lived by the credo of "freedom" made gay in that same spirit, their rollicking jubilation fertilized by an unlimited flow of bumboo, a spiced mix of water, rum and sugar, a great favorite, by all appearances. The scene came close to resembling what Cate had imagined pirates to be: carousing on a shore, wild with drink. There is a difference between revelry and drunken brawl, a fine line but a difference, nonetheless. At that point, it was still the former, but teetered precariously toward the latter.

Once supper was finished — a great boar roasted over an open pit — the pirates gathered about the fires in small intimate groups, former mates, nationality, home port, common language or mere fate the determining factor as to where they settled. With fiddles, fifes, concertinas, and hornpipes, along with a great number of exotic and homemade instruments, resulted in a dissonant din. The Scots' *bodhrans* meeting Hindi *sitars* and African pipes was backdrop to a Babel of tongues as the men sang.

Through that roistering din, Cate gravitated toward the fire from which drifted growl and gruff of Scots, and the even more enticing refrains of Highland music. Bodhrans, a Highland version of a stretched-skin drum, and tin whistles played Gaelic tunes which stirred her memories and pulsed in her veins. She sat against forage bags stuffed with dried grasses, the hay-like smell harkening back to hayfields and barn lofts of another life. She closed her eyes and allowed herself to be carried back. The palm trees, balmy air and rolling surf faded into the sharp resinous smell of pine trees, hunch-backed mountains, tumbling burns and crisp air. A familiar face awaited, one that brought a smile and quickened her heart. He beckoned her to the shadows beyond the fires with an intent blue gaze and an outstretched hand.

Cate opened her eyes to find Nathan gazing down at her, seeming to know what she was thinking.

He smiled, though a bit forced. "I wondered where you'd gotten off to."

She flushed guiltily. She thought to explain when he folded down next to her, but decided it was better left unsaid. There was no shame in missing what she had lost, she thought defensively. But Nathan's combination of resentment and suspicion indicated otherwise.

"Rumor mongers would go rabid if someone was to be seen not drinking," he said, handing her a tankard. A slight slur of speech suggested he had taken measures to avoid the same. "'Twould be outright seditious in many circles."

He watched as she took a drink, nodding in affirmation when she discovered it was ale. He had to have gone to some lengths to find something other than rum for her to drink. It was appreciated, and she said as much. He demurred and waved her away while at the same time puffed with pride.

Sitting companionably together, they watched the men dance, a scrap of cloth tied around the head of those posing as women. In a swirl of bearded, sun-weathered faces, distorted by the rictus of wild-eyed gaiety and drink, they whirled like wraiths in and out of the fire's shadows. Jets of sand spurted up from under their feet as they pounded the ground. Eyes feverishly bright with merriment, they pleaded for Cate to dance. Hesitant, she looked to Nathan, who shrugged abidingly. As she rose amid a chorus of cheers, she wondered if she would remember how, for it had been years since she had done so. As she was spun from one man to the next, exact steps proved to be of little consequence: so long as she didn't think too much, her feet remained untangled.

The faces of her partners soon blurred, no man being allowed more than a few steps, before she was whisked away by the next. Smalley, all arms and legs, resembled a child's whirligig as he cavorted around the fire. Hughes, singing in Gaelic at the top of his lungs, fell into a jig which instantly took her back to the Highlands and Hogmanay celebrations,. Towers' diminutive height brought his face—much to his pleasure—in line with the edge of her bodice, earning him admonishing glares, and ultimately his skipper's warning hand on his shoulder. MacQuarrie, normally as stoic as one of his guns, verged on giddiness. Millbridge was the surprise. He moved with surprising gentility and poise, a distant-eyed gaze indicating he saw a face other than hers.

In the midst of it all, a firmer arm took her by the waist, and she looked up into Nathan's face. Coils of energy shot through her from where his hand rested at the small of her back, quickening her heart and tightening her belly. She made a conscious effort to breathe, for at some time or another, she had stopped. As he took her other hand their wrists brushed against each other, and the throb of the music in her blood was replaced by the tempo felt there. His hip pressed against hers; realizing how closely he held her, he made a visible effort to step back. It was odd for him to have nothing to say. Instead, he winked and launched them around the fire.

Barefoot, stripped to his shirt and breeks, Nathan moved with the lithe elegance she had witnessed for weeks, now alive under her hand. With his gypsy-charmer smile, his eyes held hers as they twirled. She couldn't look away had she wished it. The world outside his arms faded; she didn't recall her feet touching the ground. She was vaguely aware of him being tapped on the shoulder again and again by her next hopeful partners, but to no avail. As long as she was indulging in dreams that night, she allowed herself another, wondering what lay behind the fire-touched eyes that held hers.

With a flourishing swirl, they stopped, leaving her to wonder if it was just them or if the music had ceased. Moisture gleaming on his cheekbones, Nathan bowed and pressed his lips to her fingers. He stepped back, and before the shock of his appearance had worn off, he was gone.

As she was swept away by her next partner, the spell was broken, the ghost of Nathan's hand at her waist lingered, a reminder that it hadn't been a dream. She shied when anyone made to touch her there, lest the feeling be erased. Through more jigs and reels, she felt Nathan's gaze following her. Catching a glimpse of his fire-lit profile as she spun past, she thought she may have seen admiration in his expression.

A Griseller, a great bear of a man, facial features buried in a ferocious mat of black hair and beard, picked her up and let out a gleeful bellow. With a vise-like grip about her middle, he whirled and stomped around the fire, all the while howling in Gaelic. She was caught between laughing and gasping for air when he put her down, the next man snatching her up before he stumbled off. After one rollicking reel and jig after another, Cate was at last too breathless to go on, her lungs boring her ribs into her stays. The men begged for her to continue, but relented when Nathan—boots, baldric and pistol in place, his hat square on his head—waved them off. They left in a chorus of jeers and cat-calls, for everyone knew what a man and woman did in the dark.

The feel of where his hand had pressed at her back was still there. She longed for him to touch her there just once more, but the respectable distance was resumed as he steered her back to their fire. Ever-hovering, ever-protecting, but never venturing those final few inches which bridged between friends and... well, never mind.

Dabbing the sweat from her temples and lifting her hair from her damp neck, Cate realized she had forgotten about Prudence. They found the girl roughly where she had been left, a short distance from their fire. She had now been joined by a young seaman. Seated a discrete distance apart, they spoke between themselves, so enraptured the earth could have fallen in around them, and they wouldn't have noticed.

"Money well-spent, don't you think?" Nathan said as they drew up a short distance away.

Cate whirled on him, gaping. "Nathan, you didn't!"

"Very well, I didn't. What? 'Tis only for tonight. Better him, than her setting her sights on someone else," he said, shuddering. "And it didn't come as readily, nor cheaply as you might be led to believe. I had to persuade one of Thomas' lads. There wasn't enough money in the Spanish Main to persuade any of our people. Ignorance can sometimes be bliss," he ended in wonderment.

"But now she thinks—"

"That a lad wishes to spend an evening with her," he said evenly.

"You sold her." She could feel her color rising at the thought that Nathan had been so callous.

"No, I bought her a gentleman caller," he said with marked patience. "I'm letting nature take its course, with a little help. What's the harm, eh? She doesn't have to sit the night alone, and the lad earns the company of someone what doesn't have hair growing out of every crevice. You'd think a soul might get a little thanks for his efforts." He displayed a small pout.

She eyed Nathan, and then the lad. Too young to have lost his lankiness, he bore a strong jaw which promised of character to come. Non-descript in his sun-drabbed clothes, he was yet to have found his identity in the way of dress or accoutrement. On second observation, it did appear to be near to what Nathan represented. Prudence's gentleman caller appeared innocent enough, indeed far too young to pose a threat. It was worth bearing in mind, however, that just as every other man on the shore, he was a pirate.

"I'll thank you, when I'm surer of what just happened," she said, and went to find a place to sit, well within sight of the young pair.

Nathan wove his way between the torches and fires, dodging the drunk-to-the-point-of-stupor men, looking for the two women who currently bracketed — and plagued — his life. One he hoped desperately to find, the other he crossed his fingers desperate not. One made his balls tighten, the other made them seize.

He'd been called off on some insignificant detail of business — a near brawl requiring careful negotiations lest there be dismemberment — and had returned to their fire to discover that not only had Creswicke's noisome wench disappeared — Thank the gods! He'd paid good money for that small blessing — but Cate and Thomas. Snuck off together was his first suspicion, but a more tempered voice offered a host of explanations.

At his inquiry, Pryce mumbled something indiscernible, but had no specifics to offer. It would appear his first mate had found the bottom of his omni-present, supposed to be secreted flask more than once that night.

Contrary to all hopes — and vehemently cursing the Fates for such foul and black luck — it was the Yellow Nemesis he encountered first, perched on a log. Following the direction of her intent gaze, he located what he truly sought. His first urge was to race forward, but stood off.

It was Cate, close enough to see, but too far to hear. She stood at the base of a tree, her slender form silhouetted against a fire's glow. Face upturned, she was laughing with Thomas. The breeze brought the sound of it, a rippling, throaty sound suggesting roughened velvet. When echoing throughout his ship, it was a pleasing sound, but brought a sickened feeling when heard intertwined with Thomas'. Could the man never laugh, without sounding like a damned old lecher?

He felt a tightness which was not the fault of his breeches. "Easy lads. I know 'tis been a time, but there will be none of that, now at any rate," he murmured.

He knew he was staring, but didn't give a rat's arse, if anyone saw. Lost in her beauty, he was. Too many times, she had caught him gaping like a sun-struck dullard. He wondered if that was normal for *friends*.

Damnation and seize my soul, I'm learning to hate that cursed word.

Cate moved, and the light caught her eyes.

Emerald blue: is there such a color?

Well, there bloody well must be, because you're looking at it, mate.

He learnt such a color meant she was at peace... happy.

About bloody time!

So rapt in watching, he stumbled into the log where the Demon Seed sat. He was obliged to catch himself by her shoulder to keep from toppling over the bloody thing. Chin propped in her hand, she barely acknowledged him. He lowered down next to her, both now engrossed in the same vignette.

Prudence dreamily sighed. "He is rather dashing, isn't he?"

Nathan sat back, brought up short by the thought. "Really? You think as much? All things considered, I hadn't really considered it."

He cocked his head and squinted, trying to imagine what a woman might see.

Well, aye, tall and blonde... and big... blue eyes, and a nice laugh, and a big smile — not unlike meself — and charming, a man with his own ship... Oh, bloody hell!

He buried his face in his hands. Many a time he and Thomas had vied for the attentions of the same woman — actually came to blows, the once — but he had never actually *saw* Thomas for all his attributes.

"Don't you think he's handsome?" Prudence tore her eyes away long enough to look to seek affirmation. It was baffling why women were constantly doing that: asking questions with answers they already knew.

'Twas like a bloody test, all the time.

"Aye, I suppose," he said, in strained off-handedness.

Cate laughed again. A purling, seductive sound on the evening air, it was. She moved into the firelight. Now he could see the angle of her body, those wide shoulders and delicious curve of collarbone. She bent toward Thomas to hear amid the surrounding merriment and then put her mouth nearer to say something in his ear.

Suffering Jesus on the cross!

Friends, remember? A chill rippled between his shoulders, and he felt sick. *So, that's what it means.*

"Aren't they enchanting together?"

Prudence's voice jerked him back to reality. "What?"

"It's perfect." Her eyes shone with romanticism. "The wild pirate comes and rescues her, then carries her away into the sunset on his ship, forever happy."

Prudence heaved another sigh. "Just look at them together."

"I'd rather not."

Thomas laughed softly and lifted his hat a fraction. "I beg your leave. My men await, but I shall return." His features gilded by the fires, a smile lurked at the corner of his mouth.

Cate watched Thomas stroll away, coattails swinging with the roll of his step, so much like Nathan's, a seaman's gait. There was another ghost shadowing his movements, however, and the sight of it made her bite her lip. She heard a faint metallic tinkling, hesitant but near. She turned to find Nathan standing half-immersed in the night shadows. He shifted and the moonlight caught his shirt. It gave off an ethereal glow, harkening to the visages just seen in Thomas' wake.

"Been there long?" she asked.

Nathan broke a crooked smile, the one which always came when he was uncertain. It disappeared quickly as he stepped forward. He cleared his throat and then made a poor attempt at nonchalance.

"Thinking I might have overheard things perhaps not intended for me ears."

She chuckled quietly. "Hardly. What could I possibly have to say to Thomas that you shouldn't hear?"

His mouth took an odd twist. "One never knows, does one?"

Folding his hands behind his back, he rocked on his feet, and cleared his throat again. A tentative smile played briefly, a nervous, failing flicker. "Nice evening, isn't it?"

It was not so much the inanity of what he said, but the strain in his voice which caught her attention. "Yes, it is," she said, curious as to where this charade would lead.

He jerked dramatically, as if just discovering a downed tree and made a wildly errant gesture toward it. "Would you care to sit?"

Cate allowed Nathan to see her seated. It was disquieting the way he hovered, as if she were an infirmed old aunt, sitting only as an afterthought. He leaned on his arms on his thighs. It might have been a casual pose, except for his heel tapping the ground, and his hands working against each other. Something was bothering him; experience had taught waiting was the best means to learn what.

A deep laugh — unmistakably Thomas' — drew their attention. Looking, she felt Nathan's eyes darting between his friend and her.

"You fancy him, don't you?"

The suddenness of his inquiry startled her, as did the solemnity with which it came. It was an unreasonable question, yet reasonable for him to ask. Looking down the beach, her gaze lingered on Thomas, now standing by a fire chatting.

"What makes you ask a silly question like that?" she asked, painfully conscious of the miserable job she did of gleaning her defensiveness.

Nathan's mustache took a wry twist. "I'm not daft, nor blind. I've seen you looking — that look."

Cate groaned inwardly. So, he had noticed. It had been foolish to think he wouldn't. In spite of his disarming and off-handed demeanor, he missed blessed little.

"You're right, but it's not what you're thinking. It's just so difficult." She sighed, vigorously rubbing her forehead, as if it might erase the images. "He reminds me so much of Brian."

Nathan swiveled to regard Thomas. "He was that tall?"

She closed her eyes to recall: Thomas' chin met just between her brows. "Actually, Thomas is a bit shorter; my head used to fit just under Brian's chin," she said to her hands in her lap.

Irresistible forces compelled her to watch as Thomas crossed his arms and cocked one hip, intently listening.

"It's not just the height. It's his walk and his smile. There's that little something at the corner of his mouth..." Her voice caught and the tears welled. Thomas' image blurred, erasing the differences and rendering him even more like Brian. There was far more to it: the way he laughed and jested, swung his arms or crossed his ankles as he sat. No matter how hard she tried to focus on the differences, the likenesses always elbowed their way to the surface.

Nathan slumped and looked to the ground between his feet. "Oh."

"My grandmother always said to marry a tall man. 'They were the most gentle' is what she used to say. She was right," Cate said, with a faint smile.

The firelight flared on tendons of Nathan's arms, now gone rigid "So, you do fancy him."

His shoulders rose and fell, and then he looked up with the expression of a man commending himself to the gallows. His throat bobbed as he swallowed. "I could put a word in for you," came in a tight rasp.

It was tempting, so very tempting.

For a moment, she allowed herself the luxury of that fantasy, but instantly saw it for what it was: a hopeless snatch at regaining a life, long lost. And yet, she had not made mention of the resemblance to Thomas for that very reason. "You remind me of my dead husband" was hardly the way to initiate anything. She hadn't made mention to Nathan for the same reason: so that she could pretend. And pretend she did, to the point that it was both a startlement and irritation, when Thomas did something out of character. To use Thomas in such a way was reprehensible, and she despised herself for it. She only need think how she would feel if Nathan was to use her the same way: as a replacement for his precious Hattie.

Ah, but would it be so terrible if he was to have you for just a little bit?

Cate batted down the voice. To chase ghosts was to throw her heart away. She had surrendered one heart—one long gone—in exchange for another.

She looked at that very heart sitting next to her just then, dejected and miserable.

"No." Regrettably, the word didn't come out as definitively as intended. She cleared her throat and tried again. "No, it wouldn't be fair."

She stiffened as another thought occurred. "Are you hinting to be rid of me?"

"No!" Nathan burst out, eyes bugging with alarm. He checked himself and softened. "No, most definitely and adamantly, no."

She dipped her head to intersect his gaze. "Then why even ask the question or even suggest it? Is this because of the other night?"

"No, upon me word! Just intuitive insertions, idle observations." He lifted a shoulder, as if to dismiss it, but it still pressed his mind. "I thought... perhaps—"

They were interrupted by Thomas' hail as he strode toward them.

"There you are!" he boomed. "You children lurking about in the dark, I see. Shame, shame!" He waggled a warning finger at them. "People will talk."

"Only about the overbearing pestilence what keeps storming up and down the beach like a pillaging Cossack," Nathan grumbled.

"Then c'mon over to the fire and sit. One of my men finally brought a chessboard. Are you ready to get beat?"

"Certainly," Nathan declared eagerly, handing Cate up. "Except, I do suffer a bit of remorse at the prospect of demeaning and humbling someone so grand as yourself... *again.*"

"Willing to put your money on that?"

Nathan swept a mocking bow which finished with an inviting arm toward their fire. "I'm your man."

Nathan and Thomas settled into what some might call "a friendly game." It was a far cry from any chess match Cate had ever witnessed. Customarily associated with long pensive silences, interspersed with quiet murmurings of appreciation of a move, Nathan and Thomas' version lacked all manner of gentlemanly restraint, bearing more resemblance to a tavern brawl than a parlor game. A player's selection of his next move was made under a barrage of taunts, bawdy jeers and derisive challenges. The move was immediately followed by a tirade of swearing and name-calling—in several languages—heavily mixed with punches, slaps and generalized fist brandishing.

Familiar enough with the game of chess to understand, but not proficient enough to pose a challenge, Cate had been goaded into a game by Nathan now and again. She had learned at her father's knee, with further tutelage from her brothers. Brian had spent innumerable winter evenings attempting to broaden her game, and ultimately she became accomplished enough to delay defeat for almost an hour. Her successes against Nathan had barely been better. Her matches with him had been nothing like this.

She sat on a cask between the two pirates and watched. There were no classical moves, no familiar gambits. This was based on nerve and cunning, bravado and bluff. Their familiarity with each other bred congenial contempt, but also an advantage, often seeming to know the other's next move before it was made.

Alike in so many ways, the two men were diametric opposites in so many others. Sitting between them, Cate became aware of being bracketed by muscle and bone, the round of a shoulder against the linen of a shirt, the pull of thigh muscles under the taut fabric of breeches, each exuding his unique aura of maleness. More often, she was lost in watching their fingers—Nathan's long and aristocratic, Thomas' broad and blunt—hover over the board in thought, and then pluck the chosen ivory piece.

A few times she glanced up to find Nathan watching her watching Thomas, dropping his attention to the board when caught. In those brief moments, she caught a glimpse of something akin to jealousy... again. It had cropped up several times, since Thomas' arrival, and Harte, too, come to think on it. It was a puzzle. On the one hand, Nathan wanted no other man near her, and yet on the other, he held no interest. She was caught between saying "Make up your mind" and "You've nothing to worry about; I've cast my lot." Surely she was reading more into it than was meant. By his own admission, Nathan was new to this concept of friendship, especially where a woman was concerned. Finding the balance between friendship and possession clearly was a struggle. This was going to require patience on both parts.

Cate looked periodically to check on Prudence. A girl in a saffron dress wasn't difficult to find among a crowd of sun-drabbed, weatherworn sailors. She now sat atop a keg, a piece of canvas chivalrously draped over it. According to Thomas, the young lad Nathan had hired was named Biggins. He was the ship's baby. Thomas represented he had only taken on the lad because he had cried so hard when he had been denied.

"Half-monkey in the tops, though," said Thomas in wonderment as he waited for Nathan to make his move. "The boy's fearless on that account. A week of bein' cabin boy taught him nothing could be worse."

To their chagrin, Prudence and Biggins had been joined by Grisellers and Morgansers, and no wonder. Young or old, fishwife or princess, women were a welcomed relief, and the pirates circled around for the sheer joy of a feminine face.

Crude laughter had drawn Cate's attention a few times. She looked again to see Prudence, ashen-faced and scandalized, Biggins next to her, stiff with indignation. Cate chuckled silently. In the face of such propriety and innocence, the men couldn't resist the temptation of being as raucous as possible. They had tried her on at the beginning, but life, a war and five brothers had already seasoned her; few things shocked her now.

Cate straightened at seeing Prudence lurch to her feet and race away, and was instantly on her own feet to give chase. Nathan called out from behind her and then darted to catch her up. Their paths down the shore in Prudence's wake converged with Squidge also in pursuit.

"What happened, man?" Nathan demanded.

Deep in his cups, the garland of dried ears swung at Squidge's neck as he splayed his hands in innocence. "Honest, Cap'n, we was just tellin' her of her intended. I guess it just went a bit too far."

"A bit," Cate shot back acidly.

Swearing, Cate took off in the direction in which she had last seen the saffron dress. She scanned the beach and nearby bushes as she jogged along, confident Prudence wouldn't have gone far. The dark wilderness would be too scary. Once away from the fires, and her eyes had grown accustomed to the night, she saw the glimmer of yellow just ahead, only a few paces into the trees. As Nathan came up beside her, the sound of muffled crying could be heard over the rattle of palm fronds and rustle of the water lapping shore. Nathan stiffened and put out a protective hand. Cate silently bid him to wait, and went closer, making a good bit of noise, lest she startle the child and upset her further.

"Prudence? Are you all right?"

"Go away!"

"We just came to—"

"Go away, all of you!" she shrieked louder, her fists balled at her sides. "I hate all of you! Leave me!"

Cate hesitated then pressed closer. "I just wanted to—"

Cate inched close enough to touch Prudence on the arm. The girl whirled around, her face contorted with rage. "I hate you. I hate you! I hate you! I hate you!"

Prudence flew at Cate like an enraged cat and pummeled her with her fists. Nathan lunged forward, but Cate waved him off, for it was more like being attacked by a kitten. Even in a fit of blind fury, Prudence's blows were pitifully ineffective, although there was a good chance Cate would be bruised by morning. She took a fist to the ear, another grazing her cheek. Overall, it was far less abuse than what her brothers had inflicted in her youth.

Exhausted at last, Prudence fell away. Turning her back, her small shoulders heaved as she gasped for breath. "You lied to me."

"I've never lied," Cate said evenly.

"Yes, you did," Prudence hissed over her shoulder. Her eyes glittered with teary hatred. "I asked inquired about Lord Creswicke and you lied. All of you lied."

"I never said—"

"Why didn't you tell me about him?"

"Because I... we hoped to spare you." Efforts which now seemed woefully inept, Cate thought ruefully.

"They said he's a horrid man, and he has done despicable, disgusting things."

Cate stood mute. Too often, the truth was regrettable. Upon reflection, it might have been better advised to have eased the child into it, rather than leaving her to the shock of finding herself married to a monster, and monster he certainly was. Cate had heard thinly-veiled allusions to Creswicke's distasteful "tastes." She didn't care to contemplate to what or where those tastes might lead.

"Anything I did or didn't say would not have made Lord Creswicke any better or worse person," Cate said, a bit defensive.

Prudence drew several shuddering breaths in an effort

to regain her composure. "They said he beat Nathan... Captain Blackthorne."

Cate looked toward Nathan. He stood half-hidden by the fronds of a head-high fern. Scowling, the vertical lines between his brows deepened: a clear message that he preferred she desist.

"Yes, he did," Cate said at length, with some reluctance.

"And he branded him."

Nathan's expression darken further, willing her to leave the subject lie.

"Yes, that as well," she said, looking back to Prudence.

Prudence turned, the petite features twisted with anguish. "Will he brand me?"

The question caught Cate so unprepared, she almost laughed. At the same time, she felt a pang of sympathy. As irrational as it might seem to everyone else, the possibility was very real to Prudence.

Cate's mouth wobbled with the urge to smile. "I doubt it."

Sniffing, Prudence twisted at the fabric of her skirt. "You should have told me. I thought you were my friend."

Cate inched close enough to lay a tentative hand on the girl's shoulder. Tremors coursed through the small body. "And sometimes friends have to do difficult things."

"You all hate me."

"That's silly, of course we don't—"

"Yes, you do! I've seen the way you all look at me. You all treat me like I'm a child... and you hate me!" Prudence's voice took a new pitch as her anger re-surged.

Cate bit back a remark to the effect that one is treated as one acts. "Prudence, you know better than that. We've all—"

"I hate you!" Prudence spun and leapt at Cate again.

The child came at her with the frenzied misdirection of having attacked, but with no real idea as to how to go about it. As they grappled, Cate absorbed the slaps and fended off several more. She ducked from the curled fingers aimed at her face. Prudence made a fortuitous snatch at the hair at Cate's temple, and she yelped. Over Prudence's shrieks, she heard a growl and saw an arm snake out. Beringed fingers dug deep into the black curls and Prudence was jerked away.

"Stand off, you shrieking strumpet." Nathan's graveled voice ripped the night air as he swung the girl by the hair in an arc. The patent leather shoes skipped over the ground, Prudence squealed like a shoat, more startled than in pain.

"Nathan, put her down!" cried Cate.

He gave Prudence a quelling shake and then released her. The small space was filled with the sound of ragged breathing.

Rubbing her head, Prudence gave them a wounded look, and then broke into a new wave of plaintive crying.

Blood pulsing still from being attacked, Cate rounded on Nathan. "You don't need to be so—"

"Belay!" Considerably calmer, he said, "I mean, quiet, luv."

He stalked toward Prudence with a vehemence that caused her to fall back several steps, half-stumbling on the low plants behind her. "Stay your claws, you cross-grained bit o' cuckoldry. You will never, *never* raise a hand to that woman *ever* again!"

"Nathan, I—" A desisting hand and a glare from Nathan cut Cate short.

He rounded on Prudence with a rigid finger in her face.

"You will treat her as if she were the Queen Mum, not your goddamned chambermaid." He dipped his head lower, denying Prudence's attempts to look away. "You touch her, or speak to her with any—I repeat, *any*—disrespect, and sink and burn me, I will bare that arse before every tar on that beach and strap it as your cursed father apparently never did."

"Nathan, you don't need to—" Cate began.

"Aye, but I do. This has been coming and little Miss Bird o' Price knows exactly of which I speak, does she not?" He fixed a gimlet eye on Prudence.

Sniffling, Prudence risked a glance toward Cate then back to the ground, pointedly avoiding Nathan.

He cleared his throat, a sound similar to ripping canvas. "Prudence?"

Prudence sniffed loudly—dramatically so, by Cate's judgment—and cringed. Twisting her hands in her dress, she batted her eyes at him, the effect greatly diminished by the tear-reddened rims.

"I can't imagine whatever you mean," she said meekly.

Nathan's eyes narrowed to slits. "Do not try me on, Missy. I'll see you rot, mark me words," he said in a low rumble.

Prudence dodged around Nathan with surprising nimbleness and flung her arms around Cate. "He hates me. He only cares for the money."

"That's not true, and you know it well." Cate said, over the top of Nathan's sputtered objections. "He's provided for you far better than elsewhere."

"He's kept you a hostage. He's kept you from the man you love." Prudence implored, her grip tightening on Cate's shoulders.

Cate held her back at arm's length. "What? Who?"

"Thomas, of course. Don't be afraid to admit it's so."

It was Cate who sputtered now. "He's done no such thing."

Prudence cringed. Cate realized that her fingers were

digging Prudence's arms and she let go, wresting herself from the girl's clutches.

"I am *exactly* where I want to be." Cate's voice quavered with both frustration and rage. "A lady does not meddle in other people's lives."

"I'm sorry." Prudence's high-pitched squeak carried only a hint of remorse. "I didn't think—"

"And that's the point, Prudence. You weren't thinking. You're due to be married, and it's high time you become the lady your mother raised you to be."

"But, Lord Creswicke—"

"Will only be the smallest of your problems if you continue to meddle in other people's lives."

Old habits were well-entrenched, Prudence snatched at her next ploy: grabbing Cate's arm, beseeching. "He still doesn't like me," she whined, with an accusing look over her shoulder toward Nathan.

"Aye! Flog her," Nathan shouted.

"See," shrieked Prudence, and clutched Cate, wailing anew.

"Hell's fury, you bloody-damned right! But by your own hand, you envenomed sprat!" Nathan shouted over the sobs. "Always blathering and snotting about. 'Tis enough to drive the saints daft."

"Nathan, how could you?" said Cate.

"How could I not?" he huffed. "Surely, you don't desire me to lie? Goes completely contradictory to me entire moral fiber. No, can't abide a liar, particularly distasteful. Flog her, I say! Hodder can lock her in the brig for the night and rig the grate for morning. Twelve lashes! Always starts out the day with the proper attitude for the crew."

Prudence's shrieks reached siren-like proportion.

"Nathan, when was the last time you flogged anyone?"

For a fleeting moment, Cate had thought she was seeing the renowned pirate. Then the corner of his eye twitched and the hook of his mustache lifted the corner of his mouth. It was Captain Nathanael Blackthorne, at his best.

"To the *Griselle* then," he cried, brightly, with a piratical gleam. "We'll bid Thomas to do it. I've seen him flay down to the bone in four strokes."

Prudence's wails built to a terrorized crescendo, Cate began to think Nathan might be overplaying just a bit.

She brought Prudence's snot-laden face up to hers and said, "Perhaps you should go back to the fire, while I speak with the Captain."

"Aye, aweigh and quick sharp about it," Nathan said, with a bit more additional growl.

Prudence hesitated. Nathan drew his sword and charged. "Scat!"

Arms over her head, Prudence let out a startled squeak and ran. Nathan lunged to slap her soundly across her bottom with the flat of his blade, slitting the silk and the first layer of petticoats.

He smiled crookedly as he watched the yellow dress fade into the dark, back toward the bonfires' friendly light. "How many more days is it until we are rid of her?"

"It's positively wondrous how you turn that off and on so readily," Cate said in awe.

Nathan smiled and gave a self-deprecating shrug.

In the wake of Prudence's wailing, the space fell eerily quiet, neither of them knowing quite what to say. Nathan looked to his feet, while Cate stared off. Eventually, the dry rattle of the palm fronds and chorus of night creatures filtered in. The trill of tree frogs came from very near. Laughter from the fires rode the shifting land breeze, along with the smell of wood and tobacco smoke. Cate felt tired and defeated. From the first, her only thought had been to help the girl, had been inexplicably driven to do so.

"You didn't believe her, did you?" Cate said.

A part of her hoped for a convincing lie which could give her ease. It was worrisome to think Nathan would have believed anything so outrageous. Judging from his reaction, however, this wasn't the first time Prudence had uttered such foolishness. She had been so wrapped up in Thomas' resemblances she hadn't considered what Nathan had seen: her mooning over his best friend.

Nathan eyed the fingernail gouge on Cate's arm with disapproval. The blood welled in a long thin stream, nearly black in the moonlight.

"Not exactly... for the most part. Had me doubts... somewhat." His attempt at nonchalance allayed none of her concerns.

He looked away and shifted uneasily, his hands working at his sides. Eventually he came around to her with an expression akin to one facing a firing squad.

"Am... I...?" he asked, in an inordinately small voice. "Am I... keeping you...?"

He fixed her with an intent gaze, as if willing her to say something, but what she couldn't tell.

"Nathan, I told you I—"

"And with a marked lack of conviction, I might observe,"

he said, barely tolerant. "The measure of a man's regard is in the price he's willing to pay, and Thomas is willing to pay quite handsomely, a king's ransom."

He sobered, his resolve solidifying. "I said before and I'll say again: what you want, I want. No more, no less. And if yon gargantuan is what holds your dreams, then..." He gulped. "Then say as much, and... let the negotiations begin."

She gaped. Panic, rage, dismay and fear all jammed to the surface, like apples in a barrel. Hurt found a different path, rising up under her ribs in a searing ember. A moment ago, he had been vehemently defending her, a bit before that, had offered to put in a word with Thomas on her behalf. A few hours ago, he had pledged her the moon. And barely a week hence, he had stood on the *Morganse's* forecastle and begged her to stay.

God, what I wouldn't give for a moment's honesty.

She rubbed her temple where a headache began to throb. She was weary of the games. Through all Nathan's evasiveness, she had the strong sense that the honesty which she longed for was just beneath the surface, dangling like a bone before a dog, waiting to be revealed, but not to her. It would take a very special woman to gain his confidence.

Like his precious Hattie?

If Nathan's purpose was to befuddle to the point that she finally threw up her hands and walked away, she could compliment him on his success. And yet, in her heart, she knew it was folly to think she could leave him. She would be with him to the end, whenever *he* desired it to be, for it would be his decision.

"Is that all I am: a matter of price?" she sighed. The night suddenly weighed like a cloak of lead.

He grimaced and then flashed a constrained smile. "A price which I've been paying since the day I saw you puking on me deck."

While she strained to comprehend his meaning, he hooked his thumbs in his belts and chuckled with smug glee.

"What's so funny?" she asked.

"I'm thinking how much that double-dealing git and Creswicke deserve each other. She will torture the hell out of him."

Still fizzing with mirth, he made to leave.

"What are you going to do with me?" she blurted.

He stopped in mid-stride, but didn't turn. Staring into the night, it was several moments before he sighed, suddenly sounding tired. "T'will require a Solomon for that."

When they returned to the fire, Thomas sat exactly as when they had left: chin propped in his hand, resting on his knee, studying the chessboard. Only his eyes moved at their approach, shifting in exaggerated question from Nathan to Cate, and back. The sandy brows arched high in mute inquiry. Cate shrugged noncommittally.

"How many of my pieces did you move while I was gone?" Nathan asked as he sat, making a great show of surveying the board.

Thomas lifted one shoulder and dropped it. "Only three; you were losing anyway."

Nathan's eyes widened in skepticism. "Really? Perhaps we should just play this out and see who the true prevaricator is, eh?"

Cate settled back in her place between them to watch as a new game developed: the My-Turn-to-Move-Three-of-Your-Pieces version. It included the If-You-Can-Move-Mine-I-Can-Move-Yours rule, which led to the Punch-You-So-I-Can-Move-Your-Man-While-You-Recover method. Oddly, that particular game ended in an impasse. Swearing heartily, the board was wiped clear, and they began anew.

As the hour grew late, the game settled into something more familiar, with long, pensive stretches between moves, murmurs of admiration and soft rumble of male laughter. A bottle of brandy appeared and they shared, regularly toasting each other for a number of reasons.

A moving shadow and stirring of air marked Artemis's passing. Swooping low, she roosted in a nearby tree to blandly observe humanity. Altogether uninteresting by owl standards, she swooped off into the island's interior. Later she returned, dipping low over the fires to show off the fruits of her labors: a large rodent dangling from her claws.

Sometime later, footsteps approached with a speed and suddenness that launched Nathan to his feet. His sword drawn and Cate shoved behind him, before he realized it was only Prudence's lad, Biggins.

He drew up before Nathan, fists curled at his sides. "I challenge you... sir!"

Sword forgotten in his hand, Nathan gaped. "Me?! What the bloody hell? Did you put him up to this?" he cried, whirling around on Thomas.

"No." Chin still propped in his hand, Thomas looked on

benignly. On closer inspection, he was visibly struggling to keep a straight face. "I wish I had, but..."

The lad swayed slightly. His eyes focused on Nathan with considerable effort. "I challenge you, sir," he cried in a quavering voice. It was unclear if the thin voice was the product of fear, drink or youth.

Cate had learned much in the way of the pirate way of life, but on the matter of dueling she was woefully uninformed. The first question which came to mind was "Were there any rules at all?" Was there such a thing among a lot who fancied themselves beyond rules? It stretched credulity to image two pirates squaring off at twenty paces and firing. One just outright killing the other in a brawl seemed more likely. "To the death" echoed in her mind, but in what context was lost. Observing the puzzled reaction of the gathering onlookers, it appeared that either rules did exist and Biggins had failed to adhere to them, or he was trying to instill rules which didn't exist.

Among the "civilized", a glove would have been dropped or a calling card delivered by a second. Something was dropped at Nathan's feet just then. Possibly intended to be a glove, the thing bore more resemblance to a sock, and a sad representation it was: a non-color brownish grey in the firelight, tattered and multi-holed.

Nathan slipped his sword back into its scabbard with a deft flourish which indicated he had no intention of drawing it again. He prodded the challenge token with the toe of his boot.

"What is this?" Nathan bent to pick up the thing and shoved it back. "Here, take this and cut along, lad, before—"

Biggins jerked it away, only to throw it again, with even more conviction. "I challenge you, sir! I'm calling you out."

"Me? Out? The poor boy's drunk," Nathan said to the increasing crowd of curious rogues.

"I'm no boy," Biggins huffed, his thin chest heaving with conviction. "I'm calling you out in defense of the honor of Miss Prudence Collingwood."

"Thomas," Nathan roared, turning. "What nursery did you pluck this one out of?"

"You defiled her, sir," Biggins cried.

"I never laid a hand on her," Nathan sputtered whirling back around. "Aye, I grabbed her by the damned hair, swung her about a bit and smacked her bum, but I never touched her."

"Then you defamed—"

"Make up your mind, lad."

"Goddamn you, sir!"

"You're a bit late on that one, mate. T'was achieved long

ago," Nathan grumbled back. A small chuckle came from those around.

"Pistols or swords?"

"Go back to your mates, lad. You're skirt-sick." By this point, Nathan was sounding quite strained.

"Pistols or swords!" Biggins insisted louder.

"Pick that bloody thing up and be done with this. Where is that insufferable wench? We'll stint this foolery..."

Said insufferable wench was, at the moment, either through luck or plan, not to be seen. Cate entertained the same need to speak with her; this smelled of her in more ways than one.

A small crowd was gathering. They were of little guidance as to what to expect next, their faces carefully impassive lest they show a favorite, until after the terms were settled. Those who knew Nathan saw a storm gathering, and had begun to inch back, taking those who knew no better with them.

"Pistols or swords?" Biggins's chin jutted in belligerence.

"Neither," shot back Nathan. At the same time, he maneuvered sideways, allowing more space between Biggins and himself. The move could have been to defuse the situation, but at the same time, he was distancing himself from Cate.

Biggins pressed closer. Planting his feet squarely before Nathan, he announced, "I'll have my satisfaction, sir!"

Thomas' blue eyes shifted from one to the other. In the flickering shadows, Cate thought she saw the corners of his mouth quivering, whether to keep from smiling or saying something the only question.

"Pistols or swords?" Biggins demanded, refusing to be ignored.

Nathan briefly regarded the lad. "Swords."

"Are you sure?" Thomas rose to stand next to Nathan. He bent as if only for Nathan's benefit, but spoke loudly enough for all to hear. "After that last time...?"

A suggestive lilt in Thomas' query caused a corner of Nathan's mouth to lift slightly.

"And that would be—?" Nathan said.

"Damnedst thing I ever seen," Thomas said more loudly to the crowd. "The last one... well, two, come to think on it, but the last one most particular," he added aiming a meaningful look toward Nathan. "One flick of the blade, the poor sod's cock was cut off, clean as you please. Well, except the blood." He frowned. "Bled like a stuck pig, he did. I saw him a year or so back. He carries it around in a jar o' gin around his neck. His mates call him Pickle-cock."

That brought a fair amount of laughter. The young challenger paled and then went an interesting shade of green visible even in the moonlight. Cate found herself wondering what on earth the boy could have seen in Prudence—and so quickly—which could have driven him to this. Or was the lad just a natural raving romantic?

Young love.

"Then pistols," Nathan cried.

Thomas' countenance clouded. "Don't you remember the last time—?"

"Lucky shot 'twas all," Nathan said with a flip of the hand.

"Providence," Thomas said significantly. He turned to the crowd. "One shot, square in the eye. Dropped like a stone. Least he never knew what hit 'im," he finished with a brief display of compassion.

"Aye, regrettable, that," Nathan said abstractedly. Then he brightened. "We could have a go at knives."

"Noo... Remember Mahon? Oh, and then, there was Porto Praya. Slow deaths are ugly deaths," Thomas said under his breath, though still heard by all.

Both gave a dramatic shudder.

"Then cudgels," Nathan offered.

Thomas squinted a thoughtful eye. "You know, I saw that last one you fought in Maritan. Hit him square upside the head," he said for the benefit of all, tapping a finger to his temple. "All he does is drool and cackle like a chicken."

Cate averted her face to hide a smile.

Thomas crossed his arms and pensively propped his chin in one hand. "There's gotta be something."

"I know, I know," Nathan grumbled. "Ease off and stand by. Blunderbuss? No, not that. Nasty mess, that was."

Still deep in thought, Thomas nodded distractedly. "Difficult to look a man in the eye with only half a face."

"Fisticuffs?"

Thomas chuckled. "Made such a mess o' that one. He's obliged to pay the blind whores extra just to have him."

Biggins followed the conversation intently. Bold at first, his conviction faded with each description.

Chin, Mute Maroi and several of the larger Morgansers pressed to the front of observers, which had now formed into a loose ring. Weapons in clear evidence, they stood arms crossed, shoulder-to-shoulder, imposing with their presence. Biggins noticed and sagged.

"Pray, don't mind them," Nathan said, seeing the lad weaken. "They took some blood oath ages ago, pledging to avenge the death of their captain, or some such nonsense. No basis to it a'tall."

"Still there was..." Thomas warned.

"I still say t'was a shark what got him," Nathan shot back.

"Bloody difficult to tell with what little was left," Thomas said with a dramatic roll of the eyes.

"Arm wrestle?" Nathan said, after a prolonged silent debate.

"I'm surprised you'd suggest that after Calcut. You swore never again after his arm came off in your hand."

They shuddered together.

"Boarding axe?" asked Nathan.

"Nay! Remember Ol' Crossjack Johnson? One swipe and guts are spilling all on the beach, baking in the sun. Too quick; no justice," Thomas concluded with a dismissive swipe.

Biggin's dulled senses finally pricked, and he realized that the two captains were having a go with him. Many of the onlookers had long seen as much and were having a good laugh at his expense. The remainder stared at Nathan and Thomas in slack-jawed wonderment.

"Very well," Nathan conceded. He sighed. "This is a bother. There has to be a way. The lad deserves his justice, field of honor and all that."

"True, true." Thomas nodded pensively. He hooked a fatherly arm around Biggins's shoulders. "Come to the fire, son, and we'll drink on it, whilst we ponder. 'Tis ill-advised it is, to go off killing, before your mates have been allowed to properly toast your success."

With a smooth bit of manipulation, Thomas handed Biggins off to several Grisellers, who shepherded him away amid a barrage of hails and hearty backslapping.

Thomas watched to assure the lad was well away, before asking the remaining crowd, "Any of you drunk or stupid enough to have declared yourself his second?"

Quiet murmurings and shaking heads was his answer.

"Then there's nay harm, unless you desire your justice now," Thomas said turning to Nathan.

"Jesus and Mary, no. Was he drunk?" Nathan asked looking in the unfortunate Biggins path.

"Not yet and not enough," Thomas said, with a half-smile. "Pitiful wretch can't hold it, either. In an hour, he'll be face down, and by dawn he won't remember a thing."

With nothing of any further interest pending, the small crowd dispersed and returned to their revelry. Thomas excused himself with a "Don't you dare touch that board" to Nathan.

When they were finally alone, Cate came up beside Nathan. "How many duels have you been in?" she asked in a low voice.

One side of his mustache lifted in an odd quirk. "Not. A. One."

His attention shifted to Biggins' direction. "Barely has hair on his balls. Tonight, I let him live, so he can curse me for it when he's old and decrepit."

"Hell's fury. A fine kettle o' fish," Nathan steamed at length. "These upstarts, nowadays can't be trusted. No upbringing. I blame Thomas for this. He's had the lad under his wing for a time. Certainly, long enough to have taught him a man's responsibilities."

With a sweep of his hand, the matter was dismissed. Nathan returned to the chess game. Studying the board with renewed interest, he glanced to see where Thomas might be, and then hunched with intensity.

"Let me see... this knight would be ever so much more advantageous over here..." he said under his breath, reaching delicately for the game piece.

Several unkind thoughts surged to the surface at the sight of Prudence some time later standing at the edge of the light, drooping with weariness, first and foremost being Nathan's suggestion to "turn her skirts and spank her as her parents apparently never did." In her less generous moments, Cate considered that the manipulative little busy-body and Creswicke deserved each other.

Cate felt Nathan stiffen beside her. Seeing the muscles in his jaws go white, visible even in the dim light, brought her to think perhaps it would be best to allow cooler heads to prevail. Berating Prudence would only serve to stir a pot which had barely ceased to boil. There had been enough excitement on for one night.

A more generous side prevailing, Cate rose; a desisting hand to Nathan bid him to stay. Under his glower from where he sat, and a series of incensed huffs and sputtering, Cate retrieved Prudence, scooped out a spot in the sand, spread the quilt and guided her to bed. The child was asleep before Cate rose to her feet.

She almost collided with Nathan when she turned around.

"Where the hell are you to sleep now? Couldn't the little —?"

"Shh." Cate pressed her fingers to her lips and pushed him several steps away. "Just allow her to sleep. I'll manage."

"That's the trouble." His shoulders jerked under his shirt. "You're always the one to *manage*."

Muttering, he disappeared into the darkness. He returned

shortly, a piece of canvas in tow. Moving nearer to where he and Thomas sat, he scooped a depression in the sand, and then spread the canvas over it. Straightening, he swept an inviting hand. Too tired to object, she did as she was bid.

"Sleep well, luv," he murmured as he knelt and spread his coat over her. His eyes gone to near black in the fire's shadows, he brushed a strand of hair from her cheek, his fingers lingering on her neck. "You're safe tonight."

Lying only a few feet away, Cate could see Nathan and Thomas, knee-to-knee, hunched over the game board. The flames gilded them in gold and flickered on their profiles as they sat dark head against light. If she was to look through one eye, with pistol and cutlass at their sides, they were like two Teutonic war gods. Looking at them through the other, they could have easily been sitting in a library before the hearth.

She closed both eyes and listened, not necessarily to the words, but their voices. Thomas' was a deep rumble, so very familiar, but Nathan's provided more warmth and comfort than his coat over her shoulders. At one point, Nathan launched into a lengthy dialogue. She drifted to sleep to his throaty gravel detailing the pros and cons of the Lucen position versus the Greco counter gambit.

Sometime in the night, Cate woke. She wriggled to get more comfortable. Sand could be insufferably hard. The fire had burned down, the embers a red-orange glow under their cape of white ash. Hushed voices and muffled laughter drifted from down the beach, Artemis's plaintive whistle coming from nearby. Cate raised her head enough to see where Prudence slept some distance behind her, the moonlight outlining her shapeless hump.

A shape in the opposite direction caught her eye. It was Nathan, barely an arm's length away. He lay on his back, sprawled like a broken rag doll, one arm flung toward her. His braids fanned in black fingers on the sand about his head and shoulders. She listened carefully. Through the distant sounds of surf and merriment came the throaty rhythmic rasp of his breathing.

She snuggled deeper under the coat redolent of him and went to sleep.

22: DESPERATE MEASURES

CATE WOKE TO A PAIR of worn, suede boot toes staring her in the face. She blinked away the sleep, the canvas beneath her rough against her cheek. The boots bent and Nathan's face came into focus, bare inches from hers.

"Joy o' the morning, luv!" he declared brightly. Wide-eyed with enthusiasm, he held forth a steaming cup. "Kirkland was already in a snit, worried you might be going without. I swear, the bloody cove fancies you drink this in your sleep."

Groaning with stiffness, she sat up. Clutching his coat around her shoulders against the morning chill, she reached for the cup, only to have it taken beyond her grasp.

"Have a care! 'Tis extra hot this morning," he warned. "I think the man has discovered a new temperature for boiling water. Pray, allow me to hold."

Face contorted with concentration, he guided the cup for her first sip. Nathan was correct: the liquid was viciously hot. She jerked back, touching her tongue to her scalded lip.

Nathan clucked his tongue, scolding. "Let me blow on it for a bit."

Balancing the cup well to the side, he lowered his buttocks onto the sand and industriously applied to the task.

Yawning, she shook out her hair. She finger-combed the larger snarls and then set to working one of the tortoise-shell combs through it. Nathan cocked a scornful eye, dubious of the likelihood of her success, but oddly said nothing.

"How long have you been up?" she asked.

He stopped blowing long enough to say, "Ages," and then resumed.

"Where's Prudence?" she asked, craning her neck.

"Huh?" He paused in mid-blow to look disinterestedly about. Finally, he jabbed a thumb over his shoulder. "Over there, still abed."

Surrendering to the reality that there was little more to be done with the mess, Cate twisted up the sides of her hair and shoved the combs in place. Settling more comfortably, she hunched the coat higher about her shoulders and scanned the beach, taking in the new day.

The scene before her appeared more like a battleground, the casualties of war strewn where they had fallen to the artillery of revelry and rum. Some of the sea rogues still rode the momentum of drunkenness: staggering and stumbling over the still bodies of their fallen comrades. Cup, mug or tankard in hand, the survivors milled about the cook fires, their lazy curls of smoke melding with the bluer ones of tobacco to spiral into the azure sky. Towering flat-bottomed, anvil-headed clouds, dark and heavy with moisture, hung threateningly far on the horizon.

"Enjoy land while you might," he said between blows. "We'll be leaving on the 'morrow tide."

"I thought the terms was four days. It's been barely three."

"Aye, but the first what arrives is the best positioned."

"You expect foul play?" Cate asked, growing uneasy.

"Duplicity is a common middle name," Nathan said sagely.

"Including you?"

"Jonathan Edward," he said at length and then added at her puzzled look. "Me middle name, or names, as it 'tis."

A brow arched expectantly under the edge of the faded blue headscarf.

"Maureen," she finally said. "Family name, from my father's side."

Nathan nodded interestedly and stopped blowing enough to say, "Then you are Scots."

"Not that they would admit to," she said smiling faintly. "Nathanael Jonathan Edward Blackthorne."

"A bit grand for a tyke what wasn't expected to live."

"You?" she asked, canting her head. Any morsel of his past she eagerly devoured.

"Aye. Small I was. Mum claimed it was because I came early, but it was a full moon," he added importantly. "The midwife claimed I was black when I came out—had a headful of black hair, for one thing. She announced me cursed and the Devil's spawn. Mum had to do everything she could to keep them from killing me straight away. She put charms all about me basket and named me Nevan."

"Nevan?"

He shrugged indifferently. "'Tis Celt for little saint or some such. As I grew up, everyone kept getting it wrong, calling me Nathan. She knew well how burdensome a Celt name might be, so she changed it... for everyone but her, that is. She called me Nevan until her dying day." The corner of his mouth drew up on a crooked smile of such tenderness it seemed a violation of his privacy to say anything further.

He gave the cup a final puff and then tested it. "Aye, 'tis ready."

"Thank you for sacrificing your safety for my pleasures, Captain," she said teasingly and batted her eyelashes.

She sipped cautiously then closed her eyes as she blissfully moaned. "Oh, that's good."

"Is there anything else what causes you to make those noises?" he asked with a suggestive waggle of his brows.

She posed careful consideration. "Come to think on it, there are a few other things which cause me to groan."

A devilment sparked his eyes, but his response was cut short by Mr. Hodder's hail. With a crooked smile and a playful roll of the eyes, he sauntered away, scarf tails wafting in the breeze behind him.

Daylight and time having resuscitated most of the stricken, the scene on the beach was much the same as the night before, although in the glare of daylight, the festive mood gave way to something appearing more in the way of drunken revelry, occasionally breaking into an outright brawl when tempers flared. There was a portion of the men whose only purpose seemed to be to achieve the same level of drunkenness as the night before. A goodly number, however, could not suffer the idleness of drinking and found other pastimes.

There were chess games, although cards and dice were more common. Betting was prohibited aboard, but ashore the pirates were free to lose or win their money at will, with ensuing arguments and fights breaking out regularly. Competitions, however, were what men do best, and there were a number of them from arm wrestling, to story-telling—a panel of judges in place—to spitting.

At one end of the beach, an impromptu play reenacting a mutiny trial was presented. Something akin to talent shows were at opposite ends of the beach: singing, magic tricks, juggling, mime and dancing a few skills on exhibit. From one of those erupted a knife-throwing contest. Distances were paced off, and a cask top, with concentric circles drawn with a charred stick, was set up as a target.

The spectators were unabashedly partisan, *Ciara Morganse*

vs. *Griselle*. The best from each was pressed forward, odds shouted and coins collected at every toss of the knife. Through a process of eliminations, it came down to Pryce against the best Griseller. To no surprise to any Morganser, Pryce handily won. The third place winner was a huge surprise, Mr. Stubbs, missing fingers and all.

Cate was called away to tend the third sliced limb of the day, a nasty-looking slash running from the inside of the man's arm to nearly his wrist. Not deep enough to require stitches, by the time she finished binding it, the knife throwing had evolved into sword fighting.

The rules were roughly the same as practices on board: a circle heeled in the sand; the first to knock the other over was the winner. Again, the best from each ship was pressed forward. Cate watched in fascination as the men lunged and parried back and forth. The sun flashing off the steel blades, and the metallic clash and grind of the metal stirred primeval blood. The carnage which could be wrought by those razor edges was a fearsome thing. But today was all in fun. At least, that is what she privately chanted.

"No worries, luv!" she growled under her breath in a graveled imitation of Nathan.

On a fervent cloud of one-up-manship, the Morgansers set to bragging that they possessed something unique to any other ship on the Caribbean, hell, the world: a sword-fighting woman. Under Nathan's watchful eye, a reluctant Cate was dragged into the ring. His dark-framed eyes scanned the Grisellers, and then glanced to Thomas, who barely lifted one shoulder in consent.

The Grisellers eyed her speculatively. They knew her only as the captain's guest. A woman pirate would have been a novelty; that she could manage a sword expected. On the surface, however, she bore the aspects of neither, and they placed their bets accordingly.

So, consumed by her apprehensions, Cate was only vaguely aware of Pryce coming up at her elbow. Grey eyes bright with the excitement of combat, he pointed with his chin toward her first opponent sidling into the ring.

"Mind what ye've lernt, lass. Keep yer elbows down and yer wrist firm. Watch them eyes; 'tis the window to his soul. Ahh, look at 'im! Scairt of ye already, he is. Two-thirds of the battle 'tis won already. But mind, he's more afraid of embarrassin' hisself. Take 'im quick, else ye won't be takin' him a'tall."

Pryce was correct. If Biggins had been the ship's baby, then this one was but a month older. He'd most likely been chosen on a wave of skepticism and reckless male pride, which meant they thought her a joke. To be dismissed so out-of-hand stirred her determination to prove them wrong. Dark of hair and eye, sweat rolled down the lad's olive-skin: he was as nervous as she. It was a good sign.

The sword shoved into Cate's hand wasn't a familiar one. This one had a thicker grip and was rough against her palm. The blade was heavier, a weapon built for labor, not finesse. She worked it in her hand, griping and re-griping, trying to gain familiarity. She struck her stance, feeling grossly disadvantaged as she touched her blade in salute.

Nervous and nearly frozen with self-consciousness, the startling swiftness of her foe's—Rafa, according to his supporters—first move took her by surprise. Within seconds, she had been driven back, until her hem brushed the line in the sand. Irked by his temerity, and determined not to be embarrassed, she counter-attacked. Rafa's eyes widened, caught unawares. She countered harder, pushing him further back. A twisting slash on her part, and his weapon fell to cheering approval.

An enthusiastic slap on the shoulder broke Cate from the astonishment of winning.

"I knew ye could do it," Pryce exclaimed, vigorously rubbing her arm and shoulder. Tucking her sword under his arm, he massaged her hand. "Well, done, sir. Yer the pride o' the *Morganse*, to be sure."

Exhilarated by the flush of battle and success, Cate dabbed the sweat from her face. She saw Nathan at the circle's margin, hip cocked and arms crossed, displaying a gold-bedecked smile of approval.

"Watch 'im," Pryce said, pulling her attention to her next opponent: a grizzled but wiry one. "Arabie, he is. He be a crafty cove. Mind his eyes; the sneakin' scug is a-tryin' to intimidate ye already."

Pryce was correct. Her new opponent's ferret-like eyes were stonily fixed on her.

Pryce nodded in affirmation as he massaged her upper arm. "I've seen his sort a'fore. He'll be desirin' to go high 'n bring ye up, so's he can cut you low."

Her abdomen knotted at the word "cut." "I thought this was supposed to be in fun."

"Aye! It 'tis! And don't be a-worryin' about the difference in swords."

Cate blinked, only then noticing the weapon: a vicious-looking instrument, with a sweeping curved edge similar to the scythes used in the hayfields.

"They fight just the same," Pryce assured, judiciously. "The curve's the better to slit yer gut in tight quarters." He patted her in a confident dismissal. "You'll do fine."

As she took up her position, the onlookers grew feverish, the hunger for battle etched on every straining face. These were pirates, blood and mayhem their bread and butter. The blood drawn in earlier exchanges had only peaked their hunger, and anticipation was a heady nectar.

Again, the Griseller took the early advantage. As predicted, he slashed high, the tip of his blade whirring past her ear. Angered at being played, she parried back. Her height was an advantage, providing a longer reach. Her opponent tried several more ploys, mostly intended to break her concentration, but to no avail. The spectator's shouts merged into a unified, multi-lingual din. Pryce's bass rang the loudest, with pointers and encouragements. At length, she drove her rival backward and over the line to win again.

As the cheers went up and winnings were collected, Nathan stepped forward and gently took the sword from Cate. Good-naturedly taking the jibes, shooting back a few of his own, he took her out of the circle and sat her down under a tree. Thomas was there, leaned against a cask, arms loosely crossed over his weapons.

"Watch her," Nathan said to Thomas, and then to Cate, "Oh, and here."

He fumbled in his pocket to extract a small leather pouch and dropped it in Cate's hand with a metallic clink.

"What's this?" she asked, still gasping for air.

Nathan sighed at her thick-wittedness. "Your share of the wagers."

"I didn't bet, especially on myself," she said as Nathan artfully dodged her attempts to give it back.

"Aye, well, 'tis a good thing at least one of us — two, actually," he qualified, with an acknowledging nod to Thomas, "have the savvy and good sense to know a sure thing when they see it. One is obliged to answer the door when Opportunity knocks, for she rarely returns."

Cate gaped at Thomas. "*You* bet on *me* against your own men?"

The lake blue eyes narrowed to knowing slits. "No man shall ever get the best of you."

Nathan made rueful snort as he pivoted and swaggered back to the circle.

"You're not bad. Nathan's been teaching you, hasn't he?" Thomas asked after Nathan was out of earshot.

Still thoroughly winded, Cate lifted the hair from her neck to cool it. "A little. How could you tell?"

Thomas pursed his lips as he regarded Nathan, now exchanging jibes with the spectators. "I recognized a few moves. He never had much formal training. It's always been a matter of survival than style."

He chuckled quietly at a memory. "There was a time—a short one, mind—when we had an opportunity to study with a master. He was on a ship we raided off Tenerife. We convinced him to trade instructions for his life."

Thomas assured himself of Nathan's location and then leaned very near her ear. "I said it before, and I'll say it again: if that damned fool ever hurts you, I will not abide it."

She stared up at him, puzzled by his low-voiced vehemence.

"If he is that blind or damned stupid then there's no help for him," Thomas went on. "But I can save you, and by the gods, I will not watch him destroy you the way—"

He was cut off by the rise of voices chanting his and Nathan's name. The latter now stood in the circle, with his arms spread in invitation.

"Seems they shan't settle for less." Nathan called over the voices. Grinning, he gave a dramatic shrug. "It would appear I'm obliged to best you again."

Thomas straightened to sketch a formal but mocking bow. "*A votre plaisir, Monsieur,*" he said, in impeccable French.

"*Le plaisir est `a moi,*" came Nathan's equally fluent reply.

As Nathan approached, Thomas turned back to her. "By the gods, I mean it."

The two men threw off everything, until they wore only shirts, breeks and boots. The rest was piled into Cate's arms, Nathan's hat poised haphazardly on her head. The two captains were virtually carried to the circle on a wave of enthusiasm. There, under a barrage of outcries and adulations, they drew their swords and squared off.

"*Morganse! Morganse! Morganse!*"

"*Griselle! Griselle! Griselle!*"

Neither man was above a little showmanship. Slowly circling each other, they allowed the suspense to build. These were pirates, who lived and died by the sword, in the most literal sense of the phrase. There were no formal stances here, no address or salute. They stood loose armed, eyeing and waiting. Cate had never given Thomas' sword much notice, before. Standing side by side, as he and Nathan often did, she had seen the hilt was heavier and more ornate than Nathan's, but little else. Now, she could see the weapon in its full glory—and a glorious weapon it was, with a basket-style grip of carved silver and intricately detailed guards. It was larger in not only breadth but length by a good third. Nathan's sword was stoic in comparison, a layman's weapon, made to impress with its lethality, not looks.

Nathan's eye imperceptibly twitched; a corner of Thomas' mouth quirked. A plan offered and accepted.

It began with such startling swiftness Cate didn't see who moved first. As they lunged and parried back and forth, the contrast between the two was striking. Thomas was big and powerful, but amazingly graceful for his size. Nearly a head shorter, Nathan was lithe and athletic, virtually gliding over the sand. The two's advantages were counter-balanced, the larger man's reach neutralized by the smaller's agility, strength countered by guile. Like their chess matches, they knew each other's game, countering effortlessly, sometimes laughingly, sometimes with a grunt of surprise and a flood of cursing.

The sun flaring on the blade edges, their steel voices rang clear, with an underlying hiss of threat. Calm and intent, each bore a faint smile. Both captains knew what the audience desired and gave it with a flair. It might have been all in fun, but neither held back. Cate was afraid to look, but unable to look away, gasping at moves which would have been fatal had it been anyone else. If there had been the slightest error in judgment, the force of their swings could easily have sliced the other from gullet to craw. She had seen such exhibitions before, but in this setting, surrounded by sea rogues cheering for blood it took on a new lethality.

Breathing heavier, shirts darkening with sweat, they fought. Their expressions sobered as they grew more absorbed and focused. Caught up in the fervor of the battle, the pirates brandished their own weapons as they clamored for victory, in a myriad of languages. Bets were made, the odds fluxing with the fight's ever-changing momentum.

With a loud grunt, Thomas reposted with a vicious slash, forcing Nathan to scramble backwards. A flick, and the back of Nathan's right hand bloomed red. Thomas lunged with a curling downward swipe, knocking Nathan's weapon away. An upper cut with his fist sent Nathan onto his rump. A victorious uproar erupted from the *Griselle's* crew and bets were settled.

Thomas pulled Nathan to his feet, and they heartily clapped each other on the back, accepting adulations as they departed. In the shade, where Cate waited, they hung onto each other, bent and gasping for air. Faces streaming with sweat, mutual compliments collided in mid-air. Cate tried to inspect Nathan's bleeding hand, but was genially waved away.

"'Tis nothing. No more than a scratch," Nathan said. He mopped his face on his sleeve and licked away the blood. "I thought it was my turn. Remember Cartagena?" he directed to Thomas.

His head hanging between his arms, Thomas' broad back heaved as he gasped for air. "Eh? Oh, forgot I suppose."

The false tone in that caused Cate to turn just as Thomas straightened. With a steady blue look, he stabbed a finger at her. "By the gods and make no mistake."

And then Thomas stalked off.

"Wonder what put the twist in his jib?" Nathan said, more to himself. Then he said louder, "Pay him no mind, luv. The ol' grandmother, he always thought he knew more than he ought."

After several minutes of persistence, Nathan at last relented to allow Cate to tend his hand and perched on a puncheon. The cut ran nearly the width of its back, its edges as cleanly sliced as if with a razor. The blood welled in a steady flow, but slowed with pressure. A bit of salve and a hastily tied bandage was all that was possible before Nathan's patience was exhausted.

After, they sat in the shade and watched the ensuing matches.

Several bouts later, the swordplay giving way to knife fights. The circle was erased with a kick of the boots and replaced with a smaller one, opponents paired up and the competition began. A goodly amount of bumboo had been consumed by then and skill gave way to brute force. Split lips, gushing noses, gashed brows, torn knuckles and swollen eyes becoming badges of honor, Cate's blood box coming in fast demand.

Cate had just finished bandaging an arm when she heard her name being called. The Morgansers had put her up as a contender. In soaring spirits, they wheedled and catcalled to encourage her, while at the same time placing their bets. By the Griseller's measure, a woman might bear a sword, but could never handle a knife, and they relished the easy wager. The implication that she was incapable stirred her blood. It was an affront which couldn't go unanswered. Nathan intercepted her at the circle's edge. Seizing her by the arm, he steered her through the crowd and away, in spite of her attempts to pull away and go back to the ring.

"I could take that little one," she said, bouncing at the end of Nathan's grasp.

"Did you see the looks on their faces?" he asked, steering her away by both shoulders. "All they desire is to grope and maul you. Absolutely not. Bye-the-bye, have you seen Princess-Pain-in-the-Arse of late?" He craned his head with exaggerated interest.

Nathan's intent to distract was poorly executed, but effective, for it drew Cate from the ring. Prudence was spotted straight away, her bright yellow dress a beacon against the lush tropical growth. She sat with a newfound suitor, notably not the noble Biggins. Cate couldn't help but wonder if this one had also been paid for by Nathan or if this was nature taking its course.

Nathan steered Cate to the water's edge. They strolled, the pirate revelry fading behind them, until there was nothing but the lap of the waves at their feet and the cries of shorebirds. It was late afternoon. The bay had gone to glass, reflecting sunset and ships in perfection. The sun's final flare gilded Nathan in a molten glow. At first, Cate reveled in having him alone. That faded, however, as he grew more preoccupied. Nathan had guided her down the shore like a man with a purpose, why or what was the question.

As they walked, Nathan drew a breath as if to say something, and then thought better. There were several such false starts. Cate glanced at him, waiting, growing more restive herself. She could think of but one reason which could have caused him to bring her there, one thing which would cause him such perturbation: he meant to tell her that he had taken Thomas up on his offer. She now belonged to Thomas. Given Thomas' sudden concern about her welfare — or whatever that outburst had been about — seemed contradictory, but what else could it be.

While she and Nathan had watched the competitions, Thomas had stood across the circle. She had felt his gaze fixed on her, grave and intent, far from his customary geniality. It was more than a little unsettling to think that Thomas had been observing her with the same keenness as she had of him. She had often caught herself gaping at him like a love-struck school girl. She ruffled at the thought of the two men bartering over her like she was a prized pistol. There was little flattery to be found in knowing one was considered worthy of a "king's ransom" as Nathan had put it, although he was known to exaggerate.

What are slightly out-of-their-prime widows going for these days?

With a pang of remorse, Cate wondered what she might have done to keep Nathan from selling her, knowing all the while the answer was "Nothing."

"You remind him of her."

Nothing to be done about that, she thought moodily.

All that only added to her irritability, which had been building since she saw Prudence cowering in the floor: there had to be a way to help the child. Granted, the child was meddlesome, and had caused an inordinate amount of disruption, but that didn't mean she deserved to be banished to a hellish marriage. Seeing Prudence with her young man had set Cate to thinking anew.

There was the argument that Prudence was about to live a dream: marrying a rich and influential man. A louder voice dwelt on the hell in which the girl was about to be flung: a cold, loveless marriage to a man who, by all accounts, possessed few admirable qualities. Granted, many marriages had started with less. On the whole, to marry for love was a romantic notion. It was a luxury which few enjoyed and was considered folly by many. After all, love faded and died; only money and position endured. At least, that was the argument Cate had been given at Prudence's age.

The exchange was the day after tomorrow; Prudence was running out of time.

"Nathan, we have to help her," Cate said into the silence.

"Help who?"

"Prudence. We have to help her."

He flicked a sidelong glance. "Help her how? She's not starving. She's not drowning — although I've been fair tempted — nor she's fallen off a cliff — another temptation resisted. What help could she possibly need?"

"Get her away from Creswicke."

"Hold off!" He halted to squint at her in confusion. "We took her so Creswicke would pay to get her back."

"I know that, but, I was thinking — "

"Do I want to hear this?" he asked, warily leaning away.

"I was thinking after he paid, perhaps we could take her back."

Nathan's face screwed. "Ransom her again? Isn't that a bit redundant?"

"No, we could take her... I don't know, somewhere." Cate was painfully conscious of her lack thorough thought, which only weakened her proposition.

Shaking his head, Nathan resumed walking. "Creswicke would be burning these waters apart searching for her."

"But you said he doesn't really want her," Cate said, striding to catch up.

"Possession, darling," he said tolerantly. "'Tis all a matter of the having."

"Would he look for her or for you?"

Nathan looked off, smiling whimsically. "T'would be a quandary, to be sure. There's no way she could be on the *Morganse*. One couldn't spell 'assume,' before he was upon us."

"Then, we could find somewhere else, the *Griselle*, perhaps," she said. That Nathan was discussing it she took as a good sign: he hadn't dismissed her out-of-hand.

"That would be a matter to take up with Thomas."

So, lost in thought, Cate looked up to find Nathan well down the beach. Running to catch up, she fell in step next to him.

"Do you realize that her first...? That Prudence going to have to—" she said.

"Give up her maidenhead to Breaston Creswicke?"

"That's not quite how I would have put it, but, yes. It's not right; it's not fair."

"And pray who do you fancy would be better?" Nathan asked conversationally.

So deep in thought, Cate slowed and eventually stalled. Noticing she wasn't at his side until several steps away, Nathan came back into her considering look and a growing smile. He scowled then his eyes rounded in horror.

"Me? Oh, no!" he cried, scrambling backward. "Not in life!" He pivoted on his heel and sped away.

"Why not?" she pleaded, running to catch up.

"I haven't... done... *that*, with a sixteen-year-old—that I knew of—since I was sixteen meself," he sputtered as he churned down the beach. "My luck, I'd get her with child, and then there would be hell to pay."

"She'll be married in less than a month; no one would know the difference."

Nathan skidded to a halt and swiveled back. He planted his fists on his hips and glared. "Lord Creswicke is blond-haired and blue-eyed. Need I say more?"

An outright laugh seemed unwise, and so she choked it down. "You think every child of yours is going to come out with black hair and a tattoo?"

Nathan built up to say something then thought better. "There is no talking to you." And he spun away.

With an exasperated gasp, Cate hitched her skirts and raced after him. She pivoted in front of him and skipped in reverse before his hasty pace. "Do you know what that poor girl is expecting? Her mother told her to close her eyes, and it would soon be over."

Nathan made a face. "That's what she thinks? 'Course with Creswicke, it probably will," he added under his breath.

"I wouldn't know." Breathless, she stopped, hoping he would, as well.

"Well, I do," he said, brushing past. "And no woman should have to go to bed with the likes of that princock just because her father desires connections. Bloody bastard!"

"Who, Creswicke or her father?"

Nathan whirled in a clatter of bells, his hair fanning wide behind him. "Both!" He pirouetted and marched on.

"So, you'll do it?" Cate called.

"No!"

"Nathan!"

Cate waited, but when he didn't, she swore under her breath and jogged to catch up.

"This is madness!" Nathan's voice cracked with acrimony. He spun around with a suddenness that caused her to skid to a halt. "Have you completely left your senses? You're more daft than I. Why are you so anxious for me to do… this?"

"Because I suspect you would be good at it."

"At what?"

Winded from running, she braced her hands on her knees. "Being a girl's first."

"Gentle and attentive" had been the kind of man she had advised Prudence. She had every reason to believe Nathan could be all that and more, if he was of a mind. In his less guarded moments—few and fleeting as they were—she had seen flashes of gentleness. She had seen him lovingly caress the wheel, run his hands along the rail as if it had been a woman's calf. She had felt the benefit of his charms and had seen eyes that could go to liquid, turning her every thought to mush and tighten her belly. Any man capable of such devotion to a ship had to be able to give the same to a person.

His jaw dropped. "*You've* been thinking on how I bed a woman?"

"Well, yes." Thankfully she was bent over, effectively hiding her flaming cheeks.

Vividly and extensively, nearly every night.

He grappled with several responses. Ultimately, he slumped and said dully, "You know nothing about me."

Nathan made to turn away, but was halted by her hand on his arm. "A girl's first time should be special," Cate said. "She should be with someone who knows how to make it wonderful— give her something to remember all those nights later, lying next to a snoring husband."

"It could be said this is a time where ignorance might be bliss," he said wryly.

Cate eyed Nathan dubiously. "And to which side of that equation would you rather find yourself?"

She ventured closer to toy with a braid at his shoulder. "I suspect under all those trappings there is a very tender and adept lover."

"Adept?"

She winced. "It was meant as a compliment."

"Oh, certainly didn't sound like one."

"I beg your leave. Out of all those women in your life, surely there have been times when it was more than just filling a need.

Surely there were times — with certain ones — that were…" She groped for a word, finally landing on "Remarkable."

"Must we talk about this?" he asked, looking thoroughly strained. "This is a subject for neither a lady nor the genteel."

She made a rude noise. "That's all well, because I am neither. Don't you dare go priggish on me now."

One hand falling to rest on the pommel of his sword, the tails of his scarf fluttered about his shoulders, Nathan stared at the water and the *Morganse* resting on her mooring. The sun flared bright on the angles of his profile.

"What makes you so sure she'd be willing?" he asked finally.

"Surely you don't question your powers of persuasion. Charm her." Cate batted her eyelashes for emphasis, at the same time hating herself for resorting to such feminine wiles.

Nathan snorted, cocking a sardonic eye. "It would seem me charms haven't been working, lately."

"Really? I hadn't noticed. Mind, I'm not suggesting you should throw her down and take her —"

Nathan made a derisive noise. "Praise God for small considerations."

He rounded on her and propped his hands on his hips. "And you see this as a fantastic idea? You're daft, completely and irrevocably, and more so than I, if that's at all possible."

"Is it so unthinkable she should have a choice? If she prefers Creswicke, then very well, but at least she had a choice."

Nathan ruffled at the suggestion Prudence might find Creswicke preferable. Then he batted a dismissive hand and continued down the beach. "No, I'll not. Get someone else."

"Who?"

"Get Thomas. He's fair with the ladies and he's younger," Nathan shouted over his shoulder.

Cate stopped to gaze thoughtfully at the water. "I never thought of him."

"You can't be serious," Nathan implored to the sky and raced back. "He's old enough to be her father!"

Thomas was indeed a consideration. He was amiable and possessed the quiet confidence which many a large man possessed. Any man who was willing to arrange a woman's hair was sure to possess great sensitivity in many other aspects.

Cate then shook her head. It would be too much like seeing Brian go with another woman.

"Maybe he has someone on the *Griselle*," Cate said aloud.

There was Prudence's current young man, or the noble Biggins. Cate instantly negated both. Youth is fine for energy, but couldn't be depended upon for the skill or finesse required.

Prudence needed to experience something more than a furtive tussle in the bushes. And to foist Prudence off on someone else would be too much like selling her.

"Will you clap a stopper on it!" Eloquent with frustration, Nathan spun and stomped away. "Stop meddling! You're worse than she is."

"But, Nathan...!"

"Suffering Jesus on the cross, now, what?" he whimpered, scuffling to a halt.

"Maybe you might think of it as an opportunity," Cate said coming around Nathan, who now stood with his shoulders slumped and his head hanging.

"Opportunity?" he said blankly, looking up. "What the bloody hell does that mean?"

"I mean, let's take the pragmatic approach: when was the last time you were with a woman?"

For the second time in as many minutes, she rendered him speechless.

"I will not stand here and discuss this," Nathan hissed and brushed past.

"C'mon, Nathan. There's no secrets on a ship," she called to his back.

When she saw that he had no intention of stopping, she jogged to catch him up.

"I know it's been a while," Cate said, now a bit breathless. "Unless you really did stop for a whore while you were looking for me last week. Are you used to going this long?"

He vacillated at an alarming rate from blenched to flushed and back. "Enough!"

She fell back a step, now thoroughly offended. "I was only trying to help."

"I don't want to hear it!" Hunching his shoulders, he strode away, the sand spurting from under his heels.

"We still haven't decided about Prudence," she called after him.

Wheeling, he stormed back to loom over her.

"I am Captain of this ship, and as Captain of this ship, I decide, and I've decided the subject is closed." He jerked a conclusive nod and spun away. "Bloody woman!"

"Any reason why Nathan is avoiding you like you have the French pox?"

Cate looked up at Thomas with a tentative half-smile. "Has he? I hadn't noticed."

Thomas laughed and gave her a teeth-jarring brotherly pat

on the back as he passed. "You're not near as good o' liar as he by half."

Still chuckling, he ambled away, leaving Cate sitting on a log. As much as she wanted to deny it, he was correct: Nathan had been avoiding her. He had not spoken, nor looked her direction since their conversation on the beach. An odd sort of avoidance-hide-and-seek-eye-tag had been transpiring all evening. Several times, he had brushed near enough for her to attempt to catch his attention, but had sped by, pointedly ignoring her. A few times, she thought to have him cornered, but he slithered away, feigning rapt fascination in a crewman sharpening a stick or a bird flying past.

She was miserable.

Every variety of regret and self-remonstration ate at her as she wondered what on earth had possessed her to suggest Nathan deflower Prudence. Impulses can be horrifying things. Heaven knew, no one should be more familiar with that phenomenon than Nathan, but that didn't render him more forgiving. That he might never speak to her again clawed at her, the prospect of being sold monumentally increasing. If it was to be the case, then fair enough, but it wouldn't come to pass without first having her say. If he wished to toss her from the ship after, there would be nothing to stop him. As miserable as she was, marooning, and a slow death from thirst and starvation would be a blessed end.

It was later that night, when she finally caught Nathan in the undulating margins of the firelight, perched atop a cask. At seeing her approach, he intensified his attention on the orange he was peeling with his knife, but for once he didn't take flight. Cate sat on a puncheon at his knee and waited. At length — long enough to cause her to think her ploy might not serve — he lowered the orange and his guard.

"What?" His tone wasn't churlish, just unsure, with a tinge of wounded-little-boy.

There had been plenty of time for her to think what she might say, if the opportunity arose. Now, with Nathan's dark-framed eyes on her, every word and sentiment she had collected became woefully inadequate. With a cautious sidelong look, she wondered what it would take to make amends. Recollections of her apologies to Brian came readily to mind. Those, however, had required long nights on the floor before a fireplace. Not much guidance there.

It brought her squarely before the motive behind her latest blunder: ruffled feelings. She had wished to inflict the same hurt Nathan had dealt her when he had trifled with her a few nights earlier, and then suggested she might be sold, again toying with her. That had been her intention, but her darts had been far less accurate than his.

Love could erase so many hurts.

Dammit! Why can't I stay angry with him?

She had agreed to remain on the *Morganse*, but it had been a deal with the Devil, her Purgatory at her elbow every day. It was torture to have him so near, and yet so very far: the smiles, the glances, or, as at that moment, his leg brushing her arm, his fingers caressing the smooth skin of the orange. Very briefly, she allowed herself the luxury of visualizing what else those fingers might be capable of.

"Are you well?"

She jerked. "What? Huh? Oh, certainly... Why?"

"You had an odd look, like you'd swallowed a bug."

She hoped the darkness obscured her flaring cheeks.

"I'm sorry, Nathan. I didn't mean to put you in such an awkward position." They were vacuous words, but the only ones available.

The bells in his mustache flared in the firelight. He made a face, acknowledging her apology, while at the same time asserting his own disapproval.

"I'm sure in all that blithering madness, there were good intentions. Most insane proposition I've ever heard." His hands stopped in mid-motion so he might regard her. "What in all that is holy ever possessed you?"

"I don't know."

Go ahead. Allow him his revenge. Your atonement is nigh.

Time can sometimes be a burden, and time was exactly what she had to realize what a blundering dolt she had been.

Absolute lunatic!

She belonged in Bedlam for such thinking, which was the very place she was likely to land, if he didn't forgive her.

"I just... I just wanted to help her... somehow. I thought maybe... I mean if she..."

"Go ahead, say it: if I bedded her, Creswicke wouldn't want her." Wielding the knife in deliberate strokes, he chuckled. "Soiled goods, is it?"

The realization was a gut punch: the dirty and vile pirates, sullying the pristine innocent. She had fallen into the same pre-judging and misjudging as those detestable people in Lady Bart's drawing room.

"Something like that," she mumbled to her lap.

He posed indignation, with enough exaggerated flair to rub salt in her wounds that bit more. "I'm not sure if you've complimented me charms or insulted me morals."

He was toying with her now, a good sign.

"I'm sorry, Nathan. I never meant... I mean, I never thought..."

He bumped her with his knee. "No worries, luv."

He slipped a section of orange into his mouth. "With all due respect," he began, checking the fruit, "there are only a few flaws, minor oversights in your grand line of thought."

He paused, ostensibly to chew, but in fact to inflict further revenge by causing her wait. "First and foremost, what you are suggesting *might* happen, will already be assumed."

"Just by virtue of being here?" She groaned at her dumbness. She had personally experienced that very phenomenon in Lady Bart's parlor. "The benefits of a reputation: no woman is safe when you're about?"

He bobbed a bow from his seat, accepting the mantle.

She had heard the stories, not only from those on the *Constancy*, but from Nathan himself. Rampaging, pillaging, plundering and ravishing — indeed!

"But Creswicke wouldn't think that, because... Oh! I forgot: his mother and sister."

The oversight left her feeling even more foolish. Nathan had indeed done — and openly admitted — to that very thing, with two Creswicke women; a third would be readily assumed.

He straightened to peer down the long edge of his nose. "As I've said, I've never taken a woman unwilling in me life."

"Just used your charms," she mused, wincing. It seemed everyone had experienced those benefits, except her.

He popped another orange segment into his mouth and offered her another. She took a piece and pensively chewed.

"The other error in this tangled thicket of thought is that Creswicke doesn't care a rat's arse about social standings nor welfare of the love of his heart. She could be pricked as a witch or branded a traitor, and it wouldn't make a wit's bit o' difference. Money and power is the motivation in this evil," he added with a sage nod.

"So, darling, it would appear your little escapade would have been unwarranted. Thank God I didn't act on that one!" he finished with a dramatic roll of the eyes and a mirthless chuckle.

Thank God, indeed!

She couldn't begin to imagine the damages which would have been wrought, if Nathan had pursued her suggestion. She knew herself well enough to know that she could never forgive him for doing something so calculated and crass. And yet, it would have been by her hand, with enough blame to endure for a very, very long time.

"So, I was wasting my efforts," she said.

He waved a casual hand, exonerating her with that single motion, the dance of the flames catching his rings. "Not wasting: misdirecting. You were only doing what you do best, luv: caring. 'Tis a bloody rare commodity in these waters," he added softly.

The compliment was his peace offering, and she accepted it with grace.

"Caring doesn't feed the dormouse," she sighed. "But I can't help but feel the need to do something to help her."

He leaned to brace his elbows on his thighs to peer at her more closely. The firelight caught in the cinnamon flecks of his walnut orbs. "What is it about this girl? Arranged marriages happen all the time. What's so different about this one?"

His question wasn't any different than what she had been asking herself for days. From the moment she had seen the cowering soul in the corner, she had experienced a maternal surge heretofore unwitnessed.

"I don't know," was all she could manage. "I just…"

Their heads turned at the sight of Prudence, strolling past at not great distance. At her side was a young, tow-headed Griseller—most notably not the noble Biggins. Smiling wistfully, Cate looked up into Nathan's ironic smirk.

"It would appear you've been replaced," she said.

Nathan scowled as he considered his competition. "Revered and copied, darling, but never replaced."

He paused for a second inspection. "Not exactly up to me high standards."

"I would say she is willing to suffer the deficiencies."

They watched Prudence and her new suitor stroll away. Heads tilted together, the two youths were a stark contrast: blonde and dark, bright and faded, refined and barbaric—but, in spite of it all, bonded by the exuberance of youth.

"Young love," Cate mused.

"Nothing like it." Nathan's countenance darkened. "Should she be going off like that? You said she doesn't know anything about lads."

"Watch; she knows exactly what to do."

As if on cue, Prudence coquettishly tilted her head and laughed, the delicate sound drifting on the breeze. Her hand fluttered to the neckline of her bodice and her hips swayed in a measured increment.

Nathan made a rude noise. "Aye, I see your point. A real man-eater that one, and the poor bugger doesn't have a clue."

Shaking his head, the frown returned. "Still don't like the idea of them going off like that."

Cate turned to give him a curious look. "Since when do you sound like the protective father?"

Growling under his breath, he lurched to his feet and stomped away.

Cate shifted in discomfort. Since the incident with Bullock, in spite of his intention to be covert, she had been aware of Nathan's increased vigilance. If there had been no secrets before, she had even less privacy now. A watchful eye was on her every move, as evidenced by Nathan's relieved look when she came out of the privy — err, roundhouse — and a "I was wondering where you were." The concern was touching, but it was a bit tiresome and extremely constraining.

When they had first landed, Nathan had been forced to tip his hand when he insisted that she was not to be alone, *ever*... even when answering the call of nature. It was irksome, not to mention embarrassing, to have to announce her needs, and then be watched over the while. Given Nathan's precise personal barriers, it was a level of intimacy for which she was not prepared, not to mention the difficulty of trying to time when she needed to go with intervals when he wasn't otherwise occupied. Granted, there were no secrets on a ship when it came to bodily functions, the seat of ease right off the salon, but having someone waiting within a whispering shout away was altogether too awkward.

Feeling the need just then, Cate checked up and down the beach. At the moment, Nathan was occupied, as was everyone with the raucous festivities. And so, she rose, confident she could sneak off and return before she was missed.

The moonlight shafted through the forest, reducing its verdant palette to tones of silver, grey and black. As Cate picked her way through the bushes, she ran through a mental litany of the "do's" and "don'ts" as given by Pickford and others. It was a delicate balance between finding the proper seclusion, while on alert for poisonous plants, insects, and reptiles, and yet not venture too far. Since childhood, she possessed a strong sense of direction, but was still careful to keep the bonfires within sight.

The snap of a twig was her only warning before a hand shot around and clamped over her mouth. She was driven forward to the ground with a *whomph!* the force of her assailant coming down on top of her knocked the air from her.

Stunned, her clarity of mind returned with the wind rushing back into her lungs. The two tumbled and thrashed, the fingers at her mouth gouging her face. His wild eyes inches from hers, he seemed roughly her size, but wiry and considerably stronger. His breath hot on her neck, she was engulfed by the smells of rum, arousal, and fish stew.

The knife in her pocket was unreachable in her tangled skirts. She clawed, gouged, elbowed and kneed. The hand drew back and clouted her across the face, and then clamped back over her mouth. She was punched once and then again in the stomach. She drew up her knees and curled into a defensive ball. The hand at her mouth gave a cruel wrench and flipped her on her back. He rose up and drove a knee into her gut. The pinpricks of light swirled before her eyes and her ears buzzed.

The hand loosened a fraction, and she bit down, until she felt the grind of bones between her teeth. He yanked free and swore. It was enough of a distraction for her to slam the flat of her palm against his ear. He yelped and swung out, his fist catching her in the jaw. Her vision reduced to a tunnel, the pinpricks now a beehive as oblivion loomed.

Don't pass out! Don't pass out!

He came down on top of her. His hips grinding against hers, his eager hardness prodded against her legs. With limbs gone as heavy as sand, she shouted at herself to do something as he pried at her knees. She wanted to scream, but like in a dream, couldn't. Against bands of iron that seemed to have seized her chest, she drew a breath and forced it out through frozen jaws. The result was but a pitiful mewling moan.

A shadow fell over them. Thinking it was another one come to join in, Cate tried again to cry out, but with the same pathetic result. The shadow shifted and a human form separated from the trees. She caught only a fleeting glimpse, but there was no mistaking Nathan's outline as he loomed over them. He moved and a band of moonlight fell across his face to reveal an expression of somewhere between black rage and dead calm. So, preoccupied with fumbling with his flies, her assailant didn't look up, until Nathan drew back a foot and drove it into his belly.

The force sent the man tumbling into the dark. Nathan kicked again and again, rolling his victim, until he flopped like a rag doll. Standing over him, Nathan calmly drew his pistol, aimed and fired. There was a crack, a blue spurt, a faint retort, and the acrid smell of gunpowder. The body bucked once, sending leaves and dirt scattering, and then went still.

So effortless, so quick, so clean, and a man was dead.

Heavy running and crashing brush marked Thomas' arrival, pistol in one hand and sword in the other. In one glance, he assessed the scene. Stowing his weapons, he moved to the lifeless form, and poked it with the toe of his boot, until the face came into the moonlight.

"He's one of yours," Nathan observed dispassionately, stuffing his pistol back into his belt.

"Aye, pity," Thomas sighed, equally impassive. "He was my best f'c'stleman. Leave him lie."

Nathan came back to where Cate huddled on the ground. He helped her to stand, steadying her by the waist when her legs wobbled dangerously. Too stunned to cry, she stumbled next to him as he took her back toward the friendly light of the fires, Thomas' heavy step behind them. She was sat on something—a keg or an up-ended log—near enough to the gangs of men for comfort, yet far enough for privacy.

"Get something to drink, *now!*" Nathan bellowed.

A water gourd arrived shortly filled with bumboo. She hated rum, but the spices made it palatable, and she was most definitely in need of a drink. She fumbled, nearly dropping it, obliging Nathan to hold it while she sipped.

"I'm fine."

Nathan's mouth quirked. "Aye, as you keep insisting."

Nathan steadied Cate by the arm as she continued to sway. Blinking stupidly, she probed through her fogged mind, trying to recall having said anything. She felt more than heard people speaking, their voices no more than dull thuds in her ears. She could hear Thomas fuming somewhere near, pausing periodically to peer over Nathan's shoulder at her.

The bumboo went to work in short order. Cate's head cleared sufficiently to put one thought in front of another. With it, the numbness gave way to sensations. The night air grew fingers of ice. Shock jolted through her body in rolling waves. Her face throbbed. The muscles in her abdomen spasmed at every breath. She twitched and jumped at hands that weren't there. Nathan's coat was wrapped about her shoulders, but she continued to quake. She hunched it higher and drank deeper, in hopes the blessed numbness might return.

In jerky, abrupt moves, Nathan plucked leaves and twigs from her hair and clothing. His inscrutable mask firmly in place, he checked her over again and again, confirming for himself that she was indeed fine. While he saw to her physically, it was notable that he didn't look at her directly. The most unnerving, however, was his silence. Swearing, chiding, berating; anything would have been better than nothing.

"I'm sorry," Cate said. At last, two different words.

"No worries, luv." Nathan intently snugged the faded coat

about her. "It would have been now or it would have been later. If a man's taken a notion, there's naught to be done about it."

"I knew he was a treacherous bastard, but I had no idea..." Thomas said, looking on over Nathan's shoulder. "Hell, I would've killed the son-of-a-bitch ahead of time, had I known."

"It's all right," she said, mechanically. It seemed almost laughable to kill someone for what they *might* do.

Cate reached for the gourd with a quivering hand to take another drink. "I'm sorry."

"There's no sorrow for a man's beastliness. Put your mind to rest. now you'll be safe. No better protection than a dead suitor," Nathan said bitterly. "I'll represent you were the one to kill him, if you like. No better insurance, aye?"

Fuzzy as she might have been, it still seemed severely wrong to take advantage of a man's death. Yet, from the moment she had been knocked to the ground, she wanted nothing more than for the bastard to be dead, and had taken cold satisfaction at seeing him prostrate in the leaves.

"Tell them what you will," she said shakily. Weariness struck her like another punch from her assailant.

There was a protracted silence. Thomas churned back and forth in the wavering margins of the firelight.

So much like Brian.

Eloquent with fury, Thomas snatched at his pistol, and then his sword, driven by the need for action. Finally, he picked something from the ground and hurtled it into the night. Swearing, he did so several times more, and then resumed steaming back and forth.

"Dammit to goddamned fucking hell! I knew this would happen," Thomas extolled to the night sky. He spun around to stab an accusing finger at the two of them. "This wasn't the first, was it?"

Nathan looked to the ground.

"No," Cate finally said.

Thomas swore in something like Germanic. He stalled to glare down at Nathan. "And it will happen again."

Nathan looked briefly up into the voice of doom. Not unlike herself, she could see him mentally calculating the odds of that very thing. Twice in less than a month she had been attacked, and twice he had been obliged to kill, four other men dying in conjunction with the first attack. A man had died just now, only because she had needed to pee. She scanned the throng of men scattered down the beach, rendered faceless by distance and darkness, and wondered how many more she had doomed to their deaths when she had agreed to remain on the *Morganse*. How many more would Nathan be obliged to kill? Only a few hours ago, he had said something about the price he had been paying since her arrival. How much longer before he said "Enough?"

Thomas looked to her, the blue eyes gone to steel. "By the gods, I will do it," he said with the same vehemence as earlier that day. Then he rose abruptly and disappeared into the night.

"You can yell at me now, if you like." She spoke in the spirit of precipitating the berating she knew was to come. How could he not blame her?

Fondling the gourd which she still couldn't manage, Nathan looked up from under the dark dashes of brows and snorted. "Would it help? Would it make any difference? Which would you prefer to hear: what the hell were you doing; silly woman; why don't you do as I say? Which one?"

"How about 'This was your fault'?"

The corner of Nathan's mouth tucked up grimly. The firelight glinted copper hairs in the plush of his beard as he looked to the ground.

"No, not that one. 'Tis another I'm saving that for."

"You?" She looked down at the crown of his hat. There was no room to place any more blame. He had taken it all and was thoroughly flogging himself.

"Do you see another? You aimed to be away from all this, and I—" he said.

"I said I wanted to stay," she said levelly. "It's not your fault."

She winced inwardly. It was so unfortunate that the most sincere sentiments come out as hollow-sounding platitudes. And yet, in many cases, there was wretchedly little else which wouldn't sound equally false.

Thomas appeared again, considerably more composed. He squatted next to Nathan and peered up at her. "You gonna be all right?"

"Yes, I'm fine." It had been dubious earlier, but now she was coming around to actually believing it.

Thomas quizzically looked to Nathan, who shrugged in deference and said, "A gentleman never argues with a lady."

Thomas rose, leaving Cate and Nathan alone once more.

"Don't tell Prudence," she said.

He made a face. "Why?"

"There's no call to alarm her."

He made a sarcastic noise. "Bloody high time she learned what the world is about."

"Not this. Not yet."

He carefully searched her face. His eye twitched, perceiving much and opting to question none. There were many lessons which awaited one so young and naïve. What it was to live among the predators was a lesson best left for another day.

She considered her own future, and a glum one it was. It was easy to envision Nathan shackling her in the most literal sense of the word, lest she wander, and justifiably so. Independence came at a price.

She felt hollow and fragile, like a soap bubble, likely to shatter at the slightest touch. And yet, she wanted nothing more than to be held; she needed the solid firmness of safety, to know not every touch was to be feared. The one she needed it most from sat hunched at her knee, much of the same condition: in need of assurance that he had done right. And yet, the gap between them was too vast for either to reach across and give what the other so desperately needed.

And so, they sat together, and yet so very apart.

At length, she shifted in discomfort. Nathan scowled with renewed concern. It was the ultimate embarrassment—the ultimate payback—but it couldn't be helped.

"I really need to go to the privy."

23: EXCHANGES

As Nathan had forecast, the next day was fair, and the *Morganse* made weigh out of the bay. She pressed on to the designated exchange point on a t'gallant breeze, her bow wearing a collar of white froth against the deep blue water.

The *Morganse* arrived at the Straits with the last rays of the retiring sun gilding her sails. Following at no great distance astern, the *Griselle* veered off to take up her post on the opposite side. It was a large cove in which the *Morganse* settled on her kedge to lay in wait, crouched like a great cat. Stealth, however, was neither vessel's intent: both desired to be seen.

As such, the two ships spent the night and the largest part of the next morning, waiting… and waiting.

The tension aboard the *Morganse* was palpable. Her people moved mechanically, their conversation brief, laughter forced. Nathan paced circuits around the quarterdeck, calling frequently up to the lookouts on the mastheads, "I'll slit the eyelids of the first slaggardly lout found napping!"

There was another source of tension, however, a source even more daunting: Prudence.

The girl ricocheted from pacing the cabin and staring for protracted periods out the aft gallery, to breaking into verbal tirades about everything and nothing. The impatience and intolerance of youth being what it was, she went outside. Advancing down the decks, her prattle parted the men like a prophet parting the Red Sea.

In the peace of Prudence's absence, Cate sat before the stern windows idly fondling her embroidery. Her thread was gone. Now, she could only dream of what she would stitch next.

The determined clump of boots broke her thoughts. She looked up as Nathan, Pryce close in tow, skidded to a halt at the cabin door and planted his hands on his hips.

"Do something!" Nathan cried.

Thinking he had been injured, Cate leaped up, looking for blood. Finding none, she assumed it must have been one of the crew. She reached for her blood box, but her path was blocked by Nathan.

"You've got to do something about the Plaguing Princess," he said. "The men are fit to start jumping ship before the glass runs out."

"Aye, sir," Pryce chimed over Nathan's shoulder. "She's babbled since a'fore the sun's cleared the gun'l, with nay so much as a breath's break. Not a moment's peace fer anyone."

"Except one," Nathan dryly interjected. "Beatrice had the wherewithal and good sense to escape; hasn't left the crosstrees since. The hands are cross-eyed in pain what with holding their water."

"Aye, sir," Pryce put in eagerly, looking a bit strained himself. "Yammer's away she does, right a'fore the pissdale."

"That's ridiculous," Cate said. "You do it every day before everyone."

"Not amid a dozen questions," sputtered Nathan, eloquent in his indignation. "A man needs to concentrate."

A shriek, female and of a pitch which could only be attained by the young, came from outside. It was the piercing sort, which stabbed the temple straight through to the back of one's eyeballs.

"Thar she blows," cried Pryce, wincing.

"What was that?" Cate asked.

"God knows," Nathan sighed, looking thoroughly haunted. "She could have just met Mr. Squidge or noticed Pickford's ear collection. Hermione looked cross-eyed, or Beatrice said something untoward. Her skirts could have flown up, or she might o' scuffed a shoe. Suffering Jesus!"

Cate was in no position to argue. She had experienced much the same scream when His Lordship had ambled past. Come to think on it, the mongoose and Hermione had been conspicuous in their absence.

"Clap 'er in irons, I say, 'n pitch 'er in the hold." Pryce's eyes rounded with delicious anticipation.

An appealing thought at first, Nathan waved it away. "Nay, allow the rats their peace. We'd be up to our knees in them in no time." He turned to Cate, beseeching. "Do something!"

"I'm not her mother."

"And I'm not her father," retorted Nathan. "There, we've settled lineage. Now, pray, might we move on to more important and pressing matters? Do something!"

"Oh, honestly, very well." Cate brushed past, painfully aware of her own testiness. The waiting had taken its toll on her as well. "Upon my word, I can't fathom why a bunch of grown *pirates* can't manage one young girl."

"Ever seen a rat terrier?"

Pryce's query stopped her in mid-stride. Her blank look prompted him to explain.

"A wee beastie, no bigger than yer foot, what can kill a wharf rat with a single shake. Saw one near tear a man's hand off... well, nearly," he qualified under Cate's dubious stare.

"I get your point, Mr. Pryce." Chastened, Cate looked to the floor to hide her smile. "I beg your leave, *gentlemen.*"

Cate found Prudence, cornering Diogo between the foremast and the scuttlebutt. Portuguese-born and with little English, he stood clutching a sheet with a stunned, quizzical look as Prudence babbled. With promises of hair ribbons and hot chocolate, Cate lured the girl away. Amid the audible sigh of her people, Cate thought she heard the *Morganse* expel the same relief as she ushered Prudence into the cabin.

Several turns of the glass later, came the cry "Sail ho!" Cate was on her feet and out on deck.

"Where away?" Nathan shouted to Damerell on the masthead. "Can you make her?"

"She's the *Resolute,* sir."

Cate was met with droll smiles from Nathan and Pryce as she mounted the quarterdeck. "I take that's good news. What is the *Resolute*?"

Pryce folded his hands behind his back and rocked on his heels, fat with smug satisfaction. "Eighty guns. 'Tis the largest what the Royal Navy plies in these waters."

The news struck Cate as alarming, and yet neither of the men, nor anyone else aboard, showed concern.

"You're pleased they sent their biggest ship?" she goggled.

"That ship," Nathan began patiently, "being the biggest, consequently and most significantly, carries the deepest draft."

Cate followed his pointed look toward the mouth of the bay, still puzzled. In her three to four months at sea, she had gained considerable knowledge of sailing, but many of the finer points still escaped her — as now.

"Soo, if they require deeper water..." she began, slowly.

"She'll not clear the reef," Nathan finished. "She draws a good four feet more than we." He draped his hands on the heels of his weapons, tapping his belts, preening in the luck. "Providence has smiled!"

"Then where are they to go?" Cate asked, still confused.

"Nowhere," Nathan and Pryce chorused.

With a flip of his fingers, Nathan yielded to Pryce. "There be no other anchorages here 'bouts, not for a ship of her draft. She can set a hook, aye, but 'twill be a fair rough go, what with wind and wave, and land in 'er lee. They'll be a-stowin' topmasts and yards in no time."

Cate nodded. It was common for topmasts to be swung down, in order to ease the weight overhead and the overworking of the planking. Wind and current funneled into the Straits' narrow space resulted in very rough seas. Both the *Morganse* and *Griselle* had ducked their heads into the waves, throwing off great sheets of water over their shoulders and waists as they came through.

"*We* are at liberty to move about as we please," Nathan said, with a sweeping gesture. "They'll be stuck, on their hooks, riding hard, whilst worrying where the *Morganse* might pop up next."

"'Tis smaller and faster we are; we can out-maneuver her in these tight waters," Pryce added with pride. "We could up anchor and be on 'er a'fore they could beat to arms."

"We could rake her, broadside to stern. What with yon Thomas lying abeam, they would be at our mercy, *if* we're of a mind," Nathan said.

"Are we of a mind?" Cate felt quite dense by this point.

Nathan waggled his eyebrows with smug glee. "They don't know, do they? We can worry them to death and never stir a hand."

Time crept. A week seemed to have passed with each bell until the *Resolute's* masts finally peeked over the treetops lining the distant arm of land. Cate watched the ship round the headlands and draw up at the cove's mouth. Sails aback, waves breaking high over her forecastle, the ship's bow rose and fell at a sickening rate. She sat with her guns presented to the pirate ships which flanked her, but distance pulled the teeth of her threat.

Towering triple masts, brilliant in her regal blue, gilded fretwork gleaming, the vessel bore a presence, as if accustomed — nay, expecting — ships to shy in her presence. The Union Jack in prominent display at her backstay, a number of other banners and pennants stood out in the stiff breeze. One was glaringly plain and white: the flag of truce.

"Well, well, well," Nathan declared, peering through the spyglass. "Dash me buttons and rip me jib. His Pompousness has blessed us with his presence."

"Commodore Harte is aboard," Pryce explained over Cate's shoulder. "'Tis his flag there, the blue with the star."

"A status achieved only through the good graces of the fair Governor of the Royal West Indies Mercantile Company, and a wholly unholy alliance it 'tis," said Nathan, the glass still to his eye.

"The Commodore's convinced he would have made Admiral several times over had it not been fer the Cap'n," Pryce sniffed.

"If it hadn't been for you?" Cate asked of Nathan.

He shrugged. "The Commodore's hubris can be of epic proportions, betimes."

"It's cost 'im promotions in spite of Creswicke's endorsements," said Pryce.

"And through no fault of yours, of course," Cate said, looking to Nathan.

A muscle twitched at the corner of his mouth. "I'm just a poor pirate, doing what I might in the way of making a living."

Nathan slapped the glass closed. "She'll lay in irons. They shan't desire to be mucking about with anchors. Sharpshooters aloft," he shouted over the quarterdeck break to Hodder. "Gun crews, Mr. MacQuarrie, at the ready, but don't open the lids. Loose the t'gall'nts and stays'ls, but don't set the braces. Let's give them every cause to believe we're at the ready."

He rounded on Cate and sobered. "You'll need to be out of sight. They may suspect you're here, but seeing would be believing, would it not? No arguments, luv," he went on over her protests as he steered her toward the cabin. "Rest assured they've spyglasses and are fixed on us as we speak. If all goes pear-shaped, I can't be worrying about you. Now stay inside."

His walnut eyes held hers, searching for the assurances he needed. "Please, luv, allow me to know you're safe."

Now at the cabin's door, Cate nodded woodenly. He winked and strode away. The cold realization of how much her presence burdened him pricked the nape of her neck.

Deep in the cabin's protective shadows, Prudence wrung her hands. "They're coming, aren't they?"

"It will be a while before they arrive, but yes, they are."

"Is Lord Creswicke with them?"

"I think not." Wishing to ease the girl's anguish, Cate fingered one of the curls at her shoulder. "Your hair is very pretty."

The sun-reddened cheeks deepened. "Thank you. I did it myself."

"And you did a lovely job of it."

Beaming under the praise one moment, Prudence threw her arms around Cate and clutched her tightly. "I don't wish to go. I'm afraid."

Cate gently pushed her back and brought the tear-streaked face up to hers. "Don't you remember how afraid you were a few days ago? And now, look."

Prudence had the grace to be ashamed. "Of the Captain most especially. He's been so kind; I'm sorry I said those bad things about him."

She brightened with the enthusiasm of an inspiration. "I'll make it up. I'll tell everyone how wonderful and kind he was, and —"

"No, no, not that," Cate blurted. Nathan could forgive a lot of things, *except* telling everyone what a wonderful person he is.

"Then what shall I do?"

Cate bit her still-sore lip. Lady Bart's had taught her how drastically one's story could be misconstrued. "Just represent that you were treated well. If experience is any indication, they won't credit anything else."

She tried to see Prudence through the eyes of those very same people. The glossy black hair was brushed and arranged, but the long curls, achieved only through hours with an iron, were gone. The porcelain skin was bright red from sun, the rounded nose glowing. Ripped, hem hanging, and slashed across the back, where Nathan had spanked her with his sword: the dress was still yellow, but streaked and soiled. Her stockings, shoes and kertch all gone missing, through some eyes, the damage could be seen as the result of rough handling. As Nathan had forecast, the worst would certainly be assumed.

The hollow thud of boats hooking on to the *Morganse's* hull and Hodder's cry of "Watch the goddamned paint, you fucking whoreson's!" broke Cate's thoughts. Footsteps scurrying on deck and climbing the ship's side announced the *Resolute's* boarding party had arrived. Cate slipped nearer the door to peek through its sidelights.

The Royal Navy came aboard with a flourish. The *Morganse* had run up a square of white on her jack-staff at the bow, but it was nowhere near the huge one displayed over the heads of the boarding party. By the time Cate took up a position, to peek from behind the door and through a sidelight, a double-file of officers — blue-coated, white breeched and laced hats — Marines and sideboys flanked the entry port. It was sobering to see the red-coated uniforms on the decks of the *Morganse*.

With a clash and stomp, the Commodore was piped aboard with all the flourish befitting his rank, and the *Morganse* — predictably — had failed to provide. One could almost hear their snap to salute. Harte came up the side ramrod-stiff. Like his ship, the Commodore's uniform was meant to impress, and it did. A ceremonial sword and a gold-laced, cockaded hat had been added to his resplendency. In honor of the moment, Nathan had squared his hat and donned his coat. Even in its infancy, the burgundy could never have equaled the naval splendor, but it was worn with the same élan as if it did.

The sea rogues had their own theater. They had on their masks: familiar faces were now contorted into the barbarous expressions she had first witnessed on the *Constancy*. With blood-dripped sails overhead, the same symbolically drooling from her deck, the *Morganse* had no goldwork, but the sun shone even brighter on the fresh-honed edges of cutlasses, boarding axes, pikes, gaffing hooks and hatchets. Chin, Mute Maori and Hodder stood at the forefront, brutish and menacing, Churchill's maniacal, cackling laugh in the background.

The Navy's brilliance only served to exemplify the pirate's sun-drab, rendering them that much more the Tartans. Several took great pleasure in singling out a Navyman, their tension evident in rigid jaw muscles and white-knuckled fists on their weapons, and fixing him with a sinister glare. Even at Cate's distance, "Steady" was quite readable on the mouths of several of their superiors.

Harte surveyed his surroundings as a warrior surveys a possible battlefield. It was done more out of habit than a precursor, for an outbreak of violence was unlikely. The odds were not in the Navy's favor—a little over a dozen among nearly two hundred—and their hands were bound by the white flag.

Harte drew up before Nathan. The green eyes which fixed on him were even more reptilian, like a hungry snake with its favorite meal dangling before it. The prize Harte sought most was within arm's reach, and it might as well have been a league.

A hush befell the deck, only the creak of the ship and the flap of the two white flags, with a cough now and again, to break it. Harte's patent-leather, silver-buckled shoes took a step forward. As distasteful as it obviously was, Harte was a slave to the Rules of Procedure: he swept off his hat and executed an overly proper bow. The obligatory "Your servant, sir," uttered through white lips, was barely audible.

The poor man probably can't help it.

So noble and honorable. She had seen men much like him before, so insufferably honorable and noble they would watch their own mother hang if duty was thought to require it. Harte might rescue her from scurrilous pirates, if she so desired. He would also arrest her, and then with that same nobility, watch her hang.

Harte stiffly gestured toward the *Griselle* across the Straits. "Might I inquire as to the identity of your accomplice?"

Nathan snorted. "You may not."

"Oh, come now, *Captain*. I am not without my resources.

It will only be a matter of time before I learn of her and her captain's identity."

"Then, I suggest you use your time more remuneratively, because that ship will be naught but a wake."

The corner of Harte's eye ticked, conceding. "Lord Creswicke sends his compliments."

"Me aged aunt's arse he does," Nathan sputtered. "And where, pray tell, is our fair Lord Pompous? Has he not chosen to honor us with his presence?"

Roger sighed imperiously. "The distances were too great, as you well know. You were the one to so brilliantly engineer this entire sordid affair within a timeframe which did not allow for word to reach His Lordship, intentionally rendering him helpless."

"Too bloody damned right. But, I pride meself on being an amicable and co-operative sort." Nathan sauntered back and forth in front of Harte with an extra flourish. "If you prefer, the Young Miss may linger to allow His Insuffurrableness the time to evaluate his options with regards to the future of his future intended."

The Commodore again scanned his surroundings, measuring and assessing. It couldn't be missed that it provided time for the pirates to be duly impressed, and no doubt, in hopes second thoughts might prevail, allowing intimidation to take root.

"I demand you produce Miss Collingwood at once, so I may verify she is well and unharmed."

His impertinent smile growing to devious, Nathan waited a lengthy interval before calling with lilting affection, "Prudence, darling. Pray, will you join us, luv?"

In the cabin, Prudence's corn-flower eyes rounded with dread. She swiveled to Cate, who waved her forward. Gripping the folds of her dress, Prudence went out with the levity of the doomed.

"Ah, there you are, luv. Come out and meet the nice man," Nathan said.

Those in official blue did a en masse intake of air at seeing Prudence's tattered and barefoot state. Harte's eyes narrowed to a contempt-laden glare. Nathan put an arm around Prudence's waist and drew her close. The insult of the act sent a shockwave of indignation through the navymen and they lurched forward. An equal reaction came from the Morgansers, poising their weapons higher. The sight of the plumed and cockaded hats on the deck had been chilling. That, however, was erased by the warmth brought at seeing Harte's eyes bulge at Nathan's arm trailing higher to the girl's shoulders.

"Pray tell the nice man, darling, of your wonderful time," prompted Nathan in sugary tones.

"I had a wonderful time." Prudence was miserably at a convincing smile.

"Ah, see there. From the mouths of babes." Nathan regarded Prudence and licked his lips. "And a babe she is, is she not? It would appear our illustrious Lordness has been particularly fortunate, wouldn't you say?"

"Get on with it, Blackthorne." Harte ground out through his teeth.

"Captain Nathanael Blackthorne, if you please, sir. I thought we might bide our time—have a bit of a chat—what with your long journey and all." Nathan clucked his tongue in mocking sympathy. "You have come so far. Would you care for a spot of tea, perhaps, and rest your weary bones?"

"Thank you, no," Harte said in measured patience. "I imagine Miss Collingwood would prefer to retire to the *Resolute*, where she will be among the civilized, as opposed to this vile and barbarous lot. I'm confident her delicate sensibilities have been accosted."

"Accosted?" Nathan rolled the word in his mouth. "Prudence, luv—?"

"*Miss* Collingwood, to you," Harte hissed.

"*Prudence*?" Nathan began again. "Have your sensibilities— stipulating, of course, that they are indeed of a delicate nature— have they... have you been accosted in any way?"

Prudence stammered. "Well, no, I—"

"I thought not!" Nathan pulled her closer in the nearest thing to a hug. "So, you see, my dear Commodore, your concerns for the safety and welfare of this fine young lady have been categorically unfounded."

"We've brought the sums demanded," Harte said.

As if on cue, a pirate cheer went up, with a suddenness and ferocity which caused Marines, sideboys and officers alike to fall back.

Nathan touched a finger to his chin and thoughtfully rolled his eyes. "Have you now? I was having reconsiderations— second thoughts, as it were—as to just how much our beloved Lord might be willing to pay. Just how much are fresh, young fiancés going for these days?" he mused, toying with a lock of Prudence's hair.

"There was an agreement." The muscles flexing in Roger's jaws were visible even at Cate's distance.

"Did we? Hmm... I don't recall that bit." Nathan counted

off on his fingers. "I recall taking her. Do you recall that, Master Pryce?"

"Aye, sir! Recall it well," the First Mate called from nearby.

"Yes, I thought so. And, I recall making a demand." Nathan twisted his face with the effort of recollection. "No. No, I don't recall an accord after that."

Nathan stood back to take in Prudence and gave his brows a salacious waggle. "I don't know; I might decide to keep her for meself. Bunks can be cold this time of year, but you would be more aware of that than I. And I shouldn't have to tell you how unlucky a woman on board can be. Insufferingly bad luck, is it not, Mr. Pryce?"

"Foul-black and terrifying, sir."

"Although," Nathan said, swiveling back on Harte, "come to shed a light on it, perhaps we've just struck upon the source of your less than fortunate fortunes of recent. One too many whores secreted away, eh?"

Harte went even more rigid—if that was at all possible—his knuckles whitening on the hilt of his sword. Cate felt a brief surge of sympathy for the man. The man knew Nathan was provoking him. Propriety wouldn't allow him to do a blessed thing but take it as a gentleman.

Gentleman. It was Harte's banner and his burden. He wore it for all to see, like a little girl with a new dress. And, like that little girl, the possession was an instant confinement, imprisoned and handcuffed by the thing they loved most.

The Commodore's nostrils flared. "You would certainly be more familiar than I."

Nathan made an unsavory face and clucked his tongue reprovingly. "Why Commodore, jealousy is certainly not a becoming color on you, a'tall!"

The green eyes sharpened to pinpoints. "Do. Not. Test. Me."

Harte gestured and a large leather pouch was tossed at Nathan's feet, landing with the clatter of coins.

Nathan regarded Harte and then turned to Prudence.

"Very well, then, darling," Nathan said in a fatherly tone. His hands fluttered about her person, arranging curls and straightening ribbons. "We must take our farewells then, my dear. Be a good girl and remember what I told you about strangers."

He shook a parental finger, while Prudence nodded, intent on his every word. "Mind your elders, say your prayers, and never eat dessert with your fish fork. Now, do you think you can remember all that?"

"Then, this is goodbye?" she asked meekly.

"Aye, luv, *adieu* it 'tis."

Her lower lip began to quiver. "Will I ever see you again?"

Nathan slid Harte a taunting leer. "One never knows, does one?"

Nathan barely had time to pat the girl on the head and nudge her forward before Harte seized her by the arm to tuck her safely behind him.

Nathan ducked a mocking bow and bared his teeth in a contemptuous smile.

"'Tis been a pleasure doing business, Commodore."

Harte's gaze travelled the deck and fixed on the cabin door. "I am in a position to offer the price of freedom for whomever *else* you might be harboring against their will."

Cate jerked back, clapping a hand over her mouth against her gasp. Since their parting, Harte would have had time to learn of her identity and the warrants for her arrest. Or, was he operating in a fog of chivalry, only intending to save her?

"Can't imagine what you're referring to, mate. You suggest we are running some sort of vessel of iniquity. Anyone here is because they wish it. There be no other hostages. Right, mates?"

The crew heartily sounded their support.

"And, as we have already so succinctly and eloquently discussed, women on a ship *are* bad luck, or have you forgotten, already?" Nathan asked.

"Then our business is complete." Harte ducked a bow and pivoted on his heel. Taking Prudence by the elbow, he headed for the accommodation gate, his boarding party in close order behind.

"By the bye," Nathan called to Harte's back. "Have a care unshipping her, mate. Her welfare is in *your* hands, now."

Nathan swaggered toward the Great Cabin. Roosting atop a cask near the doors, he lounged against the bulkhead.

"I would have paid admission to watch this," he said low enough for only Cate's benefit.

Together, Cate pressing her eye to the door jamb, they watched a commodore and men of the Royal Navy grapple with the gargantuan task of removing a sixteen-year-old girl from the *Morganse.*

"Harte doesn't appear pleased," she said.

Nathan made a caustic noise. "He always appears to have his breeches on backwards or something."

A screech pierced the air, another of the temple-stabbing nature, and Cate gasped. "They aren't actually going to do what it looks like, are they?"

Nathan cocked his head considering. "It's been me personal experience—humble as it may be," he added, touching a hand to his chest, "that a kicking and screaming woman doesn't pass well from hand to hand, under any circumstances, down the side, while at anchor, or at any time, actually, truth be told. Doesn't go well, a'tall."

Pryce sidled closer, unable to tear his eyes from the spectacle unfolding. "Shouldn't we be offerin' a hand, Cap'n?"

Nathan contemplated briefly. "No, Master Pryce. 'Tis been me perpetual experience the Royal Navy is best left to its own devices. Bloody resentful they are of interference, especially from the likes such as us."

Pryce swiveled an incredulous look. "Even if 'tis the path of destruction?"

"More's the sweetness of the result," Nathan said, with a complacent grin.

The pirates stood in a mix of sympathy and disbelief at the two Marines bellowing in pain as Prudence clawed for a more secure hold on their necks.

"Not sure they've enough skin for this task," Pryce observed, struggling to preserve his straight face.

Nathan lolled in half-lidded contentment. "Aye, Mr. Pryce, we can all tell our grandchildren of the day Royal Navy blood was drawn and spilled on the decks of the *Ciara Morganse*, and never a blade was raised."

He was correct; blood was being spilt, albeit in fine droplets, from nails raking cheeks and necks of the souls who lowered the screeching Prudence over the side. Her head eventually disappeared below the gunwale, leaving only the sound of her screaming and frantic shouts. At length, there was only the coxswains' call to the oarsmen as they pushed away.

"Ah, well," Nathan sighed. "The show is over. Prepare to make way, Master Pryce."

"Is it over?" Stepping over the coaming, Cate could see the recessional of longboats trailing toward the warship.

"Not until they've sank the horizon, but from all appearances, I'd say 'Aye'. The *Griselle* on their flank will help keep them honest." Nathan rocked on his toes, his hand resting on the butt of his pistol. "I shan't fancy they would try anything, what with Lord Creswicke's beloved betrothed aboard."

"That was cruel, you know."

He struggled to hide his satisfaction, but finally surrendered and broke into a full-fledged grin. "Only because Commodore Stick-Up-His-Britches wouldn't deign to ask for help. Besides, no two people deserved it more."

Towers ambled down the deck. He bent to pick up the leather

pouch, his eyes rolling in pleasure at the heavy clinking sound inside. "What's to do with this, Cap'n?"

Nathan waved a vague hand. "Pass the word for Mr. Pryce. 'Tis his affair."

"After all that, you're not interested in the money?" Cate asked.

Nathan cocked one hip as he leaned on the rail. He scanned the horizon and smiled crookedly. "Pryce is the quartermaster: shares are his task."

"My rewards come in other forms."

"Creswicke doesn't strike me as the type to be trifled with. What will he do when he finally finds out?"

His cheeks rounded with a grin, white laced with gold. "Everything he can, darling—*everything* he can."

END OF PART TWO

24: TWISTED FATES

CATE STOOD AT THE CABIN'S table, her honing basket and all its contents spread before her. She concentrated on the flat even strokes of Stubbs' knife across the honestone's oiled surface. She heard the clump of Nathan's boots come in and the scuff of when he stopped.

"You're upset." He spoke from somewhere near the mizzen, she thought, for she didn't look up.

"I'm fine."

"No," he said carefully. "I think not."

"I'm fine."

"I see." Sighing as one resigned to an inevitable battle he inched closer. "Then why are you in here, when you're usually out there?"

From the corner of her eye she saw a thumb jab over his shoulder toward the door.

"Beatrice represents that Hodder, Squidge and the afterguard didn't banish you from the afterdeck because of your charmingly gay company," he said reprovingly.

Cate winced. Once the exchange for Prudence had been completed, and the *Resolute's* masts had dipped the horizon, the *Morganse* had wore around through the Straits, spread her studdingsails and ran before the wind to her rendezvous with the *Griselle*. In retrospect, Cate mightn't have presented herself in the best light since. The hands' eye-rolling and grumbling behind her back hadn't gone unnoticed. Several things had weighed on her mind, none of which she was willing to put a name to.

"I'm fine," she said, sounding more bullish than was flattering.

Nathan twisted his jaw sideways in consideration. "Uh-huh. Then what are all those?"

He nodded toward the floor. A small, bristling array of knives, from rigging to pocket, were stuck in the wood at her feet, as if someone had been playing mumblypeg. She winced, vaguely recalling having flung a few things... maybe...

"I'm fine. I... Ouch! Dammit!" she said, plunging her finger into her mouth. The honing oil combined with an untimely lurch of the ship caused the knife to slip and sliced her finger.

Nathan drew the wounded digit out. The blood welled, but didn't spurt. He sucked the blood away and frowned intently as he inspected it.

"You'll do," he said.

"Since when do you carry a handkerchief?" she asked at seeing him pull one from his sleeve.

He cocked an eyebrow as he dabbed her finger with it. "Since I've been 'round you. I find an inordinate need for one heretofore never experienced."

Her gaze fixed on his right hand as he tended hers. The cut, inflicted by Thomas' blade, was now bound in a bit of rag from heavens knew where. "Your hand should be looked at."

His mouth quivered with the effort to not smile. "It's fine."

While she knotted the cloth around her finger, he collected the knives from the floor, depositing them in the basket. He stood back to regard her with an expectant fatherly look which she found altogether disquieting.

"Very well, let's have it," he finally said.

"You need to sit."

One eye narrowed, thinking it to be a jest. A scowl came with the realization that she wasn't.

"Very well." In exaggerated steps, he went to his chair and sat.

She stood over him. "I need you calm."

"I am."

"No, you've a fist, and your lip is doing that little thing it does whenever you're upset."

"I'm not upset, I'm —" He checked himself then made a great show of opening both hands, and then strained to rearrange his face.

"You're still tense," Cate said.

"I'm not —"

"Sit back and relax."

"Goddamnit, I am relaxed. See!" He drew back his lips into a smile which resembled a skull's grimace.

She stood back, but on second thought, pulled his pistol from his belt. A defiant gaze fixed on her, he reached across the table to slide the sharp-edged objects away from her.

"Now, promise you'll stay there."

"I'm not a ruddy dog... oh, very well," he said over her

objections. "Like the damned Number One anchor I'll be. On to it, then."

So overtly serene, he was more a caricature and less at ease than ever. She took a deep breath. She had come this far; there was no turning back now.

"I need to beg a great favor."

The false smile faltered and he blinked, thinking there was a trick in there somewhere. "I've bid you welcome to anything you desire," he said with measured caution.

She surreptitiously crossed her fingers in the folds of her skirts. "Yes, well, in that spirit... I wish to go fetch Prudence."

"What!" He launched to his feet. "What the goddamned hell...? Are you trying to put me in an early grave!"

Her glare reminded him of his pledge, and he sat heavily. He exhaled through his nose several times and then scrubbed his hands tiredly over his face.

"Explain to me *again* why we should be so all fired concerned with this girl? Arranged marriages happen all the time. Why are you so fixated on this one?"

"I've told you." Unable to stand still, she set to stalking the cabin. "There's something about Prudence. I can't leave her to a hopeless marriage with a—"

"Bastard," Nathan finished, shrugging a half-apology. He leaned back in his chair and drew his fingers down the curve of his mustache. "Aren't you being a tad over-dramatic?"

"No." She paced the gallery. "Well, maybe a little. I sympathize."

His frown deepened. "I thought you said your marriage wasn't arranged."

"It wasn't—sort of. We probably would have married... eventually... if Brian's uncle would have allowed it."

"Then what has all this have to do with anything?"

"Her father, my father... Her family, my family..." she ended, lamely.

He exhaled heavily and closed his eyes as he rubbed his forehead. "You're not making any sense a 'tall."

"I had a particular friend in school—you recall me telling you about it the other day by the pool?"

Nathan nodded.

"Her Uncle Naecel was the head of the Mackenzie clan, one of the biggest in the Highlands. It was through her that I came to live there. Marriages there are often arranged when the participants are very young. Mairi was six when she was promised to a cousin of the laird of the neighboring clan. There had been a border dispute of some kind or another, and she was part of the settlement."

"Tangled webs." Nathan rose and came around the table. "Here, I fear Defoe is not up to the task."

He gently pried a book from Cate's hands, one that she had no idea of having picked it up, nor that she had been worrying it to the point of threatened destruction. He pulled a length of cord from his pocket and her heart sank, fearing another lesson was in the offing. Knot tying lessons were always tedious, Nathan a dogged instructor. To her surprise, he left her to work it in her hands.

"You've no idea," she went on grimly. "He was a monster: nearly thirty years older, and looked and smelled like an old bear. He lived in a house with his prize bull on one side and his bed on the other. He treated the livestock better than her, beat them less, too. Several of Brian's uncles tried to intervene. Even Brian tried to bargain, and then outright threatened the man, but nothing helped. They found her frozen to death in the bottom of a burn. She had run away... again."

Nathan considered for several moments from his chair, his expression growing grave.

"No, I'm not buying it." He rose to circle her. "You've been at loose ends since Prudence was shipped, before, come to think on it. It's not the ladyship, nor a churlish father, nor some damned arranged marriage something or other. It's something else..."

She bristled, for no one liked their motivations questioned.

"It's the kidnapping." She drew back at her outburst. At first, she wanted to reject it out-of-hand, and yet at the same time, was relieved to have it off her chest.

"It's wrong. I was uncomfortable with it from the first, especially for someone so young."

"And how were we to have known that?" Nathan said, leaning against *Merdering Mary's* barrel.

"You didn't, but it doesn't make the deed any less," she said peevishly. "You have no idea what it's like for a woman to be taken: the terror and cold dread, being frozen with fear of what's to happen next."

Nathan reached to seize her by the arm and turn her to face him. "But it wasn't like that for you... was it?"

"The first time... Well, both times, yes," she said to the floor.

"*First?*"

"Oh, umm..." She sidled away.

Dammit! It was the hazard of giving way to one's emotions: the inadvertent inevitably tumbling out.

"I was taken once before, a year or so after we were married. Deserters... I was... It was..."

Her voice caught and she waved him away, the handkerchief on her finger like a flag of truce.

"Here, at first, yes, I was scared beyond words."

Weeks had passed, but the anguish was fresher than she had imagined. Her heart picked up that same pounding rate once more, and a cold sweat prickled her spine. That terror must have shown on her face, for Nathan came round to stand over her. So, caught up in the emotions once more, she cringed.

"You were never in danger." His voice quaked with fury.

"I know that."

"No one was going to lay hands —"

"But I had no way of knowing that, did I," she said levelly. "It was the *Ciara Morganse*, the dreaded Captain Nathan Blackthorne. Anyone would wish to escape" she said, glancing toward the windows.

They had fought her first day aboard. Thinking he sought to violate her, she had bitten him and tried to jump. It had been folly, but hindsight always came through a clearer lens.

"It was either stop you or watch you kill yourself," he said, following her thoughts. He studied her, regret knitting his brows. "You were that afraid?"

She forced a smile. "Water over the decks, as you like to say."

He was barely appeased.

"I didn't object to the kidnapping at first," she said, returning to her initial point, "because I knew there was little danger, I knew I would be here to aid and protect, save whoever it was from what I had to endure."

"Endure, eh?"

The glumness in Nathan's voice caused her to stop.

"Please, I don't mean to reproach you," she pleaded. "You're doing what you must. It's me. I can't... I can't —"

"Bear to be brought so low," he said, sinking further.

"That's not what I meant."

"Not quite, but so very, *very* near," he said, bitterly.

"I understand why you loathe Creswicke, and I am in fullest sympathy why you want to do everything in your power to make his life a misery." God, she was making such a hash of this. "But I'm uncomfortable with —"

"Being drug down and obliged to wallow in the gutters with the rest of us."

Nathan thumped his fist on the brass back of the great gun. "And so, this is what I've done: made you do what you wouldn't else, until your conscience won't allow you peace."

"No, no, I don't mean that it's your fault," she said, clutching his arm.

"Aye, but it is." The walnut eyes were sharp with hurt. He made a caustic noise. "Pirate, darling. Not much more to be said. It's what I am. It's not a pretty world, but 'tis the hand I've been dealt, and by Great Lucifer's horns and tail, I'll do what I must."

His shoulder slumped. He raised a hand and dropped it to his side in surrender. "But you... you didn't choose this. You don't deserve... this..."

He moved to the window and stared out. "I should have gotten you away from all this," he said, more to himself. He looked over his shoulder toward her. "You tried and..."

Nathan clamped his lower lip between his teeth and shook his head with a rustle of bells.

"I said I wanted to stay," Cate said evenly.

"You should be where it's..."

"I'm where I want to be." Fears began to rise that he meant to send her away. "And I'll suffer anything to..." She checked herself, for she was on the verge of making a confession which no one wanted to hear. "You declare yourself guilty of allowing me to be where I desired? That's a strange Court of Justice your running, Captain Blackthorne."

Cate touched Nathan's arm and gazed earnestly up into the dark, troubled eyes. "I'm exactly where I want. There is no place else."

He smiled faintly, somewhat appeased.

He shook off his mood to say, "But Prudence is back, safe and sound amid the fold once more. You should be skylarking in the rigging with joy. Instead, you're skulking about like we'd just sent her to Jones' Locker."

"I have to help her."

Nathan slumped in his chair and propped his head in his hand. "You're making no sense a'tall."

"You know Creswicke better than I. Can you honestly say you're comfortable with leaving her to a man like him?"

He shrugged, looking off. "I can sleep with it."

"Well, I can't."

Looking up, he smiled crookedly. "So, you propose to right the wrong, by doing another wrong, to save her for her own good from something which she might well desire to do. You've been tying too many knots, darling. That's positively convoluted; it has more turns in it than a Spanish bo'lin."

"I'm not talking about taking her again, but what's so wrong with allowing her a choice?"

He rolled his eyes to the beams overhead and said under his breath, "Where have I heard that before?"

She winced. A few days earlier, she had indeed uttered those same words in the fervor of offering a different kind of plea on the girl's behalf.

"You think I'm as half-crazed and misguided now as I was then?"

He regarded her balefully. "'Tis but a strake one way or t'other."

Heaving a sigh, he closed his eyes like a man commending himself to the gallows. "So, put a name to what's in your mind."

"I have no idea."

With an exasperated gasp, he buried his face in his hands.

"Well, have you always gone into every action, with your every move planned to the letter?" she demanded defensively.

"Of course!" Both knew that to be a blatant exaggeration. "A man without a plan is a man what plans to fail, or get himself killed, as the case might be. Be warned, you darling, best intentions are often not appreciated. They can be a sour fruit."

Cate dropped into a chair, tiredly rubbing her temple against a headache, which for a week seemed to have taken up a permanent residence. "All I know is I shan't be able to live with myself, unless I've at least tried to do something."

"Fancy it will allow you to sleep, do you?" Nathan asked. "Allow me to be so bold as to say it will help precious little. I don't expect a place in line at St. Peter's gate all for the cause of a few 'I'm sorrys.' But for you." The walnut eyes grew gentle. "For you there shall be a golden pass, for there is no badness and you shall go to the front of the line. I'll put in a word, if you like, should you think it might help, but mum might be best, all things considered."

Another crooked smile appeared; the one which came with uncertainty. The sight of it tugged her heart, as it was meant to do. It was one more coin in the price of being with him.

Nathan narrowed an accusing eye. "Putting the curse of your perpetual happiness on my shoulders, eh? Bloody heavy burden, that one. Could haunt me the rest of me days."

Drumming his fingers on the table, he slammed the flat of his hand. "Oh, very well. Deliver me from well-meaning, good-hearted, meddlesome women. They don't call me Daft Nathan for nothing. I just hope they don't call me Dead Nathan."

The late afternoon shadows of the trees crawled like fingers across the stilling water as the *Morganse* slipped into the back bay of Hopetown. Under jibs and staysails, she passed through the reef and stood in with a familiarity which almost rendered the lead lines a formality. Cate paced the forecastle while the longboat was roused over the side, for only one would be going ashore. To be there and gone before even the fish took notice was the plan.

It was a dark night, the moon yet to make its appearance. Nathan seemed unmindful. He made his way down the starlit road like a cat, never stepping a wrong foot, while catching Cate as she stumbled. There was none of his customary breeziness or witticisms, however. He had been quite open with his disapproval of this entire endeavor, but he was now quite closed, resolved to see this through.

Hopetown lay in a direct line between them and Lady Bart's. The line of his mouth growing a little grimmer, Nathan led Cate on a darting path through the town's outskirts to the road which led to the estate. Once there, he found invisible paths through the bushes and into the gardens, presumably the same ones he had used to find her shortly after Harte had brought her there.

The dark hulk of the house could be seen ahead. It and most of its inhabitants were at rest, a majority of the windows dark. The sight of a guard caused Nathan to jerk back, pushing Cate to the ground behind a dense rosebush. Standing over her, his hand poised over his sword, Nathan peered around. A dance of fingers indicated she was to stay low and quiet; the guard was coming their way.

Seeing no other option, Cate tugged at her neckline, pulling the edge of her bodice low across her bosoms.

"What are you doing?" Nathan hissed.

"Going to take care of a guard," she whispered back. Cupping an arm under her breasts, she gave them a plumping lift. "I'll be right back."

To a hoarse rasp of Nathan's objections, she stepped out into the gravel path. She tousled her hair, and then set to huffing, as if she had been running a long distance, and spurted down the path in the direction of the guard.

"Please!" She ran up to the guard, his musket brandished. She leaned heavily on his arm while she gulped for air. "Help!"

"Mum?" He was startlingly young, his voice breaking in an uneven timbre between lad and man.

"Help me!" She braced her hands on her knees. Bent ostensibly to catch her breath, the position put the full of her cleavage on display. "I need to see Lady Bart."

"No one's allowed in or…"

"Please! I've just escaped from those pirates. They could be right behind me. I need to see her about her niece."

"I heard she was returned." Somewhere in his mind, that bit of coincidence seemed to add to her veracity.

"No! Pray, I beg, I have word. I need to speak to Lady Bart, please." She gave his arm a familiar squeeze and, through the heavy breathing, batted her lashes.

He glanced into the darkness, uncertain. "Very well, then, 'tis way—"

"No, no!" She rounded her eyes as if in fear. "The pirates, they're chasing me. Someone needs to be here to protect us."

Torn between duty and a woman in distress, the former won. The lad straightened and squared his thin shoulders.

"Very well, ma'm," he said, striving to keep his voice deep. "Follow that path; it will take you 'round to the servant's entrance."

"Thank you, and please, have care. Those pirates are dangerous."

As advertised, the semi-familiar path led to the house. Cate made her way around through the cooking wing and inside. At such an hour, there were few servants about. Some recognized her and bobbed a bow, or dipped a curtsy, but most paid little attention as she made her way through the scullery and service areas. Most servants knew what to see and not see, when it came to the comings and goings of a household, and she banked on that now as she made her way up the servants' stairway. On the second floor, it opened into a room-sized linen closet, dark and smelling of cloth and starch. Groping her way along the shelves, she found the door and slipped out.

The hallway was deserted, most of the lights snuffed for the night. She knew Prudence was there, the question was where? As Cate crept down the hall, she heard a door open, and froze. Silently chanting "The best way to fit in is look like you belong," she straightened and forced her feet to move. The door closed and a woman looked up. Her eyes flew open as Cate recognized Sally at the same time.

"Mistress Cate, you shouldn't be here. The Commodore is still here—"

"Yes, I'm sure," Cate cut in. "I'm looking for Prudence. Which is her room?"

"Just there," said Sally with a tilt of her head toward the door across the hall. "Her nanny is there now, I believe. Miss Prudence downstairs with Lady Bart."

Cate's stomach griped at the thought of the salon filled with Lady Bart's guests. "How many are there, tonight?"

"Only Miss Prudence and Her Ladyship; the rest have left, for now, except the Commodore. God knows, they'll return soon enough to live off her good graces!" she declared, rolling her eyes. "We'll check her room first, just to be sure."

A scratch at the door, and Sally pushed her way in, Cate close behind. She recognized the room as the same she had occupied, flounced and laced within an inch of its life. A small woman, clad mostly in black, rose from a chair, a bit of mending dangling from her hand. Her eyes matched the fine wisps of gray hair which escaped from under her cap. Cate hung back as Sally surged forward.

"Miss Fran, do you know where Miss Prudence might be?" asked Sally.

Round-faced and well past middle-age, the top of her cap barely coming to the level of Cate's chin, the woman bobbed a curtsy while regarding Cate with suspicion. "The Young Miss is downstairs with Lady Bart, in the parlor, I believe."

Brushing past Sally, Cate moved closer to Miss Fran. "Are you Nanna?"

The woman blinked, taken back. "Why, yes, how did you know?"

"Prudence spoke a great deal and quite kindly," Cate said.

Nanna stiffened, rearing back her head to glare down her nose. "Are you Cate?" She almost spit the name.

"Why, yes—"

"A fine lot of good you did the poor girl!"

Cate jerked back as if bitten.

"You'll mind your tongue, you old biddy," hissed Sally.

"I'll not!" Nanna advanced on Cate, the little body rigid. "The *least* you could have done was protect the child from the... the... the horrible ordeal!"

"I know being kidnapped was a trial," Cate said, scrambling to recover. "I... I mean we meant to see to her comforts, but—"

"Hog wash!" Nanna burst with a withering glare. "We all know what has been done. And now the poor girl has been ruined by that... monster!"

"I beg your pardon?" Cate flared back.

"She's been violated!"

The very idea was so astoundingly absurd, Cate's first impulse was to laugh, but found she couldn't.

"No," Cate wheezed. The air seemed to have suddenly been sucked out of the room. "No! You mean... No, no, no. That's not right. That's impossible—"

"There's no sense to be had in lying to protect the blackguard," Nanna fumed. "She's been examined by a doctor. There are *no* doubts!"

The room took an odd tilt.

"That's not right," Cate implored to Sally. Of all people, she would agree. "You know it's not. Nathan wouldn't... I mean, he couldn't have—"

A guilty pang stabbed high under her ribs. She had asked Nathan to do that very thing, and yet, he had—they had—agreed it was out of the question. But this... this hadn't been her intent. Had he done it anyway?

Sally patted Cate's shoulder, crooning like a mother hen, "I know, I know. You don't have to make excuses for him. We all know how they are."

"*They* are!" Cate yanked free. Confusion fell away, and to a cold calm. "Where is she? I need to speak to her, now!"

"I'll not have you upsetting her by—" Nanna began.

Cate whirled around on her, her hands balling into fists. "She's upset things quite enough. I came here—Nathan came here—to try to help her out of this marriage."

"Is the Captain with you?" Sally ran to the window, pulled back the curtain and craned her neck.

"Yes, he is." Cate glanced nervously at the night and then the mantle-clock, painfully aware of Nathan watching the house, waiting. "I mustn't keep him waiting; he could be caught—we both could be caught. Do you really think Nathan would have come, if any of this outlandish nonsense were true?" she asked, rounding back on the *au pair*.

"What purpose would the child have in lying?"

"She's no child." Instantly regretting her outburst, Cate drew a calming breath, and began again. "Miss Fran, I beg—"

"Why are you so willing to help her?" Nanna demanded coldly.

"I've been worried for her, as should any person with any sensibilities."

The rebuke wasn't lost on Nanna, who sputtered in indignation.

With considerable effort, Cate collected herself, and ventured toward her. "You must tell me what your feelings are regarding Prudence's impending marriage. Please, be honest. Look past what may or may not have happened, if you possibly can, look to the child's future, and tell me what you think."

Cate held her breath. If Nanna agreed, something could be done for Prudence, if not... it could be a long walk to the awaiting longboat, and there would be no living with Nathan.

Like most domestics, Nanna wasn't accustomed to being asked her opinion. That shock gave way to indecision, her lips pursing into a tight bow shape.

"Trust her, woman," Sally hissed from the window. "She's only trying to do what's right for your girl."

Nanna's features compressed tighter, to the point of resembling a small black teapot set to explode.

"I think it's reprehensible the way Master Collingwood has shipped that glorious child away to marry a total stranger, knowing nothing of his family or character, and without so much as a by your leave," Nanna finally burst out.

Cate expelled a rush of relief. "Then we must help her. I'm not sure either," she said to their questioning stare. "But we have to think of something and quickly. Please, can you take me to her?"

The journey through the halls and down the stairs gave Cate time to formulate a plan and then count the near dozen holes which perforated it. Prudence stood as the next obstacle. Up until a few moments ago, it had been a struggle to imagine why the girl would object, but now, what she would do was anyone's guess. The last and biggest obstruction was Lady Bart, *grande dame* and dowager mistress of the island. If she chose to go along with Cate's plan, her word would rule. If she chose not...

Cate found herself wondering what the garrison's cells would be like, since they promised to be home for her remaining days.

She swallowed down a bilious lump, only to have it rise again. Coherent thought came with difficulty, her mind being so filled with images of Nathan's fingers entwined in Prudence's glossy curls, and his hands on that milky bosom.

"I never took a woman unwilling in me life."

"Charm her" she had begged him. She had felt the power of those eyes and that smile, inadvertent as it might have been on his part. She could barely imagine the effect of those charms when he meant it.

He wouldn't do it!

She clung to that thought like a talisman while riding a downward spiral of doubt. She had lived elbow-to-elbow with him for nearly two months. Nathan was no predator. He was no knight in shining armor, but neither was he a goatish, rapacious brute. There was no denying that he was the King of Deception, but he wasn't that good, not on that count.

Prudence was the greater puzzle. She had been on the verge of tears at the prospect of leaving the *Morganse*. A girl who had been violated wouldn't offer to tell everyone of Nathan's kindness. It defied all reason that the girl could manage that in the aftermath of something so horrific.

Damn you! she thought, without really knowing who it was meant for.

At the bottom of the stairs, Cate was surprised when Sally veered in the opposite direction of the salon, and instead led them down the hallway to another room. It was somewhat smaller than the salon. The tall windows and rows of shelves which lined the walls suggested it had once been the library or a man's study. It had been emasculated, however, with layers of frill and flower. Legions of porcelain figurines and framed silhouettes had replaced the books on the shelves. Delicate-legged velvet and crewel-worked chairs looked to be on their tip-toes on the floral-patterned carpets and polished mahogany floor. Satin and laced pillows dotted chairs and settees.

Prudence and Lady Bart sat on either side of a lamp when the small parade of women entered. Prudence was quick to rise. Freshly frocked, her hair neatly arranged underneath a pert cap, its lappets drawn under her chin, she looked considerably refreshed from the last time Cate had seen her.

"Cate, I'm so pleased to see you." Prudence lunged forward to hug Cate, but then stiffened and backed away, muttering to the floor, "Whatever are you doing here?"

"I came to help you." As Cate looked at the down-turned head, she saw something about the small shoulders she hadn't expected to see: guilt. Then she realized what she had never seen: shock, nor anything near it.

If Prudence had been brutalized as she claimed, then where had been the shock or the trauma? The attacker might well have hidden it—Nathan was indeed the Master of Deception—but the victim, especially one as young and naïve as her, could not. She had seen the aftereffects of such an attack: the incessant sobbing and shaking, or the dazed, stuporous look, or the wild vacillation between them. Where had been the torn shift or petticoats, the stains from struggling on the ground, or even tousled hair? A woman violated—no matter the age—would not be the picture of well-being, bright-eyed and pink-cheeked, the next day.

Cate eyed Prudence with new suspicion and grudging respect—Or was that contempt?—for the child was far more diabolical than previously credited.

"I should have thought the time for help would have been on the ship," Lady Bart said harshly from her chair. "There's blessed little to be done for the girl, now. I was shocked to learn you were on that ship with her... and all those... men. Shocking! I should have hoped common decency would have compelled you to do... something."

"There was nothing to do, because there was nothing done,

was there? Prudence," Cate said, swiveling back around, "what did you tell everyone?"

Prudence tried to pull away, but Cate held her firmly by the arm.

"Just the truth," the girl whimpered, the picture of virtue shamed. "What Captain Blackthorne did... one night... near the waterfalls..."

Tears dotting her lashes — *How did she manage to orchestrate that?* — Prudence turned beseechingly to Nanna and Lady Bart.

"But, he... he drug me away, into the dark and he..."

Oh, she was good! She was so very, very good!

Prudence extended her arm — appropriately trembling — and tipped her chin to display several bruises. "I fought, but he forced me."

Cate was almost sick with relief. The girl might have been violated, but there had been no violence. The incriminating bruises on her arms were from the ordeal of Harte and his men trying to get her off the *Morganse*. Those on her chin were by Cate's own hand. It meant everyone was to believe Nathan had spirited Prudence away — quietly, for the girl had slept but a few yards from Cate — and then led her through the jungle, at night, for over an hour's walk, in order to ravish her by a waterfall?

The girl had been on a beach with over three hundred men, and yet she had chosen Nathan to target in her hoax, because it was what everyone expected to hear.

The cunning behind that virtuous façade was stunning.

"That's not true and you know it, you stupid, silly fool. Do you have any idea what you've done?"

A perfectly-timed pearl of a tear slid down the China-doll cheek and her lower lip quivered.

"I only thought..." Prudence whimpered.

The bilious lump rose once more in Cate's throat. "No, that's just it, Prudence, you didn't think at all. Do you have any idea of the consequences of this?"

Prudence looked to the floor once more, her hands twisting at her middle. Nanna had sidled protectively closer. Sally stood teetering between who to believe.

"I was so afraid." Prudence's voice pinched to a small squeak, and she reached out a tremulous hand. "I didn't wish for you to be upset."

"Upset doesn't begin to describe it." To Cate's pleasure, Prudence flinched at the bite of her tone. "Lord Creswicke is not a man to be trifled with. He's dangerous and you're playing childish games with Nathan's life. This will give Creswicke the grounds to have Nathan hung, or worse."

And yes, where Creswicke was concerned, there were most certainly things worse than a quick death.

A number of unkind thoughts and words bubbled up, many which would have made Nathan proud and her mother blench.

"But he took me—" Prudence went on determinedly.

"Stop it!" Cate cringed at her volume. She lowered her voice to quaking growl. "I don't need to see any more of your crying, nor your theatrics."

"He's only a pirate!" Prudence burst out.

Rage surged, blinding Cate to everything except the cornflower-eyed face before her. Cate drew back her hand and slapped it. She heard the *crack!*, Prudence's squeal and then saw her tumble backward, patent leather slippers and petticoats to the air.

"You little selfish bitch," Cate hissed.

Lady Bart gasped, scandalized. Nanna and Sally rushed to help Prudence up from the floor. Once righted, hat askew and hair straggling, Prudence rubbed the offended cheek now brilliant. Her accusing look was accompanied with a perfectly rounded, pouting lip.

"How dare you!" Nanna cried, rounding on Cate.

"How dare you!" Cate retorted down at the diminutive nursemaid. "How dare you raise—"

"You have no right! You're nothing but a—!"

"—a child who doesn't lie just to save—!"

"I'm sorry!" Prudence shrieked. She fell against Cate and wept. "I had to do something! I can't marry Creswicke. I can't! I was so scared. Papa said I had to leave Boston because no one else would have me. Lord Creswicke was so far away, he wouldn't know—"

The delicate pearl-tears dissolved into a cascade as she clung to Cate. Fighting back tears of her own—of anger or relief, she wasn't sure—Cate put her arms around the quaking shoulders and woodenly patted her on the back.

"Prudence, please, time is of the essence—" Cate pleaded.

"There was a young man." It was Nanna who spoke. She closed her eyes with pain of the admission. "He and Prudence... well... They did what young people do."

"I loved him, Cate," Prudence moaned into her shoulder. "I honestly loved him, with all my heart."

The grey eyes going soft, Nanna lovingly stroked the back of Prudence's head. "But the boy didn't have the prospects or connections Master Collingwood sought. So, he was sent away."

"Papa meant to send me away, because I was ruined: no one of any position would have me." Prudence sniffed hugely.

Fumbling, Lady Bart produced a handkerchief and handed it to her.

"Then, a letter came from Lord Creswicke," Prudence went on, after blowing her nose, her voice thickened with crying. "A business offer, I believe. Papa said it was perfect; Lord Creswicke was too far away and had no way of knowing. So, he..."

"Sold you to Creswicke," Cate said flatly. "Damaged goods."

Lashes quivering with tears, Prudence looked up. "I knew if I had been with a man—spoiled—no other would want me. Papa had said as much. So, I thought if Creswicke knew I had been, then he wouldn't want me, and I wouldn't have to marry him. So, I told everyone—"

"That it was Nathan, and the doctor confirmed it."

The sickening knot seized Cate's gut. It was virtually her own plan, but Nathan had dissuaded her, pointing out the multitude of flaws. She regarded Nanna, wondering how much she knew. Worse yet, how long Nanna would have played along: before, or after Nathan was hung?

Cate closed her eyes and pinched the bridge of her nose, hoping the pain might wake her from this nightmare. Opening them, she instead found reality staring her in the face, and now a dull headache.

"Prudence, you silly, silly girl," Cate groaned. "Don't you understand anything? Lord Creswicke doesn't give a tinker's damn about you, or your worthiness, or anything else. He seeks connections, nothing more."

"It's true dear," Lady Bart said, tight with emotion. "Your father has been a reprehensible, money-grabbing cad most of his life."

Humored by her aunt's blunt evaluation, Prudence stifled a nervous snicker.

"What am I to do?" Guileless in innocence, Prudence looked to the surrounding women.

Lady Bart's eyes welled. "Marry Creswicke; there's aught else."

"Perhaps not." Cate pensively chewed the inside of her mouth. "What if there had been some kind of a mistake?"

Lady Bart pivoted to ask blankly. "What kind of mistake?"

"What if," Cate began haltingly, still playing it out in her mind, "since you had never seen your niece before, she had been able to put one over on you? What if she told you she was your niece, but wasn't... really?"

Cate looked from one to another, hoping for them to grasp her point quickly and save precious time. She had been in the house far too long; every minute more increased the chances of herself, or worse yet, Nathan, being discovered.

Sputtering, Lady Bart slumped in her chair and threw up her arms in abject surrender. "Of course, she's my niece," she muttered, more to convince herself. Rocking in agitation, she pleated and re-pleated the fabric of her dress. "But you *are* Prudence, aren't you, dear?"

"Yes, of course, Auntie." Prudence knelt to clutch her aunt's hand. "But, Cate means to help."

Lady Bart's mouth took a severe downward turn. "How is it helping, when she's trying to convince me you're not?"

"Not convince *you*," Cate explained, patiently. She angled her head toward the parlor door and the unseen world beyond. "We just need to convince all of *them*."

"Convince them of what?"

"That Prudence isn't… Prudence."

"Then who is she?" Lady Bart asked, her distress increasing.

"A girl on the ship." Even as Cate heard herself say it, she was struck with how desperate it sounded. The pain in her temple pounded in rhythm with her pulse. She glanced toward the window, and then the corner clock.

"That's ridiculous," exploded Nanna. "Everyone knows who she is."

"*You* know that," Cate said, facing Nanna, "because you were on the *Capricorn*. But how does anyone else know, I mean, really know? Have you ever seen a likeness of Prudence before now?" she asked of Lady Bart.

"Hardly," Lady Bart said with an unladylike snort. "My brother would have never spent that sort of money on the child. Her mother sent me a silhouette she had made, but that was years ago."

"Then how do you know *this* is really her?" Cate pressed.

"Why on earth would she lie? For heavens' sake," Lady Bart declared, her hands going to her face. "Will you stop being so circuitous!"

Cate turned to Prudence. "What if, while you were on the *Capricorn*, you made friends with a girl named Prudence Collingwood, and she had told you about the rich and powerful man she was to marry, the head of the Royal West Indies Mercantile Company? It sounded like a dream come true. Then she died, and so, you decided to take her place and no one would be the wiser."

Prudence scowled. "But what about Nanna?"

Cate turned. "What about it, Nanna? How badly do you wish

to see her married to a reprehensible man? Agree, and Prudence is free."

The clock's pendulum ticked off the seconds as Nanna looked first to Cate then Prudence. Her expression softened and her shoulders fell. "Tell me what's to be done."

Cate clasped a fist at the small victory. "Nanna should be the one to start: she used to be your niece's nanny and will be the one to suffer a sudden sense of conscious, and reveal Prudence—this one, that is—as an impostor. Then, with a little convincing," Cate went on, exchanging a sly smile with Prudence, "she could finally admit to not being your niece."

"Then, who is she?"

"Does it matter?" Cate shot back. Her patience and time was running out. "Pick a name."

The wheels of realization were beginning to turn in Lady Bart's head, albeit slowly, too slowly. "What happened to my real niece?"

"She died. A terrible sickness took her along with this girl's parents."

"But the passengers on the *Capricorn* would know," Nanna said haltingly.

Cate winced. This was the weakest part of her plan, and where it could all fall apart too readily. "We can only hope they have spread across the West Indies and are all very far away. And how would any of them *actually* know?" she said, crossing her fingers in the folds of her skirt.

Lady Bart rose. Each tick of the clock was a stabbing reminder of time passing while she paced. Hands writhing at her stomach, she made little, indecisive puffing sounds, her tiny feet clicking on the polished floors.

"Why is she telling the truth now?" Lady Bart said. "She could still marry, if she didn't say anything."

"She's had time to learn what sort Lord Creswicke is," Cate said carefully.

"He'll certainly write Father." Prudence's expression clouded as she grew to understand the implications of the plan. "He'll think me dead."

"And well enough," sighed Lady Bart, bracing her head in her hand. "For what little good that man has done you over the years."

Prudence clouded with the slow realization that the terms of her salvation: she would never see her parents again. It was the part which pained Cate the most. In saving the girl from a miserable fate, she had doomed her to the same one she had lived: losing family and home.

"And Mama?" Prudence barely squeezed out.

By then, Lady Bart, as well as everyone else, had come to the same conclusion. The matron clasped Prudence's hands. Her chin wobbled, but conspiracy touched her eye.

"Where there is a will, there is a way. Perhaps we can have a note secretly delivered." Eyes brimming, Lady Bart smoothed the dark, glossy curls at Prudence's shoulder. "Where will you go, dear?"

The question hung in the air. It was another large—perhaps the largest—hole in Cate's plan. Prudence would no longer have to marry Creswicke, but neither would she have an identity. The backs of Cate's eyes stung. She knew the paralyzing aimlessness of having no name, no family and nowhere to go. With no beginning and no end, it was like a leaf riding a gyre of pointlessness and futility: down seemed the only direction to go.

Prudence slumped. "I don't know," she said in a small voice. The red-rimmed eyes turned to Cate. "Mightn't I go with you?"

It was a painful admission—and one Cate could never share with Prudence—but she had been obliged to make a pledge to not only Nathan, but the entire crew: under no circumstances would Prudence step foot aboard again... *ever!*

"We can't take her on the *Morganse*," Cate said, firmly. "It would be too obvious; the entire Royal Navy would be after us by tomorrow. Besides, a pirate ship is no place for a young lady."

"You're living there," Prudence said.

"I'm no young lady," said Cate, dryly. She looked hopefully to Lady Bart. "Are there any other relatives or friends in these waters?"

Lady Bart shook her head. "There's no one. There's a nephew on St. Thomas, but he's an idiot and trying as desperately as he can to gamble away every penny he has." She hesitated. "Would you like to stay here, dear?"

Prudence's face lit, the blue eyes rounding. "Can I?"

"How?" Nanna demanded, with a pugnacious scowl. "We just agreed she isn't your niece."

"I'm Lady Bart Dinwoody," she announced, grandly. "I can do whatever I please! As far as anyone is to know, I'm just a silly old widow looking for companionship. You're welcomed to say here for as long as you wish."

"Are you sure?" Cate asked warily.

"Well, well, look what we have here!"

All five women jumped, startled at the unexpected male voice. Spinning, they found Roger Harte standing in the doorway, pistol in one hand and sword in the other.

The women gasped, startled, and clustered like a covey of frightened quail. Cate might have fallen back with them had her feet been willing to move. Altogether, it painted a guilty face on the scene. Quite surprisingly, it was Lady Bart who was the cooler head.

"Diggie!" Lady Bart pressed a hand to her bosom. "You gave us such a start, skulking about! You ought to announce yourself..."

In dishabille and wigless, his short hair tousled, Harte still presented an imposing figure. As he stood now, shirt hastily tucked into his breeches, features obscured in the half-shadows of the doorway, he was thoroughly ominous. Barely acknowledging the elder, he stepped farther into the room and swiveled his attention on Cate with an intensity which reminded her of Artemis spotting a rat.

"Mistress Harper, our little refugee from the pirate ship. Escaped *again*?" he said to Cate under Lady Bart's rambling.

Cate gulped and forced her frozen lips into something that she hoped resembled a smile. "Roger, what a surprise."

She strained to recall if the windows were opened or closed, envisioning a leaping escape. Air stirring against her arm gave hope. So, faint, however, it might have been only the result of someone moving. If the room had been stuffy before, it was now stifling.

"My regrets if I have discommoded you lovely ladies, in any manner." Harte's voice took a condescending dip. He took another step, bringing his humorless smile to light. "Were we looking for someone? Lost something, perhaps? Or might this be a social call?"

Given the hour, he knew damned well it wasn't that.

"Whatever are you doing down here, Diggie!" Lady Bart demanded, insinuating herself between him and Cate. She briefly squeezed Cate's arm, but if it was meant as a signal, or only another of her maternal gestures Cate couldn't tell.

"I thought you retired for the night," the elder woman said. "Oh, pray put away those weapons. One would think we're about to be attacked."

"Aren't we?" He arched a questioning brow at Cate. "Are we about to have unwelcome visitors?"

He broke his stare to address Lady Bart. "I heard voices and was alarmed for your safety, m'lady."

Lady Bart completed her indignant parade around the room and alit in a chair, like a hen settling on her nest. "I declare, there certainly are no dangers here. If you were to ask me, I would say you've over-reacted. It's only Cate, come to see that Prudence is safe. She learned Prudence was here and—"

"Yes, I would imagine she's quite aware of the whereabouts of our Miss Collingwood," Roger mused dryly.

A green-eyed look cut sideways to Cate. "I had feared perhaps you were indisposed, Mistress, when you failed to offer your compliments the other day."

"What I do hardly matters," Cate stammered. A trickle of sweat began a slow march down her ribs.

"On the contrary." The green eyes flickered to Prudence then back. "May I assume you've come in some feeble attempt to right the damage already done? A little tardy in your concerns, aren't you? The time to help would have been before the despicable act took place, not after."

"I don't understand what—" began Cate.

"Oh, I think you do," he cut in. "I don't know who you are, but I do know you are not as you represent. Of that, I am entirely sure."

There was little sense in arguing the point; Harte had obviously come to his own conclusions. How much he had overheard was the larger issue. His bland countenance showed nothing. Had he heard enough to know of Prudence's deception, or only arrived in time to learn of Cate's grander scheme? The more chilling prospect was, if he knew of Prudence's hoax, would he choose to ignore it, and use her supposed abuse as one more excuse to see Nathan hung.

With a small—very small—bit of relief, Cate noted he made no mention of the warrants against her. Her familiarity with the finer points of British law was foggy, but she believed kidnapping and defilement to be lesser offenses than murder and traitor. It was a small consolation to know that at her execution, she would only be hung, not drawn and quartered.

Harte tilted his head slightly in consideration. "You're too fine to be one of Blackthorne's whores, but neither are you a hostage, for you are unscathed."

"Compliance has its rewards," she said evenly. Containing her dislike for the man was becoming a task.

"Indeed," he said distantly, deep in his speculations. "Clearly he has yet to tire of you, for he would have sold you for his next rum."

She winced at his conclusion being so near to her own.

He regarded her with the same air as one would regard a new horse. "Although you're fair enough, he could make whoremongering worthwhile. And now he's using you, hiding behind a woman's skirts, sending you to do his dirty work."

"No differently than you sought to use me," Cate shot back in equal coldness.

"Upon my word, Diggie," exclaimed Lady Bart. "You're being rather boorish playing silly questions."

He gave his hostess only the briefest of glances.

"Two counts co-conspirator to kidnap, misrepresentation, fraud, wrongful doing: all hanging —"

"Cate had nothing to do with that. She wasn't there when I was taken," Prudence said, darting protectively to Cate's side.

"Really?" Harte's voice arced with doubt. "And where, pray tell, would our dear Mistress Harper have been, if not on the famed *Ciara Morganse*?"

"Well, I..." Cate was at a loss. The day she met him, she had confessed to being on the ship. Any further denial or explanation would only incriminate Thomas.

"It's beside the point. You can explain it all to the magistrate." Shoving the pistol into his waistband, he crooked a beckoning finger. "Come along, my dear. I've arranged for —"

He took Cate by the arm, but instantly went stiff and frozen.

"Hold off, mate."

Cate could see behind Harte, where the voice and the metallic click of a pistol being cocked came from, but she immediately recognized the voice.

Harte stiffened and drew Cate against him. "Well, well, Nathan Blackthorne."

Nathan slipped around Harte to come farther into the room. The muzzle of his pistol shifted with him, going from the back of the Commodore's head to the side. The women gasped upon seeing Nathan and scurried behind the settee. With Harte between them, Cate could only see Nathan's hat and eyes. They flicked in her direction, assuring that she was so far unharmed.

Nathan clucked his tongue with what only the most desperate could call sympathy. "*Captain* Nathanael Blackthorne. Disappointing you can't retain that bit. Gone feeble, have we? And at such an early age."

Roger held Cate so close, his pistol gouging her ribs. It was a miscalculation on his part, for now she blocked both his pistol and his sword.

Nathan pressed the muzzle harder into Harte's temple. "Leave 'er go."

"Rest assured, I will add this to your charge sheet," Harte said, coolly.

"An extensive and weighty document, already," Nathan replied, lightly.

Harte gave a short, humorless laugh. "You'll be arrested before you reach the front gate."

Nathan rolled his eyes thoughtfully. "I see it different. By my way o' thinking, you'll let us go, easy like, since the young miss over there will be with us, insurance, as it were. Her safety being your main charge and concern, you'll not desire to endanger her with something so unfortunate as a stray bullet."

"A fool's mission," Harte sneered. "There are guards just outside, in the hall. They'll —"

"Not anymore." The smile in Nathan's voice couldn't be missed.

Harte's confidence faltered a fraction. "Where are they?"

"Not here."

Harte's fingers dug deeper into Cate's arm. She felt him shift, evening his weight, readying himself. Her instincts screamed for her to do something, yet she stood, unable to breathe, afraid to move lest she distract Nathan.

"I'll have you shot before you clear the grounds," Harte said, his confidence regained.

"Mebbe." Nathan said agreeably. "On the other hand, t'would be a mite embarrassing to find it necessary to inform Lord Creswicke of the shooting of his betrothed, during your attempts to apprehend someone who had bested you *again*."

"Pray, don't —!" cried Prudence.

The outburst gave Harte the diversion he needed. He flung Cate aside with a force which sent her to the floor and whipped around with his elbow. A move intended to smash a nose and teeth, or dislocate or fracture jaw, caught Nathan in the side of the head. Nathan sprawled backwards on the floor, his pistol skating off into a corner. Harte drew his sword and spun. He came down with its heel, aiming for Nathan's head. Nathan rolled, taking the blow in the shoulder, instead.

Cate came up from the floor and lunged at Harte built up for another blow. Hitting his elbow, the momentum took her back to the polished planks. At the same time, Nathan bound to his feet, and tried to draw his sword, but was impeded by a chair. Harte kicked it from his hand to send it skittering out of sight.

Now unarmed, Nathan backed around the room as Harte slashed at him. Nathan came near enough to the fireplace to snatch up the poker and wielded it as if it was a weapon, sparks flying at every collision of steel. Nearly a half a head taller, Harte should have had the advantage of reach and weight, but the furnishings seemed to have joined Nathan's side, hindering him time and again.

"Pray, not the silk!" Lady Bart cried querulously from her

sequester behind the settee when Harte skewered a chair, "Mind the wood!" when a table was knocked over, and "Have a care with the crystal!" when a cabinet was hit.

From where she laid in the floor, Cate spotted Nathan's pistol in a corner. She lunged to seize it. Rising to her knees, she took aim at Harte, but hesitated. Granted, the fight was noisy, but the sound of a gunshot would bring everyone in the household, including the guards. A worst risk was she might hit Nathan. She lowered the pistol and hovered, desperate to do something, the poker having been knocked from Nathan's hand. She snatched up a small footstool and hurled it at Harte's feet. It tangled there for a moment and then skittered within Nathan's reach. He grabbed it just in time to use it as a shield against a viscous swipe from Harte.

Cate whirled in search of another weapon when Sally shot out from behind the settee. A fringed satin pillow poised high, she set to beating Harte about the head. Confused, Roger tried to defend himself with one arm while going at Nathan with the other, driving him farther back with each blow. Satin only able to endure so much abuse, the pillow split with an explosion of feathers.

Nathan came up against a chair. Now trapped, he hurtled the stool at Harte. It hit Harte in the right shoulder and his arm fell limp to his side. Weaponless again, Nathan dove behind the settee, his belt buckles scraping the wooden floor. Lady Bart gave a startled screech as Nathan wove under her skirts, popping up finally at the opposite end.

Feathers stuck in the sweat streaming down his face, Harte staggered as he furiously rubbed feeling back into his arm. When his back was to her, Cate took the chance and launched at him, intending to... Hold him down? Tackle? Distract? Anything! Somehow, Harte sensed her coming. He sidestepped and swung with his left arm, bellowing "Away!"

Cate was sent tumbling, the corner of a cabinet catching her in the ribs. She cried out in pain. The wind knocked from her lungs, her knees buckled and she crumpled to the floor.

"Leave off!" Nathan roared and launched up to drive a ringed fist into Harte's jaw.

Both men now unarmed, they resorted to fists. His right arm still useless, Harte staggered, and then swung his left fist. Nathan ducked and drove his shoulder into Harte's midriff, sending them both to the floor in a writhing heap.

Cate lay curled on her side, straining to force her spasmed lungs to move. The sounds of the two men fighting, grunts and curses, fell flat in her ears. Through a swirl of black spots, she watched them amidst the wreckage of furniture and feathers. Nathan got an arm around Harte's throat and squeezed, but Harte threw him off. Both men rose to their knees. The cords rigid in his neck with the effort, Harte drove a fist into Nathan's gut that sent him sprawling face-down. Dazed, Nathan braced his head on the floor as he struggled to rise.

Cate watched in horror as Harte snatched up his sword and, with a double-fisted grip, rose behind Nathan poised for a killing blow. She wanted to scream—needed to scream—to warn Nathan, but her airless lungs managed only a wheezing gasp. Fearing the sickening sound of a blade slicing flesh and shattering bone, the spots before her eyes grew to a frenzied dance as she floundered to rise.

There was a sound, but not the one expected. Shattering, yes... But, it was glass.

Amid the female shrieks, Cate's breath came back in a wrenching gasp. With it, her vision cleared enough for her to see a round-eyed Prudence standing over Harte's hunched figure, shattered china scattered at her feet. Harte staggered then collapsed on top of Nathan.

Grunting and swearing came from the swirl of feathers as Nathan struggled out from under Harte's limp weight. Cate unsteadily rose to her feet and stooped to help Nathan to his.

Eyes rolling, Nathan managed a lop-sided grin. "Nice shot, luv."

"It wasn't me," Cate said. She braced a shoulder under his when he swayed. "It was Prudence."

His unfocused eyes traveled the room, until they came upon Prudence, standing nearly at his side.

"Nice shot, darling," he said, blinking wide.

He sagged against the back of a chair and braced his head there, his shoulders heaving as he caught his breath. Cate scooped up his hat and pistol, and guided his fumbling hand to tuck the latter into his belt. He cautiously settled his hat back on his head, wincing.

Seeing Nathan was safe, Cate's anger surged. "What are you doing here? You're supposed to wait outside."

He touched his temple, checking for blood, and then glared down his nose at her. "I came looking for you."

"We agreed you would wait."

"*You* didn't come back."

"I wasn't finished."

The shouting of guards—strident with alarm as they raced down the hallway—cut them short. With a small "Eep!" and a swirl of skirts, Sally ran out to meet them, Lady Bart close behind.

"Thank heavens!" Sally exclaimed. Her feigned breathlessness was muffled by her pulling the door to behind her. "They went out through the back."

"The fiends! They broke in upon us." Lady Bart's shrill rose over the male furor. "They seek to escape through the gardens. Oh, the shock! The horror!"

"Yes, ma'm," came a deeper voice. "But we heard—?"

"No, no! The Commodore has scared them off. Pray, he begs you give chase and do not return, until you have apprehended them and we can safely rest in our beds," said Lady Bart, with a heretofore unheard tone of authority.

There was a moment of indecision, questions and answers colliding. And then they heard the thump of boots speeding away. Sally and Lady Bart slipped back into the room, closing the door and throwing the bolt behind them.

Lady Bart pressed a hand to her heaving bosom. "They've taken their leave for now."

Sally retrieved Nathan's sword from the corner. Adoration softened the stern features as she gave it back, her fingers lingering on his. "You need to take your leave."

From outside the windows came the clatter of musketry and men running.

"We need to show a leg and haul our wind," Nathan announced and headed for the door.

"There's been a change in plans," Cate said, stopping him by the sleeve.

"Suffering Jesus on the cross, now what?" he groaned.

"Prudence won't be going with us."

His mouth fell open and remained so for several seconds. "Then what the bloody hell did we come here for?"

"To help her, and we did!"

"We did," he said dully. He gave his head a shake. "I must have been hit harder than I thought."

"It's all arranged," Lady Bart cried joyously, pressing her palms to her cheeks. "She'll be staying here, with me."

Nathan whirled at the sound of her voice, feathers billowing at his knees. "Who the hell are you?"

"This is Lady Bart," Cate said. "She's Prudence's aunt—"

"Except not anymore," Prudence said with a conspiratorial smirk.

Nathan looked to the ceiling in search of guidance then closed them in search of patience.

"Look, luv, I'd love to stand here and have a gang old chat, but yon Commodore shan't stay down much longer, and here is not where I'd rather be when he wakes up, if you get me drift."

Conceding his point, Cate hugged Prudence, and then held her by the shoulders. "Prudence, it's your responsibility to set this all right. This could have very serious consequences, so you must do everything in your power to assure the Captain isn't implicated."

"What did I do?" Nathan demanded from the doorway.

"Nothing," Cate said, unwavering from Prudence.

"Then, what did she do?" he asked.

"Nothing," chorused the women.

"I shall, I promise," Prudence said earnestly. She hugged Cate tightly. "Thank you, Cate, for everything."

Prudence peeked around Cate to wave timidly at Nathan. "Thank you, also Captain."

"You're welcome," he said, and then grumbled under his breath, "Not sure what I did."

Cate lowered her eyebrows at him, jerked her head in Prudence's direction, and then arched her brows significantly.

"She just saved your life," she hissed in the face of his scowl.

Groaning, he stepped around, took Prudence by the shoulders and kissed her lightly on the cheek. The girl's eyes popped open in shock, her porcelain face going several shades of crimson.

"You're a lovely girl," he said, with surprising sincerity.

He turned to find himself encircled by women, all focused at him. Flashing a nervous grin, he shifted on his feet. Expelling a resigned sigh, he seized Nanna's hand before she could recoil and kissed it. He barely straightened before Sally had him in her arms and gave him a plunging kiss.

"Goodbye, Nathan," she said, breathless as a maid.

He pushed free of her grasp only to wind up squarely before Lady Bart. She was clearly distraught to have the renowned brigand so near. There was a brief jousting of hands, Nathan reaching while Lady Bart, caught between civility and dread, extended only to jerk away. Nathan finally caught up her hand and touched her knuckles to his lips. He then swept a bow and wheeled around on Cate.

"Can we go now or is there a skullerymaid I missed?" he asked as he propelled her toward the door.

"Wait. Wait!" Prudence cried.

Amid Nathan's sputtering protests, Cate pulled to a halt. Prudence snatched up the two sewing boxes and thrust them in Cate's arms.

"You need these," the young girl said, eyes bright with emotion.

"Thank you!" Cate shouted over her shoulder as Nathan pulled her away.

"Wait! Wait!" Lady Bart trotted to catch them up "Allow me."

"But, there's guards and —" Cate began.

Lady Bart waved her away. "Yes, yes, I know. Come!"

Exchanging uncertain glances, Cate and Nathan had no option but to follow Lady Bart down the long hallway to the foyer. Every footstep echoed like a gunshot on the polished floors, but the house was already in such high turmoil, they passed with little notice. The doorman drew open the front door for his mistress to pass, Cate and Nathan in her wake. Lady Bart stopped on the portico and craned her neck to inspect the surrounding grounds.

"It appears to be clear," she announced, red-faced with excitement. "Have no care; I'll attend the guards."

Cate hesitated, not sharing her confidence. "How are you going to explain this?"

"Pish-posh! Diggie already thinks I'm a doddering old fool; a little more so is of minor consequence. I'll manage."

She hugged Cate, a gesture of surprising familiarity. "I am in your debt; you saved my niece from an intolerable fate."

A knot of remorse twisted in Cate's gut. "And robbed her of her family."

"And given her a life. I'd call it a fair trade." Chin quivering and eyes welling, Lady Bart patted Cate on the arm. "Have a care, dear."

Nathan stood with his hands on his hips in the middle of the drive, having apparently just discovered that Cate wasn't with him.

"Forgot to exchange recipes?" he asked as she caught him up.

"A real gentleman would carry these." She pitched the sewing boxes into his arms as she passed, leaving him to fumble on his own, to keep from dropping them.

25: DECLARATIONS IN THE DARK

Suffering none of Lady Bart's confidence, Nathan steered a path sharply away from the one they had come by, and well wide of the sleeping town. Several times Nathan left Cate in a thicket, in order to circle back and confirm they weren't being pursued. Eventually, they angled back to the narrow road to the back bay.

Once on the road, they walked side-by-side. A box dangling from each hand, Nathan listened to Cate relate the resolution of Prudence's situation.

"How in bloody hell did you come up with that," he blared.

"I don't know. It just came to me."

He snorted and shook his head, wincing with the movement. "That plan has more holes in it than a fish net. And people say I'm daft."

The starlight limning his profile, she told him of Prudence's dalliances in Boston, and her father's decision to send her away.

"Why that little trollop," he said in grudging awe.

"I was thinking something considerably less kind."

"I dare say," he said, smiling tolerantly. "You curse better than a street whore."

"I suppose I should take that as a compliment?"

"In every sense of the word, darling," he said, with all sincerity. "That scheming, devious, conniving little..."

He chuckled wryly. "Blessed pity, that. I was enjoying the prospect of the misery she would cause His Bumptiousness."

Cate saw him wince as he shook his head. "Head hurt?"

"A bit. It would seem the Commodore's elbow is a mite more accurate than previously credited."

Nathan protested—more for form, she thought—but finally halted to submit to her attentions. Plucking away the lingering feathers, she probed his head and under the scarf. His scalp was wet, but it felt more like sweat than blood's stickiness.

"It's difficult to see in the dark, but it doesn't seem anything serious," she said.

The night closed in. The way was narrow and they occasionally bumped shoulders. It was remarkably warm and still for such an hour, the air like heavy velvet. Moths, some the size of small birds, hung motionless, as if suspended. Nathan had a *cantus firmus* of his own amid the nocturnal choristers of night creatures. The crunch of his boots, the creak of leather belts, the slap of his sword against his leg, and the swish of bells made a kind of music — his music, the soft rasp of his breathing adding a counterpoint.

"You owe me a 'thank you', by the way," he threw into the silence.

"For what?"

"Did you not notice? I told Princess What's-Her-Name she was pretty, just like you asked." He nodded primly.

"Yes, I noticed, and I'm proud of you. I could see she was much the better for it." She felt rather like a mother praising a child and should be patting him on the head.

"I live to serve." His attempt at a grandiose bow was hindered by his burden.

It was nearly impossible to not notice Nathan's increasing uneasiness, like a pot building up to boil. Several times, he drew a breath as if to say something, and then abruptly chose not.

"God's blood and wounds, I can't bear another minute," he burst out, drawing to a halt. "What did I do? I'm not so thick-pated as I couldn't tell I was being blamed for something. What did I do?"

"Nothing." She turned and continued on.

"No, no, no!" Striding to catch up, he pried a finger from a box handle to waggle it at her. "Don't try to pull one over on Ol' Nathan. What did I do?"

"Nothing." She clamped her lower lip between her teeth as eyes fixed straight ahead. "I thought you did something — they thought you did something — but you didn't, just like I thought."

A faint flash of gold and white showed his relieved smile. "That's good!"

His pace slowed as the smile faded. "What had I done?"

"Nothing. That's just it, nothing."

She whirled around with a suddenness that made him skid to a stop to avoid a collision. "Just as always: nothing! Isn't it?" she fumed.

He fell back a step in the face of her vehemence. "I'm being cursed for doing nothing?"

"You damned right!" Spinning around, she struck off, agitation quickening her pace.

"And, if I had done… something?" he called.

"Anything!" she shouted.

Nathan jogged to catch up and fell into step next to her. "I see," he finally said, straining to pick through her logic. "And, if I had done anything, you'd be the happier?"

"Something would have been better than nothing," Cate said tartly.

"There's an eloquently informative statement." He paused to sweep a mocking bow as if the forest was his audience. "Pray, I beg you not to hesitate but allow me the joy of knowing how I can be of greater service. If there's anything — something — *nothing* I can do, I am forever at your leisure."

"I'd be happier than I am now."

"With nothing. Bloody hell!"

Grumbling darkly under his breath, he stopped again. "All right, let's have it!" he called after her. "C'mon, something's vexing you. Let's have it!"

Scuffing to a halt, Cate stared ahead. Her legs ached, for she had been pounding the ground with every step, since they had passed through Lady Bart's gate. She had been trying to make the best of the evening — on the surface, everything had been a success — but had failed miserably.

"Very well," she said, turning back around. "Do you *really* want to hear it?"

His shirt a ghostly glow in the dark, he extended his laden arms to his sides, as if to offer a target. "Either that or I'll be doomed to spend the rest of me days in mystery of when it finally *will* come out."

A part of her screamed for her to desist, to leave it lie. Another part, larger and more boisterous, irked and angered, frayed by weeks of containment, urged her to let fly.

"You kissed every woman in that room tonight," she began, her throat tightening.

"I did." His pride faltered at the sight of her stalking toward him. "At your bidding, I might add."

"I only desired you to give Prudence a little peck on the cheek."

"Then you should have given me your peck signal, because all I got was the go-ahead-and-do-something," he shot back, eyes bulging in defiance.

The internal voice of ration screamed for her to stop.

On many occasions she had listened, but not now. A knot of impending tears grew behind her eyes; she vowed not to give him the satisfaction of seeing her cry.

"Jesus to god, woman, out with it!" he growled.

"You kissed every woman in that room tonight, except me." She gulped down a lump. "You kissed all of them, except me! Why not me?" She pounded her chest with her fist. "Am I so distasteful to you?"

With no ready answer, Nathan looked to the ground, and then away. "I was taking you with me."

"For, what?" as Cate chocked on each word.

He winced at his hollow answer being recognized for what it was.

Squarely before him now, her voice quavered dangerously. "You kissed Prudence. You kissed Sally—God knows what else you did to that poor woman! Hell, you even kissed Nanna's and Lady Bart's hand! But not me. Why...?"

The moonlight caught the glitter of resentment and accusation in his slitted eyes. Regretting having said anything, she retreated in the face of what looked to be a storm fit to erupt. Instead, he lurched forward and kissed her, firm, but quick on the mouth.

"There!"

If shock had been his intention, he had been triumphant.

He stood back. His chest heaved, rising and falling as if he was fighting someone, or something, like a long torment.

"Oh, bloody hell!" He flung the boxes aside and swept her into his arms.

Knowing he was going to kiss her was one thing. The ferocity with which he took her was something else, driving her back, until she came up against a tree and then held her there.

"Damn!" He drew a shaky breath. "I knew this would happen; I knew if I started, I could never stop."

He kissed her again, forcing her mouth open under his, hungry and demanding. A thrill verging on giddiness raced through her. The scrape of the tree at her back brought back visions of another night, but this was nowhere near the same. Her head whirled in disbelief, fearing it another of his fooleries.

He braced his forehead against hers, his voice hoarse with yearning. "Mother of Heaven, I've waited a long time to do that, since the day we pulled you from the water."

"But why...? Why so long?" she gasped, breathless.

His mouth moved wordlessly. Ultimately, he shrugged. "I was a damned cod-livered coward. God curse me sorry bones, I was afraid you'd laugh, afraid you'd leave."

"I'd never—"

He choked a mirthless laugh. His body still hard against her, the walnut eyes were but inches from hers. "Aye, but you almost did. The only thing what kept me from locking you up was the fear you'd jump the moment you were free."

He touched his lips to where her neck and shoulder met, and she shivered. "Just there," he breathed. "I've wanted to put me mouth just there and taste you."

And so, he did, a warm path from shoulder to neck, lingering at the tender skin underneath her jaw. He sucked gently on her earlobe, and flicked it with his tongue, her breath coming shorter yet. She slid a hand into the opening of his shirt and felt his skin ripple at her touch.

His body against hers strained with need and they tore furtively at each other's clothes. His hand found its way under her skirt to her bare leg. The heat of his palm followed the curve of her thigh and cupped her bottom. His knee insinuated itself between hers and he lifted her higher. Her feet no longer touching the ground, she hooked a leg around his hip. His fingers searched deeper, and she made a small almost animal sound when he found the slipperiness between her legs.

He broke off with a ragged gasp and braced his head on the trunk. "It's not right. You don't deserve me coming at you like a rutting boar."

"It doesn't—"

He turned his head enough to peer at her from the corner of his eye, and his voice softened. "Not here. Not this way. I want a bed, a place where I can serve you properly and not have to worry about Harte looking over me shoulder."

Nathan lowered Cate to the ground and, with considerable effort, withdrew his hand. He tipped her face up and kissed her again, eloquent with tenderness. The bristle of his mustache brushed her lips as a final parting.

"Properly," he whispered.

A reminder to himself, a vow to her.

He smiled, one of devilment and charm.

Cate kissed the hollow of his throat. His skin was damp with exertion, his pulse racing against her lips. He bent to kiss her again, but stopped short. Arm curling protectively around her shoulders, his gaze averted skyward.

"What is it?" she asked, looking up.

His jaw twisted sideways as he scanned the diamond-glittered velvet. "I don't know. Just a feeling. Best we push off."

"Is there something wrong?" She stooped to retrieve the boxes from the ground.

"Don't know for sure and not desirin' to see."

He took the boxes and put his arm around her. The small gesture was suddenly so natural, and yet so intimate.

He took several steps and then stopped. Screwing his face, he shifted his weight and plucked delicately at the front of his breeches.

"The lads are in a bit of disarray."

⌘

The remainder of the walk was lost to her. It was entirely possible she had floated the rest of the way, for she didn't recall her feet touching the ground. She was buoyant on a flood of emotions: joy, disbelief, elation. They tumbled past, too quick and too many to name. Besides, to do so only threatened to dampen them. With the heat of his hand still on her thigh, she played the scene over again and again in her head. If she could etch every detail to memory, then she could prove to herself that it hadn't been a dream.

How? Why? When? What? But then...?

Questions bobbed to the surface like apples in a barrel, and yet none could she seize upon with enough surety to respond.

Nathan moved next to her as if nothing was different. His face was too obscured by the night, and therefore of no guidance as to what he might have been thinking.

"...from the first..."

A part of her was furious with him for waiting so long, and yet she flogged herself with the regret of having been so blind.

He must have felt her looking, for there was the flash of ivory and gold of a smile, and she was sure he winked.

Pryce waited at the longboat, Maori and Chin resting on the oars. He gave them a long, significant look, seeming to know what had transpired. There was no disapproval, however. If anything, Cate thought she caught a glimmer of relief on the stern countenance.

"'Pears there be foul weather a-brewin'," the first mate said, casting an eye skyward.

"Aching bunions saying tomorrow next, eh?" Nathan said as he handed Cate to a thwart. A blur of brilliant blue soaring toward the ship caught his eye. "It would appear Beatrice knows it, as well."

"Aye, I've yet to see that blessed bird stray when there be a blow a-comin'. Artemis 'tis not moved the night, neither."

Following their gazes, Cate saw only night-shadowed trees, ink sky and the bay's glittering gunmetal surface. The *Morganse's* silhouette laid low against the island, her masts and spars merging with the jagged treeline. Lamps doused and sails aback, she sat like a panther coiled to spring. The two mariners stood in the boat elbow to elbow, gazing up with the wisdom which came only with a lifetime at sea.

Nathan closed his eyes and lifted his face into the freshening breeze. "We'll haul anchor at the ready."

Pryce pursed his mouth and said as they pushed off, "T'will be a dicey passage to make in the dark."

"And no easier for the waiting. At the ready, Master Pryce."

Unable to disagree, Pryce signaled the oarsmen aweigh.

❧

Conversation as they pulled across to the *Morganse* was kept to low-voiced murmurs, voices being so readily augmented by the night-glassed water.

Cate sat on the thwart next to Nathan. Pryce eyed the two of them knowingly. By some strange intuition, every hand in the boat peered at them with the same look.

Is there a damned sign on my forehead?

Feeling the weight of everyone's stare, Cate and Nathan avoided looking at each other like two north ends of a compass. While Nathan and Pryce made low-voiced plans of what was to be done once aboard, Nathan's hand crept under the cover of darkness and her skirt, seeking hers. As he directed Pryce on men and sails, his fingers brushed the dip and curve of her knuckles, and then curved in a two-fingered grasp over her hand as he gave Pryce a heading.

Darkness and damp-slickened steps made scaling the ship's side a treacherous proposition, even with Nathan guiding from behind. Cate had barely managed halfway up when two stout arms reached down to lift her up over the gunwale. As she was lightly set down on deck, she was struck with an overwhelming sense.

Home.

Something longed for, now found.

Silence was the order, stealth an utmost necessity, the urgency to make weigh sharp in the air. With no more than a gesture or nod from their superiors, the men were but dark blobs against a darker deck as they moved in a silent ballet to set sail. The flat line of the topsails and jibs bellied as they filled, inching the ship into motion. The slap of bare feet, creak of rigging, and the *Morganse's* sigh of relief to be off.

Nathan steered Cate through the scurrying crewmen to the Great Cabin. The moon was visible through the stern windows.

603

Now no more than a glow behind the island's curved back, the silver beams streaming through the glass barely reached the table. Nathan deposited the sewing boxes on the table. Glancing outdoors, he steered Cate backwards, out of the way of prying eyes, and kissed her there. He held her loosely, his lips barely brushing hers, intending a reserved parting. His resolve quickly dissolved and he grew more ardent. His arms tightened holding her closer and his mouth more demanding. She pressed her hips against his, offering, asking. A trunk pressed against the backs of her legs; he could take her there. There was plenty of room, and it wouldn't take long. She was ready, moist and full, and he was already rigid against her leg. A flick of the tongue or a touch of the fingers would be all it would require.

He broke away with a gasp. Bracing his forehead against the bulkhead, he closed his eyes and grimaced, as if waiting for a spasm to pass. He cut a sideways look, the corner of his eye pinched with a combination of regret and curiosity.

"Siren." He smiled, sly and crooked. "Always believed them to be naught but fantasies, but me thinks I've found one."

Groaning at the loss of what might have been, he pushed upright. He hesitated, making a visible effort to collect himself, and then bent to kiss her again.

"They do say duty is a heartless master," he said into her hair. "I had plans of things much greater, but I've reefs to clear and a commodore to evade."

"I'm not going anywhere."

He made a sarcastic noise in the back of his throat. "Bloody damned near did, twice, no three times. You've no idea how near I came to locking you up."

With considerable effort, he held her away at arm's length, and said, "Properly."

A pledge reiterated to himself, a vow to her.

"I could be a while." He winced at the prospect and allowed her to see his longing. "It 'tis a wonder how a moment can pose as an eternity."

⁓∽∾)(∾∿⁓

Weak-kneed, Cate sat heavily on the trunk and watched him go out and disappear into the darkness. She waited for her heart to steady and a lucid thought to return.

"I could be a while."

She took a tiny bit of skin at the back of her hand between her thumb and forefinger and pinched until she was on the verge of breaking the skin. She cautiously looked around, waiting.

Nothing had changed. The tingle of Nathan's mouth was still on her lips, the taste of him still on her tongue. It wasn't a dream.

The weight of guilt kept her seated, guilt for having made him suffer, for making herself suffer. The mind reeled at the joys which had been missed. And yet, how could she have known? She harbored a deeper appreciation of his powers of deflection, of how thick that mask of his had been.

At last, she rose. Her first steps a bit unsteady, she found her way through the room's deep shadowed to the galley steps and went down to procure a ewer of hot water from Mr. Kirkland.

Once back in the sleeping quarters, she filled the basin. Prudence had used the last bit of soap, and so for a bit of fragrance, she sprinkled a pinch of dried lavender from her blood box atop the steaming surface. Bathing was a ritual performed most every night, but this time it was done with exacting care, the hot water echoing the paths Nathan's hands had traced. She fumbled with the sponge, dropping it several times, her chest tightening until breathing was no longer a natural thing. She chided herself for being as nervous as she had been on her wedding night.

No, not Brian… not now… not ever.

She couldn't think about him now. He was gone… and Nathan was there, so very there.

From overhead came the hurried stump of footsteps. The floor beneath her feet shifted as the *Morganse* began to move out of the bay. In the moonlessness, it would be a treacherous passage. By means of lead lines and her master at her helm, the ship felt her way through the shoals and reefs like a blind person in a narrow corridor.

When finished bathing, Cate slipped naked under the quilt, feeling as fresh as a nymph. She was seized by the fear of appearing a little too eager and jumped up to snatch her shift from the stool. Slipping it on, she tied the bow at the front with extra precision, and then settled in bed once more.

It wasn't long before the ship leaned on a larboard tack. Cate shifted with well-practiced ease to wedge herself more comfortably. The *Morganse* was sailing hard, her urgency felt through the thrum of her rigging and rush of the water sliding past the hull. With Harte and his warships standing in at Hopetown, pursuit was a real threat. It was difficult to erase the image of the *Resolute* at the Straits, in all her eighty-gun glory. Cate regretted not having fully appreciated the risk under which she had placed not only Nathan, but the *Morganse* and her people, when she had pleaded for help for Prudence. Granted, Nathan had grumbled and chaffed, but with no more ire than if she had asked him to pass the salt. There had been no remonstration, nor recrimination from anyone, but then no one had been injured... yet.

She was familiar enough now to know the difference between the clamor of sailing and that which rose from eminent danger. Pryce and Hodder's bellows and the fainter hails from the fo'c'stle and topsmen all indicated they were in the clear. Nathan's destroyed voice couldn't begin to equal that of the First Mate or Boatswains, but authority compensated where volume failed. The only thing now to be heard was the all-encompassing desire to put as much sea to the ship's stern as possible.

The deck prism as her light, she lay in its ethereal greenish glow with nothing more to do than to think.

He wanted her!

The shock was as strong then as it had been on that dark road. Touching her fingers to her lips, she could still taste his kiss, and feel the press of his body against hers, urgent and needing... Yes, so very, very in need.

He wanted her... but Nathan couldn't possibly burn for her the same way as she did for him. It would mean he had suffered the same ache and need that coiled like a serpent in her belly and constricted to the point of verging on pain. It would mean he had woken in the night panting and writhing with avidity, and then walking the decks, for nothing else would appease the cries of the flesh.

It was a wonder how two people could have lived in such parallel worlds of desire and denial. She regretted for having been so blind, for having made him suffer—both suffer for that matter. A steadier thought pointed out it hadn't wholly been her fault: The King of Arcane had ruled his realm in convincing fashion.

With nothing but time, she reexamined every moment with Nathan, from the first day, when she stood dripping in the cabin, until just a few hours ago, trying to glean out the oh-so-very-subtle hints which only hindsight could illuminate. So many questions were answered, and yet from each answer rose another question.

Gradually, her racing heart slowed. Breathless anticipation eased into tempered impatience, which faded into uncertainty as the watch bell clanged its increments of time.

One hour... two... three...

"I could be a while..."

❧❧❧

Cate woke sometime later, with no way of knowing the time. To her, time was relative on a ship. Granted, the grains of sand in the glass perpetually sifted away, but there were four sizes. Beyond their increments of half minute, half-hour, hour and four hour they were of little guidance. The watch bell clanged with meticulous regularity, but the intervals tended to blur together, their intricacies lost.

As best she had been able to gather during her sojourn at sea, albeit brief, at any given time the bell rang there were five options. Six clangs of the bell could mean it was either three, seven or eleven in the morning, or three or eleven in the evening. She prided herself on her intelligence and quickness of mind, but the entire concept she found staggering.

With a finite amount of patience, Nathan attempted several times to explain. Suffice to say, the sessions never went well.

"Why can't you just ring it like any other clock?" she had argued testily.

The questioning of such a time-honored tradition caused him to puff with indignation. "It's not a bloody parlor clock."

"But it's still a clock. If it's five, why not just ring five? If it's nine, why not ring nine?"

"That makes no sense a'tall! You can't have the goddamned, ruddy thing banging away. The crew would be deaf by the end of their watch, besides not a soul having a wink of sleep."

"So, those four bells just now, meant it's...?"

"End of the dog watch," he said with a narrow look.

Cate closed her eyes, summoning patience. Sorting out the watches was even more elusive. She was yet to comprehend why the First Watch began at eight o'clock at night. "Which means...?"

He frowned as if she were dim-witted. "Six o'clock."

"Morning or night?"

"Bloody hell!" He threw his hands up as he bolted from his chair. "Any slab-sided, dutch-built fool can look up and see if 'tis day or night. Besides the fact there's no dog watch at six in the morning. Honestly, darling, I'm worried for you. A simple cabin boy can grasp it! Hell, even Hermione knows it!"

Shaking his head, he had walked away.

Consequently, Cate resorted to her own concept of time: Either it was day or night, early morning or late morning, noonish, early afternoon, late afternoon, early evening, or night. Sometimes, night could be divided into late and really late, but such distinction was rarely significant.

However, at that moment, it felt very late.

"I could be a while."

She sat up and flung back the quilt, the chill of the night air cutting through her worn shift. A sliver of light slipped under the curtain. True enough, it meant someone was in the salon, but it also meant it was okay for the light to be lit, the threat of the ship pursuit was past. Aboard a pirate ship, the captain's cabin was considered public domain, his table open to anyone who cared to dine. It was a privilege rarely exercised, but the possibility was always there. Pryce, Hodder, Kirkland, Millbridge or a number of others could be in the cabin on some manner of business. In any case, she wrapped the quilt around her before going out.

Nathan sat in the relative quiet of the ambient voice of his ship. A small collection of candles in battered holders sat on the table in a molten glow. Slouched in his chair, his bare feet were crossed on the table. His head tilted back, he stared at the beams overhead, the scar at his throat a shadowy slash. She was nearly to the table before he heard her. He jerked up, his bells jangling softly, and blinked.

"'ello, luv."

His speech was thickened, either from sleep or lack thereof. As he sat up and a bottle he held came into view. He made preparations to stand then decided against it. Instead, he hooked a chair with his foot and slid it closer, then gestured for her to sit.

"Did I wake you, darling? I'm sorry; I thought I was being quiet." It was uttered with marginal sincerity, the candlelight flashing on the gold of his teeth as he bared them ever so slightly at the end.

Cate busied with arranging the blanket in the chair around her, not from modesty, but as an excuse to avoid meeting his gaze. "No, I just woke."

It was only a small lie. A twitch of a dark brow revealed he recognized it as such.

An awkward silence filled the space. Nathan struck a blank gaze at the table. His straight-nosed profile sharp in the candlelight, he was deep within himself. There was an unfamiliar slump about the usually square-set shoulders and a mood which she couldn't identify. A gap loomed between them, now more vast than her first day aboard, when she had sat in that very chair. She propped her head in her hand and wondered.

"I could be a while."

And, indeed, he had been a while. She had waited... and waited, but apparently, not long enough. Sometime in the darkness, she had fallen asleep. In hindsight, perhaps the lavender hadn't been a wise choice. Ordinarily administered to ease headaches and minor pain, it might have had a more sedative power than credited.

Had he come back—or not? It was a question she couldn't bring herself to ask; there were no good answers. When they parted, he had shown every intention of coming to her, but did he? Or had second thoughts prevailed? In typical Nathan-fashion, was he hoping the situation would go away, forgotten? She found herself faced with the choice of where to put her faith: with six weeks of past behavior, or a flash of passion?

Nathan took a swig from the bottle, and then looked up, as if he had forgotten she was there.

"Have a nip?" He made a feeble attempt at one of those smiles intended to charm.

Cate took the proffered bottle. The rim glistened from where he had just drunk, and she made a point of turning it in order to use that same space. She winced when the raw liquor touched her throat. As she passed the bottle back, their fingers brushed, his seeming to reach for hers. It was ever so brief, but enough to make her heart jump.

"Is there a... problem?" she finally threw into the silence. It was woefully inadequate, but inane was better than the waiting.

Nathan stared at the bottle as he pensively rolled it between his palms. A smile slowly grew as if at a private joke. He looked up with an intensity that made her breath catch.

"I'm gathering courage, luv," he said so very quietly, inordinately so. "The courage to take something."

Cate was struck a bit odd. He was a pirate; rarely did she consider them to suffer the burden of restraint on taking anything they desired.

She had learned it was often necessary to be patient when trying to follow Nathan's train of thought. Often perplexing at first, he had a tendency to make sense... usually.

"Do you know what it is to want something?" he began conversationally, his gaze fixed on the bottle. "'Tis right before you, within your grasp, and yet so far from reach it might as well have been on the rings of Saturn." He ended with a skyward flair of fingers.

"It's not anything you'd considered too fancy or seek," he said without waiting for her answer. "And yet, you know from the first that it is something for which you have searched all of your days."

He stared at her with great intent as if waiting for an answer to a question unasked. Bottle in hand, he rose with startling abruptness to prowl the room like a great cat.

"And then you realize," he said, "'tis something not to be yours a'tall. Meant for another, a treasure never intended to be shared. 'Tis unworthy you are, the Fates whisper."

He drew up before the window. He leaned his arm against the frame and cocked a hip. A breeze lifted the tails of his scarf and coiled them about his shoulders. He gazed at a sea glittered with gunmetal and silver.

"But then you find yourself thinking, 'Just once,'" he said softly to the night. "Not forever, for that would be too grand. But just once, if you were to reach out and take it, and be damned the consequences."

"What led you to believe this... something wasn't—?" she began.

"'Tis the treasure of another," he sighed over his shoulder in utter defeat. "Once claimed is twice possessed."

Nathan resumed pacing. As he moved on a feral path in and out of the shadows, Cate noticed his bare feet once more. The candlelight caught the gleam of freshly shaven cheeks and glistened on droplets of water in his beard and chest hair. She surveyed the room with a new eye. His coat and sash were flung over a chair in the corner, his hat and belts tossed on the table. Boots and socks laid scattered across the floor. Under closer observation, they formed a loose trail toward the curtain.

Yes, he had come back.

She recalled awakening at one point. No one had been there, the movement of the curtain assumed to be from the motion of the ship.

Yes, he had come back. He had kept his word and she...

Cate braced her head in her hand. The regret which sickened her just then had to have paled in comparison to Nathan's abject disappointment. There was no gracious way of saying someone's arrival hadn't been sufficiently exciting to keep one awake. To many a man it would be an insult, a deep unforgivable affront.

What he was about, however, was no longer a mystery. He was afraid to ask the same awkward, humiliating question which she couldn't bring herself to pose.

"But what if...?" Cate gulped, words not being where she had expected. "I mean, what if the Fates were to, umm... change their minds?"

Nathan paused in mid-step and looked off to consider, his jaw twisted thoughtfully to the side. "Only a cuckle-headed dolt would think it possible," he said, and then added with a wistful smile, "But if I was that fortunate cove, I'd treasure it, cherish it as no other has or could."

She shifted self-consciously and wiped her suddenly damp palms on the quilt.

"What if you find you've misjudged, that this... something isn't all—?" she asked. Anticipation could be a lethal enemy, meeting expectations a daunting prospect. It was no secret that he was far more practiced than she in the art of lovemaking. One man, in her whole life, compared to how many for him?

"Noo..." Nathan said gravely. It was uttered so softly she could barely hear it over the tinkle of his bells. "Not possible. I've observed this something for a time, now. So much, so remarkable..."

His mouth moved wordlessly, and he finally surrendered. "Nay. Dreams are fulfilled in so very many ways."

A glowing rush surged up to her face and other parts below. "Once, then, is all you'd desire of this... something?" The hoarseness of her voice wasn't completely a result of the rum.

Nathan made a scornful noise. "Hardly. A lifetime wouldn't allow for what could be."

He flopped in the chair and sighed, dejected. "But, if it came to pass the once 'tis all I was allowed..." His head fell back against the chair, and he looked again to the smoke-darkened beams. "Then, I would have the once, and would be obliged to find a way to live with that."

Too restless to sit, he rose again to stand at the window.

"If you've wanted this something, why haven't you taken it before now?" Cate asked.

He turned to her with a look which turned her spine to water. Boring into her with an avidity-sparked cinnamon and amber gaze, he knew better than anyone of how to hide his thoughts, but he hid nothing now.

Nathan's voice dropped to a throaty purr. "T'was not mine to have. To take it could be to lose it, and then... " He looked away, his shoulders moving under his shirt finishing the thought.

Cate drew a deep breath. A kindred spirit had been mirrored in those eyes, one who had suffered and burned the same as she, desire and longing that neither had words for.

Words, however, had served them poorly.

Cate rose and walked purposefully to the doors. She swung them closed, the sound of the bolt sliding home punctuating an end to conversation. As she came back across the room, she allowed the quilt to slip from her shoulders, and halted as near to him as possible without touching. A breeze wafted through the cabin. Clad only in her shift, she shivered, but not from a chill.

She plucked the bottle from Nathan's hand. "Just how much of that rum have you had?"

He lowered his lids. The heavy lashes fanning dark crescent over his cheeks, he looked up through them and smiled crookedly. "Not much."

Cate set the bottle on the table and then pressed her body against his. "Then you're not so drunk, are you?"

"No." His breath stirred her hair.

"Good, because I want to show this fortunate cove something."

She plucked a taper from the table and put out her hand. As she led him toward the curtain, he reached to retrieve his baldric and pistol, and shrugged self-consciously. She nodded in mute acknowledgment of the facts of his world: above all else, one must always be on guard.

From the time she took his hand, until she put the candle into the wall sconce by the bunk, her mind was flooded with a myriad of reasons as to why she should stop. Instead, she turned into his arms and allowed his kiss—so fervent it arched her backwards—to erase them all. She thrilled as her hands splayed across his back, tracking the cords of muscle taut over bone. A stronger thrill rolled through her at the brass hardness against her leg.

"I have to warn you," she said. "I haven't done this in a very long time."

"Well, 'tis not something readily forgotten," he said dryly.

"It's been five years." She spoke with some effort as his tongue flicked her earlobe.

Nathan drew back, scowling as if he thought surely he had misunderstood. "Five years?"

"Nearly six, now." She took the brief interlude to catch her breath. It had been nearly six since she and Brian had…

No, not now. Go away!

"Five years." He angled his head and viewed her as if she was a new variety of animal. Then he straightened, ready for the challenge. "Five years. Aye, well, as I recollect, not much has changed."

He kissed her again, his braids pattering a provocative dance on her chest. "Damn, you taste good."

Nathan had his own taste: rum—strong enough to make her light-headed—musk and desire, and she drank deeply.

They undressed each other with hands that occasionally shook and fingers that fumbled. Buttons suddenly became inordinately slick, ties unmanageable. Her hand hovered at the ribbon at the neck of her shift, and she bit her lip, embarrassment heating her cheeks.

"I can't. I'm scared," she said.

"Of what?"

"You." What if it had been too long? Was it possible for the body to forget? At the moment, it didn't seem possible, but the doubt lurked.

"Me?" His disbelief dissolved, and his brows drew together. "You know I'll never hurt you."

She tried to smile, but his image blurred.

Dammit! Not tears! Not now!

She laughed mirthlessly. "No, not that way. I'm nervous as all hell, but it's because you're more... experienced."

He flushed under his tan and looked away. "Don't worry luv," he mused. "We'll move easy. If there's any part you don't recall, just let me know."

"But there's..." Her hand went reflexively to her stomach.

"Your scars?" Arching an admonishing brow, Nathan gently took her by the wrists, turned them up and kissed the inside of each one, the bristle of his mustache tickling the delicate skin. "We all carry them. You forget: I've seen them."

"But I didn't see you see them; there's a difference."

He smiled tolerantly. "And so, you shall see mine, or blow out the candle. 'Tis your choice."

Cate saw and heard his hopefulness that she would not. They both wanted something more than a furtive anonymous tumble in the dark. He would take her, flaws and all, if she would do the same.

"But, I—"

Nathan cut off her objections with his lips, as reassuring as nothing else could.

"Now then..." His eyes held hers as he pulled the ribbon free. On shaky legs, she stood transfixed on his gaze as he nudged the garment from her shoulders and it fell into a puddle at her feet. She observed him keenly for the first sign of recoil or disgust, but found nothing. His fingers dancing an air ballet around her, his eyes glistened as he took her in.

"My God." His throat moved when he gulped. He shook his head in wonderment. "You're more beautiful... How could I have ever...?"

He pressed his lips to her cheek, neck and collarbone, while at the same time sank to his knees before her. Cupping her breast, pale against his tanned hand. Lying heavy and taut in his palm, he took it deep against his tongue. She cradled his head in her arms as one would a child. Sinking lower, his lips tracing a moth wing's path over the slope of her belly, holding her by the hips to steady her when she flinched or shied. As he followed each scar, from the heaviest to the most thread-like, she could see in her mind's eye the angle and curve of each one.

Cate closed her eyes. She grew more light-headed, the room beginning to spin. She clung to him, her anchor, afraid if she were to let go he would be lost to her forever. It had been so long since she had felt the sensations which now coursed through her. Sequestered for years, the body recalled all too well the yearning, the deep-seated aching need.

At last, Nathan rose to his feet. "There now," he said, as one would soothe a child.

"Now you," Cate said, tugging at his shirttails.

Nathan took a half step back, slipped his shirt over his head, tossed it to the floor and spread his arms in display. Dark and wild, a blur of tattoos and scars, he glowed, bronze fading to ivory. The candlelight played patterns across his body, shadows defining the deep cut of bone and muscle. It was obvious he wanted her badly... very badly.

He lifted her to the bunk and lowered over her. "Don't worry. I shan't risk burdening you with a child."

He kissed her once more, this one a thorough exploration of her deepest crevices, his tongue darting, taunting and teasing.

"Show me, Kitty," he whispered. "Touch me as you would have me touch you. Use me as your chart. Give me your course."

The ship's ambient chorus of sail, rigging and plank faded. Their eyes held each other's as they played a languid game of show and tell: seeking and exploring, discovering and learning.

"Touch me here," she said, curving her hands along the spring of his ribs. And so, he did, gooseflesh following in the path of the softly callused fingers.

"And here."

Nathan's breath caught and he trembled when she touched his nipple. It came up hard, as hers rose against his palm, begging to be suckled once more.

As she directed, he followed, echoing her every move. Her fingers teasing his stiffened length were answered by beguiling fingers, which found her slippery cleft. A fingertip at the tip of his cock delicately guided him further. When her eyes closed in ultimate surrender, he chuckled softly, and then slid down. Cradling her hips in his hands, he re-traced his exploratory route, re-discovering with lips what fingers had already known. She curved her fingers into the raven hair, and guided him, until she could hold on no more.

He kissed the inside of her thigh, his breath warm on the tender skin. "When you ready, luv, and not a moment before."

Cate surprised him when she pushed him back and rose over him to track similar journeys: over the curve of his ribs, his skin rippling in response; down to the jut of his hip and the deep grove of his groin. She tasted the salty dampness at the hollow of his throat, felt the hard nub of his nipple, and smelled the deep musk of the heavy thatch between his legs.

"Succubus," Nathan hissed and pulled her to him. Crushing her mouth with his, he rolled above her.

Encircling his cock, she gave him a few more strokes and then guided him home. He gave a solid thrust and staggered with relief in her arms. She flinched, her tender flesh contracting at the invasion and he tried to pull away.

"Nathan, no, please..." Her hand at his back held him in place.

"But, I..."

"No. Please."

His body trembled with the strain of giving her time to adjust, unable to move, unable to breathe. A flex of her hips her assent, he plunged to the root. He held so very still, allowing her to set the pace. She had the impression he would have never moved had she not seized his hips and goaded him on. She discovered years of denial weren't as ready to be relieved as one might think. What had seemed so simple and imminent became an elusive taunt, teetering so very near, only to fall away, a dam impregnable. She bucked under him, urging, begging, demanding. Pain and pleasure ricocheted against each other, until they became a new glorious goal: to suffer one was to gain the other.

Her consciousness spiraled down to the point of their joining. Clawing at his flanks, she smothered her cries into his shoulder. Giving over to his own need, Nathan settled with new purpose, driving harder and faster. The pounding became a fleshy rhythm, each thrust felt to her womb.

He sought to withdraw, but her hand at his back stopped him. His final shuddering gasp was lost as her finish came in a flood of long racking spasms, one overlapping the next as she crashed against him.

Forehead buried in the pillow next to her head, Nathan limply lay on top of her. His pulse echoed through their joining, and their hearts settled into a unified beat.

Yes, the body does remember — and remembers very well, she thought, idly stroking his back.

Nathan's body began to quake and then the low rumble of a laugh finally erupted into the pillow. He pushed up, rolled his eyes back and fell away. Spread-eagle across the bunk, his chest heaved as he strove to catch his breath. He raised an arm to wipe the sweat from the side of his face and then dropped as if it was too heavy to support.

He cut her a sideways look, started to speak, gulped and tried anew. "Are you always that way?"

The flush of their love-making drained into cold mortification.

Cate scrambled for the edge of the bunk. "I'm sorry! I told you it had been a while. I didn't mean to—"

"No! No!" He groped for her arm and pulled her back. "I meant, I have never been with anyone *ever* like that."

"I'm sorry." Embarrassment still heated her cheeks. "I was nervous; I'm not usually that... that... awkward."

Nathan lifted his head to peer down his nose at her. "Awkward?" His head dropped heavily back down and he drew several more ragged breaths. "For a moment there, I thought I shan't ever breathe again."

"Suffering Jesus!" he gasped, with a lop-sided grin. "You are something!"

Cate had never experienced it, but she had heard of men who, once their needs were fulfilled, rolled away and slept. It would not have been a surprise if Nathan had fallen into that category. Once again, he proved to be unique unto himself: he gathered her close, nestling her head into the curve of his shoulder. One leg wedged between his, she toyed with one of his braids, and listened to the rush of his breathing under her cheek. The deep thud of his heart gradually steadied to an easy rhythm. His fingers languidly tracing her outline from temple to hip and back, he periodically brushed a wisp of hair from her face or pressed his lips to the side of her head.

She closed her eyes and reveled in the joy of him near. She had never thought to have a man again. Perhaps she had been too dubious and impatient of Providence. Perhaps, given sufficient time, it would smile. She brushed all the mystery and questions of the last weeks aside and sighed in contentment.

He wanted her.

It felt so good to finally know...

So good to be with him...

So good to be...

She buried her face into his shoulder and began to silently quake.

"Here now, what's this? 'Tis not flattering to say I've driven a woman to tears."

"Nothing... It's..." Shaking her head, she rooted deeper.

"Did I...? Dammit!" His alarmed concern grew as he tried to see her face. "Did I hurt you? I didn't mean... I mean, I thought you would have—"

"No, no," she moaned, now too embarrassed to be seen.

Nathan burrowed his hand between them until her chin was

found. He brought her face up to his and she cut her eyes first one way, then another to avoid him. His persistence won out and she reluctantly settled on the coffee-colored orbs directly before her. Just inches away, she could see the thick row of double lashes, the candle, now so very near to guttering out, catching the cinnamon and gold flecks.

"It's nothing..." she sniffed, looking away.

"Well, aye, 'tis most definitely not 'nothing' I'll wager very likely something," he said dryly.

"It's just... It's just... It feels so good to be held..." The rest was lost in a thin squeak as her throat constricted.

Cate sobbed, the frustration of spoiling such a joyous moment only adding to her despair. Years of never being touched in anything other than the most perfunctory of ways: accosted, yanked, barricaded or mauled, she had been touched, but never held. She clutched him until her arms shook, while Nathan held her with the fervency of one hanging on to his life.

He lifted her face once more and dabbed her eyes with the corner of the quilt. "I know, luv. I know," he said, gravely. "More times than I care to think, I have paid a fair bit o' coin just for this."

He found her hand between them and squeezed it.

"To know you live." His voice shook with sincerity. "To know you're something more than some heap of flesh stalking about."

Sniffing, she hung her head and nodded.

Nathan kissed her on the forehead and then thumbed from her cheek a fugitive tear which squeezed out. "You're alive. Know that."

Chin wobbling dangerously, she nodded again, swiping at the tears glistening on the hair of his chest.

He resettled her against him and nestled her head under his chin. "And I'll skewer the next bloody damned scrub what says different."

She gave a half-choked laugh. Once more Nathan had worked his charms.

A sputtering *pop!* And a hiss marked the death of the candle. Now cloaked in darkness, Nathan continued to hold her. Rocking her ever so gently, he stroked her neck and arms, while a thumb brushed her ear.

"Hist, now. Shh, shh... Shh, shh, shh..." he whispered so lowly at times it almost sounded like the rush of water against the ship's hull.

Sharing the single pillow, they slept entangled and entwined. Sometime in the darkness, Nathan came to her again, tender but wanting. Cradling her in his arms as he proved to be the gentle and skilled lover she had suspected. At the end, they clung to each other and shook. In the foggy margins of sleep, they rolled together, fitting like spoons, his arm around her waist, his upturned palm cupping her breast—her surrender, his possession.

Sometime in the night, the bond was broken, ties snapped.

Adrift again.

26: PARLAY

CATE LAY QUIETLY IN THE bunk the next morning listening to the ship awake.

It was as many mornings: Pryce and Hodder bellowing the men from their hammocks; the smell of wood smoke and cooking—most significantly, coffee—rising from the galley; the distant growl of holystones working their way aft; and the low rumble of male conversation and laughter, subdued by the presence of their superiors, but jovial, nonetheless. The ship's momentum picked up with the shifting of the sails, the heavier daytime versions bent in place of the fly-by-nights, the song of water and rigging raising a full chord.

From the salon came the gusty *slurp!* of Hermione taking her morning tea, a sound so close to cloven-hoofed ecstasy as could be imagined. Millbridge's footsteps were interrupted by a colorful burst of cursing, a boot hitting a small furry body, and the high-pitched, puppy-like squeal of a rat.

"Goddamned varmint-eater slouchin' again!" cried the ancient voice.

One could only hope His Lordship possessed the wisdom to remain scarce.

Weighted by Nathan's seed still heavy in her womb, Cate idly watched a gecko scurry among the beams overhead.

It had been a long time.

She had never considered herself to be a woman who needed a man to justify her existence and had little understanding of those who suffered lack of purpose without one. On the other hand, it was a grand feeling to have one in her bed.

"Properly" indeed. Just the word, uttered in Nathan's husky graveled voice was enough to cause a warm flush.

She had been nervous, at first. Patient and gentle, Nathan had eased her out of her protective shell, across the chasm of unfamiliarity, and then coaxed her to take a leap of faith. Yes, there were pangs of guilt, whispers of betrayal to pledges made before an altar over a decade ago. It was imperative for her to move on. Nathan was an unexpected gift, literally a lifeline to a drowning soul; the Fates or Providence rarely provided such opportunities.

It had been a leap of faith into his arms. He had been there to catch her the night before, but could she count on him to be there again? Her hand drifted to the space next to her on the narrow bunk. Empty; he was already gone, his spicy sharpness lingering on the pillow, and the musk of their lovemaking his only trace.

Her afterglow spiraled quickly into the cold pit of reality, where it tangled in the muddled morass of the uncertainty of the last few weeks. There had been Nathan, the elusive and evasive; and Nathan, the teasing and mocking. Nathan, the sincere and passionate had been a fleeting phenomenon, to say the least. Which one was she to believe?

His numerous conquests being well-known, she was seized by a crawling sensation that she had just become the latest in his tally book. An achievement through the oldest trick: the You're-So-Special-I-Care-For-You-As-No-Other story. And she had fallen for it like an innocent maiden. It was easy to imagine the laughter overhead was him, exchanging smug glances and jests with the afterguard. She had been very young — fifteen or sixteen — the last time someone — a boy — wooed her with such nonsense. Seeing it then as the ruse it was, she had escaped unscathed.

Unscathed hardly described her now. Her lips were puffy and her breasts still tingled; Nathan had been very attentive there. Between her legs felt full and sensitive; he had been more than gentle, but five years had left her constricted. A flush of heat spread through those same softest tissues again at the thought of him in the candlelight, hovering over her, so dark and seductive.

What came even easier to the imagination was that it had all been an act, a ploy — a skill at which Nathan exceeded — aimed to attain what he needed: relief from a pair of aching balls. Wild versions of strange Pirate Codes raced through her mind, the crew being obliged to wait until the captain finished, and lines of men now forming just outside the curtain, awaiting their turn. Bizarre, true. Ridiculous, certainly. Ludicrous, probably. But self-doubts and second thoughts were powerful demons.

Brushing a strand of hair from her face, Cate felt the cool of metal brush her cheek. She held up her hand to see her wedding ring. That and her memories were all she had of Brian. She had taken vows, given herself to one man, just as he had given himself only to her. Her subsequent chastity had been a tribute to what they had shared. Now that was shattered.

Cate rolled onto her stomach and buried her face in her hands.

"What have you done?" she groaned aloud. "Stupid. Stupid!"

She heard a sound and raised up on her elbows to find Nathan standing at the curtain, a cup and coffee pot in one hand, and a plate of orange slices and scones in the other. Something flickered across the otherwise frozen expression, too brief to be identified.

"Joy of the morning," he chimed. He swaggered to the bed stand to set down his burdens. "I fancied you might desire a bit o' sustenance."

An inexplicable surge of modesty caused Cate to snatch the quilt up around her. As he poured coffee, she watched his hands, and reddened at the recollection of the marvels they had worked so very recently.

"I know how much you like this, first of a morning." He flashed a smile that ended far more quickly than usual. He met her gaze with difficulty as he handed her the cup.

She covertly watched him as she drank, wondering if he had heard her just moments ago.

Of course, he had. No secrets on a damned ship.

She thought of how appropriate a kiss might have been about then, but he showed no inclination. Her most recent line of thought grew in veracity.

"There's cinnamon in it," she said, if for no other reason than to break the strained silence.

"I recalled you liked it," Nathan said to the floor.

His lids hooding his eyes, it was impossible to know what was going on in that raven-colored head. It was doubtful anyone would ever be allowed that privilege. Someone so very, very special to be sure.

"Well, on to it, then." he declared abruptly. Pausing at the curtain, he ducked a stiff bow. "By your leave, m'lady."

And he was gone.

Cate closed her eyes and dropped her head back against the bulkhead with a hollow thud.

Well, that didn't go so badly, but it certainly didn't go well.

While she dressed, she tried not to look back at the scrambled bunk. Contrary to popular opinion—and her mother—there was a drawback in being virtuous: lack of experience, knowing how to conduct oneself after a night of surrendering said virtue.

She had but one such morning as her reference, and it barely equated: it had been her wedding night. Brian had greeted her with smothering kisses and... Well, they didn't rise, until they were so sore there was nothing else to do. Ah, but that night...!

What the hell were you expecting? she fumed as she fumbled to fasten her skirt. You're a big girl now — and damn you, don't you dare cry!

Exasperated, she halted from struggling with the elusive ties. She drew several deep breaths, loosened her shoulders and set to it once more.

One learns by observing a master. In her case that would be Nathan. Judging by him, blasé seemed to be the word of the day. Urbane, sophisticated or worldly were never her strengths. The damned French do it all the time, if she was to believe what she had frequently heard.

Dammit! Face it like a man, or at least this man, and ignore it. Wipe it away, like... like...

Cate angrily dashed at the wetness on her cheek. The thought of looking at herself in the mirror set the sip of coffee in her stomach into a nauseous swirl. She blindly jerked the brush through her hair, twisted up the sides and shoved in the combs. Snatching up the pot and cup, she drew a deep breath and went out.

The salon was empty, Hermione's empty dish still on the floor. Nathan had been there, as evidenced by a half-drank cup of coffee. The breakfast of oranges and scones sat untouched. Neither was there any of the telltale dribbles of honey from him having dipped his finger in the jar. Apparently, Nathan had no appetite. With no taste for food either, she refilled her cup.

Beatrice marked a brilliant dash of color amid the room's walnut walls. Perched atop a spice chest on the gallery sill, she paused in her preening to regard Cate. Well aware of the irascible creature's preference to not be crowded, Cate sat on the sill at a respectable distance. In a rustle of feathers, the parrot hopped down and crab-stepped closer, her interest focused on Cate's cup. She held it out for Beatrice to peer over the edge. Hackles rising in protest, Beatrice sidled away.

"I could have told you, but you always require to see for yourself," Cate said to the accusing look she was given.

Head canted somewhat, Beatrice appeared as apologetic as a bird might. Cate tentatively reached to stroke the hyacinth-colored chest. To her surprise, Beatrice allowed it.

Nathan's footsteps passed overhead. Through the open skylight came the sound of his good-natured railing with the afterguard.

Insufferable man!

"Hang the bastard," Beatrice croaked with her customary clarity.

Cate smiled faintly. "Not quite what I was thinking, but a good flogging might answer."

Shortly after, Nathan burst into the cabin. Amiably shouting back over his shoulder to someone outside, he came only so far as the desk near the doors. There he rummaged through several drawers, grunting in satisfaction at finding what he sought. With a curt nod in Cate's general direction, he left.

"Although a hanging might answer to put one of us out of our misery," Cate said in consideration as his voice faded down the deck.

"Plague and perish the maggot," said Beatrice.

"Have a care. You're beginning to sound like him."

Cate's humiliation bloomed in the wake of Nathan's most recent performance, the horror of her predicament multiplying to near paralyzing proportions. She was stuck: no escape, no options, and no reprieve in sight, a captive audience to Nathan's gloating, and gloat he certainly would. It brought her to seriously question her judgment and the long list of assumptions she had made—and yes, they were clearly assumptions, now in the glare of day.

"Where were you last night when I needed you?" she said accusingly to the sun.

There was no surprise. This was Nathan; no more need be said. Home had just turned into a floating Hell.

Cate looked with longing out the windows at the ship's wake, its V-shape stretching into infinity, and wondered where Thomas might be.

Not much later, Nathan reappeared, stern and mute. Cate was on the sill, now feeding Beatrice bits of orange from breakfast. Stopping at the table, Nathan kept his attention fixed on the cup as he filled, and then took a drink. Setting it down, his gaze drifted her way and darted back. Shortly, his eyes crept back, and for the next few minutes, she and Nathan played a silent game of eye tag: looking and dodging away, the silence punctuated by a random cough or clearing of the throat.

He can't even bring himself to look at me. Is this the 'what-have-I-done' phase?

There was the chance that he despised her now. As always, the man was lauded for his prowess, while the woman was scorned for failing to be virtuous. A more rational voice pointed out that the picture of Nathan she pieced together in those few glimpses was other than expected. He lacked the much-dreaded vaunt, the braggadocio of the conqueror. If anything, he was quite the opposite: reserved. She considered rearranging her countenance into something more benign, but dismissed it directly. Her edges were beginning to fray. He was a considerably better actor than she, and her resolve was withering quickly.

From the corner of her eye, Cate saw him square his shoulders and assume an overt casualness as he came toward her. She fixed her attention on the sill, wondering if she should flutter her lashes or throw the plate. His boots scuffed to a stop and two luminous eyes came around into her view.

"Silence can be a deafening thing, don't you think?" He smiled, thin-lipped and brief. "Somebody should say something, or we'll be obliged to start passing notes."

He shifted and cleared his throat several times. Beatrice's "Thrice-damned princock," startled him, apparently not having noticed her prior.

"Must she be here?" he asked.

"I'd say she has a reasonable grasp of the situation," Cate said, jerking her hand back to avoid a truculent clap of a beak.

He narrowed an eye, willing the creature to leave. Parrots could be quite stubborn. True to her heritage, Beatrice cocked her head in acute birdish angles to peer at him.

Opting to ignore Beatrice, Nathan tucked his hands into his belts, his arms working triumphantly at his sides. "Open and honest, that's me motto."

Cate nearly choked. Caught so off-guard, she lost every thought — that, quite possibly, his purpose.

Something was on his mind, however, obvious in the furrowing of his brow and severe erosion of his customary amiability. His mouth worked under his mustache, struggling with some inner debate. He frowned and shook his head as he dismissed one unsatisfactory thought after another. He prepared to speak then grimaced, changing his mind. After several more false starts, he clenched a fist and closed his eyes, looking much like a man commending himself to a firing squad.

"I require to know if... if... what we... when we...?" He gritted his teeth and forged on. "Pray tell if it was to be the once or... or no," he finally burst out.

Nathan inhaled sharply as if to suck it back in. Failing, he gathered himself and pressed on. "Tis not beyond me comprehension, if you were to invite me to your bed, just for the use of me."

He assumed an off-handedness — as false as ever witnessed — as he began to pace before her. "God knows, I've been in much the same sorts meself. More than once — oh, very well, many a time — I've felt the dire need of someone warm, only for the sake of the having."

"So, if, as you say, it's been a long time — a *very* long time." His eyes rounded, mystified yet by the extent of her celibacy, "I would be more than sympathetic of you wishing — needing — to have... a source of said warmth, so to speak, long enough, at any rate, to render the necessity no longer necessary."

His parody of affecting in-consequence might have been successful had it not been for the pained wince and a white-knuckled grasp on the butt of his pistol. There was another nagging contradiction: he had shaved. Even in the dim of the sleeping quarters, she had noticed his brightly gleaming cheeks. He had gone to the effort of making himself presentable.

"Pray tell, how many men do you fancy I've been with?" she asked, rising to her feet.

Nathan faltered and smiled tenuously. "You desire a number?" he asked, clearly hoping she would say "No".

She crossed her arms. "If you please."

He winced at what he obviously had not wanted to hear. He looked to the ceiling and floor, as if the answer might be found there. She knew she had put him in a no-win situation, for there was no good answer, and yet there was great joy in watching him squirm.

Fingers flickering, his mouth worked. "Maybe...?"

"One."

"One?" came out in a strangled wheeze, his mouth failing to close.

"If all I was looking for was a warm bed, I could have found that long ago." The backs of her eyes began to sting. "I saved myself for one man, and when he was gone, I saved myself again, only to discover that I'm no more than... than one more on a long list of conquests."

Head bent, he turned and took several pensive steps. Spinning around, he came back at her, stabbing an accusing finger at her. "So then, just what, exactly, were — I mean, are — you looking for?"

"I thought we were both looking for the same thing."

"As did I!" He stalked the room with a flurry of hands. "Until I heard you in there beating yourself in the head for it, fool that I was. But don't mind what I say: I'm known to be a little balmy! Balmy Nathan, that's me, and getting balmier by the minute!"

"So, fill me full of lies, get me in bed, and then plead insanity? What's next, Captain, throw me to the crew?"

He stormed toward her, driving her back several steps. His

eyes narrowed menacingly. "Mayhap you shan't be so fortunate. I fancy keeping you here, torture you with me presence."

Cate choked back a number of retorts. She turned her back as the tears of self-loathing began to well.

"I can't believe I was so stupid, and so gullible!" She dropped her forehead in her hand with a soft smacking sound. "A few sweet words and I melt like a maid."

"Go ahead, beat yourself in the head some more! You seem *so* much the better for it!"

"It must have been a bare challenge: tell her what you think she wants to hear and she'll melt."

"I thought you *did* want to hear it."

"Fool that I was, I couldn't wait to hear it from you." Closing her eyes, she tipped her head back. "I wanted you so badly, for so long."

"No longer than I, dear woman. No longer than I."

"*Lickspittle*," called Beatrice.

"Stow it!" they cried together.

From opposite ends of the gallery, their parallel soliloquies stopped abruptly. Cate looked to him for affirmation that he had actually said what she thought she had heard, but found only the same look on him.

Cate sagged against the sill, propping her head in her hand. "Nathan, I'm sorry. I didn't mean... I mean it wasn't... I thought last night was because you were bored or... something. Never once had you given the slightest hint you were even remotely interested."

"Never once?" he echoed, gaping. "Suffering Jesus, I made every overture known to answer on seven continents. Seems me efforts were wasted then," he sighed, ruefully. "Then what the bloody hell is all this huffing about... about?"

"This morning, you were so... so... gone," she finished lamely. Her arm dropped limp at her side. "I thought you were done with me."

He sidled closer. "Pirate, eh? Naught more to be expected from such a blackguardly dog."

There was no recrimination in his voice, but his barb was deadly accurate. Nothing hurts more than the truth, especially when it's used against you.

"You said you didn't wish just once," she pleaded, looking up. "You said... I mean, I thought...? Didn't you say...?"

He cocked his head interestedly. "You claim there were negotiations, a parlay?"

She closed one eye, trying to recall. "That could be a word, I suppose."

"And pursuant to said parlay, there was an accord?" he queried, sliding nearer.

"It could be said." Suddenly she wished she had paid far more attention to the finer rules of piracy recited her first day aboard.

"I see." His jaw twisted sideways in thought as he came nearer. "A pirate is either bound by his word, or be seen as a swivel-tongued mountebank. In consideration of said parlay, might you enlighten me as to what exactly were the terms to which I agreed?"

He batted his lashes at the end, the charmer!

"You said 'treasure' and 'cherish'. That's what you said."

Her breath caught as he stalked her, his eyes, dark and avid.

"Only a base-souled dog would fail to comply," he said.

"You said more than once," she repeated with as much conviction as could be managed. Damn him, he was doing it again, rendering her as palpating and breathless as that aforementioned maid. "I distinctly remember."

"Then I must keep my word, or loose me honor as a pirate." A finger tracked up her arm, pausing to brush the delicate skin at the inside of her elbow as he asked, "Two?"

"That's more than once." Things were moving much faster than she was prepared for. Hoping to slow things down, she fell back a step, only to come up short against *Murdering Mary*.

"Twenty?" He was next to her now, close enough to feel the heat of his body radiating. His breath blew across her neck and she shivered.

"It's... that's... more than once."

An arm slipped around her waist. His hips pressing insinuatingly against hers, as he said, "I imagine, then, I shall be obliged to defer to your meticulous expertise to keep an exact record of how many more than once is managed."

"An exact count," she said with effort, those same enchanting fingers now following the curve of her ear.

"Lovely," he purred against her neck. "And exactly where, then, are we?"

"One."

The night before, they had been tentative, shadowed by doubts and fears, afraid to disappoint and of what might be discovered. Now, they rushed in eager anticipation of what was to come. Nathan undressed in snatching motions. Leaving a trail of boots and accoutrement across the floor, he bore Cate, stumbling out of her skirt, back through the curtain. In his haste, he abandoned shedding his clothing in favor of ridding Cate of hers, his fingers scrabbling at her laces. With an impatient grunt, he jerked the shift's ribbon and lifted her to take her breast in his mouth. In one more final surge, he swept her onto the bunk. She giggled in delight as he came down on top of her.

Hungrily devouring her mouth with his, he paused long enough to blindly fling aside his breeches. Weeks of pent up frustration and desire manifested as they tore at each other, demanding restitution for their mutual anguish.

They briefly retraced paths explored before. Beguiling fingers sought again her most sensitive places preparing and opening. He came up hard and quick, a silky stiffness to her touch, writhing and cursing through clenched teeth. He rose over her as she opened to him, stroking and guiding him home.

"I'm sorry, I...I can't be gentle," he gasped and plunged to the root.

Nathan clutched her close, his body straining and taut. A quick move of her hips gave him the permission he sought. Bracing a hand at the small of his back, she helped him set his motion, riding each trust, absorbing the shock with her own need.

Two. Three. Four...

His breath became more ragged. Each drive was felt all the way to her womb. She buried her mouth into the hard cords of his shoulder to stifle her cries. He sought to pull away just before his release, but she held him as he shuddered, her flesh stroking him to his end.

⚜

Nathan reclined on the bunk with his eyes closed, a sheen of moisture glistening on the bridge of his nose. His hand resting on Cate's back, he contentedly twirled a piece of her hair between his fingers. She lay with her head pillowed on his chest, toying with one of his braids. It was what she had dreamed: to lie with him, have him to herself, touching and holding.

Together.

"Why didn't you come in last night?"

He twitched at her question, but his eyes remained closed. "I did."

She ran a finger down the slope of his belly and watched it ripple with gooseflesh, delighted in seeing his body respond to her. "I didn't hear you."

"Aye, well, I was there, nonetheless," he said in quiet affirmation. His head stirred against the pillow. "You were sleeping."

Cate rose on her elbows to better see his face. "You should have woken me."

One eye cracked open in stern observation. Weighted by his afterglow, the lid closed again. "I tried... twice." One hand stirred enough to exhibit two fingers.

"I must have been more tired than I thought." She laid her head on his chest, the soft curls of hair tickling her cheek. "I'm sorry, Nathan. I never —"

He pressed the same two fingers to her lips. One brow lifted as an eye slitted open. "Is this how we are to spend our days: apologizing?"

"But I —"

"Hist! Belay." He bent to kiss her, and then re-settled, closing his eyes once more. "Sorrows come in legions, luv. We'll face them another day, together."

There was merit in what he said. Over the last weeks, words had failed them. Words had spoiled and clouded, dammed and barricaded, confused and falsely pledged. To add more would only add fuel to a fire one sought to extinguish.

"Take your shirt off; I want to see you," Cate said, sitting up.

One dubious eye barely opened. "You've seen me before; I had it off last night."

"I must have been distracted," she said, peevishly, tugging at his shirttails. "I don't remember. Take it off."

Huffing and boring a suffering look, Nathan sat up. When the garment finally cleared his head, he leaned back against the bulkhead. Cate tossed it aside then arranged herself on her knees before him.

Nathan reclined before her, one leg bent. A band of daylight through the port fell across his torso. She had seen glimpses of him, moving under the fabric of his clothing when he twisted or turned. She had thought him slight when first met; he was anything but. He was solid and beautifully made, with long taut muscles drawn across an elegant frame. Even then, in his relaxed state, his shoulders and forearms were tightly corded. There was an air of quiet strength about him, cured and hardened by years of ship and sea.

She splayed her hands across his chest, sliding up and over his angular, well-set shoulders to push back the heavy fall of braids. Any part of him touched by the sun was tanned to a tawny bronze. Elsewhere, his skin was ivory, not milky but with the antiqued patina of mellowed ivory. She was familiar with the woad tattoos at his neck, ankles and wrists, but was surprised to see another belted his waist. Older and faded, but still bright blue against the pale skin, its design was the same, yet more simplistic. It was a warrior's body, marked, but victorious. Life had taken its swipes and shots, and he had sidestepped them all, his spirit undiminished and indomitable. The tattoo over his heart said it all: "Freedom."

She slid her hand sideways to a long scar. Old but still vicious, it followed the curved of his well-sprung ribs. "This one?"

"A boarding axe off of Malacca," Nathan said in a near whisper.

She traveled a little farther down. Whorls of fine dark hair led from the mat on his chest, down the long slope of his belly, to the ferocious thatch between his legs. A shorter, thicker scar lay just above the jut of his hip bone.

"Sword." A hooked end of his mustache tucked up grimly. "Hiriam Maubrick."

She twitched at the name. Maubrick had been Nathan's First Mate, and one of the pair who shot Nathan and cast him adrift to die.

Cate continued her journey over his body, halting at each mark, while he gave his quiet litany: sword fight in Madagascar, a slave trader's knife in Singapore, a bullet's graze pirating off St. Augustine, stabbed by a whore, or bitten by an enraged boar. Splinters, knifes, pikes, fragments and blades; glass, metal, fire and bullet. The list of places was a world's atlas: Algiers, Goa, Puerto Cabellos, Mocha, Guayaquil, Havana, Campeche. Fights, battles, beatings, tortures and imprisonment, every variety of calamity, wreck and ruin which could befall a body was there. Some were old and faded, virtually erased by time. Many were interlaced, one over the other, over the other. Some appeared to have healed well, while others showed the ravages of infection. One such rested on his upper left arm.

"Broken arm; fell from a tree, trying to fly. I was six," he added as an all-encompassing explanation.

The tattoo on his forearm she knew: a swallow carrying a stabbed and bleeding heart. The swallow a mariner's symbol for thousands of miles traversed, she had seen it often, but it was still a wonder if it had been the heart which was stabbed, or the spirit? His hooded lids precluded her inquiry; it was a confidence he wasn't willing to share. Nor did she inquire as to the squarish patch of corrupted skin over his heart, just below the "Freedom" tattoo. Thomas had told her of it, for the scar had been by his hand, when he had cut away where Nathan had been branded.

His right hand laid palm up on his leg, the "S" brand in plain view.

"Lord Breaston Creswicke, of the Royal West Indies

Mercantile Company." Otherwise detached, that came through a set jaw.

Nathan looked to see Cate's reaction. He had told her of how he had come to be branded, but it had been a half-truth. His eyes hardened, desiring to know how much she knew. She dropped hers to the space between them.

Everything.

The corner of his mouth tucked up, and he sighed, displeased, but resigned.

Years at sea were revealed in the tattoos of the swallows on his knuckles. The harshness of that life could be seen in his fingers, the off-angled and enlarged joints from multiple fractures and dislocations. Violence showed in the lacework of scars and the severed tips of the last two fingers of his right hand.

On the fat of his underarm was the rounded mark of a musket ball, its twin directly across, where the ball had passed through. There were two more—on his side, another on his upper leg—in which he hadn't been so lucky: their rounded shape distorted by whatever implement had been used to dig them out. High on his right breast was another. The margins were blackened, however, the result of a weapon fired at very close range. He flinched when she touched it, not from soreness, but a sensitivity of another sort. She placed her hand lightly over it and met his gaze. Nothing further was necessary, unless he was so inclined.

He wasn't.

Even in such a moment of intimacy, she either hadn't sufficiently gained his confidence—or he couldn't bring himself to speak of it.

His thighs and calves were curved and dipped with muscle. The hair there was like that on his arms: nearly as fine on his head and not near as dense on his chest. Down the length of his left thigh ran the wickedest scar of all, thick and gnarled, cleaving deep into the muscle. She didn't have to ask; Thomas had told her. It had nearly cost Nathan his leg.

His toes curled slightly in self-consciousness, the tip of one considerably shortened.

"Frozen rounding the Horn," he said. "Lost part of me ear on another." He lifted his hair to show that a goodly portion of the top curve of his ear was missing.

"And here?" she asked.

It was the first time she had dared to touch the scar at his neck. It lay between his Adam's apple and the soft notch of his neck. The delicate skin tortured into a thick gnarl, it was a reverse branding of sorts, the curving arcs of a rope's twist permanently etched in the skin.

"Were you hung?" She bit her lip at her boldness.

The amber and cinnamon eyes held hers for the briefest bit and then fell away. He smiled grimly. "Aye, but dancing the hempen jig of a different sort."

Nathan was hesitant, taking time to form his thoughts, deciding how much to reveal. "A cabin boy I was, as fresh and hairless as a lass. You'll mind of me stowing away?"

She nodded. Living in Matelotage—a pirate haven and a place he loathed—driven by the death of his mother and a deep-seated hatred for the man who assumed his custody, he had left.

"Mark me, I'd made precious sure it was a merchant and not a pirate ship," he said, with a wag of a finger. "I'd seen enough of that postulant hellhole to know what they were about. Captain Pope was known to be fair-minded; one can't desire better than that. As for the hands, months at sea can put thoughts into a man's head, ones what can be readily seen for anyone who cares to heed. I managed to cat-and-mouse about the ship, dodging them for the first while. I took a right hazing for clinging to the captain's coattails. But then, he was taken with a fever."

Thomas had told her of Nathan's nickname, "Scupperbait." Being so small of stature at that age, he had been easily swept away by the waves washing the decks, leaving him stuck in the scuppers.

Nathan fell quiet, a number of thoughts tracking his features.

"They were thorough, I'll give the bastards that," he said in grudging admiration. "I was blindfolded, so as unable to accuse, and a rag in me mouth…"

He clamped his lip in his teeth, the muscles in his jaws flexing. "They bound me. I fought…" The hand resting on his leg curled into a fist, the knuckles going white as he shook. "God help me, I fought, but…"

Nathan's voice grew raspish, tightening with the memory, as if the rope was still about his neck. She sorely regretted having said anything. It brought back too many of her own memories. It called to mind too easily her story: the bite of the ropes, the desperation of helplessness, the struggle…

As disquieted as he was, he pressed on, as if the telling gave him ease.

"'Twas a blessing, I think" he said frowning slightly. "I was fair out of it through most of it. I have no idea how many…"

The last was choked off.

She blinked back the rising shimmer of tears when she thought he wasn't looking. "What…?" She cleared a suddenly constricted throat. "After…? I mean, what—?"

"The report to the Master was I'd tangled me foot in a sheet and tumbled down the companionway, which answered well, since I'd been thrown down it. Broke me arm in the doing," Nathan said, meditatively rubbing a spot just above his elbow.

"Cap'n Pope didn't credit a word of it. A fall doesn't leave a lad bleeding... And me neck..." He left the thought to finish itself.

"Didn't he ask...? Couldn't you tell...?" she asked.

He smiled, tolerantly. "No man before the mast betrays another. A brotherhood of silence it 'tis on the f'c'stle. I couldn't speak for nigh on to a week, and a broken arm prevents one from writing. I couldn't eat or drink. I just... cried. Made nothing more than little squeaking sounds like a half-drowned kitten," he said, looking away. "Ripped breeches, a bleeding bum, and legs slick with spunk... not much to be said. He knew."

Nathan stared off for some time. Then he shook himself as one did to rid oneself of a bad dream.

"No charges could be made, because there was no proof, other than a lad's word against those willing to speak for the bastards' character," he said. "I knew the ones what nabbed me. As for the rest—at least some—I knew by the looks after; gloating they were. And the smell of them I'd never forget," he finished in a flood vehemence.

Her stomach clenched, as the ghosts of smells rose in her nose. The sense of smell could be the most damning. No matter how valiantly one tried, one sniff, and it all came tumbling back.

When she had first come aboard, she had inquired as to why there were no cabin boys aboard, a time-honored tradition at sea, as she had been given to believe. Nathan had turned away, mumbling something under his breath. Now she understood.

"By some strange coincidence, the pair what nabbed me died within hours of each other," he said, brightening somewhat. "The ship's cirurgeon declared it bad beef."

The lilt in his voice suggested something more.

"You?" she asked.

He gave her a sidelong look, the light sparking on the burned molasses orbs. "I only said I was fresh, I didn't say I was innocent. There are benefits to be had from living in that festering hellhole Matelotage. The cirurgeon knew, and 'tis a good chance he told the Cap'n as much. The Cap'n put a pallet in his cabin floor; like a dog sleeping at its master's feet, but I slept sound, at any rate. Me voice hadn't changed before, and after I sounded like... like a man old before me time."

She wondered what the ravaged voice might have been: as soft and gentle as he, or deep and melodic, a clear tenor which might have carried from the forecastle on the night air, instead of the labored grate heard on those rare occasions when he was taken with song?

"It still bothers you, doesn't it," she said.

"Me throat? Aye. As for the rest?" he mused. "Ancient history, darling, the trials and travails of a lad growing up is all."

It was spoken with the pragmatism of a mariner with regard to anything bad: since the worst obviously hadn't happened — death — then it couldn't have been so bad.

He probed his neck, grimacing slightly, but it was unclear if it was from physical discomfort or the recollection of it all.

"Eating doesn't come so easy," he finally admitted. "Something hot to drink or rum helps ease the ache of a night."

As often as she had seen him in drink, never had she considered the physical comforts it might be affording him from the residual aches and pains of so many years at sea.

"The Cap'n knew. Those sorts can't help but brag, and there are no secrets on a ship," he said with a wry twist. "Pope wasn't one to often let the cat out of the bag, but he did so then: fifty lashes, and I the first stripe, had I wished."

"Did you... wish?"

He made a rude noise. "To what point and purpose? Flaying their skins wouldn't heal mine."

She couldn't argue that. Nothing reversed time or undid what had been done.

What color is hope when it fades?

When the innocence of youth is dissolved by the reality of life, it was rarely gentle. The question might be whether or not it was compulsory for such lessons to be particularly brutish, or otherwise go unlearned. Earlier in his boyhood, he had seen his mother beaten. Had he learned the lesson of the treachery of men then, could he have been saved from the classroom of this harsher lesson? Hindsight. Regret. Remorse. One could starve if they sought sustenance on those.

Cate touched her lips to the twisted skin in benediction for all that had happened, at the same time giving thanks that he had survived to be there now. His arm tightened around her in acknowledgement.

"S'all right, luv," Nathan said into her hair. His fingers brushed the back of her shoulder and the thick scar there. "Only bloody fools brag in Hell, and St. Peter shan't pass fools through his gates."

Coming from many, it could have come across as quite cavalier, but he bore the marks of experience to give it wisdom.

She urged him to sit up and moved around in order to see his back. Pushing his hair out of the way, she gasped.

"You've been flogged!"

It had once been a beautiful back, wide-shouldered and carved with muscle, tapering down to a narrow waist. The deep curving grove of his spine ran between the sculptured shoulders, the hard curve of his buttocks half-buried in the folds of the quilt. The once smooth skin was marked with claw-like grooves of silvery-white against the antique ivory.

Nathan grimly nodded, a dark eye over his shoulder looking mildly surprised. "You recognize the marks. When I was a cabin boy; it was me first and second voyage. The handiwork of that blighter, Beecher."

He had told her of it one day by a hot spring, and she had been shocked then. Still, knowing that he had been whipped and seeing the marks was two entirely different things.

"They flogged a cabin boy?" Cate asked in disbelief.

Nathan looked off, squinting in calculation. "Three, no four times, all tolled. First was only two strokes, and then five, the second," he rationalized then shrugged, mirth lurking around his mouth. "I was mouthy and brash."

"The mind strains to imagine," she mused.

"The others were..." Nathan looked off, his mouth working for a word, "indiscretions" being the one he finally landed upon.

What he didn't say she could see. He had been whipped as a lad, but there was a vast difference in the age of the marks. Some, the faintest and oldest, had been applied with care, light and even, meant to punish and no more. A vast number more were vivid with relative newness. Their thickness revealed the savagery with which they had been applied, their crisscrossing meant to maim and destroy, breaking the spirit if not the body. Creswicke's hand, again.

Amid all that ruin, just below his shoulder blade, laid the divot of another musket ball. The margins blackened like the one on his chest, this one was from a smaller caliber weapon, the sort a woman might carry.

How does one go about asking if a man's love—his precious Hattie—had been the one to shoot him in the back?

Overwhelmed by the horror of it all, she pressed her lips to the slope of his shoulder. His hand came to rest on hers and squeezed in silent acknowledgement.

Nathan lounged against the bulkhead once again. He looked down to scrutinize himself with an odd look. "Seems to be the map of me life," he murmured, with a mystified smile. He looked blandly at the brand and sobered. "Only a few I really mind."

Cate pressed her hand over the "S", as if somehow that simple action might erase it. "I wish I had been there for you."

His hand closed around hers and squeezed lightly. "Nay, lass. You couldn't have stopped it, and there was bloody little to be done after."

"I could have helped you heal. I could have helped you... with all of those."

Nathan clasped both of her hands between his. Holding her eyes with his, he stroked the backs with his thumbs.

"No regrets, darling. Those can cut worse than any blade. If you can't control it, you can't help it, and if you can't help it, then there's nothing to be regretting."

He angled his head toward her stomach, and then her shoulder. "Wear your marks proudly. If they are to be seen, it's because you have survived. There's no shame in living. And if it's to be laying on of the hands, I'd rather it be here in me bunk than on some wretched deck, with some cod-handed cove stitching me up."

He kissed her lightly to emphasize his point. He then ran a pensive finger along her jaw, setting off trails of goose flesh up her face and down her neck. "Come to mind, I may just have something those hands could do well by, *if* they were so inclined."

A warm rush flooded her cheeks and several other places. "Well, I do like to keep my hands busy."

"Ah, a woman after me own heart," he said with a gold-glinted grin, pulling her with him down onto the mattress.

"Why, Captain Blackthorne, I didn't think it was your heart we were speaking of."

Nathan ducked his head lower and began doing things that made her shiver. The clanging of the watch bell shattered the quiet.

"Suffering Jesus on the cross! Goddamned—!" Nathan checked himself and shifted into another language, still swearing, for the spirit of it was still to be heard.

He braced his forehead against hers. He heaved an exasperated sigh and then watched as she struggled to interpret the seven rings.

"'Tis nigh on the end of the forenoon watch," he said at last, putting an end to her suffering. "I've courses to lay and a glass to check, before I report at eight bells. They do say duty..."

"Is a heartless master," she finished. "You'd best go. We don't want anyone thinking we've been up to something."

Nathan sat on the bunk's edge, angling his head to admire the view as she bent to search through the pile of discarded clothing on the floor.

"They already know what we've been up to, darling." Sighing, he rose and began his own search.

"I'll never get used to that." Handing him a sock, she pulled on her shift.

Scrutinizing the sock for a moment, he pitched it over his shoulder. He rummaged further, making a little sound of discovery at locating his breeches.

"Used to what?" he asked as he pulled them on.

"Everyone knowing everything; eyes always on you, seeing everything."

"You get used to it," he said through the folds of his shirt. Settling the linen on his shoulders, he worked to free his braids and scarf tails from the collar.

"I don't think I'll ever get used to it," she said.

Sitting on the bunk again, his grin was a bright flash of ivory as he pulled on a stocking. "You learn to keep up a front; never let them really see."

She sat next to him and studied him intently. "That's what you've done, isn't it? A front, a mask?"

He sobered, his eyes searching hers.

"Aye," he answered softly, touching her cheek. "And you, and those cursed eyes of yours, have seen through it. You're the only one who ever *really* has."

"Does that bother you?"

Nathan thoughtfully examined her face further, taking in every detail. "No," he said softly. "No, I'm safe with you."

Cate pulled her stays free of another of Nathan's stockings and tossed it his way. He adroitly caught it one-handed.

"What do you suppose they'll say?" she asked, struggling into her stays.

"Who?"

"The crew. You said they know what we're doing."

He considered while he stuffed his shirt into his waistband. "I should imagine they'll say ''Tis about time,' and settle their bets."

"Bets!" she gaped. Her arms dropped to her sides. "Bets? They've been betting on when we... I mean, if we —?"

"From the day you were brought aboard, I should imagine."

He chuckled at her startled look as he pulled on a boot. "Darling, these are men who bet on whose spit kills the spider first, or which way a goat turd will roll. Betting on when I bedded you is a minor thing."

"Well, it wasn't minor to me! Didn't I have any say in it?"

Stomping his foot into his boot, he grinned. He came around to cup her cheek in his palm.

"Darling, you had all the say. I wouldn't take you until you'd have me. It was never going to be any other way, *ever*."

"Why, Nathan? Why did it take so long...? I mean, before you...? Why didn't you say...?"

He reddened and smiled, grim but tolerant. "Because you're his, darling."

"His?" she echoed stupidly. She had expected any number of excuses but that.

"You're married," he said with the eloquent patience of one dealing with a child.

"He's dead." It wasn't to be ghoulish or cold. It was but to state a simple fact.

"As you keep saying. You don't know that."

She brought his face around by the point of his beard in order to look into the coffee-colored orbs. "Yes, I do." The thought of Brian returning was ludicrous. She bit back a rising smile, lest she wound Nathan's already delicate pride.

"Darling, I've a lifetime of men declared dead—gunshot, lost at sea, fever or sea monsters, or whatever you desire to name—and the next thing I know, they are buying me a drink. Hell, I was given up for dead meself, and yet here I am in all me charming glory." He spread his arms in display.

To argue to the contrary would have been disingenuous for she too knew people mysteriously died and mysteriously reappeared. And yet, on Brian's death she was firm: she had woken screaming the night it had come to pass, had felt the stab in her heart and had awakened the next morning with a part of her gone. For Nathan's part, she couldn't argue either. She had heard many and widely-varied versions of him being cursed, blessed, resurrected by the hand of some sea goddess, even allusions to immortality.

"I thought it was because I reminded you of... her." She said, looking away. It was her strong belief that there should only be two in a bed—or bedchamber, as it were—at a time. But so long as it had been opened to three, it might as well be four.

"Her?" Now he was the one to sound stupid.

She willed herself to meet his gaze, but failed. "Yes, *her*. Pryce claims you said I reminded you of... of... Hattie," she finally squeezed out through a constricted throat.

"Did I now?" Nathan mused, a bit too innocently for her money. "Bloody awkward that."

"God help me, I was a spineless coward," he said on a sudden surge of self-loathing. "I was scared, mortified you'd confound and burn me for the accursed, driveling, maudlin milksop I was. And when those cursed eyes of yours failed to see, well... I knew it had to be because they didn't desire to."

"You always looked like it was torture to be in the same room—"

"And it was," he said with hearty conviction. "To have you right there..." His hand rose to her shoulder and hovered. "To have you so near, to hear your voice and smell you, and not be able to..." His clamped his lower lip between his teeth, eyes clouding and filling with anguish.

"And then, there was the fear if I was to say something, you'd jump. You damned near did, twice, nay... three times," he added to her dubious look.

Nathan had made mention of that same worry before, although for the life of her, she couldn't fathom to what or when he was referring. Still, whatever the fabrications, they were real to him.

The poor man and the tortures he had suffered, so much like her own.

"Misery enjoys company, it would seem," she said.

"And 'tis no finer company in which one could wish to suffer."

His eyes softened to the color of warm molasses. He touched his lips lightly to her forehead as a parting and swaggered to the door.

"Bye the bye," he said, pausing there. "Shall you be desiring to know who won?"

A hurtled shoe harmlessly hitting him in the shoulder was his answer.

27: STORM TOSSED

O NCE DRESSED, CATE BALKED AT the curtain as Nathan's words rang in her head. "…settling their bets…"

Mortification knotted her gut. Everyone aboard knew…

Every man, jack, tar, and mate knew what they had been doing, not only just then, but the night before, too. She tried to think back, wondering if she had cried out at any point. She wasn't usually given to doing so at those crucial moments of passion, but it had been a very long time.

Everybody knew… which meant she was going to have to face everyone, knowing they knew. From the fo'c'stlemen, to the foretopsmen, to the afterguard, to anyone slaving in the hold moving water butts… *everybody* knew.

"No secrets on a damned ship," she grumbled under her breath.

She prayed—vowed not to go bright red at the first person met and then worried as to who it might be.

When Cate came around the curtain, Nathan stood at the table leaned over a chart. He nimbly walked the brass dividers, his fingers tapping the parchment in calculation, reminding her so much of her first day aboard, and innumerable times since. His charts were his pride and justifiably so. Detailed and finely scripted in his florid handwriting, they were works of art. She had spent many an hour watching him work on them, embellishing with further details and descriptions.

He looked up, brightening at seeing her.

"We're to meet Thomas at Cogburn's Island," Nathan explained at her inquiry as to their destination.

A ringed finger indicated their current position, and then the aforementioned island. His rag bound hand reminded her of the cut he had suffered from Thomas' sword. Earlier attempts on her part to attend it had failed; hopefully he would yield this time.

"Allow me to—" she said, reaching to examine it.

"It's fine. Observe." Jerking free of her grasp, he worked his hand to illustrate. His checked wince — slight, but unmistakable — robbed the desired effect. His hands were near the color of mahogany, but she could see bright red peeking from under the binding.

"It needs to be —" she said more determinedly.

"I'm fine," he said in a tone that would brook no further discussion.

Conceding, she peered over his shoulder and pressed against him, still thrilled at being able to do so. "How far?"

"Two days." Nathan shifted his hips in acknowledgement of her nearness. His fingers sought hers where they rested on the parchment and stroked her knuckles.

"Sometimes three, if the winds are in our favor. Doesn't appear, however, as though Calypso is going to bless us today," he added with a grudging sigh.

"How bad is it going to blow?" She had endured storms on the *Constancy*, but had yet to experience a bad one on the *Morganse*. Her apprehension stemmed only from not knowing what to expect. Her faith in Nathan's seamanship was unquestioned. With Pryce and the crew, it became an impossible sum when adding up the number of years of experience represented on these decks.

"Not sure." Straightening, he cast a dubious eye over his shoulder toward the glass. It was an inconspicuous, odd-looking instrument: a long tube with a bulb at its bottom. Gimbaled on a rosewood board on the bulkhead, it was consulted with a devotion and reverence of a religious icon.

"Weather glass says bad, right nasty. The wind is steady, but I don't like the looks of that swell," he said swiveling a speculative gaze aft.

She had been vaguely aware of an increase in the action of the ship. The sea was kicking up rough. A dark and tumultuous-looking bank of clouds hung low on the east horizon.

"We're required to see what comes," Nathan went on, looking to the chart once more. "We might scud before it, if it will answer, and be taken leagues off course. If it overtakes us, then we'll take the worst of it on the stern."

It was spoken as if there was a positive to be found in that outcome.

Nathan gave Cate an encouraging grin and squeezed her arm. "Not going lily-livered on us, are you?"

Cate straightened and pasted on a smile. "Of course not! Don't you dare get hurt."

She had waited for what seemed a lifetime to have him; to

lose him to storm or injury would be too cruel. And yet, life had proven to be exactly that. Yes, she was afraid… for both of them.

He bent to kiss her, brief but meaningful.

"Now there's the motivation what a man needs," he said, grinning with devilment. Grabbing his coat from the chair, he sauntered to the door and stopped. "Stay under hatches. Don't come out, no matter what you hear."

And then, he was gone.

⌒◦⌒◦⌒

That a storm was brewing was no great surprise: cloud formations, bird sightings, coffee grounds and aching bones had all been read, the omens conflicting only with regards to severity. The glass had dipped its lowest according to many, and yet Millbridge's hip said nothing so severe. Hermione retreated to her manger below; His Lordship and the geckos were nowhere to be seen.

The swell grew to more precipitous heights, while relieving tackles on the rudder and masts were rigged, topmasts lowered and storm canvas bent. The air turned sultry and still, the world taking on a bilious green cast which rendered sky and sea inseparable. Guns were bowsed up and double secured; a half ton of iron careening across a deck could smash a man, or worse yet, pierce the hull, taking everyone to Davy Jones' depths. Hatches were bonneted, bulkheads secured. Pitch stoves sent up sharp-smelling curls of smoke as the caulking irons were put to their fullest application at every port, including the gallery windows and skylight.

As the wind stiffened, the Great Cabin was swept clear. Rugs were rolled, furniture and lockers lashed, and oil lamps tucked safely away; many a ship had burned to the waterline from an oil slick gone unnoticed. It was in that process that Cate encountered her first member of the crew, since her and Nathan's… err, tryst: Millbridge. She willed herself to put on a strong front, but her cheeks heated, nonetheless. She expected severity, at the least the old codger's customary churlishness, but was met only with benign benevolence. It was more disquieting than if he had openly pointed and laughed.

Having failed the first test, she passed the second, barely. Her blush had paled in comparison to Kirkland's. For that matter, Nathan had left with a levity in his step heretofore unseen, and she could have sworn she heard humming.

The galley fires were doused after the dog watches, allowing the men their last hot meal. As if waiting for that last meal to be finished, the blow arrived in full fury. The wind pressed a stiff arm at the *Morganse's* masts, heeling her over and holding her there.

Cate stood in the middle of the cabin as the great doors were slammed shut. Hearing the resounding *"clunk!"* of the crosspiece dropped into its brackets, she was seized by a sense of being entombed. She wasn't completely sealed in: the galley steps stood open — she could come and go as she pleased, Nathan's final orders notwithstanding — but the feeling was undeniable. So empty, so quiet, in spite of the full gale outside.

With all the furniture stowed, Cate stood wondering what to do next. She shied from the gallery, the wind and rain lashing at the thick panes. Flashes of lightning illuminated the mountainous waves of greenish-grey water just the other side of the glass, the foam at their crests hanging like snarling great teeth, seeking to devour anything in its path. The deck now at a violent pitch, she half-crawled to a locker. It was against a lee bulkhead, which meant she could sit atop and lean back against the wall with a modicum of comfort.

Beset by a chill reminiscent of the more sour days in the Highlands, she hunched on the trunk, listening to the gale tear at the windows and doors, clawing to violate her solitary bastion. The ship lurched to dizzying heights, and then sickeningly pitched downward, disorienting one to the point of doubting which way was up. The rain a hammering drone, the wind screaming through every crevice and the grind of planking combined into a din which battered one to numbness.

The gunmetal sky had given way to a Stygian night, lightening the only illumination, when Millbridge appeared at the galley companionway, reporting over the storm's clamor of men injured. Cate stirred from her torpid state and her corner. She skated helplessly on a skim of water over the slanted deck and slammed into *Merdering Mary's* carriage. Rising shakily, she crabbed across the room to follow Millbridge down the steps, the elder carrying her blood box under one arm and a watch lamp. They wove through the swaying cocoon-like hammocks, filled with sodden sleeping men, to the gunroom to where the injured waited.

A near senseless Mr. Seymour was met with first, reported to have been knocked in the head by a swinging block. Blood and rainwater glistening on his face and chest, he sat oblivious, even when spoken to directly. Afraid to appear "lily-livered", but in desperate need to know, she inquired after Nathan as she strapped Ogden, his ribs having taken the brunt of a battle with the ship's wheel.

"A fiend he is during a blow." Bald head gleaming with wetness, Ogden rolled his eyes upward with something between fear and awe. "He's up there now, a-darin' Calypso to take 'im."

Mr. Harrier appeared, cradling his arm. "Bo'lun snapped it like a dry twig." A nasty rope burn entwining the forearm gave credit to his testimony.

A table suspended over a gun her surgery, a steady trickle of injured continued. Fractures and dislocations became the mode of the day: ribs, shoulders, arms and collarbones. Millbridge stoically held the lamp, while she groped in her box for salve, splints and bandages, ignoring the water that dripped down her neck and sloshed at her feet soddening her skirts. Her station was nearly at the ship's waist, much nearer to the ship's heart than in the Great Cabin, rendering the storm that much more immediate.

"How bad is it?" she asked of Millbridge, straining for all the nonchalance she could manage.

"None so bad," he said judiciously. The seamed face was immobile and of little guidance. "Water's only knee-deep at the waist and the spars are still standing."

She looked upward at the deck overhead, uneasy at the thought of such waves washing just on the other side of those planks.

"We ain't been pooped... waves overtaking the stern," he explained semi-patiently to her puzzled look. "And I heard the Cap'n laugh a bit ago."

"Daft he is," put in Harrier with significance.

"Charmed," Millbridge countered solemnly. "And we'll all have the benefit for it."

As the injured filed in, she was kept abreast of Nathan's well-being through their reports. "Cross-braced...," "double-rigged...," "relief-tackled...," "spliced and knotted...": she had no idea as to the meaning. The wonderment mixed with the graveness with which the deeds were reported were indicative of the import.

The clang of the watch bell was barely discernible over the howl of the storm, and yet sufficient to stir the men from their sleep and to "show a leg." No one desired Hodder to come looking, nor be seen as a slacker. The relieved watch came down, half-drowned and exhausted. Some headed straight away for their hammocks, collapsing with an audible groan. The remainder perched on the guns or wherever they might. Rain and seawater dripping from their clothes, they huddled over the cups of half-warm coffee, tea or tepid portable soup and ship's biscuit, served by Kirkland and Millbridge. Hollow-eyed, their spirits were high, not a worried face among them.

And the noise... always, the noise!

At one point, Cate thought the storm to be easing, and said as much to Hallchurch — Mr. Mole, she had first christened him — as she strapped his broken collarbone, thinking it to be a good sign.

"Not if it backth on ye." Hallchurch's ominous warning came through horrifically bucked teeth and a severe lisp. "Just as bad, if not worsth, but from the opposhite direction. The seath all ahoo..." Shuddering, the rest was left to her imagination.

A galvanic crack of thunder made everyone jump. A marrow-penetrating charge, like a massive frisson, shot through her, while simultaneous explosions came from directly overhead. All eyes were fixed upward, wondering what the hell had happened, why the rush of feet and cries of alarm. Every downward tilt of the capering ship filled Cate with a rising panic that they were sinking, every lee lurch feeling like it was about to bowl over. Everyone was still deep in wonderment when three more men stumbled in. All larbolin fo'c'stlemen, they were severely shaken and their hands burned.

Mr. Heap, sat round-eyed and stunned, responding in vague monosyllables and only if spoken to. At one point he turned his head into the light. Like most f'c'stlemen, his pride was his pigtail, long and tarred, but it was no more. He was singed bald.

"Sparked and went up like a goddamned torch, beggin' yer pardon, sir," reported Fouts, one of his mates. "The sod woulda been naught but glowin' cinder had the Cap'n not doused 'im."

Heap's freshly denuded skull was livid red in the semi-dim, the sharp tang of burned hair, and a lesser of urine, stirring at his every move.

"Glowin' like a babe's bum," snickered Fouts.

"Might never grow back, neither," said Hughes, one eye closed in speculation.

"What happened?" Cate asked as she examined Heap.

"Lightning bolt hit the larboard kedge," said Hughes in restrained awe. "Set off *Lucifer* and *Beelzebub* to boot."

"Damn near blew *Bloody Bess* clean off her carriage," Fouts added.

She smiled faintly at the affection for a cannon, so tenderly named.

"Thought the Almighty was sendin' me a signal," said Heap. His blistered hand shook violently as he reached for a cup proffered by Millbridge.

"After all the drinkin' and blasphemin', ain't the Lord gonna be comin' after you," said Hallchurch.

"Ain't nothin' that damned ugly allowed in Heaven," added

Seymour. His senses finally had congealed enough to follow the conversation.

"Tossed Cheeves over," Owens announced over his cup, as flat-voiced as if asking for someone to pass the bread barge. His shoulder moved in a half-shrug at Cate's aghast. "T'weren't enough o' him left for services."

All the men fell quiet. Those manning the forecastle tended to be most seasoned seamen aboard, and were a tight-knit, proud group, and severely felt the loss of a mate. Cheeves was given his moment of silence then, with an unspoken pledge that a more official memorial would be held at a more opportune time. Cheeves was sure to be remembered fondly at the next dispensing of grog and for many months to come.

With rum liberally applied to all patients, and patients resting as comfortably as could be expected, Cate judged it a good time to resupply her blood box. Nearly all the bandages and splints were gone, the carron oil, too. The burn dressing could be mixed up readily enough—half limewater and half sweet oil, shaken well—but the middle of a storm was no time to attempt it. Honey, vinegar, or just fresh lard would serve well—sometimes better. All of which could be found in the galley. Kirkland would either have what she needed, or as keeper of the keys to the stores, could get it for her. And so, she struck off.

Groping through the lightless t'ween deck was like finding one's way through an underground cave. Cate knew the ship well enough, but navigation was rendered nigh impossible by the total darkness and wildly pitching floor. Any landmarks she might have relied upon had either been moved for the storm, or blocked by hammocks. The lamp she carried had long died, either guttered out or doused by the steady drip of water from overhead. With no flint, she clutched it anyway, if for no other reason than security, and the slim hope of light sometime in the future.

After colliding with several hammocks, eliciting rude remarks from the occupants, bumping into two guns and tripping on the training tackle of a third, she found what she hoped was the aft bulkhead. The ship took a violent lurch, and she had the sense of flying through the air. Landing hard, she lay in a crumpled heap, gasping for the wind knocked out of her. The ship tilted anew and she began to slide, discovering then that she had been lying on the bulkhead. She lay with a spinning head, not only from the collision, but the pain of still trying to draw a breath. She groped with one hand, discerning that she might be on the floor. Unable to trust her battered senses, she considered remaining there until the storm passed, in spite of the risk of being trampled in the dark.

"Cate!"

A bobbing light broke the darkness and came steadily toward her.

"Cate! Cate!"

Nathan's gruff voice rose over the racket of the storm. Each cry grew more urgent, verging on panic, as he cast about with the lamp. It was a prayer answered, proof Providence, or whatever deity, watched over her.

"Cate!"

"Here," she called in a thin wheeze.

Nathan sped to her. Lifting the lantern over her, he slumped with relief.

"Goddammit to bloody hell! You weren't there. What the hell are you doing here?"

"They were hurt," was all she could manage.

"*Tachh!*"

Rainwater dripping from every aspect, it was unclear if he understood or even gave a damn as to her excuse. Her muddled head allowed her to vaguely wonder if he was more annoyed at having to search for her, or that she had disobeyed orders. Swearing and mouthing very unflattering references, he hauled her floundering up from the floor and propelled her toward the companionway. Nathan bolstered her when she staggered or slid as they climbed, flashes of lightning from the cabin above and Nathan's lantern lighted the way topside.

"Stay here or I'll lash you to that mizzenmast," he said, once they were in the cabin.

Given his mood, it was a credible threat.

He saw her concern and smiled. He patted the mast and then clapped a startlingly warm hand on her shoulder. "No worries, luv! Neither I nor this ol' girl are ready to wait upon Jones and his Locker anytime soon."

Wet to the marrow, bright red-rimmed eyes, braced against the sickening pitch, half-hoarse from shouting over wind and water, and she believed him. He brushed her cheek with a kiss, his lips hot against her chilled skin.

The lamp's small flicker faded as he trundled down the stairs, and she was alone again.

Standing in the middle of the room, she avoided looking toward the sweep of the gallery windows. In the darting flashes of lightning, it was necessary to look up to see the wave crests. It was too easy to imagine them bursting through — the dreaded "pooped," as represented by Millbridge. *Merding Mary* and

Widower strained at their lashings. If they were to break loose, it would mean a near half ton of iron careening about. Lingering anywhere in the salon was less than appealing.

Cate made a halting path to the sleeping quarters and their bunk. There she lay, braced by both feet and hands to keep from being tossed out. In spite of those precautions, a violent lee lurch pitched her out. She landed in a rib-jarring heap where bulkhead and floor met, and there she remained. Fine sheets of water sloshed back and forth across the planks, soaking her clothing and the quilt in which she was cocooned.

Thirst and hunger gnawed. Exhaustion being an unfailing sleep potion, at last she slept.

Cate was jerked awake sometime later by a commotion at the cabin door. Its loudness and air of urgency brought her upright from the floor. Through the howl of the storm, she heard the heavy scrape of the cabin door being unbolted. As she sped into the salon, it crashed open. A burst of seawater broke over the coaming carrying Towers, lantern on high. Bazzi and Squidge were directly behind him, staggering under the weight of Nathan, slung by the shoulders between them. Pryce came tight on their heels, more grim than stern. All were grim, for that matter, alarmingly so.

"Avast! Away, you! Get your goddamned bloody hands off me, you cod-faced, motherless bastards. I'll have every one of you sons o' bitches hocked and heaved, before the night's out! I'm fine. Off, I say! I'm fine…!" Nathan growled as the small sodden parade half-dragged him toward the sleeping berth.

Shivering from the blast of cold air, Cate followed. At the bedside, Nathan was to his feet. He batted the two men away as one would an annoying insect. A puddle of water growing at his feet, he swayed precariously, while struggling to focus on her. Once her face was found, he broke into a beatific smile.

"'ello, luv!"

Nathan's eyes rolled back, and he toppled backwards onto the bed. He landed with a cry one would have expected from someone landing on the deck, not a mattress. She thought him to be drunk — an extreme curiosity, for he never drank while on watch — until she touched him.

"He's burning up!"

"Aye." Pryce glared with the irritability of someone who had just suffered a severe scare. "A wave damn near carried 'im away. Found 'im tangled in the mizzen chains, we did. If it hadn't been fer them..."

He allowed her mind to fill-in the rest: overboard, lost at sea. At night, in such savage seas, there would be no finding him.

It was a shock and a puzzle. Nathan was like a cat on deck; never a wrong foot set, nor even caught by an abrupt lee lurch that sent others scrabbling for a handhold. He seemed to possess a second sense regarding oncoming waves, never taking one unprepared. She had seen him walk the rails and yards like most would stroll the Sunday church aisle.

"But what...?" Cate looked at Nathan as she set to pulling off his water-logged boots, trying to comprehend what malady could have struck him with such sudden force. He flailed in a feeble attempt to rise, and cried out again, cursing and clutching his right hand.

The light caught the pinprick brightness in Nathan's eyes which only came with fever, the very brightness she had seen just a few hours before, when he had come to check on her. She had thought it to be excitement of the storm, the heat of his touch due to the coldness of the room.

Damned fool!

Squidge, Bazzi and Towers filed out. Millbridge hung at the door while Cate undressed Nathan. The sensation spurred him into sudden amorousness. Murmuring severely slurred street slang and vulgarities, groping at her cleavage, crying out in pain every time his hand was jostled.

"He's raving," said Millbridge, stepping in to help.

"So, it would seem," Cate said, ducking another assault of Nathan's searching tongue.

She stripped Nathan down, each item making a wet *splat!* when it hit the floor. While Cate tucked Nathan up in the quilt, Millbridge snatched up the sodden mass and took it away. She began to bid him to hang them before the galley fires, but then recalled those were long cold.

Nathan fell quiet, his breath now reduced to short bursts. Cate sat on the edge of the bed and took his hand. It lay like a hot coal in her palm, bright red in the dim light of the horn lamp. Swollen to the point of looking like a bladder blown full of air, the fingers were like sausages. She drew out her knife and slit away the ragged binding, the very one she had begged to remove that morning, and several times before that. Guilt surged, but shifted quickly to anger: anger at him for refusing; a considerably larger dose reserved for herself for not having been more insistent.

The makeshift bandage had once been crusted with dried

blood. The hours of rain had softened it, but it still required a firm tug in order to pull it free. Nathan moaned and jerked. Mumbling a curse, he settled once more. Once a mere slit, the edges of the wound were now curled back and oozed with a greenish-white pus. Her nose was met with a fetid smell. Infection, yes, she thought, sniffing delicately. Something worse? Not yet.

Initially, it had been relatively minor in the way of blade injuries: a clean slice across the back of Nathan's hand, nowhere near deep enough to consider sewing. She had suggested a sticky plaster, but Nathan had literally laughed at her. The last time she had seen it was on the road from Lady Bart's, reopened during the fight with Harte. Nathan had waved her brusquely away and bound it with a strip of cloth.

It's your fault. It's your fault...

There was no rhyme or reason to wounds or injury. The grandest and most grotesque could heal, a virtual miracle, while the smallest nick could fester to the point of death or loss of limb. She resolutely blocked the last possibility. No such thing was going to happen, so there was nothing to be gained by worrying.

"He should be bled," came Kirkland's voice from behind her.

"I haven't the tools, the training, nor the stomach for that."

Nathan cried out—a pitiful sound—at the mere act of lowering his hand on the mattress next to him. Her stomach squeezed at the thought of what must come next.

"It needs cleaning. Bring hot water and—" she began.

"There is none, sir. The fires are out."

She bit back a snappish reply. Her anger was with herself for so foolishly in forgetting.

"Then we'll have to make do," she sighed, ignoring the inner voices screaming in objection. "Bring rum, and a brush or cloth, or... or something," she said finally.

Her faith in the curative powers of whiskey was long-established, but rum was largely untested. Rum, however, was all there was to be had, and so rum it would have to be.

"Pass the word for some help. We'll need to hold him down," she called in Kirkland's wake.

As preparations were being made, she watched Nathan with increasing concern as he became more listless and less aware of the world around him.

Perhaps for this next part, it might be just as well.

Chin and Mute Maori appeared shortly, one dripping wet, the other bleary-eyed from being jerked from his hammock. Stern-faced, they resolutely took up positions, one at Nathan's legs; the other at his shoulders. Millbridge held the bowl. Cate took a deep breath and poured rum over Nathan's hand. With his scream still vibrating her ears, she set to scrubbing with a soft-bristled brush.

Like Highlanders, seamen tended to be a stoic lot in the face of injury. The fever, however, had robbed Nathan of such restraint. He twisted against the grasp of the ship's goliaths with uncommon strength, the already ragged voice going guttural as he screamed. She resolutely kept her eyes averted from Nathan's, so accusing and pleading.

It has to be done! It has to be done.

Cate scrubbed and poured, scrubbed and poured, the stench of fouled flesh was sharp through the rum's sweetness. At one point, she called for the lantern to be brought closer, and verified that nothing more remained than raw flesh, bleeding freely but cleanly.

She knocked the damp strand of hair from her face with a forearm. A stream of moisture tracked between her shoulder blades. Everyone in the room was shaken and sweating. Nathan gazed at her through dull eyes and then rolled his head away.

Kirkland arrived with a bowl containing a mix of relatively warm milk and linseed oil, a slab of bread already soaking. For a proper poultice, the milk should have been near boiling and the soft tack fresh. In order for the milk to have been as warm as it was, Kirkland had to have heated it over a candle the while. She fished out the bread, squeezed, and pressed it to Nathan's hand.

Cate drew the stool up to the bedside and settled in for the vigil.

⌦⌫

Nearly lost him. Nearly lost him, an inner voice chanted as Cate trickled a mix of water, brandy and honey into Nathan's mouth.

Cate had no recollection of where the habit had come from, but it had allowed many a person — injured, ill or otherwise incapacitated — to thrive. Her faith in it was dampened somewhat, for whiskey was the proven ingredient. Brandy, however, was all that was to be had. She ran a mental list of known febrifuges — catnip, coneflower, willow bark — with longing, for she had none. She was obliged to rely on what was to hand: a tepid poultice, a compromised potion and Nathan's spirit. Her greatest faith was in the latter.

As she sponged Nathan's head and limbs, and kept a wet cloth on his head, she tried not to think about how vital and compelling his body had been. Exactly how long ago was unclear; time had gone missing with the sun. His body was paler still than from when he had been brought in. It had been too much like watching the glow of life drain as he grew to near-bone white. The light carved deep shadows in the curves and dips rendering him almost skeletal. The ebony braids were a stark, tangled framework around a pallid face. His hand lying on his belly was a livid slash against the pale of his skin, the barest brush of the fine hair caused him to flinch. Bruises had begun to bloom on his ribs and hip from the battering of being swept off the deck.

Nearly lost him. Nearly lost him.

Voices were periodically heard outside the curtain, the men inquiring as to their captain's progress.

"The day will tell," came Millbridge's ancient creak.

Day?

She blinked and looked around. It could have been day. The gloom in the cabin had brightened somewhat. The storm still raged, however, the wind still screaming through the ship's every crevice.

In spite of her attentions, Nathan's fever deepened. His body radiated with an internal inferno, and his skin drew dry and taut over the bones of his face. The rattle of his rapid breathing was audible over the storm. He barely stirred when spoken to, and she fought the nagging sensation that she had lost him already.

Sometime, Nathan slipped into delirium. Cate called for strong hands to help tie him down. It was a precaution not only to keep him from doing himself harm, but prevent him from being tossed from the bunk by the capering ship. His brow furrowed, and his bound limbs worked against the bindings. His head jerked and eyelids twitched as he rambled, names and orders, fragmented conversation mumbled in varying degrees of lucidity. He tossed his head as his agitation grew until the cloth upon it was flung to the floor. Cate bent to pick it up and straightened to find his eyes had opened. They were fever-glazed and as vacant as a sleepwalker's.

"Hattie?" He spoke a cry croak, in a strange combination of puzzlement and hope.

With a sharp intake of air, Cate lurched back on the stool. Before she could decide how or if to respond, Nathan's eyes rolled closed, and he sank away. Bone-rattling jolts emitted from deep within, wave upon wave. She couldn't breathe, her chest seeming as bound as Nathan's arms. Through an increasing haze of wetness, she watched from a careful distance as he churned and mumbled.

In his agitation, his hand was often jostled or flexed, causing him to cry out. His moans of agony gradually gave way to ones of yearning and apprehension, some verging on sheer joy. His breath quickened, whether in arousal or fear she couldn't tell. Either way, she couldn't bring herself to touch him. Then he went rigid.

"Hattie!" Nathan arched his head back into the pillow, his graveled voice eloquent with anguish. The tortured body writhed against the soft bindings, whether in defense or desire was impossible to know.

Gasping as if she had been punched, Cate clapped a hand over her mouth. She heard a wet *splat!,* and looked down to see she had dropped the cloth, gone forgotten in her hand. She turned from the bedside and closed her eyes, tears cascading down her cheek.

He went suddenly still, deathly so. Panicked, she swung around directly into his glassy-eyed gaze. A face so recently tortured was now completely at peace.

"There's me darling. I knew you'd come," he said in utter tenderness.

Allowing him to think she was his precious Hattie seemed to provide him ease, and so she sat frozen, her heart pounding dully in her ears.

"I knew you'd come, me blessed angel. From the first... So long... needed you... needed... so long... so..." His head rolled aside and he faded once more into oblivion.

Cate clamped her lower lip between her teeth, struggling to dam the flood of emotions which washed over her: fury, hurt, shock, confusion... and hurt, unspeakable hurt. There was a small crack as her heart broke, and then the sharp pain in her chest as it was torn out.

You stupid fool. You stupid, silly, gullible... stupid fool. What the hell else did you expect?

She bent and sobbed into the linen folds of her skirt.

"He's out of his head."

Startled, she jerked up to find Pryce standing at the door, braced against the storm. With his captain incapacitated, command had fallen to him, the weight of it showed, for he was grey and haggard. Thoroughly sodden, he brought with him the smell of rain and the sea.

She dashed her face dry. "Yes, I know."

"He don't reckon—"

"Yes, I know!" she hissed, more sharply than intended. "There's always the chance that he does *reckon,* isn't there?"

"She shot him."

"He loved her," she retorted. Her gaze fixed on the divoted scar on Nathan's chest. A shadow cast across it rendered it almost a hole—the same she felt in her chest. "And still does," she added bitterly.

"She was named after Cape Hatteras." Pryce offered the innocuous detail as if it might equivocate or allay, or if nothing else, a bridge to a subject less unpleasant.

It failed on all counts.

"Really?" Cate asked, wholly disinterested.

"Aye, born there durin' a storm."

Cate gave a feeble attempt at a laugh. "I suppose she should have been grateful it hadn't been off Cape Cod."

A strained silence fell between them. Water dripping from Pryce patted on the floor where he stood at the end of the bunk. His expression darkened further as he listened to his Captain's ramble.

"'Tis possible someone..." Pryce began delicately.

Cate looked up, blinking dully. "Someone what?"

"Someone was t' put somethin' on the blade, assurin' this very thing," he said with a significant lift of his grizzled brows.

"But Thomas..." Weariness fogged her mind, turning every thought back on itself. Urinating on or sullying weapons by other means wasn't unknown to her. It meant the merest nick would doom the enemy to a torturous death from a fouled wound. She strained to think back to that day on the beach.

"That's ridiculous. There was no time for such scheming," she heard herself say.

Pryce's broad shoulders lifted under the wet shirt and dropped. "Mebbe."

"I love him, Pryce," she blurted.

It is a wonder, she thought dimly, what prompted such a confession. The dark room, the glow of the lanterns, and sense of timelessness gave the room the air of a confessional. A wholly unnecessary confession, she suspected. Surely by now it was written on her forehead. And yet it seemed an important one, if for no other reason than a rationale for her steadfastness, or as steadfast as Nathan would allow. She was resigned to that inevitable day, when she would no longer serve his needs as a substitution for the one he truly longed for, and would be set off, banished or just left.

Just like you used him for Brian?

No, it was different. Brian was... gone.

She looked at Nathan, now tranquil, and smiled faintly. It would seem the two of them were much more alike than supposed. One man: she had been prepared to remain so to the end of her days. And Nathan? Granted, he had held many a woman in his arms, but only held one in his heart.

Nathan's forearm was turned away, but she could see the tattoo there, for it was as indelibly etched in her mind as it was on his skin: a swallow bearing a heart, pierced and bleeding. Not much more need be said. It was unreasonable to expect Nathan to forget such a love, when she couldn't do the same. What a tragic lot they were: two lost people cleaving onto the first bit of flotsam to keep from drowning in the loneliness.

She gave a mirthless laugh. "I know it's the last thing anyone, especially him desires to hear, but there it is. Do you think me foolish?"

Gentleness touched the usually severe grey eyes. "Nay, to do otherwise would be akin to desirin' ye not to draw breath. And that's the pity of it. He'll hurt, ye, sir. He won't be intendin', but he'll hurt ye just the same."

❧

Bells, bells and bells.

Cate's existence narrowed down to the watch bells, changing the poultice and the space in between.

Ignoring an aching back and burning joints, she sponged Nathan's fever ravaged body and trickled her potion into his mouth with trembling hands. She swayed on the stool, desperate for sleep, but the thought of leaving his side was intolerable. The damp and chill of the storm had penetrated to her core. She jerked from a tremor and guiltily thought of lying next to Nathan's heated body to warm herself, just as she had just a few days ago.

The sound of dripping water came from somewhere. In the Highlands, it was believed the sound was the harbinger of death, a water spirit come to collect a soul.

She leaned defensively over Nathan's body. "Go gather elsewhere. There's no one to be had here."

Her nostrils twitched constantly for the first hint of mortification.

Not yet.

Only the foulness of infection was detected. She had seen the looks from Pryce, Millbridge and others, and knew what they were thinking. When changing the poultice, she had seen the red streaks, now reaching nearly to Nathan's wrist. They seemed no worse, but she couldn't trust judgment quite possibly skewed by desperate hope. To believe otherwise was to be obligated to consider the options: death, which she could not allow, or in the well-meaning spirit of avoiding that, amputation.

The sharp taste of bile rose in her throat.

She had witnessed amputations, heard the saw grind through tendon and bone, seen the blood spurt as veins were severed, and then smelled the seared flesh when the hot iron was touched to the stump. Many healed and flourished; others had withered and perished, in spirit if not in body.

Cate eyed Nathan lying there, his ribs rising and falling as he labored for each intake of air. Every cloud had a lining. Some would say Providence had just provided a salvation: remove his hand and take the "S" brand with it. Nathan would no longer be a marked man, the threat of ownership gone. He could have his life back, the freedom he so cherished.

Would it be to clip his wings, like his precious swallows, no longer be able to fly? The ends of a few fingers and toes, the top of one ear: life had taken its swipes, and he had prevailed. But how much more could his spirit take before it surrendered? With his right hand gone, he would be defenseless in a violent world. He could learn to use his sword with his left, but living long enough to do so would be the challenge. He could, however, still have his ship.

Would she? Could she stand by and watch as Nathan's hand was cut off? Or would she fight against it and watch him die in putrefying agony? What would she face when he woke: hatred or gratitude, relief or resentment? Would he wish his precious Hattie had been there? Could she have kept him alive and whole?

She rubbed her forehead wearily.

The price… always the damned price.

"No mind. We're a long way from that," she said as she mopped Nathan's fevered brow. "So, let us not dwell."

She found solace in the determination in her voice. The furrow in Nathan's brow softened, and he calmed ever so slightly, as if he might have found ease, too.

Pryce's suggestion rolled and pitched through her mind like the deck beneath her. In the long hours of darkness, hunger and exhaustion began to play tricks on her, lucid thought more elusive. Thomas' blade catching Nathan's hand couldn't have been intentional, nor something put on the blade itself. And yet, there was no denying that Nathan's fever was remarkably high.

Still Thomas' oath rode heavy.

"If that damned fool hurts you, I will not abide it."

Thomas was Nathan's best friend; he trusted him as she had seen Nathan trust no other, including herself, she thought ruefully. Thomas had become a pirate only because of Nathan.

Pirate.

And, treachery abounded in their world.

She preferred to not admit her judgment of Thomas was

skewed by his resemblance to Brian. She tried to see a darker side to the man, but couldn't find one. Perhaps Thomas was the greater actor, even better than Nathan. Ruthlessness could lurk behind that genial smile. The two men had come to blows over a woman before. It would be too cruel to think it could be happening again, all because of her. Or it could be that she flattered herself too much, that she was but a piece in an old grudge match.

A shift in her world shoved all further thoughts aside: Nathan's fever broke.

Now, he was consumed by chills with teeth-chattering violence. Sweat formed a dark circle on the canvas mattress, his braids leaving dark trails of moisture on the pillow as he tossed and churned. In between changing the poultice, she wiped his face and strove to keep the quilt about him, which he fought with the determination of the possessed.

During the brief interludes when he quieted, Cate rested a hand on his shoulder, rested her head on the raised edge of the bunk and closed her eyes. She had been dozing thusly when she woke to a deafening silence.

The storm was gone, blown itself out. Sunlight streamed under the curtain, illuminating the room in a warm flood of eye-squinting brilliance.

Joyous in the absence of one noise, she was alarmed by the absence of another.

Like the storm, Nathan had gone still, deathly still. Heart in her throat, she checked for the rise and fall of his chest, leaned her ear next to his mouth, and then sagged with relief. He still breathed, but barely so: shallow and quick, but not labored, no wetness, no death rattle. It wasn't the deep sleep of restoration, but more like his body no longer possessed the strength to fight.

She pressed her hand to his cheek, the bristle of his several day beard a soft plush against her palm. Compared to the raging fever, he was almost cold to the touch.

"How does he do?" came Millbridge's voice from the door.

"Not sure," she said frowning. Exhaustion was making it so blessedly impossible to think. "The fever's broke, but... I'm not sure."

Kirkland brushed past Millbridge bearing a bowl of now steaming milk and linseed oil. Heartened by having a fresh and proper poultice, Cate squeezed out the already soaking bread. She undid the binding and lifted away the old.

"It might have been wasted effort, Mr. Kirkland," she said. Nathan's hand shimmered in the wetness which filled her eyes.

The gash was still there, widened by corruption. Clear fluid, faintly tinged with blood, welled from the raw flesh, but the angry brilliance of inflammation gone. His hand was healthy and pink... relatively.

He would be both whole and alive.

❧❧❧

With the storm past, the *Morganse* exhaled, a long expulsion of air pressing up from her bowels. It was over.

The hatches were beaten open. Bands of sunlight stabbed through the below decks' gloom to illuminate the damage wrought, and the process of recovery was begun.

Seeing that Nathan rested comfortably, with pledges from both Kirkland and Millbridge that she would be woken at the slightest change, Cate was drawn like a compass needle to north to the stern sill. Now blazing with sunlight and warmth, she stretched out there in glorious comfort and collapsed into a deep sleep.

Cate's reprieve was brief. The storm had been violent, the injuries many: splinters—some almost as long as her hand—gashes, contusions, smashed digits, burns and battered ribs were only a sampling of what awaited. Two men had been stricken with inexplicable fevers, and two more were confined to their hammocks with busted guts.

As for the ship, before the mast was a snarled mess, her jibs and forestays a cat's-cradle of jury-rigging. The forecastle jacks and carpenters worked in ant-like fury to set their world aright. The stricken anchor was barely recognizable and quite the spectacle. Flung from its cathead by the lightning bolt, it had landed prong-down, and stuck in the forecastle planking like the sea bottom itself. The opposing hook, higher than a man's head, was contorted, as if a gargantuan had made a rude attempt at a bowline knot. The nearby kevels, nearly shoulder-wide wooden cleats mounted on the rail, had been shattered; its splinters Cate had removed from the flesh of several of the men. The tar and varnish, which coated everything, had been sparked by the lightning, leaving parts of the bowsprit, forepeak and forecastle charred. It made one thankful for the storm's deluge, which had doused the fire before the ship was consumed.

The carpenters and smith, and their respective mates, hammered out new blocks, eyes and fittings, nails, pins, bolts and pegs. Amid the flurry of splicing, knotting, reeving, and fair weather sails bent, the teeming decks were a virtual snow bank of drying hammocks, clothing and sails. A constant vigil was maintained on the rigging, lest the masts be wrung. In

658

spite of its covering of pitch, wind-driven rain could saturate a rope, causing it to stretch. Drying rope shrank, damaging her sticks and yards. The smell of tar stoves returned, as the hands furiously toiled to fill the seams loosened by the ship's working, the rap of caulking mallets a backdrop to every conversation.

"Two feet in the well, sir," was the carpenter mate's report to Pryce, "but holding," came with a sigh of relief.

"At least the scuttlebutts are full," said Millbridge in his aged pragmatism, as he scanned the ruin. Fresh drinking water was the least of their concerns.

The seas calmed, the wind freshened and steadied, and the mizzen, jury-rigged staysails and royals bellied out. A tops'l breeze, to be sure. The topmasts, however, remained on deck.

"She can't bear it just now," Pryce said, casting a concerned but loving eye upward.

A battered queen, the *Morganse* sailed, her dignity broken, but still regal.

Between mending the ill and injured, and fraying oakum, vast amounts now in desperate need, Cate was busy. As promised, Kirkland and Millbridge kept her regularly informed of Nathan's condition, but she was still compelled to see for herself. She found him the same: sleeping as peacefully as a babe, recouping and repairing, just as his ship.

It was after the second dog watch—notable because during, the hands had their first warm meal served in days—and Cate went to check on Nathan, once more. She pushed the curtain aside, careful so as not to rattle the curtain rings. A watch lamp hung, so that he might be readily observed but not disturbed. Careful not to trip on the stool, she crept closer, pressing her skirt to her legs, lest the rustle of the cloth might wake him. A reflexive, useless gesture, for it would have been lost amid the babel from outside.

There was a stillness about the room, the odd tranquility which shrouded the ill when they slept. The riot of noise outside somehow muffled and distant, the most prominent sound was the somnolent rhythm of his breathing, a slight rattle in his throat echoing the ragged of his voice. Looking up at the port, she made note of the need to pass the word for a carpenter's mate to unseal it, so that the room might be rid of the smell of sickness. The thought was immediately dismissed until after Nathan had his rest.

Nathan was inherently so animated, it was disquieting to see him so still. Stranger was to see him lying in his own bed, a rarer thing to see him sleep—she still had no idea where he had slept these weeks past. An internal voice demanded that he should drink; another, he should eat. "He should rest" won out. The rictus of pain and delirium gone, his was a peaceful face. His hand, almost mahogany against the blue and yellow quilt, rested on his belly, a sticking-plaster in place. No swelling. No redness. No smell. He would be whole. She closed her eyes in thankfulness once more.

Cate resisted the urge to straighten the quilt or brush the braid from his chest, and the even stronger ones to clasp his hand or kiss his cheek. Seeing him now, almost angelic, she regretted her earlier indignation and anger. The hurt she suffered at being called Hattie was less readily put aside, but not indispensably entrenched. She shouldn't like to be held responsible for what she might utter in fever or dreams; neither should anyone else. After all, the unconsciousness wasn't the realm of reality.

God help me, I love him.

She sat heavily on the stool with the impact. Love: an elixir, which could erase and ease more ills and hurts, than any potion or palliative. Either by his charm, the Fates, or whatever controlling powers might be, she had been drawn. She had seen the pit looming and had fallen in, from which there was now no escape.

Cate lingered for some while to watch Nathan sleep, memorizing every curve and line, odd hair and blemish. What the light didn't allow, her mind filled in. His headscarf was gone, but its ghost remained as a pale line across the high forehead, just above the sweep of sable brows. A thread-like scar ran from his temple up into his hairline. The thick copper-tipped lashes had an almost girlish curve. The color was repeated in the three bright copper hairs at one corner of his beard. The somberness caused by the downward curve of his mouth from the sharp peak in the center was softened by the hooks of his mustache lifting it in a half-smile, his cheeks rounding with it.

Sleep could be highly contagious, mere observation sufficient for one to be stricken. With a body suddenly filled with sand, Cate rose and trudged out. The cabin's furniture was yet to be released from its storm-lashings, and so she went to the sill once again. She pulled the combs and shook out her hair then stretched until her joints popped, expelling a groan of relief like she had heard her grandmother emit.

The stern window was open. The breeze brushed Cate's cheek as she lay with her head pillowed on her arm. It was a soft night, as were most in the Caribbean. With the light of a lop-sided moon glittering on the water and outlining scallop-edged clouds, she watched the phosphorescent wake of the ship reach back into eternity. She thought of all the things she should do, and all the reasons why she shouldn't: no one was seriously ill, the injured had been tended, a great mound of oakum stood before those charged with rolling it for the caulkers, and Nathan was within earshot, if he was to stir or call out.

The pounding of adzes, mallets and hammers her lullaby, she slept.

28: TROUBLE IN PARADISE

Hodder's bellow echoed up the galley companionway with sufficient force to yank Cate from a profound sleep.

"Show a leg, you pimpish, misbegotten bunch o' sluggards! Haul yer arses, ladies! Goddamned, spindle-shanked swag-bellies, the lot o' you's!"

Cate bound to her feet before realizing it was only meant for the men in their hammocks.

In spite of her unscheduled awakening, a pot of hot coffee sat steaming on the table. How Kirkland did it was a mystery for the ages. Rubbing the sleep from her eyes, she shuffled over, poured a cup and sipped, aware Kirkland's brew was always capable of scalding the unsuspecting. Once braced up, she went to see how Nathan did.

It was a mild but pleasant surprise to find him lying on his back, staring at the beams overhead.

"Get me clothes," he said without preamble, pulling the quilt closer about him.

"I give you joy of the morning as well," she said tartly. It wasn't quite the start of the day she had imagined. Nathan could be curt in the morning, but there was a particularly unpleasant edge about him.

"It's too soon for you to be abroad," she said, with reserved concern.

"I've shirked long enough." He frowned, uncertain as to how long that had been.

She reached to inspect Nathan's hand. He successfully jerked it from her grasp, but failed at concealing the pursuing wince. Crossing her arms, she stood over him, feet planted squarely. Her intention was to block him from rising, but the position also provided a fair view of his hand. It looked better, no longer inflamed and angry-looking. The swelling had gone down to where his fingers were near normal-sized, and his knuckles were once again visible.

He fixed a defiant eye up at her and bellowed, "Mr. Millbridge!" Nathan's glare held through Millbridge's arrival and, "Me clothes, if you please,"

Millbridge darted a rheumy eye at her, and then knuckled his forehead in salute, a rare and a bit mocking gesture.

"At least linger here the day," Cate pleaded after Millbridge's departure. A relapse of the fever wasn't out of the realm of possibility.

"Indolence 'tis not a virtue," Nathan said doggedly.

Clutching the quilt about him, he lurched to his feet. All color instantly drained from his face, and an odd greenish tinge set in about his nose and mouth. He looked sure to either vomit or fall out, but determination saw him through. He stood defiantly before her, weaving and catching the edge of the bed. A high-chinned glare suggested she was expected to not notice.

The clothing arrived directly. Nathan snatched, missed and snatched again at his shirt on the bunk. He drew himself to full height and growled, "A bit o' privacy, *if* you please."

"You should rest."

"Pray, mind the oars in your *own* boat," Nathan said censoriously. Only the most generous could have called his showing of teeth a smile.

Fine tremors coursed through her as his image was blurred by several shades of red. She hadn't expected effusive thanks to be lauded upon her, but a little acknowledgement would have been appreciated. Ingratitude seemed no more Nathan's nature than the dreaded "indolence."

Still deep in that same tinted haze, she didn't remember going to the curtain, but did hear the clatter of the rings when she snatched it aside.

"Then by your leave, *m'lord!*" She hoped he didn't hear the quaver in her voice. Amid another jangle of rings, the curtain was yanked shut behind her.

Once alone, she sagged against the bulkhead, tears stinging the backs of her eyes. Voices rose from the galley companionway, and she ran to the corner of the salon and locked herself in the convenience. There she sobbed into the folds of her skirt.

⌘

The day failed to improve.

Several days bed rest would be normally prescribed after what Nathan had just suffered, but a ship wasn't a normal place, especially one staggering under such storm damage. Nathan was still pale and drawn, the glow of health yet to return. There were dark smudges under his eyes and an uncommon sag to his shoulders. He flared at delicate suggestions, not only from Cate, but Pryce and Millbridge, that he should rest. Seeing Nathan periodically cradle his hand in the crook of his other arm causing everyone to make allowances. That sympathy, however, was quickly dissolved by uncharitable thoughts in the face of his ill-tempered bursts.

Cate tried to shake it off, crediting Nathan's contrary behavior to his concern for his ship. Keenly aware of the toll the last few days had taken on everyone aboard, she scolded herself for being thin-skinned and testy.

She thought it her imagination at first, but gradually came to realize Nathan was making a point of being where she was not. Over a hundred feet of ship suddenly wasn't large enough. Twice, while she mounted the windward steps, she saw him exit the quarterdeck by the leeward. When she came into the cabin, he rose abruptly and brushed past her without a word. She was left standing in his wake confused and feeling as cold and empty as the coffee cup he had left on the table.

That night, Cate glumly picked at the plate Kirkland had left. For the third time that day, Nathan had come to the cabin, saw her, pivoted and left. The report was that he now sat on the masthead — God knew how he got up there, one-handed — threatening bodily harm to anyone who ventured near. Beatrice grew quarrelsome — more so than was her usual — and Hermione declined her evening tobacco quid.

The memories of the fervor of his kiss and the warmth of his arms, his body pressing against hers, responding so readily to her touch, had faded incrementally under his cold glares and icy shoulder. It was quite clear it had all been an anomaly. It was unsettling how one could be so passionate one point, and so distant and surly the next.

She braced her head in her hands. "This is Nathan. What the hell else did you expect?"

The thing which weighed most was the one she could barely admit: Hattie.

Hattie.

The name loomed over her like a mythical being. It was like being the second wife after the untimely death of the beloved first: living in the shadows, always measured, always seen through a tinted lens.

You remind him of her.

No more chilling or damning words had ever been uttered.

It was clear that she was but a substitute. A fascination and wonder it was, as to how Nathan could continue to love the very one who had so cold-bloodedly betrayed him, but there it was. Cate stood at the curtain looking at the bunk, and wondered what pleasures he and Hattie had enjoyed there. She couldn't help but wonder if a few days earlier, when Nathan had closed his eyes, had it been his precious Hattie he made love to? It had been his precious Hattie he had called for when fevered. His disappointment at finding Cate standing there instead was evident. The whole situation was so much like a drunk after a binge, during which ugly things had been said. Now sober, the drunk didn't recall anything, and assumed everyone around him to do the same, any hurt to be forgotten. The difference here was that Nathan had been the drunk. And yet, he was the one acting hurt. Worse was a strong edge of resentment about him, as well, as if Cate had somehow sought to deceive him.

A part of her wanted to tell Nathan "Have the bitch and be damned!" Except her heart told her what she already knew: there was no leaving him. The question was how much more wretched she would become, in her desperation to be with him? How long would she allow him his illusions? Sadly, the question was more how long before he was done with her?

Neither did the second day improve.

The ship cracked on with an uncommon press of sail. Looking nearly as haggard as their captain, many of the crew cast an eye skyward at the show of canvas, and surreptitiously crossed their fingers or touched their charms.

"The Cap'n knows 'is ship better than any pigtail swingin' tar aboard, but this..." she heard Hodder mutter.

The rare times Nathan spoke to Cate—and blessedly rare they were—he was churlish and distant, often curt to the point of cutting. His most loyal, including Pryce and Millbridge, scowled in his path, as puzzled as she. Nathan's growing moodiness brought her to almost regret having nursed him to health. "Health" however, was barely applicable. He was even more slumped and hollow-eyed, the dark circles there deepening.

As Cate swung from confusion to fury, she sank deeper and deeper into misery, all the while smiling in desperate hope that it was all her imagination. When the smile failed, she locked herself in the convenience and sobbed into the towel, now kept in the corner for just such moments.

That night Nathan came up missing. Cate was seized by panic, envisioning him lying somewhere, fevered and helpless. He was at last found sprawled on the bowsprit. Arm hanging limp, a rum bottle suspended between two fingers, starring at the night sky.

The next day, the *Morganse* finally cleared a point on Blue Goat Island, Cogburn's Island, her destination, could be seen ahead. The bay, where they were to rendezvous with the *Griselle*, was to its north, but so was the wind, or nearly so. It meant a long tack: angling out as close to the wind as the *Morganse* would bear, until far enough out when she came about — wear around, that is, bringing the wind more or less behind her — it would be in a direct line back into the bay.

Cate had hoped the prospect of joining up with Thomas might sweeten Nathan's mood.

It didn't.

Nathan flew into a black rage at Mute Maori, at the helm, for turning too soon. It was now a decision made by the helmsman, but that was a minor point. Doing so had caused their course to fall short of the targeted point of land. It meant they would have to tack again.

"Goddamned current is what it is," muttered someone from behind Cate, standing at the waist. "Any blighter worth 'is salt could see it."

Cate stood at the lee rail as the *Morganse* drew nearer and near to the Cogburn, a trio of masts poked their heads above the treeline, indicating a ship sitting on the island's far side.

"Is that the *Griselle*?" she asked against the backdrop of Hodder's bellow of "Ready about!" and the pounding of feet as the hands raced to their stations.

Busy with the ship, Pryce glanced up. "Aye, 'tis her."

"How did they get here ahead of us?" If two ships departed from the same point at the same time, one would expect the fastest to arrive first, and that the *Morganse*, hands down.

Pryce shrugged. "Better winds. Shorter course. Probably wasn't obliged to scud so far a'fore the storm."

The outward leg of the tack, required two flips of the glass, during which Nathan bawled out two of the ship's most seasoned topsmen for being laggardly aloft, but the tack brought the Morganse into position. In the long rays of the late afternoon sun, she pirouetted as prettily as a ship might and angled toward the bay. It was four more turns of the glass, however, before the reef was cleared and she slipped into Cogburn Bay. A unified sigh of relief from all her people seemed to provide an extra push on the sails.

They hailed the *Griselle* as they passed, Thomas, at the taffrail, shouting back. The *Griselle* couldn't have been long arrived, for her boats were clustered at her side like chicks around a hen, and the beach stood empty.

Even with his ship settled on her mooring, Nathan's snappish mood didn't improve. He flew into tirades at minor oversights and nonexistent mistakes: the yards were crooked, reeving too sloppy, lifting tackle too high, and sheets improperly stowed. At the end of one such berating, he reeled off into the cabin.

Cate stood at the capstan when she realized every eye aboard was turned on her. From the f'c'stle to the quarterdeck, from the tops to the waist, she saw expressions in varying degrees from imploring to warning, pleading to accusation. Nearly ten score of innocent bystanders were taking the brunt of what was clearly something between her and Nathan, no matter how desperately she wished otherwise. With a nod of vague acknowledgement, she trudged into the cabin, with no clear idea of what she meant to do.

Nathan sat at the table, snatching through the charts, grumbling about a missing divider. Cate took it as a small victory that he hadn't sped from the room when she entered.

"Problems finding something?" she asked lamely.

Nathan didn't look up, but his mouth took an ugly curl. "Problems seems to be me specialty lately."

Cate was in the process of steeling her nerve when she discovered she couldn't breathe. The condition was not entirely the fault of the closed windows, a rare oddity. She moved to open them, if for no other reason than to stall further.

"Leave it!" he growled, with a tone that suggested he had been waiting for her to do exactly that.

"I just thought we might—"

"It's the same damned air what comes through the door. Leave it!"

Cate flinched at the cut in his voice. She began to pace; charity and the driving need to do something churning her gut.

"You need to eat," she said, at last drawing up to the table.

"No. Thank. You," he said without looking up.

"Allow me to pass the word for Kirkland...?"

Nathan gave a thunderous glare from under his brow. "I had one mum; I shan't be in need of another."

"But you haven't—"

Nathan slammed down the dividers with a force that sent his pencil skittering off the table. "Clap a stopper on it!"

Cate considered turning and leaving, just as she had seen him do over the last two days, but hesitated. She was driven by what some would call determination. Other less charitable souls might have flung words like "stubborn," or even "bullish," in her less stellar moments. Whatever it was, she was resolved to seeing this to a head.

In that spirit, she went to the galley for some hot broth.

"Here, I thought…" she said, and slid the mug before Nathan. She had bid Kirkland put it in a mug, so Nathan mightn't be obliged to sit, which he seemed so disinclined to do when she was about.

His eyes fixed on the chart, it was shoved aside. "Away, you meddlesome pestilence."

Her cheeks flamed. Nathan could be edgy, even brusque, at any given point in the day, but never so vicious.

"What in the hell is eating you, Nathan?" It came out more confrontational than intended, but what was done was done. "You've been prickly as an old bear. You snap—"

"Bugger off, strumpet!"

For a moment, she wasn't sure she had heard him correctly. "You meant that!"

"At last, the dull-witted dolt comprehends!" he extolled to the ceiling.

Her fist curled, but then she thought better.

"No," she said, recomposing herself. "I'm not going to—"

In a sharp jangle of bells, he lurched to his feet with a suddenness that caused her to stumble back. He stormed to the windows and stood for some moments, staring out at the evening just settled.

Nathan whirled back around, his braids arcing with the momentum. "I want to know whose it is?"

"Whose what is?" she stammered.

He crashed his fist on the table, the broth spurting up out of the mug. "Goddamn it to fucking hell, woman, do not vex me!"

"You're raving." She eyed him from a distance, thinking perhaps the fever had returned. He was not hale, by any means, but neither were there any signs of fever. If anything, his hand seemed to have gone forgotten, perhaps the result of a great quantity of rum. The air was thick with its sweet smell.

Nathan stalked toward her, his voice falling to threatening rumble. "I have been more than a gentleman. I've given you everything what could possibly be provided on this ship. I've never made so much as a gesture towards you. God knows I could have, but I never laid a finger on you."

"I'm to be grateful you didn't throw me down and take me the first night?" she asked, backing away.

"But I didn't! And this is me thanks!"

"Tell me whose it is! If he took you unwilling, by God, I'll see his balls swinging from me bowspr't. Hell, I'll hold him down so you can cut them off yourself, but you have to tell me who!"

First time since her first day aboard, Cate was afraid of him. His beard had grown to a deep ebony bush, and obscured his face, so similar to that day. The dark smudges under his eyes rendered him even more sinister. His sword and pistol were across the room. She eyed the weapons at the mizzen and urn at the door as she continued to back away. She didn't think he would use them against her, but he also looked the right tartar, and capable of anything.

"Nathan," she began levelly. "I don't understand —"

He went dead white and charged. Stumbling back, she came up against a trunk. He grabbed her by the throat and bent her back over it, slamming her head against the wall. She tore at his hand; the very one she had fought to save now squeezing the life from her. His eyes, now inches from hers, had gone as black and sightless as a shark's. His thumb gouged her windpipe, and her limbs grew heavy, too heavy to move. A roar filled her ears, and pinpricks of light began to flash at the edges of her vision. A remote voice warned she was about to be killed, and would never know why.

As suddenly as Nathan had attacked, he broke away. Cate slumped atop the chest, wincing in pain as she clutched her throat. Raggedly panting, Nathan closed his eyes in an effort to regain a level of self-control.

"You've been on this ship for nigh on to two months," he began, his voice breaking with emotion. "I've offered you safe haven. I've not asked a thing of you, not a goddamned thing."

He pivoted and kicked a chair, sending it tumbling. He took an angry swipe at another, and prowled the room like a caged cat. Grunting in effort, he threw open a gallery window. He braced his arms on the frame, his back heaving with each breath.

"I just want to know whose it is," he said. Grinding his head into his forearm in anguish, his fist pounded the wood in rhythm with each word. "I just need to know who you've been with."

It took Cate a moment to get his meaning and her mouth sagged. "You think I've been bedding someone?" she wheezed, her throat not yet fully recovered. She stood on shaky legs. "You think I've been cavorting with one of your crew?"

"I dare say 'tis fairly obvious," he said, coldly over his shoulder. "Was it someone on this ship, or was it someone on the *Constancy*? Don't tell me it was Harte or Thomas!"

Days of tension had taken its toll, and now she was the one to snap. "What do you care? You have no claim on me. It is none of your bloody, damned concern!"

Whirling, he kicked over a stand, sending the candlesticks atop it clattering to the floor. Her sewing box was sent flying next.

"It *is* my concern!" he bellowed.

"Who made you my master?" Seething, she stalked toward him. "Pray enlighten me as to which angers you the most: that I bedded someone, or that it was someone other than you? Let me tell you, Captain Blackthorne, just because you're the captain does not allow you the right to expect *anything*!"

By now they were nose to nose. Nathan was rigid with fury, the tails of his scarf curling around his shoulders like serpents.

"Pray allow me to tell you a thing or two, *madam*. As captain, I have the right to do or expect anything I damn well please. And if I had wanted to have you, I'd have goddamned had you! What with your whoring around, being a gentleman was lost on you."

"I'm obliged to defer to your expertise on whores. Unlike you, I don't swive everyone or everything that passes."

"You think if you can seduce me —"

"Seduce!?"

"*Seduce* me into stuffing your quim," Nathan continued over her sputtering objections. "And you made double-damned sure o' that."

"What are you raving about?"

"Once again I tried to be the gentleman, but oh now, you'd have none o' that. All to assure that bastard you're carrying could be passed off on me."

In an enraged blur, Cate seized the first thing within reach — an unsuspecting lantern — and hurled it. Nathan dodged and took it on the shoulder, metal and glass crashing to the floor. A candlestick was next. She pitched it, catching him in the arm. While in search of her next weapon, Nathan grabbed her by the arm and jerked her around. She brought her knee up aiming for his crotch. Easily deflecting the attempt, he gave her arm a vicious wrench, his fingers like spikes in her skin.

"Don't you ever do that again." He gave her arm a sharp twist in emphasis.

"Or what?" Cate balled her fist and swung. Nathan ducked to take the blow in the ear. Swearing, he wrenched her arm harder, eliciting a pained cry.

"Take your hands off me, you sodding bastard!"

To her surprise, he did. He stood back, chest heaving. She backed away, rubbing her arm. Hot tears welled behind her eyes, but be damned if she would let him see her cry!

"You arrogant son of a bitch. That limp codpiece couldn't sire anything. Even if there was a child, don't flatter yourself: you'd be a sorry candidate. Getting too old to take your pleasures? Have to fancy me with someone to get them? I certainly found none."

Nathan pointed a rigid arm at the door, eyes glittering with hatred. "Then away, with you. Take your bastard and be off, and be damned to you both."

"Fine! I shan't desire for you to ask twice."

As Cate whirled around, she felt the weight of the knife Nathan had given her swinging against her leg. She drew it from her pocket and hurled it. Nathan dodged, allowing it to fall harmlessly to the floor. He then glared, uncertain if she had meant to draw blood.

"There! I shouldn't desire to take anything which might lead you to think I meant to at your expense." She spread her arms in exhibition. "Take a good look. Not one copper. I know these aren't mine," she said, plucking at her skirt, "but you'll forgive me, if I decline to go naked. Rest assured, they shall be returned. Goodbye!"

The crew, gathered at the door listening, scattered like flushed quail as she burst out.

"You have a share of Creswicke's money coming," Nathan called after her.

"Stuff it up your arse alongside your head!"

She met Pryce, who stood frozen in mid-step at the bottom of the quarterdeck steps.

"Get me as far away from this stinking hulk as possible," she said loudly enough to be heard in the cabin.

Uncertain, the First Mate looked to his Captain, who now stood in the doorway, a dark, faceless blot against the cabin's lights.

"Away with her and the Devil take her!" Nathan gave a dismissive bat of the hand and disappeared inside.

Towers and Smalley were beckoned by a jerk of Pryce's head. "Take 'er as she desires."

Pryce fixed his attention on the two scampering down the side and the boat being made ready. Cate stood quivering. As rage dissolved into shock, more rational thoughts pushed their way in. She could think of nothing more than to be as far from that bastard as possible, but to where? The island was directly before her. Now dotted with campfires, the beach was a silvery gleam between the dark of water and trees. Looking across the bay, the glow of the *Griselle's* stern windows was ever so much more appealing.

The call of "Ready away," from the water drew her back. When she moved toward the gate, her eyes finally caught Pryce's.

"What did I do?" Cate asked, tears welling anew.

Pryce glanced cautiously over his shoulder to the empty cabin door. "By the devil's tail, 'n damn my eyes if I know, sir."

She nodded. His reluctance toward the suggestion of betrayal of his captain's confidence was understandable. As she turned to step over the gunwale, Pryce stopped her with a hand on her arm.

"I honestly don't know, Cate," he said in uncommon sincerity. "Ain't never see'd 'im like this a-fore. More 'n likely, 'tis nothin' of yer doin'."

She put a hand over his and squeezed gently. "Thank you."

And then, she left.

⁂

Sitting very still, Thomas slid a look toward the hour glass.

He hadn't seen his sisters in years, but their crying bouts were indelibly etched in his mind. There had been four, and each had taken generous amounts of time for such sessions.

Hunched on the hassock watching Cate pace the cabin, Thomas heaved a silent sigh. This one bore the makings of dwarfing any of his sisters' tantrums. She had already scored higher marks in volume and vehemence, and was on the verge of surpassing all competition in violence. He wasn't sure if his cabin was going to survive.

She and Nathan's caterwauling had been readily heard. It came as no surprise when the watch hailed a *Morganse* boat shortly after. One look at Cate's face and any doubts were erased as he had handed her up the side. He held her while she cried—Sweet merciful heaven, she felt good in his arms, snot-faced, blubbering and all—and now gave her a wide berth as she rampaged, alert to any harm she might do herself, or that she might need him once more.

Mired as she was in her own crisis, she had given him no notice, leaving him at his leisure. He could watch her all day. Mesmerizing she was, a sorceress who had cast a spell. A beauty she was... Well, aye, not exactly at that very moment. Face contorted like a Balinese devil mask, puffy-eyed and red-nosed, her mouth curled around oaths that probably caused the hands to blush.

Propping his chin in his hand, he tracked her path with his eyes. Only time would salve this.

Thomas wondered what in all that's holy had possessed Nathan. He grumbled silent curses at someone who could be so consistently blind to everything and everyone around him. Granted, Nathan had survived all these years by raw will, guile his steadfast partner, but it would appear those had failed him, *again*! This wasn't new; he had lived this scenario before, and could probably quote Nathan's latest bungling tirade chapter and verse. Expecting the man to change, however, was to expect the tides to do the same.

But then again, maybe not; Cate was different. Thomas had known it the moment he'd laid eyes on her. Nathan knew it, too. Poor dumb bastard just didn't know what to do. And now, Nathan might have just pissed away the best thing — the best hope — to ever have crossed his hawse.

Bruises bloomed on Cate's neck; that was damned disquieting. He'd never known Nathan to do a woman violence before... Well, other than the occasional, cod-fisted street whore who sought to lift his purse. His first urge was to go slap some sense into him, but Nathan's cup looked to runneth over with troubles already.

Thomas leaned aside as a book sailed past, ducked as another spun harmlessly to the other side, and then reached to snag a pillow from mid-air. Deep blue satin, with hummingbirds embroidered; no sense in letting that one go to ruin. As he observed Cate, seething before the stern windows, he made a mental note never to provoke her — or at the least be prepared if he did. After all, forewarned was forearmed. Knowing the kind of fury, she was capable of warranted special caution. He weighed the possibility that might have been Nathan's downfall: no warning. How could the cuckle-headed dolt have foreseen something like this?

Re-settling his chin in his palm, Thomas glanced around. So far, Cate was too gone to notice all the changes made since her last visit. Most evidence of a man living alone had been secured, stashed or stowed. There were more pillows about, particularly in the chair he had pulled closer to the windows. A stand and a hanging lamp sat next to it — she had said something about liking to sew. The sheets on the berth had been washed, and there was a new coverlet. The ewer and basin were new — well, newer than before.

When Cate's back was turned, he closed one eye and measured. Definitely going to have to get her out of those rags. She deserved better, much better, something to show off that small waist and sumptuous curve of hip. Body of a woman — all woman — buried in there. Leave it to Nathan desiring to hide it; obscuring temptation, in all likelihood.

He cringed when a bottle hit the bulkhead. Oh well, water over the decks. They drank it dry directly after she boarded.

Better than the crystal one which contained the port she favored. A lamentable loss that would be.

Aye, duration was the only remaining question to this rampage, and she gave all signs of crushing that record, too.

Thomas reached to turn the glass.

Aye, this was going to be a long one.

Cate wept as she hadn't in years. She sobbed now as she had the first night Brian was gone — and the next — and the next. It was much the same: the same pain, the same sense of every organ being ripped out and trampled, this time by a pair of worn, brown suede boots. It wasn't just the anguish wrought by coarse words and hurt feelings, but loss, a deep, gut-tearing loss.

She swung on an emotional pendulum from anger to desolation and back again, making brief visits to every increment in between. She cursed herself for having trusted, for being too damnedably eager to clutch onto something, *someone*. Self-loathing and furious, she chewed at herself like a trapped fox, and at Nathan, for being... for being himself!

That thought — that small fact — pitched her back into the pits of despair. Nathan was what he was: a pirate, pillager of the seas and women's hearts. What moment of innate stupidity made her think he would ever be anything different?

Rage would then revisit, furious at having allowed him to play her, furious with herself for falling victim to his cavalier games. She shot a tear-burred glare out the stern windows at the *Morganse* across the bay. It was easy to envision him that very moment, lounging in his chair, feet crossed on the table, laughing in smug satisfaction.

Her heart had cracked at being called Hattie. Now she gasped at the ripping sound of it being torn from her chest. If she wasn't his precious Hattie, then too damned bad! All that foolishness about a child had been just one of his hair-brained schemes to be rid of her.

"Well it worked!" she shrieked at a chair.

Her mother only raised a partial fool. Be damned if she would ever step foot on that stinking hulk. She was done with him. She didn't want to see his face or hear his voice ever again... *ever*!

A blinding fury took her afresh. In the dim reaches of her mind, she knew she hurled something, the sound of shattering glass her only clue as to what it had been. The exertion purged some of her frustration and, mindless of what it was or the direction it went, threw something else. She heard the clang and clatter of metals, but paid little heed. Screaming until her throat burned, she pitched and threw anything in her path.

Sweating and gasping, she crumpled in a chair, buried her face into a pillow and surrendered to the next wave of tear-laden despair.

She shrieked and jerked at being tapped on the shoulder. Looking up, she found Thomas standing over her, proffering a glass.

"Drink it," he said, with the tone of a person accustomed to being obeyed. "It's the port you fancied so much the other night. Maybe it will allow you a little ease."

Thomas stretched across the table to grab the bottle and plunked it emphatically in front of her. "Here, drink the whole damned bottle, if that's what it's going to take."

Sniffing loudly, Cate took it. Thomas hooked a chair with his foot and dragged it over to sit knee-to-knee. He propped his chin in his palm and looked interestedly into her face. "How much longer can we expect this to continue?"

Eyes hot knots and face throbbing, she knew she must look a wreck. She bent her head.

"I don't know." Her voice squeaked to a ridiculously high pitch. "I've been trying to stop."

"The crew is growing fair frayed. Sooner would be better."

A warm flush rose up her face at the realization the entire crew had perforce, been listening.

No secrets on a ship.

A pair of lake blue eyes, sparking with mirth, came into her view as Thomas leaned forward. "No man can possibly be worth all this."

Cate's chin wobbled as she attempted a smile between sniffs. She made a feeble attempt to dry the side of her face, but dropped her hand at seeing how badly it shook. A quick glance told her Thomas had seen, too.

"You wouldn't think so, would you?" she choked.

Cate sipped from the glass. Thomas frowned, an arched sandy brow bidding her to take a larger one. Relenting, she did and shuddered. The liquor burned her throat, raw from crying, and her eyes watered worse.

Sniffing hard, she dashed at the wetness on her cheek. Rummaging in his pockets, Thomas produced a large lace-edged handkerchief and watched, sympathetic yet bemused, as she blew her nose and wiped her face.

"I'm not sure if I'm more angry or hurt," she said. "He was a monster. I've never seen him like that before!"

Too upset to sit, Cate rose and commenced to pace. "I've

seen him drunk, or on some crazed tangent, but I've never seen him so… livid."

"Nathan can have a bit of a temper," Thomas conceded. "Although, it is rare. You must have really pushed him."

"*I* pushed him," she huffed, whirling around. "That's just it. I don't know what I did. For the last couple of days, he had been growing touchier and touchier, and then he just exploded."

Thomas pressed his palms together and watched as his fingers laced in and out among themselves. "Well, give him time; it will pass."

"No, I don't think so. I don't think it's going to be that easy. We both said some horrible things that—"

"All in the heat of anger," he said, bearing a tolerant smile.

"It was more than that."

Cate swallowed with some effort and touched her throat. The soreness there brought back the murderous look on Nathan's face as he had squeezed.

"He meant it. I could see it was something he had been waiting to say for a long time, as though it had been festering for… for… forever."

"Well, no matter." Thomas slapped his thighs and rose. "You know where everything is. I said you'd have a place here, and I meant it. You're welcome for as long as you wish."

So, caught up in her own turmoil, she had overlooked how her arrival might have appeared. "Thomas, I'm not here to—"

He broke into a self-conscious grin. "No, no, don't worry. Never entered my mind."

Under its golden tan, his fair skin flushed, his ears going pink. "Well, that's a bit of a lie. It wouldn't be Christian of me, if I didn't say that I'd love to have you—not in the biblical sense," he was quick to add. "Well, aye, in that way too—but you're too wound up in Nathan, right now. Give it time; I'll wait."

He ended with a quiet note of confidence, one which she didn't share.

"Thomas?"

He stopped at the door and looked back over his shoulder with an expectant lift to his brows.

"In all honesty, thank you," Cate said.

Waving an obliging hand, he left.

⌘

Morning broke bright, but by Thomas' judgment, the sun was the only thing which shone on the *Griselle*. Cate looked like hell and seemed to feel worse. No small wonder. It had been a fitful night for all aboard. The woman didn't suffer privately.

Cate sat brooding over a cup of coffee, looking at it as if she wished it was something else. He took a drink and winced. The word had been passed for Youssef to make it so decent people might drink it. Waste of words, by all evidence. He watched from the corner of his eye—she melted under direct eye contact—as her cup rattled against the saucer at every lift; something stronger was definitely in order.

He gave her a wide berth: saying nothing, making no gesture which might oblige her to speak. The mere utterance of "Good morning" had come with a wobbling chin and flooding eyes. Anything further came with uncommon effort. And so, they sat at opposite sides of the table in silence.

The moment he heard a boat hailed, he knew who it was. Cate heard Nathan's voice and looked up in round-eyed horror. Tears welling, she began to tremble worse.

"I don't want to see him. I don't want to hear him," she said with the coldness of a henchman. Her fist curled around the nearest thing to hand, an innocent coffee pot, and she tensed, ready to fling it. Thickened by crying, her voice was a ghost of its usual melodic self. "He can rot in hell for all I care."

The corner of Thomas' mouth curled. "Aye, well, he would probably tell you there's a good chance o' that already," he said dryly.

To give Cate ease, he took up a position at the door, shoulder against the frame and arms crossed.

Nathan's arrival was to be expected. The surprise was the hour: two bells had just rung on the forenoon watch. It was early, remarkably so.

"I give you joy o' the morning!" Nathan reeked of over-anxiousness as he bounded up over the side. It was uncommon for him to show his colors so readily.

"Joy to yourself. Too quiet on the *Morganse*, so you came here to stir things up?"

Nathan's jaunty step slowed. By some thought process known only to Nathan, clearly he had thought Thomas would be ignorant of what had transpired. Granted, Thomas didn't know everything, but he knew enough.

Nathan hesitated then pressed forward, though a bit more heavy of foot.

"I allowed you two desired a visit," Nathan began, "but now I've come to fetch her back. I know how anxious she'll be, what with how she worries about the crew. Veritable grandmother she is. Worry. Worry. Worry. I've advised she was to be old before her time, if she is to continue that-a-way, but she wouldn't..."

As Nathan chattered, he sought to pass Thomas and go inside. Thomas shifted, easily blocking his path. Nathan ducked to the other side, only to be blocked again. They jousted for several more rounds before Nathan stood back and gave him a narrow look.

"Don't you have somewhere else to be? I think I hear your crew calling."

Thomas reached inside the cabin for a small bundle atop a locker and handed it over. "Here, she said you desired these back."

Nathan looked up blankly. "Her clothes?"

Thomas grinned. "Easy, mate, I found her others. She's not running about naked."

Nathan marginally credited that statement.

"What scullerymaid did you steal those from? Couldn't you get her something decent?" Thomas asked severely.

"Wasn't time...I suppose," Nathan said, studying the bundle. He craned his head to see over Thomas' shoulder. "I need to speak with her."

"Tell him to go to hell!" called Cate vehemently from somewhere within.

Thomas cocked his head inside and then back to Nathan. "You heard the lady."

Nathan shot an accusing look. "Someone must have said something to upset her."

Ignoring Thomas' skeptical snort, Nathan rose on his toes to shout, "There are things what need saying."

"You've said quite enough," she cried shakily.

"You did your fair share," Nathan flared back. He gave Thomas a tenuous smile, "Women: an awkward lot, are they not?"

It was a question not intended to be answered; every man since Adam had pondered that one. He had known Nathan through hell and high water, seen him through his best and his worst, and this was one of the worst attempts to put on his best face ever witnessed. Hell must have been the morning's condition, for Nathan looked worse than Cate. True, he had shaved —

Damn! Forgot that, Thomas thought, passing a hand along his jaw.

Nathan looked as polished up as a school boy or at least as much as one might. Lord knew when that hair had last seen the benefit of a brush — fruitless venture, regardless — but attempts to smooth it had been made. The smell of orange oil was sharp in the air, rancid old stuff. Freshly shaven, coat and boots brushed, and hat dusted: aye, attempts had been made to render himself presentable.

Nathan straightened and squared his shoulders in the direction of where he thought Cate to be. "Very well, then, when might we speak?"

"I don't know!" Cate's voice quavered dangerously. She was on the verge of tears, *again*, a bad sign for all concerned.

Nathan's face darkened, and he charged the door. Thomas extended an arm, catching him by the throat.

Thomas leaned closer, eyeing him with cold severity. "Don't you dare start her crying again. She's barely over the last round. The cabin can't bear it."

Nathan's hands worked at his sides with the need to snatch Cate up and drag her back. The mood she was in, it was a sight Thomas would have given his purse to see Nathan try.

"Just allow me —" Nathan began.

"Thomas, don't you dare!" came a seething threat from inside.

" — only for a —"

"Never!"

Cate's virulent cry brought anyone within earshot — and a good portion of the ship it was, she having a strong set of lungs — to a halt. A deeper hush befell the decks, the hands warily circling in a wide berth.

"You can't talk your way out of this one, Nathan." Thomas glanced into the shadowed depths of his cabin and lowered his voice. "I tried to talk to her, last night — all night. I poured enough port down her to float the *Morganse*. There's no reasoning with her. Get her crying again, and by the devil's horns, I'll throw you to the sharks."

Nathan stared into the cabin. "If I could just talk to her, make her listen."

"Get the bloody hell away from me!" came a female shriek.

Nathan drew back as if struck at by a viper. He closed his eyes and swayed, looking fit to topple over. A strange calm befell him, and for the first time since Thomas had known him, he saw Nathan Blackthorne surrender.

"A gentleman always heeds the desires of a lady," Thomas suggested lightly.

"Aye, well as soon as said gentleman is found we can inquire as to how he does," Nathan said tartly.

Nathan fell quiet as he gazed into the shadows. A sadder, more dejected sight had never been seen. Haggard, drawn, dark circles under his eyes, and altogether beaten; it was a serious degeneration from when they had last met, barely a week hence.

"You look like bloody hell, man! You need a drink," Thomas said.

Nathan's shoulder moved disinterestedly under his coat. "I tried. It didn't answer."

Nathan trudged to the gangway and slumped on a step, hands dangling between his legs.

"I don't understand. I was me usual charming self. Oh, very well," he said at Thomas' derisive snort. "It was a fucking nightmare. Satisfied?"

"She hasn't stopped crying since she came up the side, except for that bit when she was throwing things. Has a bit of a temper, doesn't she?"

"She can be a terror," Nathan sighed, his gaze fixed on the cabin door. "What did she tell you?" he asked under his breath, even though they were well out of earshot.

"Everything and nothing," Thomas sighed. It had been a very long night. "'Mettlesome harlot'?"

Nathan winced and frowned with the effort of recalling. "No, t'was 'mettlesome strumpet,' I think."

"She curses better than most foremast jacks," said Thomas, duly impressed.

"Didn't learn it from me," Nathan said to his hands. "She came that way."

"What the hell were you thinking? Belay that," Thomas said with an irritated swipe. "Goddamned obvious you weren't. She's not Olivia, you know."

Nathan shot him a searing look then relented. "I know." Heaving a long exhale, he ground his forehead into his palm. "Cate's five times the woman Olivia ever was."

"Then why are you treating her as if she's half?"

Nathan twisted a grim gaze upward. "Always the friend."

"A friend is someone who helps when you're in trouble, and *you*, my friend, are in big trouble," Thomas said, clapping a hand on his shoulder.

Nathan threw off his hat and buried his face in his hands. "Suffering Jesus on the cross, this isn't going well a'tall."

"Can't argue with that."

"What do I do?" Nathan asked, rubbing his face hard.

"Get her back."

Nathan stopped to peer between his fingers. "How? You've always claimed to be the genius on women. What do I do?"

Making a disgusted sound, Nathan batted the air, but then assumed an essence of his familiar bravado. "'Tis for the best. Pryce can't bear a woman on board. The crew's grumbling..."

"Can you live knowing you let her slip away?" Thomas asked tentatively, studying his knuckles.

"I've lived with far more disturbing thoughts than that." Nathan glanced sideways to see if Thomas believed him.

He didn't.

"What if she finds someone else?" Thomas asked delicately.

Nathan wearily rubbed the back of his neck. "I don't want to even think about..." He stopped to look up. "You?"

Thomas straightened to present himself in the best light possible. "If she'll have me."

"Always the friend," Nathan muttered ruefully.

"She's too beautiful to be wasted."

Nathan thoughtfully drew his fingers down the curve of his mustache. "And has too much to give."

"She needs a man."

Nathan looked up to scowl. "And you're volunteering for the task? Mind, I shan't be about to pick up the pieces, if she won't."

Nathan rose and walked to the rail with the levity of a man heading for the gallows. Leaning heavily there, he gazed at the *Morganse* on her moorings. Standing at the rail, Thomas covertly studied Nathan and wondered whatever happened to the gentle, gregarious, nautical genius he had known years ago, whose sole desires were a ship and someone to love.

"Just keep her safe," Nathan said quietly. "Silver and gold does not all treasure make."

Thomas closed his eyes and murmured a silent *deo graci*. Nathan had just surrendered. "I know that well."

"Have a care," Nathan warned, his smile growing wistful. "She can be a handful; keep you guessing, she will. Sometimes, 'tis bloody impossible to know what she desires."

"Perhaps it's a matter of someone telling her."

Nathan chuckled mirthlessly. "She is going to tear you a new arse." "That bad?"

"Oh, yes, that bad," Nathan said heartily. "You've seen naught but the ripple over the reef."

Nathan sobered, his jaw twisted sideways in thought. "Take care of her. She likes coffee the very first thing of a morning, with milk, if you've a goat. The wise man will have it waiting before her eyes open. And with a little cinnamon, if you have it; she really likes that."

Nathan paused, pensively tracing his finger along the rail. "She likes air; keep the windows open. And scones; she likes scones," he said, looking up with a faint smile, "with bits of lemon or orange peel."

"No rum," Nathan continued, with a grimace. "She hates it;

a good whiskey or port, but no rum. Make a place for her, on the fo'c'stle; she loves it up there. She'll spend hours sitting there, while you're under sail," he said, inclining his head toward the bow.

He regarded Thomas and frowned. "And for God's sake, don't let anything get dirty. She hates dirt; the least sight sends her into a cleaning frenzy. And you'll have to start washing that shirt more... and yourself. She id the bathingest person you'll ever meet and expects the same of everyone near. Shave closer, too; she'll like that."

"Did you ever wash for her?"

Elbows braced on the rail, Nathan hung his head between his arms. "No, never did."

"Listen for her," Nathan said quietly, as he stared sightlessly across the water. His throat moved as he swallowed. "She cries, at night... for *him*. It's enough to tear your heart out. She won't remember come morning, but you'll need to be there for her."

Thomas found his throat had suddenly gone so tight he could barely squeeze out "I'll try to remember."

Nathan's smile grew distant. "Wait until you kiss her. She's like a hot coal; she comes alive in your arms—." He checked himself. Clearing his throat, he looked away. "Sorry."

Surrender. Thomas knew its cost on blood-slickened decks, but never this. He had seen Nathan in his lowest, knocking on death's door and hoping it would open. Beaten, flogged, stabbed, shot, starved, fever-wracked, scurvy-riddled, half-frozen, and half-dead from heat and thirst: none had been like this.

Thomas shifted again, telling himself this wasn't betrayal. This was picking up the pieces. If anything, he was doing them both a favor, a grand favor...

Then why the hell doesn't it feel that way?

Nathan nodded a vague appreciation. "What's your course to be?"

Thomas narrowed his eyes as he considered. This was the painful part; he'd sailed an ocean in hopes of resuming a lost friendship. "I had thought we could sail in consort for a bit. All things considered, I suppose that might not be the best idea now."

"Not bloody likely," Nathan said, with restrained vehemence.

"Probably north," Thomas said finally, looking in that direction. "Might try along the coast off the Colonies. Heard there's some good prospects along there; lots of heavy merchants and authorities willing to look the other way, for a small price, of course."

Nathan nodded interestedly. "She might fancy that. She's

from the Colonies, you know; she's kin of some sort or another there. It might be a chance for her to see home, finally."

Nathan leaned closer. "She's with child," he said, as if he was divulging the great secret of the ages.

Nathan pressed his fingers to his lips while glancing over his shoulder, oblivious to Thomas' gape. "T'would be ill-advised to speak of it. She's a mite crank on the subject. You know how they are," he added, with a conspiratorial wink.

"No, I don't," Thomas said, barely tolerant. "That would be more in the way of your expertise. Are you the—?"

"Hardly!"

"Then who...?"

Nathan slid a cutting look from the corner of his eye. "One never knows, does one?"

Thomas flinched at the barb. It was surprising how much restraint Nathan had exhibited on the matter, truth be told. Thomas had preferred to think it was all by the board, but apparently not. Contrary to all hopes, Nathan hadn't changed one goddamned bit, to the downfall of everyone around him. The outside might have changed, but the man inside was still the same bungling mess.

Nathan straightened, shook off his mood like a great dog in the rain. "Tis a grand friend you are for taking her off me hands," Nathan said, considerably louder than was necessary, probably for Cate's benefit, by Thomas' judgment.

"At a loss, I was," Nathan went on, "as to what the bloody hell I was to do with her. Nothing worse than a meddlesome, clinging woman on your hands."

Skepticism was Thomas' only reaction. The smile a bit pasted, the levity a bit forced, the gestures a bit stiff: it was another of Nathan's poorer performances.

"Damned annoying," Nathan went on, oblivious to Thomas' disgust. "Blabber, blabber, blabber. Never puts a stopper in that gob. No peace. No freedom; freedom is what it 'tis you know. Me ship, the sea and the horizon: what more could a man desire?"

Several answers came to mind, but it was a question not intended for one.

"Then you're done with her," Thomas said, straightening.

It was more a statement than a question. Nathan symbolically dusted his hands and held them up in exhibition: empty.

"Very well, then." Thomas snatched Nathan up by the front of his shirt and gave him a solid shake. "Lay hands on her again like you did yesterday, and I'll snap you like a twig."

Gazing up, Nathan went very still. "Go ahead," he said dully. "Put me out o' me misery."

Thomas let go and regarding Nathan through a narrowed eye. "Nay, I think not. It's more fitting that you should suffer."

Now Thomas was the one to dust his hands. "What are you going to do?"

Nathan brightened. "Don't rightly know. You know me: pick a spot on the chart, and I will already be there. The wind at me back and the waves at me bow..." The thought was finished with a grand swipe.

Sobering, Nathan looked off across the water toward the open sea. "Lord-on-high Creswicke will be burning the waters looking for us—me, that is—but the men will be desiring a few days at Tortuga, looking to spend their coin. After that, I dunno. Cartagena, maybe west."

Nathan's voice drifted off and he fell quiet. At length, he shook his head, as if closing off a private conversation and pushed away from the rail. "Very well, then. It's been good seeing you, old friend."

It became instantly clear a handshake wasn't insufficient, and they embraced, slapping each other heartily on the back.

"On the next horizon?"

"On the next horizon."

"Take care of yourself, Nathan. Oh, one more thing," Thomas said, just as Nathan reached the entry port. He drew back his fist and punched Nathan, his head snapping back with the impact.

"Ow!" Nathan's hand flew up to his nose. "What was that for?"

"For being such a thorough-going, bloody, fucking, goddamned fool!"

"Oh." Nathan tested his nose and examined his fingers for blood. "Can't argue that. Feeling better, are we?"

Thomas reflected as he rubbed his knuckles. "Aye, a bit."

"Then by your leave. Always desire to be of service to me friends in a time of *their* need," Nathan grumbled and swung over the gunwale.

"You want to take these?" Thomas held up the bundle of Cate's clothing.

"No! Tell her they were a gift," Nathan shouted back and disappeared down the side.

⌁

Cate stalked the cabin. She refused to look, but she could hear Thomas and Nathan talking on deck. She ducked anytime Nathan's voice threatened her ears. There were inopportune glimpses of them, and she took great satisfaction at seeing

Nathan looked positively wretched. Misery did indeed enjoy company and in a grand way!

A part of her wanted to go out there and do... something! Those urges were immediately quashed by the prospect of facing Nathan again. She vowed if he came in there she would do exactly as he had said he feared: jump. A glance reaffirmed the stern gallery stood open, just in case.

Oh, and there's that smile! She clamped her eyes shut against the pain of how it had touched her heart. He had flashed it at her, like candy to a child.

And how he had sweet-talked, with all those heart-felt confessions...

Vile... underhanded... manipulative bastard!

With that came a surge of disgust, at a level usually reserved for the likes of Creswicke and his ilk.

Nathan's look of relief was all too familiar, as was the dismissive wave of his hand. Swiping her from his life, she suspected, ruefully.

Once more, the voice of reason tried to make sense of it all. Cate slapped it away, for there was none. Was it because she wasn't his precious Hattie, or because it was just her? Had jealousy raised its ugly head, or was it as simple as Nathan was done with her, as she had always known would come to pass? Like a flash of St. Elmo's fire, the conquest made, the mystery gone. Women were his specialty, like cogs in a wheel: one in, one out; one in, one out...

Thomas' call of "You can come out now. He's gone, and too far away to shoot," cut off Cate's stream of thought. She squinted from the dim of the cabin into the glare of daylight to verify that Thomas was indeed alone.

"Are you sure?" she called back.

"Aye."

Cate repeatedly scanned the deck as she crept out, alert for the first sign of a ruse. She wouldn't put it past Nathan, or Thomas, for that matter. She rose on her toes to peer over the rail and saw the crown of a familiar leather hat no great way off. As she neared the rail, the longboat came into view.

Cate drew up alongside Thomas, his gaze as fixed as hers on the receding craft, Nathan standing at the bow like some damned figurehead. "I always knew it would come to this," she heard herself say.

Thomas stirred, as if from a deep thought. "What?"

"When he tired of me: sell me, pass me on. How much did you pay?"

He looked down at her with an odd mix of satisfaction, pleasure and wonder. "Not a farthing."

Cate closed her eyes and swayed. She wasn't even worth bartering for. Her heart was as cold and empty as the cannon next to her leg, once burning hot, but no more. She propped her head in her hand, suddenly feeling very tired, defeated and... useless.

What color was hope when it faded?

The circle was complete; she was back to where she had begun just a few weeks ago, with the clothes she stood in and strangers all around. Providence had interceded once more. It was too cruel: allowing her a shred of happiness, only to jerk it away.

She was now a pirate woman. She had scorned those who had sought to bestow the title upon her in Lady Bart's parlor. A fine fate for someone who had kept herself, one man her whole life. Purity and good intentions didn't pave the way to happiness.

First Nathan, then Thomas... and then how many more?

Homeless and penniless—she didn't even own the clothes she stood in—her only asset now was her appearance. Age and hard use would quickly take their toll, although just being a woman would always open certain doors. Her future was dim, starvation, squalid streets, and begging for a man's favor and his shilling. If she was lucky, she'd catch the pox, or a morbid fever, and die quickly. It was a desperate hope, for Fate seemed determined to deny her any relief.

She peered over the rail to the water below. Not too many weeks ago, she had done the same on the *Constancy*. The sea then had offered a reprieve, an escape, and the prospect of final peace.

Cate regarded Thomas from the corner of her eye. It could be worse, she thought philosophically. Thomas wasn't without assets. With effort, she could see him as himself and not Brian— well, not quite so much. Pretending he was Brian might prove beneficial, rendering this arrangement a little more... palatable. So long as she warmed his bed, she suspected Thomas wouldn't mind her visualizations.

She looked up to find Thomas viewing her as if she was a newly-found sea creature.

"What?" she demanded, checking to see if her skirts were turned up.

He shook his head and looked away. "Nothing."

Cate shifted away a bit. The possibility still lurked that Nathan's hand festering had been no accident. She wondered how diabolical of a mind lay behind Thomas' genial smile— Brian's smile. Scheming came natural enough: he had taken her on a moonlight stroll—a ruse, by his own admission—and then tricked her aboard his ship and set up a candle-light scene befitting of a farce.

"Did you plan this?"

Her question was met with the same blue-eyed, child-like innocence as when she had posed it that same night.

"Now why would I do a thing like that?" Finally, his bland façade crumbled. He grinned, shaking his head. "Nay, I but allowed Nathan to be Nathan."

"And I'm the prize?" The prospect of being a pawn in some grand scheme gave Cate an ill-feeling. She felt a chill, as if a cloud had just blanketed the sun. "How long until you pass me on or leave me on some island?"

His smile tightened, and he shied. "I aim to take care of you a damn site better than he did. Look at you: dressed in near rags, a rope necklace, and I can damn near count every rib."

"You shouldn't flatter me so." Never had she been made to feel so paltry so handily.

The longboat was now nearly to the *Morganse's* side. Nathan was still at the bow, his shoulder's set with determination not to look back. A bubble of panic rose as Cate realized this could be the last time she ever saw Nathan.

Pirate Captain. Damn his soul.

Cate made a derisive noise in the back of her throat. "It 'tis a wonder if that man will ever find anything he treasures more than his freedom and that precious ship."

She turned and trudged back to the cabin, home... for now.

An Excerpt from "Nor Gold,"
The continuation of "The Pirate Captain,
Chronicles of a Legend"

MRS. CRISP SCOWLED IN DISAPPROVAL as Thomas took Cate, fixing her attention in any direction but the proprietress', through the inn's public room and past the doorman. Once outside, Thomas steered a course back toward town.

Thomas ducked in under a sign marking the shop as the stays-maker, but neither the master nor apprentice was in the way. The only one there was a woman, who looked old enough to have greeted Christopher Columbus when he landed mopping the floors. She had no notion of her mistress' return.

The market square, in many ways, was much like one in another Charles Town Cate had known, long ago and so very far away. With its Turkey carpets, South American monkeys and parrots, African drums and talismans, and China lacquer-ware, one might have thought it to be the crossroads of the world.

If Cate had hoped a leisurely stroll through the market, she would have done so in vain. Their visit seemed casual enough at first, stopping at this stand or that cart. All too soon, however, she discovered Thomas was guiding her as handily as he would have steered his ship through a reef. She wasn't, however, quite sure how she had come to be standing before the straw bonnet weaver's stand and trying on broad-brimmed ones. It came as no great surprise to her when, after explaining to him what would happen, they sprang from her head, twice in as many minutes, in spite of a string tied under her chin. She stood with her arms crossed over her chest, biting her tongue as Thomas tried pins, combs and ties of every description, all to no avail. Jaw set determinedly, the parasol-maker's stand was his next stop. With the heat of the day building, Cate couldn't disagree that she needed some sort of shade. She resolutely put back Thomas' selection, with its inlaid pearl handle, pink tassel, and lace-and-ribbon edging, and selected a blue-and-white striped one with a carved ivory handle, instead.

At a goat-cart stand, Thomas picked out a modesty piece of netted lace with a vine-and-rose pattern, and insisted she put it on that moment. His big blunt fingers were surprisingly adept at arranging the delicate fabric into the edge of her bodice. She stood very aware of not only his nearness, but of his resemblance to her dead husband, one strong enough to stir her heart and tightened the pit of her belly. Guilt weighed on her, as if she was somehow taking advantage of Thomas, an odd thought toward the man who owned her. When did the slave ever feel obliging of the master for his food and shelter? Still, she couldn't shake the feeling.

As they strolled through among the carts and stands, the square was a veritable Tower of Babel. Thomas, however, shifted easily from one tongue to the next as he haggled. Between his size, heavy armament and eyes which could turn to steel if displeased, his price was usually met. The more persistent vendors seized Cate by the arm and shoved their bargains before her. Standing a head and more above the teeming mass, Thomas imposed himself between her and the intruder. Hand resting on his pistol, he edged them away. Under the draper's striped awning, several dress lengths of fabric — silks and an unfamiliar weave, light and airy, perfect for the tropics — — and fine linens for small clothes were selected.

They passed the dog and pony carts, lean-tos and tables, selling everything from charms to chickens, monkeys to melons, to find what Cate would need to create her new wardrobe: buttons, crinolines, hooks, stays tape, lace and the like. It didn't come easily, for she was unaccustomed to such grand expenditures. Thomas, however, had a second sense for what caught her eye. Bags, baskets, and bundles were sent back to Mrs. Crisp's via a pair of knob-kneed lads, Thomas' coins chinking in their pockets as they sped away.

Cate stood gape-mouthed at an apothecary's table and its staggering selection. Thomas stepped in with the pragmatism of a mariner to select skin creams, smelling of jasmine and roses, honey-almond soap, and shampoo, bright with rosemary and a spicy sweet flower she couldn't name. Taken individually, the purchases were not extravagant, but on the whole, it was overwhelming. Life aboard the *Ciara Morganse* had allowed for few luxuries; many years before that, she had lived on the scraps from others' tables. And while living in the Highlands, a life so long ago it was almost forgotten, had been very comfortable, by Scottish standards, but such luxuries were unheard of.

A good part of her discomfort rose from the knowledge that such pampering came with a double edge. It meant protection, but it also meant being controlled. Self-reliance had been her only means of survival for all those years she had lived on her own. That same independent side of hers bridled at the thought of bending to someone else's will. And yet, that independence had taken the worst of all blows: being sold by Nathan Blackthorne, peeved, fed up, or whatever his reason had been. Thomas was comely, good-natured and caring, but she was still his property. If not a slave, then what else could she be called?

Pirate's woman.

In most circles, it was a very unflattering title.

As they made their way through the market, Cate tried not to look up the residential side streets they passed. Seeing the tidy rows of homes and cottages set off a longing which left her standing and staring. Home. A place to belong. It was what she longed for, and yet she might as well have been reaching for the rings of Saturn.

Her melancholia dissolved at seeing a dry goods stand, its tables laden with spools of threads and ribbons, thimbles, hoops, frames and needles, gold, no less! There was no hesitation in Cate's part there. Thomas' smile widened in direct proportion to the mounting pile of her selections. As the proprietor filled score upon score of ivory and bone bobbins with thread, Thomas poked through the ribbons. An "Ah-ha!" in his mariner's voice marked his discovering the shade which matched her eyes. A length was cut and, he tied it about her head, a pert bow at the crown.

As they moved through the market, Thomas occasionally called out and waved to acquaintances. For many, that greeting wasn't enough, and they scurried over to shake hands. Sailing might span the Seven Seas, but the sailor's world was a small one. The greetings were mutually hearty, but the pursuant conversation was always carried on with Cate standing mute.

During one such interlude, Cate lifted the hair from her neck and dabbed the sweat at her temples. She rued the absence of the fresh, bright sea breeze, blocked by the town's buildings. Fish and vegetables lying in the sun, tobacco smoke, tightly-packed bodies, and an underfoot slurry of dung, urine and refuse rendered the air nearly unbreathable. The stuffiness combined with the heat made her go light-headed. Thomas caught her as she swayed and sat her on a bale of dried hides. He hailed an African man with a sack of coconuts slung around his shoulders and a machete in hand. The end of the great green nut was whacked off, and Thomas held the cut end to Cate's lips while she sipped.

Thomas frowned as he dabbed the milk from her chin. "I need to get you out of here. Hungry?"

"Starved." Her stomach cleaved onto the coconut milk. She felt considerably steadier, but breakfast had been a very long time ago.

Thomas rose and put out his hand. "Your wish is but my command, m'lady. To *The Crown*, it is."

A sudden rain shower broke, the mist-like rain rendering the air so thick it was almost like breathing underwater. Under the protection of her parasol, they trotted down the street toward the docks. Cate smiled as they ducked into a doorway with a sign "*The Crown*" over it, with an appropriate yellow image painted on it. The tavern wasn't the seedy hole which one expected on a waterfront. It was a typical tavern, however: a long room with rush-covered floors, filled with rows of tables and benches, and a serving counter at the far end. The low-beamed ceiling was black with wood, candle and tobacco smoke.

"Why aren't we eating at Mrs. Crisp's?" Cate asked as Thomas guided her to a table along the wall.

Thomas smiled tolerantly. "Mrs. Crisp is a slave to the application of mop and broom, almost as much as you," he added wryly. "But she has no sense of duty to pot, nor spoon, nor will she spend the money to engage someone who does. You might as well go to the cooper's or the ropewalk, for the fare would be barely different. *The Crown*, on the other hand," he went on with an admiring eye to the room, "has a clientele whose main concern is the liquid in their tankard, in spite of a kitchen which produces some of the best sea pie in the New World."

No sooner had Cate sat than she shifted uncomfortably. "I need to go to the privy," she said at Thomas' questioning eye. She rose, only to see him do the same. "Oh, for heaven's sake, I can do this much on my own."

"Are you sure?" he asked, hovering between standing and sitting.

She gave his hand splayed on the table between them a reassuring pat. "I've been doing this for some years now. I can manage."

Thomas reluctantly lowered to the bench. As Cate wove her way through the tables, however, she could feel his eyes following. A well-worn path in the floor's planks led to a door outside and a rear yard. It had stopped raining; the moist air growing steamy in the emerging sun. The yard was enclosed by a fence tall and solid enough to block any movement of air, which could have served well, for the space smelled like old vomit and a vast, overused chamber pot. The fence's sun-battered boards bore the yellowish-brown stain of years of being urinated upon, as proved by the man who stood facing it then. Doing up his breeches, he barely ducked a nod and scurried back inside.

The privy was at the rear of the yard. Cate tiptoed down the mud-puddled path as one would through a cow byre. She opened the door and reflexively ducked to avoid the cloud of flies, rankled at being disturbed. The leaning shack was as foul and rank as would be expected, and she made quick use of it.

Cate's exit, however, was blocked by a pair of women, each wearing a strained, impatient look. Their straggling hair, dragging hems on much-mended skirts, stays loosened, the dark ends of their breasts showing through the tissue-thin shifts, and shoes walked to the point of shapelessness marked them as street whores. At first, she thought them to be waiting their turn for the privy, but at the same time it seemed remarkable such a pair would stand on such formality, when any semi-secluded patch of ground would usually do.

The pair was more or less bookends. Only slight variations in coloring or build separated them: one light-headed and squat, the other dark and slim. A thick layer of powder, ostensibly applied to create an appearance of gentility, was streaked with rivulets of sweat. The powder also served to obscure the pallor of near-starvation, the blots of rouge, like cheeks on a rag doll, failing to provide the intended allure of health. Their wax patches, meant to cover pox scars or open sores, were curled at the edges.

Cate bore no complaint against whores. They were merely women who, left to their own devices, had resorted to their only means of survival. There but for the grace o' God could have gone she. Only luck had saved her and only arrogance would allow her to think she was far removed even then. If Thomas was to grow weary of her, she could easily wind up being one of those gaunt and hollow-eyed wraiths roaming the streets, begging for a man's favor like curs at a butcher's doorway.

"Bugger off, bitch. This 'ere is me n' Iris's territory," said the lighter of the pair.

This was delivered with Cate being herded backward with their shoulders and hips, until she came up against the privy door. If she had been living alone in East London, they would have never gotten her cornered. Dammit, she had grown soft-headed. As she eyed them, her fist balled at her side. Both women were at least a half-head shorter than she, but it would be further soft-headedness to underestimate them. Street life would have rendered them wiry. A simple shout would bring Thomas—hopefully—but also the entire tavern and anyone else within earshot. It was a scene Cate didn't wish to cause, if at all possible. She didn't fancy she was in immediate danger. This struck her as more the everyday strain of intimidation. Still, she squared her feet and balanced her weight in preparation should a fight ensue.

"This is first comes what's first served best 'ere," said the lighter one again, pressing Cate with her shoulder.

"Aye, 'n what we gets is best, first pick that 'tis. Newcomers go to the end o' the line," said Iris, in thick Irish. Her point was punctuated with a thumb stabbed over her shoulder. "And don't forget me n' Rose gets half o' yer earnin's," she added, ramming a finger into Cate's chest.

"I beg your pardon, but I'm not—" Cate sputtered.

"What's goin' on 'ere?"

The harlots whirled around at the male voice and jerked back like scalded cats. They shied, declawed by their apparent master, a hatchet-faced, simian-like man, with long arms, bowed legs, and a wall-eye.

Rose flashed a tense smile as he strolled nearer. "Nuthin', Squires. We wuz just advisin' the newun' here as to how we do things hereabouts."

As Squires neared, the bookends inched away from Cate, like two children seeking to distance themselves from a third about to be disciplined. He drew up and shrewdly eyed Cate as one might a new brood mare. The wall-eye made it difficult to track where he was looking, while the other peered at her with the warmth of a shark. The air grew more pungent, the stench of him overcoming the privy behind her.

"Hmm... not bad," he said, with an appreciation which made Cate's skin creep. "A mite old, but with little powder and rouge; pull down that bodice so as to show the customers you're friendly-like; do something with that hair and you'll do well......
very well, indeed."

Squires' hand casually came to rest on the hilt of the knife at his waist. "'Tis a partnership we have 'ere."

He flicked out the knife and began to track slow circles before Cate, the blade's tip periodically carving an upward arc or downward slice, the sun flashing on the steel with each turn. Cate reflexively tried to recoil—she had a deep hatred of blades—but her back was firmly against the privy door.

"Everyone works for the common good," Squires went on. "Give over your share straightway and there shan't be trouble.

Forget and I'll see that your odds o' working again are cut off, *if you get my drift.*"

You're in trouble now, girl.

Cate slid a glance toward Iris and Rose, measuring the chances of their intervention. Nothing but fear there. The pair's attention was fixed on the knife with a familiarity which meant only one thing: Squires used it, and often.

The time to scream might have passed, but Cate opted to try anyway. She drew a breath, when she heard a deep-voice calmly say, "It doesn't require much of a man to draw a knife on a lady."

Squires and the whores whirled around to where Thomas stood a short distance away, pistol in one hand, a knife in the other.

"Doesn't take much of one to pull a pistol on one what's only armed w' a knife," Squires sneered in a faltering bravado.

His gaze steady on Squires, Thomas shoved the pistol into his belt and shifted the knife into his right hand. The switch allowed for a fuller view, and an impressive weapon it was, its hilt nearly the thickness of the average man's wrist, the blade nearly as long as one's hand.

Thomas allowed Squires' eyes to follow the circular path of the knife's tip before asking, "Better?"

A breeze staggered over the fence, but only served to stir the yard's foulness, like kicking a half-dried pile of dung. A droplet of sweat began a languorous trip down between Cate's breasts.

"No harm meant. We wuz just enlightenin' the newun 'ere as to the way o' bizness 'ere. Partners we are 'ere, are we not, ladies?" Squires sharply elbowed the two whores into agreement. "Scratchin' each other's backs, that is. I let her work 'ere 'n she gives me 'alf. Fair's fair, n' all that."

One could almost hear the trio's heads nod in earnestness. If they had tails, they would have been tucked between their legs.

"Just to show what an abidin' cove I am, so as to show my goodwill n' all, I'll let you 'ave 'er at half price... free!" Squires blurted at seeing Thomas' knife tip jerk up.

The corner of Thomas' mouth quirked. Whether amused by the offer, or at the thought of paying for what he already owned, Cate couldn't tell. "The lady is my guest," he said with precision.

Squires spun around and back-handed Iris. "Stupid slut!"

The muzzle of Thomas' pistol was pressed against the side of Squires' head before he could turn back. Squires' eyes bulged at hearing the hammer cock.

"Do that again," Thomas said in a low rumble. "And I'll blow a hole in that miserable bag you use for a head."

Squires' mouth worked like a fish lying on a dock. At length, he only nodded.

Thomas stepped back and crooked a finger at Cate. "Come along, lovely."

∽≪∘≫∽

As Thomas steered her back inside the tavern, Cate half expected him to give her a good shake, or at least a berating. Instead, he only said under his breath, "Can't leave you for a minute, can I? Like a damned sign around your neck."

He looked down at her as she sputtered a response and shook his head. "Never mind. I've seen that very sign myself."

"What are you talking about?"

"You have no idea, do you? The power you have, over men most particular?" he said in amused wonderment.

"I never—!"

"You don't have to," he said, chuckling. His hand tightened on her arm as he urged her along. "It's an air, or a scent, or some damned something. Hell, I don't know what the hell it is, but there's no denying it. Makes every man wanna bed you the minute he lays eyes on you, and every woman hate you for it, that's for damned sure."

"Stand easy, lovely. To expect you to change would be to ask the trades to shift or the moon to stand still." He saw her seated at the table once more. He sat across from her and broke into a pleasured smile. "Besides, some of us downright enjoy it."

She gave him a sharp look, but was met with only his usual benign boyishness. Thomas could be as vulgar as a f'c's'tleman, but never a suggestive or lewd mark had been made toward her, until then.

The pitcher bawd came. She made no airs about bumping Thomas' shoulder with her hip. As she set their drinks on the table, she bent to allow him a full display of her bosom. A wink and a smile were cast over her shoulder as she sauntered away.

Cate was surprised to find the drink was shrub. She had expected either ale or straight rum, not the mix of lemon juice and sugar, the rum lurking amid the sweet and tart. Fresh and cool from the well, after the heat of the market and the foulness of the privy yard, it was blessedly refreshing.

"I think you have an admirer of your own," Cate said over her drink. In fact, there were several eyes cast wistfully in Thomas' direction. His earlier observations were accurate: outright resentment was aimed at her.

She looked up to see Thomas' gaze fixed over her shoulder,

as intent as a starving man with a feast just beyond his reach. A squeal of feminine laughter revealed the object, or objects of his attention. She started to tell him she wouldn't mind if he desired to sup. With a sharp stab, however, she discovered nothing could be farther from the truth.

It was a puzzle, for she had no claim on him. He was the one who possessed her. Still, Cate batted her lashes. "This shrub is wonderful." Her ploy worked. Thomas blinked and came back to the table. A blush rose from his collar, but he said nothing.

The sea pie came. It was delicious. The "sea" aspect of it was but one among several of layers of meats, onions, and currants, with flaky layers of crust between each. At first, Cate thought the great wedge which was set before her was far too large, but she ate with an industry which surprised her and clearly pleased Thomas.

The tavern's door burst open and a group barged in. Cate stiffened, the fork gone forgotten in her hand. Her back was to the room, but it wasn't necessary for her to look. There was no mistaking that voice. The sound was like a kick in the gut. She sat frozen, watching from the corner of her eye as Captain Nathanael Blackthorne brushed past, a whore under each arm and several more in tow. A small entourage of followers brought up the rear, all drunk as dukes.

"What's he doing here?" she hissed.